SUPERHEROES

BECOMING THE TRULY ELITE AND HONORABLE

DANIEL JOSEPH CYRUS

Superheroes
Copyright © 2024 by Daniel Joseph Cyrus

All rights reserved. No part of this publication may be reproduced, distributed, or transmitted in any form or by any means, including photocopying, recording, or other electronic or mechanical methods, without the prior written permission of the author, except in the case of brief quotations embodied in critical reviews and certain other non-commercial uses permitted by copyright law.

Library of Congress Control Number: 2024919850

ISBN
978-1-964982-63-2 (Paperback)
978-1-964982-64-9 (eBook)
978-1-964982-62-5 (Hardcover)

Superheroes: Becoming The Truly Elite And Honorable

When Morality, Ethics, Acknowledgement Of Unalterable Divine Birth Gender, And Respect For Each Country's Conservative And Godly Religious Society Values-Based Enlightenment, Motivation, And Inspiration Are Embraced by Every Society Member And Each Citizen Of Every Country, These "World Citizens" Will Then Inevitably Merit, Attain, And Achieve "Superhero" Status, A Realization That Is Highly Desirable, Fulfilling, Eternal, And Satisfying, That Will Be Experienced By Each and Every One Of These Transformed "World Citizens" In Every Country Throughout The World.

Daniel Joseph Cyrus

TABLE OF CONTENTS

Foreword xi

Chapter One:

Battling Freedom Of Speech And Religion Suppression Tyrants, Monopolistic Sinister Suppression Of Divinity And Nationalistic Religious And Societal Values By Biased And Unethical (e.g., "The Network" movie), Media Organizations, Technology Companies, Massive And Wealthy Corporations, And Globalists Throughout The World, And Imperative "Age Of Reason" Enlightening Remedies For Rectification And Ongoing And Never-Ending Battle Victories By Freedom Of Speech And Religion Advocates Known As "Current And Future Generation Superheroes" 1

Chapter Two:

"X" (formerly known as "Twitter") Free Speech Suppression and Unjustified, Prejudiced, and Errant "Permanent Account Closures" For Those Whose Life Perspectives Differ From Employees Monitoring Posts On The Company Website, Or From That Of The C.E.O. And Company Board Members 11

Chapter Three:

"LinkedIn" (currently known as "Fake Defender of Free Speech") Free Speech Suppression and Unjustified, Prejudiced, and Errant "Permanent Account Closures" For Those Whose Life Perspectives Differ From Employees Who Are "Monitoring" (Censoring And Restricting Freedom Of Speech) Posts On Different Company's Websites, Or From That Of The C.E.O. And Company Board Members 19

Chapter Four:

"Facebook" and "Instagram" (never known as politically unbiased media companies and never even attempting to be a "Fake Defender of Free Speech"), Free Speech Suppression and Unjustified, Prejudiced, and Errant "Permanent Account Closures" For Those Whose Life Perspectives

Differ From Employees Monitoring Posts On The Company Website, Or From That Of The C.E.O. And Company Board Members, and the Facebook Presidential Election Scandal 33

Chapter Five:

The Failure of the United States of America's National Football League (N.F.L.), National Basketball Association (N.B.A.), Amateur and Professional Soccer, Swimming, Track & Field, Other & All Sports, And All Other Countries Sports Teams & Sports Organizations Throughout The World, to Address and Denounce Individual Athletes Who Errantly and "Delusionally" Believe They Have Either The Authority Or Right To Change or Otherwise Alter Their Gender, Assigned Irreversibly At Birth, Or Those Who Pretend To Be The Opposite Sex By Inappropriately Dressing, Using Makeup or Jewelry, Or Acting Or Behaving Like The Opposite Sex That The Are Not A Member Of, Nor Ever Meant To Be A Member Of, All In Order To: "not offend potential paying audiences or consumers, place monetary gains and profits at the highest priority level and divine human gender assignments determined before birth and at birth (only two, male and female), and society ethics and morals at the lowest (or nonexistent) level, and, most disappointingly, disrespect the entire world population, which, for thousands of years, have respected and acknowledged the unique and cherished differences that exist, in reality and in perpetuity, between irrevocable and irreversible birth genders, namely, males and females. 77

Chapter Six:

Literary Agents And Book Publishers And Movie Producers/Studios Long-Standing Anti-Religious And Anti-Societal Values Bias And Monopoly And The Opportunity For Human Society Members To Transform Into Superheroes By Engaging in Ant-Trust And Anti-Bias And Anti-Monopoly Litigation And Winning Battles That Result In The Eradication and Annihilation Of Current Anti-Religious Values Bias And Monopolistic Behavior & Rejection Of Religious Authors And Their Book To Movie Adaptations So That Future Generations May Enjoy Ethical, Moral Books And Movies To Read And View (And Be Positively Impacted By), Versus Current Creepy, Immoral, Psychiatric Disease (e.g., Gender-Confused Individuals) Glorification, Violence And Criminal Behavior-Glorifying and Promoting Books And Movies That Currently Dominate The Book Selling And Movie Production Industries, And, For Over One Hundred Years, Are Being Sought And Aggressively Promoted By Literary Agents, Screenwriters, Book Publishers, and Movie Production Studios.. 105

Chapter Seven:

Fraudulent And Corrupt State Elections In The United States of America And All Countries Throughout The World. For example, when California voters resoundingly defeated, by their voting majority, the concept of "same-sex marriage" or "gay marriage," how was the Governor of California (corruptly elected but correctly voted by California voters to be removed from office, then corruptly, through election ballot manipulation and fraudulent vote counting, not removed from office during and after the recall vote, despite California voters majority intent to remove him from office on the basis of corruption and incompetence), able to single-handedly override democracy and the intent of California voters to reject the unethical and immoral concept and notion of "same-sex marriage" or "gay marriage"? This issue was never correctly addressed, in legal terms and in court, and the prosecution of the Governor for voter system fraud and corrupt ballot counting (not counting ballots from voters with opposing views) has not been addressed for decades. Why? Ethical Society Members Who Address And Correct These Fraudulent And Corrupt State Elections Via Legal Court Victories Will Be Instant Superheroes, The Truly Elite... 113

Chapter Eight:

Politically-Motivated, Fraudulent, Malicious Prosecution In The United States of America And All Countries Throughout The World. Ethical Society Members Who Address And Correct These Politically-Motivated, Fraudulent, Malicious Prosecutions Via Legal Court Victories Will Be Instant Superheroes, The Truly Elite.. 149

Chapter Nine:

The Fallacy, False Narrative, And Outright Lie Regarding The Purported "Benefit" (Actually a Detriment And Lethal Assault) to a City, State, Country, And Society" of "Sanctuary Cities." .... 170 "Sanctuary Cities" true definition: A city whose corruptly-elected, and/or unethical, and immoral politicians give preference to illegal immigrant federal law-breakers, protect them from prosecution and ethical deportation from and out of the country they illegally entered without authorization, hide them from or release them prior to prosecution for the crime(s) they committed and prior to the arrival of immigration authorities assigned to deport them, and, outrageously, often offer them state or other government photo identification cards (e.g., driver's license) so they may preferentially and fraudulently vote in upcoming election for the corrupt political party that ignored their crimes, prosecutions, deportation in all future state or federal elections, and receive food stamps, free hospital care, and be eligible for free low-income housing,

all paid for by hard-working legal citizen's tax payments to their corrupt state and federal government, who allow such "Sanctuary Cities" to exist and continue their unethical practice of using tax dollars on noncitizens and illegal immigrant criminals, law-breakers, and terrorists or other countries' non-law-abiding citizens who neither respect nor intend to follow the rules or laws of the new country they illegally crossed into, to forever be a menace and burden to that country and society, financially, ethically, morally, patriotically (they are neither patriotic nor loyal to the country they illegally entered, often without any intent to work or pay taxes or become a citizen, or obtain a social security or other identification number for any work they do such that the government can track and apply taxes to their income), and, in essence, "Sanctuary Cities" thus recruit the entire world's most unethical, non-law abiding noncitizens to destroy that city, country, and society, indefinitely into the future. 170
"Sanctuary City" means "Sinful City." Ethical Society Members Who Prosecute And/Or Annihilate/Eliminate These Fraudulent And Corrupt "Sanctuary Cities" Via Legal Court Victories Will Be Instant Superheroes, "The Truly Elite." 171

Chapter Ten:

Unjust, Unethical, Immoral Lack of Indictment And/Or Non-Prosecution Of Criminal Acts Of State Or Federal Government Politicians And Other Government Agencies' Members (e.g., Members Of Congress: Senators, House of Representative members) In The United States Of America Or Any Other Country In The World, Based Purely On The Biased Fact That The Criminals Are Members Of The Elected Political Party In Charge Of The Government, Is And Will Always Be The Most Corrupt And Blatant Insult To Democracy And The Best Evidence Of The Lack Of That Government's Leadership Skills And Worthiness To Command Or Receive The Respect Of Their Citizens, Based On Their Lack of Morality And Ethical Behavior. Ethical Society Members And Government Members Who Prosecute All Criminals By The Same Standards And Criteria And With The Same Criminal Sentences Based On The Crime They Committed, Regardless Of Political Party Affiliation, Income Level, Social Status, Skin Color, Via Legal Court Victories Will Be Instant "Superheroes, The Truly Elite And Honorable." 177

Chapter Eleven:

Raping (Figuratively), Robbing, And Embezzling (RRE) Of Payments And Reimbursements Of Physicians and Physician Groups Who Are Reverently Caring For Routine And Emergency Health Conditions Which Demand And Require Their Loving Care And Surgical Procedures As A Remedy For Their Conditions Or Diseases Throughout The World By Large Trust-Like, Monopolistic, Unimpeded, Unhindered, Unopposed

(At Least Up To The Present Time; This Needs To Change Immediately), Large Conglomerate Unethical or Criminal Health Insurance Companies Who, One To 12 months After Patient Care Is Delivered In Good Faith By Physicians and Physician Groups, Are Then Demanded, Without Ethical Justification, Recourse, Or Appropriate Consideration Of Physician Appeals (At Least Without Future Physician Unions' Lawyers Criminal Financial Scandal Law Suits Directed Toward These Sinister Health Insurance Companies), To Refund To These Monopolistic And Sinister Health Insurance Companies, Significant Percentages, e.g., 30-80%, Of Original Payments To Physicians, Or In Some Cases, The Entire Physician Exam or Surgery Fee Due. Because Honorable, Empathetic, Altruistic And Caring Physicians Have Delayed And Precariously Avoided Or Shunned To Their Detriment, For Centuries, The Formation of Ethical Legal Powered And Backed, Physician-Defending and Physician-Supporting Unions, They Continue (Hopefully Not Too Much Longer) To Experience Self-Inflicted Raping (Figuratively), Robbing, And Embezzling (RRE) Of Payments And Reimbursements By These Large, Powerful, Dictator-Like, Sinister, Criminal, Trust-Like, Monopolistic Health Care Insurance Companies Who Have Been Enabled To Continue Their Crimes And Even Supported And Facilitated By The Inaction, Lack of Unity, Insufficient Decisiveness, And Overt Lack Of Resolve By Physicians, For Centuries, To Organize Physician Unions To Defend And Protect Their Ethical, Moral, And Honest Practice Of Examining And Operating On Patients, And Their Rights and Justification To Maintain Their Respect For These Services, Freedom To Appeal Unjust Demands For Return of Just Fees Paid By Health Insurance Companies, And Fair Reimbursement For All Services Performed. 203

Chapter Twelve:

Ironically, Paradoxically, Or Fortunately, Depending On Whether You Have Agnostic, Atheistic, or Positive And Christian Perspective Or Outlook On Life And The World, The Same Perspectives, Intent, Aspirations, Motivation, Inspiration, Mentor Mindset, and God-Respecting, Bible-Based Values, Morality, and Ethics That Makes Parents Game-Changing, Miraculously Magnificent Parents Of Their Children, Also Make Politicians, Believe It Or Not, The Most Influential, Positive Life-Impacting Leaders And Stewards of God For All "World Citizens" On This And Every Planet In Our Universe, Also Known As The Cosmos! 303

Chapter Thirteen:

A Message To All Future Endeavoring Superheroes: Embrace And Cherish The Opportunity To Become The Truly Elite For Every "World Citizen," Culture, Society, And Country In This World Will Ultimately, Infinitely, Eternally, And Reverently Respect And Be Indebted And

Forever Thankful For You, In Addition To Your Certain Attainment Of God's Grace, Mercy, And Blessings While On Earth And In Heaven With God In Perpetuity!.. 447

Chapter Fourteen:

Analysis Of Fifty Superheroes Who Became The Truly Elite And Honorable During This Century Or Past Centuries And Synopses Of Their Endeavors And Life Achievements Along With Their Profile Portraits And Classic Statements, Communications, Brief Descriptions Of Their Demonstrated Superhero Perspectives, Attitudes, Actions, Behaviors, And Their Other Messages To This World For This Generations And All Future Generations! All Readers Who Seek To Learn From These Superhero Mentors To Become Superheroes During Their Own Lifetimes Have The Potential To Become Superheroes Themselves If Exceptional Steadfastness, Ethical/Moral/God-Respecting Behavior, And Earnest Effort, Work, Courage, and Resilience To Accomplish Their Benevolent Aspirations, Goals, And Glorious Superhero Destinies Are Pursued With Unwavering Determination. With Regard To Superhero Status Achievements In Life, There Has Never Been A More Succinct And Precise Synopsis Statement or Philosophy To Inspire, Motivate, And Induce Or Initiate A Gestalt And Paradigm Shift In Every Individual Who Chooses This Endeavor And To Embark On This Magnificent Zenith Goal In Life To Be A Superhero And Mentor For And To All "World Citizens" In This Generation And Future Generations: "It takes one to know one ('Superhero')." 639

Photo Gallery.. 693
Conclusion.. 780

FOREWORD

It has been my pleasure to be a friend of Daniel Joseph Cyrus for almost 30 years. I have been on long runs with him, and I have enjoyed trying to keep up with him on tennis courts and ski slopes. I have known Daniel to work long hours, study continuously and rise in a super competitive professional field. He is a consummate professional, a serious athlete, a straight A student, an accomplished musician, and a devout Christian who lives the life he writes.

In Superheroes, Daniel writes to alert the reader of numerous injustices that are plaguing the United States of America. He sees "non-leaders" pushing a dark age of deceptive, unkind, sinful, selfish, and non-world-enhancing reign of terror and corruption through suppression of speech and religion, fraudulent elections, malicious prosecutions, sanctuary cities, non-prosecution of criminal events with monopolistic technology companies, various government agencies, and criminal health insurance companies.

Be not afraid! Daniel also offers multiple "surgical solutions" rooted in Christian values that enable us to become Superheroes and push back against the evils dragging down our society. He identifies and elucidates essential vital values, principles, insights, wisdom, enlightening stories, and clever solutions to disheartening trends, dangerous plans for our society and paths that current large monopolistic companies and political organizations are inadvisably pursuing. This book is quite diverse in topics addressed, extremely pertinent to the current political chaos we are experiencing. As I was writing this foreword, we all witnessed the assassination attempt of the most high-profile person in the world, Donald J. Trump! In that attempt we saw incompetence or carelessness in how security officers were deployed on the scene. We saw shooters waiting to act until other people had been hurt and killed!

We saw people on President Trump's security detail who did not appear to know what they were doing, and it seems like they were probably hired for reasons other than their potential as Secret Service Agents. Everything is upside down and not only in this country but around the world as immoral, anti-human bombing continues in Ukraine and the Gaza Strip while our political leaders appear to be happily selling more munitions.

As I read Superheroes, I felt a little anxious about things that are going wrong in my country, but I was also encouraged that there are solutions when one lives a life in dedication to their creator and savior. The book is grandiose in its scope, aspiring in its benevolent content and goals (similar to a book entitled Father's Eyes), and meant to improve the lives of all "World Citizens" in every country and continent in the world.

Cliff Masters

CHAPTER ONE:

Battling Freedom Of Speech And Religion Suppression Tyrants, Monopolistic Sinister Suppression Of Divinity And Nationalistic Religious And Societal Values By Biased And Unethical (e.g., "The Network" movie), Media Organizations, Technology Companies, Massive And Wealthy Corporations, And Globalists Throughout The World, And Imperative "Age Of Reason" Enlightening Remedies For Rectification And Ongoing And Never-Ending Battle Victories By Freedom Of Speech And Religion Advocates Known As "Current And Future Generation Superheroes"

Winston Churchill (1874-1965) was the Prime Minister of the United Kingdom during World War II. His leadership and oratory skills were crucial in rallying the British people during the darkest days of the war. Churchill's steadfast resolve and inspiring speeches helped to maintain British morale and resistance against Nazi Germany, ultimately contributing to the Allied victory[1,2].

Globalists are determined to dismantle and destroy religious communities throughout the world and then appoint a single nonreligious "leader (antichrist)" to rule the world by parameters that acknowledge no existence of God or Godly values, principles, attitudes, perspectives, and without any semblance of a world created by God.

When Jean Harlow was in love with William Powell, and before her premature and shocking death at the young age of 26 years old from post-streptococcal glomerulonephritis (kidney disease leading to renal failure and her death), she traveled to a San Francisco hotel during the filming of the movie, "After the Thin Man," in which Myrna Loy and William Powell were starring in the film, in order to be with William Powell. In 1936, it was unacceptable for an unmarried man and an unmarried woman who were dating to share the same hotel room, so the hotel clerk assumed rightly that Jean would share a hotel room with Myrna Loy instead of William Powell, and that is precisely what occurred throughout the filming of the movie. Jean and William were then able to see each other each day while not sleeping in the same hotel room together.

What was right, moral, ethical, and Godly in 1936 has not changed, yet "Globalists," agnostics, atheists, and "religious people" who pretend to be God-respecting and Godly people but do not act accordingly during their daily life habits and activities, would have you believe that "times have changed" and unmarried individuals should sleep together before they are married. This is just one example of how Godly values and principles of living a Godly life are being compromised and, in essence, disregarded or discarded in current times and that no progress is being pursued by "Globalists" to improve this world by seeking to educate and guide each new generation to be more and more God-fearing, God-respecting, and God-loving in their daily perspectives, attitudes, motivation, inspiration, work activities, and life aspirations and goals.

The George Soros family, known to be "Globalists" (e.g., George Soros, the billionaire, and his son) have given new meaning to the concept of

"Globalists using their wealth to crush and devastate God-respecting individual citizens of countries throughout the world, especially those who favor, support, and advocate for secure national borders, nationalistic culture and religious values maintenance and growth, and all those international citizens demonstrating strong and visible faith in God and God's benevolence and, as a result, reject and oppose "Globalists" attempts to remove religious values and Godly practices, laws, and Godly behavior from every country in the world by funding fraudulent elections and financially supporting corrupt politicians (agnostics, atheists, those open to bribes), to run for leadership roles such as state leaders or court judges, such that laws will be passed that eventually annihilate all possibilities of citizens to secure their country's borders, practice and defend their faith, and live the Godly lifestyle they desire and deserve to live.

While globalists seek no country border walls, ignore human rights abuses and/or total neglect of human rights and free speech by citizens of select (and sinister) countries (sadly but true), and are proponents of no tariff free trade amongst all countries in the world, regardless of each country's behavior or lack of respect for basic human rights and respect for their citizens' right to vote and express themselves through free speech without imprisonment if that speech is contrary to the sinister activity or opinions of their country's (often corrupt or ungodly), political leaders, non-Globalist citizens of every country advocate for, desire, and expect their democratically elected government leaders to maintain secure nation border walls, deport criminal acts of illegal border invasions, maintain their nation's unique cultural identity and religious, God-respecting values and lifestyle, respect the only two birth genders (male or female) discovered at birth, not teach or be advocates of "delusional gender confusion" or "anti-national values" dishonest "lessons or classes" to naïve, young, vulnerable innocent children of God in every country on this planet.

Globalists put monetary profit and selfish, stingy wealth goals ahead of ethical, moral, Godly generosity and tithing (e.g., giving 10% of one's salary each year to the church community to help those less fortunate in the world) at every moment of their life, day and night, even dreaming of a world without God whereby semiconductor chips, oil, money, military weapons, and supplies, or any other products that could be used to attack other countries or fund evil operations of sinister governments, could be sold for an enormous profit to any evil, terrorist-spawning, or otherwise sinister country (e.g., a country showing no respect for their citizens' freedom of speech, religious freedom, or all other fundamental human rights as defined in the Bible by God and his son Jesus Christ) to achieve wealth at any cost (and detriment) to a country's citizens and humanity, specifically those countries who show no respect for their very own citizen's right to free speech, freedom to worship God, and freedom of citizens to dissent, publicly without unrighteous retribution or imprisonment by their own ungodly government leaders when they see their country's leaders act or behave in a sinful, selfish, cruel, and ungodly manner.

Due to the antiquated and outdated concept and practice of "tenure" of "teachers and professors" (liberal radicals without Godly values in many education institutions, unfortunately), in many (but thankfully not all) countries in the world, which should be abolished immediately for its sinful, disrespectful, and devastating effect on nationalistic religious practices, national culture, patriotism, and respect for the benevolent and Godly international actions and defense of Godly behavior and protection of all other country's citizens who are being disrespected, abused, and deprived of fundamental human rights and freedoms set forth and delineated in the Torah and Bible and other God-respecting manuscripts that teach benevolence for all humans on this earth.

Currently, educators undergo no rigorous background checks or screenings and are indiscriminately allowed to teach students of all levels and all ages for several years, during which they may knowingly hide their true evil intent and ungodly world views, including socialism, Marxism, pro-homosexual, pro-same-gender-marriages, "pro-gender-dysphoria-encouraging behavior and attitude toward children and adults alike," Globalism, evil intent to eliminate or discard religion from schools and communities, discouragement of children and adults to engage in prayers to God and frequent church attendance regularly, and teaching children and adult students that their nation is evil, was evil, will be evil, or always has been evil, and that their students should not trust, respect, or obey immigration laws, law enforcement, and that they should always resist arrest by immigration or law enforcement officers at all times and in any situation "where they feel uncomfortable or threatened."

Tenure in the education system throughout the world should be abolished and, as in every other occupation and profession and trade, be replaced with annual reviews and evaluations, whereby detrimental or otherwise unruly or evil educators may be removed on an annual (or shorter duration) basis and replaced with educators, teachers, and professors who teach children and adults to respect Godly and universally accepted benevolent societal values (e.g., as taught in the Bible), respect national borders, national values, cultural values, respect for all humans, respect for God-created and God-assigned birth genders (male and female only), freedom of speech, freedom from being judged solely based on their skin color, return to merit-based performance reviews and occupation job hirings, advancements and promotions versus skin-color or gender or nationality-based job hirings, advancements and promotions, which are inherently forms of prejudice that have crept into society disguised as and under the guise of "diversity, equity, and inclusion (D.E.I.)," whereby the best students, hardest workers, most qualified job and occupational promotion candidates can be excluded from their deserved hirings or promotions, in order to give those positions or promotions to those individuals who are less deserving of or unqualified to receive the designated job hiring or promotion due to their inferior work ethic, lesser qualifications, or defiant and uncooperative attitudes or willingness to perform the job function expected, all in the name of (more accurately, misleading excuse or outright lie), "diversity, equity, and inclusion (D.E.I.)," what would be called "pulling the wool over one's eyes" in past decades and centuries.

In the past several centuries, ungodly citizens throughout the world have reaped the benefits of their Godly citizen colleagues or community members in the sense that these God-respecting community members have set up communities based on human rights and equality, freedom of speech, freedom of religion, "love thy neighbor as thy self" concepts, the ten commandments (time-proven laws, principles, and keys to successful, Godly, benevolent human respect and treatment of fellow humans in society as prescribed by God, Creator and protector of, and guide for all humans, male and female, from birth to death, and resurrection to be united with God for eternity), as espoused in the Bible and other religious manuscripts written by citizens throughout the world and, most importantly, inspired by God their Creator and redeemer.

God's omniscience, omnipresence, and omnipotence in the lives of all humans created at birth allow and enable God to forgive less-than-honorable actions and sins of all humans, when those humans, individually and voluntarily (without coercement), ask for forgiveness of their bad behavior or mistakes in life, agree to not repeat their transgression, agree to read the Bible and thus learn to act and behave in a Godly manner as taught in the Torah and Bible, and in essence, be "reborn" into life of honorable, honest, ethical, moral, altruistic, generous, caring, kind, compassionate, empathetic, forgiving humans who both accept and bestow grace and mercy for themselves and other humans they interact with in this world, after which God, in divine and ephemeral brilliance, compassion, and mercy may then bestow upon that individual who has made these changes, commitments, and promises backed by corresponding Godly behavior at all times, redemption from their sins, which would otherwise have led to eternal damnation of non-repenting individuals, allowing each repenting individual to be "redeemed" or reunited with God in heaven for eternity upon their earthly physical death and during the "rapture" and "second coming" of God to earth to assemble and unite with his God-respecting, "reborn", and "repented" Godly creations.

The current crisis in this generation and century, and in every century and generation, is when ungodly citizens temporarily overtake control or monopolize the narrative in one or more or all communities throughout the world, then misguidedly attempt to manipulate or strangulate the Godly message, Godly behavior, and Godly respect that all humans benefit from in society, and attempt to substitute evil "alternatives" to God's approach to and teachings regarding world peace, God-created man and woman, marriage defined exclusively as the Godly, loving relationship, and life-long commitment of a one man to one woman, "love thy neighbor as thy self" concept, and the "ten commandments" (in the Bible) as the most wise, enlightening, and Godly, loving guidelines ever given, graciously and mercifully, by the Creator of all living creations (e.g., humans) to all citizens (humans) from all countries and universes in this galaxy and all galaxies.

When governments of various countries and societies throughout the world allow monopoly behavior and unbalanced dominance of one-sided narratives and messages by organizations and companies engaged in news and media, movies production and promotion, books production and promotion (including "literary agents" as, often, immoral and biased gatekeepers and restrictors of religious book publications and adaptations into movies), sports team coaches, owners, trainers (all levels from elementary school, university, and professional sports), while suppressing or persecuting or prosecuting citizens with opposing views regarding, e.g., religious, ethical, moral, human rights-affirming views, freedom of speech, criticizers of unethical, dishonest, greedy, sinful leadership and behavior of government or other democratically elected officials, and those promoting Godly human behavior, then the earth and its inhabitants risk returning to a dire situation and circumstance akin to the Bible's description of the ancient world (Earth) in the days of Noah's Ark and the great flood, due to the overwhelming sinfulness and wickedness and total disregard of God's creations for their Creator.

When evil behavior by this universe's humans grasps and attempts to choke out God's love for God's creations, and evil citizens throughout the universe choose sin over repenting of sin, and knowingly reject the wiser choice of being "reborn" into a Godly life described and elucidated in the Bible, despite also being informed of and knowing that their sins will lead to their eternal condemnation and suffering and separation from God their Creator for eternity, and, lastly, when evil and ungodly humans reject the option they all have been given to voluntarily repent of their sins and shortcomings in living a Godly life as taught in the Torah and Bible, and instead choose to continue living a sinful and ungodly life until the end of their life and physical death on earth, then they will have, knowingly, chosen eternal damnation and misery over eternal glory and honor and love upon their physical death and spiritual resurrection and reunification and reunion with God their Creator in heaven for eternity.

The choice is clear for those of sound judgment and wisdom and dark and nebulous for those who seek short-term ungodly pleasures in exchange for eternal suffering, misery, and damnation as a result of their irresponsible choices and actions during their transient life on earth, compared with their, now lost and past potential eternal happiness and reunion with God their Creator in heaven, despite whatever they had to endure and suffer through during their transient life on earth.

TOP TWELVE BOOKS (MUST READS) FOR IMPROVEMENT IN WORLDWIDE SOCIETIES, CULTURES, AND COMMUNITIES, HEALTHCARE IN HOSPITALS, PERSONAL HEALTH (SPIRITUAL, MENTAL, PHYSICAL), TATTOO INK CHEMICAL DANGER AND HEALTH RISKS, DRUG AND ALCOHOL ABUSE OR DEPENDENCE AVOIDANCE, ADDICTION AVOIDANCE OR REHABILITATION AND CESSATION GUIDELINES, WHICH WILL ABSOLUTELY BENEFIT ALL COUNTRIES THROUGHOUT THE WORLD AND ALL WORLD CITIZENS

1) "Two Boy's Amazing, Inspiring Journey" by William Andrew Maximus Wallace

2) "One Man's Unfathomable Adventure, Beyond Wildest Imagination" by Steven Clark Kent Thomas
3) "The Generational Assault on Christianity, Free Speech & Democracy in America" by Christopher Arthur Rockefeller
4) "Modern-Day Slave Trade in the 21st Century" By Priscilla Lisa Alvarez-Mendez
5) "The Plant Paradox" by Steven R. Gundry, MD
6) "The Longevity Paradox" by Steven R. Gundry, MD
7) "The Energy Paradox" by Steven R. Gundry, MD
8) "The End of Alzheimer's Program" by Dale E. Bredesen, MD
9) "Brain Maker" by David Perlmutter, MD
10) "Fiber Fueled" by Will Bulsiewicz, MD
11) "Father's Eyes" by Winston Anselm Irons
12) "Two Sisters, The Dynamic Duo, Pilgrimage To Eternity" by Rachel Esther Lewis

May you be inspired, motivated, and enlightened by all these enlightening books which encourage all "Superheroes, Becoming The Truly Elite And Honorable", and world citizens of diverse backgrounds, cultures, and countries (e.g., consisting of readers of all groups and categories, comprised of: atheists, agnostic, Jewish, Muslim, Christian, and all other religions and life philosophies of world citizen readers), to seek and pursue life strategies that promote personal and community and society health, safety, security, kindness, happiness, longevity, prosperity (spiritual prosperity especially), and God-respecting behavior, including respect for human rights and freedoms within the context of Bible-based values: ethical, moral, and righteous daily behavior, and demonstration of grace, mercy, and other values that have been shown to be beneficial and auspicious for countries and societies and all world citizens for thousands of years, delineated in the most published, most read, inspiring, and uplifting book ever in history, the Bible.

What are the "Imperative 'Age Of Reason' Enlightening Remedies For Rectification?"

In short, be humble enough to read the Bible, admit your sins in life, ask God for the forgiveness of your sins, request to be "reborn" in the likeness of God as described in the Torah and Bible, and sin no more (the goal) after being "reborn," accept that there is nothing you can do to "earn or deserve" to be redeemed by God and accepted and resurrected into heaven to be reunited with God your Creator. However, all humans can be reunited with God in heaven as a result of God sending his Son, Jesus Christ, to be crucified, though sinless, as a sacrifice to take on the sins of all humans on earth such that all humans may be forgiven and washed clean of their sins, if they accept Jesus Christ, God's Son, as their God-given sacrifice and pathway to being "reborn" in God's likeness and to start anew Godly behavior toward their fellow human beings while on earth, thereby gaining the opportunity for God to redeem them, and resurrect them to live with God in heaven for eternity!

CHAPTER TWO:

"X" (formerly known as "Twitter") Free Speech Suppression and Unjustified, Prejudiced, and Errant "Permanent Account Closures" For Those Whose Life Perspectives Differ From Employees Monitoring Posts On The Company Website, Or From That Of The C.E.O. And Company Board Members

Abraham Lincoln (1809-1865) served as the 16th President of the United States. He led the nation through the Civil War, preserved the Union, and issued the Emancipation Proclamation, which began the process of freedom for America's slaves. Lincoln's leadership and dedication to equality and democracy have left an enduring legacy[3][4].

In the paragraphs below, a true story is revealed regarding a shocking example of a social media company that, with a new chief executive officer who claimed to be a proponent of free speech, engaged in the harsh, excessive, and utterly intolerant suppression of free speech by another human who proposed and promoted Godly writing and manuscripts, books, and other sources of Godly insights, perspectives, family values, marital principles as created and defined by God between one man and one woman, and the existence of only two genders, male and female, in perpetuity.

This individual whose "Twitter" or "X" account was "permanently restricted from future posting on the "Twitter" or "X" website. (e.g., permanent free speech restriction by the "X" chief executive officer), was not only a Godly individual but also a true national patriot who served in the military for many years to defend and protect his country. This individual whose "Twitter" or "X" account was "permanently banned from ever making any posts online on the "X" website, was also an extremely well-balanced, healthy and fit, moral, ethical, kind, loving, caring, compassionate, merciful teacher, professor, and fantastic role model for other children and adults for the entirety of this individual's existence.

The reason this individual's "X" account was "permanently restricted from posting online forever in the future" was never justified or explained to this individual. The individual's account was restricted because of his religious and God-inspired instructive posts and references to God-inspired authors who wrote and published brilliant masterpiece novels. These novels referenced and defined marriage as a lifelong union created by God between one man and one woman.

At the time that this Godly and patriotic individual's "X" account was "permanently restricted from posting online forever in the future," the "X" company's chief executive officer, Elon Musk, spouse history consisted of two ex-wives, three marriages, and no known, current partner. Elon Musk is also the C.E.O. of Tesla, SpaceX, and other companies. Elon Musk has been divorced three times and has dated celebrities, including twins and triplets. His ex-wives are Justine Wilson and Talulah Riley (as of September 11, 2023). Elon Musk is a father of 11 children with three different women. The mother of three of the tech entrepreneur's children, the artist Grimes, recently filed a petition in court to establish parental rights after her split with Musk (as of October 5, 2023).

PARENTS
Who are Elon Musk's kids? His 11 children's names, ages and mothers

By

Brittany Miller

Updated July 24, 2023, 11:35 a.m. ET

Elon Musk's brood just keeps growing.

The Tesla mogul and one of his top Neuralink executives, Shivon Zilis, welcomed twins in November 2021, just one month before the arrival of his second child with on-again, off-again partner Grimes via surrogate.

The three newborns join Musk's seven other living children: Techno Mechanicus, Griffin, Vivian, Kai, Saxon, Damian and X.

Meet the billionaire businessman's kids and their mothers below.

Nevada Alexander Musk

After marrying in January 2000, Musk and Canadian author Justine Wilson welcomed son Nevada Alexander Musk in 2002. Nevada died of sudden infant death syndrome, or SIDS, at only 10 weeks.

Griffin and Vivian Musk

Elon Musk clowned around with his children in this 2017 photo.amberheard/Instagram

After losing their firstborn, Musk and Wilson turned to IVF to grow their family. She gave birth to twins Griffin and Vivian Musk in April 2004. Griffin and Vivian are now 18.

Vivian came out as transgender in June 2022 when she <u>filed a request to change her first name</u> and take the last name of her mom.

The filing listed the reason as "gender identity and the fact that I no longer live with or wish to be related to my biological father in any way, shape or form."

Kai, Saxon and Damian Musk

The former couple also used IVF to welcome triplet sons Kai, Saxon and Damian in January 2006. The trio are now 16.

Musk and Wilson divorced in 2008.

X AE A-XII Musk

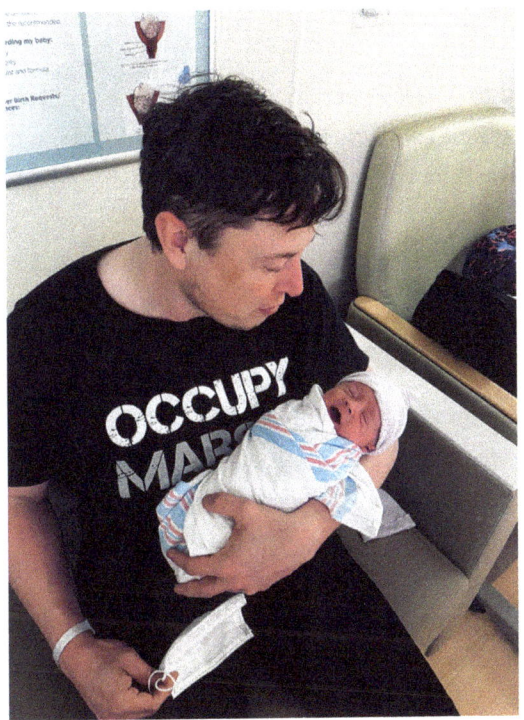

Musk welcomed his son X in 2020.

After two marriages to "Westworld" star Talulah Riley and a brief relationship with actress Amber Heard, Musk started dating singer Grimes in May 2018. She gave birth to their son, X AE A-XII, in May 2020. X is now 2.

X was originally named X Æ A-12, but "Æ" and "12" violated California law for not being part of the English alphabet, forcing his parents to change his name.

Page Six exclusively reported in September 2021 that Musk and Grimes had broken up.

Exa Dark Sideræl Musk

Grimes revealed in March 2022 that she and the SpaceX founder had welcomed his first daughter, the unusually named Exa Dark Sideræl Musk, via surrogate in December 2021. Exa was given the nickname Y after their other child being named X.

Grimes referred to Musk as her "boyfriend" in the bombshell Vanity Fair interview, though she called their relationship "fluid." Hours after the cover story was published, however, she tweeted that they had since split again.

The musician tweeted in March 2023 that her daughter goes by "Y now, or 'Why?' or just '?'" However, she admitted the "government won't recognize" the symbol.

Twins with Shivon Zilis

Musk quietly welcomed twins with Neuralink director of operations and special projects Shivon Zilis in November 2021, according to court documents obtained by Business Insider in July 2022.

The Twitter CEO and Zilis reportedly filed a petition to change the twins' names in order to "have their father's last name and contain their mother's last name as part of their middle name," which a judge in Austin, Texas, approved in May 2022.

The newborns' names are not yet known.

Techno Mechanicus

The tech giant secretly welcomed a third child with Grimes, named Techno Mechanicus, according to a book review published by the New York Times on Sept. 9, 2023, on Musk's soon-to-be-released biography, "Elon Musk."

Very little is known about the little one or when the kid might have been born.

Superheroes

The exes have nicknamed the child "Tau."

Should the free speech of this national patriot and Godly individual who was recommending God-inspired books by God-inspired authors to his friends and other contacts on the "X" website, be able to be permanently banned for life with no future ability to post on the "X" company website within the account setup on "X" by this patriotic and Godly individual, merely because the "X" company C.E.O. has a turbulent marriage history that resulted in 11 children from three different marriages and wives and has a history of 3 divorces?

The individual whose account was banned ("permanently") from future posts was never given specific reasons for banning and suppressing his constitutional right to freedom of speech nor allowed to appeal the decision. This is injustice in its purest and most raw form! Disappointing, discouraging, and disgusting suppression of freedom of speech by an American company unjustly directed at a religious and Godly American patriot and citizen! This was and is company misconduct, suppression of freedom of speech, and, devastatingly, disconnected this individual (whose account was permanently restricted from making any further posting or communicating with anyone on the company's website) from his friends, colleagues, and followers from around the world, which he had accumulated and been close friends with for many years. This was shocking, unacceptable, and blatant suppression of freedom of speech!

Another interesting and true story derives from another internet company, unrelated to "Twitter or X company," named "Doximity."

The author learned of a true account whereby a professional who created a profile on this website, after having posted a "30-year reunion weekend event" notice to approximately 200 of his past graduate school classmates, was then singled out and threatened by Doximity administrators and employees, and threatened to permanently close and delete their profile and website on their Doximity website.

They offered no opportunity for this individual to explain, justify, or account for this posting, and had this individual not succumbed to these tyrant Doximity administrators' and employees' suggestion (of course incorrect, but the only recourse available to this professional to rescue their website profile on Doximity from permanent shut down and banning closure for the remainder of the said individual's professional career, a devastating event), that this event was an "unknown spammer."

Hence, this individual then agreed to change both the username and password on the account (again, for no legitimate reason or purpose) to "prevent this spammer from sending a message to 200 people using this account in the future."

When internet companies and other large, wealthy companies can make these tyrant and dictator-like unilateral decisions and attacks on everyday and free speech communications, what makes them different from other nefarious and human rights suppressing countries "satanic, suppressive, ungodly, anti-leaders" like China's dictator and non-human rights affirming or supporting, President Xi Jinping, North Korea's dictator, Kim Jong Un, Iran's "Worldwide Terrorist Depot Anti-Leaders," and Venezuela's dictator, Nicolas Maduro?

Why are there no restrictions or laws that prevent companies, their employees, and company officers from unjust, unexplained, and "unappealable" decisions to suppress freedom of speech and "permanently restrict posts (free speech) by an individual who has violated no laws and whose intent, motivation, inspiration was to improve the life and happiness of all those being communicated with.

CHAPTER THREE:

"LinkedIn" (currently known as "Fake Defender of Free Speech") Free Speech Suppression and Unjustified, Prejudiced, and Errant "Permanent Account Closures" For Those Whose Life Perspectives Differ From Employees Who Are "Monitoring" (Censoring And Restricting Freedom Of Speech) Posts On Different Company's Websites, Or From That Of The C.E.O. And Company Board Members

George Washington (1732-1799) was the first President of the United States and is often referred to as the "Father of His Country." He led the Continental Army to victory over the British in the American Revolutionary War and presided over the Constitutional Convention of 1787. Washington's leadership set many precedents for the new nation[36].

A professional's free account on "LinkedIn" company website was rapidly and exponentially growing in popularity with a monthly increase in "followers" of approximately 20,000%, at which time, the "LinkedIn" company staff members began constantly badgering, harassing, and trying to coerce this individual to convert the account from the current free account to a paid monthly subscription account. This uncomfortable harassment continued for several months, with the free account holder declining to convert the account to a "SaaS" subscription. A "SaaS" subscription is a method of purchasing online software services where payments are made on a periodic basis, usually monthly, quarterly, or annually. This definition includes a couple of critical components: Software is being purchased as a service hosted and delivered online rather than hosted locally.

Shockingly, this individual's account was then abruptly, after multiple requests and refusals to convert the account from a free account (which was sufficient in the account owner's mind) to a paid monthly subscription account, and inappropriately permanently closed indefinitely. Again, the individual was never even given specific reasons for the banning and suppression of his constitutional right to free speech, nor was he allowed to appeal the decision. This is injustice in its purest and most raw form! Disappointing, discouraging, and disgusting suppression of freedom of speech by another American company unjustly directed at public service professionals and American citizens!

Why are there no restrictions or laws that prevent companies, their employees, and company officers from unjust, unexplained, and "unappealable" decisions to suppress freedom of speech and "permanently restrict posts (free speech) by an individual who has violated no laws and whose intent, motivation, inspiration was to improve the life and happiness of all those being communicated with.

Microsoft owns LinkedIn. Anyone who believes that Microsoft does not actively suppress free speech, especially of conservative, religious Americans, is misinformed and incorrect!

This individual was extremely disappointed that Microsoft canceled his account because it was an extremely popular ("viral" in a positive sense, especially with the benevolent frequent posts that were being created by the account owner each week, which inspired, encouraged, enlightened, and motivated his friends and colleagues on the website) and rapidly growing account, with exponential monthly growth in followers and colleagues, and because the individual refused to be "strong-armed" and coerced into paying for a different monthly subscription (which the individual did not want or need).

This was company misconduct, suppression of freedom of speech, and abruptly disconnected the individual from his friends, colleagues, and followers from around the world; in a word, unacceptable!

Microsoft must be closely monitored, especially in the artificial intelligence era, especially after witnessing the covert scandal when the chief executive officer from the company "OpenAI" was fired by the company board members, then, interestingly, the chief executive officer of Microsoft, without any hesitation or investigation, immediately offered to hire this individual (and all other employees whom he could pilfer from this suddenly disturbed, disrupted, and confused company, Open A.I., including their board members.

The reason or reasons the chief executive officer from the company "OpenAI" was fired was never openly disclosed in the initial several weeks after this chaotic event, yet the chief executive officer of Microsoft was never concerned with any potential ethical or moral violations or other criminal acts that the "OpenAI" chief executive officer (C.E.O.) may have or actually committed.

This total lack of regard for ethical, moral behavior and concomitant obsession with artificial intelligence "know-how" and experience that this "OpenAI" chief executive officer possessed, showed the world that Microsoft, and many other large technology companies often, if not always, place earnings and future profits far above (and perhaps totally out of reach from their lowest priority concern for ethical and moral behavior of their current or future prospective employees), any concern they may have for an active and ongoing allegation or investigation into possible unethical or immoral or criminal behavior by an otherwise intelligent person they have an interest or desire to hire for their company.

An executive from OpenAI, an artificial intelligence startup into which Microsoft had invested a reported thirteen billion dollars, was calling to explain that within the next twenty minutes, the company's board would announce that it had fired Sam Altman, OpenAI's C.E.O. and co-founder. (December 1, 2023)

According to multiple people familiar with the board's thinking who asked not to be identified discussing private conversations, the directors' move was the culmination of months spent mulling issues around Altman's strategic maneuvering and a perceived lack of transparency in his communications with directors. (December 9, 2023)

TECHNOLOGY UPDATED NOV. 22, 2023

Why Was Sam Altman Fired As CEO of OpenAI?

Superheroes

By Chas Danner, staff editor at Intelligencer

Sam Altman at the APEC CEO Summit in San Francisco on Thursday. Photo: Justin Sullivan/Getty Images

Sam Altman is going back to OpenAI after he was fired last week, the company announced late Tuesday. His four days of his exile were nothing short of whiplash-inducing: deposed as CEO for mysterious reasons, then almost rehired over the weekend, then poached by Microsoft to run a new artificial intelligence effort following a second leadership shakeup at OpenAI that cleared a path for him to return. Below is what we know about this still-developing situation and why it all went down.

The return of the king

Altman posted on X early Wednesday morning that he is returning to the company he co-founded, after the board of directors that booted him was replaced.

While the old board represented OpenAI's non-profit beginnings, the new board will include major names in the world of business and tech — guys like former Treasury Secretary Larry Summers, Quora CEO Adam D'Angelo, and former Salesforce co-CEO Bret Taylor, who chaired the Twitter board prior to Elon Musk's leveraged buyout.

Sign up for Dinner Party

A lively evening newsletter about everything that just happened.

Top of Form

Bottom of Form

In his statement, Altman said that he was going back to OpenAI with the support of Microsoft CEO Satya Nadella, who hired him on Sunday to lead an AI research wing at the computing giant. "We are encouraged by the changes to the OpenAI board," Nadella tweeted early Wednesday morning. "We believe this is a first essential step on a path to more stable, well-informed, and effective governance." Stable board leadership is certainly important to Microsoft, which has invested some $13 billion in OpenAI.

A shocking power-struggle roller coaster

Altman's dismissal on Friday followed what OpenAI said was a "deliberative review process by the board, which concluded that he was not consistently candid in his communications with them, hindering its ability to exercise its responsibilities." As a result, the company said at the time, "the board no longer has confidence in his ability to continue leading OpenAI." Soon after, president and Altman ally Greg Brockman — whom the board had removed as chairman — resigned, as did three senior researchers. All were set to join Altman at Microsoft, as were as many as hundreds of other employees.

But the drama wasn't over. On Tuesday, the latest interim CEO, Emmett Shear, reportedly told the board that he will step down if they do not provide a clear explanation and evidence for why Altman was fired.

On Monday, the Verge reported that Altman and Brockman were still willing to come back through those OpenAI doors, if the remaining board members who axed Altman stepped down:

The promised mass exodus of virtually every OpenAI employee — including board member and chief scientist Ilya Sutskever, who led the initial move to depose Altman! — means that there is more pressure on the board than ever, with only two of the three remaining members needing to flip. Altman posted on X that "we are all going to work together some way or other," which we are told is meant to indicate that the fight continues.

Altman, former president Brockman, and the company's investors are still trying to find a graceful exit for the board, say multiple sources with direct knowledge of the situation. The sources characterized the hiring announcement by Microsoft, which needed to have a resolution to the crisis before the stock market opened on Monday, as a "holding pattern."

During a pair of television interviews on Monday night, Microsoft CEO Satya Nadella said that whether or not Altman and OpenAI staffers would become Microsoft employees was "for the OpenAI board and management and employees to choose." He added that his company expected governance changes at OpenAI, and that the partnership between the two companies "depends on the people at OpenAI staying there or coming to Microsoft, so I'm open to both options." Nadella also spoke with Kara Swisher about the future of his partnership with Altman and OpenAI, which Microsoft is heavily invested in.

Soon after Altman was fired, OpenAI investors had launched an effort to get Altman reinstated and the board began talking to Altman about bringing him back, though he was reportedly "ambivalent" about returning and would expect significant governance changes if that happened.

Altman — backed by leading shareholders in OpenAI, including Microsoft and Thrive Capital — wanted the entire board replaced and had already started making plans to start a new company with other newly departed OpenAI employees. In-person talks between OpenAI's board and Altman continued through Sunday, and there were signs the board would agree to Altman's terms. The board balked, instead, and OpenAI announced that Shear, formerly of Twitch, would replace the interim CEO. Not long after, Nadella announced that the company had hired Altman and Brockman to launch a new advanced-AI research team with Altman as leader.

Altman responded to Nadella's announcement on X/Twitter.

On Monday, more than 500 of OpenAI's 700 employees sent an open letter to the three remaining board members who had voted to oust Altman and threatened to jump ship if they didn't resign and reinstate him. The signatories included many senior executives, including Sutskever, the chief scientist who reportedly pushed the effort to replace Altman, and CTO Mira Murati, whom the board had originally named interim CEO.

Altman subsequently published tweets heaping praise on the remaining OpenAI leaders and said he looked forward to continuing to work together "some way or other":

Altman then insisted that he and Nadella's "top priority remains to ensure OpenAI continues to thrive" — which would have been hard if more than 72 percent of the company's workforce is about to walk.

The coup

The upheaval at OpenAI has shocked the tech world given what Altman, 38, had accomplished in a few short years. While tech giants such as Google have been working for years to develop artificial intelligence, OpenAI catapulted in front of them when it unveiled ChatGPT last November. The chatbot demonstrated abilities never before released to the general public — like being capable of writing a lot more like a human. Immediately gaining 100 million users, ChatGPT helped OpenAI raise billions of dollars, sent Google reeling, and put AI at the center of the tech industry. It also made Altman an overnight celebrity, and he was happy to play the role, presenting himself as a visionary if slightly weary face of what AI might mean for humanity.

On Friday, the company initially announced that co-founder Greg Brockman would step down as chairman of the board but remain in his role as president of the company. Not long after, Brockman announced that he was quitting and tweeted that the board fired Altman minutes before announcing the leadership "transition" to the world.

There may have been other factors, but Altman's firing blindsided everyone, and the OpenAI board has not provided any additional details to curb the confusion. As Platformer's Casey Newton aptly noted on Monday night, the information vacuum clearly benefited the media savvy Altman:

In their silence, the board ensured that Altman became the protagonist and hero of this story. Altman's strategic X posts, cleverly coordinated with his many allies at the company, gave him the appearance of a deposed elected official about to be swept back into power by the sheer force of his popularity.

So why did the board turn on Altman?

Kara Swisher dug into the situation on Friday night, reporting out what she was hearing from inside the company along with her own analysis, via a series of threads on X/Twitter:

[As] I understand it, it was a "misalignment" of the profit versus nonprofit adherents at the company. The developer day was an issue. Sources tell me that the profit direction of the company under Altman and the speed of development, which could be seen as too risky, and the nonprofit side dedicated to more safety and caution were at odds. One person on the Sam side called it a "coup," while another said it was the right move. This seems more plausible, but the tech community is also rife with rumors of all kinds, some really out there. A lot of questionable incoming, for sure …

Sources tell me chief scientist Ilya Sutskever was at the center of this. Increasing tensions with Sam Altman and Greg Brockman over role and influence and he got the board on his side. The developer day and how the store was introduced was in inflection moment of Altman pushing too far, too fast. My bet: He'll have a new company up by Monday …

The board members who voted against Altman felt he was manipulative and headstrong and wanted to do what he wanted to do. That sounds like a typical Silicon Valley CEO to me, but this might not be a typical Silicon Valley company. They certainly have a lot of explaining to do. Would be eager to hear actual specifics of their concerns and also evidence that they tried to inform him if they had problems and gave him a chance to respond and change. If not, it looks cloddish.

The Verge's Alex Heath heard the same about Sutskever's role and reports that Altman has been exploring outside business endeavors for some time:

And on Tuesday, the Wall Street *Journal* reported that Sutskever was the person who told Altman that he'd been fired. The Information reports that Sutskever faced blowback from employees during an all-hands meeting after the news came out on Friday, and that he acknowledged how his actions could be interpreted as a coup, though he didn't see it that way. On Monday morning, Sutskever publicly apologized for his role in the upheaval:

On Saturday morning, OpenAI chief operating officer Brad Lightcap sent a memo to employees letting them know that the company was still talking to the board to try to understand why it axed Altman. "We can say definitively that the board's decision was not made in response to malfeasance, or anything related to our financial, business, safety, or security/privacy practices," he wrote. "This was a breakdown in communication between Sam and the board."

Shear announced in a statement on Sunday night that he would, in the next 30 days, "hire an independent investigator to dig into the entire process leading up to this point and generate a full report." (He apparently hasn't been able to obtain written documentation of why the board dismissed Altman.) Per the Verge, employees are giving Shear the cold shoulder regardless:

Employees at the company's San Francisco headquarters refused to attend an emergency all-hands scheduled on Sunday with new CEO Emmett Shear, according to a person familiar with the matter, who added that they responded to the announcement in OpenAI's Slack with a "fuck you" emoji.

The New York *Times*' Kevin Roose notes several specific factors that played a role in the drama, including how Altman didn't have the same protections that other tech founders have enjoyed:

The ouster was only possible because of OpenAI's unusual corporate governance structure. OpenAI started in 2015 as a nonprofit and in 2019 created a capped-profit subsidiary — a novel arrangement in which investors' returns are limited to a certain amount above their initial investment. But it retained the nonprofit's mission, and it gave the nonprofit's board the power to govern the activities of the capped-profit entity, including firing the chief executive. Unlike some other tech founders, who keep control of their companies via dual-class stock structures, Mr. Altman doesn't directly own any shares in OpenAI.

Roose also explains why OpenAI's board is unique:

It's small (six members before Friday, and four without Mr. Altman and Mr. Brockman) and includes several A.I. experts who hold no shares in the company. Its directors do not have the responsibility of maximizing value for shareholders, as most corporate boards do, but are instead bound to a fiduciary duty to create "safe A.G.I." — artificial general intelligence — "that is broadly beneficial." At least two of the board members, Tasha McCauley and Helen Toner, have ties to the Effective Altruism movement, a utilitarian-inspired group that has pushed for A.I. safety research and raised alarms that a powerful A.I. system could one day lead to human extinction.

How Altman initially responded

Altman, in a tweet soon after he was fired, said he "loved" his time at the company, which he called "transformative." He also praised his former colleagues:

Then later, Altman tweeted that "if i start going off, the OpenAI board should go after me for the full value of my shares." (Altman had no equity in the company.) On Saturday, the Information reported that Altman has been telling investors he intends to launch a new AI venture with Brockman expected to join him:

[Altman] has been in discussions with semiconductor executives, including chip designer Arm, on Friday morning about early efforts to design new chips that would lower costs for large-language model companies like OpenAI, a person familiar with the talks said. That effort would likely take years. It couldn't be learned whether Altman was representing OpenAI or a separate venture in the discussions …

In the past, Altman has also talked to investors about the importance of building a "full-stack" AI startup that's also involved in chip development, another person familiar with the matter said.

What others are saying

There has been plenty of speculation and commentary about what happened at OpenAI:

And of course somebody asked OpenAI's chatbot, ChatGPT, what it thought had happened — and it guessed there was likely "more to the story":

In September, *New York*'s Elizabeth Weil profiled Altman and highlighted the numerous anxieties about him and his role in the AI revolution:

By Altman's own assessment — discernible in his many blog posts, podcasts, and video events — we should feel good but not great about him as our AI leader. As he understands himself, he's a plenty-smart-but-not-genius "technology brother" with an Icarus streak and a few outlier traits. First, he possesses, he has said, "an absolutely delusional level of self-confidence." Second, he commands a prophetic grasp of "the arc of technology and societal change on a long time horizon." Third, as a Jew, he is both optimistic and expecting the worst. Fourth, he's superb at assessing risk because his brain doesn't get caught up in what other people think.

On the downside: He's neither emotionally nor demographically suited for the role into which he's been thrust. "There could be someone who enjoyed it more," he admitted on the *Lex Fridman Podcast* in March. "There could be someone who's much more charismatic." He's aware that he's "pretty disconnected from the reality of life for most people." He is also, on occasion, tone-deaf. For instance, like many in the tech bubble, Altman uses the phrase "median human," as in, "For me, AGI" — artificial general intelligence — "is the equivalent of a median human that you could hire as a co-worker."

In addition, she wrote:

[I]t can be hard to parse who Altman is, really; how much we should trust him; and the extent to which he's integrating others' concerns, even when he's on a stage with the intention of quelling them. Altman said he would try to slow the revolution down as much as he could. Still, he told the assembled, he believed that it would be okay. Or likely be okay. We — a tiny word with royal overtones that was doing a lot of work in his rhetoric — should just "decide what we want, decide we're going to enforce it, and accept the fact that the future is going to be very different and probably wonderfully better."

This post has been updated to include additional reporting and commentary.

CHAPTER FOUR:

"Facebook" and "Instagram" (never known as politically unbiased media companies and never even attempting to be a "Fake Defender of Free Speech"), Free Speech Suppression and Unjustified, Prejudiced, and Errant "Permanent Account Closures" For Those Whose Life Perspectives Differ From Employees Monitoring Posts On The Company Website, Or From That Of The C.E.O. And Company Board Members, and the Facebook Presidential Election Scandal

Martin Luther King Jr. (1929-1968) was a Baptist minister and civil rights leader who played a pivotal role in the American civil rights movement. He advocated for nonviolent resistance and led numerous campaigns to end racial segregation and promote equality. His famous "I Have a Dream" speech remains a symbol of the fight for civil rights[7][8].

Instagram Suppression of Free Speech of a God-respecting, Motivating, and Inspiring Mentor

If any human or "World Citizen" in this century and all future generations and centuries needs verification and indisputable evidence to support their daily "Superhero" perspectives, intents, endeavors, and proactive behaviors and actions to battle and defeat the everyday enemies, terrorists, and striving assassins who attempt daily to suppress God-respecting, moral, ethical, benevolent, motivating, and inspiring humans whose goals are, in direct opposition to these malevolent characters, to improve this world while, at the same time, discourage narcissism, materialistic aspirations, selfishness, liberal and radical perspectives, attitudes, goals, actions, and behaviors of individuals, politicians, and large media and "God-disrespecting fake news" agencies, then please memorize and never forget the paragraph below.

One month before the publication of the free speech masterpiece nonfiction novel, "Superheroes: Becoming The Truly Elite And Honorable" was published, an individual who was a tremendous world-enhancing mentor on Instagram (parent company, Facebook) who created an account 3 years in the past not for fame or recognition but for the opportunity to recruit all "World Citizens" from all countries, cultures, and religions to this website address, and then enlighten them with over 500 music reels promoting novels that promote health, peace, serenity, cooperation, working together in unselfish, non-narcissistic, and non-materialistic ways to improve the plights and zenith happiness of all "World Citizens" during their journeys through life, and, furthermore, this benevolent mentor amassed and endeared approximately ten thousand communicators and followers over these three years as a result of being a wise, kind, and loving mentor, and then experienced the cancellation and shut-down of this account, with no opportunity to appeal this decision, and with no communicated nor documented nor delineated reasons whatsoever.

Superheroes

A doctorate-level professional started a "Facebook" company account and website profile and was highly successful in connecting with many friends and colleagues over many years. The individual had a tremendous number of followers. Then, Facebook randomly, abruptly, and permanently shut down access to the account without explanation or the right to appeal ever being offered or otherwise given to the website's "supposed" (but apparently not in reality) owner of the website's benevolent, pro-American, moral, ethical, motivational, and inspirational masterfully written and other created content meant to benefit everyone in the world.

This was a wholly unwarranted and inappropriate action and decision by the "Facebook" company, which was the administrator of the individual's "free" (but obviously not "freedom of speech") account and professional website profile. The public service professional was a very respectful and religious man. The "Facebook" company employees (must have) despised the individual, perhaps because they were neither very respectful (definitely true) nor religious (suspected) and, therefore, unilaterally and abruptly, again without explanation, conversation, or offering any opportunity for the individual account holder to respond to the announced "permanent account closure and restriction from login forever in the future," and offered no option for the individual to appeal the account closure to re-open the account.

This individual was so frustrated and disappointed in the unethical, biased, unexplained, inappropriate account closure and disconnection of the individual from hundreds of classmates, friends, family members, and professional colleagues that this individual then vowed to perhaps never trust this company (due to their lack of principles, and absent ethical and moral behavior and actions) that acted in such a highly erratic, unpredictable, unprofessional, and absolutely "unAmerican" (but perhaps in a "pro-North Korean," "pro-Iranian," "pro-Russian," or "pro-Chinese (all of which are communist or other sinister mindset and behaving dictatorial government leadership regimes who respect no human rights or freedoms for and on behalf of their citizens)," manner.

More than a decade later, "Facebook" was justifiably labeled as a "politically-biased liberal, freedom of speech suppressing company" (especially of religious conservatives of all levels of education, even doctorate level health and experts in myriad other occupations and fields attempting to speak the truth and post their professional input, research, findings, and opinions on "Facebook" to refute false narrative being unethically espoused and shouted by radical and liberals whose goal was to suppress all logical and scientific recommendations, opinions, and other viewpoints that were contrary to these liberals false narratives and politically-biased lies that were being allowed without any restrictions by "Facebook").

"Facebook" employees disappointingly, repeatedly, and consistently refused to listen, hear, accurately read, and seriously consider new posts as possible and likely true and accurate statements or allow these postings from conservative citizens on the company's website.

Facebook was blatantly suppressing freedom of speech from religious conservative citizens of the world during campaigns and reins of terror by radical and liberal (and in some cases, anti-American) politicians, e.g., Barrack Obama, Hilary Clinton, Joseph Biden, who attempted to destroy the pride, honor, reputation, history of American benevolence and simultaneously replace these facts and qualities and descriptions with hateful, anti-American disrespect and speeches throughout the world, in addition to attempting to divide united Americans into evil and divisive and racist categories based on skin color and attempts to convince American adults and children that they can (false narrative for sure) change the sex they were assigned at birth by God.

"Facebook" employees and the C.E.O. were exceedingly corrupt in their behavior, including creating illegal ballot boxes in certain states and suppressing corruption news and coercion and embezzlement of money from foreign countries (e.g., Ukraine and China) by Hunter Biden and Joseph Biden, which in an ethical, moral country without severe corruption and election interference, would have resulted in the prosecution and imprisonment of both these corrupt and criminal individuals, effectively nullifying Joseph Biden from even being eligible to run for the United States Presidency.

Thanks to the corrupt and dishonest "Facebook" company and other large, corrupt, liberal media companies' suppression of the New York Post front page newspaper article detailing these Biden family crimes, Joseph and Hunter Biden never served prison time for their crimes, and Joseph Biden was despicably, corruptly, and fraudulently made a (dementia was evident and obvious, at the time of his utter failed and corrupt presidential "noncampaign") candidate (ineligible if our country had demonstrated any morality and ethical behavior with standards of truth and honesty versus only corrupt politics which dominated the election) for the United States Presidential election, then ballot fraud, ballot scanners fraud, and fake ballots stored in warehouses which were used during and, despicably weeks after, election day to alter and fraudulently overturn all ballot counts in states where Donald Trump was sure to win and be successfully (and "truthfully; a word despised and shunned by corrupt "democratic" politician leaders in this generation) re-elected as was the desire of the vast majority of America.

All perceptive and true American patriots and religious conservatives who possess insight and intelligence were clearly able to observe that Joseph Biden was unqualified, corrupt, demented, and more appropriate for a prison cell than the United States President's Oval Office. These perceptive and true American patriots were then crushed to see that evil politics intervened and defeated past (and fondly reminisced) traditional American values, including morality, truth, non-criminal and Godly, ethical behavior, and actions.

During political "elections, "Facebook" repeatedly chooses to side with "evil and corrupt liberal political figures" (note the word "leaders" was not used and not appropriate) to post unproven or unsubstantiated liberal individual's false narratives and lies without any valid research, and chose, conversely, to always restrict posts and true statements by expert doctorate level health leaders, government leaders, religious leaders, and all conservative leaders and individuals who attempted to post opinions that were "contrary to Facebook's C.E.O. and other employees' (unsubstantiated) opinions" or perhaps the opinions of those "evil and corrupt liberal political figures" that they were in cahoots with and who instructed them on what misinformation to post regarding their political opponents and what false narratives to repeat incessantly and promote.

Liberal and corrupt politicians were clearly embraced and promoted by "Facebook" in a disgusting, anti-religious, and anti-American manner. "Facebook" created and defended false narratives on purpose to damage the reputations of their conservative, religious, and political opponents, a genuinely evil yet highly overt, visible, historical recounting of history as seen by conservative, law-abiding, patriotic, religious citizens of every country in the world!

To this day, "Facebook" continues to limit posts daily, and restrict conservatives' accounts for days or weeks, randomly (one would like to assume but unfortunately probably politically biased instead), in order to accomplish their ongoing (non-God-respecting, unethical) goals of "controlling (their radical, liberal, anti-religious, anti-conservative, and, in essence, anti-American Christian benevolent values) the narrative (false and devastating to Americans and all religious citizens throughout the world), especially during political election times when they must choose leaders who will not investigate or prosecute them for the saboteur-like Anti-American and anti-religious activities they engage in on a daily basis via their ability and prowess in suppression of freedom of speech when it matters the most, namely, during political elections of country government officials in the United States of America and in every other country in the world!

Extremely annoying and continuing up to this present day, both Facebook and Instagram continue to restrict posts on both websites and, in both a tyrant and monopolistic manner, often subsequently and annoyingly, completely shut down posting any messages for several hours or 1 week or more depending on the fickle, prejudice, biased, and (unqualified and uncertified) judgmental nature or pet peeves or idiosyncrasies of these two company's liberal and ungodly monitoring employees who might be working that particular day or night of the week that various posts on both websites are be placed, and these frequent account posting restrictions (acts of suppression of free speech), annoying and irritating as they are, are always inflicted unilaterally, as one would expect from a despot, evil monarch, tyrant or dictator, e.g., similar to, if not identical to, the expected unilateral suppression of free speech that one would anticipate and rightfully expect from Russia's President, Vladimir Putin, China's President, Xi Jinping, North Korea's President, Kim Jong Un, or even Venezuela's President, Nicolas Maduro, and each violation of free speech (also known as "account posting restriction for many hours or days"), which occurs much more frequently for individuals posting (or at least attempting to post, prior to being restricted almost daily), Christian messages which are inspiring, uplifting, or otherwise society-improving revelations and enlightening posts.

What is the Facebook presidential scandal?

In the 2010s, personal data belonging to millions of Facebook users was collected without their consent by British consulting firm Cambridge Analytica, predominantly to be used for political advertising.

What information was leaked from Facebook?

The April 2021 leak exposed the phone numbers, locations, and birthdates of Facebook users on the platform from 2018 to 2019. (November 28, 2022)

Did Facebook break the law?

The F.T.C. argues in its suit that Facebook obtained a monopoly in social networking and maintained it illegally by acquiring rivals. The lawsuit focuses on the company's acquisitions of Instagram for $1 billion in 2012 and WhatsApp for $19 billion in 2014. (January 11, 2022)

When was the Facebook scandal?

The Facebook-Cambridge Analytica data privacy scandal details. Facebook experienced its biggest crisis ever in March of 2018 when a cache of documents inside Cambridge Analytica made its way into the hands of the New York Times.

What is the Facebook unethical scandal?

Cambridge Analytica was a political consulting firm that specialized in leveraging data mining techniques in order to help its clients expand potential voter bases. The scandal involved Cambridge Analytica's exploitation of the raw data of over 87 million Facebook profiles that Facebook negligently protected.

Why is Facebook being sued by 48 states?

WASHINGTON (A.P.) — The U.S. government and 48 states and districts sued Facebook Wednesday, accusing it of abusing its market power in social networking to crush smaller competitors and seeking remedies that could include a forced spinoff of the social network's Instagram and WhatsApp messaging services. (December 9, 2020)

Has anyone tried to sue Facebook?

In July 2022, a former Army vet and member of Facebook's escalation team sued Facebook. The lawsuit claimed that Facebook introduced a tool in 2019 to allow staff access to deleted Messenger data and that this data was sometimes shared with law enforcement.

What is the Facebook Privacy Scandal 2018?

On March 17, 2018, the Guardian and New York Times broke the story about a Cambridge Analytica whistleblower, saying that the company had utilized 50 million Facebook profiles to do their modeling. Facebook tried to pre-empt the stories by announcing it had suspended access to everything on Facebook for Cambridge (March 16, 2023)

What was Facebook sued for political?

Facebook users can apply for their portion of a $725 million lawsuit settlement. The settlement stems from a lawsuit alleging Facebook developers sold user data to Cambridge Analytica, a former political consulting firm, to target people in the 2016 U.S. presidential election. (April 20, 2023)

How many people have filed against Facebook?

Plaintiffs' co-counsel Lesley Weaver claimed the 28 million applications is "the largest number of claims ever filed in a class action in the United States." Law360 reported that Chhabria said he was "blown away" by the massive number of claims.

What did Mark Zuckerberg do that was unethical?

Over the past decade, Mark Zuckerberg's Facebook has received widespread criticism for what many characterize as unethical business practices: abusing user data, using algorithms that spread misinformation, and knowingly harming people's mental health. (April 20, 2023)

How did Facebook violate privacy?

There have been allegations by some users that Facebook's mobile app is capable of listening to conversations without consent, citing instances of the service displaying advertisements for products that they had only spoken about and had otherwise had no prior interactions with.

BY [PHILIP MARCELO](#)

Published 3:20 PM PST, November 7, 2023

Share

CLAIM: A CNN broadcast captured an Ohio woman illegally placing multiple ballots into a drop box on Election Day.

A.P.'S ASSESSMENT: Missing context. In the video, which is from October 31, 2020, the woman appears to be placing at least three ballots in a drop box as CNN is filming. Election officials and government watchdog groups in Ohio say there's nothing inherently illegal about placing that many ballots in the box. The only requirement is that the ballots all must be from family members.

THE FACTS: As Ohio voters headed to the polls Tuesday for an off-year election, social media users shared a news clip they claim captures mail ballot fraud in action in the bellwether state.

The CNN clip shows national correspondent Gary Tuchman standing in front of a ballot drop box in the parking lot of the Cuyahoga County Board of Elections office while wearing a facemask.

OTHER NEWS

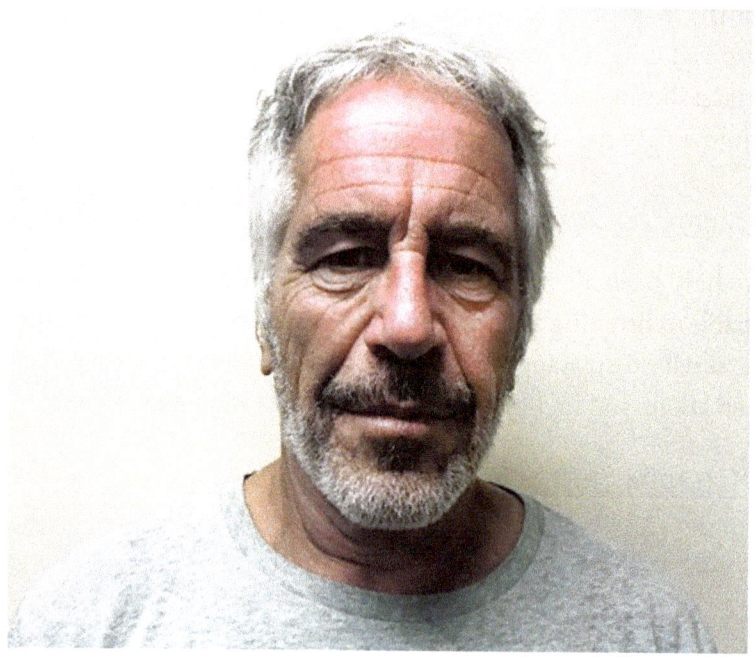

NOT REAL NEWS: A look at what didn't happen this week

Images made to look like court records circulate online amid Epstein document release

False claims question Haley's eligibility to serve as US president

As he's speaking to the camera, a woman pulls up in a minivan and begins placing some of the papers she has in her hand into the ballot box. Tuchman jokingly asks if she voted for Ronald Regan or Jimmy Carter, to which she responds, "Carter."

"CNN accidentally caught a woman stuffing a ballot box," the text over the brief clip reads. "Watch how quick they pan away when they realize what she's doing."

"Nothing to see here folks," wrote one Instagram user who shared the video.

But there's nothing to suggest the woman, who is not identified on the clip, was doing anything suspicious under state law, said local election officials and government watchdog groups.

They say she's holding at least three ballots, which is within her legal right to submit, so long as they're from approved family members.

The video also dates to 2020 and isn't from the current election, as the posts seem to imply.

Indeed CNN's chyron running along the bottom of the video reads, "Trump, Biden vie for Ohio with 2.5M+ votes already cast," showing it was from when then President Donald Trump lost his bid for re-election to Joe Biden.

Anthony Perlatti, director of the Cuyahoga County Board of Elections, said the maroon-colored design of the state's ballot return envelope can be readily seen on the paper she's holding in her right hand and the two in her left hand.

The other papers don't appear to be ballots, he said.

Ohio law permits people to hand in completed absentee, or mail, ballots for relatives, including their spouse, father, mother, father-in-law, mother-in-law, grandfather, grandmother, brother, sister, son, daughter, adopting parent, adopted child, stepparent, stepchild, uncle, aunt, nephew, or niece.

Melanie Amato, a spokesperson for Ohio Secretary of State Frank LaRose, agreed that an individual dropping off two or three absentee ballots isn't itself a crime.

"Can't say what is happening here, BUT she is not doing anything illegal IF she is returning ballots from family members," she wrote in an email.

Catherine Turcer, executive director of Common Cause Ohio, added that in 2020, while the coronavirus pandemic was at its peak, many Ohio residents opted to vote absentee with one person in a family or household dropping off the ballots.

"I wouldn't assume that the voter was doing something wrong," she wrote in an email. "Voters drop off ballots for parents, adult children, and spouses."

Tom Sutton, a political science professor at Baldwin Wallace University in Berea, a Cleveland suburb, noted that state law doesn't limit how many ballots from family members can be deposited at one time.

A person could, theoretically, deliver one or more ballots for each of the 19 categories of family members listed under state law, he said.

CNN spokesperson Emily Kuhn, meanwhile, confirmed the video was from the cable news network's election coverage in 2020.

But due to social distancing rules in effect at the time and the angle of his live shot, Tuchman didn't see the woman putting anything into the box while live on air, she said.

This is part of AP's effort to address widely shared misinformation, including work with outside companies and organizations to add factual context to misleading content that is circulating online. Learn more about fact-checking at AP.

PHILIP MARCELO

Marcelo writes for AP Fact Check and is based in New York. He was previously a general assignment reporter in AP's Boston bureau, where he focused on race and immigration.

How Private Money From Facebook's CEO Saved The 2020 Election

DECEMBER 8, 2020 5:12 AM ET

HEARD ON ALL THINGS CONSIDERED

FROM

APMreports.

By

Tom Scheck,
Geoff Hing,
Sabby Robinson,
Gracie Stockton

- LISTEN 4:46 4-Minute Listen **PLAYLIST**

Embed

Detroit election workers count absentee ballots for the 2020 general election at TCF Center on Nov. 4. Election offices around the U.S. say they couldn't have carried out this year's challenging election without help from a nonprofit tied to Facebook CEO Mark Zuckerberg.

Jeff Kowalsky/AFP via Getty Images

Bill Turner knew he had a tough job. He took over as acting director of voter services in Chester County, Pa., in September, just two months before a divisive presidential election amid a pandemic. A huge voter turnout was expected, and COVID-19 required election managers like Turner to handle mail-in ballots on a scale they'd never seen and confront the threat of their staffers becoming sick.

These challenges had forced many election offices to burn through their budgets months earlier. Turner had previously served as the county's emergency manager, experience that seemed apt for overseeing an election that many observers feared would become a catastrophe.

Mark Zuckerberg, the founder and CEO of Facebook, and Priscilla Chan, his wife, donated $350 million to a nonprofit that gave grants to election officials around the United States.

Ian Tuttle/Getty Images

With a tight budget and little help from the federal government, Chester County applied for an election grant from the Center for Tech and Civic Life, a previously small Chicago-based nonprofit that quickly amassed hundreds of millions of dollars in donations to help local election offices — most notably, $350 million from Facebook CEO Mark Zuckerberg and his wife, Priscilla Chan.

"Honestly, I don't know what we would have done without it," Turner said.

The coronavirus pandemic — and Congress' neglect — necessitated an unprecedented bailout of election offices with private money funneled through the little-known nonprofit. And the money proved indispensable.

Turner is one of 25 election directors from swing states interviewed by <u>APM Reports</u> who said the grant money was essential to preventing an election meltdown amid worries over a pandemic and a president who continues to openly question — without evidence — the legitimacy of the process.

The Center for Tech and Civic Life gave grants to more than 2,500 jurisdictions this year to help departments pay for election administration. The money arrived as historically underfunded election department budgets were sapped from unforeseen purchases during the primaries and were forced to spend money on election workers, postage and printing for the increasing number of voters who wanted to vote by mail.

The nonprofit gave Chester County $2.5 million for the election, which is more than the county's 2020 budget for voting services.

Chester County is one of several large suburban counties that ring Philadelphia — once-Republican strongholds that have shifted in Democrats' favor in recent years. Pennsylvania was pivotal to Joe Biden's victory over President Trump, and his win in the state was fueled in part by his success in Chester County. He won it by 17 percentage points — nearly double Hillary Clinton's margin four years earlier.

Turner used the grant to buy 14 drop boxes for ballots, pay staff to watch those sites and purchase body cameras that recorded employees collecting ballots from the drop boxes. He also spent a large portion of the grant on additional equipment and people to ensure that ballots were mailed out and counted quickly. The county processed 150,000 mail ballots for the November election in 36 hours. Without the new equipment and personnel, he said, it would have taken a week or longer.

YouTube

"This grant really was a lifesaver in allowing us to do more, efficiently and expeditiously," he said. "It probably would have taken a very long time if we didn't have the resources to do this."

Election precinct cases containing ballots, election materials and keys to voting machines are held under guard by the Allegheny County Police at the Allegheny County elections warehouse on Nov. 4 in Pittsburgh.

Jeff Swensen/Getty Images

The private money was needed in part because the federal government hadn't provided enough funding. Congress allocated $400 million in March for election services, but that was just a tenth of what some officials said was needed.

"Despite election officials basically begging our federal government for assistance, that money never came through," said Liz Howard, with the Brennan Center for Justice at New York University. "Congress really failed our election officials."

With little action from Congress, the private sector, led by Zuckerberg and Chan, stepped up. The couple awarded $400 million to nonprofits for election assistance — with most of it going to the Center for Tech and Civic Life.

The full extent of the grants isn't known. The Center for Tech and Civic Life declined repeated interview requests from APM Reports to discuss the funding and how it was used. In late October, the group listed the jurisdictions that received funding on its website but didn't disclose dollar amounts or funding priorities for each jurisdiction.

But through a series of interviews, public records requests and a review of public meetings, APM Reports pieced together the details of grant awards in the five swing states that decided the election. APM Reports obtained more than 30 applications and grant agreements between local election offices and the Center for Tech and Civic Life. The documents show requests mainly focused on the logistics of the election: increased pay for poll workers, expanded early voting sites and extra equipment to more quickly process millions of mailed ballots.

Some jurisdictions received grants that were a small fraction of their election budgets, while others saw theirs increase several times over. Suddenly, election administrators who had had to scrounge for resources could "fund their dream election," according to Howard.

In the weeks since the election, allies of Trump have included the Center for Tech and Civic Life's grants in their voter fraud conspiracy theories. They have challenged the legality and neutrality of the grants, claiming that the funding was aimed at boosting Democratic turnout.

But an APM Reports analysis of voter registration and voter turnout in three of the five key swing states shows the grant funding had no clear impact on who turned out to vote. Turnout increased across the U.S. from 2016. The APM Reports analysis found that counties in Pennsylvania, Georgia and Arizona that received grants didn't have consistently higher turnout rates than those that didn't receive money.

An election worker scans mail-in ballots at the Clark County Election Department on Oct. 20 in North Las Vegas, Nevada.

Ethan Miller/Getty Images

Officials with the Center for Tech and Civic Life and government officials have defended themselves in court and in written statements by saying the goal was to ensure safe voting options during the pandemic.

"In this moment of need, we feel so fortunate to be administering an open-call grant program available to every local election department in every state in the union to ensure that they have the staffing, training, and equipment necessary so that this November every eligible voter can participate in a safe and timely way and have their vote counted," the Center for Tech and Civic Life said in a statement on Sept. 24.

The nonprofit is also continuing to offer grants to communities that are holding runoff elections in Georgia in January.

While some election officials see little difference between private and government funding for elections, other officials are deeply worried about the precedent that the private grants may set. They say private donors could have a personal agenda. For example, Zuckerberg may have wanted to improve his public image after years of criticism that the misinformation and divisive rhetoric on Facebook have damaged democracies around the world.

"It's really important that it's a one-time thing," said Rachael Cobb, associate professor of political science and legal studies at Suffolk University in Boston. Cobb said the private money was critical for election administration this year, "but over time, it in and of itself is corrosive." She said continuing to use private money for such purposes "sullies [the election] in a way that we don't need it to be sullied at all."

But other election analysts say private funding is the best option if the federal government isn't going to commit to sustainable long-term funding for election offices.

They also say the grants helped avert a potential disaster where long lines, missing mail and slow counting could have led Trump to further question the integrity of results in Pennsylvania, Georgia and Arizona.

David Kimball, a political science professor at the University of Missouri-St. Louis, said that without the grants, "it certainly would have taken them a lot longer to process and count those absentee ballots, which would have only made this post-election period more unbearable."

For more, read the full story at APM Reports.

Editor's Note: Facebook is among NPR's financial supporters.

From Wikipedia, the free encyclopedia

2000 Mules	
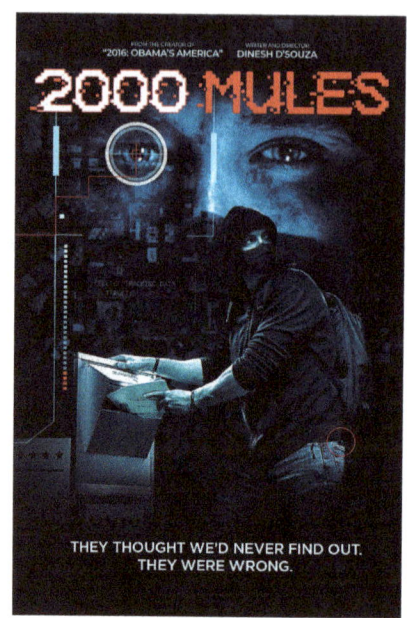 Theatrical release poster	
Directed by	Dinesh D'Souza Debbie D'Souza Bruce Schooley
Written by	Dinesh D'Souza Debbie D'Souza Bruce Schooley
Produced by	Dinesh D'Souza Gregg Phillips Catherine Englebrecht
Starring	Dinesh D'Souza
Narrated by	Dinesh D'Souza

Edited by	Dinesh D'Souza
Music by	Bryan E. Miller
Production companies	D'Souza Media Salem Media Group
Distributed by	D'Souza Media
Release date	May 20, 2022[1][2]
Running time	89 minutes
Country	United States
Language	English
Box office	$1.5 million[3]

2000 Mules is a 2022 American conspiracist[4][5][6] political film from right-wing political commentator Dinesh D'Souza. The film falsely[7][8][9] claims unnamed nonprofit organizations supposedly associated with the Democratic Party paid "mules" to illegally collect and deposit ballots into drop boxes in the swing states of Arizona, Georgia, Michigan, Pennsylvania, and Wisconsin during the 2020 presidential election. D'Souza has a history of creating and spreading false conspiracy theories.[10]

The Associated Press (AP) reported that the film relies on "faulty assumptions, anonymous accounts and improper analysis of cellphone location data" provided by conservative[11] non-profit True the Vote.[7] FactCheck.org found the film's "supposed evidence is speculative."[12] National Public Radio (NPR) reported True the Vote "made multiple misleading or false claims about its [own] work".[13] AP reported that the assertion that True the Vote identified 1,155 paid mules in Philadelphia alone was false. The film presented a single unverified anonymous witness who said she saw people picking up what she "assumed" were payments for ballot collection in Arizona; no evidence of such payments was presented in any of the other four states.[7] The film characterizes the alleged operation as "ballot trafficking" with "stash houses", but presents no evidence that ballots were illegally collected to be deposited in drop boxes.[7][14][15][16]

A companion book was set to be released in early September 2022 but was abruptly recalled amidst legal threats and edited for release late in October.[5]

Content and methodology

2000 Mules opens with a misleadingly edited clip from October 2020 of then-presidential candidate Joe Biden responding to a podcaster's question about boosting his election turnout. After replying, "Republicans are doing everything they can to make it harder for people to vote, especially people of color to vote," Biden added, "we have put together I think the most extensive and inclusive voter fraud organization in the history of American politics." His second statement was taken out of context in clips and memes that went viral on conservative media at the time, purporting to be an admission that Democrats were preparing to commit election fraud. This was debunked at the time, as Biden was actually referring to safeguarding the vote, later adding, "What [Trump] is trying to do is discourage people from voting by implying that their vote won't be counted, it can't be counted, we're going to challenge it and all these things."[17]

The film relies on data provided by True the Vote. According to NPR, "A conservative 'election integrity' group called True The Vote has made multiple misleading or false claims about its [own] work, NPR has found, including the suggestion that they helped solve the murder of an eight-year-old girl in Atlanta. The claims appear in a new pro-Trump film called *2,000 Mules*". NPR said that True the Vote's claim that it "solved a murder of a young little girl in Atlanta" was false.[13]

Analysis conducted by the AP found the film was "based on faulty assumptions, anonymous accounts and improper analysis of cellphone location data".[7][9] AP explained that in various swing counties across the five states, True the Vote used phone pings to cellphone towers to identify people who had passed near ballot drop boxes and various unnamed nonprofit organizations multiple times per day, concluding that such people were paid mules for ballot collection and deposits. Experts said such mobile phone tracking was not accurate enough to distinguish alleged mules from many other people who might walk or drive by a ballot box or nonprofit during the course of a day, such as delivery drivers, postal workers and cab drivers. True the Vote asserted it had conducted "pattern of life" filtering of such people before election season; the AP noted limitations of that approach.[7]

The film also asserts that some of the geolocated alleged mules were present at what it called "antifa riots" in Atlanta during the George Floyd protests in spring 2020. AP explained that the geolocation data could not reliably determine why people were present at that event; they could have been peaceful protesters, police or firefighters responding to the protests, or business owners in the area. The geolocation data True the Vote had purchased began on October 1, 2020.[18] D'Souza and Gregg Phillips, a True the Vote board member, asserted they had matched their geolocation data with data from the Armed Conflict Location and Event Data Project (ACLED). In the film, Phillips claims that "dozens and dozens and dozens of our mules show up on the ACLED databases" as what are characterized as "antifa rioters". ACLED said the claims were categorically false, noting it does not track cellphone data. True the Vote's leader Catherine Engelbrecht asserted Phillips was actually referring to a different organization, then mentioned ACLED, but she declined to name the different organization, saying Phillips relied on "multiple databases".[13]

To illustrate the use of phone geolocation technology, in the film D'Souza speaks with Phillips, who alleges he used it to identify two suspects in an Atlanta homicide cold case, providing his analysis to the

FBI, which he and D'Souza suggest resulted in arrests of the suspects. The homicide was not a cold case, and both suspects were arrested by state rather than federal officials, with no indication phone geolocation played a role. True the Vote stated days after *2000 Mules* was released that it had notified the FBI of its analysis more than two months after the suspects had been indicted. Promoting the film on his podcast, D'Souza said the FBI had forwarded the information to the Georgia Bureau of Investigation (GBI) and the arrests resulted shortly thereafter; the GBI denied receiving such information. NPR was unable to confirm that True the Vote had provided analysis to the FBI; Engelbrecht told NPR she would not provide names of any FBI agents she claimed to have contacted "as I do not want them harassed". Phillips had previously claimed without evidence that non-citizens illegally cast as many as five million ballots in the 2016 elections.[13]

The film likened its geolocation methodology to that used by federal investigators to identify individuals inside the U.S. Capitol during the January 6 attack, showing an image of individuals at the centers of large circles of uncertainty, fully within the building, to show they were there. Similar large circles of uncertainly would be insufficient to show someone was at, rather than near, a ballot drop box.[15]

In the film, Phillips shows a diagram on a tablet computer purporting to show a mule traveling to 28 drop boxes in Atlanta. When that diagram is superimposed over a diagram of actual drop box locations, only some of the purported locations are near actual drop boxes. Phillips told *The Washington Post* that "the movie graphics are not literal interpretations of our data." Another diagram in the film purports to show geolocations superimposed over a map of Atlanta, but the map is actually of Moscow.[19]

The film shows surveillance video of people allegedly depositing multiple ballots into drop boxes, though there was no way to match them with the geolocation data, and most states allow such ballot collection on behalf of family members and household members. In one segment, Phillips narrates that a woman deposited "a small stack" of ballots into a drop box, though it is not actually clear there was more than one ballot. The deposit allegedly occurred at 1am, after which the woman removed latex gloves and threw them away, which the film characterizes as suspicious. The incident occurred on January 5, 2021, during Georgia's runoff election, not during the 2020 presidential election. The film alleges that some of those captured in surveillance videos were wearing gloves to avoid leaving their fingerprints on ballots, but the videos are from the fall and winter of 2020, when people were taking precautions during the COVID-19 pandemic.[9][7]

Phillips narrates a surveillance video in which a man on a bicycle rides up to a drop box and deposits his ballot. Phillips characterizes the man as "sort of frustrated as he starts to leave," though there is no obvious evidence of frustration, supposedly because the man had forgotten to photograph himself depositing the ballot. Phillips speculated, "they had started requiring the mules, apparently, to take pictures of the stuffing of the ballots. It appears that that's how they get paid." The man later took a photo of his bicycle next to the drop box, leading Catherine Engelbrecht of True the Vote to ask, "If you're just casting your own ballot, what reason in the world would you have to come back and take a picture of the box?" Elections officials had encouraged voters to share their experiences on social media to boost turnout; images posted on social media included people depositing ballots at that particular drop box.[15]

Georgia Secretary of State Brad Raffensperger said his office investigated a surveillance video from the film showing a man depositing five ballots into a drop box, finding he had lawfully deposited ballots for himself and his family.[20] It was one of at least three surveillance videos from the film found by Georgia investigators to show lawful depositing of multiple ballots.[12]

2000 Mules does not inform viewers that, even if the events it depicts occurred, every absentee ballot deposited in a drop box must be inside an envelope sent to each registered voter that includes the voter's registration information, signature, and a barcode for verification. Ballots lacking the envelope are rejected. True the Vote did not assert any of the ballots involved in the alleged mule scheme were illegal, though in the film D'Souza falsely asserts the Georgia man depositing multiple ballots for himself and his family was committing a "crime" with "fraudulent" ballots. In an interview with Philip Bump of *The Washington Post*, D'Souza asserted that, despite not having shown there was any illegal ballot trafficking operation, any ballot delivered by such a process would therefore be invalid. The Republican chairman of the Georgia election board explained that a valid ballot remains so regardless of how it was received.[20][8][12]

AP reported that the film's assertion that True the Vote identified 1,155 paid mules in Philadelphia alone was false. The film presents a single anonymous witness who says she saw people picking up what she "assumed" were payments for ballot collection in Arizona; no evidence of payments was presented in any of the other four states.[7] Engelbrecht states in the film that according to unidentified "people who have shared information with us, it's generally $10 a ballot" for what is characterized as "ballot trafficking" through "stash houses," but the film presents no evidence that ballots were collected from a nonprofit to be deposited in drop boxes. The film speculates that nonprofits acquired ballots from voters who had moved or died, by stealing them from mailboxes, or by coercion of incapacitated elderly people.[15][16][12] None of the surveillance videos in the film show anyone dropping off ballots more than once.[21] True the Vote claims about video of multiple drops by an individual, "Some of that footage was shown in the first trailer. It was taken out because the video is extremely poor quality."[22]

D'Souza asserted as many as 400,000 ballots may have been involved, "more than enough to tip the balance in the 2020 presidential election," though True the Vote did not allege any of the ballots were illegal.[8]

The film shows a supercut of news clips after election day saying the results had changed from the night before. D'Souza describes what he and others consider suspicious the fact that Trump was leading in some key states early on election night, only for Biden to win the states by the next morning. This is attributable to a phenomenon known as blue shift, or red mirage: Republicans have a greater tendency to vote in person and their ballots are counted early, while Democrats have a greater tendency to vote by absentee ballots, which are counted later. This disparity was more pronounced in the 2020 election because Trump had spent months discouraging his supporters from voting by absentee ballot, which in some cases resulted in expected large jumps in Biden votes as absentee ballots were counted overnight.[17][23][24]

The last third of the film consists of a panel discussion among several conservative and right-wing pundits, all of whom have shows with conservative outlet Salem Media Group, which was an executive producer of the film.[15]

Phillips said in an interview with right-wing activist Charlie Kirk, one of the panelists in the film, that it took "12 people 16 hours a day for 15 months" to conduct their data analysis. Phillips said part of the analysis was conducted at the High Performance Computing Collaboratory at Mississippi State University. A university spokesman said he was not aware of any such analysis conducted there, noting Phillips had taken a publicly available tour and leased office space in a separate building in the same research park that "appeared to us to be sporadically used, if at all".[13]

The film conflates with its premise a case involving unlawful ballot collection by two Yuma County, Arizona, women during the August 2020 primary elections; the women had collected ballots for others, though they were not family members or caregivers as required by law, and their prosecutions were underway before the film's release. D'Souza said during a podcast that the Yuma County sheriff saw the film, "went berserk and has opened up an investigation" and "I believe there will be arrests very soon." The sheriff denied the claim, saying he had been investigating a variety of alleged voter misconduct issues for over a year, none of which were related to the film's claims.[25] He later claimed that these two women pled guilty after having watched the film 2000 Mules. Alma Juarez pled guilty on January 18, 2022[26] and Guillerma Fuentes pled guilty on April 11, 2022,[27] whereas the film had a wide release on May 25, and limited screenings May 2 and 4, 2022, making this impossible.[28]

Trump ally Patrick Byrne, who financially backed the Maricopa County, Arizona ballot audit that attempted but failed to find 2020 voting fraud in the county, also falsely said the Yuma investigation was in direct response to the film.[29][30]

True the Vote did not cooperate with investigations by Georgia election officials, refusing to disclose the names of people who allegedly collected ballots. The State Election Board issued subpoenas to the organization in April 2022, seeking documents, recordings and names of individuals involved; the Board sued the organization in July 2023 for failure to comply with the subpoenas.[20][31] The GBI examined the True the Vote allegations in fall 2021 but did not find sufficient evidence to open an investigation. In a letter to True the Vote, the bureau noted that the data it was provided counted a "visit" to a drop box as extending to a radius of 100 feet (30 m). The GBI letter also mentioned that it was given cell site location information (CSLI), which is far less accurate than GPS data; GPS was not mentioned in the letter. D'Souza told the *Post* that True the Vote "did not exclusively use CSLI data" and that they told him the GBI had misrepresented the data.[32][19][33]

In October 2022, the office of Republican Arizona attorney general Mark Brnovich referred True the Vote to the FBI and IRS for possible investigation, finding that Engelbrecht and Phillips had falsely told the office they had given their data to the Phoenix FBI office and were working as informants there, while telling the FBI office, the Arizona Senate and the public they had given their data to the attorney general's office, though they had not. Brnovich's office said True the Vote claimed to have evidence of 243 mules in Arizona, but presented no proof. The attorney general's office also suggested True the Vote's tax exempt nonprofit status should be examined.[34]

Reception

In the first day of its release, the film earned $300,000, making it the second-highest grossing documentary to date in 2022.[35] According to executive producer Salem Media, it grossed $10 million in revenue in the first two weeks of independent and streaming release, with over one million viewers. Salem said its net revenue makes it the most profitable political documentary in a decade.[36] It earned $163,331 in its second weekend,[37] and $50,696 in its third.[38]

Former president Donald Trump, who has routinely made the false claim that he was the true winner of the 2020 election (in the popular vote), praised the film as the "greatest [and] most impactful documentary of our time"[39] and as supposedly exposing "great election fraud",[7] and arranged for a screening to be held at his Mar-a-Lago resort on May 4; the screening was attended by various people affiliated with the American right, some of whom (Rudy Giuliani, Mike Lindell, and Marjorie Taylor Greene, among others) have also promoted the false claim that the 2020 election was stolen from Trump.[40] In his twelve page rebuttal to testimony and evidence that was presented in public hearings by the United States House Select Committee on the January 6 Attack, Trump cited the movie in one of its sections that focused on "ballot trafficking" claims.[41]

Media outlets such as PolitiFact, the Associated Press and The Washington Post criticized the film for its factual errors and omissions, making implausible claims, and promoting conspiracy theories about the supposed theft of the 2020 presidential election. The Post characterized the film as presenting "the least convincing election-fraud theory yet".[8][7][9][15][20][42]

Writing in *The Bulwark*, Republican author and political advisor Amanda Carpenter characterized *2000 Mules* as "a hilarious mockumentary" that "doesn't survive the most basic fact-checks to support its most important claims". Conservative commentator Ben Shapiro of *The Daily Wire* said, "I think the conclusion of the film is not justified by the premises of the film itself. There are a bunch of dots that need to be connected. Maybe they will be connected, but they haven't been connected in the film."[43] *The Dispatch*, a conservative publication,[44] wrote that "The film's ballot harvesting theory is full of holes" and that "D'Souza has a history of promoting false and misleading claims".[45] Philip Bump summarized a discussion with D'Souza as "D'Souza admits his movie does not show evidence to prove his claims about ballots being collected and submitted."[46]

Further response

On May 9, D'Souza criticized Fox News and Newsmax for not promoting the film, claiming that Fox News' Tucker Carlson instructed Engelbrecht not to mention it during his interview with her and that Newsmax had originally booked an interview with D'Souza but then canceled.[42] Trump later made similar criticisms, claiming that "Fox News is no longer Fox News" due to not showing or discussing the film, and that the outlet's silence was pleasing to what he called "Radical Left Democrats".[39]

On May 19, *The Daily Beast* reported that D'Souza continued to be frustrated that his film was not receiving much attention outside of an "election-denier movement" that already believed in Trump's false claims of a stolen election, with the movement's adherents demanding that conservative media outlets talk more about the film. Conservative talk radio host Jesse Kelly, responding to ever-increasing requests that he discuss the film on his radio show, dismissed those making such requests as "talk about *2000 Mules* guys" and "the bottom of the barrel". *2000 Mules* was initially available online for $29.99 until D'Souza lowered the price to $19.99 within days of its release. He alleged the film was being widely pirated and that someone who attended the Mar-a-Lago screening had recorded it. Kari Lake, a Trump-endorsed Arizona gubernatorial candidate who embraced the film, said she was "flabbergasted" that she had not been asked about it during an interview with a conservative network; Lake did not specify the network.[47]

Eight Arizona Republican officials held a meeting with about 200 others to hear a presentation from Phillips and Engelbrecht weeks after the film's release. Phillips called the press "journalistic terrorists" for demonstrating the film's lack of proof. Asked if he had turned over evidence to law enforcement, Phillips said he had given data to the Arizona attorney general's office a year earlier; the office said they never received it. He declined to discuss specifics of the film's methodology, saying it was proprietary. Engelbrecht declined to name any of the nonprofits allegedly involved, asserting that doing so would interfere with law enforcement.[29][30]

The editorial board of the *New York Post*, a conservative tabloid that endorsed Trump in 2020, published an editorial on June 10, 2022 stating Trump "clings to more fantastical theories, such as Dinesh D'Souza's debunked '2,000 Mules,' even as recounts in Arizona, Georgia and Wisconsin confirm Trump lost."[48]

Bill Barr, Trump's attorney general during the 2020 election, announced on December 1, 2020, that the Justice Department and FBI had investigated allegations of election fraud but found nothing significant.[49] In June 2022 testimony to the House Select Committee on the January 6 Attack, Barr laughed at the mention of *2000 Mules*, and when asked to assess it, dismissed its assertions there had been widespread election fraud,[50] calling the movie "indefensible".[51]

Jeffrey Clark, a former Trump Justice Department official who was the central figure in a Trump scheme to install Clark as acting attorney general to announce falsely that the department had found election fraud, promoted *2000 Mules* while taunting law professor Steve Vladeck and Democratic elections attorney Marc Elias on Twitter. He asked Elias, who had thwarted every lawsuit Trump's legal team had pursued after the election, "Were you part of the massive multi-State operation #TrueTheVote uncovered?".[52][53]

Three screenings were held during the Republican Party of Texas' June 2022 convention, which saw attendees approve a resolution falsely describing Biden's victory in the 2020 presidential election as illegitimate.[54][55][56]

The AP sent a survey about drop boxes to the top elections offices in each state in May 2022. Forty-five states responded, reporting no instances of the boxes being connected to voter fraud or stolen ballots, and only a handful of cases in which boxes were damaged. D'Souza responded, "This AP article contends that mail-in drop boxes are fine because: 1. Election officials say so. 2. There have been hardly any cases of dropboxes being vandalized or damaged. Everyone that has seen #2000Mules will recognize how pathetic and silly this is!".[33][57]

In October 2022, Atlanta citizen Mark Andrews sued Dinesh D'Souza, True the Vote, Gregg Phillips and Catherine Engelbrecht for defamation, conspiracy, and intrusion on seclusion.[58] The film accused him of being a "mule" who illegally harvested ballots as part of a fraud ring. Although the film had blurred his face, the film's trailer and promotional stills used his image.[59] A state investigation found that Andrews had dropped off ballots for himself, his wife, and their three adult children, who all lived at the same address. [60]

Cast

Not including people only appearing in archive footage.
Dinesh D'Souza, director, host and narrator
Debbie D'Souza
True the Vote: Catherine Engelbrecht, Gregg Phillips
Salem Radio Network hosts: Dennis Prager, Sebastian Gorka, Larry Elder, Eric Metaxas, Charlie Kirk

The Heritage Foundation: Hans von Spakovsky
Capital Research Center: Scott Walter

Book

A book based on the film was set for release in September 2022. It had been promoted by D'Souza as including new evidence supporting the film's claims, including the names of specific nonprofits supposedly involved in the conspiracies. Shortly before the scheduled release, the book's publisher, Regnery Publishing, abruptly recalled physical copies already sent to stores, and delayed the e-book release, citing an unspecified "publishing error". NPR obtained a copy, reporting that it repeated the same false claims as made in the film, and features new allegations, including naming specific nonprofits D'Souza claims were involved. Several of these groups have threatened legal action in response.[5]

The book was released in October 2022, with references to named nonprofits removed. Language regarding some were softened, and sections linking antifa and Black Lives Matter to election fraud were omitted.[61]

Legal case

A legal case of defamation against the filmmakers by an individual accused of being a ballot mule is going ahead after, in October 2023, a judge ruled against dismissing the case.[62]

See also

537 Votes
Attempts to overturn the 2020 United States presidential election
Ballot selfie
Ballot tracking in the United States
Big lie#Donald Trump's false claims of a stolen election

Blue shift (politics)
Michael Gableman#Investigation into 2020 election results
Postal voting in the 2020 United States elections
Presidential Advisory Commission on Election Integrity
Recount (film)

References

^ Palmer, Ewan (May 5, 2022). "Donald Trump holds screening of "2,000 Mules" documentary at Mar-a-Lago". *Newsweek*. Retrieved May 13, 2022.

^ "Domestic 2022 Weekend 20". *Box Office Mojo*. Retrieved May 25, 2022.

^ "2000 Mules (2022)". *Box Office Mojo*. IMDb. Retrieved June 11, 2022.

^ Downen, Robert (October 7, 2022). "How the debunked conspiracy film '2000 Mules' became Texas Republican orthodoxy". The Texas Tribune. Retrieved October 15, 2022.

^ Jump up to:[a] [b] [c] Dreisbach, Tom (September 8, 2022). "A publisher abruptly recalled the '2,000 Mules' election denial book. NPR got a copy". NPR. Retrieved November 7, 2022.

^ Rogers, Kaleigh (October 25, 2022). "Most Candidates Who Think 2020 Was Rigged Are Probably Going To Win In November". *FiveThirtyEight*. Retrieved October 25, 2022.

^ Jump up to:[a] [b] [c] [d] [e] [f] [g] [h] [i] [j] Swenson, Ali (May 3, 2022). "FACT FOCUS: Gaping holes in the claim of 2K ballot 'mules'". *Associated Press*. Praised by former President Donald Trump as exposing "great election fraud," the movie, called "2000 Mules," paints an ominous picture suggesting Democrat-aligned ballot "mules" were supposedly paid to illegally collect and drop off ballots in Arizona, Georgia, Michigan, Pennsylvania and Wisconsin. But that's based on faulty assumptions, anonymous accounts and improper analysis of cellphone location data, which is not precise enough to confirm that somebody deposited a ballot into a drop box, according to experts.

^ Jump up to:*a b c d* McCarthy, Bill; Sherman, Amy (May 4, 2022). *"The faulty premise of the '2,000 mules' trailer about voting by mail in the 2020 election"*. PolitiFact. Retrieved November 9, 2022.

^ Jump up to:*a b c d* Bump, Philip (April 29, 2022). *"Analysis | The dishonest pivot at the heart of the new voter-fraud conspiracy"*. The Washington Post. Retrieved April 30, 2022.

^ Multiple sources:

Whitfield, Stephen J. (October 2018). "The Persistence of the Protocols". Society. **55** *(5): 417–184. doi:10.1007/s12115-018-0282-6. ISSN 0147-2011. S2CID 150256723. Most recently the conspiracy theorist Dinesh D'Souza accused Soros of supporting antifa, that is, of backing 'domestic terrorism.'*

Langer, Armin (April 2, 2021). "The eternal George Soros". In Önnerfors, Andreas; Krouwel, André (eds.). (1 ed.). Abingdon, Oxon: Routledge. pp. 163–184. doi:10.4324/9781003048640-9. ISBN 978-1-003-04864-0. S2CID 233615606. The US conspiracy theorist and pro-Trump commentator Dinesh D'Souza… {{cite book}}: |journal= ignored (help); Missing or empty |title= (help)

"Trump pardons right-wing conspiracy theorist Dinesh D'Souza — World News with Matt Bevan". Radio National. June 1, 2018.

Savan, Leslie (July 8, 2014). "ABC News Helps Dinesh D'Souza Hype His Latest Conspiracy Theory". The Nation. ISSN 0027-8378. Retrieved March 1, 2021.

Jones, Sarah (May 31, 2018). "Grifters All the Way Down". The New Republic. ISSN 0028-6583. Retrieved March 1, 2021.

Rodgers, Jennifer (March 19, 2019). *"Trump is turning his pardon power into a shield"*. CNN. Retrieved March 1, 2021.

^ Eilperin, Juliet (May 21, 2013). *"Conservative group True the Vote sues IRS over being subject to heightened scrutiny"*. Washington Post. ISSN 0190-8286. Retrieved June 28, 2022.

^ Jump up to:*a b c d* Farley, Robert (June 10, 2022). *"Evidence Gaps in '2000 Mules'"*. FactCheck.org.

^ Jump up to:*a b c d e* Dreisbach, Tom (May 17, 2022). *"A pro-Trump film suggests its data are so accurate, it solved a murder. That's false"*. National Public Radio. Retrieved November 7, 2022.

^ Dreisbach, Tom (May 17, 2022). *"A pro-Trump film suggests its data are so accurate, it solved a murder. That's false"*. National Public Radio. Retrieved November 7, 2022.

^ Jump up to:*a b c d e f* Bump, Philip (May 11, 2022). *"'2000 Mules' offers the least convincing election-fraud theory yet"*. The Washington Post.

^ Jump up to:*a b* *"Fact Check-Does '2000 Mules' provide evidence of voter fraud in the 2020 U.S. presidential election?"*. Reuters. May 27, 2022. Retrieved November 7, 2022.

^ Jump up to:*a b* Himmelman, Khaya (May 21, 2022). *"Fact Checking Dinesh D'Souza's '2,000 Mules'"*. The Dispatch Fact Check. Retrieved May 21, 2022.

^ Fowler, Stephen (October 22, 2021). *"GBI says GOP's cellphone data lacks enough evidence to prove ballot harvesting"*. Georgia Public Radio. Retrieved November 9, 2022.

^ Jump up to:*a b* Bump, Philip (May 19, 2022). *"Even the geolocation maps in '2000 Mules' are misleading"*. The Washington Post.

^ Jump up to:*a b c d* Niesse, Mark (May 10, 2022). *"What '2000 Mules' leaves out of ballot harvesting claims"*. *The Atlanta Journal-Constitution*. *Archived* from the original on May 11, 2022.

^ Funke, Daniel (May 12, 2022). *"US documentary revives Trump's unproven election fraud claims"*. *Agence France-Presse*.

^ *"TTV and 2000 Mules: Frequently Asked Questions"*. *True the Vote*. May 12, 2022. Retrieved May 16, 2022.

^ Graham, David A. (August 10, 2020). *"The 'Blue Shift' Will Decide the Election"*. The Atlantic. This sort of late-breaking Democratic vote is the new, though still underappreciated, normal in national elections. Americans have become accustomed to knowing who won our elections promptly, but there are many legitimate votes that are not counted immediately every election year. For reasons that are not totally understood by election observers, these votes tend to be heavily Democratic, leading results to tilt toward Democrats as more of them are counted, in what has become known as the "blue shift." In most cases, the blue shift is relatively inconsequential, changing final vote counts but not results. But in others, as in 2018, it can materially change the outcome…But the effect could be much larger and far more consequential in 2020, as Democrats embrace voting by mail more enthusiastically than Republicans. If the public isn't prepared to wait patiently for the final results, and if politicians cynically exploit the shifting tallies to cast doubt on the integrity of the vote, the results could be catastrophic.

^ Mejia, Nathaniel Rakich, Elena (October 30, 2020). *"When To Expect Election Results In Every State"*. *FiveThirtyEight*. Retrieved May 21, 2022.

^ MacDonald-Evoy, Jerod (May 19, 2022). *"The Yuma sheriff isn't investigating election fraud because of '2000 Mules'"*. *The Arizona Mirror*. *Archived* from the original on May 19, 2022.

^ "Alma Juarez Plea" (PDF). Arizona Attorney General. Retrieved August 27, 2022.

^ "Fuentes Sentencing Agreement" (PDF). Arizona Attorney General (Press release). Archived from the original (PDF) on June 3, 2022. Retrieved August 27, 2022.

^ Palmer, Ewan (May 5, 2022). "Donald Trump holds screening of "2,000 Mules" documentary at Mar-a-Lago". Newsweek. Retrieved August 27, 2022.

^ Jump up to:[a] [b] Stern, Ray (June 1, 2022). "Arizona Capitol event with '2000 Mules' filmmakers was long on claims, short on evidence". Arizona Republic.

^ Jump up to:[a] [b] Christie, Bob; Cooper, Jonathan J. (June 1, 2022). "Arizona lawmakers hear from election conspiracy theorists". Associated Press. Retrieved November 7, 2022.

^ Niesse, Mark (July 12, 2023). "Georgia sues True the Vote over refusal to show '2000 Mules' evidence". Atlanta Journal-Constitution.

^ Niesse, Mark; Bluestein, Greg (October 21, 2021). "GBI chief" Not enough evidence to pursue GOP's ballot fraud claim". The Atlanta Journal-Constitution. ISSN 1539-7459. Archived from the original on October 23, 2021. Retrieved May 12, 2022.

^ Jump up to:[a] [b] Bump, Philip (July 18, 2022). "Claims that drop boxes were a vector for rampant fraud keep crumbling". The Washington Post.

^ Cheney, Kyle; Wu, Nicholas (October 14, 2022). "Arizona AG's office asks feds to investigate conservative nonprofit True the Vote". Politico. Retrieved November 7, 2022.

^ "Box Office Performance for Documentary Movies in 2022". Nash Information Services, LLC. Retrieved May 21, 2022.

^ Salem Media Group, Inc (May 12, 2022). "2000 Mules Becomes the Most Successful Political Documentary in a Decade, Seen by 1 Million". BusinessWire. Retrieved May 21, 2022.

^ "Domestic 2022 Weekend 21". Box Office Mojo. Retrieved June 4, 2022.

^ "Domestic 2022 Weekend 22". Box Office Mojo. Retrieved June 7, 2022.

^ Jump up to:[a] [b] Dzhanova, Yelena (May 15, 2022). "Trump rails against Fox News, saying the network hasn't aired a movie alleging widespread voter fraud in the 2020 election". Business Insider. Retrieved May 16, 2022.

^ McGraw, Meridith (May 15, 2022). "What's the hottest spot to debut your 2020 election conspiracy film? Mar-a-Lago, of course". Politico. Retrieved November 9, 2022.

^ Samuels, Brett (June 13, 2022). "Trump releases 12-page response to Jan. 6 hearing". The Hill. Retrieved June 14, 2022.

^ Jump up to:[a] [b] Baragona, Justin (May 9, 2022). "Dinesh D'Souza Claims Tucker Carlson and Newsmax Won't Promote His Batshit Movie". The Daily Beast. Retrieved May 12, 2022.

^ Carpenter, Amanda (May 17, 2022). "Dinesh D'Souza's 2000 Mules Is a Hilarious Mockumentary". The Bulwark.

^ Coppins, McKay (January 31, 2020). "The Conservatives Trying to Ditch Fake News". The Atlantic. Retrieved April 12, 2021. The Dispatch produces "serious, factually grounded journalism for a conservative audience".

^ Himmelman, Khaya (May 21, 2022). "Fact Checking Dinesh D'Souza's '2,000 Mules'". The Dispatch Fact Check. Retrieved May 21, 2022.

^ Bump, Philip (May 17, 2022). "Analysis - Discussing the gaps in '2000 Mules' with Dinesh D'Souza". The Washington Post. Retrieved May 24, 2022.

^ Will Sommer; Zachary Petrizzo (May 19, 2022). "Dinesh D'Souza's Foul New Movie Is Driving Conservatives Crazy". The Daily Beast.

^ Vakil, Caroline (June 11, 2022). "NY Post editorial board: 'Trump can't look past 2020. Let him remain there'". The Hill. Retrieved November 9, 2022.

^ Balsamo, Michael (December 1, 2020). "Disputing Trump, Barr says no widespread election fraud". Associated Press.

^ Samuels, Brett (June 13, 2022). "Trump releases 12-page response to Jan. 6 hearing". The Hill.

^ Cai, Sophia (June 13, 2022). "Barr tells Jan. 6 panel: Trump "detached from reality" on voter fraud". Axios.com. Retrieved November 7, 2022.

^ Gertz, Matt (June 23, 2022). "Jeffrey Clark, Trump's pro-coup would-be AG, praised "2000 Mules" conspiracy theory". Media Matters for America.

^ Feuer, Alan; Goldman, Adam; Haberman, Maggie (June 23, 2022). "Federal Authorities Search Home of Trump Justice Dept. Official". The New York Times. ISSN 0362-4331. Retrieved June 23, 2022.

^ Neugeboren, Eric (June 18, 2022). "Fed up and fired up: Texas Republicans meet in a climate of mistrust, conspiracy and victimhood". Texas Tribune. Retrieved November 9, 2022.

^ Sewell Chan; Eric Neugeboren (June 18, 2022). "Texas Republican Convention calls Biden win illegitimate and rebukes Cornyn over gun talks". The Texas Tribune.

^ Chappell, Bill (June 20, 2022). "Texas GOP's new platform says Biden didn't really win. It also calls for secession". National Public Radio.

^ Anthony Izaguirre; Christina A. Cassidy (July 17, 2022). "No major problems with ballot drop boxes in 2020, AP finds". Associated Press.

^ *The United States District Court For The Northern District of Georgia Atlanta Division (October 26, 2022). "Case 1:22-cv-04259-SDG" (PDF). The New York Times.*

^ *Phillip Bump (October 27, 2022). "One of Dinesh D'Souza's 2,000 alleged 'mules' sues, claiming defamation". The Washington Post.*

^ *Kate Brumback (October 28, 2022). "Georgia man sues over false ballot fraud claim in film". Associated Press.*

^ *Dreisbach, Tom (October 25, 2022). "Here's what changed in Dinesh D'Souza's '2,000 Mules' book after it was recalled". NPR. Retrieved November 7, 2022.*

^ *Bump, Philip (October 3, 2023). "Analysis | '2000 Mules,' a key piece of election misinformation, has its day in court". Washington Post. ISSN 0190-8286. Retrieved October 27, 2023.*

External links

Official website
2000 Mules at IMDb
2000 Mules at Rotten Tomatoes
2000 Mules at Box Office Mojo

Films directed by Dinesh D'Souza

2016: Obama's America (2012)
America: Imagine the World Without Her (2014)
Hillary's America: The Secret History of the Democratic Party (2016)
Death of a Nation: Can We Save America a Second Time? (2018)
Trump Card (2020)
2000 Mules (2022)

Categories:
2022 films

2020s political films
Films directed by Dinesh D'Souza
Films produced by Dinesh D'Souza
Films with screenplays by Dinesh D'Souza
Films about the 2020 United States presidential election
Conspiracist media
Documentary films about conspiracy theories
2020s English-language films
2020s American films

Electoral fraud in the United States

This page was last edited on 10 December 2023, at 17:42 (UTC).

CHAPTER FIVE:

The Failure of the United States of America's National Football League (N.F.L.), National Basketball Association (N.B.A.), Amateur and Professional Soccer, Swimming, Track & Field, Other & All Sports, And All Other Countries Sports Teams & Sports Organizations Throughout The World, to Address and Denounce Individual Athletes Who Errantly and "Delusionally" Believe They Have Either The Authority Or Right To Change or Otherwise Alter Their Gender, Assigned Irreversibly At Birth, Or Those Who Pretend To Be The Opposite Sex By Inappropriately Dressing, Using Makeup or Jewelry, Or Acting Or Behaving Like The Opposite Sex That The Are Not A Member Of, Nor Ever Meant To Be A Member Of, All In Order To: "not offend potential paying audiences or consumers, place monetary gains and profits at the highest priority level and divine human gender assignments determined before birth and at birth (only two, male and female), and society ethics and morals at the lowest (or nonexistent) level, and, most disappointingly, disrespect the entire world population, which, for thousands of years, have respected and acknowledged the unique and cherished differences that exist, in reality and in perpetuity, between irrevocable and irreversible birth genders, namely, males and females.

Nelson Mandela (1918-2013) was a South African anti-apartheid revolutionary and political leader who served as President of South Africa from 1994 to 1999. He was the country's first black head of state and the first elected in a fully representative democratic election. Mandela's leadership in dismantling apartheid and fostering reconciliation and peace earned him global admiration and the Nobel Peace Prize in 1993.

The United States of America "National Football League (N.F.L.)" showed their true priorities, money more important than patriotism and money more important than human rights, when they failed to promptly and appropriately respond to N.F.L. players who were refusing to respect their American (country) flag and the performance of their country's national anthem performance before the beginning of each N.F.L. American football game. This tradition has been around for more than fifty years. Certain disrespectful N.F.L. players, including one specific San Francisco N.F.L. team quarterback who wore socks that pictured policemen as pigs and would kneel down in protest instead of standing during the performance of the American flag and national anthem performance before each N.F.L. game he played in, and other N.F.L. players would similarly kneel down on one knee instead of standing at attention and in respect for all the similar age and strength men and women who had served in the military to obtain and maintain the freedom of all American citizens, and many of whom died in the process, during both civil and international world wars in the past several hundred years, since the United States of America's birth as a free and independent country, and creation in 1776. The money-hungry N.F.L. commissioner and team owners just sat back and watched this disrespectful and despicable behavior. They did not act rapidly or proactively to stop these few nefarious, arrogant, rude, and disrespectful N.F.L. players who were essentially "spitting in the face" of those deceased patriotic American soldiers who had fought for and ensured the independence and freedom of Americans for centuries, from other evil tyrant dictators in the world with evil aspirations and intent for all world inhabitants, e.g., burning all "non-German, non-Aryan" people in the world in ovens after cutting out their teeth that contained any valuable rare earth gold or silver fillings!

How did the Nazis construct an Aryan identity in order to annihilate non-German people throughout the world (at least that was their intent, which, thankfully and luckily, was never successfully achieved as planned)?

Adolf Hitler, the leader of the Nazi Party, argued that the Germans were somehow superior to all other races. Hitler then became atrociously obsessed with 'racial purity' and used the word 'Aryan' to describe his idea of a 'pure German race' or Herrenvolk.

The 'Aryan race' was then assigned the duty or obligation to "control the world by eliminating (by varied means of execution, including poisonous gas chamber killings, then burning their victims in incinerators or ovens) "non-Aryans," as soon as possible. The Nazis, as instructed or taught by their evil and narcissistic, and ill-advised leader, Adolf Hitler, believed that the Aryans had the most "pure blood" of all the people who inhabited planet Earth. The ideal Aryan, incorrect, but as described by Adolf Hitler, had pale skin, blond hair, and blue eyes. Non-Aryans, the majority of world citizens according to the previously described features, were then falsely described or characterized, again by the deranged, narcissistic, and evil leader of Germany, Adolf Hitler, as "impure and evil," (ironically, because Adolf Hitler himself was, in truth, the "impure and evil" human with unGodly and Satanic goals and aspirations, with no respect for other human beings who did not resemble Hitler's random and impromptu description of "perfect German people or the Aryan people concept that he described and created," endangering all people in the world who did not conform to or appear to his "perfect people appearance description, also known as the "Aryan race."

To steal the wealth and possessions of "non-Aryans" in Germany, Adolf Hitler also slandered Jews and started creating false rumors to persuade ignorant or other racist or prejudiced German citizens to embrace the "fake news," commonly used by tyrants throughout the world for centuries, that Aryan superiority was explicitly, specifically, and significantly being hindered or otherwise threatened by Jews (very specific and unjust indeed), of course with no basis or proof of these false assertions and accusations.

Thereafter, this "Aryan race" concept then metastasized like a malignant cancer to other groups, races, skin colors, and cultures, a dire, hazardous, and perilous or extremely dangerous scenario and situation that the world could no longer dismiss or ignore. As directed and recommended by Adolf Hitler, a hierarchy of 'races' was established, again errantly and in a very racist and prejudice manner, with the Aryans considered elite, worth saving, and meant to live on to the next generation versus, or in contrast to, Jews, Gypsies, darker pigmented persons throughout the world of different cultures and with "non-Aryan: facial features, facial measurements, facial or other defined physical appearance or measurements, and any persons who were non-blonde, non-blue-eyed persons, all as described, inaccurately, as evil and inferior," who were determined, falsely, to merit or be worthy of (recommended, by Adolf Hitler), execution (of course, after stealing their homes, their bank accounts, their valuable home possessions including paintings, jewelry, and other assets, and even (required as per Adolf Hitler), stealing any gold or silver tooth fillings, prior to poisoning these humans in gas chambers, then burning to death these "non-Aryans" in Adolf Hitler mandated "human ovens." These supposedly (actually errantly and mischaracterized) 'inferior' people were seen as a threat to the purity and strength of the German nation that was engaging in rapid transit to hell to move into Satan's all-inclusive underworld resort, also known as Hades or Hell.

The word "Aryan" originated in the Vedic period and was used initially and innocently by Indo-Iranian people in India with no evil implications or associations. The word referred to the noble class from the Āryāvarta parts of India. The Nazis, however, distorted the term and, in a sinister manner, inappropriately chose to link the word 'Aryan' with the similar German word 'Ehre,' which means 'honor' and then created, with malicious intent and aspirations, the word and concept, 'Aryan,' to falsely portray their (satanic, prejudice, and racist), image of what the evil German government officials, in the era of Adolf Hitler, were then to propagandize as 'elite, Aryan, honorable people,' versus all other world citizens in Germany and in every other country who "would then be eligible and more than qualified to be executed for their inferior or deleterious status as human beings that were unnecessary and not eligible or qualified, according to Adolf Hitler, to enter and proceed to live in the current century and generation, or in future generations.

The United States of America "National Basketball Association (N.B.A.)" severely underperformed, in a similar fashion to the National Football League (N.F.L.), with regard to loyalty to their country, patriotic American values, and in respecting what American soldiers sacrificed their lives to preserve in the past several centuries, fundamental human rights, freedom, and independence, and of course, the "American Dream", also known as the ability of every human to be born with equal status, and the potential to succeed in life, by accepting God's guidance, wisdom, education, and spiritual guidance, and then use these gifts to work earnestly, hard, and honestly, to achieve greatness and great success in life, based on their individual work ethic, self-education, and self-improvement attitude and aspirations, all in order to accomplish outstanding achievements, thereby potentially improving the prospects and potential success of their family members in future generations, especially if mentoring of their children and younger generations is effectively instituted and implemented, including Godly values, with acceptance by these mentor's mentees.

The N.B.A. commissioner and N.B.A. basketball team owners were tested and miserably failed their tests, especially from 2021 to 2023.

The Chinese government is engaging in modern-day slavery in China. Reports, multiple and verified, exist that have revealed that adults are currently and actively being forced to produce textiles in China. Estimates are that at least 100,000 modern-day adult slaves, up to hundreds of thousands, of Uyghurs, ethnic Kazakhs, and other Muslim minorities are being subjected to forced labor in China after being unscrupulously detained in "re-education camps," reportedly.

When several N.B.A. players, and myriad other worldwide human freedom and human rights activists protested this modern-day slave trade in China, the N.B.A. essentially ignored these actions of the China dictatorship government leaders who support and are proponents of this modern-day slave trade and slavery, and chastised these protesting N.B.A. players, and even worse, completed refused to listen or hear the message of the myriad other worldwide human freedom and human rights activists, by expanding N.B.A. games business into China, hoping to achieve enormous profits by converting the entire country of China into NBA-watching and

NBA-paying fans and customers, without any suggestion, aspiration, or intent to broach the subject of, or admonish the Chinese dictatorship government regarding their unethical and ungodly behavior toward and enslavement of the religious groups, they feel are a threat to their dictatorship, atheist, government goals and intentions for all their Chinese citizens, and, if China is allowed, their intent to metastasize their atheist, no human rights for all non-Chinese government human citizens throughout the world. Disappointingly, the N.B.A. and the entire world watched as the Chinese government imposed slavery-like lockdowns of their entire country's citizens during the COVID-19 viral pandemic, with no concern whatsoever for the optimal health and well-being of their business owners or non-business-owner citizens.

The following several paragraphs are selected paragraphs or excerpts from a public online article documenting articles and reports ranging from 2019-2020, regarding China's modern-day slavery activities, from the U.S. Department of Labor (.gov):

"Against Their Will: The Situation in Xinjiang

U.S. Department of Labor (.gov)
Bureau of International Labor Affairs

Against Their Will: The Situation in Xinjiang

Forced Labor in Xinjiang

"Xinjiang Uyghur Autonomous Region, People's Republic of China" ©Thomas Peter/Reuters

This "vocational skills education centre", situated between regional capital Urumqi and tourist spot Turpan, is among the largest known ones, and was still undergoing extensive construction and expansion at the time the photo was taken. Dabancheng, Xinjiang, China, Sept. 4, 2018.

The People's Republic of China has arbitrarily detained more than one million Uyghurs and other mostly Muslim minorities in China's far western Xinjiang Uyghur Autonomous Region. (1) It is estimated that 100,000 Uyghurs and other ethnic minority ex-detainees in China may be working in conditions of forced labor following detention in re-education camps. (2) Many more rural poor workers also may experience coercion without detention. (3; 4) China has been included on the *List of Goods Produced by Child Labor of Forced Labor* (TVPRA List) since 2009. In 2020, the Bureau of International Labor Affairs (ILAB) added five goods produced by forced labor by Muslim minorities in China to the 2020 edition of the TVPRA List. These goods include gloves, hair products, textiles, thread/yarn, and tomato products. In 2021, ILAB added an additional good, Polysilicon, produced by forced labor by Muslim minorities in China.

The production of these goods through forced labor takes place primarily in Xinjiang. (5) While previous research has focused on goods and products produced in Xinjiang, recent external reports indicate that Uyghurs also have been transported to work in other provinces in China, increasing the number of goods potentially made with forced labor and broadening the risk of forced labor in supply chains. (5; 3) Other minorities may be forced to work under the guise of "poverty alleviation" without having been detained. (6) Moreover, the government gives subsidies to companies moving to Xinjiang or employing Muslim minority workers. (2) These practices exacerbate a demand for members of Muslim ethnic minority groups that the government wants placed in work assignments where they can be controlled and watched, as well as receive Mandarin Chinese training and undergo political indoctrination. (2) Once at a work placement, workers are usually subjected to constant surveillance and isolation. Given the vast surveillance state in Xinjiang and the threat of detention, individuals have little choice but to face the difficult situations present in these work assignments. (3)

The Department of Labor's (DOL) research utilized published victims' testimonies, and media and think tank reports, to determine the various industries implicated in this system of forced labor. Given the vast state-sponsored structure in place and the control of information, it is likely that more goods also are produced with forced labor in China. (7) In July 2020, the U.S. Departments of State, Treasury, Commerce, and Homeland Security released an advisory for businesses with potential ties to Xinjiang. This business advisory, as well as the TVPRA List and ILAB's Comply Chain due diligence tool for businesses, are practical guides for raising awareness and addressing this issue. Companies with supply chains that link to China, including, but not limited to, Xinjiang, should conduct due diligence to ensure that suppliers are not engaging in forced labor. With such severe and well-documented, widespread abuses, it is important that the world remains vigilant with respect to labor and goods linked to Xinjiang, including reasonable measures to guard against complicity in these violations.

Two Stories, One Goal: Repression

The People's Republic of China officially recognizes 55 ethnic groups in addition to the Han majority. Uyghurs are one of those groups. Along with other mostly Muslim minorities in China, Uyghurs confront abuse and discrimination in places like Xinjiang and elsewhere in the country.

Uyghurs detained in camps and forced to labor in factories must endure dreadful conditions. In one internment camp in Kashgar, Xinjiang, Uyghur detainees work as forced laborers to produce textiles. They receive little pay, are not allowed to leave, and have limited or no communication with family members. If family communication and visits are allowed, they are heavily monitored or cut short. When not working, the Uyghur workers must learn Mandarin and undergo ideological indoctrination. However, these abuses are not just limited to Xinjiang.

Beyond Xinjiang, in the coastal Chinese province of Fujian, Uyghur workers at a factory in Quanzhou face similar abuses. Uyghur workers are made to live in separate dormitories from Han workers. These dormitories are surrounded by an iron gate and security cameras. When finished for the day, often working more hours than their Han co-workers, the Uyghur workers are escorted back to their dormitories by provincial police officers from Xinjiang – not Fujian. The local police say the roll call is to ensure no one is missing. Uyghur workers at this factory are not allowed to exercise their free will to leave. Even if they could leave, they would not get far, as local police have confiscated their identification materials.

Sadly, these two stories fail to capture the individual struggles of the more than one million Uyghurs and other mostly Muslim minorities arbitrarily detained in the far western region of Xinjiang and across China. These two stories are just a snapshot of the vast scale of abuse and serve as a notice for the world to ask questions, take action, and demand change.

Expand All | Collapse All

China – Gloves – Forced Labor

There are reports of glove factories forcibly training and employing 1,500 to 2,000 ethnic minority adult workers with the government's support. Victim testimonies, news media, and think tanks report that factories, including for gloves, frequently engage in coercive recruitment; limit workers' freedom of movement and communication; and subject workers to constant surveillance, retribution for religious beliefs, exclusion from community and social life, and isolation. Further, reports indicate little pay, mandatory Mandarin lessons, ideological indoctrination, and poor living conditions. In some instances, workers have been reported to be subject to torture. More broadly, according to varied estimates, at least 100,000 to hundreds of thousands of Uyghurs, ethnic Kazakhs, and other Muslim minorities are being subjected to forced labor in China following detention in re-education camps. In addition to this, poor workers in rural areas may also experience coercion without detention. Workers are either placed at factories within the Xinjiang Uyghur Autonomous Region, where the camps are located, or transferred out of Xinjiang to factories in eastern China.

Associated Press. *Rights Group: Lacoste Gloves Made in Chinese Internment Camp.* March 3, 2020.

Australian Strategic Policy Institute. *Uyghurs for Sale.* March 1, 2020.

Center for Strategic and International Studies. *Connecting the Dots in Xinjiang: Forced Labor, Forced Assimilation, and Western Supply Chains.* October 16, 2019.

Congressional-Executive Commission on China. *Global Supply Chains, Forced Labor, and the Xinjiang Uyghur Autonomous Region.* March 2020.

SupChina. *How Companies Profit From Forced Labor in Xinjiang.* September 4, 2019.

U.S. Departments of State, Treasury, Commerce, and Homeland Security. *Xinjiang Supply Chain Business Advisory*. July 1, 2020.

VanderKlippe, Nathan. *'I Felt Like a Slave': Inside China's Complex System of Incarceration and Control of Minorities*. The Globe and Mail, March 31, 2019.

Zenz, Adrian. *Beyond the Camps: Beijing's Long-Term Scheme of Coercive Labor, Poverty Alleviation and Social Control in Xinjiang*. Journal of Political Risk 7, No. 12. December 2019.

Zenz, Adrian. *Xinjiang's New Slavery. Foreign Policy*, December 11, 2019."

The N.B.A. commissioner, despite multiple N.B.A. player protests and many human rights activists' protests, proceeded to sign contracts with Chinese officials to expand N.B.A. games into different regions of China, with no mention at all of China's lack of respect for their or any other world citizen's rights to freedom of speech. Hong Kong was recently conquered (at least with respect to freedom of speech, freedom to assemble, and protest against evil and tyrant government officials' actions and behaviors) or taken over by China.

The democratic, free speech advocate and owner of the largest pro-human rights newspaper was falsely imprisoned, perhaps forever, for daring to advocate for freedom of speech, religion, and the right to assemble in protest to Satanic China dictator policies which falsely accuse, coerce, and imprison any humans who criticize their Satanic and tyrant policies and mistreatment of religious and Godly humans). Abraham Lincoln and George Washington would be so approving and proud (this is a sarcastic comment, of course, as Lincoln and Washington would genuinely be disappointed and distraught by not only the U.S.A. and N.B.A.'s actions but also by the entire world's lack of pushback by the United Nations and entire world as they watched the citizens of Hong Kong lose all their freedom, democracy, and human rights instantly after China's invasion into this formerly free, and democratically run city), of the N.B.A. commissioner, N.B.A. team owners, as well as the United States government who allowed China to dishonor their contract with the United Kingdom, regarding maintaining the democratic, human rights-affirming status of Hong Kong, after the United Kingdom agreed to give Hong Kong back to China, many years earlier.

Amateur and Professional Soccer, Swimming, Track & Field, Other & All Sports, And All Other Countries Sports Teams & Sports Organizations Throughout The World, to Address and Denounce Individual Athletes Who Errantly and "Delusionally" Believe They Have Either The Authority Or Right To Change or Otherwise Alter Their Gender, Assigned Irreversibly At Birth, Or Those Who Pretend To Be The Opposite Sex By Inappropriately Dressing, Using Makeup or Jewelry, Or Acting Or Behaving Like The Opposite Sex That The Are Not A Member Of, Nor Ever Meant To Be A Member Of, All In Order To: "not offend potential paying audiences or consumers, place monetary gains and profits at the highest priority level and divine human gender assignments determined before birth and at birth (only two, male and female), and society ethics and morals at the lowest (or nonexistent) level, and, most disappointingly, disrespect the entire world population, which, for thousands of years, have respected and acknowledged the unique and cherished differences that exist, in reality and in perpetuity, between irrevocable and irreversible birth genders, namely, males and females.

Is making money in various sports venues more important, essential, and critical than respecting and supporting Godly values, ethics, morals, and behavior that set apart and made the United States of America a great and God-blessed country?

Satan would answer yes to this question, in line with most professional sports team owners and professional sports team commissioners, as sad and disappointing as this truthful statement is (and has been confirmed for the past several decades).

Should women's basketball, soccer, and all women's sports leagues in grammar school, high school, university, and professional teams and leagues succumb to "atheist or Satanic worldly non-values" that attempt to promote and "normalize", ungodly perspectives, attitudes, aspirations, and actions, including granting, without the authority or permission from God, "non-authority" to individuals with mental illness and personality disorders, to (falsely), believe they have the power and authority to change their birth sex through surgery and hormones (mental illness or personality disorder(s) defined), or dress, act like, or behave like, the opposite sex that they were born as, all because they have mixed etiology mental illnesses or personalities disorders, that cause them to have an insecure, poor self-image and self-confidence, or perhaps anxiety and depression (e.g., bipolar I or II disease, or schizophrenia or schizoaffective disorder, or myriad other combinations of mixed, multiple etiologies of mental illness).

Is it fair to all Godly males and females growing up in grammar school, high school, university, graduate school, and in amateur and professional sports clubs, teams, and leagues to have to (unfairly) compete against an opposite-sex individual (either with mentally illness, poor or complete loss of good judgment, no moral, ethics, or intent to be a God-respecting child of God who accepts, respects, and cherishes their birth sex assigned by God, or just a selfish, greedy, Satanic individual with the sinful motives of being able to master their aspirations of being a pervert in opposite sex bathrooms and gyms, or financially and fame-obsessed (infamous, more accurately), lazy, dishonest, slacker individual to seeks to attempt to win sporting events, competing against opposite sex competitors, because they are poorly conditioned, trained, and too weak, amateur, incompetent, unathletic, and immoral to train and compete with others who are the same sex, from birth, that they are)?

In the generation in which the author grew up, and hopefully in this generation and all future generations, Christians and world citizens of every country in the world held as sacred the belief that a child's birth sex was never to be "messed with," manipulated, distorted, confused, or, most evilly, changed, because this would be, and is, child abuse, in its most overt and evil form! Guidance regarding good parenting, specifically what defines a good and Godly father and mother, is laid out or delineated most clearly and beautifully in the greatest book ever written, the Holy Bible.

The author cherishes and supports, until physical death and commencement of spiritual eternity with God, the organization entitled "Fellowship of Christian Athletes." "Fellowship of Christian Athletes" was, is, and will continue to be the most amazing and impactful organization in this past century, guiding and directing young athletes transitioning from grammar school sports to high school, college, and professional sports, to not only honor God with their philosophy that "your body is the temple of God, who created it, and you are responsible, as a child of God, to maintain, build, strengthen, and fortify that temple to endure and survive into eternity, without tattoos, unnecessary and ungodly elective (but ill-advised by a minority of healthcare providers and surgeons who are "spitting in the face of Hippocrates" and betraying the "Hippocratic Oath" that they all pledged to honor and abide by at their graduation ceremonies upon completing their medical school training), surgeries (e.g., unnecessary sex changes, breast implants, and other vanity surgeries), which are neither medically necessary nor clinically indicated to maintain their physical and mental health.

Often an excellent psychologist and psychiatrist would be the optimal treatment in many of these patients who seek and request these inappropriate and not clinically beneficial or indicated surgeries which they are requesting due to their depression, anxiety, poor self-image, or other mental illnesses or personality disorders, such as obsessive-compulsive disease and myriad other mental illness and personality disorders and diagnoses), and certainly never destroy that temple (known as the body of all children of God, who never made any mistakes or errors in assigning the sex and features of all God's children, and whom God enacted and successfully created through their earthly, motherly birth process), with body and mind-destroying, also known as temple-burning and temple-exploding, alcohol and substances (e.g., marijuana, methamphetamines, magic mushrooms [more accurately, "tragic mushrooms"], lysergic acid, "angel dust [more accurately, "devil's poison powder"], huffing, paint-sniffing, Absinthe (a toxic and poisonous form of alcohol concoction made from wormwood), and many other illicit substances [and disappointingly and shockingly, possibly soon to be legalized, by evil and ungodly politicians whose greed for tax dollars exceeds their love, concern, and care for the health and Godliness of their country's "world citizens and children of God"), abuse and dependence, which all, e.g., one hundred percent, lead to progressive brain and all bodily organs atrophy and progressive decrease in functional status, and eventual total destruction of the entire body and mind, resulting ultimately in enormous and exponential increases in the incidence of mental illness suffering and multiple various mental health diagnoses and extremely premature and often sudden death from overdoses, heart attack and heart failure, pulmonary hypertension, suicide, murder, and myriad other tragic very premature causes of death, again which evil politicians who are not proponents of securing their countries borders from illegal drug traffickers, terrorist, and other criminals entry into their (past, and hopefully future Godly) country, to protect and defend the temple health and security of all God's children within their specific country and all world citizens of all countries in the world, also known as God's family!

Just one example of how Godly societal values (which have always rightfully shunned and advised against body and mind (aka, "God's temple"), harming and devastating alcohol and substance abuse), has markedly deteriorated in the past century, Robert Mitchum (Hollywood actor), was arrested in 1949 for marijuana possession, just before filming the movie, "The Big Steal," with co-star Jane Greer (who was pregnant during the filming of this movie).

Ironically, in subsequent years, especially during and immediately after the 1960s decade of extreme atheism and extreme alcohol and substance abuse and dependence, one of the darkest and most immoral decades in American history, Robert Mitchum's reputation as a bad guy and "film noir" superstar was actually embraced and glamorized by Time Warner and other movie studios.

A true historical story that is rarely discussed is that Jack Warner, the least ethical (more accurately, most evil, Satanic, and unethical) brother of all the original Warner Brothers who created and built the Warner Brothers movie studio, stole the entire business from his brothers at an unfair, underpriced (based on the true worth and value of the movie studio at the time of his treachery and deception of his more Godly brothers), purchase price by secretly conspired with another company to buy the studio from all the Warner brothers, then resell the company, at a lower price, back to Jack Warner alone, thus embezzling and creating a fake and undervalued sale price to steal money and the studio from all his faithful, Godly, and loving brothers, whom Jack Warner was not!

Jack Warner, the unethical man that he was and should forever be clearly remembered as, then essentially made money his one and only false God, ignoring all moral and ethical priorities for movie productions, which led to the birth of the film noir category of films today, defined by their main characters who are essentially glamorized for the crimes they commit, often deficient receiving just punishment for their sinful crimes of greed, lust, and immorality.

When Warner Brothers movie studio was founded by the four brothers, the original goal of the business was established, rightfully and Godly, with the three following goals: 1] Educate, 2) Entertain, and 3) Enlighten their movie studio audiences.

Four brothers founded the company: Harry Warner (born December 12, 1881, in Poland and died July 25, 1958, in Hollywood, California, U.S.A.), Albert Warner (born July 23, 1884 in Poland and died

November 26, 1967, in Miami Beach, Florida, U.S.A) Samuel Warner (born 1887 and died on October 5, 1927 (age 42) in Los Angeles, California, and was buried in U.S.A. Burial Home of Peace Memorial Park East Los Angeles, California), and Jack Warner (born August 2, 1892, in London, Ontario, Canada and died September 9, 1978, in Los Angeles, California, U.S.A.), who were the sons of Benjamin Eichelbaum, an immigrant Polish cobbler and peddler.

The brothers began their careers showing moving pictures (traveling from town to town, renting auditoriums for showing movies, then moving on to other locations and cities with their selected movies which they owned the rights to show in each town and venue), in Ohio and Pennsylvania. In 1903, they commenced their plan of acquiring movie theatres and then entered the business of film distribution. In approximately 1913, they began producing their own films. In 1917, they moved their movie production studio and headquarters to Hollywood, California. In 1923, they named their company "Warner Brothers Pictures, Inc."

The eldest, wisest, most ethical, and moral brother, Harry, was the founding president of the company and ran its headquarters in New York City, while Albert was the company's treasurer and headed up the company's sales and distribution departments. Sam and Jack Warner managed the movie production studio in Hollywood, California.

Below is an enlightening article **By Ray Greene** Published April 5, 2023

Jack Warner

Marking 100 Years of Warner Bros. means remembering the despised studio boss who battled his brothers, fought his stars, and left a ruthless legacy

By Ray Greene Published April 5, 2023

Marilyn Monroe, Jack WarnerPhoto: Bettmann (Getty Images)

In a special series, **The A.V. Club** *looks at the legacy of Warner Bros. 100 years after the studio was founded.*

It's sad to see the once mighty Warner Bros. studio celebrate its 100th anniversary in a state of chaos and disarray. Sold to a succession of bad partners beginning in 1990 in a process that culminated with the disastrous AOL-Time Warner merger of 2000, Warner has spent the last 20 years shedding divisions and chasing the fool's gold of comic book movie dollars while the value of the whole enterprise tanked and tanked and tanked.

Related Content

Hulu announces History Of The World, Part II series from Mel Brooks

Starstruck renewed for third season at HBO Max

In 2018, AT&T paid $85.4 billion for what was then Time Warner. In 2022, they sold WarnerMedia to Discovery for just $43 billion. On March 16, the *combined* valuation for the blended entity that emerged as WarnerDiscovery was only $34.4 billion.

The Warner brothers wouldn't have stood for it.

Ah, the Warner brothers. They created a lasting enterprise that changed the course of world cinema by popularizing cinematic sound. Their list of tough-minded "golden era" classics includes *White Heat, Casablanca, The Adventures Of Robin Hood, Now, Voyager,* and *Mildred Pierce*. Their animators invented <u>Bugs Bunny and Daffy Duck</u>. For many historians, the Warners' brash motion pictures of the 1930s and '40s constitute commercial moviemaking's greatest run.

Top Stories 00:0401:12

Superheroes

11 movies to check out on Hulu in January 2024

The brothers hated each other. And everyone especially hated Jack.

Three enterprising moguls and their womanizing brother

From Left: Jack Warner, Harry Warner, Albert Warner (not pictured: Samuel Warner)Photo: Bettmann (Getty Images)

Jack was the youngest Warner, and he was the only one born in North America rather than the small Jewish village of Krasnosielc, Poland. His brothers built a burgeoning exhibition enterprise in the 1910s, and then invited Jack into it. Jack slowly infected the entire host organism, in a process that took 30-plus years to pull off. He ended up running the whole show, using business moves that were just short of mafia measures to edge out his siblings. But before that, Jack had already offended every brother in sight.

Where Harry, Albert, and Samuel Warner were characterized by moral conservatism and old world reserve, Jack was a chronic womanizer who fancied himself a song and dance man—a comedian who just happened to run a movie studio. He'd had a brief career in vaudeville, where he failed miserably. According to Jack's biographer Bob Thomas, his brother Sam told Jack to "Go out front where they pay the actors," because "that's where the money is."

It was advice Jack heeded to spectacular effect. When Sam died prematurely from a sinus infection at age 40 during post-production on the partial talkie and breakaway hit *The Jazz Singer*, Jack became the unchallenged head of Warner film production, making him an unstoppable Hollywood force. His career lasted longer than any of Hollywood's other founding moguls.

"He didn't die. Jack killed him."

From Left: Rex Harrison, Jack Warner, Audrey Hepburn Photo: Hulton Archives (Getty Images)

If you can see past the horrific addiction of lead actor Al Jolson to performing in blackface, *The Jazz Singer* is a fascinating artifact. The plot concerns a cantor's son named Jakie Rabinowitz, who shuns the old world values of tent and tabernacle for the bright lights of showbiz. It's the Jack Warner story, with Jolson as Jack, and the other brothers embodied by Jakie's old school rabbi father, slowly dying of apoplexy somewhere off camera, while Jakie lives it up on Broadway.

The analogy is imperfect of course because there were other treacheries operating within the Warner clan. At the time of his death, Sam Warner had allegedly cut a deal to migrate Warner's proprietary sound technology, called Vitaphone, over to Paramount—primarily so he could get out from under Albert's thumb.

Warner artists like Bette Davis and Jimmy Cagney clashed with Jack for decades though—mostly about money, in battles that carved years off Cagney's career, and which were fought to what amounted to a draw. The Warner directors and artists had a universally low opinion of Jack's creative abilities, and an even lower opinion of his constant jokes. But Jack did get off a quip that has lasted. Informed by the press that his old contract star Ronald Reagan had just declared his intention to run for California's governorship, Warner reportedly said, "No, no. Jimmy Stewart for governor. Ronald Reagan for *best friend*."

(Left:) Bette Davis, Jack Warner, (Right:) James Cagney, Jack Warner Photo: Archive Photos, Michael Ochs Archives (Getty Images)

It's largely understood that producer Daryl F. Zanuck was the man most responsible for the gangsters, gun molls, and gams approach of Warner's golden era, a fertile crescent from which sprouted Cagney, Edward G. Robinson, Bette Davis, Paul Muni, and Humphrey Bogart, amongst very many others. Still, Jack was obviously sympatico with the punchy product coming out in a volcanic spew under the Warner Bros. name. Brash and sassy was Jack's whole approach to life—and as for gangsters, Jack notoriously bum-rushed the stage and accepted the 1942 Best Picture Oscar for *Casablanca* before Hal Wallis—the man who actually produced the movie—could even rise to his feet.

By far Jack's greatest Don Corleone moment came in 1955, when he convinced his aging brothers Albert and Harry to sell all their shares in the company, for a windfall of $22 million, or around $250 million today. The hate between the brothers was so hot that Harry added a stipulation: Jack had to sell out too. The Warner era at Warner Bros. would have to end for them all at once.

Jack blithely agreed, then bought the studio back as soon as the deal closed, by arranging a quick million-dollar profit for his partners in collusion. He immediately installed himself as Warner's president—Harry's old job. Harry had a heart attack when he read the news in Variety, followed by a stroke a day after that. When Harry passed on in 1958, his widow Rea expressed her opinion succinctly: "He didn't die," she said, "Jack killed him."

While brother Harry should be remembered for his pioneering role in establishing the Warner brand and all it contains, his enmity toward his siblings, especially Jack, was so great it has become his legacy. He seems to have never liked Jack, whose second marriage he refused to attend, sending a note instead about how glad he was that their parents weren't alive to see the day. An enduring image of corporate lore that could be apocryphal but embodies an inner truth anyway finds Harry chasing Jack around the Burbank lot, swinging a lead pipe at Jack's head.

But Jolly Jack ultimately got the last laugh, because he lived in public, cultivated the press, and consequently wears the primary face of the Brothers Warner in the history books today. He lasted long enough at the studio that bears his name to battle with director Mike Nichols over the profane content of the Elizabeth Taylor-Richard Burton classic, *Who's Afraid Of Virginia Woolf?* and with Warren Beatty over the release strategy for *Bonnie And Clyde*. He was the only Old Hollywood mogul who could lay a justifiable claim to importance as New Hollywood took over.

New Hollywood, of course, eventually morphed into Corporate Hollywood, something that Jack would have been the best equipped of all the brothers to handle. Because Jack Warner was a survivor, after all, a trait ably demonstrated in 1958 when he lost control of his Alfa-Romeo after an evening of gambling in Cannes and was hit by a truck and thrown 40 feet from the car. With Jack in a coma, his son, Jack Jr., who worked at the studio, told the media his father was too ill for photographs, leading to reports that Jack's death was imminent. When Jack recovered he fired his own son for suggesting to the press that he'd been near death. The episode was Jack in miniature: he was ruthless, reckless, and larger than life, and while he often left a burning wreck behind him, Jack Warner always lived to fight—with his brothers or his stars or other studio executives—another day.

To be fair to the Warner Brothers movie studio (despite Jack Warner's sinister nature and sinful, immoral, unethical, and ungodly behavior toward his own brothers and family members, toward God for glamorizing criminals in order to make more money and become rich, thus creating the film noir category of movie types which again, glamorizes criminals and criminal behavior, which has been detrimental to behavior of crime-inclined humans and contrary to the teachings of Jesus Christ and the Bible, with regard to praising and encouraging Godly behavior, not criminal and Satanic behavior, that seen in film noir category movies, essentially created by Jack Warner), the Warner Brothers movie studio did, to their credit, make several movies, which helped persuade Americans to be proactive and join World War II, to prevent Adolf Hitler from taking over the entire world to execute all world citizens who did not fit his idiotic description of his idea of perfect or "Aryan" people.

For this, Warner Brothers movie studio deserves to be thanked and honored!

Fond remembrances of the past include competing in grammar school sporting events (football, baseball, water skiing, cross-country and downhill snow skiing, tennis, rock climbing, mountain climbing, high jump, long jump, relay teams, marathons (multiple), two-mile races, one-mile races, half-mile races, and 10-kilometer races (undefeated), and numerous "Boy Scouts of America Junior Olympics," or regular "Junior Olympics" sporting events that the author qualified for in various different track and field event categories, competing equitably, ethically, morally, justly, and fairly, in the competitions mentioned above with known and verified same sex athletes, which made each victory even more satisfying and fulfilling, as well as joyful and reassuring that the training regimen intensity, variety, strategy engaged in, was both well planned, successful, and verified by God my creator and Father for eternity!

It is frustrating, disappointing, and depressing to think that the current generation of children is having this remarkable, awesome, and spellbinding feeling of satisfaction stolen from them and replaced with anger, resentment, and frustration that follows each and every event that they choose to compete in which is contaminated and infiltrated by dishonest, unethical, immoral, or untreated mentally ill and unqualified (based on wrong gender participants being incorrectly enrolled in "boys versus girls," or "men versus women" athletic events), athletic competitors who are the opposite sex of others in each particular athletic competition.

Why should God and society allow these deranged, greedy, or otherwise disturbed individuals to illegitimately compete in competitions classified incorrectly by or the result of gender confusion of a mentally compromised or mentally ill athlete?

If these transgender, sex change, or other homosexual individuals pretending to be the opposite sex of what they were created as and born, by the grace and blessings of God, wish to compete honestly and ethically, achieve the true satisfaction that comes from intense, vigorous, and prolonged, strategic training and preparation, then they must do so by following race or competition gender categories and guidelines.

Society should not compromise and be sycophant to deranged, greedy, unethical, immoral, or mentally ill human athletes (or athletic event organizers) who desire or wish to be complicit in these deranged circumstances of deceit and ungodly intent and behavior by those who have inappropriately rejected their true identity and gender, as determined by God at their birth which is immutable and unchangeable, in all sane, reasonable, enlightened, and Godly societies in this universe and all universes, this generation, and all future generations.

CHAPTER SIX:

Literary Agents And Book Publishers And Movie Producers/Studios Long-Standing Anti-Religious And Anti-Societal Values Bias And Monopoly And The Opportunity For Human Society Members To Transform Into Superheroes By Engaging in Ant-Trust And Anti-Bias And Anti-Monopoly Litigation And Winning Battles That Result In The Eradication and Annihilation Of Current Anti-Religious Values Bias And Monopolistic Behavior & Rejection Of Religious Authors And Their Book To Movie Adaptations So That Future Generations May Enjoy Ethical, Moral Books And Movies To Read And View (And Be Positively Impacted By), Versus Current Creepy, Immoral, Psychiatric Disease (e.g., Gender-Confused Individuals) Glorification, Violence And Criminal Behavior-Glorifying and Promoting Books And Movies That Currently Dominate The Book Selling And Movie Production Industries, And, For Over One Hundred Years, Are Being Sought And Aggressively Promoted By Literary Agents, Screenwriters, Book Publishers, and Movie Production Studios

Mahatma Gandhi (1869-1948) was an Indian lawyer, anti-colonial nationalist, and political ethicist who employed nonviolent resistance to lead the successful campaign for India's independence from British rule. His philosophy of nonviolence and civil disobedience has inspired movements for civil rights and freedom across the world.

The literary agents in this world and book publishers in this world (currently, but hopefully not for long into the future or forever) currently demonstrate an extreme, "immorally-skewed," and ungodly disposition and aversion to Godly and divine messages submitted by religious, Godly, and spiritual authors to both literary agents and direct book publishing companies. This presently, unfortunately, applies and extends to all submitted and received new book proposal manuscripts from new and established authors, writing all genres of novels, including narrative nonfiction, fiction, motivational, inspirational, educational, historical, crime, mystery, and other various genres and different themes of novels and books.

That which follows is a true and accurate account of a talented writer shunned and disregarded by more than five-hundred book publishers, movie production studio administrators and acquisition agents, stage play production and acquisition agents, and "literary agents" (supposed academic, neutral, experts in deciphering and discovering new and fantastic book authors, though, in reality, highly biased, politically liberal and ungodly, in their websites, often seeking only gay, lesbian, transgender, murder or crime novels for publication, and undeniably anti-Christian in their immediate or often 6-12 month-delayed form letter response and declines to represent Christian authors who are writing life and world-improving, inspiring, motivational, and Godly generation-transforming remarkable novels, due to their preferences for ungodly and Satan-flavored novel manuscripts, which they believe will make them more money when and if published by them), for multiple years and after being in receipt of numerous fantastic nonfiction novel submissions sent to them by talented writers and burgeoning successful authors.

Incidentally, all the works produced by this particular author, thanks be to God and glory to God in Heaven, turned out to be fantastic novels, embraced and cherished by readers throughout the world, despite all the rejections these same, exact novels received by these monopolistic, sinister, liberal-biased, and ungodly (currently, but hopefully not for long or in the future), "Hades gatekeepers" (having no clue what the gates of heaven require in life, nor caring where they are, since they have not plan of ever passing through these gates to spend an eternal reunion with God their creator), who for the past approximately seventy-five years were and still are allowing sinister authors and their ungodly, criminal-inspiring, gay and transgender misbehavior-inspiring, and society-degrading novels, movie scripts, or Broadway play scripts to enter and pass through their, prejudiced, ungodly gates of present and future hell, while at the same time blocking all Godly values-based, ethical, moral, inspiring, motivating manuscripts for future novels submitted for worldwide publication by Christian authors.

If one has ever wondered why there is such a paucity, scarcity, and deficiency, especially in the last seventy years, of fantastic and inspiring Christian books and movies, especially coming out of Hollywood (almost none by comparison with drug abuse, crime, gay and transgender, and murder movies), and especially after the nineteen-sixty decade egregious and dreadful illegal drug abuse/dependence and alcohol abuse/dependence "young adult" cult generation that embraced, cherished, and promoted, some continuing this attitude and dark aspiration and outlook, Satan-inspired and celebrated, sadly, up to this very day.

The seemingly monopolistic or illegal trust-like behavior (a reference to Teddy Roosevelt and his "trust-busting" activities while a past president of the United States of America), inhibiting authors' freedom of speech opportunities to better this world by their writing talent, and the current monopoly power of large international book publishing companies, and their often biased and sycophant literary agents who accept little to no Christian and religious authors with Godly backgrounds and values, as well as screenwriters and movie industry executives who similarly have little to no interest, currently, in taking on new projects and making inspiring, motivating movies based on Godly values, activities, and accomplishments described in magnificently written true story books written by Christian and religious authors is alarming.

This current dilemma and travesty paints a bleak picture for the future of the United States of America and other countries worldwide. This monopolistic and illegal trust exclusion of spiritual messages and spiritual authors is incredibly disheartening to Christians worldwide who desire equal representation in the book publishing, stage play production, and movie production industries to not only glorify and acknowledge the blessing of God in their own lives but also to share God's message and blessings to all human beings on Earth!

The paragraphs and image in the following excerpt are from:

The Trust Buster [ushistory.org]
https://www.ushistory.org/us/43b.asp
The Trust Buster. **Article authored by: C. Gordon Moffat.**

Teddy Roosevelt was one American who believed a revolution was coming.

He believed **WALL STREET FINANCIERS** and powerful trust titans to be acting foolishly. While they were eating off fancy China on mahogany tables in marble dining rooms, the masses were roughing it. There seemed to be no limit to greed. If docking wages would increase profits, it was done. If higher railroad rates put more gold in their coffers, it was done. How much was enough, Roosevelt wondered?

The Sherman Anti-Trust Act

Although he himself was a man of means, he criticized the wealthy class of Americans on two counts. First, continued exploitation of the public could result in a violent uprising that could destroy the whole system. Second, the captains of industry were arrogant enough to believe themselves superior to the elected government. Now that he was President, Roosevelt went on the attack.

The President's weapon was the **SHERMAN ANTITRUST ACT**, passed by Congress in 1890. This law declared illegal all combinations "in restraint of trade." For the first twelve years of its existence, the Sherman Act was a paper tiger. United States courts routinely sided with business when any enforcement of the Act was attempted.

For example, the **AMERICAN SUGAR REFINING COMPANY** controlled 98 percent of the sugar industry. Despite this virtual monopoly, the Supreme Court refused to dissolve the corporation in an 1895 ruling. The only time an organization was deemed in restraint of trade was when the court ruled against a *labor union*.

Roosevelt knew that no new legislation was necessary. When he sensed that he had a sympathetic Court, he sprung into action.

Teddy vs. J.P.

Theodore Roosevelt was not the type to initiate major changes timidly. The first trust giant to fall victim to Roosevelt's assault was none other than the most powerful industrialist in the country — J. Pierpont Morgan.

This 1912 cartoon shows trusts smashing consumers with the tariff hammer in hopes of raising profits.

Morgan controlled a railroad company known as Northern Securities. In combination with railroad **MOGULS JAMES J. HILL** and **E. H. HARRIMAN**, Morgan controlled the bulk of railroad shipping across the northern United States.

Morgan was enjoying a peaceful dinner at his New York home on February 19, 1902, when his telephone rang. He was furious to learn that Roosevelt's Attorney General was bringing a suit against the Northern Securities Company. Stunned, he muttered to his equally shocked dinner guests about how rude it was to file such a suit without warning.

Four days later, Morgan was at the White House with the President. Morgan bellowed that he was being treated like a common criminal. The President informed Morgan that no compromise could be reached, and the matter would be settled by the courts. Morgan inquired if his other interests were at risk, too. Roosevelt told him only the ones that had done anything wrong would be prosecuted.

The Good, the Bad, and the Bully

This was the core of Theodore Roosevelt's leadership. He boiled everything down to a case of right versus wrong and good versus bad. If a trust controlled an entire industry but provided good service at reasonable rates, it was a "good" trust to be left alone. Only the "bad" trusts that jacked up rates and exploited consumers would come under attack. Who would decide the difference between right and wrong? The occupant of the White House trusted only himself to make this decision in the interests of the people.

The American public cheered Roosevelt's new offensive. The Supreme Court, in a narrow 5 to 4 decision, agreed and dissolved the Northern Securities Company. Roosevelt said confidently that no man, no matter how powerful, was above the law. As he landed blows on other "bad" trusts, his popularity grew and grew.

The paragraphs and image in the above excerpt should be both awakening and inspiring to Christians, who must battle the current liberal, Godless values, books, plays, and movie scripts being aggressively sought and produced into books, plays, and movies (while concomitantly engaging in aggressive and disparaging exclusion of well-written Christian books and stories worthy and deserving of conversions to books, plays, and movies that would definitely inspire and motivate all world citizens to behave in a Godly manner to the benefit of all cultures, societies, and countries throughout the world), by current large, wealthy, trusts, syndicates, and monopolistic "mega cap" book publishing companies, Broadway play production companies and play writes, literary agents, movie production studios and online internet streaming companies (e.g., Walt Disney whose leadership has run rogue and is continuing to ignore Godly values in its productions, and other movie studies such as Paramount, Warner Brothers Discovery, Comcast, N.B.C. Universal studio, and even Netflix).

One has only to view the current television shows, online streaming network shows and series, and current available movies in movie theaters to immediately realize that Godly values and inspirational books, plays, and films that promote a Godly, loving, and kind disposition, attitude, perspective, aspiration, and requisite actions are being totally ignored, avoided, downplayed, and cast out to back alley trash bins by the current liberal lifestyle and ungodly values-biased current literary agent employees and company directors, and production managers and chief executive officers of large, mega market capitalization companies who have made a living out of promoting premarital sex, violence, criminal and murder stories, and transgender, homosexual, and other deviant and ungodly behavior and lifestyles their money-making focus and sinister obsession, consequently leading to the constant and rapid (hopefully not irreversible), degradation and decline of society values in the past century, not only in the United States of America, but disappointingly, in cultures and countries throughout the world.

CHAPTER SEVEN:

Fraudulent And Corrupt State Elections In The United States of America And All Countries Throughout The World. For example, when California voters resoundingly defeated, by their voting majority, the concept of "same-sex marriage" or "gay marriage," how was the Governor of California (corruptly elected but correctly voted by California voters to be removed from office, then corruptly, through election ballot manipulation and fraudulent vote counting, not removed from office during and after the recall vote, despite California voters majority intent to remove him from office on the basis of corruption and incompetence), able to single-handedly override democracy and the intent of California voters to reject the unethical and immoral concept and notion of "same-sex marriage" or "gay marriage"? This issue was never correctly addressed, in legal terms and in court, and the prosecution of the Governor for voter system fraud and corrupt ballot counting (not counting ballots from voters with opposing views) has not been addressed for decades. Why? Ethical Society Members Who Address And Correct These Fraudulent And Corrupt State Elections Via Legal Court Victories Will Be Instant Superheroes, The Truly Elite

Dalai Lama is the spiritual leader of Tibetan Buddhism and a symbol of peace and compassion. The 14th Dalai Lama, Tenzin Gyatso, has been a tireless advocate for the rights and autonomy of the Tibetan people and has promoted nonviolence, interfaith dialogue, and human values globally. He was awarded the Nobel Peace Prize in 1989.

Gavin Newsom, the corruptly elected and corruptly maintained California Governor after the entire state's voters proactively voted to recall this corrupt politician, betrayed both God and the entire state of California when they voted that gay marriages should not, now or ever, be authorized. Gavin Newsom, without voter's consent, ignored the election results outlawing gay marriage.

Furthermore, the corrupt Governor of California has refused to secure the southern border of California with the country of Mexico, to prevent human trafficking, drug and illegal arms trafficking throughout his excessive and painful, morally devastating reign of terror as California's most unethical, corrupt, and ungodly (relative of corrupt fellow politician, Nancy Pelosi, responsible, in conjunction with corrupt and despicable, lying, dishonest politicians Hiliary Clinton and Adam Schiff for the unwarranted and false Russian collusion rumor and untrue scandal "mud-slinged" onto an innocent, efficient, dynamic, and pro-American standing United States of America President, who accomplished more good deeds and developments for America and American citizens despite 24 hour per day obstruction attempts by evil political opponents than, perhaps, any president since Ronald Reagan, Abraham Lincoln, and George Washington.

These presidents of the United States were an impressive cohort of like-minded strong, resilient, pro-American presidents who all left indelible marks of impressive achievements, against all odds and sinister lies and fraudulent accusations and constant attempts to obstruct his brilliant plan to protect Americans by securing the country's borders, eliminate racism, employ and raise the standard of living of all Americans willing to work honest and ethical jobs and occupations and, at the same time, care for those truly unable to work, but not necessarily those who are lazy and unwilling to work when many jobs are available, and drain the Washington D.C. swamp full of evil and Satanic crocodiles and alligators, whose only claim to fame is oversized, lying mouths, with sharp, vile tongues, espousing lies and illegitimate criticisms of an amazing, pro-American, anti-corruption, non-politician, elected by the country's citizens to be their U.S.A. President, Donald J. Trump, in response to one of the most anti-Christian and anti-American presidents the United States of America had ever witnessed or ever experienced who preceded him, namely, Barrack Obama.

Barrack Obama, one of the biggest and most infamous traitors to America, during his painful eight years as "president" (race-card playing non-leader and non-mentor who embraced corruption as though it were his best friend), gave millions of dollars to Iran, the number one terrorist country in the world, at least with regard to the United States and Israel, the two bastions of Christianity, standing strong and defending their Christian countries and heritage in a very similar manner, even while Iran was frequently and consistently chanting death to America and death to Israel, and openly burning both countries flags in public, on a regular basis long before and during Barrack Obama's weak and immoral presidency leadership attempt and test, which he repeatedly failed consecutively each year for eight years in a row.

Barrack not only criticized and disparaged the history of America as a country during his United Nations speech but also constantly and in a racist manner, always assumed that whenever Caucasian policemen had to use force to arrest Black criminals who resisted arrest, the Black criminals were always innocent victims, ignoring their crimes and resistance to being arrested.

To make matters worse, Barrack Obama's administration constantly promoted homosexual and transgender behavior, tried to force all Americans to accept this ungodly and sinful lifestyle as normal or ethical (absolutely not), and even attempted, unsuccessfully to coerce and force all businesses and schools in America to provide separate bathrooms for these mentally disturbed, sinful, and ungodly individuals, and even supported allowing these same individuals to compete in sporting events not appropriate for their birth gender, e.g., birth males fraudulently pretending to be females so they can unfairly enter, compete, and win swimming events or other sports competitions against their female opponents, a truly pathetic and anti-Christian attempt to destroy American Christian values by both these transgender mental illness patients and Barrack Obama alike, and difficult to determine who was more sinister and evil among these crazy behaving, irresponsible and disrespectful individuals.

Both had absolutely no respect for birth gender created by and assigned by God, thus no respect for God and Christian values, specifically and in general.

Barrack Obama was extremely unpopular amongst the vast majority of United States citizens after his first four-year term and terrorism against American Christian values.

However, by mastering and perfecting corrupt individual state and federal election "ballot voting" where voters were and are not verified by social security number to be citizens eligible to vote, not requiring legitimate government-issued identification to vote, using vote scanner machines that could be manipulated in any manner desired, by using pre-filled out fake ballots to alter vote totals, and delaying election results for several weeks after the election day, to allow whatever states he was behind in votes counts, to scan in sufficient numbers of fake ballots to ensure he would win, fraudulently, which he mastered, just as Gavin Newsome, and eventually Joseph Biden were also able to accomplish, without the consent or majority vote counts of the vast majority of honest, non-corrupt voting American citizens.

In California, as in most states, no signature is required on the actual ballot itself, just on the outer envelope, and voting in person is not required, nor is a valid social security number, nor proof of citizenship, nor even proof of pre-registration to vote on or before election day, a genuinely ignorant, naïve, and corrupt voting system in every state and federal election in America!

Artificial intelligence verification of social security authenticity and citizenship should be employed, voting should only be allowed in person, voting multiple times should be disallowed, dead people receiving ballots via mail so other family members can vote twice should be disallowed, vote and ballot harvesting should be outlawed and violating individuals prosecuted, all ballots should have bar codes and all voter responses should be trackable by the voter, who should be able to verify their specific vote responses were correctly received, counted, and documented exactly as they voted, all features which do not presently exist, thus the most corrupt elections ever, like a bad joke, in every aspect (without respect for ethical, moral, legitimate elections that Christian Americans expect and deserve), but loved by the forever-reigning corruptly elected politicians in power, which wrongly and inappropriately, in most cases have not term limits for how long they can continue in their mafia-like corrupt role as repeatedly, corruptly elected unethical politician.

Without non-corrupt elections, no career politician will ever merit any respect from intelligent and keen observers, who in their lifetimes, have seen multiple unelectable, unqualified, illegitimate political candidates with no support or following, and recently, without any attempts to embark on real or actual campaign trails before their supposedly "non-corrupt" election bid (for instance Hilary Clinton's non-campaign, and Joseph Biden, dementia-filled, basement teleprompter (pathetic) campaign, both with no real followers, due to their despised and unelectable status as criminal and dishonest humans or corrupt and undesirable, un-American political candidate verification based on their lack of effort to even commit to an actual campaign with visible supporters and followers. In the case of Barrack Obama's elections, Hilary Clinton's election, and Joseph Biden's "election," no astute observer could ever believe these elections were upright and honest, as there was absolutely no evidence of support or followers for these anti-American, anti-Christian corrupt politicians, known as the "triste trio" which history must accurately record and document if there is to be any truth whatsoever in this world!

Below are chapters/excerpts from a magnificent, mentoring, instructional, succinct, genuine, and truly enlightening masterpiece nonfiction novel that addresses the current corruptible and fraudulent election systems currently being utilized not only in the United States of America but worldwide to facilitate and enable corrupt politicians to constantly and assuredly be re-elected despite their misbehavior and dastardly intentions and actions carried out on a daily basis at their workplaces. This book also addresses many other societal problems throughout the world. It masterfully suggests and recommends relatively easy and practical, pragmatic fixes or solutions to these societal problems that are currently and have been, in the past, a plague and pandemic to societal health throughout all cultures and countries in this world for many centuries.

The Generational Assault on Christianity, Free Speech and Democracy in America,
A Call to Action to Preserve and Nurture American Values and Benevolent Exceptionalism

By Christopher Arthur Rockefeller

Chapter One:

The Obama, Biden, Clinton Axis of Evil: Will Democracy and Christians in America Fight Back?

The Beginning of The End of Democracy. Will Americans Stand Up for Truth, Liberty, and Justice?

"The Night Chicago Died" was a popular song in the 1970s and 1980s in the United States of America. The song was unique, special, and memorable due to the easy sing-along melody but, more importantly, for the message and history that the song conveyed about the dark times in America, which ended well with the triumph of good over evil.

On January 6, 2021, United States of America President Donald Trump's bid for four more years in office was stolen during the most blatant, unabashed, and unrepentant exhibition of evil triumphing over good in United States history since the assassination of the 16th United States President, Abraham Lincoln.

January 6, 2021, will forever in history be remembered as a major and significant setback, yet not defeat, in the crusades of Christians worldwide to disseminate the good news the Bible relates to this world and to continue to "drain the swamp" e.g., root out corruption and evil intent and malice toward the United States of America "founding fathers" who cherished the principles of, were guided by, and were protected and blessed by traditional Christian values, which the United States of America President, Donald Trump, had begun to re-establish and restore to American and World citizens, the first day he announced his candidacy for election to the highest position in government in the United States of America approximately five years earlier.

Christians must now unite like never before to defeat the evil and corrupt individual state and federal election fraud that likely has been progressively worsening, becoming more sophisticated, receiving more funding from rich and "non-elite but definitely sinister" profiteers (e.g., those who make an excessive or unfair profit, especially illegally or in a black market or by means that divert profit and employment to those outside America rather than Americans, e.g., outsourcing manufacturing to other countries to save money, but indirectly funding countries and their nuclear weapons and intercontinental ballistic missile (ICBM) manufacturing capabilities and manufacturing that may someday be used maliciously against other democracy-loving and Christian value-loving independent and free nations that respect human rights and are benevolent in world leadership roles), that are diabolically and defiantly and malevolently opposed to American Christian values and exceptionalism, freedom and independence and democracy for all citizens and traditional American Christian ethics and morals as taught in the Bible.

These same values inspired and led America's founding fathers to create one of the greatest manuscripts (perhaps second only to the Bible) ever written, the Constitution of the United States of America, which followed shortly after another miraculous and life-changing literary work of masterpiece level insight and foresight, The Declaration of Independence, written by, to, and for American citizens and addressed to England, whose abuses of the American colonies in the United States of America (a name later given to these abused settlers of America), could no longer be tolerated.

The Constitution of the United States of America was and always has been and will be a literary marvel and masterpiece that, when read aloud, sings out in one's mind like that of one of Mozart's greatest compositions being played by the world's greatest symphony. This masterpiece composition has guided American and world citizens' perspectives and behavior for the past 50 years. However, in the past ten years, the Constitution of the United States of America, which was guided by and based on traditional Christian values, is being repeatedly attacked or assaulted and not being adequately defended and protected by Christian citizens of not only the United States but the entire world. Christians worldwide must unite together to have the common, powerful, loud yet caring, and compassionate voice necessary to defend and protect Christian values when being attacked by radical atheists, agnostics, or others who would shun and mock God, their creator, and provider of peace, serenity, and purpose during their life on this planet.

Christian values have been mocked, abused, corrupted, and finally assaulted with fatal intent (this has been a progressive "ramped up" effort by radical and extremist groups in the world to unbelievably extremely high levels and have resulted in shocking consequences and events, e.g., the burning down of businesses within cities by radical "protestors" who then kill the business owners, then loot or steal all that business's inventory, only to then never be prosecuted and held accountable because they were "democratic" (crazy, corrupt, violent, unethical, ungodly extremists) political party sympathizers and voters who opposed the Republican President in office at the time!

In the past ten years, these crimes committed by unethical extremists and local terrorist organizations have largely been without prosecution if the criminals are in any way attached to (perhaps hired by) or sympathizers with the "democratic" (crazy, corrupt, violent, unethical, ungodly extremists) political party. This chaos climaxed on November 3, 2020, the most obvious, absurd, disappointing, and disgusting fraudulent United States Presidential election ever experienced and witnessed by the American people.

Not since the 1776 American Revolution against the King of England, when Americans realized their dream of beginning anew as a small but mighty nation free of misrepresentation (and no representation) in the election of their leader (Americans rejected leadership of the King of England who neither liked nor respected the common man that represented Americans in the North American continent), have Americans seen a greater assault on and insult to American citizens and world citizens and Christians values, independence, freedom of speech, and freedom from corrupt politician elections, than when the unpopular, unworthy Joseph Biden was "elected" (How are mafia union leaders "elected"?) President of the United States, without a meaningful campaign (one hour teleprompter talking, being dictated to say very little, because he had no original or intelligent things to say, does not qualify as an election campaign), and without any followers (nobody came to his campaign meetings; one could not even call them rallies because so few Americans supported him or believed he was even a worthy candidate for the position, especially after Joseph Biden took his son, Hunter, with him to China and then Hunter Biden received millions of (questionable bribe money) dollars from the Chinese and from Ukraine.

Why was Joseph Biden not imprisoned for getting the Ukraine lawyer who was in charge of investigating fraudulent Ukraine company payments to Hunter Biden? Why were the millions of dollars that China "invested" (questionable money bribe again) in the investment company that Hunter Biden was "working at or working for" never investigated as being a conflict of interest for Joseph Biden when foreign governments and companies are paying millions of dollars to the son of a corrupt politician running for the Presidency of the United States?

Why was the New York Post front-page story about these corrupt conflicts of interest and suspected foreign country bribes and interference with the United States presidential election, which was almost totally suppressed (unsuccessfully)by large technology companies, and why were Joseph Biden, Hunter Biden, and these technology companies not prosecuted for interference with free speech (e.g., deletion or blocking of New York Post front-page article about the Biden family corruption, by internet and social media companies, and by nearly every liberal and prejudiced news organizations) and election interference and corruption by suppressing truthful news of Biden family bribery and corruption that would have disqualified Joseph Biden for the election in the first place?

Every American and world citizen should seriously contemplate these questions before entertaining the idea that Donald Trump's "failure" to be re-elected President of the United States was anything more than the most overt, blatant, corrupt, and fraudulent election the United States of America has ever witnessed. If Christians in America (and throughout the world) and the common worker in America do not stand up in protest and follow through in demanding and ultimately achieving a just and verifiable voting system to replace the current inherently vulnerable, hackable, corruptible, unverifiable voting system, which currently is vulnerable to fraudulent ballot harvesting practices, ballot recounting of same ballot multiple times, scanning in fake ballots that are "pre-filled out" by the corrupt political party with no respect or regard for morality and ethical behavior, ballot replacement/swapping after discarding or other destruction of legitimate ballots, then democracy in the U.S.A. and perhaps worldwide will be dealt repeated and unending death blows…no exaggeration and no hyperbole…this is the reality this generation faces.

Voters must be able to vote (only once, in only one city and state, and only if qualified citizens, verified by social security number, official government-issued picture identification such as passports or proof of citizenship documents (not just photo identification cards or driver's licenses issued to illegal immigrants in "sanctuary" ("hades-inflicting") cities, and only if preregistered voters' ballots are received before or on election day and counting of ballots should be completed on election day with no exceptions. Ballots not arriving by election day should not be counted. This will eliminate election distrust and fraud, which peaked at the highest pinnacle of corruption and deceit on November 3, 2020.

This is not voter restriction, as many corrupt politicians and others (who wish election corruption to exist forever) assert, but, rather, the only way to ensure an organized, trustable election. Voters must then be allowed and enabled to verify online that their vote was received and registered exactly as they voted on each item. Each voter should be able (perhaps by bar codes AND each voter's personal, custom signature on each actual ballot) to then see their counted votes in the final ballot totals on the final election results website.

If we can send a rover (a planetary surface exploration device designed to move across the solid surface of a planet or other planetary mass celestial bodies, some designed to transport human spaceflight crew members, others designed to be partially or fully autonomous robots) to Mars, then we can and should be verifying who is a legitimate voter AND prosecuting those who attempt to vote numerous times or in multiple jurisdictions, e.g., by one verified bar code per verified eligible voter citizen, thereby preventing those who might otherwise be voting numerous times in multiple cities or states, eliminating ballots from deceased individuals and "last minute" unregistered, non-citizen, fraudulent criminals and eliminating the possibility of scanning of the same partisan or a particular corrupt political party's ballot repeatedly to alter election results.

Currently, certain corrupt politicians and specific corrupt states allow the counting of ballots AFTER election day so that they can calculate how many votes they need to overturn that state's election results; then they can scan in that many fake ballots to make up the difference and then add additional ballots to actually reverse the election results and thereby achieve a corrupt election victory or win...utterly ridiculous, immoral, and evil in every sense!

Artificial intelligence and quantum computer technology should and must enable same-day election-day vote tallies without errors and without exception in every state with 100% accuracy and verifiability... period! The World War Two generation dealt with and conquered the greatest and most significant threat to their generation.

Now, our generation and "true (non-corrupt) democracies" (the United States was, in the past, considered in this category...this is highly questionable now, however...sadly), and Christians worldwide must unite if Christianity and democracy without evil and tainted dishonest, non-Christian and corrupt politician misanthropes are to be prevented from usurping power and political dominance for generations to come, as a result of their lack of moral and ethical values (e.g., "moral bankruptcy") and their condoning evil, dishonest deceit in their daily embrace of corruption and disdain for an ethical, honest democracy voting system in America and all countries on this Earth!

Counting of each AMERICAN CITIZEN'S entire ballot voting entries, which should be and can be made, e.g., with a unique barcode, verifiable by that individual American voter by allowing each verified legitimate American voter (one vote per LEGAL and NON-INCARCERATED citizen) to go online with their own unique password or barcode and visualize the ENTIRE ballot that they submitted and check that each of their voted items, on each and every ballot item, was registered and counted as specified and intended by that voter, who can compare their, e.g., carbon copy, of their submitted ballot with that of the online verification system or their recorded and registered votes.

By comparing the duplicate (e.g., a carbon copy) ballot with an attached bar code that the voter can and must retain, with the ballot the voter submitted or voted in person at the voting site, with the online record, which is being recorded by the local and state and federal voting registrars, fraud can (quickly and easily, I might suggest) be eliminated for all time, again with the future help and evolution of artificial intelligence and quantum computing.

This secure voting system **must** be performed and verified by "unhackable" artificial intelligence supercomputers or quantum computer systems that instantly can confirm:

1) one legitimate vote per one verifiable state address (only one state and address even if a person has homes or addresses in multiple states or countries),

2) Eliminate multiple country citizenships (Force citizens to choose loyalty to and be able to vote in only one country if one wishes to have committed and loyal citizens and voters who have "skin in the game," otherwise risk having voters who vote for destructive policies and leaders and who are not pro-American or may even be Anti-American.)

3) Critical federal government-issued photo identification (I.D.) and/or iris registration and/or fingerprint verification of voter (one vote only per person),

4) No last-minute chaotic and corruptible registrations or voting without pre-registration.

5) Defined voting duration and deadline should be standardized for every state, and no vote should be counted before the ballot receipt deadline to prevent deficit vote calculations by those attempting to subvert truthful and accurate election results and to prevent the stuffing of ballot boxes with the corrupt and dastardly calculated and requisite number of fraudulent ballots to overthrow legitimate election votes from honest, ethical, moral, and law-abiding Americans (the only votes that count…ever!).

6) Multiple trusted cybersecurity security companies must be specifically contracted to protect all local, state, and federal elections with standardized and federally mandated security requirements and **steep and harsh federal imprisonment with prolonged incarceration for any countries, states, local governments, political parties, individual foreign or American citizens who dare to participate in election fraud,** essentially to successfully enact and achieve a "zero-tolerance policy" for election corruption or fraud.

7) Establish and enforce "pre-set," low-dollar budgets for candidates of election campaigns and contributions. This should be considered and instituted to allow any hard-working, honest, and patriotic American to compete in, survive, and win the election process. The best candidates and leaders in political elections should never be defeated merely because their election opponent is a richer socialist, communist, or fascist with more "ill-gotten gains" or funding from nefarious outsiders with ulterior motives to defeat the best candidates and replace them with corruptly-funded sycophant politicians who they can control and manipulate once they are elected into leadership roles.

Political candidates who are rich or backed by rich, radical, or liberal national or international socialists, communists, or fascists should have no advantage over American patriots during political elections. Being rich and radical does not mean you should be elected to political offices of leadership. Good leaders are defined by their moral values and their ability to be trusted by those they lead. By establishing low and equal monetary limits for political candidates' campaign funding, then candidates and future politicians will be elected based on their values and not the thickness of their wallets.

Current politicians are often evil and "amoral" political candidates (who have amassed ill-gotten gains by lying or receiving bribes from other individuals, companies, or countries, manipulating others, blackmailing others, or via dishonest personal or business dealings, or who simply inherited great wealth through gifts or inheritance that they neither deserved nor earned.

No politicians should be in financially advantageous positions to win elections purely because they "have acquired more ill-gotten gains or funds, are richer, or received outsider nefarious funding by others with ulterior motives and negative aspirations and intentions to defeat the better leadership candidate that is running for a political leadership position."

Poor, ethical, moral, hard-working, honest, educated, and Godly political candidates should be winning elections frequently based on their values and leadership qualities, and never because they possess a thicker wallet filled with biased and prejudiced currency (how currently elected politicians are being elected).

Chapter Two:

Three Antiquated Privileges (Afforded In The Past to Three Sectors of Society) That Must Now Be Abolished and Their Privileges Revoked Now and Forever

Big Technology And Biased Media And "News" Companies Who Were Granted Special Exemptions From Being Sued For Publishing Or Broadcasting Misinformation, Propagating Inaccurate And Untrue/Deceitful News To American Citizens And World Citizens, And For Censorship Or Suppression Of Free Speech

No Limits On Politician Terms (Maximum Length They Are Allowed to Remain In That Political Office And Position Of [Often Abused] Power, e.g., Senators Or House of Representatives Congress Member Or State or City Politicians), and

Tenure: A Concept That Promotes The Stifling of American Patriotism And The Stifling of Best And Optimized Outperformance Of Teachers

(At All Levels of Education) For The Duration of Their Career, Allowing Infiltration of a Country's Educational System By Socialists, Fascists, and Communists And Any And All False Narratives And Promises They May Choose To Espouse For The Remainder Of Their Career Without Remorse or Detrimental Consequence To Their Career Path And Ambitions, Which, If Go Unchecked And Are Not Eradicated From Our Education System, Will Continue To Infiltrate Our Grammar Schools, High Schools, Colleges / Universities And Forever Destroy America's Christian-Based Culture & Societal Values & Benevolent Exceptionalism That Is Necessary For American Patriotism & Loyalty To Our Country And Education System. Tenure Attempts To Destroy Democracy And Merit-Based Education Systems And Is Oppositional To Christian Values And Behavior, Which Must Be Employed Every Day And Evaluated To Ensure The Integrity Of The Educator And The Content Of Their Everyday Teachings.

Though the concept of "tenure" may have had an innocent, purposeful, and benevolent origin, all concepts or paradigms require reassessment and re-evaluation to determine the concept's relevancy and effectiveness in achieving the original intended purpose or goal. Without scrutiny, privileges granted to one or more sectors of society, e.g., big technology or media and "news" (biased and untruthful in many instances) companies, politicians with no term limits, and "tenured" educators in America may give those sectors unmatched advantages, consolidation of power and influence that these sectors and individuals may then leverage against fellow American citizens in malevolent ways and means.

Tenured professors, a select few and a minority group but unfortunately vociferous and obnoxious cohort, have, since the 1950s and into the 21st century, been able to freely promote socialism, fascism, and communism (despite thousands of years proof that these systems of government only usurp the power, freedom, and independence of their citizens and hand it over to less scrupulous, less benevolent, less moral, and less ethical "power mongers" who then use that power to inflict misery, starvation, injustice on their subjects (slave-like citizens) who misguidedly assumed their "trusted" leaders would demonstrate Christian charity and benevolence), after receiving tenure and protected status from being fired for suppressing free speech in class or on school campuses or for promoting radical anti-religious or political ideologies that are both "unpatriotic" and "un-American," in their classrooms, lectures, and publications.

Every other sector of society can be effectively held accountable for their words, actions, ideas, teachings and other inappropriate actions, biases, unjust discrimination, suppression of free speech or constitutional rights, so why should "tenured" educators, big technology companies, and politicians without term limits be allowed to gain disproportionate power and influence over other patriotic and mainstream, hard-working Christian families and American citizens, especially when these sectors have in the past century so nefariously used their undeserved or unwarranted privilege, power and influence to demean the concept of "American Exceptionalism."

What is the definition of "American Exceptionalism?" This is Luke's interpretation and definition of this aforementioned term and concept: America's belief and defense of personal freedom and liberties and acceptance that every human is created equal and with equal opportunity to work hard and achieve success that is limited only by that individual's positive attitude, hard work ethic, respect for Christian heritage, God, family, fellow humans and pride in country, America (or any other country), which is an exceptional country with regard to promoting and defending individual human liberties, freedom, and justice for all citizens in every country on this planet Earth.

"American Exceptionalism" is not an "America-only" concept or dream, but rather a dream for all citizens of all nations on all continents of this Earth. This concept could, theoretically, and probably should be renamed: "The World Dream!"

The 2020 United States Presidential Election was corruptly influenced in the twenty-first century. With all the present technology, artificial intelligence capability, and quantum computer security and sophistication that could be incorporated into the current antiquated election systems in the United States of America (and every other nation on Earth), corruption of the election process should be averted, prevented, and made impossible.

However, current corrupt "political parties" (aka anti-hard-working, honest, ethical, moral "world citizen" subverters) demonstrate no desire to and make no effort to legitimize, ensure, and verify that future elections will not be corrupt once they have been elected into office, at least up to this point in time.

This is an egregious lack of responsibility on their part and may, in fact, define their intent and goals to perpetuate and propagate their prejudiced and biased political party goal of continuing corrupt elections in the foreseeable future to ensure their sinister and corrupt politicians remain in power and protect their "sinful and law-breaking political sycophant lemmings."

The candidate whose physical and mental health were suboptimal and who should have been disqualified (due to overt dementia) was disgustingly allowed to run for political office. This was enacted, nefariously, for pure political bias reasons and ulterior malicious goals of a zenith corrupt (and "slave owner" mentality) political party who overtly has shown that they longer care for the safety, happiness, and serenity of their country's citizens, but are rather obsessed with corruptly electing any demented political party candidate in order to maintain government power and elected politicians "slave owner" status, such that they may then continue to destroy country border security, which endangers the safety and job security of ethical citizens.

By these corrupt politicians' actions, they then expect that unemployed and endangered citizens will run back to this corrupt political party (in fear, desperation, and need; again, slave-like dilemmas in life for world citizens) and vote for them. By these corrupt politicians creation of chaos (e.g., no border security and "sanctuary cities" harboring of federal law-breaking illegal immigrants, a.k.a. "humans, arms, illegal drug-trafficking mules in addition to Mexican (or any other country's) cartel/gang members or terrorists"), they then hope and have the intent and aspirations that their endangered citizens as well as illegal immigrants will then live "homeless" on city streets, sign up for food stamps and welfare programs, perpetuating their powerless "slave status" and forever disrupting or eliminating their ability to vote these corrupt politician "slave owners" out of office and out of their lives forever, as every hard-working, honest, ethical, moral "world citizen" dreams of and aspires to accomplish every day of their life! The strategy was to corruptly elect a candidate who was not qualified for the position, then let others pull his strings (like a puppet) and make all the decisions for him behind closed doors.

This individual had been a corrupt and dishonest politician his entire career (unfortunate and very sad when these are your only "outstanding" resume items), and his past performance as a life-long politician was (and is) dismal.

His entire career was (and is) defined by unethical behavior. Specific examples include repeated plagiarism, corrupt threats to the Ukraine foreign government to withhold United States financial support if that politician's son was (and is) not excluded from an ongoing financial corruption investigation, conflict of interest whereby the politician took bribes from foreign country(ies), e.g., encouraged and brought his son to China to receive payments (millions of dollars) to the business (investment firm) that the politician's son "was involved in" (despite no qualifications to be working in that occupation), all whilst the politician was active and acting Vice President of the United States. While all these disqualifying medical conditions, unethical background, criminal acts, circumstances, outright crimes (video evidence of him threatening a Ukrainian lawyer who was investigating his son for fraud and money laundering (the corrupt politician's son was paid money for "Burisma company involvement" despite having no qualifications, again, to be "involved with" that company, and thus should never have received money from the country of Ukraine), and other acts of corruption.

Only one alone, or all these combined medical issues and acts of corruption, accepting bribes and money from foreign countries (via his son) while he was a politician, should have resulted in the medical disqualification (evidence of age-related pathological dementia and memory loss), and criminal disqualification and prosecution for financial crimes (bribes from China & Ukraine). This corrupt and demented illegitimate candidate for the Presidency of the United States was corruptly elected despite all his crimes, his son's crimes, and his dementia due to the unwavering and corrupt support he was given by his corrupt "democratic (sinister) party" fellow politicians.

Suppose honest, moral, ethical politics existed in the United States of America during the 2020 presidential election. In that case, the more qualified, non-demented, businessman, resilient man, despite constant false accusations and bogus investigations, and the former United States incumbent president, should have and would have been elected.

The demented, corrupt, and criminal presidential candidate should have been "awarded" a "dishonorable discharge" and lost his pension. Then he should have been indicted and convicted of his crimes if we did not have such a world of corrupt politics and "swamp creatures" as permanent, crooked, unscrupulous politician residents in Congress and in Washington D.C.

His convictions should have been based on his criminal acts while vice president of the United States. While a federal government employee his prosecution should have been the result of his corrupt coercion and video-documented intimidation of a foreign government whereby he told the foreign government (Ukraine) to fire the lawyer who was investigating the Vice President's son's fraudulent payments from Ukraine under the false pretense that he was an officer and employee in the Burisma oil and gas company (this politician's son had no qualifications to merit a paid position in an oil and gas company).

The Vice President's son also received millions of dollars from the country of China "for his investment firm workplace" (the vice president's son possessed no qualifications or ethics and morals to work at an investment firm legitimately; you may research his personal history to verify this statement, which is highly recommended). These were all serious ethical, financial, and moral breaches and crimes that the Vice President oversaw and was directly involved in, had direct knowledge of (remember the vice president took his son to China with him on the Air Force One plane and set up the "Burisma Holdings Limited (holding company based in Kyiv, Ukraine, an energy exploration and production company) money embezzlement scam" involving corrupt Biden family members and corrupt Ukraine citizens and government officials, and was complicit in.

These were all prosecutable crimes involving world government coercions, manipulations for personal and family members' unethical financial gains and interference with justice proceedings, and a corruption investigation of the Vice President's son during Joseph Biden's election campaign that should have negated the possibility of this politician's continuing his United State Presidency candidacy. Instead, big technology companies, e.g., Google, Facebook, and liberal/anti-American Media and "News" companies (e.g., CNN, MSNBC, C.B.S., A.B.C., New York Times, others) chose to cover up, bury, edit or outright suppress and delete stories (e.g., New York Post article on Vice President and his son's Ukraine and China scandalous financial payments and Vice President's using United States tax payer money as leverage to get the Ukraine government to fire the lawyer investigating the Vice President's son for receiving corrupt payments as Burisma oil and gas company employee even though he had no knowledge or expertise in oil and gas industry and the Vice President who enabled his son to receive millions of dollars in payment to a financial firm, again, his son was supposed an employee of, despite that son having no training or experience in the financial/investment industry, all were criminal scandals that would have eliminated a corrupt and unethical United States President candidate for the 2020 United State Presidential election if big tech and media companies had not censored and deleted these findings and events from liberal media "news" outlets on tv and online. Instead, many months before the United States Presidential election, ordinary citizens were fed misleading headlines of "fake news" (altered, biased, censored, and misdirected statements of deceit).

Radical, liberal, and fake news companies (T.V. news stations and online media companies) were feeding (or more aptly described: "jamming down the throats") inaccurate news to honest, hard-working, unsuspecting American citizens who were, unfortunately, assuming that big technology and big media companies were ethically and morally reporting all the truthful (and unbiased) news that Americans are deserving of and expecting, but not getting in the twenty-first century. Liberal big media organizations, Hollywood, and big technology companies have decisively, in the past half-century, embarked on a journey and down a crooked road (perhaps "Crook's road" is more descriptive), which is emphatically anti-Christian, eschewing traditional values of man-woman marriage definition, traditional, conventional, and formal recognition that same-sex relationships and sexual partnerships are not supported by Jesus or Bible teachings.

These liberal big media organizations, Hollywood, and big technology companies are also denigrating American Patriotism. These organizations show no appreciation for the countless military lives lost in sacrifices for citizen's freedom, personal liberty, and the right to bear arms. They mock instead of supporting the notion of defending American values domestically and abroad to extend the benefits to all societies and countries the Christianity religion offers and the concept and paradigm of "American Exceptionalism" that Christianity affords to all peoples and nations that embrace it as both a concept and a way of life that is both honorable and desirable.

Never, before the 2020 United States Presidential Election, did Americans witness one candidate with memory loss, dementia, no energy, no charisma, multiple documented episodes with video evidence of inappropriate kissing or other contact with females throughout his political career and campaign, and no past performance showing any significant or above average merit or credentials, and pretend to complete an election campaign for only one hour per day from the basement of his home for over one year and expect to be elected President.

Perhaps Joseph Biden already knew the election would be corrupt, stolen, and guaranteed that he would win, so he felt no need or obligation to engage in a real campaign. Joseph even bragged in a publicly available and accessible online video clip that his political party had perfected a corrupt election for his predecessor's (Barak Obama) second term election when he was vice president and that this 2020 would be a landslide in his favor as a result of even more sophisticated plan for a corrupt election.

For a politician to admit to this means one of two things:

1) he is telling the truth, or
2) He has dementia and poor judgment, not knowing he should not reveal crimes or corruption he has participated in.

In either instance, Joseph Biden should have never been allowed to even be a legitimate candidate for the President of the United States on election day. During the 2020 presidential election campaign year, his opponent and the incumbent U.S. President was drawing full stadiums of supportive and enthusiastic Americans who were clearly pro-American and Christian conservative enthusiasts, while the former vice president challenger was dodging unstaged and spontaneous questions from reporters for his entire campaign.

This is the behavior of a candidate who is unable to field and intelligently answer or otherwise respond to unstaged questions on any topic and from any news agency or news reporter(s). The incumbent U.S. President was masterful, sharp, no-nonsense, and clearly and concisely communicated with the American people, always in a straightforward and "non-political" manner of speech (e.g., he actually told people the truth when he spoke…how refreshing). Unlike Joseph Biden or the vast majority of corrupt politicians who engage in "politician speech" on a daily basis (e.g., see all the lying done during the fake Russian collusion investigation of Trump that was a farce and completely fabricated or "made up" by the democratic party to besmirch their political opponent, Donald Trump, or otherwise telling voters what they think will get them [the corrupt politicians] re-elected, lying to citizens daily, then acting in a manner that completely disregards the American voter's wishes and desires once they are elected).

The elected and incumbent President promised to put American values first, protect United States citizens by building a border wall, and follow through on his campaign promises (until his certain re-election was shamelessly stolen in perhaps the most corrupt election ever witnessed by this generation of American citizens). Ronald Reagan, Abraham Lincoln, and George Washington come to mind when one ponders outstanding examples of United States Presidents who have put the American people and American Christian values ahead of more corrupt political party biases and self-serving political party objectives.

The corrupt and unethical former vice president's campaign in the 2020 U.S. President election began, similar to a devil's spawn of his devilish son, following Obama's stacking the "secret (corrupt) services" and "intelligence" agencies with radical leftists just before leaving office (despicable), coercion and recruitment of "Never Trump" liberal democrats, socialists, fascists, Muslim radicals and communists within the government and national security agencies (e.g., N.S.A., F.B.I., C.I.A. and other agencies) to not only falsely accuse President Trump of bogus (democrats knew the Russian collusion allegations were false the whole time they lied to American citizens on television every day, because they made up the lie themselves), unsupported, manufactured Russian collusion allegations, but also encouraged the constant sharing, leaking and collusion of the agents to launch a constant and relentless effort to smear, malign and, unjustly, destroy the character of Donald Trump and to oppose his every ambition, plan and intent to improve the plight of American workers and "even the playing field" for the American workers and American companies who were sold out by previous politicians who enabled unequal import/export opportunities for foreign countries and foreign workers and thus threatened the viability and survival of American manufacturing companies and other American businesses.

Mafia-like fat cat union leaders in America also threatened the future of American businesses and manufacturing by ensuring that the cost of manufacturing in America far exceeded foreign countries due to a lack of competition for American citizen employees to effectively negotiate their own salaries that might be lower and more affordable to and for American companies than the artificially elevated big union salaries. Many companies went bankrupt in the last half century due to union distortion of American worker wages and benefits, or were forced to outsource all manufacturing to other countries due to union-negotiated unreasonable starting salaries for American citizen workers. Companies cannot survive if labor costs exceed manufacturing product sales revenue.

It is simple math. China has been importing fentanyl into America indirectly through Mexico for many years, needlessly killing young Americans via overdoses. Donald Trump was building the southern border wall to curb not only drug but also human trafficking across the border until his re-election was stolen, and his plan to finish the border was thwarted. Democrats have no interest in preventing opioid overdose deaths in America and thus will not complete the southern border wall project that Donald J. Trump wisely and skillfully commenced during his first four-year term as the United States President. The Chinese government can then use the money that China makes from drug smuggling into America through Mexico to build missiles or create other biological weapons that may someday destroy America and the entire world. This is not a good scenario.

A biological weapon was unleashed on the world by China, suspiciously, shortly after Joe Biden and his son traveled on Air Force Two to China at the end of U.S. President Barack Obama's second term. This virus biological weapon effectively destroyed President Donald J. Trump's best American economy and lowest unemployment rate in 60 years, again suspiciously just before and during his re-election campaign at the end of 2019, and forced a shutdown of American businesses for all of 2020 (and business shutdowns worldwide).

This Chinese biological weapon effectively destroyed Trump's fantastic economy and the world economy, all to attempt to curb or minimize spread of the scientist-manipulated viruses (to make them more effective in the infection and attack on the human body, e.g., selecting and designing viruses with higher virulence) which was developed to be more virulent, made possible by indirect funding to a Chinese laboratory, from Anthony Fauci, MD, Infectious Disease Dept Head at National Institutes of Health in Bethesda, Maryland, United States who joint funded research on Chimera and viruses in conjunction and cooperation with the Wuhan, China Biologic Weapons Research Lab. Large technology companies in America, including Google, Facebook, CNN, and other "biased and prejudiced democrat news companies," did their best to suppress these stories and defend China's misbehavior rather than expose China's malicious virus attack on America and the entire world. China funded the World Health Organization (W.H.O.) President who acted as China's parrot, repeating whatever false narrative China supplied the W.H.O.

Proof of China's attack on Trump's economy and the entire world was blatant, obvious, unmasked, and unapologetic. China told the W.H.O. and the world they locked down Wuhan, China, due to the virus outbreak (after letting the Chinese ophthalmologist whistleblower about the virus outbreak die in the hospital in late 2019) but covertly and disgustingly were at the same time allowing any infected persons in Wuhan, China travel to any country outside China but to no other areas in China.

China disliked Trump's attempts to equalize trade (essentially converting Americans from (non-manufacturing, non-exporting) slaves to purposely underpriced Chinese imports (China being the Slave Owner in this scenario) into free and independent, entrepreneurial, liberated, and hard-working manufacturing non-slave "world citizens" that they had been since 1776, when American's chose to work hard and earnestly for themselves instead of Britain who cared nothing about their opinions and thus offered them no rights to vote or have any say on their plight and destiny in life, no matter how long or hard they worked each day), and level differences in import/export tariffs between America and China, and Democrats were complicit in supporting China in its efforts to ensure that Trump would not be re-elected for a second four-year term, which would have certainly brought substantial benefits to American companies and workers by having more fair competition with China who had been dumping low-cost steel and other Chinese-made products in America and underpricing American companies to put them out of business.

Anthony Fauci's attempted coverup of the human-to-human transmission of the virus and the origination of the Chimera, a man-altered virus, to make it more virulent (high human attack efficiency) from the Wuhan, China biological weapons and virus research lab was blown wide open and exposed when emails from Dr. Fauci were discovered and made available to the world by Rand Paul, ophthalmologist physician and United States politician from the state of Kentucky.

Kudos to Rand Paul for exposing the most "successful (malevolent)" China Virus Biological Weapon Attack on America and the entire world and the attempted but unsuccessful coverup by Anthony Fauci and the Democratic Party. Did the democratic party encourage and plan the attack along with China to destroy Donald Trump's booming and exceptional economy in a malevolent effort to win the 2020 United States Presidential election? This is an essential and excellent question to ponder.

Look at the pieces and reconstruct the "nightmare puzzle picture…" it's quite an atrocious picture. Hollywood, the N.B.A., CNN, and almost all politically biased "news" companies (democratic liberals who are surprisingly anti-Christian or religion-less persons and supporters of deviant lifestyles such as same-sex unions and unlawful, illegal immigration and thus human trafficking and drug smuggling, which is inseparable from illegal immigration, no borders and Mexican drug cartel enrichment and China enrichment who sell the drugs to Mexico, to then be smuggled across the [non-existent] southern border with Mexico).

United States President Trump, from 2016 through 2020, was perhaps the strongest, most robust, most capable, and fittest President ever in defending himself from the corrupt "alligator swamp" that is also known as "Washington D.C." and the unbridled corrupt and dishonest intentions and actions of what he correctly characterized as "Fake News Companies" which comprised: CNN, A.B.C., C.B.S., Google, Facebook, N.B.A. (these organizations couldn't care less about minority cultures and Muslims being placed in work and concentration camps by China, as long as China or any other European Country honored financial contracts that it made with the National Basketball Association (N.B.A.), the National Football League (N.F.L.).

The N.F.L. showed absolutely no respect for "God and Country" when N.F.L. players and N.F.L. owners were both complicit and in a coordinated effort, repeatedly disrespected the United States Flag and National Anthem song honoring the thousands of soldiers who either fought for and lived or fought for and died to allow these N.F.L. owners and players to earn exorbitant salaries playing sports games instead fighting foreign (and domestic, sad to say) wars to preserve their safety, freedom, and independence while playing games that most citizens left behind in their childhood when they had to be responsible adults, give up playing childhood games, and go to college and work to provide for their families, for much less (and much more reasonable and rational) yearly salaries, despite their occupations being much more necessary, vital, important, meaningful, and impactful to the needs of other humans on this planet.

At the beginning of football games, when the game players choose not to stand at attention and display earnest and silent respect for their country's national flag and the singing of the national anthem in remembrance of and respect for the sacrifices (e.g., wounded soldiers) or deaths of soldiers in past wars who fought for freedom, justice, independence …well this could only be described as ungrateful and truly insulting to ALL Americans.

Even other countries were shocked that "over-paid game-playing boys" could be so immature, selfish, and unpatriotic to the men and women who defend or die for their country to achieve and maintain human freedoms and independence for Americans and "world citizens" in many nations, that allow them to make a living by playing a childhood game, and with good reason, I might add.

By not standing at attention and with an attitude of gratefulness and respect for those who fought for their freedom and their very own lives (they often would kneel down on the grass instead, defiantly and disrespectfully), they were not bringing attention to social justice or any other issue, other than their own narcissism, despite the many soldiers' lives that were lost in past wars so they can "play games as adults" and make enormous sums of money that are, again, inappropriate and disproportionate to their contributions to our country, society, and world.

Unlike the soldiers and the sacrifices they made (including losing their lives) to ensure the freedom and independence of all Americans, these prima donna adult kids playing childhood games have and show no appreciation for the sacrifices made for them by soldiers now deceased. For God's sake, stand and pay respect to the soldiers who died so you can play childhood games and get paid far more than you are worth or deserve. Perhaps you should even shed some tears, while standing at attention during the display of your country's flag and the playing of the national anthem, at the beginning of your childhood and adult game commencement and recognize the grace and mercy that you are the recipient of, not because you are deserving of or entitled to grace and mercy (by definition), but because heroes of this country, in each generation fight to keep and maintain your freedom from corruption, tyranny, communism, socialism and governments that would otherwise suppress your free speech, likely imprison you rather than allow you to play games that contribute little or nothing to the overall well-being of most humans, arrest you for demonstrations, harshly punish disobedience and irreverent attitudes, stomp down protests and severely restrict your independence and freedom or, even poison you or enslave you for illegitimate reasons or under false pretenses or because you are a political opponent or political prisoner.

Think of and remember how Alexei Navalny and Brittney Griner were mistreated in Russia by that country's tyrant leader. Stand in respect and at attention, place your hand over your heart, shed a tear, and be an American who is grateful and respectful of those who suffered for you so that you, personally, did not have to fight for your life, liberty, and freedom. Show the utmost respect for these individuals who sacrificed themselves for you, are now permanently and significantly disabled or deceased, who were and are better than you in many or every respect.

By doing this, you will be setting an excellent example for young children and, at the same time, find that fans actually respect you instead of despising you for your selfishness, arrogance, and disrespectful behavior to present and past generations of persons who fought for their country's freedom and independence and universally accepted principles regarding the protection of human dignity and respect for all humans.

Why should Americans accept or believe any (fake) news organizations that care only about money, viewer ratings, advertiser revenue and no longer report the truth but rather politicize the news and delete, manipulate, suppress truthful occurrences only to support their political election candidate versus being objective and unbiased reporters of events and allowing Americans to interpret people's actions in light of the facts (truths, that are often not reported) that are evident and then make their own decision, utilizing their judgment, as to what exactly happened and why it happened.

When every event in the "fake news world" is categorized and classified based on individual(s) skin color, sex, or "sexual orientation" (always wrong and worthless categories and means of classification, incidentally), and random labels of racism, sexism, or homophobia are assigned to the perpetrator or victim by the uneducated "fake news" reporter(s).

The actual truth will not only be harder to discern but also harder, more complicated, more confused, and more challenging to see and discern outright. In this case, the actual event has now been cloaked in a distracting and unattractive grim reaper outfit, which must now be shed to assess the heart, soul, and intention of the human hidden under that cloak. The news should exist to educate and enlighten its town, city, state, and country citizens. Leave the entertainment of citizens to the movie studios who can and will, each generation… hopefully, promote movies that entertain citizens of the world with uplifting and inspiring stories versus divisive movies with characters who use profanities and engage in criminal and deviant or illegal activities.

News and other media agencies should **not** be forcing their own biased views on citizens during election time or at any other time! Citizens can then decide on their own whom they would like to support and who is worthy of being, e.g., President of the United States, based on their intelligence, ethical and moral character, benevolence, work ethic, energy level required for the job they are a candidate for or applying for, education, common sense, health and fitness to be a righteous, responsible and benevolent leader of the free, Christian, and uncorrupt world.

News organizations, media companies, big technology companies (e.g., Google and Facebook, whose C.E.O.s may be born in or from foreign countries or who may be married to a spouse that dislikes or hates America and Americans), and Hollywood celebrities or other political liberals, socialists, fascists, or communists or others who are either descendants of 1960's anti-government parents or pro-illicit drug abuse parents (e.g., the insane and deviant society members) should not be permitted or allowed to run or operate the asylum because their ideas to legalize and normalize drugs that destroy brains and other body parts are truly and genuinely insane.

Christians must step up to their responsibility, in each generation, and in a united fashion, quash the radicals, educate and make treatment and counseling available for the sexually deviant and misguided so they do not persist in self-destructive behavior and the destruction of other human's morality as was and is God's intention and purpose for every one of his human creations. A battle must be fought each day to protect and defend world citizens from the evil, the unremorseful and unapologetic fringe persons in society who seek to derail and destroy Christian families, Christian values, and ethics in small towns, cities, societies, cultures, governments and other institutions, countries, and the world. These immoral and unethical deviants who stray far from Christian societal values will never stop trying to brainwash hard-working, honest, ethical, moral, God-fearing, God-respecting citizens of the world.

Christians must, daily, honor, defend, and promote to all their friends and acquaintances the teachings of Jesus that are in the greatest book ever written, The Bible. Those who have not yet received God's message of salvation and redemption for all humans, regardless of their past sins, must be informed of their opportunity to accept Christ Jesus into their lives and live an amazing life thereafter. These individuals usually believe that if they live like Christians, they will somehow not have as much fun as if they continue down their present path of self-destruction. Christianity is a life that is rewarding, satisfying, calming, and beneficial to all humans on Earth.

Living a Christian life and lifestyle enables great benevolent success in life and provides a path, plan, and directions to find peace, develop mutual respect for others, and live in harmony with other humans, caring for and respecting all others regardless of their race, skin color, culture, country of origin, or background while striving to live the life that Jesus taught all humans to live in the Bible.

Obstacles in the paths of Christians are the evil, unethical, morally bankrupt, and sexually deviant persons who rose to positions of power and influence as a result of birthright inheritance of money or fame or wealth derived from criminal or morally and ethically corrupt business activities that contributed in no way to the betterment of their fellow human being or society in general. Christianity and the Bible provided the backbone and guiding principles of America's Founding Fathers during the birth of this nation in 1776. Christianity and the Bible should continue to be the guiding light of our country and intent to be benevolent, kind, gracious, and merciful "world citizens" and citizens of America. Christianity and the Bible should also influence daily how we introduce, support, and defend Bible guidelines to and for others to bring about and ensure ethical and moral living and to create a "more perfect" country and world, each generation of our existence.

Chapter Three:

Christianity-Based Work Ethics of Honest, Hard-Working American Families vs International Business Outsourcing of Employment Opportunities and Loyalty to American Manufacturing Ingenuity and

The Role of The Media and The Press in Propagating and Perpetuating Democratic Party Racism and Enslavement of Americans by Attempting to Divide Americans as Ancient Slave Owners Did: "Your Skin Color Determines Your Worth in Society." This Statement Never Has Been, Nor Ever Will Be True.

America is a great nation because we are "color blind." Americans, since 1776, have believed that all people are created equal. This is why American colonists rejected the idea that they were obligated to pay taxes to a British monarch they could not and did not vote for and a British monarch who was born into a "royal" family but whose resume did not include: "a leader of the people, by the people and for the people (of the American Colonies)."

Should elected leaders of America (specifically the President and Vice President of the United States of America, members of the House of Representatives and Senate, state governors and mayors, and other local city elected officials) be rewarded for predictable and despicable behavior whereby, every 2nd and 4th year during elections of politicians, they sputter racist comments and slogans reminiscent of slave owners in the past that reduce and degrade "Americans" based on their skin color only.

Should any "American" accept the racism that is implicit in being judged as a person only based on skin color? Absolutely not!

This is the behavior of past slave owners and racists of past decades, scores, and centuries ago. Yet, the Democratic party uses the "slave owner tactic" every mid-term election and every presidential election year (and, disappointingly and disgracefully, even during intervening years between election years) to stir up racism and discontent that predictably always divides family members, friends, co-workers and, in general, destroys American pride and unity as fellow "countrymates" that SHOULD BE focused on electing exceptional zenith leaders to lead our tremendous, extraordinary, and exceptional country, and to be a "beacon of light" for the world in promoting and propagating American Christian values to and for all "World Citizens" of all nations!

CHAPTER EIGHT:

Politically-Motivated, Fraudulent, Malicious Prosecution In The United States of America And All Countries Throughout The World. Ethical Society Members Who Address And Correct These Politically-Motivated, Fraudulent, Malicious Prosecutions Via Legal Court Victories Will Be Instant Superheroes, The Truly Elite

Mother Teresa (1910-1997) was a Roman Catholic nun and missionary who founded the Missionaries of Charity, a religious congregation dedicated to helping the poorest of the poor. Her selfless work in the slums of Calcutta (now Kolkata) brought her international recognition and numerous awards, including the Nobel Peace Prize in 1979.

The overtly declared malicious prosecution political party, also known as the "(non-) democratic political party" (or "nightmare fraudulent illegal aliens and illegal humans, illegal arms, and illegal drugs-trafficking, and sanctuary cities-supporting [to house, and issue fraudulent non-United States of America citizen photo identification cards to illegally vote in corrupt elections], political party who is endlessly issuing [an action that should be outlawed with issuers being prosecuted] 'state government identifications' [to fraudulently vote for present and future election criminal democrat party candidates and protect these illegal criminals from (what an ethical and Godly country would consider), a merited, warranted, and highly deserved deportation for illegally entering the United States without authorization or approval, and with criminal intent of breaking federal immigration laws and many other laws], is salvageable and may be restored to respectable if they change their attitudes, aspirations, intent, motivation, and rid themselves of their constant and yearly repetitive practice of stirring interracial discontent amongst citizens not only of the United States of America, but also throughout the world in every country.

The current and contemporary "(non-) democratic political party" is not only evilly biased and prejudicial, but also the polar extreme opposite example of, and "non-mentor" of a true and Godly democracy, as was the intent, aspiration, motivation, and Godly inspiration of the "Founding Fathers" of the United States of America constitution and country.

What would the new and dramatically or markedly improved "(non-) democratic political party" look like if they realigned their party perspectives, intent, aspirations, goals, and most importantly, actions with the original "Founding Fathers" goals for the government of the United States of America, guided by and always (every second of every day), under the auspices of God their father and creator and leader of all world citizens, also known as the children of God or God's family worldwide?

Superheroes

Below are chapters/excerpts from a magnificent, mentoring, instructional, succinct, and truly enlightening masterpiece novel addressing the "Politically Motivated, Fraudulent, Malicious Prosecution Occurring Presently In The United States of America And All Countries Throughout The World."

Ethical Society Members Who Address And Correct These Politically Motivated, Fraudulent, Malicious Prosecutions Via Legal Court Victories Will Be Instant Superheroes, And Will Be Deserving Of The Title And Will Have Truly Earned The Honor Bestowed On Them By Being Referred To, Accurately, As "The Truly Elite." Similarly, this benevolent change in the current vicious and malicious political environment throughout the United States of America and countries throughout the world will indirectly also prevent disqualification or legal distractions for Godly and Christian-supporting political election candidates who have, many times in the past, and continue to be sidelined and destroyed by the current corruptible and fraudulent election systems currently being utilized not only in the United States of America but worldwide to facilitate and enable corrupt politicians to constantly and assuredly be re-elected despite their misbehavior and dastardly intentions and actions carried out daily at their workplaces.

This book also addresses many other societal problems throughout the world and masterfully suggests and recommends quite straightforward, easy, practical, and pragmatic fixes or solutions to these societal problems that are and have been a plague and pandemic to societal health throughout all cultures and countries in this world for centuries.

The Generational Assault on Christianity, Free Speech and Democracy in America, A Call to Action to Preserve and Nurture American Values and Benevolent Exceptionalism

By Christopher Arthur Rockefeller

Chapter four:

What Are American Values? What were the November 2020 United States Presidential Election Values That Were To Be Adjudicated At The Ballot Box That Were Then Soiled, Corrupted, and Stolen?

America's founding fathers believed that the Bible is the living word of God and that the pages contained within the Bible should direct and guide the behavior, ethical, and moral principles of our nascent country and its leaders. This is evident in many ways if one closely studies the history and founding of the United States of America. Note the uppercase words in the chapter title. Is this not the ultimate goal of America and the citizens of America? Is it not a well-accepted cliché and principal: "united we stand, divided we fall?"

Why then would Americans tolerate, support, or give any votes or credibility to a political party (Democratic Party in the 2020 U.S.A. Presidential Election) that has the following agenda each and every election year: "always project on our opponent political party and anyone else who opposes our power grabs that they are: racist, misogynists, or misanthropes." The truth is that Americans went to the ballot box in November 2020, and their votes were discarded, replaced, altered, or otherwise negated by evil and maleficent ballot center workers who were malevolently organized and instructed to fraudulently alter election results by multiple scanning of single ballots for Joseph Biden, scanning ballots preprinted and transported from storage warehouses in the same state or ballots being counted that were transported across state lines by U.S. Postal Service and others. Americans emphatically and enthusiastically supported and voted for Donald J. Trump in the November 2020 United States Presidential Election. Donald J. Trump should have been elected by the widest margin of victory ever had the election not been the most overtly corrupt and blatantly stolen election in American history.

The sinister individuals who orchestrated the corrupted election completely discounted and disregarded the intent, will, desire, and love of the American people for Donald J. Trump. If anyone should doubt this fact, one need only review the multiple instances of wildly popular video footage clips filmed at the packed houses, arenas, convention centers, stadiums, and other gathering places that hosted Donald J. Trump's pre-election campaign rallies. Celebrations of American values and hard-working, God-respecting, and God-fearing everyday citizens of all occupations and from all "walks of life" who attended these celebrations of America's Christian values engender what we know as "American exceptionalism."

What is American exceptionalism? Is this a bad phrase or concept? No. Absolutely not. American exceptionalism defined: "Extraordinary power (judiciously restrained and benevolently used in times of worldwide crisis), bravery, wealth and success generated by Bible-based ethics, morals, values whereby all men and women are equally respected and believed to be created (born) equal, color-blind with regard to skin color (non-racist or judgmental regarding the opportunity afforded to all based on educational advancement in society based on work ethic and education pursued by each individual) and all individuals are given equal opportunity from birth, for each and every American legal citizen, to work hard, study hard, achieve the highest education level possible, through loans or work study programs, to advance their standing in society, all without class structure seen in other countries, past and present, where persons are born into specific poor, middle class, wealthy classes that they can never escape from, regardless of their talent, intellect, work ethic or effort or in other countries where citizens are born into peasant or royal families, never with opportunity to transition from one class to the other.

Why should someone born into a "royal family" be afforded any more respect or opportunity than someone born into a low-income family? American exceptionalism, in summary, is the opportunity to achieve any level of success, regardless of skin color, socio-economic background or upbringing, political party, or country of origin, provided that you are a legal citizen, respect and follow Bible-based ethical, moral, societal values taught in the Bible and embrace and love American values and are willing to work to achieve your goals and success through attaining the highest level of education and training possible and working earnestly and honestly each day to achieve the success opportunity afforded to you as a result your having accepted and embraced America's Christian values which engender what we know as American exceptionalism.

Donald J. Trump's campaign rallies were spied on and disrupted by evil criminal acts by the previous, corrupt "American President" Barrack Hussein Obama, who most likely did not himself honestly win his second four-year term of president when running against Mitt Romney for the highest political office in America. Arising out of a state that has long been a hotbed of state and local political corruption since the infamous days that Al Capone ruled the state, Obama was cut from the same cloth as Al Capone. This is a fact. Regardless of skin color, Godly and honest, ethical Americans are **always** color-blind.

Any skin color citizen can be unethical, morally bankrupt, dishonest, a liar, a cheater, and a disgraceful American citizen, or a so-called "bad apple" that must be plucked from the Apple tree so that other "good and healthy (for society) apples" can grow and develop to maturity and achieve Godly spirituality and zenith fulfillment and serenity in life (these apples being known as and acknowledged as "Godly world citizens").

Obama, we have learned, was, in fact, a "rotten apple." Obama premeditated treason against Trump, the candidate for President, and coordinated the greatest act of treason in the United States Presidential Campaign and Election History, with evil intent to spitefully endanger the smooth transition of presidential leadership to the democratically and duly elected people's choice for President, Donald J. Trump.

Obama committed further multiple acts of treason in setting up an enormous web of corruption and deceit of "deep state" national security agency individuals who acted as political poison pills that Obama intended to poison the effectiveness and efficiency of the next president, Donald Trump. Obama's evil intent for America had no limits. Obama supported, campaigned with, and for Hilary Clinton and flew her around to campaign events on his Air Force One Jet.

This demonstrates that Obama cared only about maintaining political power and didn't give ANY thought to supporting an ethical or moral candidate with American Christian values for the person he wanted to assume the presidency of the United States after he finished his last and disastrous, detrimental to America's survival, four-year term as president.

Hillary Clinton was the most deviant, dishonest, and unethical female candidate for United States President this country has ever seen and could not stand to listen to, especially after her comments that "Half of Trump Supporters Are In A 'Basket of Deplorables,' "which immediately (and not shockingly) grabbed the attention of all American voters. Obama, in the last months of his lame-duck presidency, appointed many skillful saboteurs to the staff of The White House and National Security Agencies and many other government organizations whom Obama instructed to attack the incoming president, Donald Trump relentlessly, and leak to "fake news agencies" any confidential information that would embarrass or be detrimental to Donald Trump during his first four-term in office or that would jeopardize the security of our nation and damage Donald Trump's reputation and ability to protect American citizens from foreign terrorists and rogue nations who chant "death to America" on frequent occasions.

The "fake news agencies" relished the opportunities to make startling headlines and received and were complicit in the constant barrage of fake news and leaked national security discussions that frequently jeopardized our country's national security. Thank you, Obama, for you and your political saboteur friends being amongst the most anti-American politicians this country has seen in its relatively short history (compared to ancient civilizations elsewhere in the world). Your corrupt eight years in office alerted America of just how corrupt American politics has become, sadly and unGodly as this realization may be.

Americans witnessed, during Trump's presidency and campaign for a second four-year term in office, despicable behavior by the news press and media companies that would be loyal to dark and evil democrat political party intentions to ruin and sabotage Donald J. Trump (an outsider to corrupt Washington D.C. politics), and his presidency every day of his presidency. Obama implanted many "Deep State Saboteurs" in "national security" (more aptly termed "politically-biased and corrupt sycophant government agencies" who lost sight of their benevolent and Godly mission to protect Americans from sinister domestic and foreign threats), the last months of his presidency, who then purposely and criminally leaked top secret and secret communications which directly harmed and endangered the security of Americans and countries worldwide. This was one of the evilest actions by an illegitimately elected United States President that has ever been so blatantly taunted and enacted despite his leaving office that American patriots have ever seen (hopefully never to be seen again in the future, if the corrupt election system can be mended and securitized).

Hillary Clinton was defeated overwhelmingly by American voters despite the election corruption tactics that Obama had successfully employed to get re-elected after his disastrous policies and racist behavior during the first four years of his presidency.

Both Obama and his racist attorney general Eric Holder, in numerous instances of criminal "resistance of arrest" cases involving black skin color criminals whom white skin color police officers confronted, immediately declared, announced rashly, irresponsibly, and inaccurately (publicly) that these incidents were "racist behavior" before any investigations or statements by direct witnesses were reviewed, or videos, or camera pictures of these incidents were analyzed in the context of the situation which occurred, and well before full investigations of the incidents had been completed.

Before Barrack Obama's "presidency," a just, time-honored concept existed in the American justice system that respected and honored the principle "Innocent until proven guilty." At the same time, these two individuals paid zero attention to the many daily murders committed by Black criminals, killing other Black citizens and Black police officers, or Black officers who killed Black criminals in Chicago, Illinois, Obama's home state. In their minds, if a Black police officer kills a Black criminal who is resisting arrest, everything is fine, and justice prevails. If the same scenario occurred but involved a white police officer, then, according to Obama and Eric Holder, this always must be a racist event.

This racism that these two individuals touted was a significant setback in race relations and the unity of America. Bill de Blasio, mayor of New York City, with his anti-law enforcement stance, lost the entire police force's support, and crime skyrocketed in New York City as a result of his radical policies and support of eliminating bail for criminals. Martin Luther King would be disappointed in all these cases where the term racism was pronounced and declared by city mayors before any investigations and the White House duo, who on multiple occasions declared racism prematurely before any investigation of these incidents had commenced. These attacks, false accusations, and premature declarations of racism against law enforcement officers of any skin color are, in fact, acts of unjustified racism and prejudice against heroes, police officers, who are endangering their lives each day to prevent or stop crimes and assaults, and who are upholding and defending justice, law, and order.

Furthermore, when actual Muslim terrorist attacks occurred at the Boston Marathon, a Florida nightclub, and a Texas military base by a real and true Muslim terrorist, Obama and Democrat party lemmings marched silently over the cliff, falling to their deaths in silence regarding these incidents, failing to name, identify and thus to attack and defeat terrorists who were daring to challenge American exceptionalism.

Further acts of treason by Barrack Obama included:

1) Releasing Islamic/Muslim terrorist prisoners in exchange for an American soldier who disgracefully abandoned his duty post and fellow soldiers only to be captured by the Taliban. Obama then proceeded, disgracefully, to maintain and restore the soldier's rank and gave the deserter and traitor soldier back pay as if he were a hero (what a face slap to that deserter and traitor's fellow soldiers who did not abandon their battle station) instead of the dishonorable discharge and deserved prosecution of the soldier abandoning his post and treason that was earned and deserved by this deserter and traitor to America and his fellow soldiers (at least one soldier died during search for this traitor who abandoned his post…where is the justice for this honorable soldier who lost his life searching for a traitor caught by the Taliban as a result of the deserter and traitor's cowardice AWOL [absence without leave] and abandoning his battle station incident). This traitor soldier, who endangered and ultimately killed one of his fellow soldiers who was obligated to search for the missing traitor soldier, deserved nothing. The Taliban must have been thrilled to receive so many of their terrorists back from Obama so they could continue killing Americans in the Middle East and throughout the world, especially when all they had to give up was a dishonorable soldier deserter, and American traitor whom they had no respect for and for whom they had grown tired of feeding and supporting each day in their terrorist camps.

2) Secretly, cowardly, clandestinely, Obama, in an additional act of treason, funded Iran's nuclear missile ambitions and hate for America with a plane packed full of American dollars (cash), which landed at night in the dark (Obama hoping Americans

would never learn that he funded a country who chants "death to America") and has ambitions to obtain nuclear missiles in the near future, which should have and should still be prosecuted for the criminal act of treason that it was and is. This event has long-term implications and is still threatening America's existence, again, due to Obama funding the nuclear weapon development by Iran, a country that chants daily: "Death to America.."

What American "President" in the history of our country, except Obama, could avoid being prosecuted for aiding and abetting a terrorist country that is a top threat to the future of America by flying an American plane to Iran (in the darkness of night to attempt to hide his blatant sin against America), and handing over to them billions in cash (united states dollars currency), the equivalent of a luxury yacht full of cash and hard-earned American tax dollars to negotiate with terrorists.

By the way, I thought, "America does not negotiate with terrorists." Is this no longer true…will honest, hard-working American voters and families please clarify this for me? Of course, this will only be possible in the future, after the nightmare and fraudulently conducted and stolen election that we all witnessed in November 2020 in the United States of America [U.S.A.] betrayed all Americans, and after the total renovation, securitization, verification, standardization of the entire U.S.A. federal, state, local election system is performed. See earlier chapters of this book for what is required to ensure that elections in all jurisdictions are not forever corrupted and stolen by the immoral and demonic behavior of the Democratic Party, flagrantly flaunted and seen on full display by all American citizens during Donald Trump's presidency.

Did all of the democratic party liars who were accusing Donald Trump of Russian collusion and treason every day for the many painful months of the investigation ever get prosecuted? The answer is no! Despicable corruption in the Democratic political party. Wake up America! We are dealing with an evil and corrupt political party that has perfected corrupt elections and the slandering of Godly and truly benevolent and capable Godly mentors and leaders who are their political opponents during election campaigns, on the scale of the Anti-Christ and if election corruption at the state and federal level is not corrected (see earlier chapters for suggested fixes to the currently easily corrupted and random election systems being employed by different states so that they can alter their elections whenever they see fit to do so).

The Democrat Party [secret] Motto/Credo is as follows:

"Ignore the Bible (if and when it serves our power grab goals) principles of ethics, morality, honesty, and integrity. Lie, cheat, steal, malign others, mischaracterize opponents to attain and maintain power by any means necessary and at all costs, regardless of endangerment to the American people and American jobs. We'll outsource all American jobs if it results in eternal and perpetual power for Democrats and political lobbyists and donations from rich international import and export businesses or other multinational businesses (i.e., pharmaceutical and large technology companies) that fund the democratic party through overt (or covert "shell" companies"; a shell company is defined as: Incorporated company that possesses no significant assets and does not perform any significant operations often used deceptively for money laundering and purports to perform some service that requires customers to pay with cash) donations of these vast profits made by outsourcing American jobs at the expense of the American worker and economy of small towns that make up the majority of America. In these cities, business owners and workers are trying to feed, educate, and raise their families by working honest and long hours, often with one or more jobs. If we can outsource jobs and employment opportunities to foreign countries, then we will have lower production costs and greater profits for multinational companies and simultaneously suppress or exterminate and eliminate American families and workers' financial independence and self-sufficiency. American citizens will then be forced to vote for and depend on the democratic party for poor quality and underfunded national healthcare and food stamps to eat."

Unfortunately, these Democratic Party Goals will also, ultimately, snuff out [like a candle] small-town hard-working Americans' freedom to achieve the American Dream of becoming wealthy via higher education and working the hardest they can advance their station in life, increase their success and earning power either as an employee or by creating a new company and generating higher income and wealth as an independent business owner. The American Dream, much like the Statue of Liberty and the American Justice System, must always be essentially "color blind" to each individual's skin color; this dream is based on Bible-based and God-fearing and respecting values and principles: honesty, ethics, morals, good work ethic, pursuing and completing the highest education level possible to accomplish one's intended goal, and creating a business product or service that is desired by others yet tempered by and qualified as ethically moral in nature (always preferred; Christian American values), good (helpful and not destructive or harmful to others), healthy (preferred) and beneficial to other humans on the planet or the planet itself.

The Democratic Party has evolved since their origin as slave owners during the pre-civil war era, into the political party that seeks only to attain more political power in order to suppress the average and hard-working honest and ethical American worker through a strategy that they have successfully employed (and dramatically ramped up during Barrack Obama's "Reign of Terror" as U.S.A. President, remember Obama's false claims that manufacturing is dead in America and is never coming back and that his reign of terror resulted in some of the highest unemployment rates and highest number of citizens on the food stamp program and receiving unemployment benefits, all of which Obama coined in such a pathetic and non-American quip: "the new normal." Balderdash, I say, this man was such a fraud and disappointment as a President and demonstrated absolutely no leadership skills whatsoever.

Does a leader or commander of a nation or army, as his first actions while in command, immediately travel to other foreign countries and armies, friends and foes, and apologize for the past actions of his country or armed forces in a disparaging manner? Does this destroy the morale of his country's citizens and "his" armed forces and their loyalty to him as (lame, unqualified, and incompetent) "commander in chief?" The answer is a resounding yes! The Democratic party's quest to destroy jobs and employment opportunities that derive from American innovation, industry, and manufacturing serves only their selfish and wicked desires to maintain power, as slave owners, over American citizens and enable them to continue to disperse unemployment checks, poor quality nationalized health insurance and food stamps, as their slave reparations and payments to American citizens they have conquered, manipulated, extorted and enslaved. The democratic party has not changed or evolved since they were fighting to maintain slave ownership in the Southern states during the Civil War, unfortunately.

Chapter Seven:

Sinister Plot of Democratic Party, Large Technology Companies with International Dominance Ambitions and Ultra-Rich Billionaires Desire to Defeat American Exceptionalism and Capitalism in Favor of Socialism and Communism and Fascism and Marxism Using Nazi Tactics of Cancel Culture, Controlling Narrative Through Takeover of Media and News and By Intimidation of Christian Conservatives, Violence, Countersuits and Attacking Family Members of Opposition Political Party Politicians.

Let's do some deep diving into these strategies employed by the sinister and radical liberal left-wing democratic party (shall we just call a spade a spade: the immoral, unethical, and corrupt democratic party that cares only about political power and could care less about the well-being and safety of American citizens) who, on myriad occasions just before and throughout the Donald J. Trump's presidency as the 45th U.S.A. President, during the worst episodes of rioting American has seen or experienced since racial conflicts and the accompanying enmity that occurred in the 1960's, chanted repeatedly "burn it all down." These anarchists and anti-authority radicals were not only embraced and incorporated into the democratic party with "loving arms," but their reckless and lawless criminal activities were completely looked upon by the democratic party with a "blind eye."

Bitcoin millionaire or billionaire investors who make money from and during world chaos and socialist, communist, fascist, or rogue Muslim terrorist or other billionaire radicals who stand to gain from turbulence in the United States economy have been exposed and must be prosecuted for the criminal activities that they have been, until recently, covertly engaging in including providing legal defense and immediate bail for criminals and violent assaulters and rioters (e.g., political campaign premeditated rioters paid by these billionaires who hate and despise American freedom and Christian values, often enacted with members of domestic terror groups: Antifa and B.L.M. (black lives matter) violence instigators, acting as accomplices in these violent political campaign riots and crimes (murders, private business looting and building burnings, etc.) and, disappointingly, making these rioters immediately available to return to peaceful Donald J. Trump campaign rallies, disguised as Trump supports, and then these same paid, bad actors then initiate repeated acts of violence and property destruction (of public property, private property, national monuments, hard-working blue-collar American business owners, even minority-owned businesses were both looted and burned to the ground in many instances). For example, one minority retired police officer's private business was broken into and looted (all store items stolen), and the owner was shot dead by these domestic terrorists.

This is the "Black Lives Matter" and "Antifa" thugs' playbook: intimidate, assault, suppress free speech, force others to chant their satanic and racist slogans, and "brainwashed" concepts of America being a tyrant throughout history. Radical and racist liberal university professors and liberal Christian-despising news and media companies (e.g., The New York Times and The New York Times Magazine) are attempting to brainwash the youth in America (from grammar school through university level of education) espousing total rubbish "fake history" aiming to inspire a false sense of guilt (when not valid or warranted) in young Americans.

What is the "1619 Project"? This "project" is nothing other than a sinister and evil attempt to rewrite American history as we know it. It is a coup attempt to overthrow America by creating a dark alternative version of American history that, at best, is invalid and inaccurate and aims to divide rather than unite Americans and create guilt in naive students who drink this poisoned punch of destructive lies about American history.

The "1619 Project" (in the unsuspecting, naïve, and gullible students who incorrectly trust that their grammar school, high school, and university teachers and professors only teach trusted and verified truth regarding American exceptionalism, bravery, benevolence, tolerance, peace-keeping and peace-loving nature of America and that all American citizens should be proud of the tremendous accomplishments the U.S.A. has achieved as a united nation of many persons of varied backgrounds (E Pluribus Unum) all positively and enthusiastically working toward the common goal of national and world peaceful coexistence and harmony) aims to revise/rewrite (with a liberal anti-American sentiment and hostility and attempts to inspire faux guilt, which is neither deserved nor appropriate) American history by placing the consequences of slavery and the contributions of black Americans at the very center of the United States of America national (fiction and false) story.

This corrupt "1619 Project" was first published in August 2019 for the 400th anniversary of the arrival of the first enslaved Africans in the Virginia colony. This project has received generally negative reviews from historians. The "1619 Project" is a false narrative.

Americans are a proud people and a nation of diversity. While the "1619 Project" tries to reincarnate racism by separating Americans into black and all others ("non-blacks"), the project's evil ulterior motive is to stimulate pity and guilt in the current generation of Americans for items in history that we will all continue to remember by classical, truthful history books and teaching. However, this generation of Americans has no interest in resurrecting demons, hate, discontent or racism based on dividing Americans into nonsensical and racist categories of colored versus uncolored (an evil and rejected concept from ancient times).

Ask any proud Black man or woman living in the 21st Century if they feel they need pity, special considerations, or privileges (that are not afforded to or provided for other Americans, regardless of skin color) to compete effectively in school, sports, work/occupation or any other endeavor. As you already know, they will immediately say that they do not want, need, or require any of these special considerations. They are both proud and competent, knowing they can compete effectively without any added crutches, training wheels, or pity-based handouts.

"Black Lives Matter" is a farce, a fake, a front for a domestic terrorist organization, as is "Antifa." The Democratic Party believes they have successfully concealed their intimate ties to these domestic terrorist groups who act on the command of and at the direction of the "Democratic (what a myth and misnomer this is)" political party to instigate violent riots and chaos in any celebrations or rallies hosted by their political opponents, these domestic terrorists go to rallies disguised as their opponents' constituents, in order to then falsely administer judgments about the bad behavior at their opponents' gatherings, which they in fact instigated with a cold, premeditated murder-like precision.

Witness the events that transpired during the presentation of objections to the final counting and certification of the electoral college votes for the November 2020 election that occurred the first week of January 2021.

What was a massive peaceful outpouring of love and admiration for perhaps the most dynamic, energetic "President by, of, and for the People of America" during the rally outside the U.S. Capital Building the first week of January 2021, which was infiltrated by "Black Lives Matter" and "Antifa" terrorists and left-wing radicals inspired by and on the payroll of the Democratic Party, who then commenced with violent destruction of the Capitol building. Interestingly, the left-wing Washington D.C. government leader(s) may have also instructed the police to allow these radicals through the barriers and allowed them inside the Capital building (see live films of incidents showing police opening barriers and allowing these radicals' entry into the Capital building).

Are slogans or mottos such as "Black Lives Matter" intended by design to be inclusive and uniting or derisive and divisive? Each American should seriously ask this question, then contemplate the answer, then definitely answer the question and explain the reasoning behind their answer. All Americans who wish to live the American dream each day of their life should answer this question after reviewing a series of phrases that are identical or analogous to the B.L.M. slogan. Hard-working, patriotic, and Godly Americans' reactions to each slogan should be clear, obvious, and unified. The B.L.M. slogan, if modified and extrapolated to other groups in society, is very offensive, racist, and prejudiced. You can decide for yourself whether the extrapolated "B.L.M. slogan," as written in the phrases listed below, perturbs and aggravates you or makes you feel that the slogan is racist, offensive, and prejudiced. Should not societies, cultures, and nations throughout the world acknowledge and conclude that the "B.L.M. slogan" is a racist, offensive, abusive, condescending, and an insulting slogan that should be immediately rejected?

There is absolutely nothing about this slogan that is "color blind, uplifting, encouraging, positive, or uniting." If you need more evidence to be convinced of this fact, then please peruse the phrases, slogans, or mottos below and analyze the negative and divisive implications and intentions (that cannot be ignored) when people pretend that this phrase is unifying, Godly, and in the best interest of making America (or any other country) unified versus more racist and divisive.

Note the negativity and Satanic nature of this phrase (see below) when only two words are substituted in the phrase "Black Lives Matter (B.L.M.)." If you are offended by the example phrases (extrapolations of the "B.L.M. slogan") in the paragraph below, then you will understand how everyone in the world feels when people "tout or offensively shout out" the slogan or phrase "Black Lives Matter (B.L.M.)."

"White Lives Matter"; "Brown Lives Matter"; "Yellow Lives Matter"; "Nazi Lives Matter"; "Communist (C.C.P.) Lives Matter"; "Socialist Lives Matter"; "Nazi Lives Matter"; "Marxist Lives Matter"; "Haters Lives Matter"; "Jim Jones Cult Members Lives Matter"

"Mega-Cap Technology Companies, Multinational Companies, And Radical Liberal International Billionaires (e.g., the George Soros family being the largest menace and agitator to democratic and benevolent, God-respecting nations) Who Wish to Crush Democracy, Outsource American Manufacturing and Make America Dependent on Foreign Medications/Steele/All Retail Products From China, Lives Matter."

Americans and all benevolent, Godly, and patriotic "world citizens" should rightfully only trust and embrace slogans, mottos, phrases, and inspiring, motivating words that have been unifying and Godly in their intent and aspirations and have thus endured and been embraced and adopted by all universal "world citizens" for more than 200 years. Examples of uplifting words (among myriad other examples not listed here) include color blind, uplifting, encouraging, positive, inspiring, motivating, and unifying. Examples of uplifting phrases (among myriad other examples not listed here) include "the pursuit of happiness," "e pluribus unum," "In God We Trust," and "One nation, under God, indivisible forever and ever."

Let's be clear, "Black Lives Matter (B.L.M.)," whatever its origin may have been, has become nothing more than a guilt engine, a tool to bludgeon non-black "world citizens," Christian conservatives in America and every nation in the world, and anyone else who dares to defy

B.L.M. assaulters, rioters, and domestic terrorists. B.LM. has also been embraced by and used, nefariously, as a "legal" (criminal and illegal in reality) way for Democrats to fund riots and destruction of property, always directed at their political opponents. Sadly and disgustingly, many businesses and companies have been intimidated by B.L.M. and other domestic terrorist organizations.

To "not be labeled as racist companies," many weak and sycophant company executives repeatedly announce and tout their "support" and "donations" or "funding" of these domestic terrorist organizations who are evil and divisive in all nations that they have infected and metastasized to, increasing the crime and violence statistics of every city they have infected with their poison and lethal behavior, similar to cancer which spreads to all organs within the body (the organs being all nations, and the body is God's world) which are all better off without "Antifa," "B.L.M." and all the other myriad society-infecting, poisoning, and cancer metastasizing misanthropic terrorist national and international terrorist groups and organizations.

The sinister "Democratic" political party has been a frequent source of funds for these terrorist groups as a strategy to cause violence or riots directed at the rallies, conventions, and other gatherings of their political opponents for many decades. The "Democratic" politicians always attempt to displace or project the blame and responsibility for the violence they funded via their sinister policies, plans, and outright conspiracies directed toward and against their political enemies and opponents. All these radical terrorist groups, funded and supported by radical and liberal "Democrats" and other America-hating individuals or families (e.g., the George Soros family), then riot and assault law officers, opposition political party members, or any individual who does not share their crazy, anti-authority, anti-American, subversive, destructive, and divisive plan for overthrowing the most remarkable and most exceptional country in the world, the United States of America.

Summary: "Black Lives Matter" is a divisive slogan and is "racist, offensive, condescending and insulting." Domestic terrorist groups, including "Antifa" and "Black Lives Matter," are nothing more than mafia-like violent extremists that have become enforcement arms of the Democratic Party that funds their riots and violent assaults on anyone who dares to confront or oppose them at otherwise peaceful gatherings and assemblies (that they purposely infiltrate to cause commotion and stir up discontent and promote and advocate violent riots and altercations and assaults) of opposing political or ideological groups.

They have become legal tax deductions for big technology, pharmaceutical companies, other Fortune 500 companies, and Russell 2000 companies or C.E.O.s who wish to secretly fund domestic terrorists and support radical, liberal "Democratic (synonymous with evil and corrupt in the current era) Party" intentions to perpetuate a cancel culture, crush American Christianity, and Traditional Conservative Family Values, continue disorganized and fraudulent elections to ensure Republicans and Independents can never be elected President or win the senate or house of representatives, pack state, federal and supreme courts with radical judges with no conservative Christian values and who make rulings that show no respect for God-ordained and God-determined sexual identity that occurs at birth and does not change, nor should it be changed thereafter for eternity.

CHAPTER NINE:

The Fallacy, False Narrative, And Outright Lie Regarding The Purported "Benefit" (Actually a Detriment And Lethal Assault) to a City, State, Country, And Society" of "Sanctuary Cities."

"Sanctuary Cities" true definition: A city whose corruptly-elected, and/or unethical, and immoral politicians give preference to illegal immigrant federal law-breakers, protect them from prosecution and ethical deportation from and out of the country they illegally entered without authorization, hide them from or release them prior to prosecution for the crime(s) they committed and prior to the arrival of immigration authorities assigned to deport them, and, outrageously, often offer them state or other government photo identification cards (e.g., driver's license) so they may preferentially and fraudulently vote in upcoming election for the corrupt political party that ignored their crimes, prosecutions, deportation in all future state or federal elections, and receive food stamps, free hospital care, and be eligible for free low-income housing, all paid for by hard-working legal citizen's tax payments to their corrupt state and federal government, who allow such "Sanctuary Cities" to exist and continue their unethical practice of using tax dollars on noncitizens and illegal immigrant criminals, law-breakers, and terrorists or other countries' non-law-abiding citizens who neither respect nor intend to follow the rules or laws of the new country they illegally crossed into, to forever be a menace and burden to that country and society, financially, ethically, morally, patriotically (they are neither patriotic nor loyal to the country they illegally entered, often without any intent to work or pay taxes or become a citizen, or obtain a social security or other identification number for any work they do such that the government can track and apply taxes to their income), and, in essence, "Sanctuary Cities" thus recruit the entire world's most unethical, non-law abiding noncitizens to destroy that city, country, and society, indefinitely into the future.

Superheroes

"Sanctuary City" means "Sinful City." Ethical Society Members Who Prosecute And/Or Annihilate/Eliminate These Fraudulent And Corrupt "Sanctuary Cities" Via Legal Court Victories Will Be Instant Superheroes, "The Truly Elite."

Dr. Albert Schweitzer (1875-1965) was a theologian, organist, writer, humanitarian, philosopher, and physician. He is best known for founding the Albert Schweitzer Hospital in Lambaréné, Gabon, where he provided medical care to the local population. Schweitzer's philosophy of "Reverence for Life" and his dedication to humanitarian work earned him the Nobel Peace Prize in 1952.

Below is a chapter/excerpt from a magnificent, mentoring, instructional, succinct, and truly enlightening masterpiece novel which addresses the current attempt by the "(non-) democratic political party" in United States of America to essentially annihilate and discard Christianity from the United States of America and pretend that the extraordinary achievements of this country over the more than 200 years of this relatively young country's existence had nothing to do with its "Founding Fathers" linking the United States of America constitution document (written by these "Founding Fathers" after much wise introspection and contemplation of what values would be most important and essential to make their country and this world a better and more Godly place to live, love, and respect until their physical death and commencement of their eternal life with the God whom they loved and respected throughout their earthly life), with Bible-based values and Christian ethics, morals, perspectives, and human freedom, human rights, and independence values, gifted and intended by God to make this world a finer place to not only live but thrive and glorify God in.

The current attempt by the "(non-) democratic political party", has been to destabilize and destroy country borders in the United States of America (ridiculously, even prosecuting Southern states for constructing and funding their own border walls, due to irresponsible and negligent behavior of the federal government to neither care for or respect these states needs for protection and security against rogue and criminal federal immigration law breakers who cross these insecure border lines daily, committing crimes such as theft, destruction of private property, rapes, murders, and other incalculable and myriad insults and violations to the safety and serenity of law-abiding and hard-working Christian American citizens), and thereby dilute and devastate American Christian culture and values, and replace these Christians with every other country's federal immigration law-breaking criminals and non-Americans that neither respect America's laws, nor have any intent to abide by or follow these laws, for if they did have this intent, they would have simply entered America through the legal immigration system already established.

The best way to destroy a country's origin, founding principles, culture, values, patriotism, respect for God, rules, order, peace, safety, and serenity is to support "no borders enforcement, protecting the rights of illegal criminals crossing the border without authorization (fake asylum seekers who travel through and past several countries to eventually arrive at American borders, then plea to be asylum seekers, who really prefer a "paid vacation in America" with free healthcare, food stamps, homeless encampments (e.g., in front of businesses who then go bankrupt or are forced to close or move their businesses), and funding by various anti-American values organization who pretend to be "pro-American" when their actual intent is to infiltrate America with so many illegal foreigners that these non-Patriotic invaders will then outnumber faithful, God-respecting and hard-working Christian Americans, vote out American values and the Christian origin of America, and, after being elected into various leadership roles, replace American Christianity, freedom, human rights, and independence with polar opposite socialism, fascism, communism, atheist or agnostic anti-religious and anti-Christian (lack of) values, and thus accomplish their goal from the very beginning, destroy all the values and principles that made America one of the greatest, independent, freedom-loving, freedom-respecting, human rights-advocating, and one of if not the most moral countries in the world over the more than two centuries of its initial existence!

The book chapter/excerpt below is a marvelous, insightful, focused, and concise summary of current problems that exist in this world of corrupt politics. The book, in general, also addresses many other societal problems, issues, and dilemmas throughout the world and around the globe and masterfully suggests and recommends relatively easy and practical, pragmatic fixes or solutions to these societal problems that are and have been a plague and pandemic to societal health throughout all cultures and countries in this world for centuries.

The Generational Assault on Christianity, Free Speech and Democracy in America, A Call to Action to Preserve and Nurture American Values and Benevolent Exceptionalism

By Christopher Arthur Rockefeller

Chapter Eight:

World War 3: Political War Has Been Declared by America's "Democratic Party" on Conservative Christian Values, Which Have Contributed Immensely to the Greatness of America Since 1776. An Attack on Democracy in The United States of America and The World Has Begun. American Christian Values, Rights And Issues That Could Be Devastated Or Lost Forever If This War Is Not Won: Fair and Honest Elections, Christian and Bible-based Ethics and Morality, Secure Borders Which Protect and Identify Legal Citizens (Versus Illegal Federal Immigration Law-Breaking Radical Extremists Who Despise and Disregard American Values, Christianity and Law and Order And Who May Threaten Or Overtake The United States of America And Forever Discard American Christian Values That Engender American Exceptionalism That Has Benefitted and Protected America and World Citizens Since 1776.

American Borders Must be Constructed, Secured And Enforced To Prevent Entry of Illegal Immigrants Who Demonstrate No Respect For American Legal Immigration Laws, Have No Loyalty to American Christian Values, Reject American History And Exceptionalism And Who Will Be Recruited and Embraced As Fraudulent Democratic Party Voters After Being Given American Worker's Tax Payer Dollars In The Form Of Welfare Benefits and Retirement Benefits That Were Paid For And Earmarked For Legal American Citizens, Thus Bankrupting Social Security Intended For Citizens.

Democrats Have Even Proposed Stealing And Reducing Social Security Benefits for American Citizen Retirees Who Sacrificed And Saved In Retirement Plans And Giving This Stolen Money To Illegal Immigrants Who Are Undeserving Foreign Nationals/Non-Americans Who Never Paid A Dime In Taxes And Who Never Worked Or Lived in America Until They Retired in Their Home Country Then Illegally Immigrated To The United States Of America To Ultimately Inflict Pain & Financial Chaos & Burdens On The Retirement System of Americans Wishing To Retire And Receive The Benefits They Were Promised After Paying

Taxes Their Entire Career When Honestly and Steadfastly Working To Enjoy A Rewarding Retirement.

How can Christians worldwide fight against devasting attacks by radical liberals, a democratic party that resembles communism, fascism, and socialism more than the Christian conservative capitalism system that made America exceptional in every way as a result of enabling all citizens the potential to experience the "American Dream": Success achievement by any legal citizen, advancement in society which is "color blind" with regard to skin color, whereby each individual may use their God-given skills, talent and intellect to pursue higher and advanced levels of university education, work as hard as possible at one or more jobs, if they desire, in order to save money, earn promotions in their occupation or job based on merit and work attitude and work ethic (not determined by gender or skin color and preferably not mandated by government overreach or intrusion into public or private work places), or start their own business to meet a need of society and produce a product or service that benefits society, enabling them to be self-sufficient and financially secure. This results in Americans being proud of their life and satisfied that their earnest effort, hard work, and steadfast striving to better themselves has resulted in happiness and contentment. This is the American Dream.

This book is not a conclusion but a rallying cry and call to action for all human beings on the planet, as well as citizens of America and every other nation, to consider and contemplate the concepts and opinions expressed in the preceding chapters. What should America and every other country on this planet look like, behave like, speak like, and most importantly, how should humans treat each other? How should humans interact with and treat other humans from countries that are not their own native countries, who undoubtedly and inevitably will have cultures, beliefs, traditions, religions, and approaches to problem-solving that are varied and diverse?

Occam's Razor (a.k.a., Ockham's razor, Occam's razor) comes to mind at this time. The idea is attributed to English Franciscan friar William of Ockham (c. 1287-1347), a scholastic philosopher and theologian who espoused a problem-solving principle that "the simplest explanation is usually the right one."

The Bible is "the simplest explanation, model, and solution of how humans in America and every country in the world can and should interact with each other and is the right one (solution)." C.S. Lewis authored many books as a Christian disciple and scholar in support of this concept, including: "The Chronicles of Narnia," "Mere Christianity," "The Great Divorce," "The Screwtape Letters," and many other phenomenal Christian apologetic genre books.

If democracy (characterized and defined, at least in part, by non-fraudulent elections with one legal vote on issues per one legal citizen), peaceful diversity (governed by Christianity and Christian-based ethics and moral behavior), independence, freedom, human rights, religious behavior, common decency in social interactions and communications, and respect for all humans and all nations, is to have any chance of survival (or preferably to flourish) in the United States and all other countries throughout the world, then Occam's Razor (a.k.a., Ockham's razor, Occam's razor) would dictate that the Bible is "the simplest explanation, model, and solution to how humans in America and every country in the world can and should interact with each other and, as such, is the most correct single solution to the dilemmas that America and all nations on Earth must address and overcome, benefitting all "world citizens."

This profound and enlightening concept should not be overlooked or ignored but instead embraced and addressed with proactive interventions to maintain and ensure future Godly and benevolent world citizen behavior in this generation and all future generations. Nations throughout the world, including the United States of America, will forever benefit from the aforementioned concept, as unity and Godliness will provide eternal spiritual fulfillment, serenity, positive social interactions and communications, unending inspiration and motivation, and benevolent goals, behavior, and actions in all "world citizens" from all nations, all of whom are members of the same family, known as "God's children."

CHAPTER TEN:

Unjust, Unethical, Immoral Lack of Indictment And/Or Non-Prosecution Of Criminal Acts Of State Or Federal Government Politicians And Other Government Agencies' Members (e.g., Members Of Congress: Senators, House of Representative members) In The United States Of America Or Any Other Country In The World, Based Purely On The Biased Fact That The Criminals Are Members Of The Elected Political Party In Charge Of The Government, Is And Will Always Be The Most Corrupt And Blatant Insult To Democracy And The Best Evidence Of The Lack Of That Government's Leadership Skills And Worthiness To Command Or Receive The Respect Of Their Citizens, Based On Their Lack of Morality And Ethical Behavior. Ethical Society Members And Government Members Who Prosecute All Criminals By The Same Standards And Criteria And With The Same Criminal Sentences Based On The Crime They Committed, Regardless Of Political Party Affiliation, Income Level, Social Status, Skin Color, Via Legal Court Victories Will Be Instant "Superheroes, The Truly Elite And Honorable."

Bonhoeffer Dietrich Bonhoeffer (1906-1945) was a German Lutheran pastor, theologian, and anti-Nazi dissident. He was a founding member of the Confessing Church, which opposed the Nazi regime.

Below are chapters/excerpts from a magnificent, mentoring, instructional, succinct, and truly enlightening masterpiece novel that addresses: Politically-Motivated, Fraudulent, Malicious "Non-Prosecutions" Occurring Presently In The United States of America And All Countries Throughout The World. Ethical Society Members Who Address And Correct These Politically-Motivated, Fraudulent, Malicious "Non-Prosecutions" Via Legal Court Victories Will Be Instant Superheroes And Will Be Deserving Of The Title And Will

Have Truly Earned The Honor Bestowed On Them By Being Referred To, Accurately, As "The Truly Elite And Honorable."

Similarly, this benevolent change in the current vicious and malicious political environment throughout the United States of America and countries throughout the world will indirectly benefit all cultures and society by eliminating "evil and criminal perpetrators of the justice system, which can neither be respected nor trusted when they cover up true crimes and do not prosecute deserving criminals purely based on their biased and prejudiced political views and/or wealthy social status.

Such "Non-Prosecutions" allow these "immoral, unethical, ungodly, anti-Christian, and anti-American Patriot individuals" to continue their biased and prejudiced malevolent practice patterns, political corruption, premeditated crimes, false accusations, malicious prosecutions, and most devastating of all, allow these criminals to actually run for first term political elections or second term re-elections to continue their business of being "political tyrants and demagogues of corruption," as we recently witnessed firsthand with and by the families of Barrack Obama, Bill and Hilary Clinton, and Joseph and Hunter Biden, who all should have been prosecuted for being traitors and for their crimes inflicted on America, American Christian values, American Patriotism, and Benevolent Exceptionalism, and for destroying the Godly reputation and standards America has always striven, in the past, to uphold, support, improve, and strengthen, generation to generation.

By not prosecuting criminals and traitors of American Christian values, standards, ethics, morals, and law-abiding behavior as defined in the American constitution and amendments and "bill of rights" all established by the "Founding Fathers" of America and ethical, American patriots thereafter, the current and extremely corrupt and anti-American "(non-) democratic political party" has not only exploded the integrity and respect for American politicians and leaders in this generation and country, the United States of America, but has also disheartened, discouraged, saddened, and disappointed the countries throughout the world, who had hoped that America would be a shining example of Godly justice, equality, human rights, human freedom, non-discrimination based on birth families, skin color, culture or country of origin, such that all countries could both legally immigrate their citizens to partake in the forever cherished "American Dream" but also that all countries could learn and be enlightened by the Godly values and God's blessing that occurred in America's young history due to their reverence and respect for God, thus enabling other countries to mimic the benevolent behavior of America, to the betterment and benefit of their own country's citizens.

Through "Non-Prosecution" of criminals, you empower these satanic and immoral criminals to commit more offenses and crimes against moral and ethical "world citizens" who are "rules followers" (who are thus presumed or perceived to be disadvantaged opponents because of their unwillingness, based on their moral upbringing, to break laws and defy rules), unlike their corrupt, law-breaking, criminal, unethical, and evil opponents in political elections, and other professions, occupations, and various leadership roles.

These "Non-Prosecuted Criminals" are then "allowed" to slander and attack (or win political elections against) Godly and Christian values-supporting political election candidates who, unfortunately, as we have all witnessed, sadly, many times in the past and recently, continue to have both their Christian background or new Christian values attacked and, ironically and Satan-approved to be sure, continue to be consequentially sidelined and destroyed, unrightfully and unjustly, by the current corrupt and fraudulent "(non-) democratic political party" and their easily corruptible election systems, overt, unabashed, and flagrantly flaunted in the past two decades. These corrupt and unreliable or verifiable election systems and methods are currently being utilized not only in the United States of America but worldwide to facilitate and enable corrupt politicians to constantly and assuredly be re-elected despite their misbehavior and dastardly intentions, criminal accomplishments (all unprosecuted) and "non-prosecuted" sinister, politically prejudiced, biased, and law-violating actions carried out daily at their workplaces.

This book also addresses many other societal problems throughout the world and masterfully suggests and recommends relatively easy and practical, pragmatic fixes or solutions to these societal problems that are and have been a plague and pandemic to societal health throughout all cultures and countries in this world for centuries.

The Generational Assault on Christianity, Free Speech and Democracy in America, A Call to Action to Preserve and Nurture American Values and Benevolent Exceptionalism

By Christopher Arthur Rockefeller

Chapter Five:

What Are the Responsibilities of Local, State, and Federal "Leaders" and Politicians ("Anti-Leaders")?

We must address the most immediate and urgent concern, the "elephant in the room," that must be rectified to ever even pretend, immediately and in the future, to have a "democratic" (i.e., non-corrupt and non-manipulated count of LEGAL votes) election. The monstrosity and blatantly fraudulent November 2020 Presidential election must never be recorded as anything but a giant fraud election event. It may be likened to one battle won by the evil and dishonest Darth Vader (Star Wars Movie analogy), whose only concern is selfish aggrandizement, manipulation, and conquering the universe, and an unquenchable thirst for power which is acquired by evil means of any sort to achieve this goal. In this Star Wars Movie analogy, Donald J. Trump was Luke Skywalker.

When Trump announced his candidacy for the United States of America presidency, he was entering a political swamp of alligators who are ancient, ruthless, crafty, brutally cruel, and unethical in their approach to problem-solving and, least expected by Trump, members of the opposing Democrat party AND his very own party (remember the R.I.N.O.S. [republicans in name only]; one such anti-hero, just before death, thwarted Donald Trump effort to reform healthcare in a meaningful way and reverse the devastation that "Obama[non-care by your present and past M.D.]care" inflicted on the American people, including unfair penalties, struck down by the Supreme Court, eventually as unconstitutional), the Republican party.

We'll analogize this "democratic corrupt and poisonous swamp water in Washington D.C." to the galaxy which Darth Vader (Barack Obama) tried to manipulate, control and cast his dark and dreary shadow of oppression, misdirection, promotion of sex change and gender confusion and incorrectly trying to change the definition of marriage that is (uneditable and cannot be altered) in the Bible, manipulation of the press and big media companies, at the time Luke Skywalker (Donald Trump) arrived to liberate the galaxy from the Death Star (Washington D.C. swamp) and Darth Vader (Racist and Anti-American "President" Obama who was both corruptly given a second four year term after an abysmal reign of terror and racism his first four year term and inappropriately awarded a "Noble Peace Prize" after his pathetic "America Apology Tour" mischaracterizing America as a tyrant instead of the Magnificent, Tolerant, Most Responsible and Magnanimous and Generous Country Ever to Exist and Cheerfully Contribute to the United Nations and Disaster Relief Operations and Rebuild War-Torn Nations

Throughout Its Existence and Since America's birth as a relatively new nation in 1776, successful and magnificent due entirely to United States of America founding fathers Christian values which were inseparably intertwined and written into the Constitution of the United States of America.)

Luke Skywalker (Donald J. Trump) entered a Galaxy that Darth Vader (Barrack Hussein Obama) had demonized by falsely and inaccurately portraying America as a sinful yet repentant (Obama being the apologizer for America's entire history during his United Nations speech) tyrant nation.

Barrack Obama, with no authority whatsoever to criticize the United States and its long history in the manner in which he did, errantly and inexcusably distorted the world's opinion of America from being a benevolent, peace-maintaining, tolerant, and generous country (that is the correct and deserved reputation of this young and exceptional nation, the United States of America) to that of country who (according to the speech made by Barrack Obama) made more mistakes and offended more nations throughout its history than it ever helped or supported (a wildly inaccurate, negative, and unacceptable portrayal of the history of the United States of America since its formation in 1776). Should anyone dispute these facts and characterizations, one needs only to listen to the speeches each president gave at the "United Nations" conference. Since its formation, this organization has had a reputation for demonstrating anti-American sentiment and voting patterns. Member nations agreed to pay a set percentage of their country's gross domestic product to support the United Nations. However, they neglected to pay their fair share for years until Donald Trump insisted that each member faithfully pay their share of expenses. No president, including Barrack Obama, had demanded financial accountability from this organization for many years.

Luke Skywalker (Donald Trump) acted to strengthen galaxy nations and planets in order to prepare them in their defense against rogue and evil galaxy planets and nations who threaten freedom and liberty in the galaxy and universe (e.g., China, Russia, Venezuela, Syria, North Korea who, presently, demonstrate no or very little knowledge of or respect for Christian values, human rights, liberty, freedom, independence and all these nations have a distinct disinterest or hate for free market capitalism that offers hope and inspiration for rising from rags (poverty) to riches (great wealth) based not on inheritance, race, class, skin color but instead on: individual motivation, pursuit of education and professional training, honesty, hard work, integrity that allows citizens of a country to rise to unlimited heights of intellectual, socioeconomic and other positions of leadership and power as business owners or valuable and indispensable employees who then have the potential to be appointed chief executive officers of companies.)

Should local, state, and federal democratic leaders be held personally responsible when they abrogate their responsibilities and allow their cities to become derelict, on life support, and near death? The average American instinctually knows the answer to this question. The answer is yes. If you want to live in nightmare cities with incredibly dangerous criminals and the highest crime rates in the country, just seek out a city in America that Democratic leaders have run for many consecutive and continuous years. I don't have to name these cities; you already know them or can easily and quickly look them up on the internet for online details and crime rates for all these cities…enough said.

Let's examine some case studies, all of which are glaring and hideous crime scenes perpetrated by irresponsible and incompetent Democratic leadership who, most likely due to many years of fraudulent and tainted election systems in states overflowing with corruption, deceit, mafia corruption, other organized criminal organizations and bribe-tainted politicians and local, state, federal leaders, lawyers, judges, Supreme Court Justices, have let their respective states or cities become derelict and on a slow, inevitable path to death and destruction.

Specifically, the Chicago, Illinois; Detroit, Michigan; New York City, New York; Los Angeles, California; San Francisco, California; Seattle, Washington; Portland, Oregon, and, after the fraudulent November 2020 U.S.A. Presidential election steal perpetrated by state and local officials who refused even to consider evidence of election fraud, which was overwhelming and rampant. The states of Georgia, Pennsylvania, Arizona, and Nevada must now be included in this list of incompetent, irresponsible, and uncouth leaders not interested in truth, justice, and non-fraudulent or legitimate elections.

Should the governor of Washington State and the mayor of Seattle, Washington allow domestic terrorists (e.g., "Black Lives Matter" terrorist group and "Antifa" group, both criminal and violent arms of the democratic party and radical, rich, leftist tyrants that are contributors to "The Bail Project" which according to Fox News Host Tucker Carlson, "sends money to rioters and other violent criminals to help get them back on the streets as quickly as possible" and whose companies (e.g., cryptocurrency companies and investments, whose value may increase, significantly when chaos rises in a country) benefit tremendously from anarchy, chaos and currency volatility that inevitably results from bailouts from democrats to and in radical democrat cities and states who, during the four years of Donald J. Trump's presidency, allowed rioters to burn down their cities and states and instigate irreparable damage to national history statues which were systematically and unjustly pulled down or vandalized by domestic terrorist and rioters or removed by cowardly city or state leaders who caved in to radical extremists in the cancel culture promulgated by the racist and intolerant democratic party who raised no objections to millions of dollars be given or donated to radical left rioters who killed or assaulted many citizens and business owners and police officers in democratic states and cities who embraced a blind eye policy toward these domestic terrorist groups in order to then turn around later and project blame on President Donald J. Trump, as if he was somehow in a magical and mysterious way responsible for these democrat and George Soros-sponsored and funded riots.

International radical leftist billionaires, such as George Soros, who funded radical domestic and international terrorist organizations to further his corrupt empire, have done more to attempt to destroy America than the average or uninformed (or misinformed due to untruthful "fake news" organization broadcasts) American citizen could possibly fathom.

The Jussie Smollett fake enactment of a "racist, homophobic attack" (wasting Chicago police time, resources, and money to investigate his nonsense) was used to demean and launch false accusations about a political attack by "Trump supporters." The lawyer who failed to prosecute this loser human being was corruptly connected to both Michelle Obama and George Soros. George Soros also has funded myriad rioters throughout Trump's campaign year by paying violent protestors to disrupt his campaign events before Trump's election and throughout Trump's presidency and re-election campaign leading up to the November 2020 U.S.A. Presidential Election.

The mayor of Seattle and the Governor of Washington state allowed many city blocks of businesses and residents to be taken over, walled off, and terrorized, including rapes and other assaults, for weeks before taking action to end this coup.

Disgraceful lack of leadership and dereliction of their city accurately defines the behavior and actions of this city mayor and other city officials who acted as sycophants to and for these domestic terrorists. They deserve to be prosecuted and disgraced for the pain and suffering they explicitly condoned and allowed the business owners and resident citizens to experience during these domestic terrorist group coups and reigns of terror and chaos.

Similarly, the mayor of Portland, Oregon and Governor of Oregon, some might say, deserve a good old fashioned "tarring and feathering" ceremony to recognize and reward them for the despicable "blind eye" policy and instructing police not to arrest and prosecute all violent and intimidating rioters assaulting conservatives, Christians, Trump supporters and journalists who exposed the radical domestic terrorists who commandeered the City of Portland for months and years (still a dangerous, violent, intolerant city who supports cancel culture and the assaulting of anyone whose viewpoint is different from their own Socialist/Communist/fascist/Crazy liberal, leftist, non-Bible-based city reminiscent of Sodom and Gomora in their lawlessness and uncouth leadership.

Governor and City Mayor policies that chose to negotiate with (unsuccessfully, I might add) these local home-grown domestic terrorist groups, "Black Lives Matter (B.L.M.) and "Antifa" (violent crazy cowards hiding behind their evil masks) instead of immediately incarcerating and charging them with assaults and hate crimes, demonstrated their incompetence and negligence in their sworn duties to protect and defend the welfare and safety of their city citizens.

They should be prosecuted for negligence and held directly responsible for the assault on Andy Ngo, a Portland-based journalist, who was assaulted on June 2, 2019. Andy Ngo was walking down the street peacefully and was then attacked by multiple rioters who caused an orbital skull fracture around one of Andy Ngo's eyes.

Consider the cities of Baltimore, San Francisco, Chicago, and Los Angeles, which are cities with Democratic leadership through many years of fraudulent and tainted elections that ensure Democrat candidate victories for decades that are rift with crime, homelessness, IV drug abuse, and multiple drug addictions and alcoholism, high taxes, excessively stringent and unreasonable gun laws that have only enhanced the ability of criminals to be unopposed and fearless in committing heinous murders and crimes without being prosecuted or even retained (especially in the "sanctuary cities" whereby criminals and violent illegal aliens are not incarcerated and retained for I.C.E. officials to deport from the country and are instead released without prosecution for these violent persons to then commit multiple future crimes such as rape, murder, robberies to name just a few.

Remember or google search the "Murder of Kate Steinle by an illegal immigrant, Jose Ines Garcia Zarate, with a history of multiple crimes who was repeatedly released by Democrat authorities and never fully or appropriately confined, imprisoned, or prosecuted in San Francisco on July 1, 2015" if you want a good cry regarding the inhumanity of San Francisco's corrupt government leaders who fraudulently re-elect themselves each election year so they can perpetuate "Sanctuary City" policy which affords more safety, protection and humanity to illegal federal immigration law breakers and international illegal alien criminals and terrorists than law-abiding American citizens who pay the highest local and state taxes in the country to be treated with hostility and disdain because they are hard-working, law-abiding, Christian, God-respecting, God-fearing California citizens who faithfully (but naively) expect their votes are counted accurately and honestly to remove crazy and irresponsible leaders like Gavin Newsome (nephew on Nancy Pelosi) from power, only to be disappointed each election cycle that their votes have been fraudulently discarded or replaced with altered ballots and these crazy radical leftists have once again retained the ability to destroy our once great cities such as San Francisco and Los Angeles, which are derelict and dying cities on life support and near death due to lack of Republican leadership, lack of fiscal responsibility with city budgets (and excessive taxes), and disregard for criminal prosecutions (e.g., "Sanctuary Cities" which are actually "violent criminal all-inclusive vacation resort cities," in reality) responsibilities for decades.

Without national standardization and securitization of election systems in local, state, and federal elections in all states of the United States of America and all nations, our elections will continue to be despicable and insulting farces, worthy only of ridicule and not "democratic" in any sense.

One only has to analyze the last corrupt 2020 United States Presidential Election of a demented, criminal politician, with no ability to run his own campaign except out of his home with a teleprompter for less than an hour each day, who was clearly physically, mentally, morally, ethically, and even socially unqualified to be a candidate for the United States Presidency, in fact, he was only fully qualified to be incarcerated for interference with a Ukrainian lawers investigation of Hunter Biden, his son, for money laundering from the Ukraine government, and for embezzling money from China to Hunter Biden's "investment firm," and Joseph Biden even gave a video confession in person stating that his election corruption was greater than that of Barrack Obama! Perhaps one of the greatest impacts that Donald J. Trump's Presidency has had on the American people and voters is that he exposed the incredibly evil and malevolent fraud that is found in the swampy Washington D. C media companies, Congress members of both the non-cohesive, non-loyal republican party (a.k.a., party of back stabbers and traitors, remember John McCain (republican in name only aka R.I.N.O.) and Kelly Loeffler as the ultimate insider or deep state traitor when she reversed her decision to call out obvious Georgia voter and election fraud perpetrated to ensure a fraudulent Joseph Biden Presidential win), and the diffusely cohesive democratic party who are all Charles Manson-like cult members who engage in evil premeditated murders (think Randy Epstein and Wall Street Journal writers who exposed or were about to expose the evil and criminal activities of the Democrat Party lies, fraud and other criminal activities (underage child molestations by many democratic members and democratic donors would have been exposed and prosecuted, had not Randy Epstein been murdered before he could testify about all the democratic "visitors (child molesters)" that repeatedly frequented (visited) his island to have sex with underage girls that were victims of human trafficking and lured to Randy Epstein's privately owned island of iniquity (aka, "Sodom and Gomorrah, part II") that are so numerous that if a fan was powered by them, a Republican could live through a summer in Yuma, Arizona mistakenly thinking he was living in the Swiss Alps during winter!

Is a congress member who was reported to be a "civil rights leader" racist when that person fails to attend the election of democratically elected United States of America Caucasian president and instead, unjustly and falsely accuses that president of being racist, simply because his skin color is different than that congress member's own skin color? Should that same congress member be held accountable and responsible for neglecting his duty as a leader for his city and district when that member has, for many years, presided over the city, which is derelict and fraught with corruption and unbridled criminal activity and holds one of the worst records in the country concerning failing to perform (based on competency testing), at the expected and appropriate grade level in math and English and other subjects in school?

This is such a common occurrence and theme, especially in Democrat-led cities that utilize taxpayer dollars only to perfect corrupt election systems rather than for the benefit, education, and safety of their city citizens, that recurs repeatedly (like in the movie "Groundhog Day" with Bill Murray) in numerous Democratic-leader dominated states and cities, who demonstrate very little interest in improving the plight of their city residents but choose instead to pursue their more narcissistic dreams of power and prestige, much to the chagrin and disenchantment of their city residents, but in line with their fellow Democrat colleagues in the House of Representatives and Senate. Do you want to be happy and safe in life? Find a city not led by a democratic party politician.

Has anyone ever actually thought how interesting it would be to see an Excel spreadsheet that listed what politicians, both "Democrats (more accurately "demonstrated rats")" and Republicans, promise their constituents (in column one) and what promises they actually and truthfully complete and fulfill (in column two)? In this respect, Donald J. Trump, a non-politician "outsider" (note: more intelligent and informed American citizens might well consider this designation, ultimately, the highest compliment Trump's critics ever bestowed upon him), in my estimation, might rank the highest Q.B.R. (quarterback rating, for an excellent N.F.L. football analogy for all you sports fans) or highest basketball shooting percentage and most valuable player status (think Michael Jordan, excellent and accurate under pressure when it was most important and necessary during N.B.A. playoffs and championship series), than any other United States President since Abraham Lincoln and George Washington.

In fact, if there were an award for the greatest United States of America President performance during a constant (nonsense) deluge of evil, vindictive, fraudulent accusations of treason, racism and other myriad false accusations that were mere projections from a deeply satanic and Charles Manson-like evil opposing democratic political party, billionaire tech chief executive officers, hateful and politically liberal, leftist "fake news and fake liberal left media companies" and their malevolent leaders such as Jeff Zucker of CNN ("Communist Neo-Nazi network") or Jeff Bezos, owner of the Washington Post newspaper, who spewed vitriol tainted with negativity and overall hatred toward President Donald

J. Trump, who was perhaps the most popular and populist "America First" attitude President and advocate for the American wage-earner who had been severely disenfranchised by decades of "sell-out the American wage-earners and American manufacturing companies and other companies" who were told by both past republican, but mostly democratic Presidents (Barrack Hussein Obama's 8 year reign of terror, who did his best to destroy the legacy and exceptionalism reputation of America as a great and benevolent leading country on this planet, being the worst uncouth and flagrant and fraudulent example) that American manufacturing dominance is dead and extinct and cannot be resurrected. All filthy, negative, un-American lies.

Should an American president who claimed to be a champion for minorities of his own skin color, but who instead stirred up the country deliberately in a "slave owner-like manner" by claiming that citizens should be judged only by their skin color to be determined worthy and eligible to receive special privilege, funding, opportunities, again, purely because they are a single skin color, be considered racist? The answer, for eternity, will always be yes. No one should ever judge a person based solely on skin color.

Does this attitude and perspective sound eerily similar to a past German leader who fancied incinerating (burning) all those books written by persons he did not agree with, and incinerating (burning) all persons he neither liked nor agreed with then, in a paranoid state of chaos, sought to destroy and banish from this earth, all his political enemies through the use of espionage (spying) and wiretapping of phones and buildings, and weaponizing multiple persons including children and nearly everyone associated with his "reign of terror" to, out of fear for their life, either comply with his compulsory insistence that they engage in spying on fellow workers, friends and even family members to maintain domination and control of propaganda being fed to citizens, while they were simultaneously being lied to and exterminated from the planet in order to achieve Aryan goals of a single skin color (and eye color and facial feature dimension that conformed to a desired and predetermined parameters considered most beautiful for the appearance of the surviving single Aryan race [Adolf Hitler thought that people of Northern European descent were a superior race to all others, known as the Aryan Race) that is to be rewarded with all the spoils of the world war two that was being fought to achieve world dominance.

Here are several questions for the American wage-earner who was any skin color different from that of President Obama: "Did you feel that President Obama represented you fairly and justly and assumed your innocence first and foremost when there were any racial conflicts or riots? Did you feel like Obama was "color blind" with regard working toward the employment and career advancement of all skin colors or focused only on "Black Lives Matter" and "Antifa" during and after his presidency, and during Donald J. Trumps four-year term as President?

Was Obama supportive of Donald Trump because he cared more about the well-being of American citizens than his "Democratic" party's political power and evil influence (e.g., besmirching the United States President who followed him in office and installing many saboteurs in political and government offices and roles whose mission was to lie about Donald Trump and falsely accuse him of everything that is wrong in and with this world)? We all know the answer to this question, and history books, if truthful (this is no longer a guarantee, sadly, and a reason this book was written, for the truth to be revealed, at least to those interested in true, genuine, authentic, accurate, and real history books), will record that Donald Trump was one of the most amazing, dynamic, and energetic United States Presidents (perhaps ever, and despite intense and constant evil opposing forces constantly and unjustifiably attacking his character [reminiscent of Abraham Lincoln, for sure]), and history books should summarize Obama's reign of terror as follows:

"One of the most disappointing, racist, and corrupt United States Presidents to ever have been corruptly "deposited" into the office, then fraudulently re-elected for a second term, despite his exceedingly low popularity, disastrous policies, disrespect for Chrisitan values, attempts to ignore male and female genders as God-assigned and unalterable creations, and disrespect for the American people and the history and legacy of the

United States of America. The president who did the most in history to sabotage the functioning and success of America and all nations of the world by his weak or entirely absent responses to international tyrant dictator nation activities and invasions, and of the next United States President, who would be a truly remarkable leader, unlike the "saboteur and domestic terrorist (non-)president who was his predecessor."

How many times do you recall hearing President Obama, Vice President Joseph Biden, Eric Holder, Susan Rice, and Loretta Lynch openly denounce the activities of the violent left-wing arms of the Democratic Political Party: "Antifa" and "Black Lives Matter"? An eerie silence fills the air. Answer: Never.

Chapter Six:

Who are the heroes that assisted President Donald J. Trump in navigating the most treacherous United States Presidency four-year term and yet accomplish more in those four years than most of the evil and ancient "deep state" criminal operatives in Congress that work not for the American people but rather to ensure, at all costs and above all other concerns, that their positions in Congress are secure and their narcissistic needs for camera face shots, prestige and power are met on a daily, monthly and yearly basis?

There are innumerable unsung heroes and even more and, as yet unidentified and unprosecuted for the many crimes, evil swamp creatures that have yet to be elucidated, discovered, or drained from the filthy and corrupt Washington D.C. poisonous swamp water that Donald Trump was forced to walk through to rescue America from Obama's devastating reign of terror and destruction of America's reputation and Christian values. Donald Trump's arrival at the swamp and single-handed rescue of all of America's citizens from the disaster railroad leading to a cliff of destruction that Obama had been loading Americans onto so that he could send all Americans to their moral death and destruction was one of the greatest rescues in American history.

This rogue, non-politician (Donald J. Trump) "People's President" was so loved and admired for his courage to stand up and confront the many grotesque swamp creatures he had to deal with and endure and then overcome and defeat, a fight to the death of sorts. The swamp creatures' maleficence and hatred toward this President were eerily similar that launched at a former great Republican hero president who was also a "non-politician" (perhaps this is why they were both so great!) and who was also considered a "People's President," namely, Ronald Reagan (God rest his soul which was as humorous as it was positive, pure and golden). Ronald Reagan advocated Christian values, and his wife, Nancy Reagan, started and promoted the "Just Say No to Drugs" program to prevent America from becoming the next opium dens-destroyed country that, throughout history, has set back many foreign countries, perhaps hundreds of years of progress, due to their citizen's mind be destroyed and addicted, beyond the possibility of recovery, by their country-wide addiction to opium and numerous other opioid drugs and non-opioid hallucinogenic drugs that destroyed many genius minds throughout these countries, sadly enough, a path that the United States of America seems comfortable going down if the radical and liberal left-wing politicians remain in power via continuing corrupt elections and ignoring Christian values which do not and will never advocate for illicit drug abuse which destroys human bodies and human minds.

God refers to his human body creations as temples that should be built up to be strong and healthy and, as such, poisonous drugs, tobacco, marijuana, alcohol, and skin tattoos are never to be placed into or onto the surface of these body temples created and owned by God.

Republican Heroes Supporting and Defending Donald J. Trump ("The People's President") From Maleficent Evildoers (Democrat Party Slanderers, Saboteurs, Anti-Americans Working Only for Political Power And Influence And Not For The Happiness, Well-Being And Safety Of The American People)

Superheroes

Harmeet Dhillon Esq., Corey Lewandowski, Charlie Kirk, Laura Ingraham, Esq, Scott Hannity, Marc Levin, Rush Limbaugh, Matt Schlapp, Ari Fleischer, Michael Meyers, Candace Owens, Mark Meadows, Tom Fitton, Sara Carter, Ken Starr, Victor Davis Hanson, Devin Nunez, Dan Bongino, Judge Jeanine Pirro, Greg Jarret, John Yoo, Matt Whitaker, Joe Digenova, Matt Gates.

Evil Politicians With Un-American and Non-Christian Values Who Participated In Slanderous Defamation and Evil Coercion, Much Like A Gang of Murderous Mobsters / Mafia, Whose Anti-Trump Behavior and Lack of Support For This Non-Corrupt Elected Leader of the United States of America Was Destructive to Every Hard-Working, Christian American Wage-Earner and Legal Citizens of the United States Who Love and Support Their Country, God, Family, and Non-Corrupt Government Leadership: (Note this list is incomplete because the list of deep state evil swamp creatures in Washington D.C., if listed here, each individual end to end, would span from planet earth to the planet Jupiter and back.)

Below is an imaginary list of fictional (not real) characters that might be imagined (incorrectly) to have been supporting the Presidency of Donald J. Trump, when they were, in fact, "Benedict Arnold-like" traitors who attempted, daily, to inflict knife-in-the-back stabbings and death by myriad knife wounds to perhaps the most dynamic, energetic, non-corrupt President in many years, who pursued and achieved his primary roles of: 1) Protecting American Citizens, and 2) Maximizing the color-blind opportunities for all Americans for: A) Employment (lowest unemployment rate for all races of Americans in decades), B) Equal Opportunity For All Americans (Regardless of Skin Color or Original Country of Origin, Prior to American Citizenship), C) Restoring and Supporting Christian Traditional American Values, D) Restoring Free Speech (Denouncing Fascism and Communism which only foster loss of human rights, human dignity, human freedom, human equal opportunity to achieve success through honest and hard work to achieve unlimited success and advancement into leadership positions in private capitalist businesses or in city, state, and federal government based on their ethical and moral character and hard-working, positive attitude, 3) Restored United States Manufacturing and Technology Innovation (e.g., Restart Vital National Defense and Vital Infrastructure Semiconductor Chip Manufacturing in United States) and Emphasized Employment of Americans in Manufacturing Goods and National Defense Structures (e.g., building national border walls to defeat human and drug trafficking or those countries/individuals who seek to bankrupt American taxpayer-funded social security, welfare, food stamps, medi-cal or Medicaid benefit programs meant for legal American citizens (not for illegal immigrant federal law-breakers who never did and may never commit to becoming lawful citizens or to support and defend United States founding fathers' Christian American Heritage and Values) and Weapons to Maintain Benevolent, Christianity Values-Based United States of America and World Peace and Keep Malevolent Foreign Country Leader Tyrants From Infiltrating Spies/Foreign Country Advocates/Malevolent Activists/Terrorists Into the United States of America and/or Inflicting Undue Harm On Other Smaller or Otherwise Vulnerable, Peaceful and Democratic Countries, seriously.

All below characters are hypothetical or fictional, and any attempt to relate or associate them to actual or real individuals would be inaccurate and invalid:

"The Un-President and Criminal in Chief" Definition: Any president who prioritizes the safety and welfare of non-Americans or attacks American Christian Values or monetarily supports or sends financial assistance to Muslim, Communist, Fascist, or other "tyrant leader countries" (who are professed enemies or haters of the United States of America and it's Christian-based origins and values) who have taken away human rights from their citizens or countries whose citizens chant "death to America (or any other country's citizens), or an American President or Politician who pays American taxpayer money to purchase American military traitors who abandoned their military post and were captured by enemy country military or terrorists or any President who allows discovered (domestic born or foreign-born) spies and traitors who have endangered American national security to flee the country or be pardoned or released from jail early and without American justice system and voter approval.

"Vice President Criminal Facilitator" Definition: Any American Vice President who threatens foreign country prosecutors who are investigating his son or other family members or relatives of the Vice President or any other United States Politician's family member(s) for fraud, embezzlement, bribery, illicit funds transfers for political or other Anti-American or illegal favors or actions promised. Any Vice President or other politician who overtly or covertly takes family members (or government or civilian planes or flights) to foreign rogue, anti-American opponent countries or any other countries, and arranges for fund transfers, by using United States government leadership role to harass and intimidate another country or prosecutors of another country, or anyone who arranges for one or more their family members to take fake jobs or fake leadership roles for or in companies (that they have no training or qualifications for and should therefore not be associated with that company) merely for the purpose of facilitating illegal bribes that may then be transferred to that company from foreign countries that have been asked to "invest in" (aka pay bribe to the recipient) by transferring large sums of money (e.g., bribery or extortion activities by any United States Vice President or other United States politician; e.g., see the American movie entitled: "Shooter (2007, starring mark Wahlberg).

"Attorney General of Corruption and Political Evil Biased Prejudice Against Opposing Political Party" Definition: See American History in the 21st Century.

Female(s) Politicians who criticize half of the country's voters (e.g., opposing political party voters that do not approve of "democratic" politicians' efforts to create election fraud and steal elections from honest voters) or corrupt democratic politicians who assassinate individuals (e.g., Randy Epstein) who have records of illegal and inappropriate conduct with underage individuals (e.g., child molesters) by that politician's spouse and other same democratic political party corrupt members, too numerous to count), should **never** even be considered for election to political offices where they might further expand their vile nexus of evil traitors and terrorist (to Christian American Values) or murderous, evil, cruel, dishonest, immoral, unethical, unchristian and un-American activities. (Honest, Christian value-respecting American Political Leaders Should Always Be Triumphant Over Corrupt and Rigged Nominations of Corrupt Political Opponents Who Never Even Bothered to Attempt Campaigning to Become a Legitimately Elected United States of America President Because They Are So Confident They Will Win (By Corrupt Election) Without Campaigning Due to Premeditated Election Corruption Guaranteed by Evil and Sinister Election Fraud.

Corruption Within National Security Agencies Definition

(Imagine This Hypothetical Scenario Below [a.k.a., the playbook of the "opposition non-Christian political party" and communists, socialists, fascists, or any misanthropic individual or country which otherwise hates: American Christian Values and The Founding Fathers' Vision For America, American Freedom, Independence, Human Rights, Freedom of Speech, Ignoring Skin Color and Instead Focusing on "The American Dream" (which ignores preferential treatment based on skin color and instead promotes and elevates individuals who achieve greatness by honesty, integrity, hard work, education and ethical, moral conduct and improving themselves from birth until death)):

"The Corrupt Democratic Playbook: How to Destroy the Reputation, Potential Game-Changing Effectiveness and Efficiency of a Proven Energetic, Dynamic Business-Smart, Pragmatic, Realistic and True American Christian Values-Loving, Legitimately Elected United States of America President"

Appoint, Cover-up, and Shield Leaders of the F.B.I., C.I.A., and N.S.A. (who are corrupt, partisan politicians who are liberal, anti-American, unethical, lying, deceptive, fraudulent, biased, prejudiced, anti-Christian "unleaders"). Stack the deck with these saboteurs in the last months of your presidency (as done by "Obama the Abomination").

Falsely accuse the opposing political party's legitimately elected United States of America President and all his most loyal and other supporters of being (in America, this has been the playbook of the original "slave owners" political party since 1776 and probably will continue to be their playbook until year 3776, due to their ignoring the Bible and American Christian Values of honesty, integrity, the "Ten Commandments," and their lack of intelligence, imagination, and their perpetual state of guaranteed "Moral Bankruptcy" every election season (and every day of each year in perpetuity), corrupt with any and as many lies as you can think of (project your evil on the ethical opponents you hate so much because they believe in and apply Christian values to their politics, which is always beneficial to their voting citizens, and make you look bad as the opposing political party).

Attack The "Christian American Majority" Citizens and Propagandize and Pretend They Are Actually The Minority And Call Them Racists, Misogynists, and Other Derogatory Terms to Vilify the American Christian Citizens Majority When They Exercise Their Rights to Free Speech, Defense of Their Right to Bear Arms (United States of America Constitutional Rights and Freedoms, among many others) and Freedom to Protect and Defend Their Christian Faith.

Appoint, Cover-up, And Shield Partisan Democratic Corrupt Internal Revenue Service "Leaders" (who are liberal, anti-American, unethical, engage in lying, are deceptive and fraudulent, are biased and prejudiced, are anti-Christian "unleaders"). Instruct them to block approval for Political Action Committees (P.A.C.) or any other (e.g., Christian Organizations) Businesses or Nonprofit Groups that might somehow support the opposing political party or candidate or who might be advocates for non-corrupt American political system and other business C.E.O. elections and leadership changes.

Appoint or elect/vote for "Fake, Pseudo-Prosecutors or Investigators" Who Will Not Justly Prosecute Politicians for Inexcusable, Criminal, Fraudulent, Slanderous, and Otherwise Injurious Actions, Lies, Cover-ups, Conspiracies, Unchristian Acts Deserving of Punishment, Termination of Employment and, in many cases, prolonged or life-long imprisonment or even execution.

Hypothetical Examples Might Include the Following:

No prosecution of an American Presidential Candidate and Son (and President) and allowing that candidate to campaign for President when he and son should have been prosecuted before the election for, e.g., videotape evidence of threatening foreign country prosecutor(s) that if they don't terminate money fraud investigation of the politician's son, then that politician (whose son is being investigated) will withdraw American taxpayer funds or military support that was previously promised to that country (e.g., extortion, intimidation, bribery)

Politicians and other traitor Americans or foreign-born individuals exposing American Intelligence agent identities to other countries, thus endangering their lives and the lives of their family members. Not prosecuting these individuals is absurd and threatens the existence of America and all American citizens at home and living abroad.

Allowing Individuals at the Internal Revenue Service or U.S. presidential candidates to Lose, Destroy, or Otherwise Erase Data on Computers, Cellular Phones, and Other Devices That Prove Corruption, Evil Intent, or Premeditation of Crimes is Absurd. It threatens the existence of America and all American citizens at home and living abroad. This lack of prosecution of evildoers also demolishes the faith that Christian American citizens would like to have in their government that prosecution for crimes is not only for one political party (often the opposite party, which was not elected to office the previous election).

When liberal media, "so-call (pseudo and partisan) news organizations" (too often political weapon organizations for anti-Christian values and megaphones for liberal, radical domestic and/or foreign terrorists groups such as B.L.M. (black lives matter) and antifa and Ku Klux Klan and other unchristian and/or violent gangs, organizations or political hitmen groups) are allowed to shame or silence or assault the President or supporters of the President or Christian Americans who desire and intend to exercise and defend their freedom of religion and freedom of speech and condemnation of immoral sexual behavior or refusing service (in their private business) to individuals who are acting in a non-Christian or immoral manner or with intentions to violate that Christian business owners code of ethics and conduct and business intent, then all Americans are losers and all the wars fought to gain American freedom and independence (and soldiers' lives lost in the process) are negated and relegated to a status of nonexistence, especially if moral, ethical Americans do not revolt against this tyranny, defend America's Christian values and Bible-based moral guidelines and teachings and refuse to have their voices, opinions, Christian ideas and guidance ignored or otherwise suppressed unjustly. The Christian voice of Americans must never be suppressed or relegated to a state of nonexistence by corrupt, liberal, unethical, lying, slanderous, dismissive media personnel, politicians, company chief executive officers (C.E.O.s), foreign individuals who are not pro-American or even hate American ideals, ethics, morality, Christian heritage (e.g., Fascists, Communists, Socialists, atheists, agnostics, other radical or violent militias or militant groups wishing to impose their evil intent or actions on weaker individuals or countries that are weaker or somehow more vulnerable to evil, malevolent tyrants or dictator "leaders (or questionable antichrist-like individuals; see Bible, Chapter: Revelations)."

Irrespective of a Prosecutable Crime: Do Not Prosecute the Criminal.

Should a United States leader who secretly flew a plane loaded with money (millions of American dollars), at night and in the dark, to a country recognized as a leading terrorist country that frequently chants:

"Death to America or Death to Israel (or other non-Muslim, Christian democratic countries)" be prosecuted for being a traitor to America for freeing terrorists from enemy countries to exchange or trade for an American soldier deserter and traitor (who left his assigned duty station) or for funding a rogue anti-American country (e.g., Iran) with money (that the hostile country can then use to build nuclear weapons and missiles to attack America in the future) secretly and without United States voter approval? This generation and every generation of Americans should contemplate these questions.

When a country starts building military island(s) in an international shipping lane of the ocean between many different countries who use that international shipping lane, should that country be able to bribe politicians (e.g., Barrack Obama and Joseph Biden and, of course, Hunter Biden, not unexpectedly) with millions of dollars to not act militarily to prevent the building of that illegitimate (e.g., China military island) island in international waters and in the middle of a busy commercial international shipping lane through the ocean?

Should a rogue foreign country be allowed to release a biological weapon with the approval and collusion of the "Democratic" (aka anti-American political party; remember Anthony Fauci and his attempts to cover up the fact that he funded the Wuhan province biological weapons lab where the COVID-19 virus biological weapon was created and unleashed by China on the entire world and specifically with the intent to derail Donald J. Trump's phenomenal economy and planned re-election for a second four-year term as the United States President?) political party, defeated in the most recent United States of America Presidential election, with the sole purpose of destroying the incumbent President's economy and presidency? This generation and every generation of Americans should contemplate these questions.

CHAPTER ELEVEN:

Raping (Figuratively), Robbing, And Embezzling (RRE) Of Payments And Reimbursements Of Physicians and Physician Groups Who Are Reverently Caring For Routine And Emergency Health Conditions Which Demand And Require Their Loving Care And Surgical Procedures As A Remedy For Their Conditions Or Diseases Throughout The World By Large Trust-Like, Monopolistic, Unimpeded, Unhindered, Unopposed (At Least Up To The Present Time; This Needs To Change Immediately), Large Conglomerate Unethical or Criminal Health Insurance Companies Who, One To 12 months After Patient Care Is Delivered In Good Faith By Physicians and Physician Groups, Are Then Demanded, Without Ethical Justification, Recourse, Or Appropriate Consideration Of Physician Appeals (At Least Without Future Physician Unions' Lawyers Criminal Financial Scandal Law Suits Directed Toward These Sinister Health Insurance Companies), To Refund To These Monopolistic And Sinister Health Insurance Companies, Significant Percentages, e.g., 30-80%, Of Original Payments To Physicians, Or In Some Cases, The Entire Physician Exam or Surgery Fee Due. Because Honorable, Empathetic, Altruistic And Caring Physicians Have Delayed And Precariously Avoided Or Shunned To Their Detriment, For Centuries, The Formation of Ethical Legal Powered And Backed, Physician-Defending and Physician-Supporting Unions, They Continue (Hopefully Not Too Much Longer) To Experience Self-Inflicted Raping (Figuratively), Robbing, And Embezzling (RRE) Of Payments And Reimbursements By These Large, Powerful, Dictator-Like, Sinister, Criminal, Trust-Like, Monopolistic Health Care Insurance Companies Who Have Been Enabled To Continue Their Crimes And Even Supported And Facilitated By The Inaction, Lack of Unity, Insufficient Decisiveness, And Overt Lack Of Resolve By Physicians, For Centuries, To Organize Physician Unions To Defend And Protect Their Ethical, Moral,

And Honest Practice Of Examining And Operating On Patients, And Their Rights and Justification To Maintain Their Respect For These Services, Freedom To Appeal Unjust Demands For Return of Just Fees Paid By Health Insurance Companies, And Fair Reimbursement For All Services Performed.

C. S. Lewis (1898-1963) was a British writer and lay theologian, best known for his works of fiction, including "The Chronicles of Narnia," and his Christian apologetics, such as "Mere Christianity." Lewis's writings have inspired millions and continue to be influential in both literary and religious circles.

For more centuries now, severely worse and more prevalent in the past three decades, large and sinister health insurance companies have been allowed to commit heinous crimes on altruistic physicians who have naively hoped and wished to only focus on caring for their patients through earnest and honest work of performing patient examinations and surgeries each day or week when clinically indicated and necessary or warranted.

However, this naivety and innocent perspective and outlook over several centuries has allowed greedy and money-focused (the sole and only focus within many health insurance companies, unfortunately), nefarious large corporations, also known as health insurance companies, to take complete control of physician sound and ethical judgment, discretion and freedom to directly bill for their patient examination services and surgeries provided to and for their patients. This naive transfer of control, discretion, and monetary fee reimbursement calculations to these large and unethical, money-focused, non-patient care and well-being, non-optimal patient outcome, and companies who have, over the past several centuries, perfected and legalized their crimes of raping (figuratively), robbing, and embezzling physicians and other health care providers and workers of fair and due reimbursement for their daily work, or more accurately, pretending to make fair, honest, warranted, reasonable, and appropriate payments to them for patient exams and surgeries, then covertly and hidden, perhaps from health insurance government regulators which should be but are not regularly and repeated bring law suits against them to prosecute their constant yearly theft of physician reimbursements, one to twelve months AFTER legitimate and just payments were originally and initially paid for these arduous and tiring care exams and surgeries performed in good faith that they will be paid and able to retain these payments for the services rendered by these physicians and surgeons!

Like a lethal plague or metastatic cancer, and because physicians throughout the world have been detrimentally (to themselves) passive, laid back, naïve, gullible, or whatever term you prefer to use, the bottom line being and is that physicians in the past several centuries have failed to evolve, update, and modernize their direct billing practices for the services they provide to their patients and failed to maintain the authority, respect, dignity, freedom, and professionalism they earned through their education, and deserve based on the altruistic, and patients life-improving results that are achieved by them performing their patient exam services and surgeries.

Centene health insurance company, as just one of many examples of numerous dishonest and unethical health insurance companies, was notoriously stealing physician payments paid to physician and surgeon providers credentialed for their "health insurance company" (more accurately, raping [figuratively speaking], robbing, and embezzling company), one to 24 months after initially, appropriately, and justly paying all their provider physicians and surgeons for the patient examinations, procedures, and surgeries they were performing on their shared patients.

When they unilaterally (like a sinister dictator or the head of the gestapo, or even more accurately, like Adolf Hitler himself), demand to be reimbursed for partial or full patient visit or surgery fees, that had been, in the recent past, rightly and justly paid fees to physicians, denied each and every physician appeal on a shockingly consistent and routine basis, all without any reason or justification given for this criminal theft of previous health insurance company payments rightly and justly due to their physicians, until they were finally and thankfully (by the action of **"Superheroes, Becoming The Truly Elite And Honorable"**), sued in legal battles fought in the court room, which effectively stopped or caused the cessation of these long, ongoing, and previously unopposed (again due to the impotence and lack of legal power possessed by individual physicians, who can barely afford their extremely high monthly malpractice insurance payments and monthly office and office staff overhead expenses, and physician groups who perceive their groups (inaccurately) of being too busy to take on and sue criminal and law-breaking large monopolistic, trust-like, health insurance companies who have been for decades, progressively becoming more brazen and bold, and criminal in intent and actions, to steal back as much physician fee payment, from all physician practices possible, to greater and greater extent, which both devastates the bottom line income and ability of physician to pay their monthly bills to stay afloat and in practice, and sadly and disappointingly, concomitantly "fills the coffers" or pockets (with money due to but stolen back from physicians originally and rightfully paid for their services), of these rich, Satanic, unethical, monopolistic and trust-like (incidentally, where is Teddy Roosevelt when all physicians need him, especially in this last century), "money-only focused" health insurance (tyrant dictator), companies!

United Healthcare is perhaps the health insurance that needs to be sued in court every month of its existence to rectify and remedy the millions of dollars they have stolen from physicians, again 1 to 24 months after patients were originally and initially examined or procedures performed, or surgeries performed on these shared patients.

Anthem Blue Cross and Blue Shield and other various large monopolistic, unethical, and criminal robbing and embezzling health insurance companies have created all these covert and supposedly hidden and secret methods to appear like they are ethically paying all physician and surgeon fees due to them, then, in the dark of night, one to 24 months later, randomly sending physician practices letters or emails, with long lists of patients "for chart reviews," enabling and facilitating the onset of their criminal actions of stealing back payments or surgical fees from their "in-network" or "out-of-network" physicians who trustingly provided emergency and urgent, needed care for their patients either in the urgent care clinic, their private physician practice office, the emergency room, the trauma bay area of the emergency room, or when called to perform an inpatient consultation exam or surgery on hospitalized patients.

<u>A recent lawsuit was filed by patients and physicians against **Cigna** for intentionally underpaying patients' medical claims</u>. The American Medical Association, the Medical Society of New Jersey, and the Washington State Medical Association are among the plaintiffs in the case. The lawsuit alleges that Cigna failed to pay medical claims based

on physicians' contracts with MultiPlan Corp. <u>Instead, Cigna applied its own, lower payment methodology for nonparticipating physicians and other health professionals, leaving patients exposed to balance billing for physician and other health service fees.</u>

From AMA Website:

Patients, doctors sue to hold Cigna accountable for underpayments
SEP 28, 2022

By <u>Tanya Albert Henry</u>, Contributing News Writer

In an effort to shed light on misconduct by one of the nation's largest health insurance plans, patients and physicians have filed a proposed <u>class-action lawsuit</u> (PDF) alleging the company intentionally underpaid patients' medical claims.

Your Powerful Ally

The AMA helps physicians build a better future for medicine, advocating in the courts and on the Hill to remove obstacles to patient care and confront today's greatest health crises.

The <u>Litigation Center of the American Medical Association and State Medical Societies</u>, the Medical Society of New Jersey (MSNJ), and the Washington State Medical Association (WSMA) in September became plaintiffs in the lawsuit alleging that Cigna failed to pay the medical claims based on physicians' contracts with MultiPlan Corp. Instead, Cigna applied its own lower payment methodology for nonparticipating physicians and other health professionals. That move left patients exposed to balance billing for physician and other health service fees.

"Patients and physicians have a right to expect health insurers to uphold their promise to provide fair and accurate payment for medical services. But alleged misconduct by Cigna has allowed the insurer's economic self-interest to be prioritized ahead of their promises to physicians in the MultiPlan Network and their patients," said AMA President <u>Jack Resneck Jr., MD</u>.

The AMA, MSNJ, and WSMA "allege that Cigna's misconduct is riddled with conflicts of interest and manipulations that routinely shortchanged payments to MultiPlan Network physicians and interfered with the patient-physician relationship."

The AMA Litigation Center and others filed the lawsuit, *AMA/Stewart v. Cigna*, in the U.S. District Court for the District of Connecticut, and they seek a jury trial.

Find out more about the cases in which the AMA Litigation Center is providing assistance and learn about the Litigation Center's case-selection criteria.

Related Coverage Proposed 2023 physician pay schedule deepens Medicare's instability.

Patients, physicians shortchanged

With more than 1.2 million physicians and other health professionals, MultiPlan is the nation's largest "third-party network" company. Doctors and other health professionals sign contracts with MultiPlan, agreeing to accept a set percentage of their billed charges as full payment. In other words, they agree not to hold the patient liable for the difference between the original amount charged for the service and the discounted rate, a practice commonly known as balance billing.

In turn, MultiPlan enters into contracts with its clients and health benefit plan issuers and claims administrators like Cigna to provide them with access to a MultiPlan network. Providers who join a MultiPlan network indirectly contract with MultiPlan's clients, such as Cigna.

Cigna advertises its relationship with MultiPlan to its insured by, among other things, placing a MultiPlan logo on insurance cards that Cigna plan members receive. The lawsuit notes that Cigna sometimes applies the MultiPlan contracted rates when it processes claims, but not always.

It's the claims that they say Cigna failed to apply the contracted rates to that the AMA, MSNJ, WSMA, and patients are challenging in court.

By not paying claims based on the MultiPlan contracts, Cigna "breached its fiduciary duties, including its duty to honor written plan terms and its duty to loyalty, because its conduct serves Cigna's own economic self-interest and elevates Cigna's interest above the interests of plan member patients," the lawsuit alleges.

That, physicians and patients claim, violates the Employee Retirement and Income Security Act of 1974 (ERISA). That federal law requires Cigna to pay benefits for services based on the MultiPlan contracts.

Related Coverage

<u>How doctors can use No Surprises Act to resolve billing disputes</u>

The lawsuit also alleges that Cigna's actions violated laws in New Jersey and Washington.

"Not only does Cigna ignore the MultiPlan Contracts that providers have entered into when processing claims, but it falsely tells patients that their providers have agreed to reimbursement rates below the MultiPlan Contract rate, when providers have not so agreed," the lawsuit says.

"Cigna uses misrepresentations to patients about their providers as a means to pressure providers to agree to those discounted rates. Cigna does so, at the expense of its insureds and their providers, in order to maximize its own profits through exorbitant and unreasonable 'savings fees' (as to self-funded plans) and reduced benefit payments (as to fully insured plans)."

Time to "shed light"

The lawsuit provides three detailed examples of patients and their physicians who say they were victims of Cigna's improper billing. Each patient exhausted their appeals within Cigna.

Dr. Resneck said that by joining the case as a plaintiff, "the AMA hopes to shed light on Cigna's misconduct and create remedies so that patients and physicians can look forward to getting what they are promised."

Another recent class-action lawsuit was filed in a federal district court in Orlando for health care providers and individual plaintiffs against several insurance companies, arguing that their clients are fed up with the "illegal hurdles" to avoid paying up on COVID-19 services.

dbr DAILY BUSINESS REVIEW

- ☐ Legal News
- ☐ Real Estate News
- ☐ Public Notices
- ☐ Small Business Adviser(current)

©

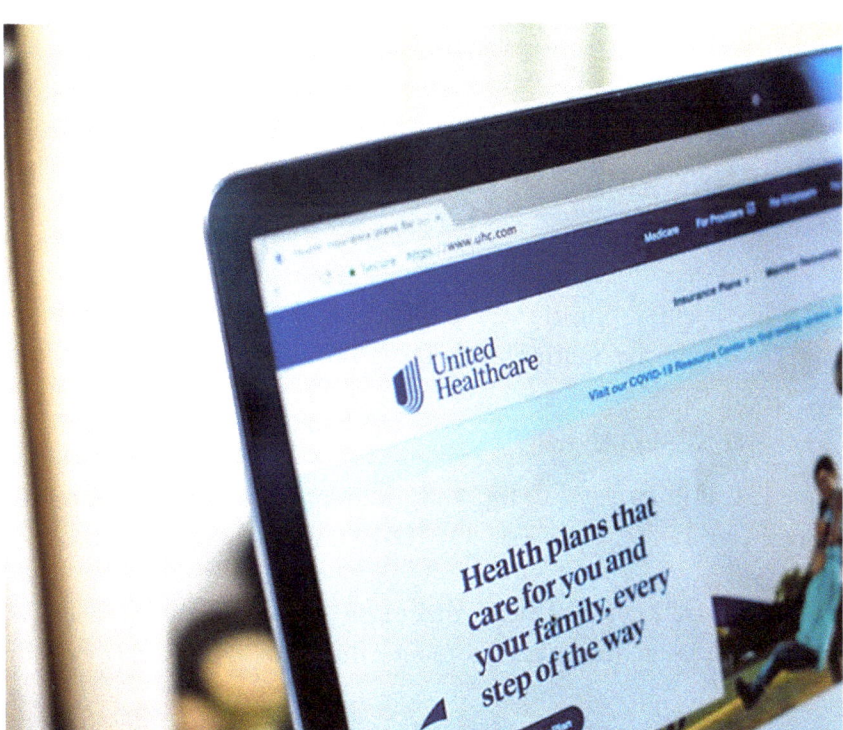

The United Healthcare Inc. website on a laptop computer. (Credit: Tiffany Hagler-Geard/Bloomberg)

NEWS

'They've Done Every Trick in the Book': Providers File Class Action Against Health Insurers

"Our strategy is to send a message to other insurance companies that they have an obligation to pay under those statutes," said Steven Adler, a partner at Mandelbaum Barrett.

December 30, 2022, at 01:50 PM

Class Actions
Michael A. Mora

Michael is a litigation editor at ALM, as well as a reporter for the South Florida Daily Business Review.

What You Need to Know

United Healthcare Services Inc. and additional defendants failed to pay more than 34,000 claims for COVID-19 tests, plaintiffs argued.

Defendants are accused of tactics that made it nearly impossible to appeal denials, such as internal appeals procedures that plaintiffs labeled a mockery.

Since defendants failed to negotiate the claims rate, the CARES Act mandates insurers must reimburse the claims pursuant to prices listed on the provider's website, plaintiffs asserted.

Attorneys have filed a class action lawsuit in a federal district court in Orlando for health care providers and individual plaintiffs, arguing that their clients are fed up with the "illegal hurdles" by several insurance companies to avoid paying up on COVID-19 services.

Steven Teppler and Steven Adler, of counsel and partner at Mandelbaum Barrett in Boca Raton, Florida, and Roseland, New Jersey, respectively, represent plaintiffs Aventus Health LLC and multiple laboratories, along with proposed class representative Sean Bygrave. They filed suit against several defendants, including United Healthcare Inc. and OptumHealth Care Solutions.

RELATED STORIES

Broward Lawyer Beats United Healthcare Again, With at Least 3 Trials Set for 2023

dbr DAILY BUSINESS REVIEW

- ☐ Legal News
- ☐ Real Estate News
- ☐ Public Notices
- ☐ Small Business Adviser(current)

©

UnitedHealthcare corporate headquarters in Minnetonka, MN. (Credit: Ken Wolter/Shutterstock.com)

NEWS

Broward Lawyer Beats United Healthcare Again, With at Least 3 Trials Set for 2023

- ☐ Legal News
- ☐ Real Estate News
- ☐ Public Notices
- ☐ Small Business Adviser(current)

UnitedHealthcare corporate headquarters in Minnetonka, MN. (Credit: Ken Wolter/Shutterstock.com)

NEWS

Broward Lawyer Beats United Healthcare Again, With at Least 3 Trials Set for 2023

"This ruling sends a strong message that doctors should be treated fairly, and it is time for insurance companies to pay up," said Justin C. Fineberg, a partner at Lash & Goldberg.

December 06, 2022 at 02:37 PM
Litigation

Michael A. Mora →

What You Need to Know

A Tampa arbitration panel entered a nearly $11M judgment against United Healthcare Insurance Co. and its Florida subsidiary.

The lead attorney convinced a jury in Nevada to return an over **$62 million** verdict in December 2021 against United, with at least three more cases set for trial next year.

The attorney's team conducted over 30 depositions, including multiple out-of-state witnesses, third-party depositions, and expert depositions.

A Fort Lauderdale attorney appeared to crack the code after beating a major insurance company for the second time in less than a year, with a Tampa arbitration panel entering a nearly $11 million judgment.

Justin C. Fineberg, a partner at Lash & Goldberg, led attorneys for Team Health Holdings Inc.'s affiliate, plaintiff Gulf-to-Bay Anesthesiology Associates LLC, against defendants, United Healthcare of Florida Inc. and United Healthcare Insurance Co.

Justin C. Fineberg partner with Lash Goldberg. (Courtesy photo)

RELATED STORIES

South Florida Attorney Co-Leads Team That Scored Nearly $63M Jury Verdict in Nevada State Court

dbr DAILY BUSINESS REVIEW

- ☐ Legal News
- ☐ Real Estate News
- ☐ Public Notices
- ☐ Small Business Adviser(current)

©

Superheroes

Justin C. Fineberg partner with Lash Goldberg. Courtesy photo

NEWS

South Florida Attorney Co-Leads Team That Scored Nearly $63M Jury Verdict in Nevada State Court

Justin C. Fineberg, a partner at Lash & Goldberg, said he has over 10 upcoming trials in several states against United Healthcare Insurance Company, potentially exposing the defendant to hundreds of millions of dollars in losses.

December 10, 2021 at 03:28 PM
3 minute read

Verdicts-Settlements

Michael A. Mora →

What You Need to Know

Justin C. Fineberg, a partner at Lash & Goldberg, was co-counsel in the Nevada state court litigation.

Getting the case trial-ready included completing more than 50 depositions in 90 days.

The jury found $2.65 million in compensatory damages and $60 million in punitive damages.

A Fort Lauderdale litigator led a team of attorneys in Nevada state court to score a nearly $63 million jury verdict. But the litigator noted he has a long road ahead of him before he can adequately celebrate the verdict.

Justin C. Fineberg, a partner at Lash & Goldberg, along with his colleagues Martin B. Goldberg and Rachel H. LeBlanc, brought the lawsuit against United Healthcare Insurance Co. and its affiliates on behalf of their emergency services clients, Team Health, Fremont Emergency Services, and Ruby Crest Emergency Medicine.

"Physician Unions" must be urgently formed or created to ensure the survival of private practice physicians, physician groups, and to emancipate and free the physicians, who for the past several centuries, have been progressively and more harshly and frequently been beaten down, financially, and from a respect and dignity viewpoint, and had the independence, freedom, and professionalism authority ripped from their superman-like (benevolent) chests, and defeated in every effort to appeal, overcome, and overturn, trust-like, monopolistic, large, prominent, wealthy, greedy, health insurance companies' "white collar" business executives and administrators betrayal of their contracted, trustingly signed by all their physician providers, physicians who perform all the work that has made this sinister large, uncontrolled, unmonitored, criminal companies filthy and disgustingly rich, causing their publicly-traded stocks to surge in price and value over the past century, while at the same time torturing and stealing (e.g., demanding partial or full refunds, one to twenty-four months after physician paid for due services), from the "peasants in the field whose honest, hard, and earnest work each day," enabled they dishonest large company to become rich as a result of their company's criminal behavior and crimes, unhindered and with no viable or effective pushback from physician who have (at least to date), no effective, practical, defensive, assertive, decisive, or powerful legal department in the future, extremely necessary and urgent "Physician Unions" that absolutely are critical, necessary, essential, required, and vital to the future of ethical care of patients worldwide!

Another vivid example of physician betrayal and rape (again, figuratively speaking) is Anthem Blue Cross health insurance company, whose Satanic and abusive, inappropriate (yet allowed to remain in place and intact by insurance regulators [or sleepers], who fail to outlaw this egregious and dishonest practice), policy of never paying more than a sixty-minute visit fee for many of its insured patients, cared for by physician providers for their patients, **regardless** of the severity of the condition or prolonged, sometimes several hours or more, examination, procedures, or surgery required to appropriately treat the emergent condition their patients presenting to the private physician office or hospital. In what other profession would this criminal reimbursement limitation for services provided be acceptable or tolerated? The quick and easy answer is none.

No other profession would accept one hour of payment for two, three, or six hours of labor and services performed, often complex and organ-saving or life-saving procedures, not just having your car brakes replaced or your car engine repaired!

Other asinine healthcare insurance company policies or healthcare industry abusive and ignorantly ignored and non-prosecuted criminal intent and actions by health insurance companies include the two scenarios described below that are daily insults to practicing physicians and surgeons and all other healthcare professionals and providers.

Only "Physician Unions" powerful and influential attorney-staffed legal counsel and departments will be able to correct these ridiculous and absurd currently practiced "dictator policies" of current "trust-like, monopolistic, sinister, and all-powerful (to the detriment and devastation of prisoner physicians and other detained and underpaid healthcare providers), health care insurance companies", who must be defeated in court, especially because current "health insurance company regulatory agencies (nonexistent in reality and professional "sleepers" for the past one century, of little to no assistance to individual honest, hard-working physicians and other health professionals), and stolen and withheld due payments by insurance companies, must be returned to the honest and ethical physicians they stole these withheld or illegally "taken back" payments from.

A succinct description of one such commonly employed and unethically "allowed" crime against physicians and surgeons, and other health care providers of emergency health care follows below. In the past, when a physician examined a new patient who also needed an emergency removal of a foreign object from their injured body or another emergency surgical procedure that very same day as their new patient's comprehensive examination visit, the health care provider performing both the extended new patient examination and the urgent required (and compassionate, to relieve the pain and anxiety of the that injured patient requiring an urgent procedure performed, in addition to the new patient exam), procedure that was discovered during the course of their examination, would be, rightfully and reasonably, paid for BOTH the new patient examination AND the surgical or other procedure or procedures that were necessarily performed at that same visit and on that same day.

Now, with the terrible and unhelpful "sleepers (health care insurance company "regulators," who have been unsupportive to physicians for the past three decades and longer, allowing the current dilemma of no righteous and just reimbursement of physicians throughout the world, who wish to do the right thing, but are now punished with half of more of their deserved exam and procedures being paid, instead of both their exam and procedure(s) being paid in full, as would be the ethical standard in any other profession throughout the world! Insurers now, as their common practice, **only** pay for a procedure or an examination fee but not both fees that they should be paying for. This is a crime and defies reason and logic.

Malpractice insurance companies and insurance companies both expect and demand that healthcare providers always perform comprehensive new patient examinations and histories to most accurately and effectively assess each patient and derive the most appropriate and beneficial treatment plan for each patient. At the same time, and only in the health care arena or professional world, do both health insurance regulators ("sleepers") and sinister, "greedy and money-only-concerned" trust-like, monopolistic large health care insurance companies and executives get away with their crimes of only paying for a small or minority portion of the total labor performed by these physicians and other healthcare providers (paying only for a procedure or a patient exam fee, but not for both, nor for the total time spent and required to care for the patient that same day visit).

Another travesty and disappointing technology-based degradation in the focused, succinct, concise evaluation and treatment of patients, specifically in the healthcare professional world, and again, unfairly singling out physicians and healthcare professionals to be the only professionals hurt and stolen from in this specific scenario, is the practice, now, of health insurance company's criminal practices and behavior of purposely intending to steal back money paid to healthcare providers, if after review of handwritten or electronic health records, they are able to find even one category of healthcare history or the examination section which is slightly (but clinically insignificant), "under-documented" (for instance did not list Family History negative for heart disease, stroke, diabetes, psychiatric disease, gastrointestinal disease, skin disease, etcetera), or even undocumented, even though it may have no connection to the current injury or illness being examined or surgery performed that same day, in order to deny full and rightful labor time spent on the examination and treatment that same day.

This crime of decreasing payment for demanded, obsessive-compulsive 100 percent complete patient histories and examination categories, despite the insurance companies knowing they will successfully attempt and achieve the lowest payment possible, e.g., only pay for one procedure on one examination fee for that one day visit, places an enormous electronic health record documentation burden on that healthcare provider and forces that same provider to be less focused on the emergency exam and procedure most relevant to each specific injury or system of the body that is most sick and in need of help, and instead causes both the care and focus to be on (an insult to all physicians focused on the most urgent and dire exam and treatment items) not being reimbursed for 80 percent of the time and labor that healthcare provider spent, due to missing, e.g., not sufficiently documenting the social history of the patient such as do they drink alcohol, smoke tobacco, use illicit drugs, had a blood transfusion, and when and for how long?

Many healthcare providers are completely disappointed and even leaving the profession, due to the discrimination against them in how they are paid, and the fact that they have to wait one to three months in many case to be pain by health insurance companies, and then find out, shockingly, that they were either denied payment, or paid one-third of billed fees (for reasons listed above), or were for the past many years (several decades for those still living and practicing in the healthcare industry), "raped (figuratively speaking), robbed, and embezzled from by these UNREGULATED, TRUST-LIKE, MONOPOLISTIC, WEALTHY, GREEDY, MONEY-HUNGREY, PUBLICALLY-TRADED, FORTUNE 500 HEALTH INSURANCE COMPANIES WHO ARE ACTIVELY, CURRENTLY, AND HAVE BEEN FOR DECADES, RAPING (FIGURATIVELY SPEAKING), ROBBING, AND EXBEZZLING MONEY FROM PHYSICIANS AND HEALTHCARE PROVIDERS, ALL AS A RESULT OF THE LACK OF (AND DIRE AS SOON AS POSSIBLE NEED FOR) PHYSICAN UNIONS WITH POWERFUL LEGAL DEPARTMENTS THAT MAY AND WILL BATTLE AND DEFEAT THESE FORTUNE 500 SINISTER AND TRUST-LIKE, MONOPOLISTIC HEALTH INSURANCE COMPANIES WHO ARE BOTH ENSLAVING AND STEALING FROM HEALTHCARE PROVIDERS, "SUPERHEROES, BECOMING THE TRULY ELITE AND HONORABLE", BUT IN DIRE NEED OF IMMEDIATE FORMATION OF PHYSICIAN UNIONS.

Below are chapters/excepts from an amazing, inspiring, motivational, and masterpiece entitled "Father's Eyes" by Winston Anselm Irons, which masterfully and sagaciously addresses different yet similar deficiencies and travesties needing a remedy in the healthcare provider training programs throughout the world. Treasure and enjoy the wisdom and insight from this masterpiece, "Father's Eyes," which are included in the paragraphs below to complete the comprehensive analysis and remedies available and possible to vastly improve the healthcare provided to every "world citizen" in this generation and every future generation!

(Below are Chapters/Excerpts from the books "Father's Eyes" by the author Winston Anselm Irons, and "Modern-Day Slave Trade In The 21st Century" by the author Priscilla Lisa Alvarez-Mendez.)

Chapter Eight:

Current Glaring Deficiencies and Travesties in the Training & Treatment of Medical Professionals by University Training Programs and Hospital Administrators? What are Solutions?

Below are salient excerpts or selected chapters from the new and outstanding author, Priscilla Lisa Alvarez-Mendez, who also graciously consented to and allowed these below-selected chapters to be included in this life-changing "Age of Reason" book and who has proved herself to be an honest, accurate, true, authentic, trustworthy, and genuine champion of human rights, particularly that of medical professionals in training programs and independent physician and physician groups that are working in or for hospitals as independent contractors or consultants in various medical specialties throughout the world.

Priscilla Lisa Alvarez-Mendez has written a paradigm-shifting historical, nonfiction, earth-shaking novel that should result in an immediate, necessary gestalt in the mindset and actions of physicians and all medical professionals in training programs and in post-training professional roles throughout the world, prompting and motivating their immediate, justified and long overdue, organization of physician-advocate unions to battle for and regain the dignity and respect they need be afforded but have been deprived of for generations and hundreds of years in an ongoing era of modern slave trade attitudes and behavior perpetrated by powerful universities with large endowments or hospital-owning corporations, limited partnerships, or other business entities that have emphasized and enforced profit motives over respect, protection and displayed dignity and gratitude for their medical professionals involved in daily patient care.

The brilliance of this author's work includes not only the pointing out of these modern slave practices with vivid, true stories of injustices by university medical professional training programs and public or private hospitals that contract with these professional and direct patient care providers, but also the author's keen insight, willingness, and courage to, beyond alerting the public of these well-hidden and covert practices, offer solutions as to how these unethical attitudes, behavior, and actions may be, once and for all, reversed and defeated, thus improving patient care worldwide and restoring happiness, job fulfillment, and respect for physicians and all other medical professionals who provide daily direct patient care for these institutions.

The reader might initially be shocked by the truth and disappointing reality of these stories but will then be encouraged, inspired, and motivated to support the effort of the author to establish a fair, equal, and balanced "playing field" for medical professionals caring for patients each day, by encouraging unionization of these medical professionals, so that corrupt or otherwise dishonest, deceitful, and abusive "slave-owners" (powerful universities with large endowments or hospital-owning corporations, limited partnerships, or other business entities, whose only interests might be monetary or covering up patient care errors or scandals, to avoid being rightfully held responsible and liable for poor patient care or irresponsible policies that hurt patients but make hospitals more profitable), may be defeated in court by physician-friendly union lawyers when necessary.

Currently, physicians and other direct patient care providers are restricted from making honest comments that will improve patient care, especially if hospital administrations do not want to hear these comments or suggestions or if the comments include any criticism of that hospital's employees or attending staff members, and may be threatened with inappropriate punishments, restrictions of practice [e.g., removal from on-call panels], or even firing if such undesired comments or suggestions are made by these "slaves" (medical professionals providing daily direct patient care or contracted services or consultations).

Currently, nonexistent Physician-friendly and Physician-Advocating Unions must be established and given the top legal minds in the country to defend and support honest medical professionals who seek to improve patient care and constantly rid the hospital and hospital administrations of those members whose motives and intents are not aligned with optimal, zenith patient care standards, but rather create irresponsible hospital policies that make the hospital money but hinder or ignore optimal and timely patient care altogether, or display inappropriate attitudes, perspectives, actions, inactions, and negligence that adversely affect patient care outcomes. The below chapters are a poignant reminder that modern slavery still exists.

Modern-Day Slave Trade in the 21st Century:

Synopsis:

Why Physicians Must Unite And Agree To Commence A Revolution, Achieve And Restore Balance of Power, Physician Independence And Freedoms Relinquished Centuries Ago, By Defeating Slave Owner Corporate Hospital "AdminisTraitors" Whilst Concomitantly Effecting And Facilitating: Abolition Of Slave Trade Practices, Physicians Emancipation, Restoral Of Dignity And Respect For Individual Physicians And Zenith Patient Care

How and Why Physicians-In-Training & Individual Physicians ("Slaves") Must Battle And Defeat Large, Powerful Hospital Corporations & Hospital "AdminisTraitors" ("Slave Owners") To Achieve And Maintain Emancipation of Physician Slaves Stripped of Their Basic Human Rights And Freedom of Speech, Restore Physician vs Administration Balance of Powers, And Bolster Honesty And Integrity Within The Healthcare System Worldwide, Fostering And Enabling Zenith Quality Patient Health Care While Equally Recognizing And Respecting The Dignity of Patients And Physicians

There Is A Dire Need For Independent Physicians (a.k.a. "The Slaves") To Stand United And Unionize To Wage Battle Against Tyrant And Unethical Large Hospital Corporations And Their Sycophant Hospital

"AdminisTraitors" (Hospital Administrators, a.k.a. "Slave Owners") To Achieve Emancipation of Physician Slaves, Restoral Of Christian, Bible-Based Ethics And Morality In Care Of Hospital Patients, Balance Of Power Between Physicians And Hospital "AdminisTraitors" And Achieve Zenith, Highest Standard Of Patient Care In So Doing.

Introduction:

The Battle That Individuals, Independent Physicians, And Physicians-In-Training Must Wage Against Hospital "AdminisTraitors" (Administrators) That Have, For Over 200 Years, Stripped Freedom, Human Dignity, Basic Human Rights And The Voice Of Individuals From Their Slaves And The Call to Unite, Unionize, Consolidate Collective Power And Influence Together For Victorious, Glorious Emancipation, Now And Forever.

Entrenched Taxation Without Representation Mentality And Dark, Dastardly Underpinnings Perpetuating Slavery-like Practices in the Medical Professional Training System Worldwide Include No Regard or Intent For Equal Representation And No Assumption of Innocence Until Proven Guilty (e.g., Justice), No Respect For Human Dignity And No Options Or Avenues For Reporting Leadership Abuse Without Consequential Retribution And/Or Loss Of Training Opportunity. Without Restoration Of Physicians/Hospital Administrators Balance Of Powers, These Current Malevolent Policies And Tyrant Attitudes Of Hospital AdminisTraitors (a.k.a., Slave Owners) Will Continue To Suppress, Torment, And Torture Individual Physicians And Physicians-In-Training, As Has Been The Case For The Past Two Centuries. Only By Standing United And Establishing Physician Advocate Union(s), Will Independent Contractor Physicians And Physicians-In-Training Ever Be Able To Maintain Constitutional Rights And Freedoms Which Are Currently Nonexistent In The Isolated Galaxies And Microcosms Known As Medical Training Hospitals And Current Hospital Administrations And Their Subservient, Sycophant AdminisTraitors

Who Are Neither Advocates For Nor Loyal To Individual Physicians And Physicians-In-Training.

Physician-Owned And Physician-Defending Union(s) Are Now Essential If The Fierce Battle For The Emancipation of Modern-Day Slaves Is To Be Fought And Won. Freedom (Of Speech & In General, Per The United States Constitution), Justice And Respect For Slaves (e.g., Medical Professionals in Training and Independent Contractor Physicians Working In Hospitals) Can Only Be Achieved With The Defeat Of Hospital Administrations (e.g., Slave Owner Plantations With Sycophant [Anti-Slave, Anti-Physician] Hospital AdminisTraitors Who Are Constantly Falsely Attacking Physicians Without Due Process And Covering Up Sinister Behavior And Harmful Actions of Hospital Employees, Akin To A Brutal Slave Owner Abusing A Slave Without Reason or Justification But Rather At The Whim Of The Slave Owner's Dark Disposition Or Bad Attitude That Day), Emancipation of Physician Slaves Worldwide, Ultimately Resulting In, Now And In The Future, Free And Satisfied Physicians, Restoration Of Balance Of Powers, And The Highest Level Of Patient Care.

Chapter One:

Dark Dastardly Non-Evolution of Medical Training & Origin of Species: Monstrous & Demeaning Rules & Regulations That Subvert Humanity, Abandon Christian Morals & Ethics of Bible, Take Hostage Physician Freedom of Speech, Equality & Justice For All in Medical Training And Independent Physicians Working As Slaves For Hospital Administrators Worldwide

As a young child, Lisa was a prodigy in multiple areas of expertise, e.g., in academics, music performance, athletic performance, and other areas. She was considered, by definition, and payments received for her musical performances, a professional musician while a grammar school student. She was the first student from her class selected for the "Gifted and Talented Education (GATE) program. She excelled in most, if not all, endeavors she pursued. Lisa graduated with top honors from grammar school, high school, university, medical school, Ivy League postdoctoral eye surgery residency medical training program, and postdoctoral fellowship subspecialty training and became an established expert physician within her specific subspecialty field of expertise.

Lisa, for the first two-thirds of her life (only a guess as she is still living), was never a fan of worker or employee unions or a detractor or critic of unions and their role in defending and protecting their constituents' and members' freedom and rights.

After many years of experience and manipulative experiences whereby bad actors in the medical field not only fail to admit their mistakes and acts of misconduct but go further to hide or deflect or reflect/project their misconduct on innocent bystanders or colleagues to hide or cover up their misconduct, Lisa now admits that she sees the essential and all-important role that unions, if conducted with ethical intent and led by physician-friendly advocates, may play in the defeat of, perhaps, the most extended and longest surviving instance of modern-day (medical trainees & independent physicians in practice) slavery, defined as follows in the paragraph below:

"Hospital Training Programs & Administrators (aka The Slave Owners) versus Physicians-in-Training & Independent Contractor Physician Specialists and Subspecialist Who Support Hospitals By Providing On-Call Emergency Care and Inpatient Emergency Care Yet Are Treated As Powerless (and "Lawyerless") Slaves Who Cannot And Will Not Defend Themselves By Creating New Physician-Friendly And Supportive Special Unions That Will Battle & Defeat Hospital Administrators Perpetuation, For Over 100+ Years, Of Medical Slave Trading, Intimidation, Incarceration & Unjust Punishment & Abuse. A Battle Must Be Fought Via Physician Unification & Creation of Powerful, New Physician Unions That:

1) Elect And Appoint Representatives in Hospital Administrations Whose Sole Purpose Is To Represent Independent Contractor Physicians (Non-Salaried Physicians Who Are Not Employed Directly As "Employees" By Hospitals), And

2) Elect All Subspecialty Department Heads (True Leaders and Strong Physician Advocates Capable of Leading Battles Against Hospital Administrators When Necessary & Indicated to Support And Defend The Physicians Who Elected Them. These Leaders Cannot And Must Not Be Chosen By Or Paid Incentives By Hospital Administrators (Thereby Enslaving Them). This Will Lead To The Permanent And Final Emancipation (Freeing the Slaves) of Physicians-in-training And Independent Contractor Hospital Physicians, Who May Then Engage In Regular and Free Constructive Criticism of Misguided Hospital Policies or Actions or Nefarious Hospital Employee Actions or Acts of Malpractice Without Fear of Unjust Retribution by Hospital Administrators, Because These Physicians Will Be Protected and Supported by Unions With Robust and Top Legal Minds Whose Expertise Is Focused On Justice In Defense Of Honest, Ethical, And Hard-Working, Brilliant Young Physicians-In-Training And Older Independent Contractor Specialist And Subspecialist Physicians Supporting On-Call Services & Inpatient Emergency Care Services And Consultation Exam Requests.

On a dark and snowy winter evening, Lisa was on-call for emergency eye conditions or injuries that presented to hospital emergency rooms in the city of Philadelphia, Pennsylvania, and were then admitted to hospital inpatient floors by these emergency departments, specifically at two hospitals on this particular evening. Lisa's pager rang out suddenly at 1100 pm, with those dreaded, high-pitched, annoying, squealing beeps that alert Batman that not all is well in Gotham. Upon calling the number listed on her pager, Lisa learned that the emergency department physician was calling about a patient who needed an immediate / emergency ophthalmology (and trauma surgeon and ear, nose, throat specialist (ENT Specialist) consult) after an explosion injury to a patient's head and neck. Although the incident sounded like a premeditated (with suboptimal execution of intended purpose), Philadelphia mafia hit job to Lisa, the history given by the patient to the medical doctor in the emergency room was: "Had a blow torch which was leaking in my car trunk, so when I opened my car door my car exploded." (In general, we always write down the history given by a patient, whether we believe that is what actually happened or not.)

Lisa immediately went to complete an ophthalmology consultation. She learned that both eyes had been ruptured and both eyes had car windshield and passenger doors shattered glass fragments as intraocular foreign bodies that were visible on head C.T. scans performed that evening on admission to the E.R. (emergency room). Trauma surgeons and the ENT specialist were nearly finished achieving hemostasis of multiple bleeding vessels from jaw, neck, and chest explosion wounds when Lisa completed her consultation examination on the patient. Lisa, a second-year ophthalmology resident physician at the time, proceeded to call the attending Eye MD physician who was on-call that evening to discuss the patient's history, exam, and workup findings and anticipated intraocular foreign bodies removal from both eyes and surgical repair of both ruptured eyes.

Shock and awe followed Lisa's telephone consult call to the on-call attending Eye MD physician (and chief of that hospital's ophthalmology department and second in command of the ophthalmology department and residency training program) that evening. The attending Eye MD / Eye Surgeon was intoxicated/inebriated with marked slurred speech and could barely produce intelligible speech during the telephone consult call. Shocking, a dilemma, for sure. Was the attending, who could barely talk with marked slurring of speech from alcohol abuse or dependence in any shape or form, ready (and able?) to perform emergency eye trauma surgery immediately that evening…absolutely not!

Lisa, with the patient under general anesthesia and in the operating room awaiting bilateral eye trauma surgery, was told repeatedly all night by the attending Eye MD that the attending would be coming in to staff Lisa's opportunity to perform glass foreign bodies removal from both eyes and subsequently the ruptured globe repairs necessary in both eyes of this patient. Instead, Lisa stayed up all night, the attending never came in, and Lisa had to leave at 700 am for eye surgery residency lectures, then proceed to see her scheduled patients in her assigned eye clinic the remainder of that day, all without sleeping or with the promised eye surgery training that she was eager to participate in the night before, but was, instead, denied as a result of the attending Eye MD (who was to assist and teach Lisa the subtleties of bilateral eye trauma surgery) being irresponsible and flat-out drunk.

The "Medical Residency (& Fellowship) Training System Worldwide, during Lisa's training, offered no avenue or recourse to address this egregious act of malpractice, dereliction of attending Eye MD on-call duty to staff the surgery needed urgently and emergently to both serve the patient's best interest of repaired bilateral ruptured eyes and to deliver the surgical training to the on-call resident taking care of the patient (and being misled by the attending intent to never come in for surgery all night long, even though the patient was under general anesthesia waiting for the attending Eye MD to arrive) that was promised when Lisa started her eye surgery residency training at that Philadelphia, Pennsylvania hospital system.

Chapter Two: The Powerless Resident Without Recourse And Without Support: Is This Ideal or Necessary?

When a Powerful, Senior Attending Physician Prostitutes Himself (or Herself) to "Paid Expert Witness" Depositions for Opposing Prosecutor Attorneys In Which He (or She) Attacks Other Eye Physicians & Surgeons During Daytime Clinic Hours (as a salaried employee of the hospital system), Acts with Prejudice & Preferential Treatment For Rich (vs Uninsured or Homeless) Patients During Eye Clinic Hours, and Refuses to Update His Eye Surgery Technique 25-50 years After Safer Surgery Techniques Have Replaced Older Techniques That Subjected

Patient to Increased Risks: Vision Loss, Bleeding, Astigmatism, Unnecessary Suturing of Larger Than Required Surgical Wounds, Delayed Healing and Recovery, Then What is a Resident in Training who Witnessed These Occurrences to do? Do residents-in-training have anyone or any organization (e.g., union) to report these unfortunate and undesirable circumstances? In short, no.

The current system, when Lisa was in the eye surgery training program in Philadelphia, rules were as follows: complainers get beat up and then shot (not literally, but figuratively). In fact, one eye surgery resident who was a benevolent genius with fantastic compassion and bedside manner, and who was an extremely capable and competent second-year-in-training eye surgery resident when Lisa was a first-year resident and taking on-call with this second-year mentor resident, was so disheartened, disappointed (and frankly disgusted) by the attending Eye MD's on-call verbal demeaning tone and condescending attitude and lack of interest or enthusiasm in advising and teaching residents on-call re: patient care and coming in to perform on-call surgery training of residents, that this particular second-year resident shockingly quit our eye surgery residency training program.

This same resident then elected instead to pursue an occupation where he was not verbally abused, neglected, and unjustly slandered and bullied by lazy, intoxicated, or otherwise misanthropic attending Eye MDs whose job was to enthusiastically teach and ensure eye surgery residents receive outstanding surgical training and become empathetic, caring eye physicians and surgeons able to deal with and surgically address any eye conditions, eye emergencies or eye trauma with fantastic medical or surgical remedies to optimize their patient's visual functioning far into the future.

Multiple upper echelon Eye MD attendings in Lisa's eye surgery residency training were shameless in their preferential neglect of lower-income patients with, often, markedly more severe eye diseases and conditions needing immediate treatment or urgent surgery who were forced to wait in their exam room in the eye clinic or up on one of the various inpatient hospital floors until the very end of clinic hours. Meanwhile, cash pay and patients with excellent insurance were catered to and chatted up by the senior attending eye surgeon until late afternoon or evening clinic hours, clearly demonstrating preferential and prejudice-motivated full attention and optimal care to private patients and extremely long (often several hours) wait times in the eye clinic for uninsured or Medicaid patients.

Ironically, private patients and patients with excellent health insurance plans who were new or long-time patients of many of these senior and elderly eye surgery attendings (instructors) placed 100% of their trust in these surgeons, leading to eventual, e.g., cataract surgery or other eye surgeries (glaucoma surgery, retina surgery or others), only to have a procedure performed that was not even the most elegant and up-to-date, advanced technique with known lowest complications rate, all because several of these most senior administrative eye surgeons never bothered to update their surgery techniques in the past 30 years or more after completing their residency training program.

Nobody was allowed to discuss this "Huge Elephant in the Room." However, all the younger attending eye surgeons on staff at all four hospitals and eye surgery first-year, second-year, and third-year residents and fellows saw the "Elephant" and pretended the "Elephant" was neither visible nor present (recklessly endangering all patients) in the eye clinic exam rooms and in the operating room. To put a somewhat more positive spin on this uncomfortable daily occurrence, all residents did, in fact, learn treatment philosophies, strategies, and surgical techniques that were used 20-40 years in the past and saw these techniques being employed in the operating room every time a resident scrubbed in with these selected attending faculty eye surgeons.

Luckily, younger attending eye surgeons transiently came to our Ivy League eye surgery training hospitals (trained at other eye surgery programs throughout the United States and other countries) and taught residents the latest, most elegant, bloodless, sutureless eye surgery techniques, often using only topical anesthesia with a touch of fentanyl and versed, resulting in operated eyes on postoperative day one that often saw the 20/20 perfect vision line and eyes that looked, on postoperative day one, as though they had not even had surgery the previous day. These advanced techniques, taught by the younger attending eye surgeons, were priceless and made the agony and neglect from the senior attending Eye MD faculty surgeons, who were often emotionally detached and unavailable to residents on-call and only taught outdated surgery techniques in the operating room more tolerable.

Chapter 3: Impact of Prejudice Attitudes Within Medical Residency or Fellowship Medical or Surgical Training Programs & Lost Opportunities: Research, Respect, Publications, Research Presentations

Lisa attended a fantastic, "elite," top-rated, highly esteemed medical school in the United States. She received excellent medical and surgical education and training, which she benefitted for the remainder of her life, and she is eternally grateful for this "once-in-a-lifetime experience" she was so lucky to be blessed with, after having been selected for admission to this medical school, which was her number one choice of medical schools that she wished to be admitted to and attend for her medical school education. Lisa's first choice of the fourteen medical schools she was offered admission to was the medical school she proudly attended and graduated from four years later. It lived up to its reputation as an elite medical school and is one of Lisa's most fond memories and accomplishments in life. Lisa is forever grateful to God for the gift he bestowed and honored her with. It was a dream come true for Lisa that she would remember and cherish up to the last minute of her life. This elite medical school granted her admission to become a physician, and four years later, at graduation, instructed Lisa to recite, memorize, and forever implement and abide by "The Hippocratic Oath" every day of her life thereafter, as a physician caring for patients, throughout her long and successful career.

Lisa's medical school education was completely or utterly free of prejudiced perspectives, attitudes, and actions, and, perhaps, the best clinical teaching program in the United States, emphasizing Christian values, caring for patients in a wholistic manner, and encouraging all medical students and attendings to cooperate in a non-competitive, mutually instructive (e.g., sharing information & insights) manner. This philosophy and paradigm raises the level of motivation, cooperative (vs. competitive) learning, wisdom, and medical and surgical training expertise to levels not otherwise achievable. Everyone at Lisa's medical school realized that glorifying God as the creator of the human body not only made the thousands of hours of studying and surgical training worthwhile but also was the ultimate source of inspiration and energy to acquire as much knowledge and necessary physician diagnostic and treatment skills and expertise to maintain the zenith of each patient's health and body function, thus ultimately honoring God & God's unique creations, our patients.

Lisa read and memorized all eleven ophthalmology textbooks the year before starting her eye surgery residency training program. During her first year of residency training, she wrote two ophthalmology textbooks. During her second year of residency, Lisa authored a clinical research case report, which was also published on a very specific topic regarding a very specific type of corneal refractive surgery, recommending the optimal technique to prevent postoperative corneal scarring. She required minor surgery on an extremity during her eye surgery residency training. However, she was not allowed any time off for her surgery, being told by the chairman to complete her morning and afternoon clinics immediately after her early morning extremity surgery. Lisa was not a complainer her whole life and was not about to start during her eye surgery residency training program, despite whatever mistreatment, verbal abuse, neglect, prejudice, jealousy, exclusion, or other neglect or inattention she experienced during her eye surgery training experience.

The truth is that Lisa never experienced outright and overt discrimination until she entered and completed her eye surgery residency training program. The program had a Jewish leader, ousted from another prestigious eye surgery program, that unabashedly gave every best research opportunity to only the Jewish residents, the majority of each selected class and year of residents, and overtly and shamelessly ignored and neglected other non-Jewish eye surgery residents requests to participate in research studies & research publication opportunities that would not only benefit patients but also establish expertise in each resident's future desired fellowship subspecialty choice. Lisa asked to join multiple research projects but was not once offered an opportunity by the Jewish chairman of the department.

As Lisa says, "If you are not welcomed and offered entry through the front door of your rightful home, find your entrance through the open window at the side or back of your rightful home."

After no inclusion offers to perform research with the permission and blessing of the chairman of the eye surgery program, Lisa successfully sought out a research project, resulting in a professional journal publication, with one of the coolest eye surgery attendings (ever) in the residency program who was a Cornea Specialist and an overall well-balanced human, a father & faithful husband with a charming wife and well-mannered and intelligent children.

When Lisa's clinical publication was accepted for presentation at a world-renowned eye research conference, the chairman (Jewish) refused to let Lisa present her paper and instead told the Cornea attending to present Lisa's research publication, very disappointing and insulting indeed. At the same time, the chairman (Jewish) allowed all the Jewish residents (whom he had hand-picked to be included in all the ongoing research projects in the ophthalmology department) to attend the same research conference and present their accepted papers and research findings; very disappointing and insulting indeed.

Lisa had a friend and MD colleague from her medical school class who was getting married in another state. She asked the department chairman for permission to attend her friend's wedding and was immediately told no, without any rational or reasonable explanation being given for why she could not attend her very good friend's wedding ceremony. All the Jewish residents were not only allowed to attend any and all weddings of their friends and family members, but they were also given all Jewish holidays off and allowed to use up every "sick day" allowed each and every year of their residency training (3 years total), while the non-Jewish residents were assigned to cover the short-staffed resident clinics during the Jewish residents' myriad absences (again, with no sick days allowed). This policy, stance, and disposition of the department chief and the entire department was disgusting, unabashed prejudiced behavior at its worst, a first and genuinely distasteful experience for Lisa, and a negative experience that she will never forget (perhaps forgive, but unforgettable).

Chapter Four:

Inexcusable Coverups And Covering for Harmful, Organ-Threatening &/or Life-Threatening Mismanagement or Prideful Neglect by Jewish Residents & Attempted (But Not Successful) Displacement of Blame or Negligence on Non-Jewish Residents And No Punishment For Negligent And Irresponsible Behavior of Jewish Residents, All Needlessly Endangered Patients

Lisa, along with her favorite Cornea Attending eye surgeon, performed gorgeous and elegant cataract surgery in both eyes on a patient with extremely long (abnormally long) eyes due to staphyloma posticum and a history of congestive heart failure and bilateral glaucoma. When Lisa was at another eye surgery facility performing surgery on other patients, the chief resident of Lisa's residency class saw Lisa's patient in clinic, did not bother to obtain patient's chart from the medical records department, and decided to add a beta blocker to better control the patient's glaucoma-related eye pressures which were minimally elevated but not measured to be at dangerously high levels and probably did not need to be treated with additional glaucoma drops other than the "heart-safe glaucoma drops" that the patient was already using. Lisa sadly learned that the patient died approximately two weeks later from congestive heart failure. There was no support for any reports of this type of incident and no consequences for the resident who negligently failed to get the patient's medical record and review the record to discover the patient had severe congestive heart failure and to therefore not prescribe (unnecessary, in this patient) beta blocker glaucoma eye drops in this patient.

Another incident involving a protected/favored (by the chairman and residency director) Jewish resident physician in the class one year ahead of Lisa was a stark example of prejudice and attempted coverup (successful in this case, to Lisa's dismay) and blaming Lisa for irresponsible and prideful negligence and a pompous, condescending attitude displayed by this Jewish resident. When the second-year resident, Lisa, was on-call at three hospitals, she was called into the VA hospital to see one of the third-year (Jewish) resident's recent cataract surgery patients complaining of total vision loss in the most recently operated eye. Lisa determined there was severe vision loss to "light perception only" in the patient and was concerned about suspected endophthalmitis in this patient.

She called the third-year resident who performed surgery on this patient, explained the history and exam findings, and she was told by the resident: "I don't care, I am not on-call, and my wife is having a party that I am at, and I am not coming in to see the patient." Lisa then called the excellent retina fellow and explained the same history and exam findings. The retina fellow kindly, appropriately, and responsibly came in immediately to examine and treat the patient with Lisa and performed a "tap & squirt" for suspected endophthalmitis. Instead of the Chairman and Residency Director chastising, reprimanding, or disciplining the irresponsible third-year resident whose attitude was atrocious, despicable, and inappropriate, both aforementioned faculty members inappropriately proceeded to attempt to displace, blame, and falsely accuse and assign guilt on and to Lisa for the incident.

Furthermore, when Lisa was working in the pediatric eye clinic several weeks later, the same irresponsible (and probably filled with guilt and regret resident) third-year resident who neglected to appropriately care for his postoperative patient who developed an eye-threatening endophthalmitis bacterial eye infection, then stormed into the room where Lisa was in the pediatric eye clinic, grabbed Lisa and took her into a conference room and began incessantly swearing with filthy language and disparaging words, which continued for approximately 30 minutes, all so that irresponsible resident could work through his guilt and regret, for his irresponsible, reckless, and unprofessional decision, and pompous attitude, by swearing at Lisa with his entire repertoire of cuss words, a disgusting and unacceptable action on his part. Again, Lisa may forgive this individual for his unprofessional and inappropriate episodes of misconduct (twice now). However, Lisa will never forget these egregious acts of irresponsible, unprofessional, and inappropriate behavior that, in essence, stabbed the "Hippocratic Oath" in the back until "Hippocrates's murder was achieved."

Chapter Five:

Lisa Completed A Fellowship Subspecialty Eye Surgery Training Program At A Fantastic Academic University But Was Distraught And Disappointed By The Inter-Department Animosity That Existed Between The Different Eye Surgery Subspecialty Departments Before Lisa's Arrival And After Lisa's Completion of Her Eye Surgery Subspecialty Surgical Training.

One year after Lisa successfully completed her eye surgery fellowship subspecialty training, her eye training program attending surgeons had an explosive power struggle for the new chairman of the ophthalmology department, resulting in one faculty member leaving the department when he was not selected to be the new chairman. This faculty member had been ousted from his previous university position and had been very abusive and inappropriate in his non-benevolent treatment of his cornea fellows for many years before that attending eye surgeon faculty member ultimately left or was requested to leave the university ophthalmology department and then join another private ophthalmology practice in town.

This Cornea attending, halfway through Lisa's fellowship eye surgery training, forced both Lisa and the other Cornea fellow-in-training into his office one night after eye clinic was finished, placed both fellows in one corner of his office and interrogated both fellows, demanding they both tell the attending eye surgeon what their post-fellowship plans are, including where they wish to or will be practicing (e.g., what city and what state or what country) and would not allow either resident to leave his office until both residents gave a detailed answer and response. Lisa was 100% honest and forthright in her answer, stating she planned to stay in town and practice ophthalmology as a subspecialist-trained eye physician and surgeon. The other fellow told a 100% lie (the other fellow had already informed Lisa that their spouse was in Texas but had just accepted a job in town and was coming to the same town where Lisa would be starting her private practice), stating they would be leaving town and the state to join their spouse in Texas.

Inappropriately and unprofessionally, the attending then terminated his now completed inquisition and interrogation and malevolently decided, for the next six months, to be kind and respectful and polite to the fellow who lied, because that fellow would not be staying in town to compete with this same subspecialty attending professor and faculty eye surgeon, and to, conversely, disrespect, attack, disparage (suddenly and unexpectedly, the next day and for the next 6 months of fellowship completion) Lisa solely because she honestly answered the faculty and attending eye surgeon and admitted that she would be staying in town, which was apparently a perceived threat of legitimate competition (same eye surgery subspecialty) to this faculty member attending eye surgeon, who in retrospect, must have had a most inappropriately and disappointingly insecure self-image of his eye surgery skills and knowledge as an attending professor eye surgeon (who should never feel threatened from a competition standpoint from someone just getting started that he, himself trained).

Lisa was astounded and perplexed by this behavior that ensued by this attending faculty eye surgeon, who cast dispersion and derogatory remarks frequently on her and suddenly despised her wealth of subspecialty knowledge and fantastic eye surgery skills and techniques that she demonstrated during each eye surgery as a result of her exceptional eye surgery training during her Ivy League residency eye surgery training program completion.

Starting the very next day and persisting until fellowship graduation day six months later, Lisa had a tyrant leader who suddenly despised her because that attending now knew this excellent and knowledgeable trainee subspecialist eye surgeon would stay in town and be competition with that faculty attending surgeon for many years into the future. Similar to patients with bipolar disease, this attending's behavior was often bizarre, irrational, and unpredictable, with dramatic and inappropriate, violent mood swings (unlike the department chairman, during Lisa's fellowship training, who was predictable, consistent, faithful, reliable, cool, calm, collective, rational and fair in his equal treatment and respect for all fellows and residents in training).

This bizarre, unpredictable behavior by the eye surgery subspecialty fellowship director and attending eye surgeon professor was devastating to Lisa's perception of academic medicine. The same attending was involved in specialty intraocular lens implant studies. During Lisa's fellowship, she learned of an incident where, during one study, multiple patient files were misplaced; data was then fabricated for these lost charts and patients to complete the study, and the files were subsequently found months later. This incident of dishonesty and fraud was disheartening to Lisa.

Lisa realized six months into her subspecialty eye surgery training that she could not rely on this attending physician for any support or letters of recommendation from this attending faculty member, who was corrupt, insecure, and abusive, now or in the future. Lisa was disgusted by the attending faculty eye surgeon's fraudulent and vindictive behavior and anti-competitive interrogation that occurred six months after the start of Lisa's fellowship. Lisa had always been a positive person and was confident that she could and would overcome this obstacle and pursue her career goals with or without this specific attending surgeon's approval or support. Lisa's positive attitude and strong, resilient work ethic had never failed her in the past, and she was confident that it would lead her to great opportunities and success in the future. Lisa was correct.

Residency and fellowship medical and surgical training programs offer no resources to physicians-in-training to approach or deal satisfactorily with these conflicts of interest or aberrant, inappropriate, bizarre, or abusive behavior by attending (professor) surgeons and no recourse or protection from such tyrants and bullies. Those in training may be severely punished, neglected, mistreated, or fired for minor or no legitimate reason, solely at the whim or discretion of the "teaching" attending physician and surgeon. What is the difference between the past slave trade and slave ownership and current medical training programs worldwide when the slave owners (attending physicians and surgeons) mistreat or abuse slaves (residents or fellows in training) and the slaves can neither report abuses nor seek justice without the expectation that their future will be destroyed by their vengeful and vindictive "Slave Owners."

Chapter Six:

Origins of Modern-Day Slavery in Medicine: Hospital & Medical Training Program Administrators Brainwashing Of Young, Intelligent Minds Who Have Achieved Great Academic Accomplishments And Success And Who Choose To Wear Rose-Colored Glasses & Exhibit Eternal Optimism That Those Selecting Them For Medical Education & Training Have Only Those Individual's Best Interests In Mind.

Even before the altruistic, though naïve, medical students arrive for the first day of medical school training, the slave-trade practice is evident and overt. One might even argue that the slave-trade attitude is not only proudly displayed by interviewing hospital administrators and senior-level physicians conducting interviews of college graduates applying to medical schools, but that their excessive power and malevolence are outright flaunted for all the interviewing college graduates (hoping to be admitted to that particular medical school) to hear, see and be humbled by, or crushed by, for those of weak character. Let's get to several interesting, disappointing, and true accounts of such behavior: Slave owners inspect their potential slaves during medical school application interviews and decide which slaves they want to be subjected to forced labor at their training program in the future, but not before disparaging remarks are made to each slave and never before that slave is made fully aware, via demeaning language during the interviews, that the slave has no power or influence and that any selection will be purely based on the whims or idiosyncratic impressions of that, oftentimes quirky interviewer who, as you will realize in the true life examples below, is unfit to objectively and effectively conduct a meaningful interview to assess critical and essential qualities of each slave (future medical student) and determine if that/those individual(s) possess qualities that will lead to their being excellent, caring, competent physicians in the future.

In one interview at Harvard, the interviewer was a top-tier hospital and training program administrator and physician who was flamboyantly homosexual, with no intent to hide or disguise his sexual orientation during the interview.

He read Lisa's curriculum vitae, which was outstanding, packed with extracurricular activities and leadership roles, top academic achievements, highest academic honors, and an outstanding grade point average in grammar school, high school, and university studies. He had read that Lisa was a Christian as well. Lisa had paid application fees, filled out primary and secondary application forms with separate fees, purchased a plane ticket, and reserved a hotel for the interview.

She was expected to be asked questions pertinent to her potential future medical training and career aspirations as an outstanding future physician subspecialist. Instead, the interview was approximately 12 minutes long, and the only question was whether Lisa liked the philosophy of science course in college. Would the interview have been 30 minutes or longer if Lisa had been homosexual, as was Lisa's interviewer? Lisa wonders to this day what the answer to this theoretical question is, was, could have, or should have been. Interviewers ("Slave-Traders") ethically and morally are not (theoretically) supposed to or authorized to ask applicants to medical schools (future slaves) what other medical schools the slaves are flying to and applying to and/or have been accepted to.

Do you think these interviewers ("Slave Traders") follow and abide by these guidelines and rules, written or unwritten? Heck no. At 100% of Lisa's fourteen medical school interviews, the Slave-Traders (hospital administrators and/or senior training program attending physicians) asked not only where else Lisa was interviewing, but what her top choices were, where she wanted to live in the future, whether she was married or not, and other sundry private and personal questions that were inappropriate, but not for slaves (medical school applicants) who possess no rights and no protections for invasions of privacy or unprofessional interview questions, all because medical school applicants, physicians-in-training, resident physicians, fellowship physicians and independent physicians on medical staff at hospitals ("slaves") have no union to protect their rights and defend their freedom and just treatment and therefore no recourse to report inappropriate treatment or interrogation or to correctly point out, identify malpractice or unethical behavior by hospital staff and assign blame (projected on them, e.g., "the slaves") to hospital administrators, hospital staff or hospital employees who are the actual and truthful perpetrators of acts of negligence, errors and omissions, inappropriateness, unethical behavior leading to patient endangerment or outright harmful, abusive, prejudice, slanderous or other activities constituting overt malpractice by hospital personnel.

For this reason, unions or other large corporate entities that are physician advocates and defenders who are both large enough and financially fit to battle and fight Corporate Hospital Administrations (aka Slave Owners) to achieve slave emancipation, maintain the freedom of slaves, and preserve and defend slaves right to defend their roles in hospital patient care without fear of unjust punishment and to afford them the right and opportunity to deflect hospital administrators repeated attempts to project and misplace blame onto independent physicians rather than punish and appropriately rebuke and punish their own hospital employees who acted in deviant, irresponsible, inappropriate or other undesirable manner resulting in poor patient care, poor outcomes, negligence, "errors and omissions," or other acts constituting medical malpractice.

Currently, Lisa, an independent contractor physician who cares for hospital patients during on-call duties and admits patients to the hospital, has never, in over 30 years, received a letter of apology from a hospital employee who acted inappropriately when a complaint was filed, yet has been forced to (as "slaves" are forced into inappropriate actions) write letters of apologies, by the hospital administrators, to the offending hospital personnel in every case where the independent physician filed a legitimate complaint against hospital personnel who endangered patients as a result of their irresponsible or negligence or refusal to provide appropriate care (e.g., acts of malpractice), completely ignoring and disregarding the legitimacy of the filed complaint. Hospital lawyers and hospital administrators (aka "Slave Owners") always project their own acts of malpractice on independent physicians ("Slaves") who they know have no union membership to battle rich hospital corporations, hospital administrators, and hospital Lawyers.

Thus, negligence, errors and omissions, and malpractice acts can always be displaced on powerless physician slaves because, without union defense or until independent physicians gather together and form unions that will free them from tyranny and emancipate them from their slave status by battling unjust Slave Owner nefarious activity and lies and displacement of blame on those slaves who are innocent but cannot prove their innocence because they, without unions, have no court of justice in the hospital where there can be equal representation of both sides of the story and the innocent can be proved innocent.

Therefore pro-physician unions must be created by physicians-in-training and independent physicians and must have no connection or allegiance to hospital administrators or physician training program administrators and should be available to medical school applicants, physicians-in-training at all levels, and independent physician staff at all private hospitals, state and federal government hospitals so there can be a system of checks and balances, without which, physicians at all levels will continue to be intimidated, threatened with firing or dismissal from the training programs or hospital staff on-call service, admission privileges, or revocation of entire medical staff privileges (unjust intimidation and threats by slave owner toward the falsely accused slave).

Furthermore, without unions, no retribution for unethical behavior by Slave Owners ever occurs. All deaths and loss of organ function that resulted from inappropriate acts and malpractice by hospital employees continues to hidden, lied about, swept under the rug by hospital staff and hospital administrators because any independent physician (slave) who files complaint letters gets labeled (unjustly) a "problem physician" (when the correct term or phrase should be: ethical and honest physician who would otherwise be helping hospital to correct deficiencies or inappropriate hospital policies or hospital personnel problems by suggesting fixes and remedies) and then is forced to write letters of apologies to evil or malevolent bad actor hospital staff members who, e.g., cursed at patients, refused to perform procedures that could have promptly diagnosed a critical illness or converted a urgent emergency to a routine healing situation, were too lazy to perform a procedure they are capable of then accuse another specialty of not performing the procedure they themselves should have completed and chose not to complete out of sheer laziness.

A rigid slave-like attitude is assumed from day one of medical school training. Without physician-in-training protection that would result from union membership of all medical students in the world, each medical student is, at every second of existence, throughout their medical school training and until and, sadly, long after graduation day, the slave of that medical school training program.

One may or may not realize that, without a union to protect and defend the individual benevolent graduate student in medical schools throughout the world against biased, racist, prejudiced, seductive, misleading, slanderous, or completely false and vindictive accusation(s) of wrongdoing, each medical student is a virtually a slave with absolutely no rights, no representation of significant influence or negotiating power to have their opinion expressed, considered or heard and no chance whatsoever of being able to comment on or make true accusations of misbehavior, misconduct, patient endangerment, bullying or abusive behavior and actions, and outright malpractice that is witnessed by physicians-in-training without the legitimate and 100% accurate acknowledgment that they may be fired from training. Unfortunately, the concepts and realities in this chapter likely extend to and apply to all graduate-level training programs in medicine and outside the field of medicine.

Sadly, physicians-in-training currently have no recourse when hospital administrators or attending physicians (senior physicians charged with the education and training of younger physicians-in-training [e.g., medical students, resident physicians completing specialty training, or subspecialty fellowship physicians completing their subspecialty medical or surgical training to be a subspecialist or expert physician in a particular specialty of medicine]) exhibit or manifest prejudice, favoritism, sexual or sexual orientation bias, sexual harassment, dishonesty, fraud, lying, submit fraudulent research results or student evaluations, are verbally or physically abusive or are unavailable (emotionally, physically or as an advisor or instructor, often due to poor attitude or inebriation or just plain unwillingness to be called into hospital from home when requested by physicians-in-training who deserve to be supported and taught medical or surgical skills when patients come in with conditions requiring immediate treatment or surgery) when these attendings are on-call and assigned to advise and assist physicians-in-training in the medical management or surgical treatment of patients seen in the clinic during office hours or in the emergency room or on inpatient hospital floors after office hours (e.g., evenings, early morning or weekends). There are many real-life examples of bad behavior by hospital administrators, attending physicians, or other hospital staff physicians.

In one instance, the physician on-call for emergencies at one hospital went to a baseball game, turned off his pager and cellular phone, and was unavailable to perform an emergency procedure on a patient who presented to the emergency room. Hospital administrators at that hospital then forced a physician (of the same specialty as that of the physician who could not be reached yet was on-call that day for emergencies) who was on-call at a nearby hospital to come in and perform surgery on that patient, despite not being on physician staff at that hospital (she was given emergency staff privileges just for that day), instead of calling all the other same specialty physicians on staff at that hospital and requesting one of them to come in and perform necessary emergency surgery on the patient.

A second example was a gay/homosexual attending physician who preferentially approved gay physicians-in-training that he had a hand in selecting for admission to his medical training program and ensured they received top priority in doing rotations with him during their training program, to the exclusion of others (e.g., heterosexual physicians-in-training) who wished to perform an elective with this individual but were denied the opportunity, purely based on their distinct and different sexual orientation.

A third and ridiculous but true example is as follows: An attending at a hospital training program, in one instance, was jealous of a physician-in-training and her success and having written several professional textbooks while in the training program as well as publishing research papers that were accepted for live, in-person presentation at various professional research conferences. The physician-in-training had also read and made detailed notes on all eleven residency textbooks the year before she started her training program. When this physician-in-training rotated to the pathology elective with this attending physician (aka slave owner), the physician-in-training (aka the slave) had also already read all three pathology textbooks just before starting the rotation.

For this reason, the slave was extraordinarily well-prepared and astute, answering almost every question correctly when reviewing pathology slides daily, correctly interpreting the findings, and stating the correct differential diagnosis for the condition, based on the pathology sections and different tissue stains used on the various pathology slides. This fact aggravated the attending physician to no end. There were others in the group who were not as well prepared and who were often unable to answer questions during the pathology rotation.

The slave owner (director of pathology rotation) then targeted the brightest student during that rotation instead of embracing her astute and enthusiastic attitude. She (the slave owner) then persisted in acting in a prejudiced and abusive manner toward this slave for the remaining years of this slave's training program, all the result of jealousy and a prejudiced attitude and perspective. Had there been a physician-in-training union this slave could have been a member of, the slave could have reported the highly inappropriate behavior of this attending physician ("slave owner") and the abuse that she ("the slave") subsequently experienced for years after this first-year rotation.

Without any organized union to emancipate and protect the slaves, the slave owner inflicted serious injuries on the slave for the remaining years of the slave's training program. The slave, however, had to put up or shut up due to the constant and unbridled malevolent power bestowed on slave owners running the training program who, on a whim, could fire a slave for any unsubstantiated reason or concocted cause, regardless of the truth of lack of any proof. Is there any better analogy than this to describe how an evil slave owner can loom over, like a cumulus nimbus storm cloud, their slave, and rain torment and torture on that slave throughout their training program with no recourse for "the slave," in the absence of a union to protect and defend the common and fundamental rights of the slave?

Chapter Seven:

Folly of the Residency Match Day System of Slave Sales To One & Only One Future Slave Owner Despite Forcing The Slave to Make Applications to Many Programs, Pay Application Fees, Purchase Many Airline Tickets, Make Many Hotel Reservations In Different Cities and States, All In Order To Obtain Only One (or None for Certain "Unlucky Slaves") Residency Program Match (aka Future Slave Owner for 3-6 years)

What better describes the medical residency match system than the analogy of a "Slave Trade Purchase Auction"?

Case in point: When you complete medical school, you must then complete a one-year internship, then a 2–6-year residency training program to become a specialist in a particular field of medicine, e.g., family practice, internal medicine, cardiac surgery, neurosurgery, pediatrics, etc.

If you were a slave owner and sought to design a system whereby you could force all your slaves to travel and visit many future potential slave owners at the individual slave's expense (even though the slave may be penniless or in much debt with university and/or medical school loans) and all without the slave owner incurring any cost and, at the same time, take away all the slaves freedom, independence, and ability to choose which final slave owner the slave will be matched with, but instead assign her to only one slave owner, even though many slave owners may have wanted that particular slave but were not allowed to make an offer for that slave or notify the slave and the slave is never allowed to have multiple offers from which to choose where the Slave would like to live and work. In summary, a medical student, in the last year (4th year) of medical school, must fly all over the country to apply and interview for residency programs (e.g., 14 programs in different states), then rank all 14 programs she or he interviewed at, and hope to be randomly ranked by those programs, so that she or he may "match" (aka be sold as a slave) to only one possible program (or not match at any program).

The physician (a.k.a., "Slave"), by the Slave Owners' design and rules, is only allowed to match at one (or none) program. In any other profession, e.g., business school, law school, or engineering school, and when applying for postgraduate school jobs, etc., if you apply to 14 jobs and have 14 offers in these other specialty fields or professions (who are not engaged in modern-day slave trade ("medical training program slave trading"), then you are allowed to choose between all fourteen offers, then freely and independently choose which location, job offer, or position you desire to work for or at, and you are then paid a reasonable wage/salary.

Wages in medicine during training are also ridiculously low or meager, insulting, and unlike any other non-medical profession (e.g., business professional starting salary or engineering starting salary). For a real-life example, when Lisa completed her subspecialty fellowship training in a medical subspecialty (postgraduate year nine), she was, as the slave with no rights and no say in her starting salary, offered (aka told) a starting salary of $19,000 for the entire year that she would be performing highly skilled and specialized surgery on one year's worth of hospital training program patients, during which her "slave owner hospital training program" would be billing for the slave's medical exams and surgeries performed which undoubtedly totaled hundreds of thousands of dollars in billable revenue for the hospital.

What is further evidence of modern-day slave trade in medical training than when a slave owner can work a slave with 80-100 hour work weeks (e.g., every other day on-call for one year and long 7-day work weeks), pay that slave a salary that does not cover the slave's rent, car expenses, gas expenses, food expenses without racking up huge credit card debt to survive each day and week throughout their physician-in-training years. Slave trade indeed.

Chapter Eight:

Fellowship Match Day During Last Year of Residency Training: Perpetuation of Modern-Day Slave Trading & Denial of Subspecialist (Physicians-In-Training, aka Slaves) Freedom To Review Multiple Job Offers (from Slave Owners, aka Hospital Administrators at Hospital Fellowship Training Centers) Then Select Where The Slave Would Like to Work & Live.

Upon completing subspecialty physician residency training, those slaves seeking to be subspecialist experts in their particular subspecialty apply to many programs, again incurring all costs of application fees, plane flights, and hotel costs while interviewing at, e.g., twenty programs (or as many programs you are invited to interview at). However, the rules made by hospital administrators & physician training hospitals only allow a slave to be matched (assigned) to just one program and allow no opportunity for (disallow) the slave to choose from all the programs she or he interviewed with and thereafter decide where the slave would like to work and live.

No other profession treats their most highly skilled and highly trained professionals like slaves as does the medical profession world of malevolent hospital administrators and physician-training programs that have, for over 200 years, suppressed, restrained, and enslaved their physicians-in-training by preventing them from establishing pro-physician unions which would re-establish balance of power and equality to independent physicians, allowing them to attack and destroy Slave Owner traditions handed-down for generations by one hospital administration to the next, without being fired without cause by their slave owners.

Physician-friendly unions, if embraced in a collective and unified manner by all physicians-in-training and independent physicians, can and will empower the final destruction of the modern-day slave trade in medicine and hospitals throughout the world, emancipating physician slaves and purging corrupt, dishonest, intimidating, and abusive behavior by hospital administrators worldwide so that the overall level of patient care can be elevated to its zenith by proper reporting of truthful occurrences within the hospital to achieve the highest level of care, without retribution or unjust punishment of physicians who make possible honest feedback to improve patient care and hospital performance of duties in an ethical, honest, moral, open manner without hesitation.

In summary, without the backing, support, armamentarium, large, rich and powerful corporation-like union support of individual, independent medical students, physicians-in-training (at all levels: medical school, residency, fellowship), and individual & independent specialist & subspecialist physicians agreeing to join hospital medical staff membership (&/or on-call panels for emergencies in that particular specialty that present to the hospital emergency room or admitted patients on inpatient hospital floors) in their respective specialty departments (e.g., internists/internal medicine, pediatrics, neurology, general surgery, urology, psychiatry, otolaryngology, ophthalmology, dermatology, rheumatology, other specialties), then these physicians-in-training or independent contractor specialist physicians who join hospital medical staff membership and assume on-call service responsibilities will not be able to survive the false accusations and hospital administrators/hospital legal department lawyers constant onslaught of deflecting and projecting onto others (e.g., the slaves, aka independent physicians who execute their responsibilities with earnest resolve & integrity) the wrong-doings of hospital staff employees whose acts of negligence, unwillingness to complete recommended procedures, or outright irresponsible errors of omission or acts of malpractice, that are neither acknowledged nor related/communicated to the involved patients at the hospital and never admitted by hospital administrators & their hospital legal department lawyers.

Superheroes

Lisa has never received a letter of apology from hospital staff members involved in inappropriate behavior or acts of egregious negligence, errors or omissions, or frank acts of malpractice and/or lying or deceit or other repetitive unethical behavior that adversely impacted patient care in multiple different hospitals. This is why the current system must be burned down.

The slaves must be emancipated by unions that have well-funded legal department lawyers who can and will support and defend honest, ethical, and hard-working independent physicians and physicians-in-training who are collectively working for the common good of hospital patients and unions must eradicate the pestilence and constant plagues created and projected onto (non-hospital employee) physicians that they premeditate and plan to slander, unjustly intimidate and threaten the loss of medical staff privileges or on-call duty privileges, and, in essence, use as scapegoats to deflect attention away from the original egregious erroneous acts of harm to patients committed by hospital staff employees.

Manipulation, distortion, distraction, misdirection, counterattacks, projection, intimidation, threats to fire that individual, and myriad other deceitful, evil tactics are both the playbook and successful strategy hospital administrators, hospital training programs, and hospital legal department lawyers have repeatedly used over the past 200+ years to keep the herded and caged slaves from lodging legitimate and constructive criticism and suggestions that would ultimately improve patient care, rectify improper and abuse, slanderous hospital attitudes and policies and, finally, emancipate the slaves & preserve their freedom to work and generate constructive feedback to improve patient care in hospitals without fearing they will be unjustly attacked, penalized, assigned nonsense tasks or courses to complete, and without being fired or dismissed from hospital medical staff membership, solely because they choose to use and preserve their right to freedom of speech as an emancipated slave. While these simple suggestions seem obvious, they have been deftly covered up and obscured by hospital administrators and hospital legal department lawyers for over 200+ years.

Hospitals (aka "Slave Owners") know that if physicians never embrace physician-friendly unions, then their physicians-in-training and independent, individual powerless physicians who are extremely well-trained and competent independent contractors with the hospital (aka "The Slaves") will remain as "Slaves," owned by the hospitals. There is an urgent and critical need for these "Slaves" to be immediately emancipated by union representation and defended by union legal departments to preserve and maintain integrity and honesty in the proper treatment of hospital patients forever in the future.

Chapter Nine:

Why is it that in the Training of Physicians and Hospital Contracting of Independent, Individual Physicians to Provide Specialty Care And Subspecialty Care for Their Hospitalized Patients, For The Past 200+ Years, There Is Still No Trustworthy, Honest Feedback System Whereby The Honest Truth (Though Difficult Truth For Hospital Administrations & Administrators To Hear or Listen To), And Suggested Solutions (By Independent Physicians Working Within The Hospital) To Ongoing Problems In The Care Of Hospitalized Patients, May Be Aired, Discussed, And (Hopefully) Implemented to Improve Both Patient Care in the Hospital and to Improve Hospital Administration-Independent Physician Relationships Which Would Then Generate And Maintain Positive Communications And Feelings That Ultimately and Auspiciously Result in Physicians Feeling Appreciated (vs. Persecuted) For Their Arduous And Faithful Daily Work To Improve Patient Care in Hospitals Worldwide?

Just a smattering of real-life examples that will either result in shock and dismay or severe disappointment to the public and the reader that the easy fix and suggested action(s) was/were ignored all together or instantly swept under the carpet (hidden and covered up, like a thief or criminal that covers his tracks and wipes clean all the fingerprint that would identify them as the murderer) and a counter-attack immediately planned then employed without hast by hospital administrators, weak subspecialty department heads (paid by hospital for their (weak, ineffectual) "leadership" role over other specialists (aka slaves) in their own specialty) or hospital legal department lawyers whose only loyalty is to the hospital that butter's their bread (e.g., pays them enormous sums to crush any independent, brilliant physician on staff who even dares to complain about the performance of any hospital staff member whose action or intent or errors of neglect or omission were harmful to a patient being cared for in the hospital).

When a physician who performs hospital patient admissions in a single instance, or repeatedly, neglects the examination of all organ systems, e.g., fails to perform a complete and comprehensive history and physical exam, due to their lack of interest in or fear of evaluating and examining specific and particular body parts/organs or organ systems, this is a negligent act of malpractice and endangers the patient and all subsequent physician specialist consultants (due to a delayed or wholly, completely missed dangerous diagnoses and delayed preventive or therapeutic treatment initiation, which could have and should have been initiated in the emergency room by the admitting physician, if they had done their job and performed a competent and complete history and physical exam, as is the patient's and hospital's expectation).

When major organ systems were not examined at all by the admitting physician who was derelict in their duty of performing a comprehensive exam of all organs to determine the most significant and dangerous diagnoses of the patient being admitted, then the patient may have in-hospital adverse events and outcomes (from previously unrevealed diagnoses and conditions that were not correctly identified and immediate treatments not initiated in the emergency room during their admission to the hospital) and delayed evaluation by appropriate specialist for all the most dire and dangerous, life-threatening, or organ-threatening diagnoses and conditions that were supposed to be (and should have been) diagnosed and discovered during the initial patient admission history and examination (H&P) in the emergency room.

Some emergency physicians or other admitting physician specialists refuse to carry their own necessary H&P diagnostic tools or use available equipment in the hospital or emergency room, such as an otoscope, ophthalmoscope, or stethoscope, verifying that they are disinterested in completing a proper (and expected) history and physical examination.

In medical school, Lisa recalled that, in multiple different hospitals, psychiatry attending physicians admitted patients and performed history and physical exams routinely without even possessing a stethoscope around their neck or in their doctor's coat pocket(s) and often never even touched, much less used the otoscope and ophthalmoscope attached to the wall within the patient exam room. This occurred regardless of whether the psychiatric patient being admitted complained of headaches, severe hypertension, heart disease, new vision changes or vision loss, ear pain, new or marked hearing loss, dizziness or vertigo, and other symptoms.

Surgeons who have antiquated techniques that have not been updated for 40 years and that subject patients to poor outcomes, higher incidence complications, require longer than necessary surgery and anesthesia times, result in delayed healing, or require suture(s) removal at a later date when newer techniques are sutureless as a result of the smaller wound sizes that are either self-sealing in the manner the surgical wounds are constructed (performed) by the surgeon or wounds that may be closed with surgical-grade wound closure tissue glue or surgical staples. Often, these surgeons are hidden, shielded, or even disguised as being the "premier" or "elite" surgeons (again by malevolent and deceptive hospital administrators, or, in many cases, these past-prime surgeons are themselves the specialty department heads, paid handsomely and nefariously by the hospital for their feckless (anti-leader) "leadership" duties, or these compromised (ethically) physicians are the hospital administrators themselves (aka Slave Owners) who sacrifice their slaves, as serves their underhanded purpose and covert whimsical prejudiced intent, to stave off criticism, more often than not from their younger cohort of independent physicians who performance and results are superior to their senior colleagues (aka Slave Owners) who perpetuate and reinforce policies that are no longer relevant or sensible or in the best interest of patients in the hospital.

How often and how many times must a physician hear the phrase: "Well, that may be true, but that is not the policy in this hospital, and that is not the way we do things here"? Myriad is the best approximation of an answer to this non-rhetorical question that must be addressed by every generation of new physicians facing impractical and nonsense policies that are made by out-of-date physicians or other (non-medical professionals) that make hospital policies from their ivory towers where they are "protected" or "shielded" from the irrelevance and impractical demands or policies they propose and that are often "set in stone," that they themselves would not even agree to if they were actively in the trenches doing the work of patient care or, in other words, the "man in the arena" accomplishing outstanding patient care despite constant obstruction and no evidence what so ever of appreciation for the outstanding and exceptional patient care, medical and surgical, the independent physician specialist (aka "The Slaves") are performing for and in behalf of the hospital. Luckily, most independent physician slaves are self-confident, capable, and not in need of constant adoration and appreciation by others, including hospital administrators, because positive feedback from hospital administrators (aka Slave Owners) may only be expressed upon each slave's death, often and ironically, only with a chalkboard short paragraph in the doctors' lounge or surgeons' lounge… so sad but so accurate and true…this is the norm and not the exception in Lisa's experience, having worked at over twenty or more hospitals during her training and post-training professional physician career experience.

Chapter Ten:

Hospital Administrators (aka "Slave Owners") Know Very Well That Because They Are Hand-Picking Weak And Corruptible Leaders And Paying These Individuals Extra Money (Legal Bribes That Are Tax

Deductible As Salary Expenses For The Hospitals?) To Be Hospital Administrators And Specialty Department Heads, So That They Have Unlimited Power, Leverage, And Control Of These Individuals to Distance Themselves And Disguise Their Dishonest And Slanderous Attacks On Any Physicians ("Slaves") Who Speak Up And Out Against Mistreatment Or Who Criticize Dangerous or Patient-Harming Hospital Policies or Hospital Employee Actions That Seriously Endanger Hospital Patients Being Cared For.

The devastation and irreparable harm that weak and unethical or greedy physician (or non-physician) hospital administrators or department heads (aka Slave Owners) can inflict on their slaves (non-hospital employed/salaried, independent contractor physicians who are caring for hospital patients when on-call for their specific subspecialty patients in the hospital) who, on average are exceptionally intelligent and with an impeccable past history, past record, and outstanding resume characterized by honesty, ethical behavior, trustworthiness, a hard-working attitude and perspective, and a reputation for being caring physicians who are altruistic, often of Christian or of other religious upbringing or background, and generally averse to and nonparticipants in "back-biting," generating untrue or slanderous rumors or false allegations of misconduct, or even filing complaints against or about other co-workers, is currently unlimited.

Physician-friendly unions are critical and urgently needed to support, defend, and protect the freedom and respect due to each "Man in the Arena." These physician unions must be financially able and willing to hire top-notch legal department lawyers who can and will be physician-friendly advocates and supporters of the "Man in the Arena" who performs all the work, performing examinations on both pleasant and vicious patients and during peaceful hospital environments and wildly out-of-control hospital environments dominated by erratic patient behavior and chaos, always completing their necessary requested evaluations and consultations despite often hostile patient attitudes or hostile hospital environments that they encounter and have to complete their consults in, regardless of their chaotic surroundings.

Hospital administrations and administrators often, if not always, assume responsibility for and take (steal?) credit for but never give thanks to the "Man in the Arena" who is being injured or burdened on a weekly or monthly basis in one way or another (lost or little to no sleep the week they are continuously on-call or unappreciated by the gangsters or drunk individuals who started a fight and were seriously injured or drug dealers who sustained critical injuries, were treated medically and surgically when indicated, but these patient were and are often unappreciative of the care being provided to them, totally abusive verbally, physically (or otherwise) to the provider who cared for them or operated on them at 1:00 am or 3:00 am or 7:00 am despite having a full schedule of patients that same morning and all day after staying up all night to complete their emergency on-call duties.

Self-sacrificing hero independent contractor on-call service physicians who are willing to take on-call for hospitals when almost no other physicians are willing, keen, or eager to disrupt their private practice schedules or sleep schedules or put up with the chaos and nonsense and abusive trauma patients who are often, but not always, disrespectful and unappreciative of the care they were provided at insane hours of the day (almost always after bars have closed and when they realize their bar fight injuries are worse than they thought), should be praised and appreciated out loud and publicly on a weekly or monthly basis (if not daily) for doing the undesirable work each week of the year, while the overpaid Slave Owner Hospital Administrators are sleeping uninterrupted at home, but when awakened in the morning are never willing to give credit and thanks due to the "Slave Heroes (on-call physician specialists)," yet always willing and instantly ready to believe and swallow in one gulp (like an arrogant king guzzling down poisoned wine from the chalice given him by his "frenemies") one-sided accounts of purported misdeeds by the on-call physician, who is only trying to do what is best for each patient for which she was contacted and asked to offer her experience and expertise on how, what & when the patient needs treatment or surgical intervention.

Chapter Eleven:

Without "Witness Protection Program (W.P.P.)" Protection, Physicians-in-Training and Physicians Who Are Not Salaried Full-Time Hospital Groups or Employees Hired By The Hospital Can And Will Never Achieve The Dream of Independence/Freedom/Emancipation From Their Current Slave Status And Will Forever Be Vulnerable to Unprovoked & Erroneous Attacks From Their Slave Owners (aka Hospital Administrators) Who Will Always Be Biased & Prejudiced By Hospital Employee "Stories" That Are Believed To Be The Truth Despite No Input or Investigation or Attempt Even To Discover The Situation (And Truth) From The Slave. Furthermore, If Any Slave Is So Brazen and Brash Even to Imply Any Wrongdoing or Iniquity Committed By Any Hospital Employee, Then That Slave Will Have Their Face Ripped Off or Extricated From Their Skull In A Fashion Similar to What a Gorilla Would Do To A Zoo Visitor Who Randomly Jumped Into The Restricted Off-Limits Area Of The Caged Gorilla.

There is long-standing myth that any physician who wishes to air a grievance or complaint against a hospital administration policy, hospital administrator, specialty department head (in cahoots with slave owner hospital administrators who hand-pick and pay these individuals, who are often but not always, weak (?non-leaders) and specifically selected not because they will most fervently defend other specialists who are their colleagues and are falsely accused of substandard care or inappropriate decision-making, based on the training and expertise as a subspecialist, by clueless hospital administration staff (seeking only to shield hospital employees from malpractice lawsuits) but rather these department heads are selected in or on the basis of consanguineous relation or inbreeding-like fashion (which can eventually spoil the species) but instead they are selected on the basis that the hospital administrator can be guaranteed, confident, certain, and sure that the department head will always agree with and be complicit (sycophant) in any opinions, impressions or one-sided (the Slave Owner Hospital Administration side only and always) slanderous letters or email sent to the independent on-call physician (aka Slave(s)) who recently completed a week of chaos while on-call caring for the hospital's "problem child patients" (e.g. injured gangsters, drug dealers, incarcerated criminals and others) and other accidental injury or acute stroke patients or patients with post-surgery complications.

Another myth, not swallowed or believed by most intelligent independent contractor physicians working on-call for hospitals where they require admitting privileges, is that: "The Joint Commission on Accreditation of Healthcare Organizations (JCAHO, sometimes pronounced "JACO") enforces the standards that another group, Accreditation Commission for Health Care, Inc (ACHA), sets forth for how hospitals and healthcare facilities have to operate, and that physicians may send their complaints to these organizations when necessary to report misconduct or outright outrageous actions or acts of malpractice or otherwise evil or unjust behavior by Slave Owners (aka Hospital Administrators and Administrations or Hospital-Selected Department Heads, again who are designated parrots for hospital administrators unending intent to always side with hospital employees to avoid being caught or exposed for acts of malpractice by hospital personnel, especially when pointed out by independent physicians (aka Slaves) who are not salaried direct daily employees of the hospital), which is totally false and sets one's course on a path to self-destruction.

To file a report with JCAHO, a physician must give sufficient detailed information that will almost certainly require that the independent contractor physician identify herself (as a legitimate source of the complaint being filed) and must identify the offenders (Slave Owners & Hospital Salaried Workers or Sycophant Department Heads Who Cannot, By Design, Adequately Defend His Specialist Colleague Physicians (his supposed job, on paper only but not in reality) Without Themselves Being Fired From Their Designation of "Special Sycophant Privilege [And Additional Payments They Receive] From The Hospital Slave Owner").

Once a complaint is filed, an investigation will be opened by both JCAHO and the Hospital Administrators (Slave Owners), ultimately resulting in the Slave who filed the complaint being taken out to the whipping pole, shackled, then whipped to the point of death (e.g., put on probation, removed from the on-call schedule or, in essence, fired and slandered, solely because the Slave dared to report the truth and offer constructive criticism to their Slave Owner, who has no incentive or intent to make any changes, but only to hide acts of malpractice and always project blame for any filed complaint on the powerless (a.k.a., physician without union support and legal representation that can battle and defeat lies and slander by rich hospital business models (L.L.C., corporations, or other) that have unlimited money to spend on lawyers and legal defense, who have collected forced, coerced letters of apologies for nonexistent false claims of misconduct by physician in all instances where the physician themselves filed the complaints against misconduct by hospital employees.

Without physician-friendly unions, independent contractors are as vulnerable to unjust Slave whippings as are patients with "severe combined immune deficiency" (a rare syndrome with severe deficiencies in T-cell and B-cell function, a type of Primary Immunodeficiency [P.I.]) likelihood of having to live in fear every day and in a bubble their whole life to avoid any and all otherwise benign infections that are potentially lethal to them, without a normal functioning immune system, vulnerable and living a life of fear every day for lack of defense against infectious agents (e.g., Slave Owners) and immune support and potential death that may ensue as a result of these undesirable and dangerous conditions.

Chapter Twelve:

A Vivid Picture of a Typical Day in the Life of a Slave (Physician-in-training or Individual Physician) Working For the Slave Owner (Teaching Hospitals or Private Hospitals Dominated by Corporation or Other Business Entity Ownership Structure(s) With Powerful

Financial And Legal Department Backing And Support) And How Total Dictatorship And Domination (By "Slave Owners") of the Physicians ("Slaves") Exists Currently And, Like A Deadly Plague, Has Persisted And Tormented It's Victims For Two Centuries, With No Hope of Slave Emancipation, Now or in Future, Unless The Imperative Step of Forming Physician-Created, Physician-Supported, Physician-Friendly, And Physician-Advocating Organized And Powerful Unions Is Embraced With Unanimous Physician Membership To Achieve, Protect, And Preserve Physician Emancipation Forever in the Future Worldwide

More often than not, real-life examples are the best teaching venues. In one instance, a physician "slave" was performing an inpatient consult exam on a patient, which was requested by the "slave owner (or their sycophant contracted group or salaried employee)" (a.k.a., "Hospital AdminisTraitors"), on a patient in a room with two patient beds and two patients in the room. The "roommate patient," who was not a part of the patient consultation examination, suddenly started ranting, raving, and swearing profanities inappropriately at both the "roommate patient" receiving the history and examination and the physician performing the consultation examination.

When the individual physician, independently contracted with the slave owner to provide subspecialty medical and surgical services to patients requiring that specific subspecialty group of diagnoses or diseases care and treatment, reported the verbally abusive and highly inappropriate conduct of the "roommate patient" (which not only upset the patient receiving the consult exam but significant impaired and delayed the successful completion of an efficient & timely examination of the patient by the subspecialist physician provider of care), to the nurse and hospital unit clerk on that inpatient floor, the physician (slave) believed that the report would be preemptive and provide safety and warning to the nurse caring for the disturbed, inappropriate and verbally insulting and abusive "roommate patient." The physician slave (always assumed by the slave owner, "Hospital AdminisTraitors," to be guilty, regardless of the filed complaint or "report facts," and always deemed worthy for another whipping at the whipping post in the public square to deflect and project any blame or responsibility for inappropriate patient or hospital staff members" misconduct, instead of receiving thanks for identifying a threatening, inappropriate patient conduct incident (to protect and warn other care providers, thus ensuring their safety), was notified several weeks later that the physician ("Slave") would have a letter of reprimand placed in the slave's covert physician staff hospital medical file on that slave. The slave was never interviewed and no query was ever attempted by the slave owner to elicit or discover the true facts of what happened during the incident, prior to the slave receiving an inaccurate and harshly judgmental prejudiced condemnation email and letter that was slanderous, damning, and unjust in its dishonest characterization of the incident, and displaced, projected blame on the slave rather than the instigating culprit, the patient, who should have been reprimanded by the "slave owner hospital administration" but NEVER WILL BE BECAUSE THE SLAVE OWNER (HOSPITAL "ADMINISTRAITORS") ALWAYS ARE 100% CONCERNED ONLY WITH: 1) FINANCIAL GAIN AND AVOIDING PATIENT LAWSUITS BY PLEASING PATIENTS (REGARDLESS OF THEIR DESPICABLE BEHAVIOR) IN HOSPITAL, 2) NEVER DISCIPLINING OR REPRIMANDING INAPPROPRIATE PATIENT OR HOSPITAL EMPLOYEE BEHAVIOR, AND 3) HIDING, COVERING UP, DISPLACING OR PROJECTING (KNOWINGLY ASSIGNING BLAME TO WRONG PERSON) INAPPROPRIATE BEHAVIOR OR ACTS OF DESPICABLE, UNETHICAL OR OTHERWISE NONOPTIMAL PERFORMANCE (NEGLIGENCE, ERRORS, OMISSIONS, OR MALPRACTICE) ONTO INDIVIDUAL PHYSICIANS (SLAVES) WHO CANNOT COMPLAIN OR DEFEND THEIR INNOCENCE (IN CURRENT PREDICAMENTS AND IN THE CURRENT ERA, WITHOUT PHYSICIAN UNION LEGAL AND FINANCIAL BACKING AND SUPPORT OF THEIR RIGHTS TO FREEDOM OF SPEECH & DEFENSE OF INNOCENCE WITHOUT FEAR OF BEING REPEATEDLY AND UNJUSTLY

WHIPPED, DISCIPLINED OR FIRED FROM HOSPITAL WORK BY SLAVE OWNER (HOSPITAL "ADMINISTRAITORS").

Because slave owner hospital business organizations get paid for each day a patient is hospitalized (e.g., financially corrupted and incentivized to side with patient and project blame always to a physician slave), the hospital administration (Hospital AdminisTraitors) currently always are malevolently biased and prejudice in siding always with patients being cared for as an outpatient or inpatient in the hospital or siding with the one-sided and inaccurate hospital employee reports who often, in an effort to diffuse and cover up their dark & dastardly acts of inappropriate care or outright malpractice race to be first in filing a complaint against the physician (slave) who first identified either the patient's inappropriate behavior or the hospital employee's egregious, inappropriate, suboptimal or other acts of malpractice (most convenient (C.Y.A.) stance for hospital to appease patients or hospital employees rather than appropriately reprimand those patients or hospital employees who engage is highly disruptive, inappropriate or physically &/or verbally abusive behavior or, in the case of hospital employees, acts of unethical or poor care or malpractice).

For the past two hundred or more years and existing unto this very day, the perspective, mentality, theme, strategy, and "philosophy" that patients, hospital employees, and hospital administrators have embraced and accepted as the norm, with regard to those in the hospital who engage in unethical, inappropriate, or otherwise harmful behavior toward others while within the hospital, is and has been as follows: "If I am the first person to report an incident or file a complaint, then perhaps my inappropriate behavior will be missed, ignored, displaced or projected onto the physician ("slave") who first objected to my inappropriate actions or abusive behavior or act of malpractice."

Sadly, "Slave Owner Hospital AdminisTraitors" use, support, and enforce this exact playbook on a daily and weekly basis to unjustly project blame for these incidents of inappropriate behavior away from patients and hospital-salaried-employees (who pay the "Slave Owner's" bills), and onto the (should be) faultless and blameless "Slaves" (independent physicians or physicians-in-training, who first tolerated and endured, then identified legitimate deficiencies in the corporate hospital care system. "Slaves" (on-call and independently contracted physician specialists, not receiving a salary from the hospital as the hospital's direct employees) strive daily to provide zenith patient care during their consults and surgeries performed, and in so doing, optimize the level of patient care being delivered at the hospital). For over two hundred years now, individual physicians have been slaves to this slave owner bias, prejudice, and mentality.

It is therefore imperative and of dire importance that individual physicians unite, unionize, establish physician union(s) that are financially strong and large enough to hire the brightest legal minds in the business of defending and supporting physicians from illegitimate and unjust, slanderous claims manufactured by current Slave Owner Hospital AdminisTraitors purporting to be physician advocates, when they are and have been for two hundred years, just the opposite: cloaked, covert traitors who are most willing, at the first and weakest claim of wrongdoing by a sycophant work colleague or inappropriately behaving patient, to thrust the dagger in their pocket into the slave's back, who always has been and continues to be the hardest working "Man in the Arena", seeking, benevolently, only to improve patient safety and realize zenith optimal level of patient care, without being slandered, disciplined, whipped or fired from their hospital patient care duties as a result of their exercising their freedom of speech and professional training and discretion to offer suggestions or constructive criticism to those in charge of providing hospital-based patient care.

"Physician Slaves" (individual independent contractors, physician groups, physicians-in-training) must immediately and urgently unionize, defeat Slave Owners, Annihilate And Make Illegal Their Slave Ownership And Slave-Trading Business Practices, Permanently Emancipate And Perpetually Defend The Freedoms of Speech,

Physician Union Formation & Maintenance and Physician Freedom To Constructively Criticize Rich Corporate Public & Private Hospital Business Organizations & Hospital "AdminisTraitors"/Administrators, And Freely Report Adverse Events or Behaviors Witnessed / Realized in Hospitals That Are Committed By Hospital Employees or Inappropriate or Bad-Acting, Abusive Patients Who Seek or Intend to Disrupt Delivery of Optimal Patient Care Within The Hospital. "Physician Slaves" Can and Must, Accomplish All These Goals, To Eternally Eradicate The Currently Existing Slave Owner Practices And Abuses That Slaves Are Subjected To Daily Intimidation And Threats By Hospital Slave Owners To Inflict Maximum Pain On Slaves Who Dare To Identify, Defy, or Question The Slave Owners Bias, Prejudice, Preferential Treatment, One-Sided Investigations & Edicts Issued Based On Only One Side of Each Story, Acts of Malpractice/Errors/Omissions/Negligence in Patient Care That Are (for 200 years?) Committed By The Slave Owners (Hospital Owners & AdminisTraitors or Hospital Employees) And Hospital's Salaried, Dependent, Non-Objective, Biased, And Sycophant Employees, Then Immediately And Without Guilt or Remorse Being Covered Up or Hidden, Then Packaged, Wrapped With Threatening Letters That Unfairly Assign Responsibility And Blame To The Slave Which Is Then Placed In The Slaves Hospital Medical Staff File By Slave Owners.

Without a Physician Union (to protect physicians working at hospitals), physicians face the threat of being slaves in perpetuity. Unions created by and led by physicians and physician lawyers or other expert lawyers for the sole purpose of the protection of physicians' professional and fundamental, constitutional human rights, due process, fair representations of the truth, and who can provide legal representation from competent expert union lawyers hired to protect and maintain physician freedoms and restore the balance of powers between physicians ("slaves") and "slave owners" (hospital owners who are white-collar administrators/owners who are only concerned about and obsessed with: "profits are top priority" and "avoid-patient lawsuits at all costs" (in essence, "Throw physicians under each oncoming, 55 mile per hour bus driving down the road."). These biased and prejudiced "AdminisTraitors" whose only priorities, purposes, and goals are monetary gain and do not include "physician slave freedoms acknowledgment or respect, physician slave dignity nor emancipation from their 200-year-old predicament of being sold into and traded, whipped, tortured as slaves in the hospital training systems in public and private hospitals practiced worldwide for over two hundred years," must be conquered and "dethroned" from their current "Slave Owner" unmerited monarchy status, which is unwarranted.

It is imperative and dire that physicians unite, create one or more unions specializing in freeing physicians from current slavery in hospitals, and then ensure these slaves are never sold out or sold into slavery ever again in the future.

What are possible avenues to the Abolition of "Modern Day Slaves in Medicine"?

Over thirty years of experience as a "modern day slave in medicine (i.e., definition: an independent subspecialist physician with no powerful employee union or rich corporation or LLC that can:

1. Emancipate or free this slave [or other subspecialists slaves from other subspecialties who perform on-call subspecialty care for Level I trauma center hospitals or Level II trauma hospitals and other private, public, county, state or federal hospitals and other medical facilities, e.g., assisted living, hospice care, urgent care, workers compensation clinics, ambulatory surgery centers, pain clinics and other medical facilities] and

2. Afford the "modern day slave in medicine" the guarantee, assurance, and protection that, if the slave should have the desire and leadership courage, skills, and self-confidence to defend herself or himself against medical facility "AdminisTraitors" untruthful/false allegations, slanderous accusations or outright inappropriate punishment, restrictions or other limitations of freedom, justice,

independence to practice and deliver ethical, appropriate subspecialty medical care to patients in the hospital or other medical facilities, then that "modern day slave" will not be immediately terminated (figuratively: killed by her or his slave owner) or that Slave's career at the hospital or other medical facility will not be terminated, restricted or otherwise irreparably damaged or that Slave's reputation will not be slandered by the misanthropic Slave Owners (Weak or Cowardly Subspecialty Department Heads chosen for sycophant qualities that will subserve Slave Owners [hospital or other medical facility staff members and/or administrators] at the expense of their subspecialist physicians just and democratic defense and support) has afforded me the wisdom and insight to realize and know what steps are prerequisite to effectively: 1) Emancipate modern day individual physician slaves in medicine, and 2) Ensure future sustained freedom from tyranny for these modern day slaves in medicine.

Chapter Thirteen:

Why Revolution & The Defeat Of Current Slave Owner Medical Facility "AdminisTraitors" In Medical Training Hospitals & Private/Private Hospitals & Other Medical Facilities is Not Only Imperative & Imminent But Dire To Restore Individual Physician Dignity & Freedoms, Improve Patient Care To Highest, Zenith Level And How Physician-Advocate, Physician-Friendly Union(s) Must Be Created, Funded & Defended to Win The Revolution, Realize Abolition Of Physician Slave Trade & Ultimately Celebrate Victorious Emancipation of Individual Physicians From Current Enslavement.

Physicians who currently pay annual membership dues to organizations (e.g., the "American Medical Association" and other city, county, state, or federal medical associations that issue meaningless certificates or titles to those who pay their dues, often return no recognizable support or defense for its member physicians. For the past two centuries, these organizations have been completely ineffective in assisting, defending, and emancipating individual physicians ("Slaves") from daily "Slave Owner Hospital AdminisTraitors."

Therefore, the time has come to embrace, create, and forever support and fund "Physician-Advocate Unions" that can then effectively battle and defeat "Slave Owner Hospital AdminisTraitors" who continue their inflicted abuses, false allegations, and other indefensible acts of malfeasance to this day. Physicians should instead "cease and desist" from paying these meaningless professional dues to hospitals and instead pay these dues to physician-advocating and supporting unions that respect, protect, and defend their honor.

Individual physicians would be best served by agreeing to revolt, rebel, and distinguish themselves from "Slave Owner Hospital AdminisTraitors," then unite, stand tall and strong, and create critical and essential "Physician-Advocate, Physician-Friendly Union(s)."

These unions' purpose should (in the near or immediate future) and shall always be, by Union charter or contract, to hire the best lawyers who then serve the physician community at large and advocate for, advise, propose, and draft contract negotiations for individual independent contractor physicians and physician specialty groups when dealing with hospitals, urgent care clinics, or other medical facilities for whom they work or provide medical services to (e.g., on-call payments negotiations & annual raises for subspecialists providing care to after-hours or daytime patient care consults requested in hospital), and defend physicians who are slandered or falsely accused or assigned unwarranted blame or fault by the hospitals.

Hospitals, for centuries, have enjoyed and relished the projection (blame assigned to incorrect individuals) of all adverse events in the hospital onto the (non-salaried, non-hospital employee) physician "Slaves," This includes a vast array of incidents (hospital errors or hospital employee errors and omissions or acts of malpractice) including any and all undesirable patient outcomes or adverse treatment outcomes and complications, which the "Slave Owner Hospital or Other Medical Facility AdminisTraitors" always prefer (or almost always, sadly, with rare exception) and enact in a purely evil and deceptive manner to displace blame and responsibility from inappropriate, abusive, belligerent or otherwise outrageous behavior of medical facility employees (or patients being treated) or hospital employees' nefarious acts of irresponsibility, sub-optimal care delivery or negligent care or withholding of clinically urgent, indicated, necessary, and assigned care duties, or other outright malpractice actions (e.g., refusal to provide appropriate or clinically indicated care within their scope of practice & hospital-granted privileges list of procedures that they are capable of and should be performing when their patient's need these interventions and procedures performed urgently.

Other various inappropriate hospital employees' negligent acts, malpractice behaviors, or errors and omissions are often, in a premeditated manner, errantly assigned (by "Hospital AdminisTraitors") to or projected onto individual physicians (a.k.a., "Slaves") rather than the irresponsible or inappropriate patients or hospital employees. These "Slave Owner Hospital AdminisTraitors," again, have as their only goals, daily and weekly, to evilly deceive, cover up, hide, not document in the medical records or operative reports any instances of malpractice or negligence, errors or omissions, or alternatively, never reprimand a patient (who's daily hospitalization fees and charges fill the Slave Owner Hospital AdminisTraitors' coffers [strong boxes or small chests for holding valuables]) who abused or swore profanities at or otherwise derided or even physically attempted or successfully assaulted a medical care provider while the patient was hospitalized, all because the "Slave Owner Hospital AdminisTraitors" have neither the moral fortitude, ethical upbringing nor honest intention to optimize patient care.

Instead "Slave Owner Hospital AdminisTraitors" have as their top priorities:

1) Avoid and escape malpractice lawsuits at any and all moral costs (no limits in acts of deception and malfeasance to accomplish this goal, including blaming innocent slave physicians who they know cannot defend themselves without physician-created and physician-advocate union lawyers to back them up), 2) Pretend the patient is always right and justified in abusing any and all care providers during their hospital or other medical facility admission or outpatient procedure visit and, in all cases, always assume the patient is honest, justified and accurate in their one-sided account in any questionable abusive encounter, in essence, always take the accused slave to the whipping post in the public square, whip the slave to death minus one whip (just short of death), then, of course, never let the slave speak, defend herself, before the whipping, during, after or forever in the future, by intimidating and threatening the Slave with letters of reprimand being placed in medical staff file of that slave or punishments (unjust as they are) such a requiring extra online courses be completed, restricting slaves from usual hospital duties or on-call schedules.

Further nefarious intentions and goals of "Slave Owner Hospital AdminisTraitors" include:

1. deflecting any responsibility or blame or accountability for poor hospital care of patients by hospital employees onto non-hospital independent-contractor subspecialist physicians and other non-salaried healthcare providers,

2. negligent declination of "Slave Owners" to discipline abusive patients and concomitantly thank, support, and commend the respective, involved medical care providers who responsibly cared for and treated these abusive patients, despite being transiently or constantly derided or verbally (or physically, in certain cases) insulted/abused physicians that were faithful in providing care to these abusive and misanthropic patients. Because hospitals or medical facilities are paid enormous and outrageous facility fees by private and public or government health organizations and insurance companies, the "Slave

Owner Hospital AdminisTraitors" will never act responsibly and honestly in reporting the true incidence of errors and malpractice events that result from its own salaried employees. This behavior, for the past two centuries, has been "fostered and sponsored" by "Hospital AdminisTraitors" misguided and deceitful, dishonest hospital policies of litigation avoidance strategies which are deployed daily to protect and cover up wildly inappropriate actions by either abusive patients or hospital employees' acts of malpractice, at all costs (or from the hospital's perspective, at no cost, if they successfully lie about and cover-up their daily, weekly, and monthly errors). Blame for these acts is then conveniently assigned to the "Slaves" (innocent non-salaried physicians and other healthcare providers) whom "Slave Owner Hospital AdminisTraitors" see as being expendable and replaceable, especially if they continually point out errors and inappropriate policies of the hospitals which are detrimental to zenith patient care. In July of each calendar year, a new crop of physician slaves will be graduating from or entering medical professional training programs, matched and assigned to only one "Slave Owner" Hospital AdminisTraitors/Administration Team (e.g., "Slave" Physicians are generated from internship, residency or fellowship training program or new fellowship graduate physician slave who applies for "hospital staff membership or on-call hospital services privileges" (indentured servant physician slave contract for physicians who are desperate to sign any contract, due to medical training loans and massive debt incurred during their training: the perfect storm of desperation for the Slave Owner to achieve permanent and lasting commitment from the slaves who will agree to no on-call fees or inappropriately low underpayment for after-hours on-call services because they need patients and money to start their new physician slave private practices). When Lisa, who has worked in over 15 different hospital systems in over 30 years as a practicing physician, first applied for hospital privileges and to be an on-call emergency services panel physician for her subspecialty, she was told by all her different, various Slave Owner Hospital AdminisTraitors / Hospital Administration Teams & Weak Sycophant Subspecialty Dept Head "Leaders" (Selected, Blessed, Ordained, Appointed by Hospital Slave Owner To Guarantee Hospital AdminisTraitors Victories In Any Future Physician Versus Hospital or Hospital Employees Dispute(s)) that, as a prerequisite for being accepted to medical staff full privileges, Lisa would have to serve as an on-call physician for her subspecialty for twenty years (there it is, the forced slave contract and loss of freedom for 20 years) before she could voluntarily choose to not be on-call but, at the same time, maintain full admitting and medical staff privileges at all the various hospitals where she joined on as an independent contractor subspecialist physician for hospital outpatients and inpatients. For the first ten years or more, Lisa was offered no daily on-call payment stipend (remember, slaves don't get paid; they enjoy working themselves to the bone and without sleep for weeks at a time [on-call was always for seven days continuous or one week in duration where the slave could be (and would be) called anytime 24 hours per day, for the week of on-call, often resulting in little or no significant or restful sleep that week due to constant calls from the hospital all day and all night, including requests to perform emergency consultation examinations or surgeries at all hours of day or night, again, continuously for one week.

Furthermore, independent contractor physician slaves that are coerced and intimidated into on-call service for 20 years without any on-call daily stipend or payment (definition of slave or slavery) as a condition to be accepted onto the Slave Owner Hospital AdminisTraitors / Hospital Administration Teams' hospital staff membership, were also informed they would have to attempt to bill all uninsured patients they treated or operated on during their on-call duties at the hospital and the hospital would not reimburse the physician slaves for their services or surgeries performed on all these (more often than not) uninsured patients seen while completing on-call weeks the next twenty years. When daily on-call stipends later mysteriously arrived, after 10-15 years of nonpayment for on-call weeks, there was no yearly raise in the minuscule (underpayments by any reasonable assessment) daily stipend payments received for another ten years.

Union(s) designed, created by, supported by, and specifically chartered or contracted to support and defend independent contractor physicians' daily appropriate and reasonable work conditions that respect and honor physician dignity, freedom of speech, democratic rights to defend against slanderous and false accusations by the hospital or medical facilities AdminisTraitors (or their weak sycophant appointee subspecialty department heads who are virtual extensions of the strong arm of Slave Owner Hospital AdminisTraitors/Hospital Administration Teams), negotiate physician-friendly contract terms & enforce physician-friendly and physician-freedom-respecting contractual agreements, eradicate and refuse unreasonable on-call requirements or obligations which are not adequately or fairly paid for or accompanied with appropriately high daily on-call stipend payments for being on-call. Physician-Advocate Unions must assign, pay, and install physician-union-elected "subspecialty physician department heads" that have physician freedom of speech protection (from potential "Hospital AdminisTraitor" attacks and attempts to fire or remove them from the hospital on-call schedule or medical staff) as the first and top priority. In stark contrast, the "Slave Owner Hospital AdminisTraitors" and Hospital Administration Teams' have as their top priorities:

Monetary reimbursement/income.

Hide errors & malpractice acts of the salaried employees of the hospital.

The (Misguided) Philosophy: "The patient is always right, and all patient complaints are undisputable truths (whether the patient was witnessed by one or many others as being wrong, or deceitful, abusive, or otherwise inappropriate in their actions and behavior)."

Physician unions must declare war on, battle, and defeat Slave Owner Hospital AdminisTraitors / Hospital Administration Teams & Modern-Day Slave Trade Practices Perpetuated by Slave Owners who want to maintain the status quo slave trade that has persisted over the past centuries. Unions by and for physicians can and will garner the respect and dignity that physicians-in-training (the most vulnerable subgroup) and independent contractor physician specialists and subspecialists working at but not directly employed by hospitals and protect physicians against discrimination, bias, prejudice, and modern-day enslavement, torture and abuse.

Chapter Fourteen:

Independent Physicians-in-training And Physicians ("Slaves") vs Hospital Administrators (Large, wealthy corporate "Slave Owners") With No Respect or Regard For Slaves' Rights Because These "Slaves" Have No Union or Other Equivalent Corporate Sponsor or Defender of Slaves' Rights, And To Defend Themselves Against False Accusations, Slander, and "Bad Actor Attacks" By Those Within The "Nefarious Corporate Slave Owner Network"

The Disastrous Consequences & Lethality (Figuratively And Literally) of Cowardice & Weak Physician "Leaders" With Poor And Succumbing "Non-Leaderships Skills" Who Fail to Fight For And Defend the Rights, Freedom, And Assumption of Innocence Until Proven Guilty of Their Specialist Physicians or for other Physicians-in-training (e.g., medical students, residents, fellows, and attending subspecialist consulting physicians covering hospital emergency on-call patients), Thus Not Only Inevitably Perpetuating But Also Enabling & Reinforcing "Modern-Day Slavery Practices And Attitudes of Hospital Administrations And Residency, Internship, And Medical School Training Programs" Ultimately Culminating in Imminent Danger to "Slaves" (Physician or Physicians-in-training), A Vicious Cycle From Which the "Slaves" Can Never Escape, The Truth Now for Centuries. Should Not Every Physician Strive To Be A Modern Day Abolitionist,

Fix The Broken & Misguided Medical Training Systems & Hospital Administrations & Administrators Who Believe Themselves To Be Rightful Slave Owners And Who Are Unwilling to Afford Or Agree To Equal Rights And Respect For Physicians ("Slaves"), Equal Justice, Equal Representation of Physicians-in-training & Consulting (Non-salaried, Non-hospital physician employees) Physicians to be Afforded the Right To Critique & Equitably Judge The Performance, Competence, Integrity and Moral versus Immoral, Liable or Criminal Behavior of Hospital Administrations & Administrators And Other "Leaders" in Physician Training Programs Without Unjust Retaliation, Retribution, Firing, or Dismissal (For Physician Suggestions To Improve Patient Care Which Hospital Administrators Dislike Due To Truth, Loss of Money, or Identification Of Acts of Misconduct By Hospital Employees Which Would Then Be Exposed To Malpractice Lawsuits), from Physician-in-training Programs or Hospital Staff Privileges & Hospital Staff Membership Merely Because Independent Specialist Physician Consultants are Functionally And Practically Naked, Isolated, Exposed, And Vulnerable (e.g., "Slaves") With No Union Support or Defense of Their Freedom, Right to Speak Their Truth And Tell Their Side of Every Storied Complaint Registered Against Them By Hospital Staff Members Or Unruly And Inappropriately Communicating or Acting Patients Within The Hospital. When the Independent Contractor "Slave Physicians" are Falsely Accused of Wrongdoing by Hospital or Hospital Training Program "Leaders" (who might also be referred to or given the titles of "Intimidators & Bullies," "Dishonest or Unethical Liars," "False Accusers or Projectors," "Vindictive or Outright Prejudice or Unfair AdminisTraitors" (Regarding Their Decisions, Judgement or Actions), All Made Possible And Feasible For These "Hospital AdminisTraitors" ("Slave Owners") Because Physicians ("Slaves"), Have Unsuccessfully (for 200+ years) Attempted To Emancipate Themselves Without Union Support. Without "Independent Physicians And Physicians-in-training" Unions, The Individual Slaves Have No Hope For Justice And Have No Recourse to Retaliate Against "Unethical, Unjust, Immoral And/Or Abusive Slave Owners" (large corporations with unlimited financial resources who have no ethical, moral, or financial limits which might restrain them from attempting to cover up their hospital employees' acts of malpractice resulting in myriad patient deaths, poor outcomes or other atrocious patient care, especially when identified by an independent physician hospital staff member [who is not a salaried hospital employee] who is contradicting a false complaint or attack by a hospital employee or administrator [who most often takes the hospital employee's complaint at 100% truth, without even asking the recipient of the alleged complaint for their version of what actually transpired to find the actual truth of what exactly happened, and not just assume truth from one-sided hearsay, often an attempt to cover-up the accusers unwillingness to perform a physician function they were capable of doing, and instructed to perform but negligently chose not to perform but instead blamed someone else for not performing the procedure the accuser should have, could have, but did not perform, thus jeopardizing zenith and optimal patient care] against such independent contractor physicians and/or physicians-in-training.) Below Are Specific Examples of Slave Owners' Atrocious Behavior and Abuse And Suggestions For Immediate Abolition of Modern Day Slavery In Medical Training Programs And Hospital Staff Independent Contractor Physicians' Need For Unionization or Other Corporate Defense Strategy to 1) Abolish Their Slave Status In Hospital Administrators' Eyes And Minds and 2) Establish & Defend a System Whereby They Can Identify, Attack, And Defeat False Accusers & Accusations of Hospital Employees or Administrators Without Fear of Dismissal From On-Call Services/Duty and Without Fear of Being Fired From Medical Staff Membership. As of the Writing of This Book, There is no Such Union for Independent Contractor Physicians or Individual Physicians, Physicians-in-training and These Groups Are "Modern-Day Slaves" With No Rights or Protections and are Living in Fear Daily That Their Non-Benevolent And Selfish "Slave Owners" May At Any Moment Dismiss or Fire Them at the Whim of Any Hospital Salaried Employee or "Hospital AdminisTraitor" Based on any Unsubstantiated Claim, True or False (Most Often False), Which the "Slave Owner Hospital AdminisTraitor" Often Never Even Bothers to Investigate by Obtaining Even A Statement of What Occurred/

Transpired From Both Involved Individuals. This Is Truly Despicable "Slave Owner" Behavior for the Past Two Centuries in the United States of America and Worldwide.

Example One:

An independent subspecialty physician is on-call for emergency patients within her specialty who are admitted through the emergency room or are inpatients within the hospital being treated for one or more medical conditions. The discretion of that subspecialist is relied upon, based on her many years of training and experience, to determine when the patient can be treated by the hospital staff members in the emergency room directly, without the subspecialist needing to drive into the hospital to perform the procedure, and also to determine the urgency with which the treatment needs to be performed or completed (e.g., instantly, within 24 hours, 48 hours or within several days or weeks). This is the input that is necessary for different medical conditions and specialties of medicine and is why different physicians receive intense training within their specific subspecialty: to be able to determine what conditions need immediate treatment and which conditions might actually benefit from waiting until the conditions are optimal for surgery (e.g. after acute inflammation has improved or resolved) or until the right subspecialist is available & willing to perform a procedure which is best & optimally performed by the most qualified & specific subspecialist for that particular condition or surgical procedure.

When a subspecialist physician informs an emergency department emergency physician that the emergency physician can and should be performed by the emergency physician (and is not necessary for the procedure to be performed or completed by the specialist), then that emergency physician should perform the procedure. Unfortunately, many emergency physicians desire to whimsically pick and choose which patients they want to treat themselves versus patients they decide they do not wish to treat long before they call a subspecialist on-call whom they think they have the best chance of delegating or outsourcing the treatment or procedure to, that they themselves could have completed or performed but wished or desired not to complete or perform.

This occurrence happens daily in hospitals worldwide.

The subspecialists on-call are confident in their training and experience to know their advice is sound, correct, and expeditious in accomplishing and achieving the best and immediate patient care outcome when giving their recommendations. If that emergency physician is lazy, negligent, afraid or otherwise has an aversion or phobia to perform the procedure that is a common and standard privileged procedure within his scope of care and specialty and refuses to perform the procedure or treatment plan recommended by the subspecialist physician by telephone consultation, more often than not, that emergency physician will unjustly and untruthfully file a complaint with hospital administrators / administration (biased Slave Owners that always side with lies that appear to protect or project a cloak of innocence on or at the hospital from blatant acts of negligence in patient care by their emergency room personnel) that the subspecialty physician refused to come in and treat the patient (to cover-up the actual fact that the emergency failed to perform the procedure they could and should have performed either without evening calling or consulting with the subspecialist physician on-call or after consulting with the subspecialist and being instructed to perform the treatment or procedure in the emergency department or on the patient floor, after the input or other advice of the subspecialist on-call physician.

Specific examples of procedures that are neglected, or not performed promptly, or altogether ignored or refused to be performed by hospitalists, internal medicine physicians, other surgeons, or anesthesiologists (on hospital operating room or recovery room patients or inpatient floor patients or by emergency room hospital staff (e.g., nurse practitioners, physician assistants or emergency room physicians with quirky aversions or phobias to particular patients or specific patient conditions presenting to the hospital emergency room) follow in the paragraphs below.

Hospitalists or other inpatient floor attending physicians who decline to perform complete admission history and physical exams, neglecting to examine all systems and obtain adequate or appropriate histories to discover conditions that are either chronic, long-standing, and preexisting and instead mistakenly and inappropriately requesting an immediate consult on a patient with a preexisting condition which, in many cases has been stable and unchanged for many years. Special senses are often not evaluated by admitting physicians, even when part of or the entire chief complaint reason for admission.

At one particular hospital, an emergency physician had a phobia for every patient he encountered with diseases affecting a specific organ. Whenever these patients were assigned to him, he repeatedly, without fail, lied and stated that the equipment routinely used by all other emergency physicians to evaluate patients with that particular organ disease or dysfunction or injury was not functioning correctly, so that is why he did not use these diagnostic instruments.

He would lie incessantly and repeatedly to the subspecialists on-call by telephone consult, more often than not, calling the subspecialist to see the patient before he had even attempted to examine the patient, therefore repeatedly being unable to answer any questions asked by the subspecialist consultant physician on the phone. He would only read what the triage nurse had documented because he repeatedly made zero effort to examine these patients.

The chief of staff at this particular hospital and during this period of blatant malpractice by this emergency room physician (incidentally, whom multiple trauma and surgical specialists complained about repeatedly to no avail and no hospital action was ever taken toward or against this grossly negligent, lying /dishonest, despicable fraud of a physician), was also an emergency room physician and totally and completely orchestrated a cover-up for this co-worker of his, banishing all the subspecialists who repeatedly alerted the administration of this physician's incompetence and unethical behavior and refusal to examine all patient's with the specific organ disease or injury which that physician refused to provide care for, by removing them from the on-call schedule or from the hospital staff entirely—the unforgivable sin of an abusive, egotistical Slave Owner hospital administrator.

At a different hospital, an operating room nurse, during a routine surgery, failed to gather proper implant material for the surgery being performed. The surgeon in the room astutely and routinely checked the implant material present in the room before the case started and noted that the implants in the room were incorrect and from or for another case, unrelated to the current case being performed. The surgeon politely and respectfully asked the nurse to gather/retrieve the correct implants (on a cart outside the operating room) for the patient being prepped and draped for surgery. The physician then scrubbed for the case and placed the surgical drapes on the patient to prepare to commence the surgery. The nurse rudely refused to obtain the requested and correct implants for the right patient undergoing surgery.

She, in fact, was swearing profanities (with the patient awake) in the operating room. The surgeon eventually had to break scrub, remove her surgical gown, and obtain the correct implant material for the case being performed, by herself and with no assistance from that outrageous, unruly, inappropriate, unprofessional, and cantankerous operating room nurse, whose deviant behavior persisted throughout the entire surgical procedure.

After the surgery case was successfully completed, with no credit to or assistance from the inappropriate nurse assigned to that operating room, the surgeon, who has never been a complainer in life and never sought to purposely attack or destroy another individual's career out of spite or jealousy or any other reason, was so disappointed with the inexcusable swearing & belligerent disposition and deplorable attitude of this particular nurse, that she immediately filed a detailed complaint about the inappropriateness of this nurse's behavior to the nursing supervisor & hospital administration (e.g., the Slave submitted a legitimate complaint to her Slave Owner hospital administrator).

The result was shocking. Because the operating room nurse was near retirement age and a hospital employee, she received no punishment whatsoever for her dastardly, disdainful, and totally inappropriate behavior. However, the surgeon who filed the complaint was inappropriately assigned fault or blame for the incident, asked to write a letter of apology to the nurse, and, to pour salt into the open wound, assigned online courses to complete. In a word, absurd. Vindictive and biased Slave Owner score= 1. Abused and beaten (badly) Slave score=Zero (0).

Physicians need either unions or other large, well-funded corporations or companies who will represent, support, and fiercely defend physician's interests and allow independent subspecialty physicians to vote for strong, robust, and non-sycophant subspecialty department heads that will protect, defend, and support their medical activities and surgeries within the hospital. These department heads must be elected by newly created physician unions whose sole purpose and essential function is to emancipate and maintain the future freedom of speech (and all other physician freedoms) and independence of "physician slaves." These department heads must also make pledges (or recite oaths) to not be pro-hospital administration sycophant sympathizers, submissive, weak, or cowardly "non-leaders" who immediately succumb to unreasonable or abusive or biased hospital-suggested inappropriate judgments without researching both sides of each incident story.

These "physician-union-elected department head leaders" must similarly not immediately acquiesce to ridiculous hospital administration cover-ups for irresponsible hospital actions, errors and omissions, and acts of outright negligence or patient endangerment and patient abuse. The subspecialist physician department heads, again elected by the physician union or corporation devoted solely to independent physician freedom, respect, and defense against malevolent Slave Owner hospital administrations and administrators, must be supremely loyal and devoted to protecting their designated subspecialists from unwarranted and unsubstantiated abuse, punishment, or slandering of reputation or disparaging and untrue comments about the level and quality of the care provided by that individual physician who may have an independent contractor consultant relationship with one or more different hospitals.

An additional example of a Slave Owner (hospital administration dereliction of ethical duty and biased cover-up for hospital physician irresponsible behavior and patient neglect) abuse and beating of a Slave (i.e., modern-day medical professional slave) involves an emergency room provider who prefers certain patients with certain illnesses who receive standard of care diagnosis and treatment for these small select group of patients with specified diagnoses.

However, suppose you happen to be assigned to this particular emergency room provider and have a condition that is not interesting to this individual provider. In that case, you will go unexamined, admitted needlessly, and then called by the inpatient physician providers to examine and treat a patient who never even underwent a basic history and physical examination and treatment in the emergency room which, if performed, likely would have averted the necessity for admission and expedited immediate treatment and improvement in the patient's condition or averted potential devastating sequelae from delaying or ignoring the appropriate action of performing an immediate, urgent, and necessary comprehensive history and physical examination, treatment to ensure safest and more expedient recovery of the patient from a specific condition which was not performed by, but in a distraught sense, punted by the emergency physician provider, without any concern or intent to treat, from the minute the patient entered the triage area.

When a subspecialist individual on-call physician complains about this repetitive behavior by a particular provider working for the hospital, that physician inevitably gets labeled as a problem physician by the hospital administration, a letter is placed in their medical staff folder, and no consequences or punishment is realized by irresponsible and negligent or abusive withholder of care to their patients, whimsical and irrational, dangerous and devastating, should that patient experience loss of organ function secondary to inappropriate immediate correct diagnosis and treatment of their specified condition which the emergency provider has no interest or enthusiasm or intent to investigate, diagnose or treat.

There is yet another example of "real-life slave abuse" by the "slave owner (hospital administration). Lisa recalls that at one hospital where she was a member of the medical staff as an independent contractor subspecialist for more than twenty years, the entire group of specialists whom Lisa was a member of and friendly colleague to all her other colleagues of this same subspecialty group of physicians, all uniformly and equally disliked and despised the verbally abusive and disorganized sycophant nurse assigned to them by the "Slave Owner Hospital AdminisTraitors." The nurse was cantankerous at every single subspecialty meeting (four meetings per year) for over twenty years. Instead of representing our subspecialty as a friendly, strong, and supportive ambassador to our "Slave Owners/Hospital AdminisTraitors," she was constantly defiant.

She produced illogical reasons why our requests for new and updated subspecialty equipment for performing subspecialty-specific procedures, or software updates for our subspecialty diagnostic equipment "could not and would not" be considered or accommodated, repeatedly, to the chagrin of our entire subspecialty physician department members. For the entire career of this nurse supervisor, the "Slave Owner Hospital AdminisTraitors" parceled more and more power and influence on and to this particular nurse. This nurse was single-handedly responsible for the gross disorganization of the entire hospital department, which Lisa and her colleagues had to endure, survive, and function in, all in order to complete their subspecialty tasks of seeing patients and affecting healing and recovery in our patients despite one nurse's constant chaos & disorganization. There are numerous specific examples, but only several will be described in detail.

For over twenty years, procedures and orders for the hospital would be scheduled by subspecialists and faxed 1 to 2 months before the procedure date by subspecialist office staff or the physicians themselves. For over twenty years, the faxed procedure documents and orders for the hospital staff for upcoming patient procedures at the hospital would be lost or misplaced, then requested urgently by the hospital nurses the morning of surgery (not the day before or the week before because chaos ruled and no one was held responsible for lost or misplaced faxed procedure notes and pre-op or post-op orders and no one checked if all paperwork had been received for each case until the very last minute and on the day of a patient's procedure), which stressed not only the physician (unreasonably and unnecessarily) but also the hospital nurses and, in some instances, the patients.

Myriad complaints by subspecialist physician offices would be filed, legitimately and with fax confirmation receipts, from the physician offices sending the faxes, including the number of pages faxed with the date and time that scheduled cases were faxed successfully to the hospital. Yet, neither the nurse supervisor (irresponsible and pathetic), who commanded and perpetuated the chaos and lack of accountability or responsibility for maintaining faxed records and orders for procedures, nor the "Hospital AdminisTraitors" ever agreed to make any changes in how faxes were received, responsibly processed, and stored securely.

Instead, this disorganized nurse would repeatedly attack and file complaints against all physicians who made suggestions for improvement to her or complained to or about her. Because the misanthropic supervisor nurse assigned to our subspecialty physician group was a salaried hospital employee and sycophant to the hospital administration and clearly not a physician-friendly advocate for the physicians in Lisa's subspecialty, our highly educated independent subspecialty physicians were, for over twenty years, treated no better than slaves, with no rights of free speech, no freedom to criticize the haphazard and lackluster (or outright irresponsible and malpractice) performance of this nurse without the expectation that any physician (possibly every single subspecialty physician in our group complained multiple times) who complained about her would then subsequently receive a letter from the "Slave Owner Hospital AdminisTraitors (Administration)" that they were being labeled a "difficult or problematic physician" and that this notification letter would be made a part of their "hospital file." There were never attempts to inquire if physicians' suggestions or complaints were valid, legitimate, or justified. Furthermore, "Slave Owners (Hospital AdminisTraitors)" seldom, if ever, suggested that changes would be considered or made to resolve identified deficient or negligent hospital policies or actions. Only the threat of retribution toward and on the Slave (a physician who dared to file a complaint or suggestion to improve, rectify, or cure a problem or disease in the hospital administration process or system) could be expected, without exception, one hundred percent of the time!

Though hard to believe, many hospitals systematically advise and counsel surgeons and nurses not to document or discuss with patients when mistakes are made in operating rooms, intensive care units, or on hospital inpatient floors. Specifically, when, e.g., the aorta, pulmonary artery, or abdominal cavity blood vessel is nicked (cut) unintentionally and by mistake by a surgeon during surgery, some hospital administrations or specialty department heads demand that these events never be documented in patient charts by the surgeon or nurses caring for these patients and never be discussed with the patients or their families (especially if the complication resulted in the death of the patient).

This is highly unethical. However, physicians and physicians-in-training who have no union lawyers to protect them from being fired from their medical school, residency, or fellowship hospital training program are enslaved by this moral dilemma. Their desire to report such unethical policies is conflicted by their lack of protection and vulnerability to being fired if they divulge that such an event occurred but was never ethically documented or explained honestly to the patient or the patient's family. Without physician-created unions to support and defend such physicians from being fired by hospitals solely because they honestly reported a scandalous (attempted) cover-up of an adverse outcome by a physician, department, or hospital administration (or all of the above in many instances), many if not most physicians will, sadly, choose to adhere to their slave existence and loss of free speech during their training, to successfully be eligible to complete their training and successfully graduate to the next level of their physician slave training.

Shocking but true, another real-life example of how many unethical hospital administrations and hospital staff employees are complicit in fraud, waste and abuse, deception, cover-ups, and, in truth, total disregard for Bible-based morality, ethical conduct, and honest characterization and recognition of outstanding (e.g., never recognizing or applauding fantastic consult quality and medical or surgical care by consulting physicians who have worked in the hospital for 20 or more years) physician consults performed daily and weekly, and other positive events and joyous patient outcomes that result from the outstanding care provided by these consulting physician subspecialists. In contrast, bad events that occur daily in hospitals throughout the world have become an "insurance reimbursement game" in a deviant, malevolent, and unethical (and indeed not based on morality and ethical behavior as taught in the Bible) manner which, to the casual reader who does not work or live in the medical profession world, will seem shocking and unbelievable, which is appropriate and justified, especially to Christians who attempt to live their life as Jesus taught in the greatest book ever, the Bible.

One additional real life example should be bring this grave concern to the forefront of every righteous and ethical human being on this planet and will serve as a prime example of why it is imperative that physicians immediately rise in revolution, embrace and create physician unions that have Bible-based morality and ethical conduct as their guiding principles and charter organization purpose, who can empower them to cast away and defeat their "Hospital Slave Owners And Hospital AdminisTraitors And Hospital-Chosen, Hospital-Paid Sycophant (e.g., Slave Master Foreman) Subspecialist Department Heads," and replace them with physician union elected and paid: administrators and subspecialist department heads, that are not sycophant loyalists to tyrant hospital administrations but rather loyalists to physicians who will defend their integrity, dignity and freedoms of speech and to practice their specialty in medicine, unimpeded and unrestricted, confident that they cannot and will not be unjustly restricted or fired merely for relating the truth (which may disturb hospital administrators, but also force necessary policy changes that usher in a new era of ethical and honest practice of medicine in hospitals worldwide, benefiting both physicians and patients), ultimately guaranteeing emancipation of physicians and zenith patient care, because physician union lawyers, guided by Bible-based morality and ethics, will protect & defend these physician and patient rights to honest, truthful, care while in the hospital environment.

Case in point. Hospitals currently may, after a patient's death, continue full, comprehensive life support, e.g., for four days after the patient's death (or whatever period necessary to receive full reimbursement for a surgical procedure performed and to meet whatever definition is required per the insurance company or medical organization guidelines), so that the patient's immediate death after surgery or admission, may not be registered, reported or recorded as either a non-reimbursable encounter or an immediate postoperative complication after surgery, at that hospital.

Other hospitals may have policies or systems in place where they communicate with patients by telephone at home after discharge by nurses or other hospital employees and ensure patients do not return to their hospital within a certain number of days after discharge to receive full reimbursement for a prior visit or for reasons of not having to report statistics that may indicate the hospital discharged patient too early before clinical improvement in the patient's condition.

By "doctoring" these situations, hospitals may appear to be better than they are or to have lower surgical complication rates than reality would be able to verify; in essence, fraudulent statistics can and are being submitted to regulatory agencies or hospital rating agencies that are neither accurate, ethical or moral, and based on fraud and deceit rather than Bible-based morality and ethical conduct at hospitals.

It is painful for Lisa to relate these truths, but her conscience demands the revelation of these truths. Lisa, therefore, believes now and has always thought it is better to live an honest and truthful life so that one has no regrets or a guilty conscience. This is what Jesus taught in the Bible. Lisa is neither perfect nor without regrets due to her imperfections; however, she possesses a clear conscience due to her life-long, since seventh grade, acceptance of Jesus as her savior and acceptance of the Bible as her source of life guidance principles. As a result of Lisa's adhering to Biblical principles throughout her life, she has been used by God to bless many other humans on this planet according to the intelligence and skills God graciously and mercifully equipped Lisa with. God empowered and enabled Lisa to live a Godly life without limits with regard to successes and victories achieved during Lisa's life.

As a result, Lisa has been able to donate back or make innumerable benevolent contributions through her daily work and surgeries to all those humans she has encountered and treated despite the many obstructions and hindrances she encountered along her journey through life. Lisa is forever grateful for God's guidance and credits God for all Lisa's outstanding accomplishments and blessings, benevolence, humanity, humility, grace, and mercy that Lisa was granted and received, despite Lisa's imperfections and falling short of the life example that Jesus provided in the Bible regarding how all men and women are to live, under the jurisdiction, protection, and blessings of God while on this earth, from life until death. If God is accepted and acknowledged by all human beings as our savior, we may be reunited with Jesus, the Holy Spirit, and God (a.k.a., the "Holy Trinity") in heaven for eternity. This is a remarkable, spellbinding, and eternal win, no matter how you analyze or critique this concept, in a biased and prejudiced manner or an objective and rational manner.

Can a physician-in-training or independent contractor physician in any public, private, county, state, or federal hospital or any other medical facility ever feel like anything other than a slave when they can never honestly report or provide constructive criticism to hospital administrations without being immediately targeted by that administration as a problem physician for making said report? In over thirty years of experience, the answer is emphatically no!

Another example, true but hard to believe nevertheless, was a simple problem that was identified by an organized subspecialist physician, rectified by the physician's suggestion, but when the fact was pointed out that the subspecialist physician had scheduled a procedure and faxed the pre-op orders to the hospital over one month in advance of the procedure date with a successful fax confirmation receipt retained by the subspecialist physician office, the orders for the procedure had, once again, been lost or misplaced by the hospital and the unorganized supervisor nurse that was the supreme commander of department chaos and disorganization.

Simply put, a patient's information on the patient's hospital-generated wristband had an incorrect name and date of birth, even though the patient had undergone a similar surgery on the opposite side a month earlier in the same hospital. When the physician arrived to examine the patient and mark the surgery site the morning of surgery, the physician noted the incorrect wristband information and requested that the wristband be reprinted with the correct name and date of birth.

The disorganized Slave Owner (hospital administration sycophant hospital employee nurse supervisor) then manipulated the facts of the situation (e.g., failed to acknowledge that she and her disorganized department once again discarded, misplaced, or lost all the faxed procedure orders and consents for this patient, printed a wristband for the patient with inaccurate/wrong name and date of birth, and had to reprint a corrected patient information wristband, with ultimately resulted in a delayed surgery start time for the patient's case) and, perhaps out of guilt for her own haphazard performance, projected her dismal department performance on the physician who correctly identified the wrong wristband patient information. In seeking to beat up and perform a severe whipping of the Slave (e.g., a physician who complained about the nurse employee of the hospital and the error that was identified), retribution was enacted to punish the Slave. The physician was then, as a result of the nurse's lying and misrepresentation of what occurred that morning of surgery, taken off the on-call subspecialty call schedule for the hospital and again sent a threatening letter by the "Slave Owner Hospital AdminisTraitors" [Hospital Administration]) falsely stating that the physician specialist was somehow (in a bizarre, "make-believe," warped, and distorted world & universe) responsible for the inaccurate surgery wristband that was incorrectly typed up, printed out and placed on the patient's wrist before their planned surgery that bizarre morning.

The definition of slavery must be recognizable in these short, sad, and true stories. When a physician is not allowed to identify problems or inaccuracies or blatant acts of malpractice that occur within a hospital, then unnecessary poor patient outcomes or loss of limb or other organs or loss of life may and do occur which would otherwise not have happened if the physician (Slave, deprived of freedom of speech and deprived of the freedom to make constructive criticism complaints and suggest solutions to the problems identified by the physician [slave]) had the freedom to file complaints without fear of (and sadly, near 100% chance and likelihood of) retribution and whipping (unjustified of course) by the Slave Owner (nefarious hospital administrations, whose only incentive each day is to hide errors and acts of omission or negligence or malpractice and, whenever possible and whenever they believe they can get away with it, project blame onto any non-union physicians-in-training or independent contractor physicians providing care to hospital patients, because they know that individuals who have no union to defend their rights and freedom and justice will be easily intimidated (e.g., Slave Owner can threaten to fire, punish, or otherwise restrict that Slave from performing activities in the hospital) and silenced, despite the injustice inflicted on that Slave (physician).

Once again, the imperative solution is that physicians stand up in unity, establish, create, support and join a "Physician Union", created and designed specifically to battle against Slave Owners (a.k.a., Tyrant Hospital Administrations and Hospital "AdminisTraitors") worldwide, Defeat Slavery in Modern-Day Medicine, Emancipate Slaves (Physicians-in-Training and Independent Contractor Specialist and Subspecialist Physicians working at hospitals but not direct hospital salaried employees for these hospitals), Restore Balance of Power (e.g., Physicians should be in charge of patient care and be completely free to identify problems and suggest solutions to substandard or negligent or errant care being delivered in hospitals to maintain the highest standard of patient care without any concern that they will fired (or whipped like a slave) by hospital administrations (slave owners who deliver whippings to falsely accused slaves based on unsubstantiated claims or projection of acts of malpractice by hospital employees that are then blamed on non-hospital employee, independent physicians who are vulnerable targets due to no union membership and union legal defense of rights and due process). Similarly, hospital administrators should not be allowed to continue to lie and cover up patient deaths that resulted from acts of malpractice by hospital employees, as is the norm currently.

When all physicians are supported by Physician Advocate Unions who have battled and defeated corruption in hospital administrations and enabled and facilitated the emancipation of the slaves, patient care will exponentially improve because ALL physicians will have the assurance that they can have an equal voice which can be heard and believed, if the facts can be presented and not ignored by hospital administrators (a.k.a., Hospital AdminisTraitors), with the presumption of "innocent until proven guilty" which has not existed in medicine for 200+ years.

One last fascinating dilemma, wrapped in an enigma, is when "Slave Owner Hospital AdminisTraitors" (Hospital Administrations) worldwide engage in crazy and absurd policies (e.g., the patient is always right, no matter what they say, how they say it, when or why they say it and no matter what actions the patient engages in, the patient is always right…implying the care providers or physician will always be found to be guilty and wrong when encountering inappropriate or wild, out-of-control patients.

Physicians must have "physician-friendly union backing and support" in all these instances for the simple and obvious reasons that follow below. Physician Unions must have the financial security and power to hire the best and most competent physician defense lawyers who are committed not only to defending honest and hard-working ethical independent contractor physicians providing care for hospital patients but also engage successfully and victoriously in battling and defeating outrageous and false allegations from dishonest patients and current "Slave Owners (a.k.a., hospital administrations [or Hospital AdminisTraitors])."

Physician unions must, in addition, be committed to defending and protecting physician reputations and defining and defending the concept of "standard of care," which all physicians strive toward and have as their goal and mission to reach, even when being forced to examine, treat, or operate (emergently) on "unrealistic, unreasonable, paranoid, insane, or outright pathologic lying patients" which, unfortunately, occurs more often that anyone would like to imagine or admit.

Sadly, in over thirty years of Lisa's experience in the medical profession, "Slave Owners" (a.k.a., "Hospital AdminisTraitors" or Administrations) make policies that are selfishly written by their contracted hospital sycophant lawyers that are always designed to be "pro-patient" and "pro-hospital" but never "pro-independent contractor physician specialist or subspecialist." For this reason, policies at Slave Owner Plantations (Hospitals) will allow patients to verbally abuse and physically abuse physician providers up to the point of murder and death without punishment or consequence.

In contrast, "Slaves" (a.k.a. hard-working, ethical independent contractor physicians providing care for hospital patients and who must battle outrageous and false allegations from dishonest patients and current Slave Owners (a.k.a., hospital administrations [or Hospital AdminisTraitors]) are expected to be whipped or flogged on a routine basis by unreasonable, dishonest or unruly abusive patients or hospital employees (nurses, physicians, others), as designed and intended by "Slave Plantation/Hospital Policy," and, furthermore, these Slaves (physicians) are then not only expected but required never to file a complaint or concern when egregious acts of fraud, waste, abuse, errors and omissions, acts of negligence or unethical behavior, dishonest behavior or lies, slander or outright acts of malpractice are witnessed by the Slave (aka physician), committed by either a hospital patient or hospital employee. In every case, the hospital (a.k.a., Slave Owner or Plantation Owner) has, in Lisa's experience, reacted in a manner and with the inappropriate and unethical attitude: "Every woman (or man) for herself (or himself)" (e.g., hide negligence to protect hospital & hospital employees first, defend hospital employees always [whether they acted appropriately or inappropriately], defend patient's behavior [whether they acted appropriately or inappropriately] "so the patients will not bring law suits against the hospital or hospital employees", and be damned the Slaves (independent contractor physicians [a.k.a., "The Woman (Women) In The Arena (or The Man (Men) In The Arena"], who are defenseless, not backed by a physician-friendly union who will defend & support them against false & unsubstantiated allegations and prevent Slave Owners ("Hospital AdminisTraitors") from inappropriately imposing hospital inpatient or on-call duty restrictions or limitations, assigning unreasonable &/or unnecessary online courses (which should instead be assigned to inappropriately behaving hospital salaried employees) and prevent harassing and threatening letters from Slave Owners to Slaves, threatening hangings or whippings (e.g., revoking hospital privileges or firing the physician who dared to file a complaint about inappropriate hospital policies or actions or about a hospital salaried staff member or employee) in order to unjustly punish or silence the Slave with the goal of preventing the Slave from ever filing a complaint or concern in the future.

In summary, all physicians must unite, stand tall and strong together, and create physician-advocating and physician-friendly unions that are financially fit, able, and willing to effectively battle and defeat rich corporation hospital systems and hospital administrations (a.k.a. Slave Plantation Owners), and forever take away their Slave Owner power & titles, successfully liberate & preserve (forever) the emancipation of Slaves ((independent contractor physicians and physicians-in-training). These urgently needed actions and battles must be fought and won. The dire need for the emancipation of these physician slaves is perhaps one of the most critical and pressing issues of our century. Successful emancipation of physician slaves from their slave owners (teaching hospitals and private hospitals) will immediately result in safer hospital care for all patients worldwide and restore the balance of power to the honest, altruistic, hard-working physicians (a.k.a. "The Man [Men] In The Arena"), who have dedicated their lives and existence to improving the health and lives of others and who deserve the freedom, respect, dignity that they have earned.

Chapter Fifteen:

Imperative Battle That Must Be Waged & Victoriously Won With Christian Values & Physician Union(s)

Summary: Eternal Guiding Principles & Ethics That With Physician-Created Unions Guided By Bible-Based Moral & Ethics, Will Defeat Current Tyrant, Abhorrent Betrayal of Hospitals & Hospital AdminisTraitors Who Have For Centuries Abandoned Bible-Based Morality & Ethics in Their Approach To Patient Care And, In So Doing, Enslaved Physicians-In-Training And Independent Contractor Physician Caring For Hospital Patients Worldwide: The Revolution & Battle, Imperative & Essential, Must Be Fought Until Victorious & Emancipation Of Physicians is Achieved And Physician Dignity

Restored Whilst Zenith Patient Care Realized, Raising The Standard & Level of Patient Care Worldwide

How to Optimize And Provide Zenith Patient Care in Hospitals Worldwide & Concomitantly Restore Physician Freedom, Dignity, and Respect Via Battling & Defeating Current Physician Slave Owners & Hospital AdminisTraitors Who Have For Over One Century Abhorrently Betrayed Physician Trust & Usurped Physician Independence & Freedom & Enslaved Independent Contractor Physicians Who Are Currently Defenseless & Unsupported (Without Physician Union(s) At Present) in Their Daily Activities of Providing Subspecialty Care To Hospital Patients. The Long Overdue Emancipation of Physician Slaves Working In Hospitals Must Be A Top Priority For All Physicians Worldwide And Accomplished With Dire Urgency. Restoration of Christian Values & Attitudes Must Be Incorporated Into Models of Providing Compassionate Care For Hospitalized Patients. Physician Union(s) Whose Sole Purpose, Charter & Contractual Obligation Is To Defend & Support Daily Physician Activity & Functioning in Hospitals Must Not Only Be Created By & For Physicians, But Must Also Employ Lawyers Who Are Staunch & Fiercely Committed To Physicians Welfare, Defense, Dignity And Freedoms Whilst Embracing Christian Values & Attitudes, Ultimately Raising The Standard & Level of Care That Hospitalized Patients Receive Far Above Levels of Care Currently Being Provided By Corrupt & Tyrant Hospital AdminisTraitors Who Currently Focus Solely On: 1) Patient Reimbursement To Hospital Slave Owners (money gotten from patients hospitalized), 2) Deceptive practices of covering up all salaried employees or physician employees acts of negligence, errors and omissions, and acts of malpractice, 3) Deflecting and projecting blame, willfully and intentionally in a premeditated manner, from hospital employees irresponsible acts onto non-hospital, non-salaried independent contractor physicians who are defenseless without physician-created and physician supported unions who have lawyers that, with Christian values as their guiding principles and guidelines, are fervently committed to and fiercely effective in accomplishing swift

& immediate responses, defense and support to physicians who are falsely accused or slandered by Hospital AdminisTraitors.

All hospital physicians of every race, religion, and culture, including physicians from every country in the world, will benefit from the defeat of Modern-Day Slave Trading & Slave Owners (Teaching Hospitals & Private, Public, City, County, State, and Federal Hospitals) Who Have For Over One Century Abhorrently Betrayed Physician Trust & Usurped Physician Independence & Freedom & Enslaved Independent Contractor Physicians Who Are Currently Defenseless & Unsupported (Without Physician Union(s) At Present) in Their Daily Activities of Providing Subspecialty Care To Hospital Patients.

By embracing physician-created and physician-supporting union(s) and emphasizing Bible teachings and Christian values as guiding principles for union leadership, all union member physicians who embrace these Bible principles will better themselves and provide better and more compassionate care to their patients. When unionized physicians care for and treat patients because they know that God has blessed them and chosen them to be capable and responsible extensions of God's presence and power to heal patients, the level of care provided is immediately raised to the highest level. The patient and physician can then experience this phenomenal situation and realize and appreciate zenith patient care outcomes.

Lisa hopes to see the defeat of Physician Slave Owners And Hospital AdminisTraitors engaging in the modern-day slave trade in medicine, unionization of physicians-in-training, and unionization of independent contractor physicians in all hospitals and other medical facilities worldwide in her lifetime and as soon as possible.

All physicians will live a more satisfied, content and fulfilled life, knowing that their work each day is fully appreciated and respected by hospital administrations, ordained by God who enabled each physician to receive the education and training necessary to be a blessed and fantastic provided of healthcare, and having the assurance and peace of mind that whenever they offer suggestions or constructive criticism (to improve patient care) to hospital administrators or are inappropriately or falsely accused or wrongdoing, they will not be unjustly punished, restricted or otherwise limited in their physician duties or fired, because of their physician union membership involvement, support and capable union defense lawyers who both defeated modern-day slave owners and slave trading practices and continue to fervently defend, respect and support their emancipated (former slaves) independent, hard-working (a.k.a., "The Man (or Woman) In The Arena"), moral, ethical, Christian values-based physicians who had the courage and resolve to create the very union(s) that assisted and enabled their eventual overwhelming victory and abolition of slavery in modern-day medicine, that had existed for centuries, merely from the lack of unification, consolidation, ratification and proactive effort that was necessary to create & support union(s) whose sole purpose is to support and defend physician freedom, dignity and respect.

In God We Trust And In God We Must Entrust The Care Of Our Patients To Ensure Optimal, Zenith Level Of Care For All Patients Within The Hospital System. Physician-Created, Physician-Friendly Unions That Can And Will Defend Physicians, Respect And Use Bible-Based Guidelines Of Morality and Ethical Conduct Can And Will Defeat Current Tyrant, Unethical Hospitals & AdminisTraitors Who Abhorrently Betrayed And Enslaved Physicians, Usurped Physician Power, Influence, Disrupted And Distorted Balance of Powers Within Hospitals (Physicians versus AdminisTraitors) And Outlawed & Suppressed / Silenced Freedom of Speech & Physician Reporting Of Unethical Hospital Acts of Misconduct Via Intimidation And Unjust Threats of Discipline or Firing, Will Emancipate Physicians & Realize Zenith Standard of Care for Hospital Patients Worldwide For Eternity.

(The above Chapters/Excerpts were from "Father's Eyes" by the author Winston Anselm Irons, and "Modern-Day Slave Trade In The 21st Century" by the author Priscilla Lisa Alvarez-Mendez)

In Summary:

Raping (Figuratively), Robbing, And Embezzling (R.R.E.) Of Payments And Reimbursements Of Physicians and Physician Groups Who Are Reverently Caring For Routine And Emergency Health Conditions Which Demand And Require Their Loving Care And Surgical Procedures As A Remedy For Their Conditions Or Diseases Throughout The World By Large Trust-Like, Monopolistic, Unimpeded, Unhindered, Unopposed (At Least Up To The Present Time; This Needs To Change Immediately), Large Conglomerate Unethical or Criminal Health Insurance Companies Who, One To 12 months After Patient Care Is Delivered In Good Faith By Physicians and Physician Groups, Are Then Demanded, Without Ethical Justification, Recourse, Or Appropriate Consideration Of Physician Appeals (At Least Without Future Physician Unions' Lawyers Criminal Financial Scandal Law Suits Directed Toward These Sinister Health Insurance Companies), To Refund To These Monopolistic And Sinister Health Insurance Companies, Significant Percentages, e.g., 30-80%, Of Original Payments To Physicians, Or In Some Cases, The Entire Physician Exam or Surgery Fee Due. Because Honorable, Empathetic, Altruistic And Caring Physicians Have Delayed And Precariously Avoided Or Shunned To Their Detriment, For Centuries, The Formation of Ethical Legal Powered And Backed, Physician-Defending and Physician-Supporting Unions, They Continue (Hopefully Not Too Much Longer) To Experience Self-Inflicted Raping (Figuratively), Robbing, And Embezzling (R.R.E.) Of Payments And Reimbursements By These Large, Powerful, Dictator-Like, Sinister, Criminal, Trust-Like, Monopolistic Health Care Insurance Companies Who Have Been Enabled To Continue Their Crimes And Even Supported And Facilitated By The Inaction, Lack of Unity, Insufficient Decisiveness, And Overt Lack Of Resolve By Physicians, For Centuries, To Organize Physician Unions To Defend And Protect Their Ethical, Moral, And Honest Practice Of Examining And Operating On Patients, And Their Rights and Justification To Maintain Their Respect For These Services, Freedom To Appeal Unjust Demands For Return of Just Fees Paid By Health Insurance Companies, And Fair Reimbursement For All Services Performed.

CHAPTER TWELVE:

Ironically, Paradoxically, Or Fortunately, Depending On Whether You Have Agnostic, Atheistic, or Positive And Christian Perspective Or Outlook On Life And The World, The Same Perspectives, Intent, Aspirations, Motivation, Inspiration, Mentor Mindset, and God-Respecting, Bible-Based Values, Morality, and Ethics That Makes Parents Game-Changing, Miraculously Magnificent Parents Of Their Children, Also Make Politicians, Believe It Or Not, The Most Influential, Positive Life-Impacting Leaders And Stewards of God For All "World Citizens" On This And Every Planet In Our Universe, Also Known As The Cosmos!

Billy Graham (1918-2018) was an American evangelist and a prominent Christian figure of the 20th century. He conducted numerous crusades, preaching to millions around the world and reaching even more through radio and television. Graham's message of salvation and his efforts to promote social justice and racial equality have left a significant legacy.

Below are enlightening chapters/excerpts from a tremendous book, regarded by many as a true masterpiece and "once-in-a-generation" outstanding novel, and one of this century's most influential Christian apologetic creations. A motivating, inspirational nonfiction novel that this generation's "world citizens" will derive tremendous wisdom, guidance, and enlightenment from reading, memorizing, and living out the principles taught and following the recommendations in this masterful guide to happiness, health, and serenity. This creation gives pearls of wisdom unselfishly to all humans so that they may achieve and experience unparalleled success in all their Godly life endeavors. Others have stated that this novel is the most complete, comprehensive, intimate, introspective, thought-provoking, life-illuminating, and God-inspired masterpiece, second in brilliance and profound enlightenment only to the Holy Bible. "Father's Eyes," by Winston Anselm Irons, accomplishes its intent and mission of improving the plight and pilgrimage of all world citizens to have the most joyful, fulfilling, satisfying, rewarding, safe, confident, and serene life possible in this tempestuous and tumultuous world.

As is the theme of all masterpiece novels, and in the greatest book ever written, the Holy Bible, this novel, **"Father's Eyes," educates, entertains, and enlightens all its readers and those who seek and relish the author's generous offering up of "the formula to success and happiness in one's life and one's afterlife.**

This book's intent, accomplished in every aspect and every respect is to gently and safely navigate all readers of this book, also known as world citizens, throughout every moment of their existence, from birth to death and resurrection, and during their journey through life's many perfect storms or hurricanes and tidal waves encountered during their journey and adventurous travels through time and life and then gently guide these tried and tested pioneers, explorers, and survivors of life's trials and tribulations, back to their Godly Father and creator, via Jesus Christ, God's son, who died for the sins of all world citizens so that they could be allowed to be imperfect, as all humans are, yet if willing to repent of their sins, be redeemed if they openly accept Jesus Christ's sacrifice of his perfect life for all world citizen's sinful lives, so they may then (counter-intuitively, unexpectedly, undeservingly), gracefully, and mercifully be forgiven of their human transgressions, and in conjunction with the Holy Spirit (acting to support and guide them to a Christian values-based existence and daily actions worthy of God's grace and mercy, and very similar to the life demonstrated by Jesus Christ in the Bible), be guided by Godly wisdom, compassion, empathy, kindness, and forgiveness, again as demonstrated by Jesus Christ's example of how all humans may and should live to respect all other God's children and family members (e.g., all world citizens who acknowledge and praise God in their life attitudes and actions), to achieve redemption from their sins and realize the resurrection of their bodies and souls into heaven upon their physical, earthly death, and eternal existence in heaven via God's merciful forgiveness of their sins, and effecting their resurrection, if they adequately demonstrated and enacted their Christian faith during their life on earth.

Relish and forever cherish the remembrances all readers will have indelibly imprinted on their hearts, minds, and souls after reading the below chapters/excerpts (or the entire book for those seeking ultimate and immeasurable wisdom and enlightenment), from "Father's Eyes" by Winston Anselm Irons, which follow in the paragraphs below, which will make all those who read this message the most non-corrupt politicians, other leaders, parents, friends, coworkers, and colleagues, but much more, will transform them and enact a metamorphosis of their heart, mind, body, and soul, which enables them to become the most likely to succeed in life, to be the ultimate and most Godly and wise mentors for others in their lives, and to, at the earliest age possible, be an advocate for God, an advocate and mentor for all their fellow world citizens, also known as all God's children and creations, and have the most profound and impactful, only in positive ways and means, existence for the duration of their lives on earth, and eternal existence in heaven with (and as a result of the impact and influence that the

Holy Trinity had and will forever have in their lives), Jesus Christ their savior and redeemer, the Holy Spirit (guiding, daily, all "world citizen" human beings or "God's children" who ask forgiveness for their sins and profess their faith in Jesus Christ, the Holy Spirit, and God the Father), and God the Father and their creator (the "Holy Trinity")!

Father's Eyes
Enlightening principles and true stories of positivity triumphing over negativity, strategies to optimize life success, achievements, fitness, and health (physical, mental, social, and spiritual), and sagacious guidance and perspectives in this tumultuous and tempestuous world to benefit all generations in perpetuity.

By Winston Anselm Irons

Chapter One:

The Essential Perspectives All Individuals Must Acquire & Utilize Daily to Achieve Success in All Endeavors

The Immensely Satisfying, Adventurous Journey to Identify Your Strengths and Weaknesses As Early As Possible In Life, Enabling You To Develop a Successful Life Path And Strategy to Reach and Realize Your Wishes, Dreams, Goals, and Ultimate Glorious (e.g., God-glorifying and God-honoring) and Adventurous Path Through Life

What is it that sets apart individuals who achieve great satisfaction and contentment in their life and success in this world from those individuals who intend to but fall short of their goals and aspirations? Initially and importantly, the answer is a purpose for living which is ethical, moral, generous and benevolent in nature, believable and learned, reinforced, substantiated, and embraced by that individual at the earliest possible age. Parents who are educated to the greatest extent possible (e.g., grammar school, high school, college or university, and trade/professional school) might have the most significant opportunity, wisdom, and enlightenment to be reasonably helpful to a young child at the earliest age possible after birth to advise and guide each child as to why that child was born and that each child has unlimited potential for an outstanding purpose-driven life that will make everyone around them glad and rejoice that they were born. These children may then make the world a more pleasant, peaceful, sane, ethical, moral, and exciting place to live, thrive, and enjoy as 'world citizens' who are rated A+ regarding their tolerant yet discerning moral code and attitude toward others and generous, positive, and inspirational role-model behavior throughout their path in life toward all those they encounter, life to death.

The Time Machine (author H.G. Wells) was a novel adapted into a movie and quite a fantastic book and movie! The book and movie should be read and seen by all readers! While I am not willing to give away the plot for those who wish to read the book and see the movie in the near future, I will point out that one of the most profound concepts in the book and movie alike (of which there are many), is when, at the conclusion of the story, the main character must choose a single book to guide present and future young children and adults to build self-esteem and confidence, to enable and empower them to rebuild an entire society (which was destroyed by lack of education, intolerance, evil, lethargy, anger, and hate), which can thereafter be respectful, ethical, moral, generous, kind, caring, compassionate and cooperative for the shared respect, freedom, and independence yet togetherness of that new society.

What single book would be taken off the bookshelf by you in your home in such a scenario? Do you even have such a bookshelf in your home? The likelihood of having a bookshelf of enlightening and empowering classic books of value, meaning, and societal importance (e.g., how to make society and this world a better place to live for everyone) is undoubtedly higher if the parents (children of the past) strove to stay in school as long as possible and reasonable to equip themselves with the most essential wardrobe or armor to ensure their safety, success, pride in their work ethic or occupation, and happiness for the entirety of their physical life on planet Earth and thereafter in their spiritual life that continues after the death of their finite, non-eternal duration, existence, and survival of their physical body, the precursor of each human's eternal holy spirit and soul, created by God.

What books will you take with you to rebuild a society destroyed by greed, selfishness, intolerance, and no moral, ethical, or spiritual framework, no faith in other humans or God (creator of all universes and universe inhabitants), and no religion being embraced by or guiding people to self-improvement, kindness, caring attitudes and actions, sympathy, empathy, forgiveness. What books and messages contained in these books can and will counter and reverse a trend toward the destruction and neglect of spirituality in the world? The Bible and Father's Eyes are books that are and will be for all future generations, essential to stabilize, energize, inspire, and motivate society members to "do your best each and every day of your existence on Earth" and to work for the wellness, happiness, health, and fulfillment of all humans and not just for the benefit of one person. Can any other single book match the Bible? No. However, can other books support the Bible's message and reinforce the message with real-life examples that are enlightening, practical, and, at the same time, very inspiring? Yes. These critical and essential questions must be answered at the earliest possible age to optimize one's life. The sooner one finds the most valuable and life-enhancing collection of books and reads them, taking their messages to heart, body, and soul, the sooner one may find that a gestalt and paradigm shift has occurred in their life and they have become a superhero, truly elite and honorable. Those who have not yet researched, explored, and compiled their life-changing book stacks to read, memorize, and transform themselves into the superheroes and the truly elite and honorable world citizens that all humans have the potential to be may start with the reading of this book to commence their amazing journey and metamorphosis into superheroes, becoming the truly elite and honorable.

Does early, frequent, and lifelong (e.g., birth to death) vigorous and aerobically challenging physical activities such as individual and team sports positively influence or shape life perspectives, perseverance, and resilience attitudes and perspectives (e.g., "I will train hard so that no individual can defeat me." and "I am never defeated until the last second of each sporting event expires.") of highly dynamic and successful individuals?

Vigorously exercising muscles during intense aerobic activities releases myosin from muscle cells into the blood, which crosses the blood-brain barrier and stimulates increased production of B.D.N.F. (brain-derived neurotrophic factor) or, perhaps, more accurately, "regular and frequent vigorous exercise-induced increased brain fitness, health, and functioning." B.D.N.F. (brain-derived neurotrophic factor) is known to optimize neurons (brain cells) functioning and overall health. One might now know why the phrase "no pain, no gain" is more truth than myth!

Does frequent and vigorous exercise make an individual happier, more confident, stronger, more assertive, less depressed, and, at the same, increase valuable and essential oxygenated blood flow to every organ in the body that depends on oxygen for survival every second of every day to operate with maximum accuracy, functionality, and precision? Would the entire individual whose every organ was operating at maximum efficiency outperform, in one or every task attempted, those individuals whose muscles were not vigorously exercising on a repeated and frequent basis or schedule? I think all readers can surmise the correct answers to these rhetorical questions.

Here is a story to illustrate some insightful tips on how to be an independent thinker, a fantastic listener and learner, worker, and problem solver who is both grounded in knowing who they are, where they came from, where they are going, why they are going there, and who to acknowledge, recognize, and credit with glory, their achievements in life each day, week, month, and year.

Mom and Dad had two children approximately two years apart. From the first week after birth, the children were brought to church one day per week during church services. Both children were introduced to extended family members (a.k.a., "church congregation members") whom these two children saw, communicated with, became close friends with, learned many lessons from, and acquired a great deal of wisdom from selected mentors within this church congregation community to emulate and replicate the positive outlook, attitude, friendliness, generosity, empathy, compassion, calm nature, and outstanding altruist nature and proactive participation in the encouragement of others in the church community while performing at the "top of their game" in their respective supportive or leadership roles at the church and in their trade, occupation, or profession within the community or greater metropolitan area. Early days in the church would begin with weekly attendance in the church daycare center where both children got exposed to every germ on the planet to stimulate B-cells, T-cells, and an infinite cascade of immune responses to these bacteria, viruses, and fungi to protect them later in life from these same infectious agents due to their having developed a stronger, healthier, and more robust immune system at very young ages. Friend-making skills, development of tough exteriors (physically, mentally, socially, and spiritually) and expertise in polite and appropriate introductions are similarly learned (and in some cases, low-grade enemy evasion or conquering skills are also learned, hopefully) and implemented and perfected in these daycare center learning sessions long before these children are even candidates to start preschool or Kindergarten (first year of public or private school).

The church congregation friendships and fellowship develop a "sense of self" in each child. Each child develops an inner sense of identity, security, peace, morality, and ethical basis for speech and behavior. Each child is also allowed or given the opportunity to admire and emulate their most admirable and heroic, dynamic role models in the church community. Parents can steer these children to admire, respect, and emulate ("copycat") the most outstanding role models of Godly living in each church community.

Receiving weekly sermons and lessons from the church community pastors (and other members of the church community) based on the single most important book on this planet, e.g., the Bible, to create, maintain, support, and ensure an ethical, moral, benevolent society, can immeasurably and permanently instill both confidence and peace in these children. If you initially disagree with or are averse to this concept or belief, please try it with your children. You will be astonished by the truth you encounter and the subsequent blessings you and your children will experience due to your overcoming your hesitation or fear of entrusting your children to the church community! The education, enlightenment, and quality of friends they make in the church community are often unsurpassed. Through their formative years of mentoring these young children, these church mentors can have a benevolent and long-lasting positive impact on these individuals that benefits them throughout their lifetime.

When these children later enter preschool or the first year of public or private school, they will have the inner peace, calmness, listening skills, reading skills, singing skills, friendship-making skills, and immune system of an ambassador (with twenty years of experience in the job) traveling by transatlantic or transpacific airline from one country to another, at a surprisingly precocious age!

As a parent interested in preparing your children for whatever chaos the world throws at them, what would be the most subtle, uplifting, fascinating, motivating, inspirational way to interest them in reading a classic, masterful, heavenly author's manuscript, which has continued to stir the imagination and creativity of all its readers and is the number one best-selling and educational book ever written for thousands of years? Well, the answer is easy. The parents can study the book one or more times per week at Church and Sunday School, then read chapters from this book each evening prior to bedtime.

As a fantastic combination of history, battles, victories, defeats, temptations and their consequences if indulged in, steadfast courage in the face of near-catastrophe, famines, battles, and health risks that can be and should be avoided to maintain optimal health and fitness, parables and teachings of kindness without wish of return in kind, faithfulness to divine purposes, unwavering loyalty and defense of one's spiritual beliefs are just several examples of what these children can be reading about and inspired by in their reading a single (and the greatest) society-building book, e.g., the Bible. All this learning can be assimilated starting with the singing of worship songs, picture books of stories and parables in the Bible, and listening carefully in Sunday School and during church sermons. Children can and should own their own individual Bible that might start as a children's Bible and escalate in later years to an adult version of the Bible (e.g., New International Version).

These habits and weekly activities of studying history, other individual's errors, sins, or transgressions and their negative consequences and travesties, in addition to learning stories of what made very holy and successful people so blessed, content, happy, and fulfilled in their lives can result in children who have amassed great wisdom, unequaled good judgment and discretion, and immovable faith, hope, and energetic proactiveness in their attitudes and ambitions to better the world they live in until their physical death and spiritual birth and eternal existence alongside their creator.

No one is available to young children, aside from their parents, relatives, and friends, to give them the immediate and most comprehensive perspective on what they will need to do in life to be successful. Life without the earliest positive perspective, constant support, and enlightening guiding principles from worthy mentors, which can then be instituted and acted upon at the earliest possible age to avoid other peoples' common errors and mistakes (most, if not all, which are regrettable by the individuals experiencing or making these errors), can only be expected to proceed sluggishly and with many painful trial and errors, resulting more often than not in highly undesirable outcomes and experiences. This process, method, or strategy of "trial and error" learning in life, and trying to learn from "non-mentors" or attempting to learn valuable life lessons via figuring out the perils, evil, deceptive, disappointing, treacherous, or otherwise misanthropic attitudes and behaviors of the least-honorable members of society is highly inefficient and sadly ineffective.

Moreover, learning only by trial and error is as annoying and frustrating as being assigned to sit and watch a flower blooming or even a pot of water until it reaches boiling temperature while holding only a single match under a full steel pot of water, a near-hopeless endeavor that wastes so much time and results in little or no satisfaction or sense of self-worth and contributes nothing beneficial to others in society or to the development of that individual. Furthermore, the "trials and errors" philosophy of life learning may devastate an individual's self-confidence and self-esteem and misdirect them toward non-benevolent goals and aspirations instead of more honorable and sacred goals in life, or even be lethal at a startlingly young age. Children and young adults who perish from the "trials and errors" philosophy of life is and always will be a travesty and should be prevented at all costs, whenever possible. Parents who seek the highest education level possible before, during, or after having their children, have and will always be the best parents possible by passing on the wisdom they have acquired to their infants and developing young adults, starting at the birth of each child. No human with a heart and good soul relishes or is made happy by hearing stories of young children or young adults that met their maker (e.g., perished prematurely in an abrupt, unexpected, or tragic manner due to circumstances that were avoidable with better insight or wisdom or enlightenment that may have been offered and afforded to that individual by books, parents, relatives, friends, and spiritual guidance) before that individual had time to develop into the responsible and caring adult that all good parents aspire to raise after giving life to their children, to guide the next generation with the values their parents thought were most important (after years of experience and eventual discernment and wisdom they obtained in an eclectic manner), and instilled and reinforced in their children's life perspectives while communicating with and teaching them through both their speech and actions while "bringing up" their children.

From the very first day each of us is born into this world, this is the most obvious and simple, single solution and answer to the most common question every one of us should ask at birth, just after asking for a Kleenex and drying our eyes from having our buttocks slapped by the delivering obstetrician, who brought the first breath to our lungs and the first tears to our eyes! The question and answer on day one is as follows: What can and will I do to achieve the most fulfilling and honorable life before my eventual physical death (but not spiritual death, because spiritual life is eternal if one accepts Jesus Christ as their savior and lives a Godly life as delineated in the Bible) in the indeterminable future? The answer is as simple as the most important first day of life question above: Educate yourself as expeditiously as possible and have as your primary goals: 1) Seek maximum wisdom from as many sources as possible (starting by reading the Bible, say one to five times, cover to cover), 2) Study history and learn from as many other's successful endeavors (and even more importantly, poignantly observe the myriad mistakes of others whose intentions may or may not have initially been benevolent, then veered left or evil with time to evolve into malevolent or evil aspirations and intent, with dire consequences and damnation of that individual's reputation and termination of their spiritual eternal life that was possible then intentionally and willfully self-jeopardized and crucified by their evil behavior) as possible, so as not to repeat other's common and/or lethal mistakes, but to also exceed other's success and accomplishments by learning what made them outstanding, and having a long-term and long-distance perspective by standing atop the shoulders of great achievers and role models in life, and seeing the present and future more clearly and with an enlightening, brilliant, innovative, life-changing perspective that allows "out-of-the-box" but sane (not insane or unreasonable or exceeding dangerous with no realistic chance of safety or success goals), reasonable, and miraculous accomplishments that extend and exceed the knowledge, innovations, goals, and achievements (in their finite lifetime, which your efforts and accomplishments will carry on to the next generation of fantastic innovations and discoveries and life accomplishments) of the great minds of those whose shoulders you stand upon. 3) Strive to develop and maintain and enhance the power and strength of your brain ("mind, spirit, and soul"), and body from your day of birth until the very last day of your physical death, attempting (hopefully with 100% steadfastness and success) to never once compromise or sacrifice your wise goals and inspiring aspirations to achieve personal and societal greatness and Godly spiritual zenith happiness, contentment, and spiritual eternal life, by poisoning or polluting your mind, body, or soul with harmful chemicals (alcohol, illicit or ill-advised chemical substance abuse that destroy the brain and entire body's organs, e.g., marijuana, methamphetamines, magic mushrooms, opioid pain medicines abuse, benzodiazepine medicines abuse, cocaine and/or "crack" abuse, lysergic acid or L.S.D., or myriad other synthetic or hallucinogenic agents and chemicals (huffing, for example), or destroying the perfect body you were blessed and created to have, e.g., with disastrous graffiti like negative imaging and signaling represented by tattoos or other unnecessary cosmetic or genitalia-altering or mutilating surgery that is not clinically necessary, e.g., prostate or testicular removal for prostate or testicular cancer, respectively (including never engaging in, accepting, or undergoing misguided and evil gender/genitalia-mutilating surgeries), surgeries to change who God (your creator and savior) intended you to be from birth to death.

What are the skills, habits, personality traits, characteristics, communication skills, and mindsets that enable one individual to learn the most valuable lessons in life at the earliest possible age? The answers to these questions will facilitate "compounding dividends and capital gains" one individual may achieve and realize long before their death.

Starting at birth, by seeking and finding the answers to this question above, individuals, regardless of young or old age, may accomplish numerous dreams or even exceed their dreams, realize unparalleled success, achievements, enlightenment, find existing or create new altruistic life perspectives, and, lastly, to maximize the "compounded growth" of these life qualities and individual and societal perspectives, values, intentions, and aspirations to achieve zenith benevolence and Godly characteristics (not necessarily monetary wealth, but often, this is an additional fringe benefit received and realized by those who work hard and earnestly to benefit others and their local and other worldwide societies), which, in this world, is the truest and most valuable "wealth accumulation" measure that one must analyze and then come to terms with (regret or fulfillment) on (and hopefully long before) the final day of one's physical life.

What are the skills, habits, personality traits, characteristics, communication skills, and mindsets that enable one individual to learn the most valuable lessons in life at the earliest possible age?

1) Flexibility. Flexibility does not mean "caving in" to lack of morality, lack of ethical behavior, or standards by others, succumbing to peer pressure, or letting others determine your potential and outlook on what you can achieve in life. It simply means, after educating yourself by reading, writing, spelling, communicating efficiently and effectively each and every day of your life, then retaining a proper amount of humility, grace, and mercy in your communications with others who have different backgrounds, education, and perspectives about life due to their different upbringing, goals, and pursuits in life, for better or worse. By remaining flexible in life, you may continue to learn every day from those less fortunate and less educated than you who still can teach you positive and negative life lessons from their own life or their friend's life or lives, and you may discover that those you misjudged during your initial assessment or impression of them may teach you fantastic and insightful lessons that you could not learn elsewhere. Conversely, highly successful people you meet in life may enlighten you

with their successful strategies employed or frustrate and discourage you once you find out or determine their "success" was obtained or achieved by or through dishonorable means, actions, or illicit sources or even by manipulating or deceiving others to achieve "ill-gotten" riches, after which you can conclude that evil behavior enriched these "pseudo-successful" individuals." What is true, genuine, and authentic success? Have you achieved success in your life if, during your last breaths of existence, you recollect, regret, and feel a great deal of guilt for hurting other people to achieve your monetary gains? Manipulating, harming, or otherwise abusing other people to enhance your own life defines "pseudo-successful individuals." Flexibility allows congenial communication and interactions with every human on the planet, enabling you to learn positive and negative features and aspects of every human's life, all without compromising your own inner code of ethics, morality, and God-inspired benevolence and kindness. Flexibility is key to a successful life.

2) Listening Skills. Just like the well-known cliché: A fantastic, detailed, comprehensive history is ninety-nine percent of what is needed to determine the correct medical diagnosis in each patient with a new or otherwise unknown diagnosis, active and engaging listening skills are ninety-nine percent responsible for how early one individual can start amassing great wisdom lessons and exponentially increase their knowledge database to genius level at the earliest possible age. This is surprising to most people. Spend one to three days focused on how poor the average person listens to what others are saying, and you, too, will be convinced that to be among the top ten percent of academic student classmates at every level of education, one needs to listen with nearly one hundred percent focus and attention to lectures being given. Speed reading and effective lecture note-taking will only enhance one's performance on every test to ensure you exceed and surpass the scores of those individuals and constituents of the top ten percent of students group in grammar or elementary school, high school, university, graduate school (master's or doctoral degree). Perhaps one of THE greatest skills at least one (or, ideally, both) parents should have (or strive to develop)

is supreme listening skills, then teach this immeasurably important skill to each child, starting at birth! Brilliant people listen intensely ninety-nine percent of the time during educational class lectures and in conversations, and speak or ask questions less than one percent of the time. If more speaking interaction is deemed necessary, then more questions and discussions can be requested after the lectures or classes!

3) Mentor. Every human, whether an atheist, agnostic, or person of faith by background and upbringing, on this planet and in this universe requires a mentor at the earliest age to maximize successful accomplishments and avoid myriad pitfalls and potential disasters that often result from inexperience, lack of knowledge, and wisdom that is still in development stage, especially in younger aged children.

How can a one-day-old infant, a one-month-old infant, a two-year-old child, a six-year-old child, a twelve-year-old child, or a nineteen-year-old teenager determine who would be the best mentor or have any confidence that the person they choose to be a mentor is the highest quality mentor that is giving only fantastic advice that will help them become the most amazing human possible on this earth, from birth to physical (not spiritual, again a life well-lived can and will result in eternal spiritual life "for them who have ears to hear" [or in deaf persons: for those who have eyes to read and learn, or in blind persons: for those who have hands to read Braille]) death?

By attending church from birth, all children can receive the optimal age-adjusted education and mentoring, regardless of the beliefs, education, guidance, and background of the parents by learning the content and teachings from "The Greatest Mentor: God/Jesus Christ/The Holy Spirit (a.k.a., the holy trinity)" as taught in the most remarkable and most read book that was ever written, the Bible, at the earliest possible age!

A) Proverbs Chapter One, Verses 2-6: Proverbs 1:2-6
New International Version

2 for gaining wisdom and instruction;
for understanding words of insight;
3 for receiving instruction in prudent behavior,
doing what is right and just and fair;
4 for giving prudence to those who are simple,[a]
knowledge and discretion to the young—
5 let the wise listen and add to their learning,
and let the discerning get guidance—
6 for understanding proverbs and parables,
the sayings and riddles of the wise.

B) James Chapter Three, Verses 3-18: James 3
New International Version

Taming the Tongue

3 Not many of you should become teachers, my fellow believers, because you know that we who teach will be judged more strictly. **2** We all stumble in many ways. Anyone who is never at fault in what they say is perfect, able to keep their whole body in check.

3 When we put bits into the mouths of horses to make them obey us, we can turn the whole animal. **4** Or take ships as an example. Although they are so large and are driven by strong winds, they are steered by a very small rudder wherever the pilot wants to go. **5** Likewise, the tongue is a small part of the body, but it makes great boasts. Consider what a great forest is set on fire by a small spark. **6** The tongue also is a fire, a world of evil among the parts of the body. It corrupts the whole body, sets the whole course of one's life on fire, and is itself set on fire by hell.

7 All kinds of animals, birds, reptiles, and sea creatures are being tamed and have been tamed by mankind, **8** but no human being can tame the tongue. It is a restless evil, full of deadly poison.

9 With the tongue, we praise our Lord and Father, and with it, we curse human beings who have been made in God's likeness. **10** Out of the same mouth come praise and cursing. My brothers and sisters, this should not be. **11** Can both fresh water and salt water flow from the same spring? **12** My brothers and sisters, can a fig tree bear olives, or a grapevine bear figs? Neither can a salt spring produce fresh water.

Two Kinds of Wisdom

13 Who is wise and understanding among you? Let them show it by their good life, by deeds done in the humility that comes from wisdom. **14** But if you harbor bitter envy and selfish ambition in your hearts, do not boast about it or deny the truth. **15** Such "wisdom" does not come down from heaven but is earthly, unspiritual, and demonic. **16** For where you have envy and selfish ambition, there you find disorder and every evil practice.

17 But the wisdom that comes from heaven is first of all pure; then peace-loving, considerate, submissive, full of mercy and good fruit, impartial and sincere. **18** Peacemakers who sow in peace reap a harvest of righteousness.

Without the best mentor in life, e.g., the holy trinity and Bible teachings, from birth and throughout life, an individual can still, potentially, achieve maximum success, benevolence, and Godly behavior toward other world citizens in societies and countries throughout the world, but the path becomes much more uncertain, anxiety-provoking, treacherous, challenging, stressful, slower, and less efficient and effective, to put it most simply! Why, then, would it be wise or advised to follow a treacherous, uncertain, dangerous path through life? Unfortunately, the most common answer is probably that many children may have parents, communities, cultures, and societies where the Bible and The Holy Trinity are not introduced to each young infant, child, and young adult until many years later in those individuals' lives. Thus, the most important decision that individuals who are lucky enough to grow up with Christian parents or discover the miraculous power of the message of the Bible and The Holy Trinity is to immediately share with as many people as possible their faith and beliefs to allow others to experience the serenity, reassurance, peace, tranquility, confidence, and phenomenal transformation and success of individuals who surrender their life to God at the earliest ages and let God guide them to immense success, accomplishments, and works of God that not only enhance the life of that individual, but also their entire family, community, society, and country.

4) Importance of Exercise to Mental and Physical Health and Zenith Existence Few people actually realize the true benefits and existential importance to life vitality, exceptional athletic performance, positive self-image, and self-confidence in all life endeavors that derive from regular daily exercise. For example, from birth to physical death, moderate aerobic exercise, or vigorous (not minimal or mild) exercising muscles in the body release myosin into the blood, which circulates up to the brain, crossing the blood-brain barrier, and upregulates or increases production of brain-derived neurotrophic factor (B.D.N.F. or B.D.N.F.), which acts as a "super vitamin to brain cells (neurons)." A common and misinformed, inaccurate "wives' tale" (or "husband's tale," if you prefer, which is a story or supposed truth that is actually spurious or a superstition or urban (or rural) legend believed and passed down through many generations from parents to their children), is that in order to become the smartest and academically most astute, capable, and genius student in school, each young child and progressively older student, while advancing through higher grades of school and university education levels must be singularly hyper-focused on studying extensive and excessive hours, shunning all other distracting activities, such as physical education classes and school sports participation, which might subtract from an individual's tally of total hours of vital study time each day, at school, at home, the library, or at other places (after-school programs or academies for advanced counseling or teaching) determined to be optimal places of study and reading and completing homework assigned by their teachers and professors, and, by doing this and following this "wives' tale," all students will excel and surpass the academic performance of their other classmates at every level of education (e.g., grammar school, high school, university, graduate school, and in future professional or academic lifetime endeavors and pursuits).

In a word, this is the most common misconception and perhaps the oldest iniquity and vice a parent could unknowingly burden a young child with, simply from an uninformed background or lack of experience in the parent or parents' own life or lives! The purpose of this book, and all magnificent literary works, is to enlighten and inform both young children and all ages of readers. If a reader can read as many books as possible from birth to death and find just a handful of books that contain 50-100 years of life experience from the wise authors of those few books, then those readers will see life with eyes of infinite focal lengths and clarity.

The resulting wisdom will afford immeasurable benefits to those readers if accepting and open to new and diverse wisdom from other life explorers, conquerors, or just keen, eclectic, insightful, and hardworking humans who find it is crucial and essential to pass their collective and acquired wisdom on to the next generation to satisfy their hope and aspiration that each generation become more peaceful, tolerant (but not compromise societal and religious values in the name of tolerance), ethical, moral, God-fearing, God-respecting, and more cooperative in helping all humans less fortunate, educated, less healthy, or more mentally impaired, anxious, depressed, or otherwise less capable of navigating a treacherous and tempestuous world alone by themselves, without the support and guidance of other capable, competent, qualified, and worthy mentors.

The author, rather than fabricating some hypothetical theory or opinion that is neither true, substantiated, plausible, or believable, instead relates to the reader what he realizes and experienced first-hand, in real life, as being true. In essence, the author wishes to convey to his beloved readers and those who seek to be the best they can be in this life at the earliest possible age, the following insight: The individuals the author was classmates with, early in school, and at the highest levels of education, doctoral level programs, flight school, and even among future NASA/astronaut candidates (these options were given to top students in classes of flight school graduates), and who were all top academic students, as was the author, in grammar school, high school, graduate school, doctoral university program, had one common feature that led them to the greatest satisfaction, happiness, and academic achievements. This common feature was that they all had a lifetime balance of activities where exercise enabled them to study shorter periods of time, and budget their time more effectively while not sacrificing their top student status! Exercise eliminates the pain (mental, physical, and social) of rigorous studying, breaks up the monotony of excessively long study sessions, and gives the student many legitimate, researched, proven reasons (or excuses, if you prefer) to stop studying briefly (say one to two hours): enhances and increases blood flow throughout the body and to the brain, releases mood-elevating and pain-killing endorphins, also known as "runner's high" feelings (e.g., makes you feel happier from non-exercise baseline status and makes you feel like Superman (males) or Wonder Woman (females) in addition to feeling that you are less sore or less stiff [e.g., from sitting still in the same chair (at home or in the library or other study location) or position for excessive and uninterrupted hours] while studying in the manner that many parents or instructors propose and often advise, ill-advised as it is, thereby heaping enormous weight or burden (e.g., "yoke upon the oxen") upon the shoulders of their loved children or older students their entire life.

While the author serendipitously learned this life-changing truth about exercise breaks in the fourth grade, which developed into a lifelong passion for running and working out amid any school or work environment he encountered, which enabled him to exceed others' expectations for him in every case. Many other individuals may be less fortunate merely by not realizing these benefits of exercise, even in the saddest situations, or until much later in life and at older ages, beyond which this knowledge could have benefitted them in early school years and early life achievement opportunities!

Imagine this scenario:

One young child learns to budget their schedule each day that is devoted to balancing their academic studies with equal devotion to scheduled times for regular vigorous exercise, sports, fun activities, and athletic outings [e.g., with church youth group activities], e.g., rock climbing, water skiing, snow skiing, 100-mile bike ride trips, climbing mountains (winter and summer), playing every sport in school (with the exceptions of brain contusion high-risk sports: tackle football, boxing, mixed martial arts, etc.): baseball, flag football, outdoor & indoor track events and cross-country running. Participation in these athletic activities and sports may then motivate and inspire these young children and students to undergo a metamorphosis into professional (unpaid or paid, with endurance of solid steel and mental and physical enriching payments, regardless of whether payment in dollars or other world currencies ever occurs) athletes expanding their superhuman physical (and mental) fitness to include: power-lifting in the gym, gym workout goals such as 100 pull-ups each session, 400-600 abdominal crunches each session, eventual chest and back (thorax workouts) machine sets of 100-150 of lifting the entire stack of weights on the gym weight machines, and outside runs on the street of 4 miles, up to 8, 16, or 26.2 miles (to be prepared to run a marathon for recreation or necessary survival, e.g., in the mountains on a camping trip, when one is lost, or in a situation requiring superhuman endurance, "I cannot be discouraged or defeated attitude and resilience," and to maximize, through all these lifetime exercise goals and workouts, the massive amount of exercise-induced and created, excess levels of: A) endorphins (that supply "runners high" and superman-like, increased pain tolerance (from whatever baseline level of pain tolerance an individual possesses) which remains with that individual as long as they continue daily or multiple times per week vigorous aerobic exercising [running, biking, gym workouts, "Stairmaster" machine sessions, treadmill), and B) B.D.N.F. ("Brain-Derived Neurotrophic"), which will enable that child and eventual adult to "raise their mental capacity and intelligence and brain health and maximize their brain's neurons' zenith functioning throughout their academic and physical life as the superhuman they have the potential to be and are realizing through their wise health and study choices and decisions!

Child Two: Let's say this child does as his parents or school instructors may advise, without a more informed and enlightened education or perspective on the vital importance of exercise to achieve a superhuman life existence and performance level, and is adherent to a life and academic plan that involves only studying as many hours per day until "burnt out" and "brain dead" and eventually develops a dislike for school and all academic excellence pursuits because that young child innately senses that his life is imbalanced (e.g., all work and no play makes Jack (boy) or Jill (girl) a dull student [and human]"), simply resulting from and due directly to "catering to" and succumbing to parents, instructors, fellow student's peer pressure to study all the time and not to "waste time exercising or playing sports with the dumb athletes, who will do worse when examination time comes, because they did not devote every awake hour to studying versus exercising for each pending school examination." Shockingly, this attitude and sentiment is more common than you think or than anyone would like to admit and is a recipe for disappointment and not achieving maximum potential and success in school and life!

Which child do you think will be happier, healthier, and desire to achieve or obtain or become the longest, enduring, or near-impossible feats or recognitions of being the very best in their field or a professional in occupations in life that require academic or other advanced training that may require half their life to achieve or may only be available to the top ten percent of academic or athletic performers in school or sports, respectively! This is a rhetorical question for ninety-nine percent of readers…I hope!

5) Importance of Sleep (Cliché "8 hours per night is optimal" may or may not apply) What is true for one person may not be true for another person. Some individuals require more sleep than others to achieve maximal and 100% alert performance of activities and to have complete functional status of memory acquisition and storage of new information encountered daily. However, all children, adolescents, and adults have one thing in common: The quality of sleep that reaches deep sleep stages

(stages 3, 4, and R.E.M. sleep) determines the effectiveness, ability to learn new concepts, ability to memorize and transfer new information from short-term to intermediate-term, and ultimately to long-term memory in the brain. Fascinatingly, without daily or several times weekly vigorous aerobic exercise, an individual can reasonably expect to have impaired or non-optimal sleep, excessive anxiety, excessive depression, sub-optimal physical strength, coordination, balance, athleticism, less healthy self-esteem, and less self-confidence.

6) The Importance of Ensuring World Citizens' Safety (Decreasing Anxiety, Stress, Depression, Illegal Immigration And Human/Arms/Drugs Trafficking, Assaults, Trauma, and Murder) Via Enforced and Secure Country Border Walls, Healthy Diet, Improvements in Healthcare, and Updating Past Generations' Knowledge of Changes Necessary to Improve World Citizens Well-Being, Safety, Security, and Health, Individual's Responsibility to Perform and Constantly Update Personal Healthy Diet Research And Then Act-On And Incorporate This Up-To-Date Diet and Exercise Research Into Daily Life Routine and Schedules.

7) Concept, Paradigm, Gestalt, Credo, Philosophy (Whichever term you wish to use is acceptable.):

"One must learn to lose (with grace, humility, respect), to learn to win in life (preferably at the youngest age possible [birth and thereafter])."

Seldom mentioned but widely prevalent, with exceptions, as always, is the enlightening truth that families with multiple children, versus only one child families, may indeed find that their children learn formulas to succeed and have the most tremendous success in life with greater ease than a child with no siblings. One must wonder and contemplate why this would be true (again, with exceptions and depending on resources sought by the parents and the child, mentors, desire and exerted effort for self-improvement and education by children without siblings, and the resulting wisdom developed or attained by children without siblings), and what exactly enhances all children's and young adult's ability to achieve highly significant life lessons at an earlier age for single children and make their success potential equal to those children growing up with one or more siblings.

Myriad examples and anecdotes exist that illustrate this truth. Perhaps the "Occam's razor" principle that most vividly illustrate this truth can be summarized in one word: sports. Sports (e.g., competition between siblings and classmates in school) and public (or private, I suppose) school competitions (band "tryouts" and marching band competitions, chess club, mock (lawyer practice) trials, academic decathlons, student body officer elections, others) are perhaps the lowest risk and highest return on tangible investment activities that parents (and their children) could never hope for and wish for, especially and explicitly regarding: "One must learn to lose (with grace, humility, respect), to learn to win in life (preferably at the youngest age possible [birth and thereafter])."

A real-life account follows in the paragraph below. Imagine a family with multiple children, all with different strengths and weaknesses, some more handsome than others, some smarter than others, some not as smart but willing to work harder to "catch up" and eventually, be more intelligent than others; some "rapid bloomers" versus "slow and delayed bloomers" (e.g., horses that get out of the gate fast and run the first half of the race quickly, then slow down or maintain their speed versus other horses that get out of gate slower, gradually increase speed, and finish the fastest and strongest as the champion of the horse race), some children are introverts versus other children who are extroverts. Genius may cloak itself in any or all of these initial childhood costumes, which are later, in adult life, replaced with grown-up wardrobes and attire.

Let's get into some specifics. Imagine brothers or sisters, usually different ages although identical or fraternal twins also possible, who, at different maturity levels based on personalities, pace of development, education, and age (note that older age is not necessarily indicative of the most advanced maturity level, in kids or adults, and may be superseded by a wiser, younger, more cool, calm, collective, introspective and contemplative sibling, a.k.a., most mature sibling, by appropriate and meritorious behavior and actions), will, in fact, be better instructors (perhaps with the exceptions of an exceptional parent or parents) of life realities, revelations, teachings, realities, and realistic expectations to and for their siblings than any other relative, friend, teacher, sports coach, or any other instructor or mentor that is eventually found and able to be verified, and trusted as a mentor later in life.

Immense wisdom is derived solely from being around your siblings and interacting with them your entire life. From birth, celebrating siblings' distinct Christmas gifts, birthdays, or other honorary celebrations for their accomplishments in school, church, sports, or academic pursuits and victories teach the siblings who are being celebrated at that moment in time, how to gracefully step back into the shadows, grab the nearest spotlight and graciously shine it on that sibling being celebrated, preferably without jealousy, spite, or malice, and learning to celebrate other's achievements, irrespective of your own, perhaps lesser, achievements or failure to be victorious in a head-to-head competition with that sibling or any other friend, relative, or classmate in similar scenarios.

If a child is lucky enough, they can add exponentially to their social skills development at the earliest infant age (and competitive losses to other children column) starting in the church nursery from birth (learning bible songs and teachings), then continue to learn how to take competition losses in stride in preschool, Kindergarten, and beyond. These experiences ingrain resilience, survival, the ability to lose then win one day or week later, all invaluable life lessons that can benefit that child and adult the rest of their physical life. Depression, anxiety, discouragement, and a " non-winner" attitudes can become apparent in children and adults who fail (or failed in the past) to get out of their comfort zone and engage in competitive academics, other childhood activities and sports as young children and never learned how to be a "good loser." The definition of a "good loser" is simple and essential to know and memorize to achieve superhero status in your life endeavors and accomplishments: learning, realizing, and knowing that you are never to give up during competitions, and always should have the perspective, will, and resolve to "regroup" after each and every loss, and then be motivated, inspired, and determined to improve your future performances of the task or activity being performed at a higher and more sophisticated or accomplished level of performance from and as a result of your earnest desire to practice and work (or "workout" with regard to lifetime exercise training sessions) harder, faster, more efficiently, more effectively, and to reach winning or superhero levels of expertise or brilliance or genius status as a result. The most outstanding and remarkable performance and amazing unlimited potential of each child and eventual adult may be missed by those who have not sufficiently experienced or learned first-hand, in real time, that a loss is only one loss, in one instance, and that life goes on into eternity, long after a meaningless and insignificant (or significant, obviously more painful but unavoidable in life) loss in any category, e.g., in academics, musical, athletic, or any other performance or performances.

Chapter Twelve:

What are characteristics and traits of "Father's Eyes" that every human being and world citizen should strive to understand, demonstrate, elicit, exhibit, and share with this generation and every future generation, regardless of whether they are an actual parent (mother or father) of children? What are the admirable, eternal, and universal common and standard features and traits of those who possess and responsibly advocate for "Father's Eyes" life behavior, protection and safety of self and others, and zenith-life positive performance? What are the common traits and characteristics of outstanding fathers in this universe?

How do you define father?

A father is a male parent. Everyone has a biological father, even if they're not raised directly by him. You might call or refer to your father as Dad, Daddy, Papa, Pops, or even Father or "Father's Eyes" (for excellent reasons). A man who creates, discovers, or invents something may be called the "father" of that person, creation, entity, or other invention.

What has been the stereotype role in the past or present of the father in the field of psychology? In general, both parents are considered attachment figures in attachment theory and the child-father attachment is autonomous from the child-mother attachment. In this attachment theory and perspective, traditionally, mothers are commonly involved in caregiving and providing emotional refuge, while fathers emphasize play and exploratory undertakings. In the current era, "Father's Eyes" would generally, in an ideal world, mandate that both parents become proactively and equally involved in caregiving, providing emotional refuge, emphasizing play, adventurous and exploratory hobbies, sports, and other life experiences, provided they are well-planned, safe, character-building, confidence-building, resiliency-creating, endurance-training, health and fitness enhancing, godly, and healthy (physical, mental, social, spiritual), in nature, intent, and goal.

What is the responsibility of a father and husband? With regard to physical and financial needs, a father or "Father's Eyes" mentor and role model or role player seeks and cherishes taking on the responsibility to provide income or money and food for his children and wife. He is to ensure that there is always a functional physical (and figuratively speaking, spiritual and Godly) roof over the head of the family at all times. He is also to ensure that the family is clothed, again, physically, mentally, socially, and spiritually (e.g., wearing the armor and helmet of God in the constant, daily battles each individual in this world must fight against evil intentions, temptations, sinful peer pressure from others, drug and alcohol use (abuse), inappropriate sexual activity or behavior outside the realm of marriage between a man and a woman). In addition, the individual undertaking the role and responsibility of "Father's Eyes" or father, generally in this modern world, would be expected to pays bills such as electricity, water, phone, and internet connectivity if possible and able, although these tasks may also be shared by both husband and wife when appropriate and agreed upon, depending on each family's unique situation (e.g., if one or both parents are employed and working to accumulate income to afford and pay for necessary bills). In general, family happiness is maximized when the father avoids unnecessary or excessive luxury purchases and expenses that exceed budget guidelines and requirements or that disallow the adequate funding and maintenance of an emergency cash savings fund or reserve for future unexpected but critical or necessary expenses which may randomly rear their ugly head at the most inopportune times in life, which may also lead to arguments between family members or undue stress on the wage-earner (especially in families with only one working spouse), who may not be able to afford the (e.g., unnecessary luxury items) items that were not essential and required for family meals, health, education, and Godly lifestyle and well-being.)

What is a strong father figure?

"Father's Eyes" concept individuals or ideal fathers will protect children by intelligently and thoughtfully establishing and enforcing boundaries, consider their children's best interests, communicate effectively (e.g., strive to be what the author George Bernard Shaw referred to as a "linguistic colorist" in his masterful literary work "Pygmalion"), with every child and kindly instruct or educate them daily with lessons regarding how to be kind, responsible, ethical, moral, respectful, righteous, and God-guided in their intent, attitudes, speech, behavior, and all other various actions.

"Father's Eyes" mentoring also includes teaching children, spouses, and all human colleagues about the consequences of making wrong, immoral, unethical, evil, or otherwise sinful (in "Father's Eyes") choices and instill a sense of character development in all these individuals.

Can "Father's Eyes" mentors and fathers in all families role model healthy behaviors?

The answer is yes, absolutely! For instance, when a father accompanies one or more children on a walk, the child or children learn to enjoy walks. In a similar fashion, when a father leads by example, eats a healthy diet, abstains from alcohol use (abuse), and shuns abuse of tobacco, illicit and mind/body poisoning marijuana, or other illicit, illegal, or ill-advised drugs that are, in reality, poisons and toxic progressive killers of all body and brain cells with continued and repetitive misuse and abuse, slowly (or in some instances instantly, as is often the case with cocaine) and gradually, leading to their eventual development of psychiatric or neurologic disease diagnoses (e.g., bipolar disease, schizophrenia, anxiety, depression, alcohol or illicit drug-related progressive dementia and brain atrophy, progressive worsening, and correlating to the frequency and duration of alcohol or drug abuse), then this "Father's Eyes" mentor or father teaches and encourages, in the most effective manner possible by direct example and his own behavior, this same healthy pattern and practice of eating only healthy foods (and avoiding toxic alcoholic beverages and ill-advised, lethal illicit drug abuse), all his children how to live a healthy, Godly, drug and alcohol-free, healthy, and nutritious foods-only diet, which will benefit their brain and body in perpetuity. Godly "Father's Eyes" mentoring instructs all humans that God, when he created and allowed the birth of every human being, wishes all his creations to treat their bodies and minds as "Temples of God" (which can then be pillars of light and enlightenment to all those humans around them or in their presence and communities), keeping their bodies athletic, muscular and strong, fit, and their minds thinking clearly and praising their creator for the blessings in their lives every minute of every day and drug-free (illicit drugs) and alcohol-free, and this can and should be accomplished via learning to eat only the healthiest foods, drinking the healthiest and most nutritional beverages (e.g., matcha green tea in the morning, water, one or two cups of (polyphenol-rich) caffeinated coffee in the morning or mid-day), and through life-long participation in aerobic sports and vigorous individual exercising (e.g., a combination of rapid sequential circuit training and powerlifting, weight training, and jogging or running). It is a well-known fact that children of fathers who are "healthy diet and exercise-conscious" engage in vigorously performed aerobic sports or other exercise routines and training several times each week throughout their life, are more likely to be active, mentally and physically fit, strong, confident, emotionally stable, happier, less anxious, less depressed, and highly successful and "over-achievers," academically and in most or all other categories, regarding their endeavors attempted, goals accomplished, and dreams realized.

What Inspirational Quotes Define In Common Terms The Concept of "Father's Eyes?"

What are the common types or classification categories of different fathers?

What is a spiritual father in Christianity, and what is the difference between the Holy Spirit and God the Father?

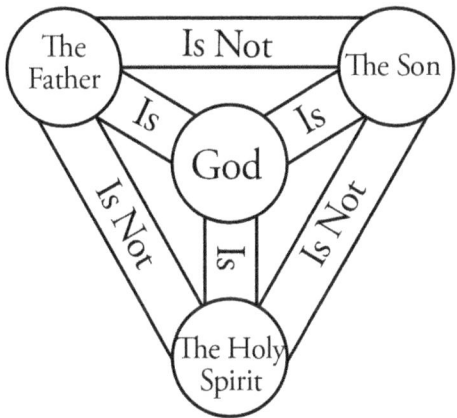

"The Father and the Son and the Holy Spirit" are not names for different parts of God, but one name for God because three persons exist in God as one entity. They cannot be separated from one another. Each person is understood as having the identical essence or nature, not merely similar natures.

What are the characteristics of the father in the Holy Trinity? As a member of the Trinity, God the Father is one with, co-equal to, co-eternal, and consubstantial with the Son and the Holy Spirit, each person being the one eternal God and in no way separated: all alike are uncreated and omnipotent. The Trinity is beyond reason and can only be known by revelation and faith by "those who have ears to hear," as so aptly and succinctly stated and sung by the amazing, Godly, American songwriter, singer, and famous Christian evangelist Keith Green.

What does it mean to worship the God the Father "in spirit"? When a "Father's Eyes" mentor or father on earth acknowledges and worships God "in spirit," this essentially means that they are giving thanks to God for his having created them and their family members (children and spouse), and this worship shall and must originate from within the heart and soul (e.g., God-shaped vacuum within every human being, that may only be filled by God in those who first acknowledge God as their creator and redeemer of their sins by faith alone, without physical proof or evidence, other than their spiritual transformation, which makes God's existence known to them, as explained in great detail in the Bible, the greatest, most-read, and most-published book ever known to, appreciated, and most respected by humanity). Worshiping God the Father "in spirit," thus, means openly displaying, demonstrating and sharing with others our love and gratitude for God and for all he is and all he has done for us, with humility and sincerity.

What role do fathers play in the development of personality and emotions? Interestingly and very predictably, higher levels of father involvement in their children's development from young ages into adulthood, are correlated with higher levels of sociability, self-confidence, and self-control in children. These same children with intimately or highly involved fathers who create sound and reasonable guidelines and limitations to ensure the safety and health of their children, and who give or demonstrate care, kindness, protection, guidance, positive affirmation, warranted or deserved reassurance and praise to their children who are making significant and remarkable progress in maturing each year and completing assigned learning tasks with outstanding results and maturing, growing, and evolving in their physical health and athleticism, mental health, social skills development, spiritual health and growth, and are also then less likely (with rare exceptions) to act out in school or engage in risky behaviors in adolescence, and thereafter as adults throughout their lives.

What influence does a father have on a child's development? Fathers definitely and without any doubt have a significant influence and effect on a child's emotional and social development while growing up from infancy to young adulthood. The child or children of a supportive and world-expanding father who encourages and pushes (figuratively and lovingly) his children to proactively volunteer for, join, and work to be the best in varied and diverse healthy activities, such as many different or distinct young children organizations (e.g., "Kiddy College" [pre-kindergarten schools], Cub Scouts, Webelos (e.g., stands for "We'll Be Loyal Scouts"), Boy Scouts of America (BSA), every possible grammar school club and sports team (e.g., chess club, ping pong club, airplanes club, academic decathlons, outdoorsmen club, jazz band, concert band, orchestra, swimming, junior lifeguard training & certification, bowling, surfing, windsurfing, rock climbing, water skiing, cross-country skiing, downhill snow skiing, "little league baseball," basketball, volleyball, flag football (e.g., non-tackle football in grammar school), apply for and compete to be a track and field multiple events participant/competitor, student government candidate and electee, chorus member, yearbook club member, school newspaper club member, to name a few examples), are assuredly and ultimately much more likely to be socially competent, create more positive friendships, be in greater control of and better able to manage and temper their emotions, be much more adventurous, more self-confident, possess a higher self-esteem level, and manifest much lower incidences of stress, anxiety, and depression.

What further defines the essence of "Father's Eyes" and makes a man a dynamic and impactful father? In simple terms, one who cares deeply and sincerely for the daily well-being of every one of his family members, one who shows and steers his children down the perhaps not shortest, safest, or risk-free path, but the most educational, adventurous, instructional, challenging, most fulfilling path that will safely, efficiently, and most effectively educate, train, and equip each child with the most valuable and relevant life skills and preparation, such that they will be able to pursue any of the most significant challenges or goals they wish and have the highest chance of success in ultimately, though painstakingly in certain situations, surmounting any obstacles in their pathway to completing the challenges they chose for themselves and victoriously realizing their dreams and accomplishing their highest and most difficult and most challenging goals for themselves in this lifetime. He works diligently and hard for the sake of education, maximum opportunities of, recreation and happiness of, and protection of his family, always striving to be the best role model and example for both his spouse and children, hoping to ensure that his family never has to suffer from the lack of opportunities to better themselves or to be deprived of the primary or common essential elements of a happy and secure, safe life, even if he, himself, has to make extraordinary sacrifices or suffer transiently to ensure these goals are met.

What qualities make a good husband and father? Dependability, trustworthiness, actively engaged in all aspects of family life all the time (to the greatest and most realistic extent possible), demonstrates self-control in his intent, attitudes, words, and actions, seeks and finds a healthy balance between his roles of being a marriage participant and being one of two (or one of one in some cases) parents of his child or children, he is and always desires to be a great role model, is a generous person and provider for the needs of his spouse and children, he desires and aspires to be a progressively wiser and more effective, accurate financial planner for the present and future of his family members, and, lastly, respects and loves his spouse's original family members (e.g., parents, siblings, and other family relatives), with sincerity, tolerance, benevolence, forgiveness, grace, mercy, and appreciation for providing him with the blessing that changed his life in a positive and uplifting manner, namely, his wife!

What are the four types of fatherhood?

Although it has been stated that there are four types of fatherhood, the author suggests that each of the below types merely focus on the negative overbearing, annoying, or negligent features that some fathers, unfortunately, may exhibit in their ungodly and incomplete fatherhood responsibilities. No father should be permanently labeled. All fathers should be afforded the hope and faith that they can always change and be better or ideal fathers if and when they seek and accept the guidance of God. God-guided and God-directed will always be blessed and made whole and complete such that they should never be mislabeled and slandered with the above (supposedly permanent stigma or derogatory title types), one through four, which are listed above. What are the characteristics of a good father?

What is the definition of an ideal father?

An "ideal father" is someone who is a "father," "friend," and "mentor", and as such, is expected and to be held accountable and responsible to work honestly and ethically, to the greatest and best extent possible, to provide the necessities (note that the word luxuries is not included in this definition) of life, including the highest quality, deep, introspective, meaningful, educational, and insightful father-child mentoring and other various interactions and interventions, when necessary or indicated, with sensitivity, affection, patience, love, and kindness How might an ideal "Father" or the concept of "Father's Eyes" be defined in several select words or phrases? Answer: protector, provider, teacher, mentor, friend, emotional stabilizer or anchor, celebrant (e.g., celebrating minor or major positive and significant events, successes, or victories instead of only being a feared or otherwise disrespected parent who is only seen by the child as being the protector, the provider, and the disciplinarian of that child, and who otherwise ignores that child and fails to celebrate each and every positive accomplishment and each step of progress that child is making in every aspect of their life, such as learning to read, increasing reading speed and comprehension, learning to be an excellent listener, overcoming stuttering, fear, anxiety, improving performance in various sports or other school and church activities or clubs, and many other achievements throughout a child's life and until their death),

Father or "Father's Eyes" individuals in our world act always toward their children, the mother of their children, and all other human beings, as protectors providing their children and others the ability and luxury of feeling safe, relaxed, and secure when their father or "Father's Eyes" are physically (or mentally, socially, spiritually) present, Outstanding fathers also open up and expand the world of their children to encompass all potential positive learning experiences and adventures that will develop courage, confidence, an adventurous spirit, athleticism, academic success, spiritual fulfillment, mental health with minimal anxiety, stress, or depression, so each child may "break out of their shy and introspective eggshell," and one day in the future, "fly out of the nest" with shrewdness, sagacity, strength, confidence, and the knowledge of how to pursue and achieve benevolent goals and success, essentially, as "Eagles" in life.

Fantastic fathers and "Father's Eyes" mentors and education principles teach and enforce healthy guidelines and discipline, ensuring values, morality, ethical, respectful, courteous, and kind behavior are both learned and employed daily by all children or other human beings, who will then have also learned to be accountable and responsible for their actions or inactions and reasonably expect to suffer negative consequences for any and all bad behavior and actions and appropriate thanks and praise for any and all good behavior and actions.

Exceptional fathers and "Father's Eyes" mentors will be enthusiastically engaged in the education, health, fitness, sports, clubs, church classes, youth groups, high school trips and all life education and training of their children with the common goal of protecting their health and fitness, ensuring the most outstanding education and wisdom development, supporting the mental and spiritual health, and alleviating and minimizing all anger, stress, anxiety, and depression in their children. Sports and team events or competitions are extremely valuable in accomplishing many of the above-stated goals, especially when engaged at the earliest age possible. Learning to prepare, train, and plan for sports, academic tests, music, and other adventures and competitions as a young child, and then repeatedly lose (and win) games or competitions as a young child, teaches priceless lessons about how to deal with adversity, disappointment, stress, anxiety, depression in life, while still maintaining a positive outlook on life by knowing that one loss is only that, one loss, and that life can be successfully improved and skills honed and perfected by repeated efforts or more vigorous or intense preparation and training to learn from losses and disappointments and then change the method or technique which one is using if found to be ineffective or unsuccessful so that the individual may enhance, improve, or perfect the next performance.

Use the words you want your children to use (e.g., never swear, for this corrupts your children)

Role model how you solve problems, make correct, wise, ethical choices, and teach "problem-solving" skills.

Lead by example (e.g., promises without fulfillment of pledges and promises by actions are meaningless)

Always maintain a positive attitude (a negative attitude is both unwise and unproductive in life)

Show your children how you want them to behave through your behavior ("stupid is as stupid does;" preferably, your children will admire and respect your good behavior instead of growing up and telling others, as an adult, that they learned how not to behave in life by observing their father or mother or both and doing the exact opposite in life, in order to achieve their success)

What are the spiritual roles of a father? Answer: "Father's Eyes" should take the lead in spiritually guiding the family and therefore neither delegate nor abrogate his responsibilities solely to the mother, although the role of providing spiritual guidance to children may be shared by both parents. He should encourage family prayer by all children and parents, participate in scripture reading with children and spouse, and encourage all children at the very earliest age possible, to practice and perfect reading skills, speed, and to increase their vocabulary by looking up in a dictionary any and all words they are not familiar with, practice memorizing the content of what they read, practice and perfect their ever-increasing vocabulary (by looking up all unknown words) and reading speed, all of which can be achieved most effectively by reading the Bible (first children's versions, then adult versions such as the "New International Version of the Bible"), cover to cover, as many times as possible and as early as possible in life. This will bring the blessings of unparalleled wisdom and Godly behavior to each child at the earliest age and allow them to excel in academic school classes and be ethical, moral, spiritual, Godly role models for all their friends and classmates, and colleagues for the remainder of their long and God-blessed life on this earth!

What is a spiritual father? A spiritual father comes alongside another human in love, helps that human find and follow Jesus, and is there for that human as that individual learns to love, serve, and give (versus hate, take, and steal) in this life to achieve Godly behavior and limitless happiness in life.

13 If I speak in the tongues of men or of angels, but do not have love, I am only a resounding gong or a clanging cymbal. **2** If I have the gift of prophecy and can fathom all mysteries and all knowledge, and if I have a faith that can move mountains but do not have love, I am nothing.

3 If I give all I possess to the poor and give over my body to hardship that I may boast, but do not have love, I gain nothing.

4 Love is patient, love is kind. It does not envy, it does not boast, it is not proud. **5** It does not dishonor others, it is not self-seeking, it is not easily angered, it keeps no record of wrongs. **6** Love does not delight in evil but rejoices with the truth. **7** It always protects, always trusts, always hopes, always perseveres.

8 Love never fails. But where there are prophecies, they will cease; where there are tongues, they will be stilled; where there is knowledge, it will pass away. **9** For we know in part, and we prophesy in part, **10** but when completeness comes, what is in part disappears. **11** When I was a child, I talked like a child, I thought like a child, I reasoned like a child. When I became a man, I put the ways of childhood behind me. **12** For now we see only a reflection as in a mirror; then we shall see face to face. Now I know in part; then I shall know fully, even as I am fully known.

13 And now these three remain: faith, hope and love. But the greatest of these is love.

What is the role of and what are the essential or all-important responsibilities or traits of an ideal father (e.g., "Father's Eyes")?

Answer: Responsibilities or traits include: kindness, nurturing, spending quality time to bond with each distinct child, and most critical, without distractions, openly and generously expressing love in ways or by methods that are healthy, ethical, moral, supportive, and always, whenever possible, positive, even during periods of discipline or reprimand that will be necessary intermittently, modeling good fitness, a healthy diet, healthy lifestyle, and appropriate (mild, moderate, or severe) reactions to surprises (good and bad), and irresponsible, selfish, or otherwise unacceptable or ungodly behavior, or in any other scenario or circumstance when help is needed by a child, demonstrating an understanding, caring, graceful, merciful, forgiving perspective and attitude in communications with a child's mother and all children within the family.

Chapter Fifteen:

The Quintessential Importance of Discovering Enlightened And Wise Mentors, Godly And Faithful Friends, Siblings, Neighbors, and Community Members Who Are Motivated And Superb Role Models With High Aspirations And Altruistic Life Perspectives, Mentors Whose Goal Is To Live Their Life On Earth In A Fantastic And Godly Manner That Emulates The Life of Jesus Christ, Creating Life Satisfaction And Happiness That Exceeds All Human Expectations On Earth And Leads Ultimately to Inspiration Which Bring Tears of Joy to "Father's Eyes" God, And All Family Member "World Citizens" and All "God's Children" Whom God Created With Equal Value, Worth, And Unlimited God-Inspired and God-Directed Potential For Greatness In This Life and Universe.

Below are enlightening and God-inspired selected excerpts, chapters, and insights from a remarkable and life-changing masterpiece nonfiction novel by a truly and genuinely gifted and Godly author, who blesses this generation and all future generations of humanity with his poignant, awakening, motivational and inspirational observations, recommendations, and spiritual health and life aspirations, intentions, and wishes for benevolent enhancements in human interactions to bolster and create a world in which all God's children are known to have equal value and worth as "World Citizens" of God's Kingdom with unlimited potential for happiness and life fulfillment, William Andrew Maximus Wallace, "Two Boy's Amazing, Inspiring Journey."

Chapter One – Early Days in Small Town America and the Origin of American Community Values.

One cool evening in January 1966 in a small town in California, a small miracle occurred. The captain of the men's swim team met the fastest and most capable woman on the women's swim team. This unlikely meeting would have great meaning months later.

Luke was about to be born minutes before midnight. Luke was prevented from being delivered and born on time because he was forbidden by both his mother and her obstetrician. It seems, in retrospect, almost but not quite acceptable.

You see, Luke's mother was about to have her dream come true: delivering her baby boy on her birthday! Yet this could only be accomplished via subverting Luke's original plan and intention to be born immediately when ready. Instead, Luke was prevented from being born for four or more minutes until his mother's birthday arrived at 12 midnight. Luke's first challenge in life was getting to and beginning his life with a first breath after a swift slap to Luke's buttocks, and life on earth began with his first breath of oxygen, four or more minutes later than Luke's (and God's) original plan and destiny.

Luke was just four years old.

Two years earlier, he had the distinct pleasure of entering preschool with his older brother, Peter. Preschool was Cambridge and Oxford to Luke and his brother, for at this age, prestigious institution names were not important or meaningful. The opportunity to learn and begin writing on our "tabula rasa," our intellectual awakening or birthing moment had commenced. Peter, while quiet and reserved, had a voracious appetite for learning and reading as many new books as possible in the preschool library and, on weekends, the library across the street from our small, rented home in the small, sleepy central California town where time, even now, stands constant and hidden from the continuum that rapidly changes other parts of this world. Comforting in a way, this town can be relied upon to provide a stable and safe place to raise children and move into the home you build several city blocks or a few miles from your parent's home who can always be relied upon as the most faithful and economical babysitters for growing children of nascent married couples. The neighborhood is predominantly hard-working, honorable, honest,

God-fearing and God-respecting citizens often mischaracterized by more radical and left-leaning extremists as "blue-collar, gun-toting, country folk." Farmers, dairy owners, industrial workers, athletes, scholars, business persons, and other professionals all sprout from this tiny town, a sort of incubator for diversity in imagination, motivation, and innovation to embrace all the world has to offer, then to change, influence, and mediate world affairs as grown adults. Being raised in modest, small, obscure American towns with traditional values of respecting God, family, and country and treating other humans as you wish to be treated, including mercy, grace, second/third/fourth chances if necessary, make these small towns incubators for great leaders. Humble and respectful leaders who derive from such small towns are constantly replenishing the constant need for great leaders throughout this great country, in large metropolis areas as they migrate out from small towns and, for those who stay local or migrate to other small towns, they positively impact all those around them whilst pursuing the American Dream, deeply ingrained in them by their parent's values and beliefs of hard work and earning honest wages to advance your development and maturation as a Christian or other religion which supports equality and respect for all humans, the result of be given, as a long-term infinite loan, to God and the church community during the first 18 years of their upbringing. After high school, these small-town wonders are confident and aware of their worth, value, and uniqueness, created in the image of God, then enter the workplace or institutions of trade learning or higher educational institutions/universities with a zeal for self-improvement and enlightenment via first climbing up to, then standing on the shoulders of enlightened world citizens who acquired wisdom, knowledge, hardships and heartbreaks long before them then, as a gift from heaven, were anointed into positions of teachers, educators, and professors. As many have said in the past, among the noble professions are teaching, God-inspired and directed Church leaders, medical professionals, local leaders, good co-workers and town/city citizens who are selfless and generous with their time and assistance and nurturing behavior. By this definition, all professions, individuals, and citizens have the potential to be noble. With nobility, however, comes great responsibility. Individuals may be identified throughout the world each day who, though not irredeemable or hopeless, have lost their way and betrayed the innate goodness and Godliness that is in them from birth. These individuals may betray their unique God-inspired goodness and, instead, choose to divide and deceive others or cheat and manipulate others to achieve their selfish, greedy or other evil desires and maleficent goals or aspirations. Some individuals even believe, misguidedly, that they may change the sex that God gifted to them and intended for them to retain and be proud of the entirety of their life. How arrogant and misguided, though still loved by God in every way, are those individuals who errantly believe that God created them but assigned them the incorrect sex that they must now change in order to be happy. Happiness derives not from changing one's sex or pretending to be someone you are not, but rather from embracing and accepting that God created you exactly as intended and will always support, love, and protect you so that you become the amazing person God intended you to be.

The astonishing, priceless, and irreplaceable gift one derives from community living, whether it be in a large metropolis, medium-sized city/suburb, or small towns throughout the world (universe?) and especially in the melting pot we call the United States of America (U.S.A.) is the diversity of religious values/beliefs, perspectives, and problem-solving skills, which may be radically different yet equally unique, innovative, and creative solutions to community enigmas and common interests/desires that, through teamwork, can benefit the community at large. Atheists, agnostics, and myriad God-centered religions worldwide exist in all communities, large, medium, and small. Seemingly shocking, obtuse, cutting, or biting perspectives and difference of opinions in communities demand that each individual evaluate whether their individual ideas, philosophies, religion, world/universe perspective are merely acquired or derived by parental guidance (not a bad thing if manners, respect for others, compassion, mercy, and grace are taught by parents at home) or indeed examined through deep introspection and accepted based on the individual's personal research, search for truth, and religious faith, which is personal and intimate with God. Pascal, the genius mathematician, was an avid gambler, alcohol and tobacco abuser as a young man until he had a near-death experience (better late than never), at which time he sought out a deep and meaningful trust contract with God, whom he could neither see nor touch but only communicate with via faith in God. No mathematical theorem or formula could prove God's existence, and this genius mathematician knew this. Yet through sheer brilliance, Pascal derived/arrived at the following obvious conclusions: God exists, God is real, and God is outside of our finite concept of time (past, present, future) and rather exists in all times, seeing all past, present, future simultaneously, God is omnipotent, omnipresent, and omniscient, and God can only be acknowledged, accepted, and recognized by having faith in that which is unseen. Faith in God's existence is the only path to a personal relationship with God. In a book entitled Pascal's Pensées, written by French 17th-century child prodigy/genius who was educated by his father, a tax collector in Rouen, who blossomed into a young adult with many titles and accomplishments, not usually confined to one man: philosopher, physicist, mathematician, inventor, writer and Catholic theologian Blaise Pascal. Pascal's religious conversion led him to a life of asceticism, and his Pensées were the culmination of his genius insight into our temporary existence on this planet Earth and God's omnipotence, omnipresence, omniscience, total protection, compassion, grace and mercy that God grants and bestows on all his creations, namely, humankind. Pascal's Wager was Pascal's solution to convince his most atheist or agnostic (pre-conversion to Christianity) gambling and carousing cohort of friends and acquaintances to deeply consider the true peace that comes from having a personal relationship with God. Pascal's Wager was as follows: Choices and Consequences For Gamblers and Others (e.g., the wager): A) Believe there is no God (atheist) or Be Unsure of God's Existence (agnostics) or B) Believe in God's Existence. The wager, interpreted by Pascal's friends, must be contemplated to assess the risk of each bet and the potential odds for winning the bet to achieve the most desirable outcome for the risk being taken and to limit the downside or loss of value or loss of life or loss of the object(s) put up for collateral in the bet or wager being placed by the gambler. Pascal explained, in his famous "Pascal's Wager," and in great detail his odds analysis for the choices being made in whether to wager that God does not exist or to believe that God does exist, and the consequences of each wager included the risks, benefits, and potential for eternal damnation versus eternal loving relationship with God. "Pascal's Wager" was, for Pascal, an intellectual gambler's analysis to convert his friends to Christianity so they could experience that same inner peace Pascal had after his conversion experience. For Pascal, any individual in this world who could know and have faith in the existence of God who created them and loves them, could also realize the inner peace that Pascal had for the remainder of his life. Pascal desired that all his friends and acquaintances could have the inner peace that he had as a Christian and as a result of knowing that an omnipresent, omniscient, omnipotent God loves, guides, and protects him. Pascal Wager, concisely, to friends was that if you wager: A) If you believe there is no God, live irresponsibly, selfishly, evil, etc. and then die and there is no God or heaven or hell, then you derive only the satisfaction that your guess was right, which will never be realized by you because you died and cannot celebrate your lucky guess. B) If you believe there is no God, when in fact, God does exist, and then you die, then you realize the worst-case scenario: your lack of faith in God and unscrupulous and evil life of immorality, selfishness, greed, conceit, or other otherwise malevolent behavior toward friends and family will ultimately result in your eternal damnation in hell or purgatory or simply not gaining acceptance or entry into heaven or an eternity in the presence of God, your savior and the one who created you from the day you were conceived and born in this world. C) Believe and have faith in the existence of God. If you live a righteous and moral life (e.g., "The Ten Commandments" and other myriad wise teachings of Jesus Christ in the Bible) and then you die. If there is no God, then you could theoretically be disappointed that you were wrong, but never realize this because you died before you found out. However, while dying you have peace and satisfaction in knowing that as a result of your following and abiding by God-guiding principles and your ethical, moral, righteous behavior toward fellow humans you encountered, you experience the serenity that results from being a humble, modest, loving member of the world and positively impacted all those around you as a result of believing in God. If there is a God, when you die, you live in eternal harmony and love in heaven with the God who created, guided, and nurtured your journey through life. Pascal's Wager would then conclude, in his discussion with his friends, that even a gambler who embraces atheism or is an agnostic would be best to gamble on the existence of God. God rejoices in those who have faith in God and live their life accordingly as modeled by the life of Jesus Christ and his teachings in the Bible.

The United States of America is a unique country. "In God We Trust" (new national motto since 1956) and "E Pluribus Unum (Latin for "out of many, one"; or more loosely translated as: "one from many")" (the U.S.A. National Motto pre-1956), are both printed on various U.S.A. currency and are both symbolic and thematic for the belief in the possibility of diversity of thought, culture, religion, and the perspective of individuals in this world, yet the unity of all diverse people who choose to become citizens of this country. For instance, Christianity guided and directed the founding fathers of the United States of America in completing the Declaration of Independence from Britain and the Constitution with the Bill of Rights and constitution amendments, which allowed these inspired and pivotal masterpieces/master plans to accept and adapt to future eras, allowing for progress and refining of these broad precepts as time elapses and changes are necessary. While the early United States of America (U.S.A.) struggled as a nascent republic for the people, by the people, and of the people, diversity was the key to adopting guidelines that incorporated and respected diverse and different religions and values in a symbiotic and peaceful manner.

Peter was 18 months older than Luke. Peter was born in northern California in the hospital where his father and paternal grandmother were born. His first son's status was a privileged position, and, as such, the first son was spoiled rotten by his grandparents and their friends, relatives, and other acquaintances. His celebrity status was certain and sure, at least until his younger brother arrived on the scene 18 months later and thereafter arear. After Peter acclimatized to northern California, where his father completed university studies in English in route to obtaining a teaching credential, and Peter's mother completed occupational therapy postgraduate internship training programs, his father distributed resumes in a shotgun fashion to pursue his American Dream of teaching at the high school level and raising a God-fearing/respecting/loving family in a small or large city, wherever and with whoever would endorse and support his career aspirations. Shortly after the father and mother married and had their first son, Peter, in northern California, they embraced the offer to live with the father's parents to allow both young new parents to complete their professional education and for the benefit of the grandparents to bond with Peter. My father took a job with the Fuller Brush Company selling door-to-door company products while awaiting job offers for a high school teaching position in California. Mother completed postgraduate occupational therapist internships at various hospitals in California and sent out job applications in towns where father was applying for teaching jobs. Every day was exciting, seeing job application responses return to the mailbox and teaching Peter to read, speak, and ambulate during his infancy. Father's parents took a great interest in gardening and had a beautiful home in Oakland Hills, California. Their home and garden were featured in the magazine "Home and Garden." Father developed a life-long passion for outside yard and garden work as a result of the passion his own father (Peter's paternal grandfather) had for these hobbies. Peter's great-grandfather was president of the American Fuchsia Society (perhaps this is a D.N.A. thing). Peter developed a love for dogs in his grandparents' home during his infancy after giving and receiving love from their Dalmatian dog, who was a beautiful, loving, and gentle dog that would have made any firetruck and fire station proud to pose with their fire station vehicles (Dalmatian dogs in days past posed with fire station vehicles in paintings and advertisements).

Chapter 3 – Soul Brothers:

The Melding of Hearts, Minds, Spirits and Eternal Best Friends and Moses Years Luke was a surprise. Who (other than God) knew this gift would be mother's most unique birthday gift ever? A happy (and exhausting) birthday indeed. Peter was thrilled to have a playmate and partner in crime (not literally) at last! Peter's mother was thrilled and delighted that now, with two sons, she could accept handed-down clothes from her older sister, Angelica, who had four children: two sons and two daughters, which could then be worn by her two children. Peter and Luke's mother's older sister was as loving and saintly as their mother was, "two peas in a pod," you might say. Angelica was raised along with Peter and Luke's mother in a small town in New Hampshire with two brothers. Angelica, Peter and Luke's mother's older sister, attended the University of Southern California (U.S.C.) University after graduating from high school and was a pre-medicine major. She taught dance at U.S.C. (for spending money while in university), an opportunity she was afforded due to her having been an excellent dancer in high school, and taught Peter and Luke's future mother and their mother's fraternal twin brother to dance as partners while they were in high school leading to many dance competition championship titles for Peter and Luke's mother and her fraternal twin brother in high school. A dynamic dance duo to be reckoned with, indeed!

Luke's adventure began with a slap on the buttocks and a momentary cry for freedom (and relief!) Luke was and is not a frequent crier, following in his older brother's footsteps in this respect and myriad other respects throughout life. Luke followed in Peter's glide path and in his trail-blazing dynamic wind draft, cruising through life on the trails prepared and arduously forged by his pioneer older brother Peter. Luke enjoyed, right or wrong, the privilege of seeing what mistakes (these were few and far between for Peter) and consequences Peter would have to endure after his pioneering path through life and negotiations that he engaged in on a daily basis with mother and father. Having a pioneer older brother can be a blessing or curse, depending on whether the older brother is angelic or saint-like or hero role model or a discontented, rebellious demagogue or disobedient rabble-rouser. With regard to Peter, he is the closest example I have known in this world to reaching angelic, "superhero" role-model or saint-like status as both a brother and best friend. Some saints suffer tremendous hardship in this life and world, which only sharpens their resolve and faith, allowing them to further hone in on what is truly important in this life and strengthening their dependence on and loving/nurturing/trusting relationship with God, who they acknowledge and accept has only allowed them to endure such hardship in this life because their omnipotent, omniscient, and omnipresent God "has their back" and ultimately has a masterplan for their life to inspire and motivate others in this world, then enjoy eternal life with God thereafter.

As Peter and Luke became acquainted, they realized immediately that they were destined to become not just brothers who liked each other and could function as a very close and effective team navigating through the wild kingdom that we call life, but also soulmates in the truest sense of the word. What a blessing this revelation is to both Peter and Luke. While not twins in reality, functionally Peter and Luke have immediate twin potential even though they are not the same age, but rather as a result of their same likes, dislikes, interests, reverence for and of God, and God's role in shaping who they are and who they will develop into in this world/universe, and in the love and respect they both have for their parents whilst realizing they will never be perfect or sinless (just as all humans will disappoint but should never be discarded or abandoned for imperfections), and knowing that all humans display (unlike Jesus Christ, who was, is, and will be the only flawless role model and sinless and perfect martyr for humans' redemption of their sins in this life), sins in their life regardless of who they are.

As a child, Peter set the standard for responsible and reverent childhood behavior and obedience, which Luke could only hope (or dream) to emulate. Talk about a hard act to follow… Peter set **the standard**… with only one exception, which is both humorous and bold, again displaying his first/oldest son pioneer status and preeminence. As a sixth-grade student, Peter was the model and brilliant, if not a genius, student and beyond reproach. He was singled out one day in class by his Mormon teacher and told that his punishment would be coming into the classroom and being read [by the teacher] the Book of Mormons during Peter's lunch break, which in fact did occur, much to Peter's chagrin, as Peter was raised in the Presbyterian Church as a protestant Christian. Peter proceeded in a future classroom session to strategically place a thumb tack in the sharp end upright position on this Mormon homeroom teacher's chair, which was effective, e.g., the mission was successfully implemented and an utterly successful mission indeed! Luke was not as thrilled with the tremendous success of this covert mission of his older brother Peter when Luke found that his homeroom teacher the following year would be this same teacher whose idea of student punishment was reading the Book of Mormons to students during their recreation or lunch breaks.

Luke somehow persevered and successfully navigated this minefield and uncomfortable situation the entire next year, when he had this same "homeroom" teacher for 365 days (after the thumb tack attack mission had been completed one year prior by his soulmate brother, Peter)!

Peter throughout his grammar (elementary) school years (kindergarten to grade 8 (13 years old)) spent most of his otherwise unscheduled Saturday mornings sitting in the library across the street in the children's books section, reading (literally) every single book in that library's childrens' books section. Luke, in contrast, preferred to ride his bike or big wheel (remember this coolest ever predominately all-plastic 3-wheel children's toy vehicle…awesome fun!) on most otherwise unscheduled Saturdays (definition of "otherwise unscheduled Saturdays": after Peter and Luke finished their house cleaning assignments, e.g., dusting, mopping or vacuuming, or finished their outside assigned yard work, e.g., weeding (with a "hula ho") or irrigation of the orchard, and other tasks assigned in the backyard by their father. Father enjoyed his two sons "willingness" (not much choice in the matter, to be honest) and effort in spending thousands (perhaps actually tens of thousands of hours) of hours, with much sweat on the brow, in "erecting his many pyramids to appease his impeccable garden and yard deity." It was not until much later in our childhood that "Moses and Moses II arrived in the forms of a paper delivery route and a landscaping/lawn mowing gig (both wrapped in a cloth and sent adrift in a basket down the river, of course) to emancipate two young Egyptians." Luke took a substitute role to the neighbor's oldest boy, Mit, who was in possession of the local city paper, the Onsreef Hornet, paper delivery business in our small town, Notsaeville. The population of Notaseville was modest, with less than 2400 people. As children in a very small town, Peter and Luke came to learn early on, that secrets are akin to the Holy Grail and a unicorn. As any young children would be inclined, the local Jiffy Mart was a popular destination for young entrepreneurs to spend their great wealth (was it 50 cents allowance per Saturday for a half day's chores of mopping all floors and vacuuming all room carpets, then dusting all furniture (payment only and ever made by Peter and Luke's mother and never by "Pharoah," incidentally). Again, and to emphasize this all-important observation and glaring and disappointing realization and fact, no payment or allowance was ever disbursed for the yeoman's work performed Monday through Sunday for thousands of hours by Pharoah (Peter and Luke's father) to his pyramid-building laborers (Peter and Luke), as this was assumed (by the Pharoah) to be the work of joyful and grateful subjects, Peter (a.k.a., Moses) and Luke (a.k.a., Moses II). Any savings accumulated by these two young boys were promptly "invested" in assets that would ensure immediate gains in the form of satisfaction (e.g., Icee flavored ice drinks, bubble gum, baseball trading cards, Abba-Zaba candy bars and mint candy fake cigarettes) and recreational distraction (new "asteroids and Scrambler video game machines controlled with joysticks where you fly through space destroying meteorites and asteroids or other impediments or aliens shooting at you while protecting their city from your spaceship's attempted attacks, remember these miraculous inventions for children) from their otherwise quite serious duties and responsibilities as servants and garden/groundskeepers initially at what was affectionately called the "Old Manse" (home rented to father by

Presbyterian church owner in exchange for church maintenance, door-locking, church security/surveillance duties, and other tasks; the pastor of the church had preferred and selected a more modern home, not far away in the community). After being raised in the "old manse" from 1966-1975, the family moved into a castle which was both designed and constructed with the help of a local city architect by Peter and Luke's mother and father. The rental home (bought from a math teacher father worked with at the local high school and a gift to mother and father as sort of "wedding present" to the young, fiscally strapped couple, aka newlyweds, was from Peter and Luke's father's parents) was eventually sold to fund the new construction of Peter and Luke's new "castle" (more modern style home which was the result of many frugal years of living and earnestly working and saving money whenever possible to build this new home). Castle in the sense that now the chores of Peter and Luke now not only included going over each evening after school to the festive activities of the castle construction grounds to joyfully participate with our parents in "cleaning up after the construction crews after they had left to have relaxing evenings with their families, but no such luck for the future castle dwellers. This so-called "castle" that we eventually moved into March 5, 1975, was like any other dwelling in a tiny country town except in the sense, most deeply felt and painfully experienced for years to come by Peter and Luke, that castles are larger, more grandiose, and more spacious (unfortunately) with more floors to mop, rooms requiring vacuuming of carpets, and items to dust, all to be "joyfully accomplished or completed" every week by young Peter and Luke, thus Peter and Luke's "castle"…brought to mind, in a weird and warped sort of way, the cliché "To those who are afforded much power and privilege is also the burden of much responsibility." In short, this best defines our new "castle" in 1975. Of course, the "castle" had a larger (one-quarter acre) garden and castle grounds area to maintain, oh the joy and splendor in the grass, fully experienced in thousands of hours of bliss with "hula hoe" and irrigation shovel in hands at all times during indentured servant activity time in the castle grounds' front and back yard and garden areas. Perhaps, in retrospect, the many thousands of hours in indentured servant activities that Peter and

Luke were assigned to complete by "Pharoah to his faithful Egyptian Slave Subjects", indeed, kept them from more devious and delinquent activities that many of their schoolmates engaged in, as idle youth with too much freedom and unoccupied hours entice their prey to activities such as excess eating without requisite balanced and equal exercise, underage and premarital sexual activity, experimentation with smoking, alcohol abuse, and other illicit substance abuse. Peter and Luke would wait years for their emancipation and symbolic proclamation of freedom and independence in the truest sense of these words, specifically until the plagues vanquished the Pharoah and loosed young Peter and subsequently Luke, to cross the Red Sea into the promised land, also known as college or university.

Chapter 4 – Community Activities and The Church Family and Childhood Vices and Temptations.

All small or tiny country towns share one common denominator: the shaping and development of its inhabitants in the first two decades and the moral belief system that is ingrained into these individuals is and will be forever a part of who they become and what aspirations they pursue, including the inspiration and motives they develop to accomplish their goals. While no individuals from these small country towns are infallible, somehow they depart and disperse into the world with a heightened and enlightened sense of who they are, from birth and beyond, and, more importantly, who they should be as a result of being raised in the local Church and being known and raised by each and every community member, in a sense, that occurs for better or worse in tiny towns. Again, secrets in such towns are akin to "The Holy Grail" and unicorns. The local store owners in the community may remember, for instance, when young children attempt and then quickly abandon a career or life of crime or substance abuse in children who are actually classmates of their own children. For better or worse, subtle or more often than not, widespread rumors (truths disguised in vagaries and paucity of details in many cases) then spread and reputations are then formed which, if reinforced with repeated bad behavior, may ultimately label individuals in that community with quite sticky post-it notes to and on these individuals' foreheads. The the joy of small-town living. At the same time, these seemingly innocuous events and life experiences shape the values of not only these young children being raised by and in the community but of the community itself. Small town inhabitants are constantly and instantly being scrutinized, and behavioral modification is subconsciously and often overtly being instituted on a daily basis. For instance, young impressionable children might happen to find a local town's mechanic shop and discover a magazine in that business, say in the restroom, which displays the opposite sex in new and revealing ways that the child possibly, as yet, has neither seen nor thought about in that less-than-innocent way. When that child or those children then frequent that restroom excessively for the next few weeks or months, depending on how savvy that merchant is, to further explore such magazines with evocative photographs, that business owner then forms an impression that may or may not stick (e.g., as a post-it note, figuratively speaking) to that child's or those children's heads, again who are the classmates of that business owner's own child or children. This is how small town America works. What's more is that, in small towns, since everybody knows everybody, successes, and mistakes or bad/evil deeds are greatly magnified, and scrutinized like a gram-negative rod-shaped bacterium (let's say E. coli for this example) under a microscope slide under the 40x ocular lens. You may, in small towns, be among the most gifted trumpet musicians in the country, as was Peter, and only be regarded by home community members as "that boy who practices so many hours and makes all that noise" by neighbors or, when performing at the high school band show concert, scrutinized after selecting the most challenging, complex, and difficult composition or piece of music to perform (e.g., "Carnival of Venice" for the trumpet) and then unfavorably reviewed or compared to other performers at the same concert who purposely selected simple music compositions or performance selections (think "Somewhere Over The Rainbow," a melody that all community members recognize and appreciate for its simplicity rather than the technical expertise and difficulty demonstrated by a trumpet player introducing the "Carnival of Venice" for the first time to the audience who often shuns any new or unfamiliar music compositions, especially when the performance of these compositions is exceptionally complex and of the highest level of technical difficulty to perform flawlessly (as was always the situation with Peter and Luke's musical performances of new, complex, and unknown, at least to the audience, musical compositions), right or wrong.

Neighborhood families became best friends and second to infinity homes that we "owned" (or at least occupied with great frequency and enjoyment) and spent the most hours possible at or in during our youth. It is these bonds of friendship and trust with neighbors and friends in small communities that are most valuable, if not priceless. These relationships involved seeing an individual's development from young children to young adults, including all the exposed and embarrassing moments, along with the teaching moments or peer-to-peer competitions, which inevitably teaches individuals (hopefully at young children ages) the so-called: "thrill of victory (always through earnest and staunchly devoted dedication and thousands of hours of practice [to be a champion, that is… let's not fool ourselves by thinking otherwise]) and, conversely, the agony of defeat."

Peter was a miler. He excelled at the one-mile race distance. He also excelled and was accomplished in the long jump and the high jump (preferring the Dick Fosbury [1968 Mexico Summer Olympics Gold Medalist] "Fosbury Flop" to the Western roll technique after adequate trials and research as to the effectiveness of both methods to achieve his goal of becoming champion of this sport). Luke participated in the same sports as Peter with similar prowess and success, but not quite or entirely up to the level of his older brother. Luke became interested in life-long running as a result of his local Presbyterian pastor. When both Pastor Black and Pastor Cast left our local church to pastor other churches assigned to them by the Presbytery, a life-long friendship blossomed with our family and the new pastor and his family. The new Presbyterian Church pastor had two grown sons (e.g., adults) and two young, adopted daughters, one daughter who was just older than Peter and the other daughter who was the same age as Peter and attended grammar and high school, along with Peter and Luke. We would spend countless holidays together with endless hours of fellowship and playing card games such "Uno" and others. One of Luke's most memorable if not in the same sense darkest or most dangerous moments at the pastor's home, our neighbor and closest of family friends, was when he almost accidentally burned down their home. Of course, a detailed explanation of this event is necessary. Having purchased fireworks, illegal in our town at this time, from a neighbor (a much older student who was in high school), including items such as "Firecrackers, M80s, and Cherry Bombs" (all of which had the potential to severely damage or destroy a finger, mailbox, or toilet if misplaced in these locations, do not ask me how I might have become aware of these facts…these were darker days in my childhood, which were fleeting but at the same time memorable and exciting moments and experiences, few and far between, in tiny country towns, like the small town that Peter and Luke grew up in. Other moments of youthful indiscretion which were similarly fleeting and brief (two days over two weeks to my recollection) were trying to smoke cigarettes obtained from the older brother of one of my Mexican schoolmates in grammar school, hiding behind bushes briefly on the way to and before school started in the morning on the neighborhood Lutheran church grounds (ironic, of all clandestine sites to pick, we chose a church as the site of our planned rebellion and iniquity experimentation, dually agreed upon as the most convenient site by both of us to meet and engage in our unwise and health-destroying experimentation phase of childhood stupidity). Suffice it to say, to this day, neither Peter nor Luke became smokers. My father engaged in a somewhat risky but very instructive activity which cemented, in both Peter and Luke's minds, that smoking is scary and destructive and leads to a path ending in ruins. The Barnburns were a married couple who lived adjacent to the one small drugstore that served our whole town. They were very simple and somewhat pleasant people who, unfortunately, whether the result of a harsh life journey or poor parental education and guidance regarding the value of exercise and healthy living (aka learning from other's mistakes to avoid patterns of behavior that are self-destructive to one's health and lead to ruins), both became morbidly obese and chain smokers with end-stage chronic obstructive pulmonary disease and emphysema. Father would often take us to talk with them briefly after church services concluded on Sundays, truly frightening experiences but very instructive (these were not random visits planned by Father but rather experiences meant to scare the living daylights out of Peter and Luke so they would **never** smoke, drink alcohol, or stop exercising and eating healthy and right to avoid having this married couple as mentors for extremely unhealthy and unhappy (or at least sad) future). To this day, both Peter and Luke have the following scene permanently etched into our minds' eyes: The Barnburns, a married husband and wife couple, were morbidly obese (guessing 300 pounds each) and sat daily, all day, at the kitchen table with a clear view of the television in the living room, each with a six-foot-tall green metal oxygen tank to the side of each individual (placed at the ends of the kitchen table), with Oxygen facemasks and attached plastic tubing leading from each metal tank to the nose and face of each married couple member. They would converse with Peter and Luke's father, Peter. and Luke with their O2 masks on, then transiently, say every 20-30 minutes, remove their masks after turning off the oxygen flow from their individual oxygen tanks to smoke one to two cigarettes, every 20-30 minutes, and unfortunately, around the clock 24 hours per day. There, now you have the same image in your head as Peter and Luke had about: smoking, drinking, and consequences (potential) of not eating right and exercising until the 6-foot cedar (why not… smells excellent) or other wood box or chest one day houses your lifeless physical body/being and divine powers transport your spirit/soul to the cedar chest warehouse in the sky (heaven), where life begins afresh with your creator. At that time, only audio recordings were made of church service sermons (video recorders not yet in existence) and deacons, elders, and Steven's (the apostle) Ministry members of the Presbyterian Church would volunteer to take recordings to members throughout the community who were unable (or unwilling to attend church in person) to get to services on Sundays or to special musical concerts or holiday cantata performances or special guest lecturers speaking at our church or, in special cases, at other local churches/denominations (e.g., Lutheran, Baptist or Catholic churches) in our small but religiously mighty, caring, compassionate, empathetic and faithful town. People in this small town truly cared about each other and watched out for each other. Though diverse people with sundry religious beliefs, everyone functions as part of the community and in a cooperative manner through participation in school events, sports, business relationships and unwritten or written contracts with the community to supply goods (e.g., farm, dairy, produce) or services to the community which were required or desired.

Chapter 5 – A Year Characterizing and Prototypical Of Life in Small Town (e.g., 1400 people) America for Best Friends and Brothers One Year Difference In Age But Of Identical Mindset, Work Ethic, and Ambition for Achieving Success In Life Without Limits.

Traditional American Holidays are most special and memorable in small American towns and communities. Why? Because in small communities, everyone knows their neighbors and learns to live with, interact with, and peacefully coexist with their neighbors and coworkers because instead of "six degrees of separation," there likely is "1-to 3 degrees of separation" in small communities, figuratively and literally. This a reference to: "I read somewhere that everybody on this planet is separated by only six other people," Stockard Channing says in a 1993 (the same year Luke graduated from medical school as a young adult) movie that only "six degrees of separation exist between us and everyone else on this planet. The president of the United States, a gondolier in Venice, just fill in the names." The concept was originally outlined and set forth in a 1929 short story by the author Frigyes Karinthy, whereby a group of individuals engage in a game of sorts in which they attempt to connect each person in the world to themselves by a link of five others. The idea was further popularized in 1990 in a play entitled, "Six Degrees of Separation" by John Guare. In other words, the theory or concept is that all human beings in the world are just six or fewer social connections away from one another and thus intimately connected as fellow human beings and, in abstract terms, "relatives." Some people have argued further that "six degrees of separation" does indeed exist, however, not through just friends but via people's random interactions and acquaintances, which are the key to this concept or theory.

The Siwel family amply demonstrates this concept or theory and Peter and Luke both would argue that only one (or more) such family(ies) become an anchor during life storms and transitions in world calamities and ultimately are the "Super Glue" that unites and harmonizes interactions between members of small towns that is not only priceless in value but the birthplace of confidence and sense of self-worth that emanates and blooms via a miraculous metamorphosis in young children in grammar school and early high school years, e.g., Peter and Luke, enabling their transformation into loving, generous, honest, altruistic, responsible, God-fearing/respecting adults that then enter the treacherous adult world with ambitions and motivation to transform the world into the best world (planet Earth and all galaxies included) of generosity and respect and kindness to self and others that God intended during the creation of the Earth.

Let's explore how one family in a community can interweave fantastic morals, family values, teamwork, kindness, tolerance, Godly values, respect and reverence for God, and a sense of relatedness in their community, and then intimately interconnect members of their small town (less than 1400 members) that are divided by "six degrees of separation" or, in the specific tiny town inhabited by Peter and Luke, more realistically, divided by "1 to 3 degrees of separation."

When Peter and Luke were five and four years old, respectively, the Siwels family was the oldest and most revered married couple in Notsaen (small town of primarily farmers, ranchers, and other country town members who enjoyed one gas station, one doctor's office, one pharmacy, one burger drive-up restaurant, one Mexican restaurant, one pizza place, one donut shop, one butcher shop, no public gyms, and only three television channels to watch (pre-cable television days and pre-internet days of existence) to their credit). This was the simple and peaceful small town, a fertile ground for blooming and blossoming young children that Peter and Luke were and are so grateful to have grown up in and fully immerse themselves in while determining who they would become as adults, later in life.

Why was the Siwel couple also known and respected as the "pillars of the community"? Simple but complex is the answer due to the myriad reasons, which are all easily understandable. Let's delineate some (but not an inclusive list, which would be a separate book of its own) of the most critical reasons that were overt and shined excessively bright throughout the community like that beam projected by the most intense lighthouse one can imagine. The Siwels had recently been recognized during a local church service on Sunday as having celebrated, recently, their 75th wedding anniversary. Should I stop with that single reason…perhaps. Each Mother's Day, again in the Sunday worship service, Mrs. Siwel would be honored, revered, and celebrated as having the most great-grandchildren, grandchildren, and children in our small community. The Siwels attended church services in the same local community Christian church from grammar school, high school, college and until they were too old to attend in person due to falling risks, after which they subscribed to the cassette sermon tapes program that recorded sermons each Sunday and then delivered the sermon cassette tapes to members of the community who were hospitalized or otherwise too frail or fragile to venture transportation to and from the Church which they eagerly desired to attend but could not for one or more reasons. As a matter of fact, Peter and Luke, ages 5 and 4, would often walk to and from church and, more often than not, knock on the door of the Siwel home on the way home from church on Sunday and briefly visit the Siwels, the Patriarch and Matriarch (honorary title bestowed on this couple) of our small town/community to, from Peter and Luke's perspective, get a small dose of Godly wisdom and history lesson from this endearing, lovely couple and role models of a life well-lived and well-navigated through stormy and clear weather conditions, which Peter and Luke found priceless each Sunday and relished this once-per-week opportunity to be entertained, educated, and enlightened by the many years of life experiences this couple possessed and remembered clearly and by the magical recounting of their life lessons learned amidst their legacy of "living, loving history-makers and community-embracers," aka, the Siwels!

Mrs. Siwel had attended college and been an educator (teacher) in the community for over 40 years before retiring. Mr. Siwel had been a patriotic American, having served in the military during World War I, surviving to be fully content on saving up for and purchasing a plot of land in the community on which he could grow crops, feed his family, and live a life of peace and serenity after experiencing the most horrific scenes during World War I that are imaginable. God had somehow seen fit to protect him throughout the war, so that he could return to his high school sweetheart after the war, who was now an educated young teacher and beautiful bride for Mr. Siwel (a decorated WWI veteran and hero from small-town America). The movie with Gary Cooper, "Sergeant York" (a classic and must-see movie for all who read this book and wish to know what it means to be an American [or faithful citizen of any other country] and God-revering, human rights-respecting, kind human being while alive on this planet, until death reunites us all with our heavenly creator in heaven) comes to mind, now as an adult, when both Peter and Luke reflect back on the many stories told to us as children of Mr. Siwel's trials, tribulations, travesties and all the close acquaintances, fellow soldiers, and friends that he lost from both his grammar and high school classmates and new military fellow soldiers that he served with, side by side in frequent and dire circumstances for multiple years during World War I.

Mrs. Siwel was a gift from God to Mr. Siwel after returning home from the war. From her birth until her death at approximately 100 years old, Mrs. Siwel was an inquisitive child who loved to learn by reading books available from the local town library, located across the street from Peter and Luke's home and the local Presbyterian Church, and was a fabulous listener, loved (her own and others) children, loved God, loved her community, and loved the country, the United States of America that gave her unlimited/unrestricted opportunities in life to educate herself, excel in her university education program, and marry the "Gary Cooper-like hero" of her "Sergeant York movie-like life and community," and thereafter fill the community with their God-blessed and God-revering descendants after bestowing on all their children the Christian work ethic and values that had resulted in their being so blessed and thankful for God's mercy and grace in their lives, acknowledging God daily in their prayers.

If Mrs. Siwel was the diamond role model in the community, then Mr. Siwel was the ruby that shined no less brightly in our small town. Mr. Siwel, early after the war, was the only person in his tiny town who was able to save up and purchase a farming tractor (diesel or gas-powered). While he could have extracted hefty fees from his community members and neighbors in need of tractor services, Mr. Siwel always freely offered his services with a happy and kind heart, accepting only what was donated or otherwise offered by requesting neighbors for tractor-plowing tasks or maintenance of ditch banks used throughout our small farming town. He continued this service well into his late 80's (e.g., 86 years old)…truly amazing and God's blessing to our small town's inhabitants. Needless to say, he garnered much love and respect for his generosity throughout the community and was always regarded as the honorary grandfather of our town of 1400 people, and his wife, similarly, was regarded as the honorary grandmother of our tiny but unbelievably awesome small town and community.

Any town can and should have this same type of influential couple that not only can provide historical insight and wisdom to all its members, but if identified and honored, such a couple can teach all members of the society they live in, why and how to respect and revere your elders and mentors, not because they are perfect (none are), but because they have striven toward Godly perfection as Jesus taught in the Bible and have lived their lives to the best of their ability and achieved near-perfection, in God's eyes, which are the only eyes (note: God's eyes or "Father's Eyes" are the opposite of selfish, self-serving "Is" or "Mes" that world citizens pursue to choose to be blind to God's intentions for all humans on this Earth) that matter during our lives and into eternity when we are reunited with God in heaven after our physical (but not spiritual) deaths here on planet Earth.

Peter and Luke's development as children and adults were immeasurably impacted by our weekly short visits and chats with this Siwel couple, God's translators from one generation to the next generation. We both have only fond and tender memories of the wisdom these "pillars of the community" bestowed upon us and, to this day and eternally, consider them our (honorary) fourth set of parents or relatives, thus "1-3 degrees of separation" (versus perhaps "6 degrees of separation" in larger cities) realized in real life.

Peter's best friend's parents were our "second set of honorary parents," and Luke's best friend's parents were our "third set of honorary parents," with the Siwels being our earliest and most Godly influencers and "fourth set of honorary parents." Both Peter and Luke acknowledge that number rankings mean nothing in life or in God's eyes. God only intends for us to do our best every day, demonstrating love, kindness, and appreciation for those God allows us to interact with during our lives and bring those we interact with closer to God by our acts of love, kindness, generosity, forgiveness, and Jesus-like existence and behavior before our eventual physical death and ascent into heaven and family reunion with God and fellow God believers, worshipers and messengers of God's love for all his creations, especially human beings on planet earth.

The Alexandria family were Peter and Luke's "fifth set of honorary parents," and the Alexandria children were moderately older than Peter and Luke but young enough to serve as ideal role models in the church and the community of fourteen hundred that we were raised in and flourished in as young children due to the density of rich and vibrant

God-worshipping community members who expected that nothing in life would be free or easy, and who preferred to be receptive of and to God's grace and mercy, knowing that each individual may then flourish if they try their best each and every day to better himself or herself (only two options acknowledged by God) via education, physical fitness (your body is your temple in God's Eyes or "Father's Eyes"; the temple should neither be desecrated, allowed to disintegrate from neglect, nor covered with graffiti such as tattoos), positive attitude, learning to work peacefully as a team member with others and work hard and for honest wages whilst always acknowledging that God is responsible for your victories and successes in life at each step and phase of your development. This is a simple formula to success in life which, if neglected or ignored, results in a less-fulfilling life and a life which is secluded and distant from what God intends for the life of all his creations, namely each human being he has created and allowed to be born into this amazing, unique, and fantastic life of limitless possibilities and eternal hope for an ever-improving future made possible by God-motivated and God-inspired humans.

The children of the Alexandria family, again both older and wiser than Peter and Luke, were very important and fundamental role models in our local church and community, not because they were better than others but because they were more kind, generous, understanding, patient and better listeners than many or most other children in the community, due largely to their parents who both were dynamic spiritual leaders in the church. Their father was always a deacon and elder in the church, a decorated WWII veteran, active in the "Men's' Bible Study Group" at church, and an amazingly humble and soft-spoken yet imposing figure at six feet 3 inches in height. Their mother was as close to the Virgin Mary (mother of Jesus in the Bible) or Mother Theresa (Nun in Calcutta, India) as is imaginable. She had been dating her husband in high school when he was called away to serve in World War II. While he was away, she contracted polio and became paralyzed from the waist down (paraplegia). She never blamed God for her polio diagnosis nor her disability (paraplegia). She refused to feel sorry for herself and became a pillar of her community and the local church, and most significantly, an inspiring "Women's Bible Study" leader for over 50 years and role model for how to live life, deal with adversity, overcome adversity, and move on with your life, being thankful every moment of every day FOR WHAT YOU HAVE IN LIFE, not focusing (negatively) on what you do not have. The Alexandria family had one son and one daughter. The son, Mit, was very tall with marked near-sightedness which enabled him to be enamored, as a young child, with reading the Bible and books in school, resulting in his becoming a well-educated and Godly man later in life and an excellent and faithful friend and work colleague of Peter later in life. Tenajia, their daughter, was a beautiful young blond girl who never had an attitude of superiority and, to her mother's credit, always seemed unaware of how beautiful, humble, kind, and inspiring she was to her parents, fellow children in the church and schools and in the community. To his chagrin, she was six years older than Luke. Luke often thought that he would happily marry Tenajia or the church's organ player's daughter, another beautiful young Godly girl in the church (who later became a registered nurse, caring for hospitalized patients), again and disappointingly approximately six years older than Luke. Although these two young girls romantically inspired Luke, they were two lessons for Luke to learn how to deal with unrealistic goals, make new and realistic goals, how to deal with and overcome disappointments or losses in life, and move on with your other goals without regret. We all must learn to deal with disappointments in every aspect of life and treat them like grammar school baseball team game losses. One game loss is only one team loss and nothing more. Practice resumes the next day for the next upcoming scheduled game, and your focus must immediately shift to the next team you will be playing. If you do not learn to move on and immediately shift your laser focus to preparing for your next opponent team, you will likely lose your next game and all future games in grammar school and in life! This is why both Peter and Luke strongly or firmly believe that a crucial part of childhood development is engaging in and participating in as many sporting events and teams as you are able to join or be selected to be a member of. Learning early in life what sports teach you is astonishingly beneficial to human development beyond one's imagination and so many valuable lessons, life skills, perseverance, concentration, focus, compartmentalization, resilience, "never give up, and I will never be defeated" attitude (e.g., I may lose a battle, but I will win the war.") These character traits learned from playing sports continue to develop and mature throughout a young child's progression from young to older children's sporting events and team league competitions. These character traits then segue (segue is a smooth transition) seamlessly to all other aspects, aspirations, and endeavors in that child's life, such as school courses in grammar school, middle school, high school, university studies, master's degree, and doctorate degree (postgraduate education), decisions on college major or graduate schools to apply to, Musician (amateur vs. professional) pursuits and aspirations, Athlete (amateur vs professional) pursuits and aspirations, decisions to climb Mountains (e.g., Mt Everest, Mt Fuji, Mt Whitney, Mt Shasta, Mt Kilimanjaro, or others), become an airplane or helicopter pilot, become a scuba diver or hang glider, and/or mastery of any skill that individuals choose to endeavor after learning to work toward goals, winning and losing battles along the way yet focusing on preparation to "win the war" ultimately, as a result of playing sports as children.

Tenajia later happily married a wonderful man who published the local community newspaper. Ironically, Tenajia's husband would later interview Luke for the newspaper and author a complimentary article with Luke's picture about Luke being "The Perfect Salutatorian." Luke was, at that point, content in knowing that the young girl he had been so enamored with was safe, content, and happily married to a man with a heart of gold and a solid community member. Luke was the Salutatorian in grammar school (number 2 academic student, losing out to a woman who would become head cheerleader in high school and whom Luke would surpass as Valedictorian of high school, relegating her to his former role and title of Salutatorian of high school) but somehow, the local community newspaper realized that Luke was a bright and rising, shining star who was just beginning his blaze through the sky of this life and world. Luke did not disappoint that newspaper's publisher, and the article emphasized that Luke attributed all his accomplishments and successes up to that point to his faith in God and inspiration to excel in all that he does as a result of inspiration derived from his study of the Bible and God's purpose for all his life and the life of all God's creations (humanity).

The most God-like, God-inspired, God-guided communities, such as the 1400-person small town that Peter and Luke grew up in, are color blind. Peter and Luke's sixth "honorary parents" in their community were an African American farmer couple who, again, were pillars of the church and community. The Husband of the Servilo family, again with children 3-5 years older than Peter and Luke, owned 60 acres of raisin (grape) vines and was a fantastic mentor, a hard-working, humble, soft-spoken, yet in size, imposing, tall man 6 feet 2 inches in height. He played football in high school and likely relocated many opposing team players to exactly where he intended them to be to help his team win repeatedly. His wife was a beautiful, educated, eloquent woman who was a vital member of all church activities and proactively involved in the success of all planned church gatherings and events; in short, a dynamic and remarkably energetic, God-inspired, God-energized woman. Peter and Luke sought out their wisdom frequently with random visits to their house via skateboarding or bike trips (their home was a "good distance (many miles far away)" from Peter and Luke's home, approximately 8-10 miles away, yet a mere short trip, in the minds of Peter and Luke (by skateboard or bicycle), who were quite athletic and extremely energetic (superhero-like) as children (and adults). Their Servilo family's children were similarly energetic, enthusiastic about life's promising opportunities, intelligent, motivated, patriotic Americans, and developed altruistic traits and life ambitions as a direct result of the outstanding parenting they received while growing up. The Servilo family's oldest daughter became a registered nurse and was an active high school band member and church member. Their second child and son was an athletic and intelligent individual who entered the law enforcement field and has been protecting the safety and security of law-abiding citizens his entire life after high school when he was also an active band member, excellent student, and church family member. Peter and Luke both worked for Mr. Servilo during the raisin harvest seasons and for several other raisin, prune, and almond ranch owners throughout grammar school and high school (with W2 wages, contributing to and qualifying for social security benefits, with such an early start to their continuous working lives and careers [throughout grammar school, high school, college, and beyond] that both Peter and Luke qualified for social security, meeting the minimum number of quarters and years worked requirements, while Peter and Luke were still in college…amazing yet true.) Children should start working while in school as early as possible (e.g., as a newspaper delivery route worker, as a self-employed lawn mowing business owner, or as farm workers receiving minimum wage earnings) so they may learn that money is earned, honestly, via hard work, resilience, persistence, and perseverance and that money does not grow on trees or just continually flow from parents' pockets or billfolds (wallets), in some magical, mysterious, whimsical (and inaccurate) manner or notion. Work, play, study in school and sporting event team participation in school all force and demand that children learn valuable skills of multitasking, time and schedule management, prioritizing, delegation, teamwork, and perhaps, in Peter and Luke's opinion, the most critical childhood and adult life skill is compartmentalization (the ability to hyperfocus on the particular task at hand to the exclusion of all distractions in order to achieve mastery and expertise in the task despite multitasking, such that each of the multitasking events may be accomplished with the greatest and most incredible precision, accuracy, and performance (e.g., sports, music, examinations in school), expertise or mastery level of accomplishment).

Is physical fitness and strength/power training optional or essential during childhood development to achieve a child's and adult's maximum potential, develop and maintain an extremely high level of self-confidence, and to excel or ascend to previously unachievable or unimagined levels of mastery of multiple, diverse skills or realize exceptional or miraculous accomplishments? Peter and Luke agree that physical fitness and strength/power training are never optional and should always be striven for to achieve greatness in this life. When a child is strong, that child is confident. When an adult is strong and muscular, that adult is confident. When a child or adult is confident, they will be more motivated to venture out and take calculated chances to pursue greatness and prepare, train, persevere until greatness is achieved.

Luke had a fantastic science teacher that convinced him to never use drugs, and that alcohol definitely and rapidly kills brain cells with every ounce consumed. Peter learned this at the same time Luke did as a result of Luke's education of all his classmates, friends, and relatives of these facts for the remainder of Luke's life, in fact, it is an essential teaching component of his current profession every day.

Humans (if not disabled from congenital or acquired conditions, infections or trauma) were designed to run, jog, move vigorously, start performing push-ups, pull-ups, or otherwise performing a variety of lifting exercises of low weights and progressively increase weights to higher levels to break down or partially tear muscle fibers so they can expand and undergo hypertrophy and heal to larger, more powerful, hyper-developed muscles that perform at professional athlete levels. This is God's desire for the human body. The human body, made precisely as God intended, is also God's temple and represents God's greatness. Thus, all human beings should, after birth, nurture and fortify their bodies (aka God temples). Each individual, by maintaining and increasing the health and fitness of their body may, in the present and future, better withstand and survive all-natural disasters and storms in life that they encounter, especially compared with those who choose early in life to destroy their body, mind, and soul with alcohol and substance (e.g., marijuana, methamphetamines, magic mushrooms, cocaine, lysergic acid, "Angel Dust" (more accurately, "Devil Dust"), and tobacco) abuse.

Peter was Valedictorian (the number one academic student in his class) in both grammar school and high school. His superhero superpowers might have resulted from (at least partially) body and brain-healthy factors, including riding his bike for 45 minutes to 1 hour every day throughout grammar school and high school education years, and his love for reading books and mastering the techniques of speed reading in his early grammar school years. Luke was the Salutatorian of grammar school (number two academic student in his class) and the Valedictorian of high school. His superhero superpowers might have resulted from (at least partially) from body and brain-healthy factors including observing and learning from the actions and behavior of his older brother Peter (a fantastic role model and soulmate of Luke), a strong passion for distance running starting in fourth grade of grammar school (Luke will be running until the day of his death, the last run ending in a long jump into his casket!), working out and beginning powerlifting in 6th grade at home with his own weight set in his bedroom (there were no commercial gyms in his local, small town of 1400 people, and the school gym was only open during regular school hours) when he received the item on his Santa Claus Christmas wish list: a set of weights, barbels and dumbbells and bench press bar, and then began before school workouts, including push-ups, sit-ups, and weight-lifting followed by a shower and a brisk run to school, then, starting in eighth grade, brisk runs to the high school Jazz Band practices from his home (as a grammar school student guest invited by the high school band instructor to sit in and play with the high school band as a special guest; Luke was very honored by this vote of confidence and inspired to perfect his craft of trombone playing so as to not disappoint the high school trombonists and band instructor who bestowed this honor on him!) which started promptly at 720 am every day and ended at 820 am, prior to Luke's grammar school class start time at 830 am. Luke had daily sprint runs first to Jazz Band, then to the grammar school campus and classroom, in addition to 4-6 miles runs 3-5 days per week around his home neighborhood (5-10 laps around a four-block area of homes with many unchained dogs; Luke learned to be invincible and fearless of dogs constantly chasing him and attempting to bite him, never successfully except, ironically, once, upon visiting the church assistant pastor's home, whose dog bit him on his leg once…go figure… life is unpredictable and exciting). Luke never stopped (and will never stop) running or powerlifting since starting in his grammar school days. Luke later was undefeated in his age group in 10-kilometer races and ran three marathon races with times consistently 2-5 minutes different in all three marathons. Luke, after his 55th birthday, lifts personal records at his local gym, most often lifting the entire stacks of weight bars on multiple distinct exercise machines and performs 100 pull-ups each gym session, multiple sets of biceps/triceps exercises (e.g., curls 45 total divided into three sets), and bar dips (minimum of 100 total bar dips) and 400-800 "abdominal rectus muscle crunch exercises" (similar to sit-ups) each gym session, and moves from machine to machine or sit-up bench in a circuit training style (finish set of 20 to 50 at one machine, then transition or move to the next machine after a 2-5 minute rest period). Luke learned this method over the years and after deploying with United States Navy Seals, Marine Corps Forced Recon Special Forces and British Royal Air Force and Commandos as a Marine Corps Helicopter and Fighter-Attack (F/A-18) Jet Pilot and Flight Surgeon on multiple land deployments throughout the world and on aircraft carriers during special operations capable western Pacific Ocean (WESTPAC) deployments to the Middle East, Australia, Thailand, Hawaii, and other regions.

What is a WESTPAC Deployment? The **Unit Deployment Program** (U.D.P.) is a system for assigning deployments of the United States Marine Corps. To reduce the number of unaccompanied tours and improve unit continuity, the Commandant of the Marine Corps, (C.M.C.) established it to provide for the deployment of units to the Western Pacific (WESTPAC) for periods of approximately six to nine months. The initial program was a six-phased evolution that sequenced infantry battalions and aircraft squadrons/detachments into WESTPAC deployments, thus eliminating the 12-month permanent change of station assignments for personnel assigned to these units. The program commenced in October 1977 and has proceeded through the six phases. In August 1985, tank companies began phasing into the program but, following Southwest Asia, were discontinued. In Fiscal Year 1987 (FY87) and FY88, Amphibious Assault Vehicle (AAV) companies and direct support artillery batteries were phased in, and later, Light Armored Reconnaissance (L.A.R.) companies were also included in the program. The Marine Corps' objective is to adhere as closely as possible to a six-month period of deployment away from a unit's Continental United States (CONUS) home base. In the case of Hawaii-based infantry battalions, which employ a three-battalion rotation base, a seven-month period of deployment is executed to support the Unit Cohesion Program and efficient staffing of first-term Marines. It must be understood, however, that shipping or airlift schedule variations and exercise or contingency operations will occasionally necessitate longer or shorter deployments for participating units. It is imperative that all personnel involved in these deployments be kept fully informed of planned deployment duration and subsequent deployment schedule changes.

Visualization and imagination are essential childhood development skills to acquire at the earliest age possible. Sports is the most obvious access to these skills, but music performance or other avenues might also give access to the development of these essential childhood and adulthood skills to achieve mastery or perfection (near-perfection) or to enhance the likelihood of being the best at what you do in at least one field (one should never limit your potential to be the best in multiple or unlimited fields or areas of expertise) or unlimited areas of expertise. People often are quick to judge and disparage the potential impact or power of visualization, imagination, concentration, and compartmentalization in achieving superhero accomplishments and performances in life. The books "The Inner Game of Tennis" by Timothy Gallwey, "How to Win Friends And Influence People" by Dale Carnegie and "Remember Everything You Read (The Evelyn Wood Speed Reading And Learning Program" by Stanley D Frank, Ed. D. are fantastic books for children to read at the earliest age and opportunity possible for the assimilation of skills that will allow them to achieve greatness and mastery of many skills, maximize educational and leadership opportunities throughout their life and will enable them to study and acquire new information in the most rapid and efficient manner possible so they may balance their life, studies, and sporting endeavors to pursue and accomplish their highest aspirations and goals in life and be the champion in as many areas of pursued interests as possible.

Children such as Peter and Luke, whether being raised in small towns or communities or in a large metropolis or big city can and should take advantage of learning everything possible from both the positive and negative attributes and positive and negative strengths or weaknesses of both their parents, their classmates, acquaintances in every group, and their church family members. Peter and Luke learned much from being above-average keen listeners and observers of other children's and adults' actions, strengths, weaknesses, and various and sundry ideas of others and the positive and negative attributes of other individuals' perspectives, attitudes, aspirations, behaviors, and actions.

The father of Peter and Luke serves as an excellent example of the above paragraph. Children should strive to learn something new (or many new things per day, if possible) every day of their existence. After all, life is a cumulative experience, and if you are eclectic and retain and put into long-term memory valuable and otherwise helpful and practical lessons learned each day, you will be considered precocious and wiser than your age group at a very young age, as was the case with both Peter and Luke. Both Peter and Luke were designated and accepted into the "Gifted and Talented Education Program," which was in the pioneer early days of the program's existence. In truth, Peter and Luke's mother was responsible for both sons being given this designation and honor. Peter and Luke's mother was the best active listener Peter and Luke ever encountered in their lifetime! She taught both her sons that listening, photographic memory skills, speed reading, and taking succinct and concise notes in class (and in life, in general!) were 99% of intelligence and that, in contrast, proper intelligible, non-rushed clear speech communication, adjusted or modified to accommodate the person to whom you are communicating (very important), was the remaining but vital 1% of intelligence, and this last 1% flows naturally and effortlessly from the 99% that has been accumulated each day of that individual's existence.

Mother was a fantastic student in grammar school, high school, and university and very popular among her female (and male) classmates because she was kind, an active listener, humble (and beautiful). In fact, she was elected prom queen in high school and college! Mother enjoyed math. I know all these facts seem to be exaggerated or unbelievable, even to Peter and Luke initially, then they were later confirmed by Mother's grammar school, high school, college, and adult coworkers in later years and by those who attended her memorial service and funeral/burial ceremony. Mother was an extremely remarkable and dynamic woman whose many gifts from God included, amongst many other gifts, being an amazing, unsurpassed, angelic (#1 rank in Peter and Luke's voting) mother with unmatched kindness, who was the best-ever proactive listener, and last but not least and remarkable, a truly and honestly humble woman created and perfected by God's design and intent. Peter and Luke attempted to emulate these skills and attributes of their Mother the best they could throughout their lives. Father taught Peter and Luke myriad lessons in life in a paradoxical yet very effective manner. All children on this planet earth have different parents with different attributes and should pay attention to the points delineated in this paragraph to maximize what they can and should learn from their parents, good and bad. No parents are perfect, just as no individual humans are perfect with the exception of God and Jesus Christ, and Peter and Luke realized this very early in life, and other children should accept and acknowledge this fact at the earliest age possible and adjust their expectations accordingly so that they not be surprised and so that they can continue to acquire knowledge and wisdom from their parents each and every day of their life.

This is how Peter and Luke's father indirectly influenced and educated his sons, Peter and Luke. Father was a high school teacher. Peter and Luke's father taught at the local high school that both Peter and Luke would attend later in their childhood (this was both awkward and uncomfortable for both Peter and Luke). As keen observers and active listeners at very early and young ages, Peter and Luke surmised, then concluded that their father grew up as an only child and, as a result, somehow failed to learn or lacked sharing characteristics that children learn when they grow up with siblings and lacked the confidence that comes with early childhood competitive sports team participation, never played or learned to play a musical instrument as a child, was often ignored and neglected by his parents, all resulting in Peter and Luke's father's lack of confidence that he could be the very best in one, multiple, or myriad endeavors in life and, thus, he neither pursued nor accomplished these feats of accomplishment. Despite these facts, he was an honorable young man, attended church on Sundays, engaged in church youth group member activities and special events. Peter and Luke's father attended the University of California Berkeley briefly but then dropped out and transferred to another university due to his lack of confidence in himself and because he had not engaged in enough sports team events or learned to have the patience, persistence, and the necessary extreme dedication to studying, practice, preparation for performances in every attempted endeavor (academic and in other fields of or categories of life endeavors), and the work ethic required to become the very best at endeavors you undertake and wish to complete by being the very best at what you are doing. All or most of these aspects and traits may be acquired as a child by becoming a musician and athlete in many different sports. Peter and Luke's father either did not have the opportunity or did not wish to become an accomplished musician as a child and did not become a dedicated athlete during his participation in sports to a significant enough extent to acquire the traits of an individual who never gives up, attempts to be the best at everything he does, and completes all endeavors started to achieve his goals with outstanding performance and dedication to those goals with unwavering determination and resolve. Peter and Luke's father had none of the following mottos as part of his being, soul, or constitution: "Never say die", "I will not be defeated," or "I lost this battle, but I will win the war." Father quickly gave up on almost every endeavor he pursued if he did not immediately experience success and refused to dedicate and devote himself to the painful, persistent, "blood, sweat, and tears" type of practice, preparation, or studying that is required to be the best student in his classes and all the schools that he attended (e.g., he started a Master's degree program but quickly dropped out of the program and did not complete his Master's degree), best athlete in the track events he engaged in, or the best and most devoted and loving husband that he promised to be to his intelligent, devoted, caring, beautiful, and angelic wife. While Peter and Luke were both disappointed and saddened by these revelations and realizations about their father, they proceeded to "make lemonade out of lemons." Peter decided, as a young child, that he would attempt (successfully) to realize and accomplish all the broken dreams that his father had attempted, with less than optimal and less than 100% dedication and commitment to invest the time and 10,000+ hours of practice to accomplish his goal of being the best in each endeavor that he pursued, for both Peter and as a gift to and out of Peter's love for his father. Peter dedicated much more than 10,000 hours to each endeavor to ensure he became the very best in each endeavor he pursued. Peter became and accomplished the following tasks, goals, and endeavors that he pursued with extreme dedication, practice, preparation, and unparalleled work ethic to ensure he became the very best that he could be in all the endeavors he chose to pursue and accomplish with great success. Peter was the highest-ranked Cub Scout, Weblo (Order of Arrow), Boy Scout, Boy Scouts Junior Olympics Participant: Number one student in grammar school and high school, number one trumpet player in high school and regional and city honor Jazz bands, honor bands, honor orchestras every year, and the number-one trumpet player in the city Junior Philharmonic Orchestra, Jazz Band Leader, Band Leader, Gifted And Talented Education (GATE) Program Membership, High School Mock Trials (Pre-Law) Competitions Number One High School Participant Representing His High School, number one Varsity Singles Tennis Player in High School, Academic All-American, National Honor Society, California Scholarship Federation Member every quarter of all four years of high school, the second-ranked trumpet player in the state of California during his California State Honor Band performance, number one or two ranked mile runner in grammar school, and Peter was also an accomplished and highly rated grammar school long jumper and high jumper. Peter was selected to the High School All-American Band (a prestigious honor) that toured Europe for six weeks after high school graduation as the number one high school trumpet player for this particular select and prestigious honor band tour. Peter accumulated multiple scholarships that paid off his first two years of college and received the "Honors at Entrance" designation upon starting his college education. I believe father was at least somewhat proud of his first son's accomplishments.

Luke had an easier, more manageable, and less stressful path through life as a result of the pioneering accomplishments and path blazed by his all-star and genius brother and soulmate for life. Luke was motivated by and learned to emulate every desirable attribute of his mother and brother (many indeed) and was motivated and inspired inexplicably by his father not to repeat the mistakes of his father (e.g., failure to totally dedicate and devote himself through persistence, myriad hours of practice until perfection is not the exception, but instead the rule, and faithful devotion to friends and family, at all costs, though never condoning or encouraging inappropriate or improper behavior or alcohol or other drug substance abuse). Luke learned more from his father about what mistakes not to repeat or make in life than by or from father's proactive teaching (by life example) how to live life and accomplish goals. Although this may seem like a rather negative statement at first glance, but all children will, at some point, find that their parents (and all humans) will disappoint them periodically and are not always perfect or, in some instances, may be frequently imperfect. Only Jesus Christ, The Holy Spirit, and God are perfect and will never disappoint or "let you down" in this life. Those who expect perfection and unwavering support and faithfulness from other humans are bound to be disappointed and will eventually come to the realization that they need only Jesus Christ, The Holy Spirit, and God for serenity and unwavering faithfulness. Choose to be positive every day and learn from everyone how to be a better and more humble, generous, and intelligent person who respects and follows God's teachings in the Bible. All humans who aspire to these goals can be a genius or near-genius in God's heart, mind, and eyes ("Father's Eyes") early in their life and long before their ultimate and joyful reunion with God in the future.

Luke recalls being jumped after school while walking home one day by one of his classmates. The attack was unprovoked. Luke informed his father that night. His father errored in not taking Luke with him to the attacker's home to discuss the matter with the attacking student's father. The attacking student lied to Luke's father, saying untruthfully that Luke had provoked the attack by calling the classmate a derogatory name in the play yard earlier that day (untrue), yet Father, having not brought Luke to the false accuser's house, could not verify with Luke whether this false accusation was true or not, so Father instead chose to believe that Luke was at fault for the unprovoked attack, and then returned home and interrogated Luke for over one hour, demanding Luke recall what names he had called the other boy, and, of course, Luke was unable to comply due to his having never called the other boy any derogatory names whatsoever. Luke realized that day that his father was not only not perfect but had assumed the worst of his second son and was not even interested in hearing Luke's side of the story. Luke lost a significant amount of faith and trust in his father's interest in and ability to protect him in life, for better or for worse. Luke chose that very same day to "make lemonade out of lemons." Luke resolved, from that day forward, to transform himself (in spirit) and his body (by brutal and dedicated powerlifting and multiple varied training exercises and running) into a warrior. By this action, Luke decided that he would no longer depend on and certainly not rely on his father for any further protection or guidance in life, a decision that proved invaluable in Luke's life and a decision that Luke does not regret to this very day, and Luke was forever changed by that experience, making him more independent and resolute to accomplish his goals of warrior spirit, warrior physical training, and limitless confidence through strength and power training whilst still pursuing his goals of academic and leadership excellence and outperformance in grammar school, high school, and during university studies in undergraduate school, graduate and doctoral degree completion, flight school completion, and obtaining Luke's flight wings, years of military service as a helicopter pilot and fighter-attack jet pilot deployments with United States Marine Corps, Navy Seals Special Forces, Marine Forced Recon Special Forces, and British Royal Air Force and British Commandos throughout the world during Luke's military service years, post-military service private surgical residency training/postgraduate training and subspecialty surgical postdoctoral/postgraduate surgical fellowship subspecialty training later as an adult.

In retrospect, Luke believes that the violent adversity he experienced on more than the one occasion noted above actually propelled him down a path or "road less traveled," but a road that led him to believe that he must radically alter his path to achieve a more satisfying, secure, self-confident and self-sufficient life, which ultimately resulted in his being a more fierce and powerful human, a more confident human, fearing no one or no danger (within reason, of course) and ultimately led him, later in life and after childhood, to pursue and be awarded with a full four-year all-expenses-paid military scholarship to attend, at the time, one of, if not the most prestigious and the most expensive medical school in the United States. Luke also was accepted at and attended the oldest medical school in the United States, an "Ivy League University," and prestigious eye institute for postdoctoral/postgraduate surgical residency training, then was selected for a prestigious and competitive post-residency surgical subspecialty fellowship surgery training at a third prestigious university training program.

Children must remember, as Luke can attest to, that negative events or circumstances can be a blessing in disguise and force one to make decisions that lead to greater confidence, resilience, determination to excel and overachieve in life and ultimately make available greater and more significant opportunities and adventures that the child (or children) is/are now prepared for and willing to accept as a result of their unique background and physical training, which qualifies them for extremely exciting and adventurous undertakings (e.g., scuba diving, wilderness survival course completion, underwater survival training course completion and obstacle course completion in flight school, flying helicopters, flying fighter-attack jets (F/A-18 Hornet Jets specifically), climbing Mt Fuji in Japan, snow skiing down double diamond ski resort runs in Aspen, Colorado, Vail, Colorado, Jackson Hole, Wyoming, and Niseko, Japan ski resorts), all of which Luke has been able to accomplish and enjoy as a result of his life-long power weight training and 15-30 miles per week running activities that are now a routine part of his life and desire to remain an exceptional athlete until his life's end.

Chapter 6 – Roman Numerals, Elite Definition, and the Making of Child Prodigy Professional Musicians before Age 11: Formulas for Success in Life and After Physical Death and Thereafter in Spiritual Eternal Life.

"Hey, maggot, get over here." This was the nickname given to Luke at a young age by the tuba player in the high school marching band, who also played baritone saxophone in the high school marching band and was among the most popular students in high school and was elected student body president that same year he bestowed upon Luke the nickname "Maggot." Luke, at the time, was in eighth grade, 12 years old, in grammar school, but had been invited to sit in with the high school jazz band before school started on weekdays, Monday through Friday. For those who are uncertain what a maggot is or if this is a complimentary nickname, let me clarify that this is a nickname that no one should ever be enamored with. A "maggot" is the larva of a fly. This term or word is applied in particular to the larvae of Brachycera flies, such as houseflies, cheese flies, and blowflies, rather than larvae of the Nematocera, such as mosquitoes and crane flies. A 2012 study estimated the population of maggots in North America to be more than 3×10^{17}. Maggots are disgusting worm-like organisms that feast on food waste or dead human tissue.
Nevertheless, because the "Big Man On Campus (BMOC)" and most respected, well-rounded, gregarious, athletic, intelligent high school senior class student member and Student Body President (who also played offense and defense on the Varsity high school football team)

labeled Luke with this derogatory nickname, it stuck on and with Luke for years. Luckily for Luke, this reference and nickname bounced off Luke like a bullet ricocheting off Superman's chest! Luke had a positive self-image at a very young age as a result of growing up in the church, attending services every Sunday with his older brother, Peter, and his parents. Luke was confident that he was a miracle created by God to achieve great things while on this planet and to positively impact other humans before his eventual death someday, after which he would return to heaven to be reunited with God and his family and friends of faith, aka, Christians worldwide. He learned in Kindergarten, the phrase which he found truth in immediately and never forgot the lesson that this phrase taught him: "Sticks and stones may break my bones (until I beat the crap out of the thrower), but words will (always be cast by evildoers and persons with evil intent) never hurt me." Luke thus carried the nickname throughout his grammar school and high school years until the nickname eventually faded out of his classmates' memories after the BMOC and Student Body President and "stud football player" graduated (he went on to the University of Southern California (USC) University, completing a bachelor's degree in accounting, became a certified public accountant, and established an extremely successful real estate and investment empire in Atlanta, Georgia, as an adult.) Despite the derogatory (but endearing, in Luke's mind at least) "maggot" label, Luke, inexplicably, would closely observe what made the BMOC so likable and popular and follow eerily in his exact steps and near identical path through high school with minor exceptions such as choosing different sports to excel in and achieve greatness and mastery to the greatest extent possible, including academic performance and great success in university and postgraduate studies, and life accomplishments.

Luke was always fascinated by Roman Numerals and was astonished at how most children and adults never received adequate education about how to interpret the symbols to know what number or year was being referenced, e.g., during Super Bowl 55 (instead of 55, the number for an American football game is always listed in Roman Numerals and thus mysterious to everyone watching the game, unless interpreted or audibly spoken by the game commentator).

Roman Numerals use a numbering technique based on seven letters:

I, V, X, L, C, D, M.
I represents a value of one (1);
V represents five (5);
X represents ten (10);
L represents fifty (50);
C represents one-hundred (100);
D represents five-hundred (500);
M represents one-thousand (1000);

Conversion Rules:

A)
When the symbol has a greater value than the symbol after it, add the symbols, such as: XI = X +1 = 10 + 1 =11.

B)
When the symbol has a lesser value than the symbol after it, subtract the symbol with the lesser value from the symbol with the greater value: IX = X – 1 = 10 – 1 = 9.

C)
When the symbols have equal value, add them:
XX = X + X = 10 + 10 = 20.

Roman Numerals to Decimals: (Converting large Roman Numeral Numbers to Decimal Numbers)

A)
To convert, e.g., MCMLXXXVI to decimal

numbers: Starting with VI, move from right to left and apply the rules (see
above rules): I + V + X + X + X + L + M – C + M (Solution / Answer = 1 + 5 + 10
+ 10 + 10 + 50 + 1000 – 100 + 1000 = 1986)

B)
To convert, e.g., DCCLXXXIV again apply above rules: V – I + X + X + X + L + C + C + D (Solution / Answer = 5 – 1 + 10 + 10 + 10 + 50 + 100 + 100 + 500 =784)

Decimals to Roman Numerals: (Converting Regular Numbers to Roman Numerals)

A)
Break down the decimal number into: 1,000's, 100's, 10's and 1's (one's): e.g., to convert 2014 into Roman Numerals: 1) break it down into 2000, 10, and 4. 2) Then convert: 2000 = MM, 10 = X, 4 = IV. Thus, the year 2014 (converted) = MMIV.

While learning to read, calculate, and convert Roman Numerals to Decimal Numbers and vice versa are seemingly a trivial pursuit or a waste of time or effort, it surprisingly places the child or adult who pursues and masters the skill and knowledge in an elite and tiny upper percentile of humans on this planet who have mastered and can quickly grasp the dates, years, or other events (e.g., when movies were made dating back to the 1920's or 1930's or earlier, when dinosaurs or ancient fossils or cities or pyramids were built by past rulers or pharaohs; what Super Bowl (American Football) highlights you are watching each year before each Super Bowl event (traditionally, the game is every January of each new year). Why not strive to be elite (in the positive sense of this word; too often, this word has incorrectly, falsely, inaccurately been used in association with liberal, socialist, communist, super-rich anti-American individuals who infiltrate American politics and government so as to subvert or sabotage traditional Christian American values that have, in the past, currently, and will, in the future, continue to be the backbone of what has made America the greatest country in the world, all because traditional Christian American values are: color-blind, reward good work ethic, honesty, kindness, mutual respect for fellow humans, respect for God and Godly values as taught by Jesus in The Bible, thereby allowing equal opportunity for success regardless of birthplace or birth family, whether they be peasants or royalty, thus "elite" is rather and instead, the American Dream (and world citizen dream) that a human being, from birth, may achieve any level of greatness that is humanly possible and via God's guidance, grace, mercy, and protection if they are kind, hard-working, generous, motivated, dedicated, directed by Godly values of making the world a better, safer, more Godly place of respect and nurturing of all humans from birth to death as God's miracle creations. The term and word "elite" has now been defined correctly for this generation and future generations in perpetuity.

Peter and Luke's parents demonstrated the flexibility and listening skills to allow adaptability and give their children the opportunity for trial and error or, more specifically, trial to see if an inner spark of passion for their first assigned musical instrument, the piano, would become a blazing fire of passion, challenge, and channel for focused devotion, expression of one's inner soul and perfecting a practiced skill that would be the basis for learning how to start any task in life, devote time and effort to that task, establish goals that may be achieved, and then accomplish those goals with laser-sharp focus and steadfast dedication until perfection (or near-perfection on the rarest occasion, after all…we are human) is achieved, and that goal has been attained and realized. At young ages, approximately eight years old, both Peter and Luke were encouraged by their mother, a flautist (flute player) in grammar school and high school, and father (never played any wind instruments or piano as a child or adult) to take piano lessons for at least three months. Peter and Luke agreed to this verbal contract "of sorts." Both brothers were assigned lessons and piano playing skills to practice before attending lessons with the private piano lesson instructor. Peter and

Luke had an old "player piano" in their home that was previously owned by their paternal grandparents, which would play itself if you inserted a piano roll (roll of paper with patterns of holes in it that would program the piano as to what keys to play, resulting in a song) and continuously used both pedals, pumping them with both feet to ensure continuous unrolling and rolling of the piano roll onto another roll holder. When the song and piano roll were completed, you would then have to rewind the role, a truly ingenious and innovative invention. The piano could also be played in the ordinary and usual manner as a routine functional piano. Peter and Luke labored at piano practice after each weekly lesson for 3-6 months, acquiring finger positioning skills and reading treble and bass clef simultaneously for using both hands to play simple scales and melodies or songs. The treble clef, or G Clef, is used for the higher-sounding notes, usually played with the right hand. The bass clef, or F clef, is used for the lower sounding notes, usually played with the left hand. When the two clefs are put together by a brace, they are called a grand staff. In Peter and Luke's grammar school days, one period every day was entitled choir, where children learned to read music notes and sing, a subtle but enormous benefit to the brain development and brain integration and coordination, interpretation, communication neuron development in children, which has been largely ignored by grammar and high schools in America, but not in Asia, which has been disadvantageous to American children's brain development (read the book, "The Mozart Effect" for more details). If you are skeptical and require more convincing, then look at a "PET scan" of a person's brain when they are reading music, singing, playing a piano or other percussion or wind instrument, and note the innumerable or myriad brain integration and simultaneous and concomitant areas of the brain that all light up with activity instantaneously and simultaneously. It's one of the true medical wonders of the world if you have never seen how the brain is stimulated, taught, trained, coordinated, organized, challenged and thrilled by these experiences. Music training of the brain to function better is analogous to an Olympic athlete's physical training to attain "world-best" status and receive the gold medal in their respective event.

Neither Peter nor Luke developed a passion for continuing with piano lessons and perfecting their piano playing skills. Luckily, their parents, instead of just calling it quits with all musical instrument-playing aspirations, elected to suggest that both Peter and Luke contemplate then decide what other instruments they would have a greater passion for and to practice and play until they became the best that they could be. Genius parenting! Peter chose the trumpet. Luke chose the slide trombone. Neither Peter nor Luke ever looked back nor resented their choice because THEY were allowed to make their own personal choice…again, genius parenting. We started taking lessons just after obtaining our new Christmas present musical instrument gifts "from Santa Claus," of course. Peter's initial trumpet was a student model trumpet, as was Luke's first slide trombone. Both Peter and Luke slowly acquired practice books recommended by our trumpet and trombone private lesson instructors (and later by ourselves and our own desires and preferences), such as: "Rubank Elementary Method: Trombone or Baritone for Luke (or Trumpet, for Peter) by Newell H. Long, Rubank Advanced Method practice books for Trombone and Trumpet by W.M. Gower and H. Voxman, Jean Baptiste Arban's Complete Conservatory Method For Trombone for Luke (or Trumpet, for Peter) and jazz, wind instrument duets and popular songs practice books for trumpet and Trombone (Luke recalls the several specific titles and specific practice books that kept him interested in practicing his Trombone in the early days of his professional musician journey: "101 Hit Songs: for Trombone," and "Rubank (Hal Leonard): Concert and Contest Collection for Trombone with piano accompaniment, Compiled and Edited by H. Voxman," and many others.

Peter and Luke embarked on an amazing journey of 10,000 +++ hours each of: 1) school studying / performance (on testing), 2) music practicing/performance (as professional musicians before age 11) and 3) athletic sports practicing /playing (and frequent, more often than not, winning athletic individual and team sport events: all sports that Peter and Luke were eligible to apply or be selected for, and that were available to them; Luke recalls being one year younger than all his classmates, having started Kindergarten one year earlier than his classmates, thus he was underweight and very disappointed after being excluded from "Pop Warner" grammar school tackle football team eligibility for "not weighing enough to be eligible for team membership.") Luke recovered from this disappointment by playing "flag football" (which involves a flag worn on a strap around the waist, and the opponent must grab and remove the detachable flag from the waist strap to "tackle" you) instead of playing "Pop Warner" tackle football involving contusion-frequent contact football tackles, which might cause traumatic brain injury and concussions, bone fractures, or other organ or soft tissue injuries, e.g., spleen rupture, liver laceration, kidney contusions, ligament, tendon, or joint injuries, throughout grammar school (age 5-13)) instead of tackle football in grammar school and high school. Perhaps this missed opportunity was instead a blessing in disguise, as both Peter and Luke avoided devastating injuries while growing up (exceptions being Peter's rib fractures after catching a football during a "flag football" game and Luke's rib fractures sustained during extreme skiing on double black diamond ski runs and during speed ice skating hobbies). No traumatic brain injuries that we recall (funny sentence when you contemplate what is implied but not stated outright in this short sentence or statement)!

Peter and Luke became top-tier, highly accomplished and "well-rounded" students, participating in numerous school clubs, many different track and field events, and as team members of many different sports teams throughout their education years. Peter was Valedictorian of grammar school and high school, and Luke was Salutatorian of grammar school and Valedictorian of high school. Luke's outperformance in high school bested his past academic colleague (and "theoretical past academic opponent," at least in the mind of Yman and as per her comment and words written in Luke's grammar school yearbook, which Luke, ironically and amusingly, never read until many years after completing flight school, military service, medical school, and earning his doctorate degree!) and female classmate, Yman, from grammar school, who was the Valedictorian in grammar school while Luke was the Salutatorian in grammar school. Both Peter and Luke were professional musicians before the age of 11. Peter and Luke were both offered and accepted multiple opportunities to participate as professional musicians in many paid "gigs" throughout grammar school and high school. A "gig" ("gigs" is a plural term for a "gig," which is a single music performance event) is slang for a live musical performance, a paid engagement of a musician or ensemble. Peter and Luke had multiple opportunities as accomplished and professional musicians, both as individuals and as groups (brass ensembles, orchestras, bands, individual soloists with accompaniment piano or orchestra, etcetera). Luke recalls being invited to a gig involving the 100 best trombonists in California, who were paid to play original music compositions that were composed only for this event at St Mary's Cathedral Services with organ accompaniment in San Francisco, CA. In Luke's opinion, this was one of the most memorable, unique, special, and magical professional musical performances of his life. Luke will always remember and never forget these multiple magical and spellbinding concerts. Luke was also, later in his professional musician career yet still only in high school, judged and determined to be the "principal" trombonist (in bands, orchestras, and other musical groups, this term is synonymous with "number one") for the California State Honor Orchestra and the California State Honor Band concerts in the same calendar year and recorded four albums total during the multiple state honor band years of performances. Peter was the second-best trumpet player in the state of California and recorded two albums during his performances. The trumpet player who bested Peter was and is an unbelievably talented professional trumpet player and Los Angeles studio musician with multiple solo albums to his credit.

Luke and Peter found early on in their professional musician formative years that accumulating, listening to, memorizing classic albums and songs played by myriad other professional musicians, e.g., famous trombone and trumpet players of all music genres, expedited ear-training and subtle wind instrument performance sounds and playing techniques by standing on the shoulders of predecessor great musicians to see clearer and farther and to achieve outstanding performances. Becoming a musician early in life may rapidly "hyper develop" the brain and body of that individual and bestow myriad unanticipated life skills, abilities, critical reasoning expertise (and other mental benefits), creative perspectives, imaginative aspirations, perfection attitudes/aspirations (especially regarding practicing and preparing for future perfect or near-perfect musical performances which will then "spill over" into all phases of that musician's future life and even their non-musician future profession and career accomplishments), and strategies for repeated success in all endeavors that are both unknown and unexpected by individuals choosing to be a child musician. Read the book "The Mozart Effect" for additional enlightenment. In Peter and Luke's specific circumstances, their "professional child musician era" empowered them to achieve optimal, zenith success for the rest of their lives, including every phase of school/education and future occupations or professions pursued, accomplished, and being performed each day of their respective careers until their well-deserved retirement. These learning principles can and should be applied to every aspect of life and in every discipline that one encounters and pursues in one's life journey, whether it be in the arts, academics, sports, spirituality, or any other field, aspiration, or endeavor.

What simple facts are near-universally ignored, yet so important and essential to know at the earliest age possible until the last minute of a human's physical existence on this Earth? That God created you, each human creation is an "Olympic Champion and Miracle," each human has been given the ultimate mentor or role model of how to live the most satisfying and God-pleasing life (Jesus/God's life and death on Earth and resurrection to heaven), and that all humans should treat each other with kindness, respect, and reverence as God's creations until they pass from their physical bodies and existence into their spiritual existence and reunion with God, their creator. Good and evil must be distinguished, and good behavior must be encouraged and rewarded, while bad behavior must always be discouraged and punished.

Chapter 7 – The Paradoxical POTENTIAL

Benefits of Injuries, Physical Altercations / Battles, Self-Defense Situations / Stances That Occur Early in Childhood and Appropriate Attitudes, Adjustments, Responses Necessary to Convert POTENTIAL Benefits Into ABSOLUTE STRENGTHS: Character, Confidence, Physical Prowess, Preparedness and Strength Dominance Into Infinity Future Existence.

Nobody gets through life without physical harm, injury (ies), fights, self-defense trials, assaults or threats of one or all of the above. This is a fact of life. It is how you respond to these events that will define who you become in this world and the limitations you self-define regarding your future versus the limitless future you afford yourself by introspection and reflection on the negative or adverse events you encountered, then devising a plan for the future prevention, defense, offense, and only if required and absolutely necessary, overwhelming aggression that will enable you to maintain a positive self-image, strength of character, 24-hour security each day, indomitable confidence and self-defense skills, and unmatched physical fitness and muscular strength that will enable you to encounter any potential or actual physical danger or threat of harm/danger emanating from an individual or physical feat or physical task or obstacle, and respond, in kind, with not only equal but excessive force, again if the situation demands it, to ensure your own personal safety and the safety of all those in your presence or vicinity. In short, there are good and evil people in this world (and every shade between these two extremes), and the earlier young children learn this and devise a plan to deal with these non-Christian evildoers and overcome fears, anxiety, and depression regarding "non-person" activities, events, conditions, or ill-advised, irrational, and unproductive "state of mind" circumstances or "mindsets" (e.g., dealing with irrational fears, phobias, or poor self-esteem/poor self-confidence issues), the earlier those young children can experience and aspire to plan, work towards, and achieve limitless future aspirations and dreams, if their motivation is to help or otherwise inspire others to do good deeds and help other humans on this planet, and if guided by God and positive, constructive and proactive attitude. Real-life examples can be very instructive.

Peter experienced very few physical threats and was involved in very few physical altercations as a child and was thus considered an excellent role model by his parents, teachers, and his younger brother Luke. Was this paucity or lack of adversity and physical threats or altercations a good thing or a bad thing? Conventional wisdom would argue that this was a good thing. Conventional wisdom would be wrong; in Luke's opinion, which is now a retrospective and seasoned view of past circumstances. Adversity, e.g., fights and skirmishes and defense of one's character where and when necessary and early in life can be very beneficial to any human child on this planet and can be an invaluable learning and developmental metamorphosis. Luke now believes that his older brother Peter would have significantly benefited from a bit more adversity (as delineated above), which would have: 1) Forced or necessitated adaptation skills at an earlier childhood age, resulting in superior future adult coping skills and strategies, 2) Inspired Peter to greater strength and physical fitness goals and aspirations, 3) Instilled Peter with greater self-confidence and ability to deal with adversity and resilience to overcome adversity and press on in life. In summary, Peter would have had the opportunity and motivation to develop greater physical fitness through exercise, weightlifting, and other strength training, which might then have resulted in an indomitable self-confidence, a 'never say die' attitude, and a very healthy self-esteem. Luke believes this because this was Luke's experience. Now for specific examples with regard to Peter and Luke's distinct development through near identical upbringing in the same family, schools, and community.

Luke was involved in multiple fights for justice and defense of defamation of character in school. He and his grammar school "Principals" ("administrative leaders of the school") were well-acquainted. Luke, being one year younger and smaller than all his classmates, was a frequent target for bullying, ridicule, defamation of character, or just unchristian behavior such as swearing, name-calling, or "sucker punches" from classmates. Luke decided early in life that if you do not immediately decide and choose to defend yourself when urgent and necessary, nobody else will, and certainly not promptly or in a timely manner that might prevent your personal destruction or demise. Thus, self-defense was learned as an early childhood skill and deterrent to prevent other potential assailants or attackers from "copycat" assaults. If Luke were to be attacked or maligned, his classmates were made aware that there would be significant consequences and both a verbal and physical response to back up those words of warning(s). Luke was thus familiar with all the instruments and enforcement techniques of his multiple school principals throughout his "life education era," some Principals being ethical, moral, and not excessively verbally or physically abusive. In contrast, other Principals took pride in their creativity and innovation of brutal, new verbal and physically abusive punishments, which, in retrospect, were unnecessary and evil in nature (and in real life for Luke!). The armamentarium of the nefarious "Emperor Nero Principals" (who would rather burn down Rome than hear the story of why a child had to fight to defend himself) used wood paddles, belts, wood sticks or wood or metal "rulers," or even the act of lifting a child who was seated, up in the air (e.g., while in the cafeteria eating lunch and talking while a principal was making an announcement), by pinching and pulling up both ears) all witnessed or experienced by Luke in "those good ol' days" of being a powerless and voiceless grammar school (astute) student, apparently with a good memory of many such bad, despicable past events and occurrences. These events, inflicted by grammar school Principals, occurred when Luke was in grammar school without any warnings, student notifications, or permission from parents, and without any mercy, at least that Luke can remember, during each and every occurrence of Principal physical abuse after school yard altercations or fights. In one instance, Luke was in a grammar school basketball game during an outside "yard break period" when one of his classmates suddenly became angered and punched Luke 6-10 times in the abdomen. Such lack of sportsmanship in the loss was shocking to Luke and caught him entirely by surprise. Luke resolved to work out to develop the strongest core abdominal muscles of anyone he ever knew (much like all boxers know they must do if they are going to have a successful boxing career), and Luke accomplished this goal and continues, to this very day, gym workouts with 400 to 600 abdominal muscle crunches per workout session. Later in life, during flight school, Luke increased this abdominal muscle crunches regimen to twice daily (during the twice daily workout sessions of flight school). In a second instance, Luke was attacked by a classmate from behind, dragged behind a sign so that nobody could see the assault, and then the classmate lied to both Luke's father and the school Principal, saying that the attack was due to a derogatory remark made by Luke in the school yard (this was a complete fabrication or lie, but nevertheless this lie was swallowed like a fish that swallows a hook, line and sinker weight, to the shock, awe and chagrin of Luke who knew that the truth was that he had been the victim of a unprovoked and vicious attack by his classmate), and this schoolmate of Luke went unpunished. Nothing motivated Luke more than this event and this unjust assault that went unpunished. Luke thereafter resolved to work out and become the strongest pound-for-pound student in his classes at school for the remainder of his life, which Luke, in fact, accomplished. After this unprovoked assault, Luke realized that the world is full of sheep, wolves, and shepherds. Luke, at the moment of his first physical assault, resolved to be that shepherd in the future whose strength was so dominant and overwhelming that all the sheep in his care could and would be protected from one or myriad wolves, if necessary, fighting and defeating each wolf to the death of every wolf if required. Luke dedicated the remainder of his life to this goal of attaining supreme physical fitness, maintaining maximum strength and overall health, and always being the "justice shepherd" whenever and wherever needed or necessary. Luke was similarly amazed that the grammar school Principal never really cared to listen nor showed any interest in hearing precisely what led to the fight, such as another student's egregious insults or acts of violence that led to Luke's responses. It seemed that Principals instead thought that the more time-efficient response to fights was simply to strike both children involved, assign equal blame to both children and then send both kids back to class. Luke learned to "roll with the punches" early in life…an invaluable lesson and opportunity to develop "life coping skills" of resilience, perseverance, strength, motivation, and inspiration. These occurrences in Luke's early childhood life turned out to be the opportunity, motivation, and aspiration that Luke would have to develop supreme superhero physical fitness through exercise, weightlifting, and other strength-training exercises and activities for the remainder of his unfathomable life. Also, they resulted in Luke's development of an indomitable self-confidence, a "never say die attitude," and a very healthy self-esteem that remained with and in Luke's mind, body, and soul for the rest of his life.

Peter was unprepared for a traumatic event that would befall him as an older student. He was confronted by the high school center on the varsity high school basketball team and threatened with physical violence if he did not comply with the dastardly request that he give his wallet to this student. Peter never told his parents, the high school Principal, other high school administration staff members, or even Luke, his brother, of this event until many years after high school and after university (a very significant but delayed revelation from Peter indeed!). Luke was greatly saddened by this revelation from Peter and immediately realized that Peter had somehow missed out on a part of his development during early childhood and had been unprepared to defend himself in that moment of urgent need for self-defense.

Luke, later in life, had a similar experience in Philadelphia, where he was walking home from a coffee shop when it closed at 2 am to his apartment approximately six blocks away. A 6 feet 4 inch unknown man confronted Luke and demanded Luke give him Luke's backpack (with all Luke's textbooks and computer laptop enclosed). Luke refused. Luke decided he was fit, strong, and fast enough to defend himself against his assailant if necessary, and a tense 10-15 minute standoff ensued. Eventually several other adults unrelated to the criminal walked around the corner onto the deserted street that Luke and the would-be criminal were on and engaged in a stare-down contest of wills. Luke was determined to fight to the death if necessary (of the criminal, of course, and not Luke's death!) which eventually became unnecessary when the other adults asked if everything was OK and the would-be (potential) criminal scampered off like a rabbit into the open grass field (on a dark, low-luminance night at 2 am, as previously stated). Luke, before this incident occurred in graduate school, had previously spent thousands of hours working out alongside United States Navy Seals (professional assassins in the military special forces), United States Marine Corps Forced Recon (Marine Corps assassins) and regular Marine Corps and Navy soldiers while deploying with all these fellow military personnel on special operations throughout the world, and Luke had also completed flight school, underwater helicopter water survival training, wilderness survival training. Luke was in fantastic shape as a very recent veteran with these special forces and was certain and confident that, if forced to defend himself, he could defend and protect himself and simultaneously inflict devastating injury or death, only if necessary, to his misguided, amateur, and thankfully unprepared and unarmed criminal assailant. Luke's attitude and confidence at the moment of attempted assault and theft was: "The bigger they are, the harder they fall." Luke never considered giving up his backpack but was happy that he was not forced to inflict devastating and lethal injuries to his would-be attacker and was instead able to return home to his apartment one block away and have a lovely night of sleep (not even a nightmare I might add).

In summary, early childhood fights and altercations, if in defense of justice or for a just cause such as self-defense, may equip that child with confidence, resolve, and determination to become more fit and strong so as to serve that child later in life as an adult to protect and defend himself or herself and those around them as just and righteous shepherds, rather than relegate that child to an eventual adult life without strength, fitness, confidence, or the ability to be anything other than an "appetizer sheep" that is repeatedly the prey of vicious wolves with an unrelenting appetite for weak, vulnerable, yet tasty sheep.

Chapter 8 – Elementary School Years: Athletics, Academics and Music, Neighbor Families

The Lowetts were the neighbors whose parents and children were most similar in age to Mother, Father, Peter, and Luke and somehow, almost like soulmates, our families took an immediate liking to each other and almost as if by destiny, our life paths intertwined most intimately based largely on our shared and similar interests, values, and reverence for spiritual closeness to God, enabling our families to contribute to our community in many different beneficial aspects and ways.

Nelag, the Lowetts patriarch, and his beautiful and regal Queen/wife Loreina (even rhymes with la Reina, Spanish for queen or empress) were regal in every respect. They were blessed with four beautiful, intelligent, thoughtful children who were raised in the church with Peter, Luke, and our parents. Their oldest son, Nairb, was like the Bible character Peter, a rock of moderation and dependability (absent the three denials of the Bible character). Nairb was the first Boy Scout of the family and was an overall great role model for Peter and Luke when they were growing up. Although Nairb was not in the high school band and played no musical instruments, he "fell in love at first sight" with one of the female tuba players in the band who was angelic in both looks, personality, and as a person of great innate qualities: caring, nurturing, and a positive outlook (sunny disposition). They dated throughout high school and were married immediately after that and together to this day. The Lowetts family's second oldest son, Matthew, was perhaps named after a Bible apostle, or at least could have or should have been. At a very young age, Matthew became both a classmate and Peter's best friend throughout grammar, high school, and thereafter. They played in grammar school and high school bands together (Peter the trumpet, Matthew the saxophone), raised heifers (to show and compete amongst other FFA ("Future Farmers of America" clubs or chapters at many different country grammar and high schools in America), and interacted, as a result, with other classmates and other different surrounding schools' FFA members, all whom performed presentations of their animals that they raised cared for, bathed, and worked with, in addition to walking alongside and showing or presenting to judges (during animal presentation county fair contests) other animal types (if they advanced into upper-level rounds of the competition), a privilege that was extended to and for those individuals who excelled at lower level rounds in presenting or walking alongside their own animals that they raised, fed, and become "animal-human soulmates" with, and in this manner, top-performing FFA animal raisers and presenters at the county fairs would compete with each other with the hope of advancing into the Grand Champion final round. To make a long story short, Peter, Luke's older brother, advanced to the "Grand Champion" final round even though he was only an FFA member for one year in high school ("Grand Champion" could have easily been the nickname of Peter as this term accurately described Peter's outperformance and exceptional performance of every task he chose to participate in and dedicate himself to. This nickname also accurately characterized every other phase and aspect of Peter's amazing, inspiring, and genius life!). Mathew and Peter, who were best friends, fed and housed their heifers and worked together with their young female cows (that had not borne a calf) at Mathew's home, where both animals were free to roam in a large, fenced-off, and contained area where they could walk them, wash and brush them as they matured into full-grown dairy cows to be auctioned off at the county fair to the highest bidder dairy owner. Peter and Matthew were avid students and have maintained their passions for reading and learning new ideas and concepts about world/universe history and science to this day. Peter, along with another classmate Mike Jorner studied history passionately and became known to their classmates as the history professors. Mathew, interestingly, went on to study veterinary science and married a classmate in vet school, became a veterinarian, and both he and his wife are currently practicing as partners in a clinic that they bought from the owner who hired them after their brief (several years) stint in Vietnam with the World Health Organization, teaching rural communities sustainable farming and irrigation technology and crop seed advances leading to more dependable crops each season regardless of unpredictable storms, flooding, other natural disasters, and crop threats in nature, as a married couple upon graduation from veterinarian school. They have two children, live in Oregon and have continued to raise fine, God-revering, warm-hearted young Christian adults who will change the world for the better just as their parents have in myriad ways and through the many human interactions throughout the world they will have, creating tiny ripples in the ocean waves that will turn into tidal waves of goodwill toward others' hearts, minds, and souls. Put another way, these loving neighbors and friends began as classmates of Peter and Luke, tiny muster seeds if you will, that grew into large muster plants, a thousand-fold larger and of great importance in providing refuge, comfort, and shade to many of nature's living creatures that have sought out or taken shelter under the expansive muster seed tree. Though mustard seeds are the smallest of seeds (e.g., 1-2 mm in diameter or around 1/10 of an inch in size), when they grow, they are the largest of garden plants and then become a tree that may become a perch for birds on its ever-expanding branches. Within 30 days of germination, mustard will develop a mature canopy and then begin to bud within 35-40 days of germination, entering the flowering period lasting 7-15 days or more, and pods develop from the flowers over the next 35-45 days. The The kingdom of heaven is like a grain of mustard seed, in one parable told by Jesus. Citizens of small towns in America and other countries worldwide, if nurtured and raised in the church for the first 1-2 decades of their lives, become mustard trees and a source of wisdom, understanding, compassion, empathy and refuge for other individuals in this universe whose seeds fell on deaf ears or hardened hearts/spirits akin to unfertilized, rugged, desolate, dry or otherwise unfarmable land or in regions of the world where frigid cold or suffocating heat or otherwise stormy weather precludes the development of the mustard seed into full-grown trees "so that the birds of the air (e.g., our world and universe) come and lodge in its branches (from the greatest book ever inspired by God, the Bible)."

Peter, Luke, and Mathew (and Mathew's entire family) were friends from the outset with our family, and continued in their many leadership roles in the community, including the Vikings Club for the youngest children,

Indian Guides for young children, Cub Scouts, Webelos (Webelos stands for "We'll BE Loyal Scouts." The Webelos/Arrow of Light (AOL) Program is a two-year program for Fourth and Fifth Grade Boys), Boy Scouts, and "Arrow of Light" distinction (the only cub scout badge that can be worn on the Boy Scout uniform (a true honor for only those who remained dedicated to meet the many requirements necessary for this badge); Luke's older brother, Peter, and Peter's best friend, Mathew, were both honored with and awarded the Arrow of Light (AOL) distinction as Webelos; Luke did not achieve this distinction but rejoiced in his brother's accomplishments). Peter and Mathew achieved the "Arrow of Light" distinction (the highest award in Cub Scouts) through teamwork and persistence as best friends. This "Arrow of Light" distinction was not in Luke's destiny (perhaps too many big wheel rides on the church sidewalks and too few community service projects that had to be planned and executed with great precision and with a willing heart at such a young age…kudos to Mathew and Peter), who also somehow steered a path distinct from Future Farmers of America (FFA) animal-raising endeavors. The "Arrow of Light" Cub Scout merit badge is awarded to cub scouts that display great community values and attitudes of service-oriented ambitions in life and act on them while scouts and amidst their many other academic and family obligations. In essence, cub scouts who have achieved outstanding performance and balance in their life, service-oriented attitudes, and, most importantly, actions much like that of a performer who walks the tightrope across bustling water rapids flowing over the Niagara Falls in upstate New York, achieve and are awarded one of the highest achievements in scouting, other than Eagle Scout status, at a very young age as a Boy Scout before graduating into a Boy Scouts of America troop (now called "Scouts BSA (formerly Boy Scouts) and allowing the path to Eagle Scout for both boys and girls)". Scouts BSA is currently for older children, ten years old (if Arrow of Light award) or 11-18 years old for all other children. I am most proud of my brother, Peter, and his best friend, Mathew, for achieving this "Arrow of Light" award for teamwork, cooperation, leadership skills at such a young age, portending auspicious futures for children on the verge of young adulthood before becoming adult leaders and outstanding citizens of their tight-knit communities and the world they live in. In short, mustard seeds to trees of refuge for birds of a feather flocking together to make this world most pleasant for our generation and the next and future generations.

Peter and Luke participated in the "Boy Scouts of America Junior Olympics," qualifying in multiple events. Mathew, Peter's best friend, had asthma as a child yet was as fast as a Gazelle (Blackbuck up to 70 miles per hour or 80-110 km/hour maximum speed in short bursts) or, at least, seemed to run that fast during short distance races. While in grammar school, Luke qualified for the Junior Olympics event in his specialty track and field event, the 880-yard dash (now the 800-meter race). It was on a Saturday in a distant city. However, on race day, Luke awoke to find that both mother and father had left in the car to complete weekend errands. They returned shortly before Luke's scheduled racing event start time. Despite the hopelessness of attempting to get in the car and arrive at Luke's event prior to the starting gun sounding, we arrived in the distant city, just outside the stadium, only to hear the announcement of Luke's race and the starting gun fire. To make matters worse, at least for personally for Luke, he found out that his grammar school's same-grade women's 4 x 100 relay team won their event at this stadium. Bitter-sweet indeed. He was happy about the school's team victory, but Luke suffered to the "core of his being" due to the lost opportunity to showcase his diligent training and dedication to his sport and the opportunity to compete for the 880-yard dash championship. With dignity and silence, Luke swallowed his pride and defeat without the opportunity to compete in the lane he had earned at earlier qualifying track meets. Luke's participation in sports, as a child, taught him (and should teach all children who participate in sports) to graciously accept victories and defeats in the same or similar manner and with the following philosophy: each game, event, or competition in sports (and in life) is an opportunity to assess and re-evaluate the effectiveness of your preparation and preparedness for that event and whether you have put in the requisite hours (10,000 + seems quite effective to be excellent or greater in many events, e.g., see Malcolm

Gladwell's books such as "Outliers," "The Tipping Point," David and Goliath" and "Endure" for both motivation and inspiration. See also books read by Luke, which greatly inspired and motivated him: The Bible (he read this book five times, cover to cover throughout grammar school and high school, several chapters per night at bedtime, as a source of: reality about dark times in world history (see Old Testament) for numerous examples of: battles, incest, shocking revelations, and battles to preserve cultural and religious principles and guidelines inspired by God and handed down through the generations), wisdom (see Luke's favorite book of The Bible for this topic: Proverbs), basic principles for healthy and happy living and loving thy neighbor as thy self, e.g., The Ten Commandments, The Sermon On The Mount (Matthew Chapter 5), The New Testament for Modern Living Guidelines As Demonstrated and Lived by Jesus Christ (truly the best guide to living a Godly life), and how to have the most positive and meaningful impact on other human beings during our lifetime, in the few short moments we reside on Earth, in comparison to the eternal life we can and will share with God, upon the death of our physical body and subsequent entry into a timeless, blissful eternity with God in heaven. Luke enjoyed other quick reads which had profound and lasting benefits in his life, such as "The Inner Game of Tennis," "Evelyn Wood's Seven-Day Speed Reading and Learning Program," "Plato's Republic," "Einstein's Special Theory of Relativity," "The Hobbit," "The Lord of The Rings series," "The Chronicles of Narnia series," "Moby Dick," "Tom Sawyer," "How To Win Friends And Influence People by Dale Carnegie," to name a few fantastic books, among myriad other books that Luke eventually read.

Luke, though not much of a book-reading enthusiast during his earliest childhood years may have at least come close to catching up with Peter's record-breaking run of reading innumerable books and racking up a fabulous "books read and understood" tally and totals on Peter's path to the Guinness Book of Records (not achieved by Peter, but Peter did, in fact, come closer to this goal of his than probably the majority of the population, at least on this planet Earth and in this universe, in Luke's estimation).

Because Peter and Luke developed excellent listening skills (credit their mother, who was an exceptional human being and, perhaps, unparalleled, as a "life teacher" and expert in this life skill, namely, being a supremely proactive and excellent listener) early in life, they both derived immense benefits and wisdom via their constant and careful listening to those offering sound and supremely wise mentoring, namely advice that was parental, pastoral, school education/school performance-enhancing, and "words of wisdom" from other friends and diverse various life teachers/counselors, and lastly, teachings, philosophies, and wisdom from prestigious university professors whom you have the opportunity and privilege to learn from as a result of your numerous years of study, preparation for examinations, and outperformance in school and life, all the result of the phenomenal listening skills your angelic mother demonstrated during your upbringing and taught to both you and your brother, enabling both of you to be the consecutive, one year apart, valedictorians of your respective high school graduating classes, and deliver graduation speeches to your classmates and the audiences, that were packed full of wisdom, enlightenment, and gratitude to and for your mother, all your teachers, and your entire class, who all enabled you to perfect your listening skills by learning from everyone you interacted with each day of your lives, up to that moment in time.

Luke feels that he would be remiss in not clearly emphasizing the incalculable value and benefits that these listening skills afforded both Peter and Luke and significantly aided their development as human beings. Peter and Luke both believe all children and adults in the world will or would be sadly lacking efficient, effective, and outstanding learning opportunities throughout their lives if exceptional listening skills are not emphasized in all schools at the earliest possible grade levels. The above-mentioned attitudes of Christian work ethic and responsibility to educate the human mind and strengthen the human body (e.g., reinstating the physical exercise period in grammar and high school curriculum, that was sadly eliminated in many California schools in years past, to teach humans the importance and interdependence of body health, mind health, and brain intelligence), do not endure through time eternal or, for some sinister reason, are neglected or ignored, or not implemented and continued forever in the future.

Advice that both Peter and Luke would like to impart and suggest to all parents, teachers, and professors are as follows: teach with enthusiasm and passion, lecture with variation in tone, volume, inflection in your voice to demonstrate conviction, passion, and commitment to your subject and emphasize during lectures, what is most important to your students, and what they should take from your class teachings out into the world and use a cloak or armor around their body, mind, and soul to battle the evil and discontented citizens of the world they will encounter who manifest qualities which are a threat to peaceful existence of all humans on this planet, lessons best taught by Jesus Christ in the Bible.

The red flags and philosophies dangerous to the continued existence of the universe include:

1) Failure to accept the teachings of Jesus Christ as principles to live by daily, by everyone on the planet, and not just professed and committed Christians that have been handed down to mankind or humankind by God, specifically as demonstrated and taught by Jesus Christ (an innocent mankind or humankind figure without sin) who is one and the same as God the Father in heaven and the Holy Spirit, which dwells in all men and women, is a gift from God our creator.

The inner peace that one derives from this acceptance and acknowledgment will reduce or eliminate daily stresses, anxiety, depression, drug or alcohol abuse or desire for body tattoos that destroy the magnificent appearance and beauty of God's creations, the human body's appearance as bestowed on each of us at our birth. God teaches that our bodies are our temples and should be treated as such. No graffiti, abusive poisons, or toxic substances should be introduced or injected (e.g., tattoos) into the body except in those situations in which the body might be healed by such chemicals or toxins, e.g., in the case of chemotherapy to arrest or slow the progression of an otherwise destructive cancer or disease that threatens the continued existence of the body as one's temple created and owned by God, who created us.

2) Professors and Teachers Should Themselves Attempt to Be Beyond Reproach and Likewise Teach Their Students to Be Beyond Reproach Whenever Possible and Seek to Discourage, Avoid, or Not Associate With Individuals Who Are: Negative, Dishonest, Divisive, Sycophant Persons, Boastful, Loud and Arrogant, And Racist individuals.

Those who lack a good conscience or the ability to feel remorse, compassion, empathy, sympathy, guilt for wrong deeds done, and those who are unwilling or unable to respect others as they would like to be respected should not be professors in our grammar schools, high schools, or universities, and "tenure" should not ever be able to protect these individuals from poisoning the minds of their life students.

Simple phrases such as: "Thank You, I Am Sorry, Excuse Me, Pardon Me, Would You Help Me and Can I Help You" not only make us human but make others aware that we acknowledge we are human and imperfect and not always self-sufficient and that we all, at various times in our lives, have benefitted from the assistance or help from others or, hopefully, have been in a position where we were open to, willing, and able to offer assistance or help to other fellow human beings while remaining functionally blind to the upbringing, language, skin color, and from whence came that other human being.

3) There are times in this life when reproaching of deviant and evil individuals whose intent is to harm or defile their communities or fellow man/woman through deceit, theft, manipulation, or other means must be dealt with. We must strive for equal opportunity (not necessarily equality for all, as we know, incentivizing honest and faithful effort by those who seek to serve their fellow man/woman and benefit their community in one or myriad ways by working as a teammate or as an individual towards one's goal should allow for those who show commitment and dedication to achieving honest and worthy goals

within the legal confines of their society should be rewarded for their steadfast labor and toiling to make this world a better place). Liberty and justice for all should always be the goal of humanity as we pass through eternity, occupying only the equivalent of a split second in the grand scheme of eternity, as God sees the universe, simultaneously in controlling and seeing time as the past, present, and future concomitantly and simultaneously.

4) Mother and Father wished to teach both Peter and Luke how important our education was to them and that they truly and genuinely cared and desired that we, every day at school, put forth our very best effort to learn as much as possible and not only pass but exceed each teacher's or professor's expectations for the depth of knowledge we acquire and the rapidity with which we acquire new knowledge and rapidly assimilate and incorporate these new concepts and paradigms in our thinking, writing, and analysis of the ever-expanding knowledge base that attempts to describe the world and universe that we live in. God surely joyfully and enthusiastically wishes for us to acknowledge him in all that we learn and accomplish on our journey through life. One seemingly simple but extremely powerful and effective technique our parents employed to show us they cared about our grades in school was as follows: starting in Kindergarten, we received, e.g., one quarter (25 cents or one-quarter of one United States currency dollar) for each highest grade, we received (e.g., an A grade), one dime (e.g., one-tenth of one U.S.A. dollar) for each, e.g., B grade (second highest grade or above average testing result), one nickel (e.g., 1/20 of one U.S.A. dollar) for each average grade, and no monetary reward whatsoever for any below-average grade. Though this system was/is overly simplistic, as some or many might argue, it also rings clear as a bell that our parents care about what effort we make to obtain good marks or grades in school and, more importantly, that they will/would/will continue to always closely scrutinize our reports each and every quarter that we receive evaluations. In two words: accountability and consequences. This method taught my brother and me that through preparedness and hard work, we would have the ability to earn a smile and acceptance

from our parents of a job well done and also earn, perhaps, a small treat such as a pack of bubble gum, a candy bar, or a pack of professional baseball player trading cards (this was a big deal when we were kids… not so much the collector items of value at this time).

Other neighborhood families with children the same age as Peter and Luke in the community greatly influenced their development. Peter's classmate and the youngest daughter of our Pastor was a beautiful and intelligent child who grew up and attended grammar school and high school and church every Sunday with Peter and Luke. Mathew and his family also attended school and church each Sunday. Our next-door neighbors, the Slevocs, had one boy and two girls. Mit gave his newspaper delivery business first to Luke, who, after a short time, he gave it to his older brother Peter. Luke preferred to start his own business in the sixth grade (approximately ten years of age), mowing all the lawns and doing landscaping work for all the neighbors who preferred not to do the work themselves (a surprisingly large number of homes opted in), and thus, Luke's entrepreneurial business idea rapidly took off and grew at an alarming rate to the point that Luke had to focus on time management at a very young age to balance studies in school, home chores, and his private business on weekday afternoons/evenings and on weekends.

At about this same time period, Peter (11 years old) and Luke (10 years old) were getting heavily interested in the wind instruments they personally selected after failing to maintain any long-term interest in continuing to practice for piano lessons that our parents encouraged us to begin several years earlier. (Cessation of piano playing is one of the few regrets that both Peter and Luke have in life. The brothers now know how this activity develops the brain in myriad indescribable ways which are highly desirable in a young child and likely will result in higher intelligence and the integration and coordination of many brain functions that are required to play the piano well.) Nevertheless, without passion for the piano as an instrument to express ourselves and because we were forced and not necessarily asked if we wished to play the piano prior to the scheduling of our lessons, both Peter and Luke declined to continue with their piano lessons. In summary, thanks, but no thanks. Instead of giving up on musical instruments altogether, Peter and Luke's mother, who was a flautist in school, encouraged both Peter and Luke to choose their own instruments so that they might agree to play and continue with music lessons if they found a new passion for their chosen instruments, trumpet for Peter and slide trombone for Luke, which they did, and both boys immediately became interested, motivated, and extremely dedicated to practicing their instruments, and undoubtedly become the best musicians they were capable of being.

These are magic words and concepts to young children: freedom of choice, freedom of expression, and parents vowing their support (in the form of buying the initial instruments to be played by their children and taking their children to biweekly lessons [and later on, weekly lessons], then most astonishingly, their willingness to put up with loud wind instruments being played in the family home up to 5-6 hours per day and late evenings on many occasions. In retrospect, this is still a shocker to Peter and Luke, even many years later!

Peter and Luke's parents were, mysteriously, willing to transport their children to band practices, honor band/honor orchestra practices and performances, and Junior Philharmonic Orchestra practices when necessary or when Peter and Luke were unable to drive themselves. Incredible.

Peter, while a high school student, was the second-best (#2) trumpet player in the California State Honor Band and was selected after high school to an All-American Band that toured throughout Europe, a once in a lifetime experience for Peter, which he will never forget.

Luke, also while a high school student, was the best (#1) trombone player in the California State Honor Band and California State Honor Orchestra in later years.

Both Peter and Luke became professional musicians starting in the sixth grade as a result of their aggressive practice schedule and lessons from fabulous professional musicians residing in the closest big city that they traveled to for personal wind instrument lessons. The most magical and most important ingredient to both Peter and Luke's precocious development as both professional musicians and superb academic students throughout their educational development was quite simple and inexpensive: parental support, encouragement, and participation in the activities of their children while they were growing up and open to positive suggestions of wisdom, e.g., "influenceable."

Luke and Peter both had, figuratively and not literally, "three loving mothers" and "three pairs of parents" in the local town and community in which they grew up as children and young adults, and, in retrospect, this was an enormous advantage to them throughout the course of both their lives. Let's focus on our three mothers. Our own "genetic and angelic mother" was incredibly supportive, the best listener I have ever met to date and phenomenally selfless and generous. She taught everything the Bible instructed us to be as young children and young adults, as modeled and demonstrated by the life Jesus Christ lived, which is described in great detail in the Bible. Compassion, sympathy, empathy, kindness, forgiveness, and love were just several of the greatest and Godly qualities that she possessed and demonstrated for and to her family in all that she did every day. I have spoken of Peter's best friend, Mathew, whose mother (our second, non-genetic mother) demonstrated the same qualities possessed by our genetic mother. Luke's best friend since the fifth grade was Garett. Garett's mother, Maggie, functionally served as Peter and Luke's third (non-genetic) mother in so many ways. The free and unconditional love that each of our three functional mothers bestowed on Peter and Luke was neither earned nor deserved but humbly accepted, greatly appreciated, and will be remembered by Peter and Luke until the day they die. Both Peter and Luke remained soulmates with all three mothers up until their deaths in later years. Peter and Luke both had three fathers, clearly an uneven playing field when compared to other individuals in life who had only one or no father for guidance, encouragement, and to set an example of how to live life in the manner that Jesus Christ lived and then died blameless on the cross to atone for our sins so that all individuals on this planet have the opportunity to sin no more and be forgiven in order to live eternal life in heaven with God, our creator. Knowing that God is watching over you and is with you at all times is a huge advantage in life because all your anxiety, depression, and uncertainty melt away and allow you to live a "purpose-driven life" (incidentally, this phrase and concept brings to mind a fabulous book "The Purpose Driven Life" by author Rick Warren, read by both Peter and Luke in the past, which should also be read, perhaps more than once, by every human on this planet who desires superhero credibility and status as a benevolent and God-guided superhero on Earth) focusing on performing at your very best each day, helping others, treating and respecting your body as a "Temple for God," striving to attain and maintain essential human qualities and attributes, including wisdom, compassion, empathy, forgiveness, tolerance, patience, humble and quiet spirit, peaceful resolution of conflicts (whenever possible, with exceptions in situations where great evil threatens God's children (humanity)).

Both Peter and Luke were blessed throughout their childhood and into adulthood, not because they were perfect or near-perfect, but as a result of God's mercy, grace, and love for them. God continues to protect and guide them, not allowing either of them to be tested beyond their abilities to withstand the tests in life that they encounter. This fact is true for all God's children (all humanity). Peter graduated from both grammar school and high school as the Valedictorian of his class. Luke graduated from grammar school as the Salutatorian. The young female who graduated as the grammar school Valedictorian signed Luke's school yearbook with the following inscription: "…Better luck next time…" Was this cruel inscription some kind of test? Luke was not sure but resolved to place his trust in God no matter what happened in life. Luke said nothing to his classmate. God may test us to the limit of our ability to handle each test, but you can be assured he has promised never to test us beyond or over and above our ability to handle stress, depression, or other trials or tribulations in this world. Four years after Luke graduated from grammar school, he graduated Valedictorian of high school. The young female who made the mocking and gloating inscription in Luke's grammar school yearbook finished high school, the Salutatorian, just behind Luke. If you trust in God and are constantly trying to live your life in the manner Jesus Christ lived his life on Earth, suffering all the hardships and anguish we face as humans and more (sinless, as God's son and dying on the cross for our sins), good things will happen in your life, and God will bless you in many ways and with amazing frequency, not only meeting but exceeding your expectations. God is great!

Luke was elected Student Body President in his senior year of high school by his high school classmates and was also elected "Most Likely To Succeed" (a final high school yearbook special honor) by his senior-year classmates. Only God may someday judge if Luke lived up to the promise, vote of confidence, and goodwill shown by his high school classmates who both inspired and motivated Luke to accomplish God's will for his life and seek out a profession that would both help and serve others and, if possible, improve their lives and communicate, humbly, his great appreciation and thankfulness for this opportunity to serve others, which was afforded to him by his creator and protector, God Almighty.

Chapter 9 – Luke's Formative Reading List, Quotes and Famous Sayings That Shaped His Future, Dramatically Influenced And/Or Shocked Luke And, Perhaps, All Individuals (In Some Cases to The Core of One's Soul) During Development and Should Stimulate Introspection and Contemplation Of Why We Were Created and Placed On This Earth and How We Can and Should Use Our Words In A Select, Concise and Kind Manner To Most Effectively Optimize Communication, Call Out And Acknowledge Foul and Undesirable Behavior Even When Dangerous and May Lead To Criticism That Is Projected Back Toward The Sentinel / Messenger and Inspire Kindness, Harmony, and Serenity Whenever Possible. Kindness and truth in communication is always possible and desirable.

Luke and his older brother, Peter, began life wearing identical and matching (ridiculous-looking) wardrobes selected by their mother, including "Winnie The Poo" red, white, and blue striped pants, cute matching cowboy pants, shirts, boots, and cowboy hats. Luke and Peter shared a "Big Wheel" three wheeled (all plastic wheels with a single large wheel in front and two smaller wheels in the rear and a dragster-like "fun-looking" design) tricycle and enjoyed many hours of speeding down the cement walkways throughout the next-door Presbyterian Church grounds adjacent to their home, an old manse (former home for the church's pastors), that was rented to Luke and Peter's parents because the manse was too old (of note, and interestingly, a newer home was offered to and accepted by the pastor of the church at that time) and on the condition that Luke and Peter's father would assist in locking up all the doors at the church facility and later on, after John Narom retired, maintain and mow the large grass lawn all around the entire church. In return, Luke and Peter's young parents received the benefit of (needed at that time in Peter and Luke's parents' lives) reasonable and discounted monthly rent payments that were due to and paid on time to the Presbyterian Church each month.

Luke and Peter had to be quite innovative and imaginative in a small town of 1400 persons to fill the hours of each day and night starting day one after their big and significant birth events, approximately one-and-a-half years apart for, first, Peter, then Luke, Peter's second-born sibling brother. Peter and Luke spent hundreds of hours walking along "dirt-only-walled irrigation ditch banks," looking for and at interesting, at least to otherwise bored very young children raised in small country towns in this world, water spiders, pollywogs, frogs, and Lady Bugs. They were and are soulmate brothers from birth. Hundreds of hours were spent by Luke and Peter (as often as possible) riding bikes, riding skateboards, playing tennis for 1-5 hours per session at the local high school tennis courts (first with "Shorty Tennis Racquets [short handle racquets for small children], then transitioned to adult tennis racquets, initially Jack Kramer wood racquets, then metal small-head Jimmy Conner racquets, then "Prince" racquets [metal initially, then graphite racquets]), and in fifth grade, Peter commenced trumpet playing/practicing (1-6 hours per day throughout high school and college), and Luke commenced slide trombone playing/practicing (1-6 hours per day throughout high school, none in College, then joined a professional big band after completing medical school and flight school, and while an active duty military flight surgeon pilot flying military helicopters and fighter-attack jets, and before returning to and commencing postdoctoral eye surgery residency training, subspecialty eye surgery fellowship training, and then commencing his private practice as an eye surgeon. Interestingly, few people realize that each eye is actually an outgrowth from the brain (study embryology for the details of eye formation in embryos). Thus, all eye surgeons are, technically and accurately, neurosurgeons by trade and in the work they accomplish each day in their practice of medicine! Luke achieved the number one and highest score on the Embryology final exam in medical school (100% certain). Both Luke and Peter excelled in sports, music, and academics as a result of thousands of hours of preparation, practice, sacrifices, studying, and NOT "innate or congenital genius status" for Peter or Luke, nor from having "world-class athlete parents" or "genius parents." Stress, struggle, learning to lose often and with grace, composure, resilience, and with the perspective, aspiration, and will to try harder and perform better next time, improving and perfecting all future performances were the guiding principles first for Peter, then Luke (who lost myriad contests in every category of activity to Peter growing up). Common traits that characterized Peter and Luke's endeavors, innumerable losses and, eventually, multiple wins and victories were: "blood, sweat, and tears" practice and preparation mentality for all events they participated in and in all their endeavors, and the "never give up" mentality that their mother had and generously passed on to both her sons. Mother's repeated statement to her two sons from the time each son was born until her death many years later, were: "Peter [or Luke]... Your best is always good enough!" These simple words strung together, and this simple statement of fact, encouragement, inspiration, approval of an exam/task/sporting event/music event/acting or singing event being well done, the best that Peter [or Luke] could muster at that time, engendered mother's credo: "Never give up." Mother was a "Big Women On Campus" (figuratively but literally, as she was never physically large, intimidating, nor imposing, but rather sweet, petite, gregarious, and very kind, which enamored her with all her classmates, male (not surprisingly) and female (very surprising, jealousy and "cat fights" usually are expected between beautiful, educated women in school at any level yet these were not issues for mother because of her docile, generous, kind interactions with her classmates and coworkers throughout her life, which was innate to her character and resulted from her upbringing in the Methodist (protestant) Church in her hometown and her trust and belief that God was her creator, protector, and savior). Luke and Peter were largely unaware of their mother's distinguished accomplishments and good deeds done in high school and college up until her marriage to Peter and Luke's father because their mother was neither a sycophant nor braggadocious but was an "A+ mother," the likes of which may never be replicated in history. Mother was neither perfect nor a saint, but respected and feared God and always sought to comfort others and find a kind resolution to conflict when possible or stand up and defend those who could but/or would not defend and protect themselves if they had been wronged or unjustly treated or accused by false witnesses. Mother was a champion from birth to death and a revered hero and loving mother and lifelong source of happiness and inspiration to both her professional musicians, all-American, and valedictorian sons.

Only after mother's death and upon finding mother's high school yearbook and college yearbook and personal communications to mother from her classmates and coworkers, did Luke and Peter learn, amongst many other amazing accomplishments, that mother was: A) a multi-sport athlete in field hockey, track, basketball, and softball, B) voted Prom Queen by her high school and college classmates, C) Flautist in band and orchestra, D) All-state (New Hampshire) band and orchestra participant, E) Champion Dance Couple Member (with her twin brother) in dance competitions throughout all of the New England region of the United States, F) Marching Band member participant in the United States Presidential Inauguration Parade (traveled to Washington D.C. for this honor and event) while in high school, and

G) Amazing, caring, compassionate, empathetic occupational therapist throughout her working professional life. One of Peter and Luke's mother's coworkers, a male occupational therapist who had worked many years with mother then moved to another city and job, returned to visit mother when Peter and Luke were in high school and came out to Peter and Luke's mother's home and informed and revealed to Luke, Peter (and our father) the following: "Your mother was the most kind person and occupational therapist I have ever known and worked with throughout my long and satisfying career in the field of occupational therapy." Luke, Peter, and their father would never forget this "highest of compliments" remark from their mother's former coworker.

As Peter and Luke aged to the ripe teenage years of late childhood, they reflected on the kind of men they sought to emulate as they grew older, and a fascinating list of individuals came to mind. The list below is anything but a complete list of the individuals that came up and were discussed and favored; rather, it is a very abbreviated sampling of the list. The list for Peter was decidedly distinct and different from that of Luke as one would and should expect from any two individuals, despite their being decidedly eternal soulmate brothers.

Peter's list included: Jesus Christ, Billy Graham (American Christian Evangelist), C.S. Lewis (Clives Staples Lewis was a British writer and lay theologian. He held academic positions in English literature at both Oxford University and Cambridge University, whose many notable and exceptional works include: The Chronicles of Narnia, Mere Christianity, The Allegory of Love, The Screwtape Letters, The Great Divorce, Miracles, Out of the Silent Planet, Daily Devotionals, The C.S. Lewis Bible, The Abolition of Man, El Peso de la Gloria; C.S. Lewis was a contemporary of J.R.R. Tolkien), J.R.R. Tolkien (John Ronald Reuel Tolkien DBE FRSL was an English writer, poet, philologist, and academic, best known as the author of the high fantasy works: The Hobbit and The Lord of the Rings.), Charles Stanley (Atlanta, Georgia, United States church pastor), Wynton Marsalis, Doc Severinsen, Al Hirt, Maurice Andre, Maynard Ferguson, Allen Vizzutti, Gregory Peck (To Kill A Mockingbird movie role), Perry Mason (1957 TV series in the United States of America, prosecutor lawyer role played by Raymond Burr).

Luke's list, somewhat more influenced by his passion for classical movies, included: Jesus Christ, Billy Graham, C.S. Lewis, J.R.R. Tolkien, Keith Green (Christian Singer with many spellbinding and mesmerizing albums, including, amongst others, So You Wanna Go Back To Egypt, The Prodigal Son, For Him Who Has Ears To Hear, No Compromise, The Ministry Years 1977-1979, Keith Green: The Greatest Hits Piano, Vocal and Guitar Chords, Horbuch, Keith Green – Icon (Audio CD), Songs For The Shepherd, Keith Green: Ministry Years Vol. 2,), Charles Stanley (pastor Atlanta, GA church), David Jeremiah (pastor of El Cajon, CA church), All James Bond Movies and Actors, e.g., Sean Connery (1962-67, 1971, 1983), David Niven (1967), George Lazenby (1969), Roger Moore (1973-1985), Timothy Dalton (1987-1989), Pierce Brosnan (1995-2002), Daniel Craig (2006-2021); Gary Cooper, Cary Grant, Robert Taylor, John Wayne, Clint Eastwood, Charles Bronson, Charlton Heston, Errol Flynn, Gregory Peck, Randolph Scott, Fredric March, Steve McQueen, Charles Chaplin, Harold Lloyd, Buster Keaton, The Marx Brothers (movie comedians), Bud Abbott and Lou Costello, Joe E. Brown, Trombone Musicians: Bill Watrous (William Russell Watrous II [June 8, 1939-July 2, 2018] was an American jazz trombonist. He is perhaps best known for his rendition of Sammy Nestico's arrangement of the Johnny Mandel ballad "A Time For Love," which he recorded on a 1993 album of the same name. A self-described "bop-oriented" player, he was well-known among trombonists as a master technician and for his mellifluous sound. Notable albums: "I'll Play For You," "In Love Again," "Plays Love Themes for the Underground, the Establishment and Other Sub Cultures Not Yet Known, Bone Straight Ahead, Manhattan Wildlife Refuge, The Tiger of San Pedro, Funk 'n' Fun, Watrous in Hollywood, Coronary Trombossa!, La Zorra, Bill Watrous in London, Roaring Back to New York, New York, Bill Watrous and Carl Fontana, Someplace Else, Reflections, Bone-Ified, Time for Love, Space Available, Live at the Blue Note, Living in the Moment with The Gary Urwin Jazz Orchestra, Live in Living Comfort,

Mad to the Bone with The Rob Stoneback Big Band, Kindred Spirits with The Gary Urwin Jazz Orchestra), Kai Winding, Urbie Green, J.J. Johnson, Carl Fontana, Glenn Miller, Tommy Dorsey, Jack Teagarden, Fred Wesley, Curtis Fuller, Wycliffe Gordon, Joseph Alessi, Frank Rosolino, and many others.

"I Never Met A Man I Didn't Like" (Will Rogers); Luke particularly appreciates the profoundness and subtle meaning in the following simple quote he discovered in his life's journey regarding "off-piste skiing" (definition: [comes from French and is commonly used by skiers or snowboarders to describe mountain snow terrain that is off the groomed trails, where you can encounter a wide variety of exciting/unknown/potentially dangerous or unpredictable snow conditions and terrain features, hazards, and perils, including deep snow, crud, large moguls or bumps, steep slopes, ledges, drop-offs or cliffs, and narrow chutes), which has been a lifelong passion of Luke's since grammar school, where one meets skiing terrain and conditions that have the power to convert the most passionate atheists into God-seeking, Bible verse-reading, daily praying Christians in a single mountain slope and conversion experience whereby the rider makes a pact or treaty with God mid-slope that if he/she survives the treacherous terrain journey down the mountain, then they will unconditionally thank God and be grateful and respectful of God's presence and protection during their (perhaps in certain instances, ill-advised) descent decision to, as some might say, "Go where no man has (or should not have gone?) gone before": "It's better to go skiing and think of God than go to church and think of sport. (Fridtjof Nansen)," "Into each life, a little rain must fall" (movie, 1951, The Flying Leathernecks, John Wayne), "The world is a tragedy to those who feel, but a comedy to those who think." Horace Walpole 1717-1797, Connoisseur and Art Historian; Reporter to Babe Ruth "How is it that you made 80k and President Hoover made only 75k? Answer: "What does Hoover have to do with it…plus…I had a better year than he did!"; "We've been having trouble making 'ends meet'…sometimes they meet in the middle…sometimes they don't meet at all" (Art Carney in the movie: "Billy Rose's Jumbo" [Doris

Day, Art Carney]), "Begin at once to live, and count each separate day as a separate life. –Seneca;" "I'm going to tell the judge that 'you would have to get better to be crazy'" (Tyler Perry and Dr Phil movie ending), "That's the pot calling the kettle black," "If you don't stick up for yourself, nobody else will." Jim Cramer's Mother during a live appearance on CNBC Mad Money television show (11-27-18). Ataraxia: imperturbability, a desirable quality for stock investing as per Benjamin Graham's classic book "The Intelligent Investor"; He was described as having: "unruffled serenity," "certain aloofness," "humane, but not human," "There are two things that are certain in life, death and taxes." and "The best thing to give to your enemy is forgiveness; to an opponent, tolerance; to a friend, your heart; to your child, a good example." Benjamin Franklin, Robert Taylor (Hollywood actor, 1950s) quote: "I'm a man of few virtues, and patience isn't one of them." from the 1954 movie: "The Valley of the Kings." "Be polite and courteous, but have a plan to kill everyone you meet"-- United States of America Marine Corps General James Mattis (2003). "Diner" Movie with Director Jerry Weintraub, quote from the movie: "I'll hit you so hard, I'll kill your whole family.", "Every person born into this world has a natural right to sustain, preserve and defend his (their) own life to the best of his (their) ability." -- Giovanni Boccaccio; "Comparison is the thief of joy." --Theodore Roosevelt (United States of America President); Quotes about the motivating value of deadlines ("The Deadline Effect" book by Christopher Cox): A) Hofstadter's Law: It always takes longer than you expect, even when you take into account Hofstadter's Law. B) Parkinson's Law: Work expands to fill the time available for its completion. C) Horstman's Corollary: Work contracts to fit in the time we give it. D) 100* Stock-Sanford's Corollary: If you wait until the last minute, it only takes a minute to do. (Funny!); "You have been weighed, you have been measured…and you have been found wanting." (From the movie: "A Knight's Tale"); "Without things to overcome, you don't become much of a person, do you?" -- Bette Davis; "Work never hurt anyone, but lack of it destroys people." Katharine Hepburn; 100* Desiderata (by Max Ehrmann, copyright 1927, renewed 1954 by Bertha Ehrmann); 100* Rudyard Kipling saying entitled: "If." 1000*

"The most important yardstick of your success is how you treat others." Barbara Pierce Bush (wife of George Herbert Bush, former President of the United States of America).

Chapter 10 – Luke's List of Interesting Words and Definitions That Motivate and Inspire an Individual to Look up New and Unfamiliar Words and Fully Appreciate How a Diverse Vocabulary Can Enhance Communication Skills and Satisfy Inquisitive Minds, Both of Which Can Lead to More Effective and Satisfying Communication.

Several books, book series, films/movies, television series/shows that Luke saw and/or read during his young, formative years that somehow impressed or inspired his imagination, dreams, aspirations, and desire to explore, be adventurous, and take outsized chances in life to reap outsized amazing, unique experiences and opportunities unimaginable were, amongst many other books not listed in this manuscript, the following list: The Bible (Luke read this one cover-to-cover five times in grammar school and high school; the greatest book and source of wisdom, history, guidance, and inspiration ever written [and God's Gift To Mankind/The Planet Earth and All It's Human Inhabitants]), Mere Christianity (by C.S. Lewis), The Chronicles of Narnia (by C.S. Lewis), The Space Trilogy (by C.S. Lewis), The Screwtape Letters (by C.S. Lewis), The Great Divorce (by C.S. Lewis), Miracles (by C.S. Lewis), Plato's Republic by Socrates, Einstein's Special Theory of Relativity (by Albert Einstein), Sigmund Freud Primer, All "James Bond" Movies (A distinct favorite of Luke's from birth to present), Wild West TV series, The Waltons TV series, Little House On The Prairie (by Laura Ingalls Wilder, based on her best-selling series of Little House books. These books are eerily but perhaps not unsurprisingly similar to the small town and community that Peter and Luke were born and raised in (typical small-town life in non-urban regions of the world), with almost every situation and circumstance in the television series, also experienced by Luke and Peter…very strange indeed…if Peter and Luke had been born female sisters (as in this television series), Peter would clearly have been Mary, and Luke would have most likely and accurately been Laura's character. It is fascinating and mysterious how Peter and Luke's upbringing so closely paralleled the "Ingalls family" in this television series from the 1970s.), The Walton's TV series, Get Smart TV series, Grizzly Adams TV series, Chips TV Series, Emergency TV Series (about paramedics everyday encounters and experiences), Roots (TV mini-series; narrated by James Earl Jones), Gun Smoke TV Series, Bonanza TV series, The Munsters TV series, Baa Baa Black Sheep TV Series, Hogan's Heroes TV Series, All War Movies, Seeing Astronauts On The Moon on TV as a young child, All Cowboy Western Movies, All Olympics TV Coverage (Peter and Luke's entire family would unite to watch as much content as possible until we could no longer keep our eyes open, then we would all go to bed!), Star Trek and Star Wars (All movies and the TV series of Star Trek [with William Shatner as Captain James Kirk]), The Hiding Place (by Corrie Ten Boom), The Other Side of The Mountain (true stories of paraplegic snow skiing professional who followed Peter and Luke's mother's credo: "Never give up.")

Luke believes that every human should compile a personal list of interesting words or phrases that are fascinating, unique, or otherwise interesting that one had encountered and had to look up to expand their vocabulary or otherwise broaden their comprehension of their non-native language or native or local language or dialect. Luke's list includes, amongst many others not able to be included in this manuscript, the following words of interest and fascination: besmirch, smidgeon, stupefying, conundrum, cogent (convincing or believable by virtue of forcible, clear presentation), imbroglio "entanglement" (Italian), messy, complicated misunderstanding, sycophant (person who acts obsequiously [too willing to serve someone or something] toward powerful or influential person seeking self-gain or false accuser [original definition], aka "brown-noser," "suck-ups," "teacher's pets"), metonymy (figure of speech where something takes the name of a related thing, e.g., Congress and "Capitol Hill"), kerfuffle, mea culpa, kowtow; prurience: prurient: marked by or arousing an immoderate or unwholesome interest or desire (e.g., sexual desire); apotheosis: the highest point in the development of something; culmination, climax, or zenith; skeeziest: [skeez: sex], sleazeball, skanky; bellicose: demonstrating aggression and willingness to fight; kerfuffle: disturbance or commotion typically caused by a dispute or conflict; mea culpa: from Latin "through my fault" ["culpa" = "guilt"] phrase means: "It was my fault," "I apologize"; culpable: "meriting condemnation or blame especially as wrong or harmful; kowtow: [derived from Cantonese Chinese: kau tau, from Mandarin Chinese: koutou], definition: act in an excessively subservient manner, behave obsequiously, be servile, be sycophantic; Chinese custom of: kneel and touch ground with forehead in worship or submission; demagoguery: Political activity/practices that seek support by appealing to desires/prejudices of ordinary people rather than by using rational argument ("the d. of political opportunists"), Rube Goldberg's Inventions; scurrilous: something that is very abusive or is scandalous and potentially harmful rumors spread to ruin someone's reputation. A nasty, verbal, abusive attack on a teacher is an example of a scurrilous attack. An untrue rumor spread for the purpose of making a politician look bad to vote for, imbroglio (embroilment) definition (dfn.): an extremely confused, complicated, or embarrassing situation or misunderstanding or disagreement of a bitter nature as between persons or nations; Chicanery : the use of trickery to achieve a political, financial, or legal purpose: "an underhanded person who schemes corruption and political chicanery behind closed doors", Apostate: one who abandons his cause or religion or a political party or friend, etc., deserter, ratter, turncoat, recreant, renegade quitter; behest: a person's orders or command; Parley: 1) noun: a conference between opposing sides in a dispute, especially a discussion of terms for an armistice; synonyms: negotiation, talk(s), conference, summit, discussion, powwow; 2) verb: hold a conference with the opposing side to discuss terms; "they disagreed over whether to parley with the enemy", synonyms: discuss terms, talk, hold talks, negotiate, deliberate; informal powwow. Ataraxia: imperturbability (desirable quality for stock investing as per Benjamin Graham's classic book "The Intelligent Investor"; he was described as having "unruffled serenity," "certain aloofness," "humane, but not human"), ukulele small guitar; Chicanery: the use of trickery to achieve a political, financial, or legal purpose: "an underhanded person who schemes corruption and political chicanery behind closed doors", Apostate: one who abandons his cause or religion or political party or friend, etc., deserter, ratter, turncoat, recreant, renegade quitter; behest: a person's orders or command; Parley: 1) noun: a conference between opposing sides in a dispute, especially a discussion of terms for an armistice; synonyms: negotiation, talk(s), conference, summit, discussion, powwow; 2) verb: hold a conference with the opposing side to discuss terms; "they disagreed over whether to parley with the enemy", synonyms: discuss terms, talk, hold talks, negotiate, deliberate; informal powwow. Ataraxia: imperturbability (desirable quality for stock investing as per Benjamin Graham's classic book "The Intelligent Investor"; he was described as having "unruffled serenity," "certain aloofness," "humane, but not human"), ukulele: small guitar; the word sabe is defined as: "Apaches," and kemo is defined as "friend." Kendall suggests that this list could have been seen; Kemosabe word meaning/origin:

There's one other theory of note, though it's not as well-known as the first two. Alan Shaterian of the University of California, Berkeley told Kendall that the word could have its roots in the Yavapai language spoken in Arizona. Striker, Shaterian says could have visited a reservation in the state and asked people there what their word was for "a white person" or someone who dresses in white, like the Lone Ranger. According to Shaterian, a typical Yavapai speaker would answer with kinmasaba or kinmasabeh. Kemosabe: J.P. Harrington's "The Ethnogeography of the Tewa Indians\," from 1916. That article includes a list of Tewa words used to denote other tribes and cultures; the word sabe is defined as "Apaches," and kemo is defined as "friend." Kendall suggests that this list could have been seen by Striker himself or a research assistant. At the time that the series was first developed, she says, "there was a variable glut of these Smithsonian volumes in used book shops since they were distributed free to various politicians who clearly had no use for them."; mendacity: untruthfulness; eschew: (əs'CHo͞o,i'SHo͞o): verb: deliberately avoid using; abstain from (e.g., "he appealed to the crowd to eschew violence"), Tardigrades: resilient multicellular eight-legged microscopic "animals" discovered in 1777; cudgel

(/ˈkəjəl/): (noun) a short, thick stick used as a weapon. There is another theory that gives the word an entirely different meaning. Noting that tonto in Spanish means "stupid" or "crazy," some people have pointed out that kemosabe sounds a lot like the Spanish phrase quien no sabe, "he who doesn't understand." (In Spanish-language versions of The Lone Ranger, Tonto is called Toro, Spanish for bull.) This suggests a whole different dynamic between the two characters. Is the Lone Ranger a racist who calls his partner an idiot? Is Tonto, in turn, being subversive when he addresses his white companion as an ignoramus? Levee (barrier preventing river overflow), Cacophonous: (adjective) involving or producing a harsh, discordant mixture of sounds (e.g., the cacophonous sound of slot machines (synonyms: loud, noisy, ear-splitting, blaring, booming, thunderous, deafening); Tranche: (noun) a portion of something, especially money; "Judas Priest": is a "swear." It's used on the theory that it is better to swear using the name of Judas Iscariot (see below), who betrayed Jesus, rather than saying "Jesus Christ," taking the Lord's name in vain.; Datant: date (romantic); Kerfuffle: noun (informal British term): a commotion or fuss, especially one caused by conflicting views: e.g., "there was a kerfuffle over the chairmanship"; quid pro quo: (noun) a favor or advantage granted or expected in return for something, e.g., "the pardon was a quid pro quo for their help in releasing hostages"; proviso: (prəˈvīzō, noun) condition or stipulation attached to an agreement: "he left his unborn grandchild a trust fund with the proviso that he be named after the old man"; aurevoir: goodbye until we meet again. "here's hoping it is au revoir and not goodbye"; "1) Exculpatory evidence is evidence favorable to the defendant in a criminal trial that exonerates or tends to exonerate the defendant of guilt. It is the opposite of inculpatory evidence, which tends to present guilt; 2) Rapscallion: By the century's end, rascallion had been further altered to create rapscallion. Today, rapscallion is still commonly used as a synonym for blackguard, scoundrel, and miscreant; laissez-faire: a policy or attitude of letting things take their own course without interfering. Economics dfn.: abstention by governments from interfering in the workings of the free market: "laissez-faire capitalism," Wingman Dfn (noun): a pilot whose aircraft is positioned behind and outside the leading aircraft in a formation. 3) quis·ling /ˈkwizliNG/ noun; a traitor who collaborates with an enemy force occupying their country. "He had the Quisling owner of the factory arrested." 4) The slang term is "four-flusher," meaning "a bluffer, a cheat, a worthless, dishonest person. Betwixt definition: archaic term for between, encomium dfn: a speech or piece of writing that praises someone or something highly, Moxie dfn: , Hankering dfn: noun, a strong desire to have or do something: "a hankering for family life," modicum dfn: a small quantity of a particular thing, especially something considered desirable or valuable: "his statement had more than a modicum of truth," Doused dfn.: verb past tense: Doused, pour a liquid over; drench: "he doused the car with gasoline and set it on fire," tranches: tran(t)SH/noun, plural noun: tranches, a portion of something, especially money.: "they released the first tranche of the loan," hegemony: leadership or dominance, especially by one country or social group over others. "Germany was united under Prussian hegemony after 1871."; Smorgasbord definition: a buffet offering a variety of hot and cold meats, salads, hors d'oeuvres, etc., or a wide range of something; a variety. "The album is a smorgasbord of different musical styles"; Hegemony: leadership or dominance, especially by one country or social group over others. "Germany was united under Prussian hegemony after 1871"; "e.g., China aspires to geopolitical hegemony. Gallant: giving special respect to women; chivalrous; brave or heroic; Acolyte: a person assisting the celebrant in a religious service or procession or an assistant or follower.

Chapter 11 – "The Years of Living Dangerously": Moments or Periods of "Near-Demise" or Potential Traumatic Loss of Limb(s) or Life That, If Survived, Shape The Adventure Seeker, and Allow The Adventurer to Live and Seek Other Adventures In The Future With An Ever-Increasing Sense of The Reality of Life and Death And Its Eventual Inevitability, Accentuating The Vibrancy Of What It Means To Be Fully Alive Experiencing The Full Extent of The Amazing Journey We All Take Through Life on Planet Earth: Hardship, Rejection And/Or Acceptance, Goals Achieved and Not Achieved, Fear and Doubt versus Faith In One's Training and Preparation, False Sense of Security versus Confidence Honed By Exceptional and Arduous Physical Conditioning, Mental Compartmentalization, and Mental Focus To Achieve Physical Feats and Personal Best Athletic

Performances Beyond One's Wildest Imagination And For Victory In All Endeavors and Adventures Embarked Upon.

Luke, at four years old, was enjoying a family trip to the snow organized by the Presbyterian church for all families in the church and any non-church members of Luke's small town and community who wished to join in on a fun trip to the snow (with ice skating, snow inner tubing, snow saucers (hard, curved plastic discs or saucers young kids sit on for speeding down snow slopes), singing songs as a church community by the fireplace in the main lodge each evening, bible studies, and sharing stories of how God has been good to each family that year, sharing wonderful meals together with other children of other church families, all activities that participants enjoyed at the annual winter "Presbyterian Church Snow-Go Retreat."

On this particular trip and as a four-year-old young, dashing, daring and fearless (to a fault) boy, Luke relished the opportunity to show his school and church youth group classmates his adventurous spirit and fearless "need for speed." Luke had been enjoying a wonderful trip to the snow with everyone from his small town church and the opportunity to get to know his age group and every other age group, younger and older members of his church family. On one late afternoon, and on the verge of early evening, Luke obtained a large hard plastic snow saucer or disc (to sit on and ride down the mountain on) and took it to the very top of the mountain and decided to show everyone he could set a "land-snow speed record" for this particular "snow-go" trip. The setting was perfect as every church family and their children were present on the mountain and enjoying a beautiful snow day, although now the sun was setting and dusk (the darkest stage of twilight, or at the very end of astronomical twilight after sunset and just before night) setting in, the dark of night was soon to begin his/her shift in the day/night cycle of God's 24-hour day. Luke launched himself after a speedy sprint for momentum onto the hard plastic snow saucer or disc and embarked on his speedy, adventurous journey down the mountain straight down the middle of the slope and through all the church families and their children, in full view of his entire church community. Unfortunately, Luke had neglected to perform requisite pre-flight planning, route planning (e.g., mapping out the route and identifying any obstacles or hazards in the flight route being planned, and contingency planning [e.g., if a flight route has to be changed or altered in-flight to avoid obstacles and collisions, potentially resulting in flight mishap(s)]) before launching his mission down the snowy mountain, on this particular day. Luke gained more and more speed as he descended from the mountain top. Without the ability to steer his snow saucer, gravity became Luke's malevolent and unrelenting evil master of potential disaster as Luke sped down through many trees and eventually down toward the highway road. At this point, Luke poignantly realized his mortality was both possible and/or imminent, yet could do nothing to alter his course nor his progressively increasing out-of-control speed as he accelerated down the mountain and toward the two-lane highway (leading to the mountain top) below at the bottom of the mountain. Luke's first "high-speed flight" in life was both ill-advised and poorly planned and embarked upon without any flight training, usually requisite, before any flight mission; in this case, the "flight mission" was traveling down a mountain of snow and across a busy road at an uncontrolled velocity with no steering capability or ability to slow down or stop if necessary. A treacherous journey comes to mind and was all-consuming in the mind of Luke during his journey or "flight" down the mountain, at which time Luke had an epiphany that his arms and legs were at risk of being fractured or ripped off his body violently or crashing into one of many trees or one of the many cars on the busy road below in his path, upon impact, might dislodge or sever his head or limbs from his body or crush any part of his body beyond recognition or in a manner so devastating that recovery and healing might not be an option or possible without a divine or miraculous intercession/intervention by God to auspiciously alter the plight of Luke's wild adventure down the mountain. Luke introspectively (and rapidly) prayed a prayer of protection and God's guidance during his first high speed flight in life and trusted that God might show mercy and grace to Luke and protect him until gravity lost its grip on Luke's life (or death) during this life-threatening and perilous journey. Luke darted across the road, just narrowly or barely-missing (there was a near-direct impact of Luke's head with the front car bumper, car axle, and tires) being hit by a car traveling up the road whose driver never even saw Luke speeding across the road and in front of his car like a rocket launched into space. When Luke's parents were informed of this event, let's just say Luke was severely chastised and possibly spanked for this endeavor (Luke has tried to forget and erase that latter form of punishment and thus the uncertainty over whether it indeed happened…more likely than not…Luke surmises).

Luke has always been "up for an adventure." During an early family trip to Yosemite, Luke, now being a ripe age of six years old, truly a man at this point (at least in Luke's mind), the trip's climax was to be a rigorous six-mile hike, followed by a trek up to the top of "Half Dome" (Half Dome is a granite dome at the eastern end of Yosemite Valley in Yosemite National Park, California. It is a famous rock formation in the park and is named for its distinct form or shape. One side is a sheer face, while the other three sides are smooth and round, giving it the appearance of a dome cut in half.) Luke's Yosemite family trip commenced with mini hikes and multiple photos with Dad's vintage Nikon camera (that he would only pull out for significant family vacations each summer, when dad had two months off from teaching high school English and Geography classes) of: Yosemite Native American / Indian Village, Yosemite Falls, Bridal Veil Falls, Vernal Falls, Nevada Falls, The Ahwahnee Hotel/Lodge (our family only admired the hotel and toured the inside beauty). Luke's father had a passion for backpacking trips in many national parks throughout the United States (and later throughout Europe whenever campsites were an option and could be located). We always camped out using backpacks to hike into areas (e.g., one week hike in, then one week hike out of an area) and sleep in tents during our annual 2-3 week summer mountain backpacking trips to Yosemite, Yellowstone, the Black Hills of South Dakota, Wyoming, and other states and national parks.

During this adventure, Luke, a 6-year-old brave (in Luke's mind) and robust young man (again, in Luke's mind), the trip climaxed with the Half Dome ascent. Luke's older brother, Peter, who was seven years old, began the ascent with his father leading the way up the back side of "Half Dome." At that time, the only way up for amateurs (non-professional climbers) versus the more extreme route that rock climbers going up the vertical steep side of half dome would aspire to, was to carefully step on each wood plank that was bolted into the side of the mountain's granite rock steep surface. There were also wire cables for hand gripping, which were out of reach for Luke, whose arms were not yet long enough to reach up to and hold on to these wire cables during ascent up the steep rock surface. Luke followed his father and older brother Peter, followed by his mother. One-quarter the way up the mountain, both Luke and his mother decided this adventure would inevitably end in tragedy should Luke falter and fall left or right while ascending using only the unsecured foot grip of his hiking boots on each and every (many to get to the zenith of Half Dome) bolted down wood two by four wood plank bolted into the angled, smooth, steep granite rock that is known as "Half Dome." Once Luke realized he was unable to reach the wire cables above while stepping from one wood step to the next to accomplish the successful ascent of Half Dome, he was forced to make the tough decision to terminate his ascent (his mother also determined that the risk was too significant and followed Luke down) and live to complete this adventure and other adventures when he was taller, with longer arms and legs and a firmer grip to hold the wire cables securely to ascend Half Dome safely. Sound judgment, Luke learned this day and during his snow-go near-calamity/near-death experience, always "trumps" or supersedes and should preclude embarking or completing an adventure for which one is neither properly prepared nor has properly and adequately thought out, planned, and memorized a contingency plan for aborting the adventure or mission if circumstances are recognized or realized that make the adventure inordinately dangerous and life-threatening to the adventurist. Luke is thankful to this day that he was able to demonstrate and act on his excellent instinct to live another day and adventure and not engage in unreasonable risky behavior that day at Half Dome. This experience also gave Luke, the resolve and inspiration to commence a physical training program, life-long, that would open his world to any "extreme physical-fitness-requiring adventure" in the future so that he could, at any moment, accept an offer from any group or individual to join an adventure (e.g., climbing Mt Fuji, running multiple marathons [26.2 miles each], rock climbing in Yosemite with his church youth group and climbing instructor, scuba diving, wilderness survival training, helicopter under-water escape training, flight school, flying rotary wing aircraft (e.g., helicopters such as the CH-46, Cobra, and Huey models of military helicopters) and fixed-wing (e.g., Fighter-Attack (F/A-18) "Hornet" Jets, Cross-Country Skiing Trip and Ascent Up Shell Mountain, War Games in Australia with countries: Australia, New Zealand, Canada, United Kingdom, Japan, others, 10 Kilometer Races (undefeated), qualified for Boy Scouts of American Junior Olympics, Regular Junior Olympic Qualifier in 880 yards race (but missed race when Luke's parents went shopping that Saturday of Luke's race…accidents happen), all events that Luke was able to participate in and accomplish as a result of his extraordinary physical training and fitness, which he commenced in the fourth grade. In fourth-grade grammar school, recess breaks between classes, Luke chose to run around the schoolyard's four baseball diamond backstops at each of the four corners of the immense football and baseball grass field and playground, counting how many laps around the field he could finish, ever-increasing his speed to set new personal records throughout grammar school until he later qualified for the 880-yard dash/run in the Junior Olympics. Despite missing the last race as a no-show (stranded at home with no parents to drive him to the race), Luke was only further motivated to engage in powerlifting and weight training and to continue running (until his future death) so that future extreme physical fitness adventures were always an option, regardless of what or where the adventure is to be held or what mountain is to be ascended, skied upon, or as Luke prefers to say, "I train every day and week so that I may conquer any mountain or obstacle any day of the week."

Superheroes

Luke was eleven years old when driving to the city honor band rehearsal with his older brother Peter and fellow high school band trombone player, Yendor, who was two years older than Luke. While driving early morning on Saturday on a foggy day in Central California to the honor band practice, just after rain on a cold and dreary weather day, we experienced a life-threatening phenomenon. The small Ford pickup truck Yendor was driving and Peter and Luke were passengers in, suddenly hit a patch of black ice and hydroplaned, and our truck started spinning uncontrolled at 540 degrees on the the highway we were driving on (with oncoming traffic coming from the opposite direction, mind you, a potentially disastrous or fatal impending accident in the making), finally coming to rest approximately 4 inches away from smashing into a cement wall on the edge of the highway road (miraculously without a head-on collision from oncoming traffic on the highway road). This additional near-death experience again impressed Luke that God somehow had a purpose and plan for his life that did not involve dying or being paralyzed from the neck or waist down from a devastating head-on car collision while we were spinning like a toy spinning top in the middle of a two-lane, two-direction busy highway road with oncoming vehicles traveling at greater than 60 miles per hour that morning. Luke committed to being the best musician he could be that day and decided that he had been granted a second and new life for this purpose. Luke, shortly thereafter, was invited, as an 11-year-old grammar school student, to play with the local high school Jazz Band, whose practices were conveniently Monday through Friday from 720 am to 820 am (a several city blocks sprint/run at 700 am to begin each day for Luke), before Luke's grammar school, several blocks away (the second sprint for Luke each day), whose grammar school classes started at 830 am each day. This was an incredible honor and privilege for Luke, and he remains grateful and thankful to this day for the generous offer made by the high school band director, an eccentric and incredible band director who produced many of the top musicians in the state of California through his supportive and energetic efforts to encourage grammar school and high school musicians to achieve their zenith potential as musicians, many of whom were phenoms who became professional musicians while still in grammar school or as high school students, and who were number one or number two musicians for their respective and specific instrument types (e.g., trombone for Luke, trumpet for Peter, trumpet for Kram, and saxophone for Evets (just to name a few of the top musicians in California who were all from Peter and Luke's high school and classmates); all top musicians in the state of California during Peter and Luke's high school years and professional musician years/careers. Luke and Peter both achieved professional musician status (and were handsomely rewarded with cash payments for each performance) beginning in seventh grade (at approximately age 11 for Luke and age 12 for Peter). At annual performances at the California State Honor Band and California State Honor Orchestra, both of which selected (by audition tapes) only the top musicians from the entire state of California to comprise two large bands (top-rated "symphonic band" for top ten musicians per instrument type and the second-rated concert band for musicians rated #11-20 by specific musical instrument type in the state of California and only one state honor orchestra existed (thus only the top ten high school musicians in California for each instrument type) each year. Usually only one, two, or no students would be selected per year per individual or distinct high school (only California high schools could have their students submit audition tapes for selection into the California State Honor Bands or Orchestra each year) based on audition tapes that were submitted or sent in by each high school to the California Band Directors Association (CBDA) and/or California Music Educators Association (CMEA) for the California State Honor Band or Orchestra honor and live concert performances each year. After the initial acceptance based on the outstanding audition tape musical composition performance by each high school musician, each student had to then re-audition in person (live performance in front of judges) to confirm their eligibility and ranking in each California State Honor Band or Orchestra before the week of practice followed by the concert performance and album recording of these phenomenal concerts by prodigy young brilliant musicians from the entire state of California. Each musician is then ranked #1 through 20, and the top ten musicians for each instrument type are assigned to the "Symphonic Band" of California State Honor Band. That "Symphonic Band" then performs two concerts and two record albums, one album for each separate performance in different California cities and with distinct band (or orchestra) directors for each concert, approximately 3-6 months apart. The musicians ranked #11-20 are assigned to the "Concert Band" of the California State Honor Band and play one concert per year, which is made into a record album. Luke was the #1 trombonist in the California State Honor Band (Symphonic Band) and the #1 trombonist in California State Honor Orchestra his senior year of high school (and #6 trombonist in the Symphonic Band his sophomore (2nd year) of high school, miraculously, after getting new metal braces on his teeth his freshman year of high school and being rejected (not selected at all) by the California State Honor Band his freshman year of high school (perplexing to Luke to this very day). Luke was again rejected during his junior (3rd) year of high school. Luke never understood how he could be the top #1 or #2 trombonist in central California honor bands yet not be selected for California State Honor Band all four consecutive years during high school (there will always be unanswered questions and mysteries in life, and this is just one example). Luke was only selected in his second and fourth year of high school and ranked #6 and #1, respectively, in California for those years that he was selected to the California State Honor Band (and Orchestra when he applied to the Orchestra only during his senior year of high school). Nevertheless, Luke is grateful to God that he was selected those two different years and thoroughly enjoyed the four recorded albums he was able to record during the live concert performances, which were truly fabulous performances and among the greatest highlights of his life. Some occurrences in life or circumstances in life cannot be well understood and will remain mysteries forever; the sooner one can come to terms with this simple fact, the sooner one can purposely put aside this fact and dose of reality (forget about it) and move on with life (and not let past disappointing events or circumstances impede your glorious future) without regret or obstruction. Luke's mother would always say to Peter and Luke when they were growing up: "Your best is always good enough." Luke's older brother and life mentor to this day), Peter, was selected to the California State Honor Band (Symphonic Band) and after the in-person, live performance audition, was honored with being ranked or rated the #2 (second best) trumpet player in California, behind only the phenom Ralph Alessi, an American jazz trumpeter who was, like Peter, a professional-level musician despite being a high school student. Peter was mysteriously not selected in his first, third, or fourth year of high school for the California State Honor Band despite being rated the second-best trumpet player in California. Some life occurrences just cannot be explained. Peter, the best brother Luke could have ever had and a fantastic mentor in every respect, took these disappointments in stride. He continued to be an elite and gifted high school trumpet musician ranked #1 (most frequently), 2 or 3 in Central California local honor bands throughout high school and was invited to play with the local college jazz band while he was still in high school (his 3rd and 4th year of high school), an honor and offer he gladly accepted and remembers fondly to this day. Peter never let disappointments slow down his progress in life and always strove to be the very best version of himself each and every day. Peter graduated from both grammar school and high school as Valedictorian of his class and received the John Phillip Souza Music Award and Academic All-American Honor and Designation / Selection for his exceptional performances (top tier in California) in Music, Tennis, Academic Performance while a high school phenom student, a sort of master of his universe or Big Man On Campus (BMOC) with a larger-than-life personality and unparalleled integrity and work ethic. What more could Luke possibly want for a role model than his very own older (by approximately one-and-a-half years) brother? Peter was also elected Jazz Band Director/Leader and Band President in high school and was the "Mock Trials Pre-Law" and "Chess Club's" top-rated high school student from our high school.

Luke worked summers between school years in jobs that varied in the level of (unanticipated) danger. As a young boy, Luke obtained a push mower (for cutting yard grass in neighbors' front and back yards) and started this original occupation as a sixth grader in grammar school (approximately 11 years old). As he built the business to approximately 14 accounts with every two week mowings, Luke eventually replaced his faithful push mower with gas or gas/oil 5 horsepower Professional Trimmer Motorized Mower, 2.5 horsepower Professional Motorized Edger, Power Blower (oil-gas powered), Power Weed-Wacker tool and various rakes, shovels other landscaping accessory tools and equipment to transform his business into a serious and profitable after school on weekdays and weekends business that would teach him responsibility and accountability and provide him with enough money to purchase books for school and music and musical equipment that would propel Luke to excel in music performance and become a professional musician, along with his older brother Peter, while both brothers were still in grammar school (ages 12 and 13). Of course, some earnings were spent on going to James Bond movies, buying hamburgers and root beer floats, bowling, buying an Atari football game for vacation road trips, and playing arcade and video games such as Asteroids, Scramble, Missile Command, Pac-Man and others. The boy and his brother had to live a little and have some fun with best friends and neighbors… it's only natural…and healthy. All work and no play would have made (but didn't) Luke and Peter dull boys.

Danger Job One:

Believe it or not, one may lose fingers, hands, toes, feet, or other body parts if one does not pay close attention when working every other day with sharp and curved metal blades rotating at high speed (e.g., gas powered lawn mower). Similarly, one may easily and rapidly lose vision in one or both eyes or hearing in one or both ears when using various power tools with high noise pollution features and high speed, very sharp, rotating metal blades and fishing string-like long threads or strings rotating at high speed which, the tools themselves may consume various body parts alone on their own, or propel dirt, rocks, glass, small metal fragments, wood, or other less desirable or unanticipated material (e.g., dog or cat excrement) at high velocity at the machine or tool operator's own organs, resulting in potential or actual (if not adequately protected with ear plugs, work goggles, gloves, or other protective measures and great vigilance and caution, focus, and compartmentalization such that one is alert and aware at all times to avoid calamitous injury and maiming of one's self) contusions/injuries to eyes, ears, hands, fingers, toes, facial skin, mouth, arms, abdomen, back (much bending over and lifting heavy loads of cut grass or raked leaves in trash barrels etc.), or legs. The miracle of miracles is that Luke experienced near-tragedy on multiple occasions but had a guardian angel (on loan from God) throughout his young life that protected and preserved most body parts, what a relief!

Danger Job Two:

Luke was a shelf stocker and would mark various items with price tags, etcetera, at Long's Drug Store one summer, in addition to other jobs or taking summer classes. Unexpectedly, part of Luke's job description was also to be alert when a theft code was initiated or announced over the load speaker system in the drug store, at which time, our instructions, along with the store manager was to run down thieves leaving our store, tackle or otherwise detain them until police arrived, and then return the stolen items to our store. Believe it or not, Luke actually enjoyed this rather competitive and athletic pursuit, and each theft event was a welcome adventure to break up what were often otherwise somewhat monotonous days at work that summer. However, tackling such strangers and thieves in and on asphalt parking lots or on cement roads, sidewalks or alleys was not a dangerless job, and with no helmet, shoulder pads, rugby shirt, mouth guard, or any other protective equipment (only our Long's Drug Store uniform; the pharmacy was later bought by CVS pharmacy) other than our determination not to be stolen from, the thrill of pursuit, the victory of the cattle roping and leg tying, the satisfaction of seeing police arrive and escort the criminal to the police vehicle and future prosecution, and returning stocked items to the shelves (that we so meticulously stocked and made beautiful for our faithful and otherwise law-abiding customers. Ironically, some of the smallest employees in the store, Luke and others, became the most proficient tacklers and could run down the most athletic, supposedly faster, and often much taller or older thieves. Luke, as a former wrestler with only 2 match losses in his career, was very proficient and dominant in sequestering criminals until the store manager would eventually arrive on the scene, where we would all "chat" with the criminal until the police arrived in their magic pumpkin carriage to escort these "Cinderellas" to their jail homes. Luke never discussed these activities with his brother, mother, or father because Luke knew these adventurous stories would only stir up angst, anxiety, and possibly result in Luke's not being able to continue to work all summer until the school year started up again.

Danger Job Three:

Luke took two semesters of physics one summer during weekdays and obtained what he thought would be a fun pizza delivery boy job that he could do during weekday evenings and on weekends. Unexpected adventures, surprises, joys, and unprecedented dangers presented themselves that summer of living dangerously. On a lighter note, Luke recognized one of his high school classmates (misbehaving, snorting cocaine with many others at the party that Luke delivered Italian food to) during a food delivery and, due to the uncomfortable circumstance and awkwardness of the moment, both Luke and his high school classmate both pretended (unconvincingly) to not know or recognize each other, the food was delivered, and Luke accepted the delivery two dollar tip and departed from the apartment where the delivery was made. More dangerously, Luke learned from the other full-time delivery boy at the Italian restaurant that there were specific delivery addresses that the other delivery boy never wanted to deliver to, and he would, thus, insist that Luke make deliveries to these select few addresses. Though Luke was never given a reason why the other delivery person would not deliver to these addresses, Luke eventually learned the obvious reasons on his own. When people hear the phrase: "They come from the wrong side of the tracks," most people know that this means that there are neighborhoods where very bad or evil things happen and where very bad people reside/live (who, of course, do very bad things) negatively influencing all their neighbors in the neighborhood. One such location that Luke made multiple deliveries to (of pizza and many other Italian entrees) that summer of living dangerously was, Luke learned at the summer's end, called "Chemical City." So-named because every time Luke drove up to that neighborhood (ironically, it was actually a run-down large apartment complex just adjacent to a set of railroad tracks), especially at night (the most dangerous time to be in that neighborhood), multiple strangers would walk up to Luke's car, surround it, and ask Luke if he wanted to purchase crack cocaine, heroin, Lysergic acid ("LSD"), methamphetamines, PCP ("Angel Dust"), Magic Mushrooms, Marijuana, or any other commonly abused prescription drugs such as fentanyl, Percodan, Percocet, or other opioids to get high with. Luke would, in each case and during each delivery, then respectfully decline the multiple offers of sale and politely state that he was there only to make a delivery of Italian food to those residents who ordered their food delivered. During the pitch-black of these night deliveries, Luke, though an accomplished wrestler, was further equipped (after a rather dangerous maiden voyage to this abyss), with a pre-opened pocket knife in his back pocket but hidden under his shirt, should a good wrestle or scuffle ensue that might require that Luke defend himself, if his life was in danger or otherwise being threatened, with more than a few wrestling moves or punches, or if attacked by many individuals instead of just one individual, in a "battle of life or death." Of course, Luke also realized that one or more guns used by one or more assailants would be the end of Luke and no match for a simple pocket knife. Such were the odds of the "life-death game" being played during each delivery to these "special" neighborhoods.

These were but a few of the summers and years of living dangerously that Luke experienced as a boy.

Chapter 12 – Neighborhood, Church Friends, Schoolmates, And Their Influence in "Small-Town America"

The Fannuchi neighbors had a great pool in their backyard. It was the only pool on the block…what a God-send. Their oldest daughter, Twila, was our small town's famous (and fabulously cute) solo majorette for our local grammar school, marching band, and our local high school. Our regional high school received students from six grammar schools spread throughout the countryside that made up our country community. This countryside was essentially the shell (much like the famous birth of Venus painting) that each small child emerged from in our community, much as Venus emerged from her shell, with each child (and Venus) then displaying the development and maturity nurtured by community members throughout their upbringing as young adults. Just as Venus is depicted in a raw, exposed yet innocent, beautiful manner emerging from the shell behind her, our small town's boys and girls all grew up with each community member having a role in the development and maturation of each boy and girl in our small town, often filing off and thus smoothing rough edges, attitudes and aberrant behaviors of every raw, exposed yet innocent and beautiful child growing up into mature young men and women in our small town. The Fannuchi family had two younger boys who complemented their older, cute sister. The older boy, Tommy, was Peter's classmate throughout grammar school and high school and Tommy had a short and brilliant career as a race car driver and then settled down with his family taking up carpentry as a profession. The Fannuchi's youngest boy, Michael, was two years younger than Luke, and also had a short and brilliant race car driver career, and then raised a beautiful family not more than three blocks from his parents' home. Throughout grammar school and high school, the Fannuchi family was the second home of both Peter and Luke. Having two parents who worked, back in simpler and safer times, Peter and Luke were both "Latch Key Kids." Until about third grade (or eight years old), we had a modest, caring female church member who would meet Peter and Luke at home after they walked home from grammar school, which was approximately two blocks away. Starting from about fourth grade, when Luke was nine years old, both Peter and Luke were issued keys to our home door locks so that we could enter our home after school ended at 3 pm and entertain ourselves until our parents arrived home between 400 pm and 630 pm or 8 pm at the latest if grocery or other shopping by mother after work was necessary.

Father was a teacher at our region/community sole high school and would matriculate home after he finished grading papers or preparing for his next day of class(es) or after finishing up as tennis coach for the high school tennis team during the second (Spring) semester tennis season each year. Some nights, father would not return until after 8 or 9 pm if away tennis matches were extended late or the "The Free Outdoorsmen Club" (which father also led at the high school) had an out-of-town excursion, mountain trip, or other trip to the beach or other exciting locations. Peter and Luke relished and appreciated the implicit trust bestowed on them by their parents at such a young age and the freedom, the opportunity, and the responsibility that came with being "latchkey kids." Peter and Luke spent as many days as possible after school playing football, swimming, playing croquet, and playing basketball at the Fanucchi's home, two houses away on the same block, with Tommy and Michael.

Our next-door neighbors on one side, the Skornycks, had two beautiful older daughters, four and two years older than Peter. The Skornyck's youngest son was four years younger than Luke. We had great fun whenever the Skornyck's neighbor kids joined all the other neighborhood kids on the block at the big summer swim parties at the Fanucchi neighbor's home. The neighborhood boys were incredibly grateful. Peter and Luke spent over 10 thousand hours swimming at the Fanucchi home backyard pool and over 10 thousand hours skateboarding on the long semilunar driveway of our next-door neighbor's home of the Skornycks, with (and most often without) the neighbor's kids. We skateboarded all over our small town and, on some weekends, we would skateboard to neighboring towns 15 -25 miles away. These were exhausting but exhilarating skateboarding mini-adventures.

Our next-door neighbors on the other side of our home had an oldest son, three years older than Peter, a middle daughter the same age as Peter (both were 1 ½ years older than Luke) who was Peter's classmate in grammar school and high school, and the youngest daughter, who was three years younger than Luke. The neighbor's son often went hunting with his father, Mort. On one trip, they brought back a bobcat, and Luke was fascinated to see that Mort and his son had the deceased animal on their driveway and were removing bullets so they could take the animal to the taxidermist to mount the animal in one of the rooms in their home. These neighbors had an above-ground pool, and our entire family enjoyed many summer days at pool parties with these next-door neighbors and at the Fanucci's home two doors down the street. What great pool/block parties we enjoyed many summer days when temperatures often exceeded 100 degrees Fahrenheit, sometimes for up to 21 days consecutively.

Our neighbors, two doors down on the other side of our house, were the Pastor's Kids (PKs). The oldest daughter was adopted and a joyful, exuberant, energetic child and teenager. She was four years older than Peter. The younger daughter was the same age as Peter and was Peter's classmate in grammar school and high school. Three of the five houses on our block all attended the same Presbyterian Church in our small community. We were raised as young children in "Sunday School" (children's activities and Bible-based teaching and learning activities) while our parents attended adult Sunday Church Services and Sermons by Pastor Ary Sieres. Pastor Sieres was our neighbor two houses away. His wife, Theresa, was a spiritual pillar in our community. She was a natural-born leader and willing participant in women's Bible study groups in the community on Sundays and weeknights. Along with several other women leaders in the church, she both inspired and guided younger married and single women in the community to become actively involved in church activities, including:

Women's prison ministry, Sunday and weeknight bible studies, vacation bible school during school summer vacation months, church-sponsored day care for community families, church ice cream socials, special concerts by Christian music groups, bands or orchestras, and other events. Peter, Luke, Mother, and Father spent many holidays in fellowship at our Pastor's home enjoying fresh apple, pumpkin, rhubarb, pecan, strawberry, and many other pie types, cakes, and other deserts after several spirited rounds of card games (e.g., Uno and "oh hell," pinochle.

Michigan Rummy, Boardwalk, Candy Land, and many others. Ironically, when we played card games and other games with our church pastor, his wife, and his daughters (aka Pastor's Kids or "PKs"), the individual who required the most monitoring and scrutiny was…you guessed it…the pastor! Many games of Uno (card game) were played and won by the pastor and then ceded to the runner-up after discovering cards present in the pastor's hand that were not played when necessary or required (according to the card game rules), "a simple oversight," we all concluded…over and over again! This was very amusing to observe! We enjoyed each other's company and shared many joyful holidays together. These holidays spent in fellowship with our neighbor and pastor's family were some of the fondest memories Peter, Luke, and their parents ever had and forever reinforced in their mind, body, and soul the true and magical value of socialization with friends, neighbors, and other members of God's family. Remember, all humans are God's children, and as such, we are all members of God's family.

Luke's best friend, Yargi, lived several miles from our house and his family, the Zevaches. Yargi was the youngest of three boys. The oldest son "played a mean Saxophone" (he was a great saxophone player). He met and married his high school sweetheart and watched his daughter and son graduate from the same high school he attended. He gave his prized 1954 Ford to Yargi when he started high school so Yargi could drive himself to school each day. A great brother and role model for Yargi. He was almost ten years older than Yargi. The Zevaches second oldest son was a passionate man, hardworking, and a great father of three after high school.

Yargi and Luke became best friends in fifth grade during grammar school recess under a shade tree at lunch recess on a day which was many degrees over 100 Fahrenheit. We discussed and questioned what kind of men we would become one day in the future, what occupations we would eventually gravitate toward, and we also speculated what kind of women/wives we would, one day in the future, marry and promise to be spouses and soulmates with "until death do us part." As all humans aspire to, we hoped that we would work hard and do our best each and every day and thereby have the assurance and peace that comes with knowing, as mother taught and recited to Peter and Luke a thousand times during our youth era and upbringing, those magical words that every parent should be mandated to repeat to all their children incessantly and repeatedly until all their children reach adulthood (and thereafter): "Your best is always good enough." Always work hard and do your best each day in all that you do, and you will never have regrets in this life (you will make mistakes and suffer disappointments, as we all have, however)…whatever your best is that day…you did your best… and your best is always good enough." Under that shade tree during lunch recess, we concluded, honestly, that we had no way of knowing the answers to any of the questions we contemplated that day. It was just too early in life and our school careers to know what interests we would develop regarding career choices, how well we would perform in our classes and academic endeavors, and if this would enable us the opportunity to pursue the career choice we were interested in and/or if we would ever be sufficiently qualified and accepted in the career field that we wished to enter. The only conclusion and contract/pact that we ratified that lunch recess was that life was going to be a great adventure, and we would remain best friends for life and see what life brings to both of us. Thus, it was the beginning of a "life-long best friendship" that continues to this day. Despite living with our families in separate cities hundreds of miles apart and less frequent communications than in earlier years, there is silent and deep respect in the sacred vow we took that day under the shade tree in scorching heat to become and remain best friends for life, until death, and thereafter.

When Yargi and Luke first met, in fifth grade, Luke's family attended the community Presbyterian (John Calvin Protestant who broke away after the Spanish Inquisition and founded the Presbyterian Church for Christians) church every Sunday. Yargi's family, the Zevaches, rarely attended church at that time except maybe on religious holidays when they might attend a service at the community Catholic church. Nevertheless, the Zevaches were and are an amazing, loving, caring, and close-knit family that has always and will always support each other and their friends. Luke and Peter both had the distinct pleasure of growing up with Yargi and all the Zevaches, whom we both, to this day, consider our second pair of parents. The love and respect we have for this family and the love and respect they showed and demonstrated toward our family, and specifically toward Peter and Luke, have never and will never be forgotten and will always be cherished. There are certain neighbor friends and families, especially in small communities that make up the heart and soul of a country, and which are so gracious, caring, kind, considerate, and loving that you, the individual in that neighborhood community, undergo a spiritual transformation as a result of these mentors who have so touched your mind, heart, and soul, and taught you how to see what is truly important in life.

Take, for example, the Siwels. They were married for over 75 years and lived their entire lives in our small community. The husband had been a farmer his whole life. He was a man of few yet choice and concise words and sentences of wise advice, only and always choosing to see the positive and potential good in each circumstance, conflict, or situation. His wife had been a school teacher for years before eventually retiring. They attended our community Presbyterian church every Sunday until they both reached 95 years old, after which they remained home on Sundays, relaxing in their rocking chairs or sitting on their modest couch in the living room and listened to sermons recorded on cassette tapes from each Sunday sermon. They had 22 family members in the community (if in-laws are included) who loved and adored them, as our family did. Luke had a special love and respect for this couple, the Patriarch and Matriarch, in our community. What the Siwels taught Luke was: What is most important in life? Answer: Working hard and putting forth honest and earnest effort in whatever occupation God gives you the opportunity to participate in and excel in, and always gracefully accept changes that occur throughout life and know that

God will guide you through each change and different situation or circumstances in life. Study God's word: the Bible, cover to cover, Old Testament to New Testament, for it is life's best guidebook on how to navigate this life, learn from your own mistakes and others mistakes, and do not be fearful of new mistakes (they will happen), acknowledge God in all your successes, and rejoice equally in the successes and achievements of others. Learn all that you can from the many stories and teachings in the Bible, and give love to and find love in all those around you. Keep God in your life every day, and allow God to be in charge of all your relationships and your marriage if you are blessed with a loving spouse. If married, then nurture and care for your spouse and grow and strengthen your marital relationship with God's daily help and guidance.

The Siwels were Luke's fourth pair of parents in many senses. Luke visited and had living room chats with the Siwels from birth and continuously throughout school and into adulthood and beyond this loving married couple's platinum wedding anniversary. Peter, our parents, and the entire community benefitted from the example this loving couple was to the community. Although none of us thought we could ever live up to their standard and brilliant execution of a life well-lived, we all derived inspiration and hope that our own lives could, at least in some respects, resemble their relationship, harmony, love for each other, and total serenity in knowing God led them, calmed them, and perfected each of them and their relationship over the more than 75 years that they were married. News of their deaths brought tears of sorrow to Luke and the entire community.

Church Sunday school and church youth groups instilled a sense of morality and ethical behavior principles and values that stuck with and guided Peter and Luke the rest of their lives. Perhaps you have heard (or should hear and listen to) the maxim: "Give your children to God the first two decades of life, and they will be God's children forever." Now, we all know this is only a theory or concept. In reality, children may stray from God early or late in life. However, if brought up in the church, they will always know right from wrong, especially if they have studied the Bible, front cover to back cover. There is so much wisdom to be gained in this most worthy task. Peter and Luke, as very young children, began studying the Bible and were both quite diligent and successful in earnestly attempting to incorporate these principles and teachings from God's Word in the Bible, into their individual lives, and both Peter and Luke believe to this day that God has sustained and blessed their path through this life and world as a result of their acceptance of Jesus Christ as their Lord and Savior, who died on the cross as a sinless man (God's sacrifice for man's sins), to atone for world citizens' imperfections, and sins or transgressions so that those who accept God as their savior can be forgiven of their sins and live for eternity, upon their death (of body only; spirit ascends into heaven to be in community with God and other believers), with God in heaven. God is, has been, and will be good to Peter, Luke, and all those who are born again (spiritual acceptance of God and faith in God; living Christian life as delineated in the Bible), during their life on this Earth.

CHAPTER THIRTEEN:

A Message To All Future Endeavoring Superheroes: Embrace And Cherish The Opportunity To Become The Truly Elite For Every "World Citizen," Culture, Society, And Country In This World Will Ultimately, Infinitely, Eternally, And Reverently Respect And Be Indebted And Forever Thankful For You, In Addition To Your Certain Attainment Of God's Grace, Mercy, And Blessings While On Earth And In Heaven With God In Perpetuity!

Dwight L. Moody (1837-1899) was an American evangelist and publisher who founded the Moody Church, Northfield School, and Mount Hermon School in Massachusetts, as well as the Moody Bible Institute and Moody Publishers in Chicago. His dynamic preaching and commitment to education and evangelism had a profound impact on American Christianity.

Synopsis:

Greatness By Virtuous, Honest, Earnest Daily Work Effort Is Currently Being Discouraged, Suppressed, Shunned, Or Discarded Altogether To Supplant Morality With Immorality By Globalists, Media And Entertainment Companies, Including Television/Cable/Satellite Companies, Movie Production Studios, Screenwriters, Book Publishers, Literary Agents, Universities, Large, Wealthy, And Monopolistic And Tyrant Health Care Companies and Hospital-Owning Corporations or Other Organizations, And Professional Sports Team Owners And Sports Organizations Worldwide.

Ethical Society Members Who Prosecute Immoral Society Members And/Or Otherwise Annihilate/Eliminate Fraudulent, Corrupt, Immoral, Unethical Perspectives, Attitudes, Trust-Like And/Or Monopolistic Bullying Manipulation, Behavior, And Actions, Persecution or Malicious Prosecution of Non-Criminals, Political Opponents, Or Religious, Honest, Ethical, Moral, Hard-Working And Tax-Paying Citizens, Or Unjust Non-Acknowledgement Of Certain Citizens Existence And Right To Express Their Opinions And Beliefs And To Be Heard or Acknowledged (e.g., In Book Publishing or Movie Production or Acknowledging That Athletic Competitions Should Be Strictly Male Or Female Only Athletic Events), Or Neglect Of Citizens Espousing (e.g., in the form of writing books or producing movies, or even athlete individuals expecting to compete in athletic events with only their same actual birth gender/sex athletes competing in the same competition with them), Religious, Nationalistic, And Other Country-Specific Society Values (Rightfully and Righteously), Via Legal Court Victories Will Be Instant "Superheroes, The Truly Elite."

A true account of a real life occurrence can be both educational and enlightening, though not always encouraging nor uplifting when one analyzes the details of the decision-making process and sinister intent of a particular large, manipulative, monopolistic, and wealthy business, e.g., corporations or other business organizations, that unfortunately often disrespectfully and selfishly leverage their size, monetary wealth, and out-of-balance administrative power to manipulate and mistreat others, even when the final result of these ill-intended, one-sided decisions may not only hurt those intended to be hurt by the large monopolistic business, but may even come back to hurt that manipulative and monopolistic business, as a result of the poor judgement, non-constructive perspective and intent, negative attitude, intent to harm that company's employees, ultimately invoking rage, dissatisfaction, discontent, and the feelings of abandonment by those employees, who may then choose to refer future potential customers to other companies after learning their company is both unfaithful to its employees and perhaps even leave that company, in order to find a more supportive and trustworthy employer that they may depend and rely on to treat them with respect and dignity in the future!

One of the largest (and previously), most respected health care organizations in Southern California, in the United States of America, had for more than 30 years supported all of their distinct specialty physician departments by ensuring the hospital possessed the most up-to-date and highest quality, "state-of-the-art" diagnostic and surgical equipment, to ensure optimal and zenith patient outcomes for all their hospital staff various specialty physicians and surgeons, and equally important, to recruit and maintain new physicians who are and would continue to be motivated to remain on staff to utilize all the highest quality diagnostic and surgical equipment maintained and upgraded when needed by the hospital and on the behalf of both the hospitals working, on-staff physician, and for the benefit of that hospital's optimal and zenith patient outcomes, all achieved as a result of the constant and continuing investments of the hospital to maintain both their reputation and actual optimal performance of medical and surgical care of their patients by supporting their physician staff and maintaining the diagnostic and surgical equipment essential to the mutual goal of zenith patient care, delivered on a daily basis.

After three years of the hospital organization's informing one particular medical specialty department repeatedly, every three months at their quarterly meetings each year, that they might move the diagnostic and surgical equipment essential to that specialty's patient care, diagnostic precision of diagnoses, and surgical equipment necessary to achieve precise, accurate, and safe surgical outcomes for every patient they treat in the hospital and for the patients they treat in their outpatient offices to another building, outside the main hospital, a shocking, sudden, unanticipated, completely unexpected decree was made by two of the dictator-like hospital administration staff members, one of which was a physician in a completely different specialty that demonstrated no understanding of the other specialty's vital and essential hospital equipment necessary to practice their specialty in the hospital setting. Every distinct specialist physician in a hospital is a member of that specialty department encompassing all the on-staff attendings of the same specialty, who work in that hospital to care for their patients with diseases or surgeries necessary to cure or heal these diseases that are very specific to their specialty.

All specialty attending physicians on staff daily and weekly require outpatient diagnostic tests performed at the hospital to arrive at accurate diagnoses and precise, safe, and intended surgical outcomes after surgery is performed. The hospital suddenly informed every specialist physician in this particular specialty that they intended ("to save money and decrease their expenses") to close down the department in the hospital that performed all the vital, necessary, and essential diagnostic and surgical equipment required by all this particular specialty's attending physicians on staff at the hospital, without any input, feedback, discussion, or without any meetings to discuss this ill-advised intent and plan to devastate to safety and care of this particular specialty's patients being treated in this specific hospital. In fact the hospital administration even went as far as purposely canceling this specialty department's regularly scheduled quarterly (every 3 month meetings typically), meeting in hopes of averting any pushback or negative feedback or non-consent or discontent by this specialty department's attending specialist physicians on staff at this hospital, which, incidentally, is a hospital member in a large network with a group of many different hospitals, all owned by a bullying, manipulative, monopolistic, abusive (with regard to their disrespectful and inconsiderate, sinister abusive attitudes, behavior, and treacherous actions toward their own hospital staff specialist physicians and surgeons), large wealth business entity, that has repeatedly over the last 30+ years leveraged its size, wealth, administrative and legal power (extremely out of balance with the power that physician providers should have that is equal to that of money-only focused hospital administrators whose fiscal and monetary ambitions and desires far outweigh the priority they give to the quality and safety of patient care), to abuse the dignity, respect, and proper treatment and distribution of equal power and influence deserved and necessary to be delegated or given to the physician who are responsible for the large majority of their income and earnings.

The insult to the dignity, respect, and honor of these specialty physicians, inflicted by this poor judgment and intended action by the hospital administration, was shocking to the core heart and soul of all the physicians of that specialty working for that hospital. This is just one more vivid, stunning, shocking, accurate, factual account of, and an example of large, monopolistic corporations and other business entities in this world abusing honest and hard-working employees. Incidentally, the physicians had and, very disappointingly, have no union support or legal defense to regain the respect, deserved dignity, and merited balance of power (relative to the sinister, money-obsessed hospital administrators) due to them now and sadly, for the past two hundred years, within the practice of medicine in general, and in the hospital setting specifically!

An extremely insightful, introspective, masterfully written history novel has been written which specifically, precisely, and succinctly addresses all these particular abuses (and many others), in the healthcare industry that have been allowed to persist and metastasize into larger and more difficult malignancies (in the worldwide healthcare system of employee and staff member abuse, disrespect, and torture), to deal with, seek a remedy for, or cure, however, this particular author with keen insight, wisdom, and brilliance, lays out a legitimate, viable, promising, and accomplishable plan to correct these iniquities currently being perpetrated against all healthcare employees, staff, and physicians who are working outside or within hospitals, as independent contracting subspecialist consultants or regular hospital staff, which not only restores balance of power back to the rightful owners (equal administrative power or greater being restored to hospital contracting physician providers), but also restoration of the independent behavior and freedom of truthful speech, dignity, and respect that is due to physician staff members, and has been due but unpaid for over two centuries, that will ultimately improve physician satisfaction with their daily employment in or at hospitals, and most importantly, improve patient care by facilitating honest and truthful discussions by physicians with hospital administrators, once these hospital-contracted physician are backed, defended, and supported by Godly and physician advocate unions that have both the financial and legal power to take on necessary battles with unethical hospitals and hospital administrators or administrations, who have in the past, and continue in present times, to ignore moral and ethical approaches to maximize the happiness, health, and safe patient outcomes after being admitted or treated as an outpatient in the hospital, of both their physician and other hospital employees, as well as their patients, who inevitably will benefit immensely when these physician regain and restore the balance of power, freedom of truthful and patient care-improving speech and recommendations, all without the fear or consequences of being the victim of sinister hospital administration retribution, unwarranted punishment, and revenge, solely because these physician's suggestions were aimed at improving patient care in the future, but rejected by the administrators of the hospital who were more concerned about covering up errors, mistakes, or omissions by their employees, than achieving optimal and zenith care for their hospital-treated patients.

Literary Agents currently run an exclusive and highly liberal, radical, largely atheistic, agnostic, racist, sexist, and prejudiced business, preferring, as evidenced by one's review of their business website profiles, where each literary agent describes in great detail the sex, skin color, gender confusion or psychiatric illness that they prefer their ideal authors to have, for them to accept a new author and represent that new and unknown author as their "literary agent" who supposedly have exclusive and monopolistic relationships with similar radical, liberal (e.g., no Godly values or intent to publish Christian or other religious, honest, hard-working, Caucasian, normal (without psychiatric disease or gender identity confusion), moral, ethical, brilliant authors), large, wealthy, manipulative, Godly author and Godly narrative and novel-suppressing, and monopolistic large, prominent (infamous, not famous) publishing companies, that everyone knows of and has heard of, throughout the world.

One account from a story obtained directly from honorable, trustworthy scholar and genius-level new author was that this individual received top grades in language and writing classes throughout grammar school, high school, university, post-graduate school, and throughout this individual's doctoral program, finishing this program, again, with top honors, yet his brilliant, multiple, novel manuscripts submitted to all known literary agents and listed infamous liberal publishers throughout the world all declined his numerous brilliant books for literary agent assignment or book publisher company book publication.

The "catch 22" here is that all these large liberal publishers repeatedly refuse, as noted on their websites, to accept new book submissions from authors without a "literary agent" (gestapo agent, with Godly values hatred and intent to suppress all Godly, moral, ethical messages and society-improving novels that are not written by these literary agents biased, prejudiced, and ungodly targeted new authors, namely, authors who have psychiatric disease, gender confusion, are openly homosexual, e.g., gay, lesbian, or transgender, or authors writing only fiction novels, murder stories, crime stories, or film noir, or, flouting their incredibly racist or sexist disposition, bias, or prejudice nature, before even reading or reviewing a new author manuscript and book, rejecting to even review an author book submission, detailed in their websites, if the author is not a non-Caucasian or "diversity, equity, inclusion (dark skin color or minority person)", or if the author is a man (versus "preferred women author", or vice versa), and, what should be most shocking to the entire world of "literary (gestapo) agents" and large publishers (biased, prejudiced, and monopolistic in their suppression of free speech and books written by normal ethical authors, and Godly, religious, and spiritual author book submissions for publication), and the whole world and all "world citizens" who are normal and Caucasian, have no mental illness or gender identity confusion, who also should have the equal opportunity to publish their messages and books for the overall support, encouragement, motivation, inspiration, and ultimately, the betterment of the world in general, and specifically!

Until these radical, leftist, and ungodly literary agents and large, rich, powerful, Godly message-suppressing large publishing companies are confronted, taken to court and defeated for their steering societies, countries, and "world citizens" to veer off the road and tumble to their death and destruction off the mountain cliff side they were attempting to drive up, without success, due to the distraction, misdirection, and Godly guidance suppression, and then, to make matters worse, these same "bad actors" enable and effectuate daily by rejecting all normal and sane author's books for publication, and enthusiastically not only encouraging writers to write society values-destroying books, but evening pushing mentally ill authors and gender identity confusion authors, and atheists, agnostics, and transgender or crime-obsessed or murder-obsessed authors to flood the new book reading markets and audiences with trash, society-destroying thoughts and aspirations, and child-abusing thoughts (e.g., sex change surgeries in young vulnerable, innocent, and Godly children whose sex should remain their birth sex for life), which are currently and despicably being touted and flaunted (Satan is extremely proud and very approving of this literary agent and prominent book publishing companies trend and tendency to side with Satan regarding all these issues and topics), as books worthy or deserving of publication and reading, when in truth, these aberrant authors' books should instead, most sensibly and reasonably, be used as tinder for Satan's fireplace and log burning in Hades or hell.

Television series and cable television producers who prejudicially promote, produce, and attempt to glamorize and normalize the use of profanity, nudity, and evil criminal activity including murders and rapes, are just as nefarious and evil as their "most hated and disrespected" predecessor movie studio stealer (embezzled and stolen from his brothers), and Satan incarnate, Jack Warner, who started the promotion of profanity, nudity, murder, crime stories, all to satisfy his greed and thirst for dishonestly obtained wealth through the manipulation, monopolization, and degradation of the world by promoting movies glamorizing criminals, murderers, rapists, and movies with actors whose speech is infected and contaminated with diffuse profanities, which are all ungodly and unnecessary actions and behaviors.

School administrators, track & field authorities, amateur and professional sports authorities and sports organization owners who both fail to restrict gender confused and mentally ill patients from invading the opposite sex sports that they have no business or pleasure joining, competing with, nor participating in at all, or who fail to protect and defend "American Christian Origin Values And Principles" when deciding whether or not to make new business deals or contracts with evil or sinister countries or country (anti-) leaders who abuse, imprison, maliciously prosecute all their political opponents or other enemies, or who knowingly and openly enslave, or steal all the human freedoms, human rights, human dignity and respect, from their countries very own citizens or from the citizens of other countries that they unlawfully invaded, attacked, or destroyed without any reasonable or ethical or Godly approval or any other believable justification, should be outlawed, restricted, severely punished, and any deals made with any of the above described tyrants or dictators or slave owners should be immediately be forbidden and cancelled retroactively if necessary, to honor both God and American

Christian values that have made America one of the greatest countries in the world in the past two centuries, all because of the fact that the Bible, the greatest book ever written, has been and must continue to be both the beacon of guiding light to America, and the inspiration, motivation, and guide to America's God-blessed behavior and actions, just as must be the case for every other country in the world, who desires and seeks the blessings of God for their country and all their "world citizens", also known as the "children of God" or "God's family."

Below are concluding, summarizing, and Godly positive and loving chapters/excerpts for this book, Superheroes, Becoming The Truly Elite, yet from an even greater masterpiece, entitled "Father's Eyes," an eternal blessing and formula for success, happiness, and Godly serenity and confidence in this life on earth and for one's eternal afterlife, for this generation and all future generations, written by Winston Anselm Irons.

Chapter Four:

How Does An Individual Develop Hercules-like Strength, Fortitude, And Determination to Accomplish All Goals And Concomitantly Gain Ever-Increasing Positive Self-Confidence, Self-Esteem, And Motivation For Benevolent Purpose-Driven Occupational And Family or Friend Relationships Strengthening Aspirations?

Synopsis: From birth, or at the earliest age possible, obtain a "weightlifting set of weights" that includes a weightlifting bar and barbells and also start doing pushups, pull-ups, and abdominal crunches. Purchase a lifetime gym membership at the lowest price possible from the best gym that is closest to your house. When Winston was growing up in a tiny country town, there were no commercial gyms available to workout in or to sign up and become a member of. There was only the weight room at the local high school, which was only available to high school students and too crowded to ever accommodate outside town and community members. This was very disappointing to Winston.

Winston's philosophy from birth was as follows: If the whole house, all doors, all windows, and even the dog flap in the back door is all locked up and inaccessible, forget trying to enter that silly house and build your own house which is available and accessible twenty-four hours a day, seven days per week, and 52 weeks per year! Winston entered kindergarten one year earlier than 96% of his classmates, at four years of age. Thus, the majority of his classmates were 1-2 years older than Winston and 1-2 years physically taller and (supposedly, but never in reality) stronger and smarter (the latter being always more dependent on work ethic and ability to focus on that being studied, more than age, and thus was not a significant disadvantage for Winston despite his being 1-2 years younger than all his classmates). Winston immediately realized the advantages of working out as a very young child.

Winston completed thousands of bench presses, upper extremities curls for biceps and triceps, sit ups (now Winston recommends abdominal crunches instead, with thighs held up 90 degrees [perpendicular to back/spine] and legs maintained at this elevated position and parallel to the back/spine), and pushups on his bedroom carpet in his home from about 5 years old and thereafter, when he woke up in the morning, before school each weekday and on weekends, then showered, and went to grammar school or proceeded with his weekend chores (mopping all the floors in the house and dusting everything in every room or vacuuming all the carpets in every room of the house; these chore choices alternated each weekend with Winston's older [eighteen months older] brother who shared in these pleasurable (not) chores, but enabled both Winston and his older with measly allowances, so that we could at least buy a soda and candy bar once a week at one of the only two tiny food stores in town that were both walking distance from out small and humble dwelling (home).

Winston felt and looked stronger (at least in his very young mind!) after every workout session each day. He also noted he had a more positive and upbeat attitude, was more energetic, and could concentrate on and memorize more of what he was studying and supposed to be learning in school each day! Winston also joined his church pastor on morning runs whenever Winston was free to join him at the 700 am start time. These runs were usually about 5 miles long and involved running around an approximately four-city block route, multiple tabulated or calculated times until the 5-mile distance had been successfully achieved or completed! Winston found these runs exciting and exhilarating and had many great communications with the pastor throughout the duration of these runs.

What a great learning and exercising opportunity for young Winston as a grammar school student of only single-digit ages in grammar school, until Winston graduated from university years later! Brain-derived neurotrophic Factor (BDNF) and Endorphins are created within the body due to regular or daily vigorous aerobic exercises (e.g., jogging, running, running upstairs, circuit weight training). If you haven't heard of circuit training, it's a combination of six or more exercises performed with short rest periods between them for either a set number of repetitions or a prescribed amount of time. Circuits can also be a great way to build muscle mass. Circuits that incorporate strength training can help you build lean muscle while keeping your heart rate up at the same time. Usually, there will be 8-10 exercises in a circuit, although this number can vary depending on how much time you have. You can perform a certain number of reps for each exercise (8-20 reps), or you can time each exercise (30-60 seconds per exercise).

Circuit training may be shorter and faster, but it is not easy. It requires stamina and may not be suitable for beginners or people with low fitness levels. Disadvantages of circuit weight training include exhaustion from the rapid workout, which, if not careful and monitored by you, can make your form suffer or even increase the risks of an injury, again if you are not paying attention to performing the exercise with optimal form to maximize muscles fitness and decrease the risk of injuries. Circuit training is a mixture of and combines strength and cardiovascular, or cardio, training. The average circuit training workout usually involves 8 to 12 different workout stations where you work different muscle groups. Since circuit training is a particularly high-intensity workout that quickly pushes your entire body to its limits, it shouldn't be done too many times a week. Two or three times a week is a good benchmark to aim towards. Anywhere from 10–45 minutes is ideal for circuit training. The shorter the workout, the harder you should be pushing. And since you're alternating which body part you're working on during each move, there's no need to rest for excessive periods between exercises. One or two minutes of rest between sets is usually more than enough.

- **Strength training.** Strength training is also called anaerobic exercise, a short burst of energy for movement. Think of a pushup or pull-up. These exercises help build and tone muscles.

- **Aerobic Exercise.** "Aerobic" means "needs oxygen." Your heart rate increases to get oxygen where your body needs it, thus the word "cardio." Running, biking, or jumping jacks would be examples of aerobic exercise.

The thing about a circuit is that you actually do both categories. Presses and lunges fall into strength training. Jumping jacks are cardio. **With circuit training, you build muscle and burn fat while building stamina.**

If you're limited on time and can only pick one, I would pick strength training: when you strength train, you break your muscles down, and your body needs to work extra hard over the next 24-48 hours to rebuild those muscles (with increased calories burned).

Individuals should choose their own various workout machines or exercises to include in their circuit weight training, suited to their desires and body parts that need the most strengthening and maximal functioning or rehabilitation after minor or major injuries. Winston's own preferences for circuit training exercises in the gym (please work up gradually and slowly to these levels if you wish to copy Winston's circuit training routine) include.

A minimum of 100 total pull-ups each session (e.g., five sets of twenty or any other pattern, such as a tapering pattern, is acceptable), 100 bar dips per session, three sets of maximum weight biceps curling (15 curls per set), 150 chest pectoralis major and minor (3 sets of 50 each), 21 (3 sets of the maximum stack of weights tolerable, and keep progressively increasing weight amount until the entire stack of weights is being used for back exercises, seven repetitions per set) of the back (trapezius, deltoids, rhomboids, and rotator cuff muscles), 400-600 crunches per session (either sets of 200 each or 100 each x 6 sets).

Winston performs workouts approximately three days per week, then runs 18 to 30 miles (about 6 miles per day) per week on days when he is not working out in the gym. Winston considers the running days an additional exercise type or component of his circuit exercise training overall program! Add hobby sports that are unpredictable or expensive vacation-type sports (e.g., tennis, volleyball, water skiing, snow skiing, rock climbing, hiking, or others) to this regular weekly exercise routine, and you will have the most amazing brain function and physical strength you could ever hope for!

Chapter Six:

Living Life to the Fullest: Happy, Successful, Supportive, Safe, Secure, Content, Ambitious, and Healthy.

What is it that makes people happy in life?

Psychological flexibility is a critical factor to greater happiness and well-being. For instance, allowing yourself to be open to emotional experiences and learning to experience and gracefully adapt to, tolerate, and then overcome or recover from periods of discomfort can allow you to be more resilient and less fearful in life, empowering and enabling you to move more rapidly towards your goals and aspirations, resulting in a richer, more meaningful existence. The author and reader of this book should realize and know that there is no single answer to this question.

There are myriad factors to consider.

Top Ten Factors Determining Differences In What Makes People Most Fulfilled in Life:

1) Age: Goals that transition from early life, to mid-life, to late-life ages
2) Parenting (Mother & Father combination, Single Mother, Single Father)
3) Education
4) Exercise
5) Diet
6) Health
7) Religion, Church Community, and Friends
8) Sleep
9) Music, Sports, Healthy Hobbies, and Other Recreational Activities
10) Love

What Makes People Most Fulfilled in Life?

Goals which transition from early life, to mid-life, to late-life ages.

Age and realistic goals are all important, but they are different in every stage of life. Infants, young children, adolescents, teenagers, young single adults, young married couples, middle-aged individuals, retired and senior citizen individuals will have vastly different priorities, goals, and aspirations, often determined by what they have already done or not done, goals they have accomplished or not accomplished, and their expected life duration and time they have or expect to have to prepare for and accomplish those distinct age-related goals. Infants and young children have age-related goals that are quite simple but labor-intensive for those around them who are raising them. Among their top priorities are safety, security, and help with tasks they do not yet realize or know are important, essential, and vital to existence, or dangerous and a legitimate threat to their survival and existence. They require visual, audible, and actionable benevolent role models as parents, siblings, relatives, and other contacts to show them, teach them, and demonstrate to them what a daily routine life looks like, feels like, and how it ends with a good night of sleep. They require mentors who are supreme listeners, wise and succinct responders, slow to anger, and rapid to teach all life lessons required each day, such that the child learns that learning something new and helpful about living a good life is not only possible but expected and achievable, each and every day until that infant or young child dies one-hundred or more years later, hopefully!

Adolescents require additional distinct goals that must be transitioned to from prior infant and young children goals. When adolescents interact for the first time with church school classmates, regular school classmates, older classmates or adults, or any of these groups that have one or more members with poor discretion, poor judgment, non-Christian or otherwise sinful or evil intent, attitudes, and immoral behavior, suggestions, or peer pressure, it is vitally important, ideally, that each child already possesses (or develops as soon as possible), an inner set of moral, ethical, Godly values.

These age-related goals and priorities will then allow that individual adolescent to have an inner sense of self-worth, self-confidence, and a sense of who they are, want to be, and need to be to implement and achieve a successful Jesus Christ-like magical and benevolent existence in this world. These age-related goals and priorities will also enable that adolescent to avoid being negatively or adversely affected or swayed to emulate, join in, or deceptively be convinced by evil influencers that whatever bad behavior is being touted is anything other than immoral, illegal, ill-advised, wrong, dishonest, or a threat to the integrity and health of that individual or others.

The adolescent may then avoid distractions or distractors who intend to hinder that individual's honest and ethical attitude, education, behavior, improving self-esteem and self-confidence, all of which would have potentially been detrimental to that adolescent and counterproductive to the most desirable goal of being an outstanding adolescent student, church, and family member who is a role model for others (of all ages) by the moral, ethical, honest, and Godly behavior demonstrated by that adolescent child. Peer pressure is a significant risk factor for adolescents who are not taught Godly values by reading a traditional children's (non-woke) Bible at the earliest age possible and for children who have not been schooled in and educated about Godly values in church school or during regular church services by the pastor of the church.

Adolescents also greatly benefit from strong, moral, and ethical male fathers and female mothers, who may serve as parental role models and mentors who teach these young developing humans who are transitioning from children to adolescents, and eventually teenagers, many essential life skills, differences in males and females, puberty education, menstruation education, and God's definition of males, females, and marriage which is defined as the lifelong union, blessed by God, of a male to a female. In single-parent families, adolescents may learn these essential definitions of males and females and their differences, as defined by God, by other male and female role models and mentors within the church community by attending church youth group classes, campouts, summer and winter church gatherings and retreats, weekly Bible studies, and "Fellowship of Christian Athletes" weekly or monthly meetings in grammar school and high school.

A single mother with children or a single father with children may and should seek out mentors within the church who can and are willing to be strong father or mother replacement role models for their children, which is easier than one might expect, simply by becoming more involved in weekly church youth group gatherings, Bible studies, church choir, church brass ensemble, church ministries in the local community and abroad, and various church summer camps, winter snow retreats,

"Vacation Bible School" during summer school breaks, or any other church activities or sports (softball team, baseball team, basketball team, church ski group trips, church rock climbing, bike rides, water skiing, or various other church ministries: nursing home ministry, juvenile hall ministry, prison ministry, and many others.

Teenagers are a whole different ball game! Anyone who has either been a teenager (most of us) or raised teenagers, or even watched others who have or are raising teenagers knows very well that this age group is an extremely unique and independent, yet dependent, group of individuals who are deeply in need of guidance and reassurance that the path they are pursuing is the right, straight, and narrow Godly path for their life, but often too proud, independent (or at least hoping to be), or overwhelmed by school classmate's peer pressure being applied upon their shoulders like the yoke upon an ox's back to agree to sound logic, reason, or Godly principles of life, hopefully being taught to them each Sunday in church. With proper and constant reassurance that a Godly lifestyle and Christian teachings and principles, as taught in the Bible and church, are the ultimate, optimal, and most efficient means of having a fulfilling, benevolent, purpose-driven life, developing and maintaining a lifelong positive and caring attitude, and the most accurate and enduring life guide to achieving the happiest, fulfilling, and successful life, parents and mentors in the church may rescue their teenagers from unwise and unsuccessful rebellions based on misleading or deviant peer pressure from other non-God revering classmate or evil influencers, or better yet, prevent their teenagers altogether from being distracted or diverted from God's loving, caring, protective path and guidance for their life!

College-age (teenagers and soon-to-be young adults, young professionals, or other trade specialists) individuals encounter immense peer pressure to abandon their Christian upbringing, lifestyle, and Bible-based life perspective and principles. Understanding that no human is perfect or sinless in this life (the author included), parent's best hope for their child or children should always be that the Christian and Bible principles taught to their children and young developing adults, both directly by the parents and with the assistance and guidance provided by the church community, will help guide their college or professional or other job trade specialist-bound high school graduates to make wise, reverent, holy decisions with regard to all the temptations that arrive at and within this new age group. Decisions about sexual behavior (or, per the Bible, misbehavior if before marriage), alcohol and illicit drug abuse (which destroy the brain, body, and Godly soul of all individuals rapidly and progressively with continued abuse), kind, honest, ethical, moral behavior, and caring, loving, compassionate, merciful, humble behavior versus alternative or opposite behavior and attitudes, all become poignant and highly relevant issues and guiding life principles in this age group, all depending on whether these choices are made with Bible-based education and wisdom and God's guiding principles in mind, or whether this age group chooses to shun all the wisdom, knowledge, and guidance available in the greatest book ever written and most widely published and read book in the world, the Bible!

Young married couples or young unmarried couples have age-related goals that are amazingly similar overall. If both groups follow the path of seeking out God's direction and guidance by attending church each week, enrolling their children in church youth group classes and activities, and, preferably, getting married if parents are not married initially with the birth of their first or multiple children, then both group can receive God's richest blessings, safety, and guidance for their entire family throughout their lives.

Middle-aged individuals, single, married, or divorced, have unique and varied goals depending on their marital or widow status, the stability and success of their children, and the strength of God's influence on their life and whether they feel thankful and grateful for God's guidance or resentful and bitter for what they might interpret as God's ignoring them, neglecting them, or God's absence from their life, either by their own choice, or if they feel that God purposely abandoned them or neglected to come to their rescue or fulfill their needs at the lowest time or period in the life when they needed God the most.

Some middle-aged individuals look at the "first half" of life with regret that they made bad choices (e.g., sexual, alcohol or drug abuse, criminal, atheist, agnostic) and missed out on God's blessings. Others look back on the "first half" of their life with immense satisfaction, contentment, joy, and without regret due to their feeling blessed by God's guidance and protection throughout their tumultuous and tempestuous trials and temptations they were faced with and overcame via the grace, mercy, and loving-kindness of their God and creator, whom they placed all their trust and loyalty in and with, in hopes of having a God-blessed life of happiness to the greatest extent possible, as determined by God.

Senior citizens and individuals who sense they are near the end of their life, young or very old or middle-aged, have the difficult decision to make, if not made years earlier or as a young child, to either believe God is and always has been their creator and savior, or to firmly believe, as agnostics or atheists, that God is a myth, neither created them nor has any power over their life, death, or afterlife.

Blaise Pascal was a genius. In the first half of his life, he lived a wild life of drinking, carousing, and gambling. During and after a near-death experience, Blaise Pascal underwent a conversion experience and found God. He lived the remainder of his life as a God-respecting, God-fearing, and Godly man. He abandoned his past wild, reckless, unhealthy, and Godless lifestyle and sinful behavior and activities. He then created or developed an argument ("Pascal's Wager") in hopes of converting as many of his past friends and colleagues who were continuing on a downward spiral of ungodly and unhealthy alcohol abuse, not sleeping, and excessive gambling to the Godly conversion and transformation that brought Blaise Pascal so much joy and peace in the second half of his life.

Pascal's Wager was explicitly focused on gambling odds and his hopes of convincing and persuading even his most stubborn atheist or agnostic past gambling, alcoholic, drug-abusing, sexually inappropriate or abusive, and sleep-deprived friends, who were rapidly killing themselves progressively each day by their ungodly life activities, habits, addictions, self-destructive behavior, negative attitude, lack of God's guidance and blessings in their lives, and overall unhealthy life choices that results from this sad and disappointing path in life that Blaise Pascal was once on with these friends, but then, by God's grace and mercy, was saved by God in a conversion experience that brought even more wisdom and enlightenment to Blaise Pascal, adding spiritual genius to Pascal's already impressive academic accomplishments and genius status that God blessed him with earlier in his life.

Blaise Pascal: The Penseés is a collection of philosophical fragments, notes, and essays in which Blaise Pascal explores the contradictions of human nature in psychological, social, metaphysical, and, above all, theological terms.

Pascal's Wager is a philosophical argument presented by the seventeenth-century French mathematician, philosopher, physicist, and theologian Blaise Pascal (1623–1662). It posits that human beings wager with their lives that God either exists or does not. Pascal's Wager, originally proposed by Blaise Pascal (1623–1662), takes a more pragmatic approach. Pascal thought that evidence cannot settle the question of whether God exists, so he proposes that you should bet, or Wager, on God because of what's at stake: you have lots to gain and not much to lose. Pascal was a French philosopher, scientist, mathematician, and probability theorist (1623-1662) and argued that if we do not know whether God exists, then we should play it safe rather than risk being sorry. Blaise Pascal suggested that God is infinite and eternal. Human understanding is incapable of grasping these concepts through reason. Therefore, God cannot be understood by reason. "If one submits everything to reason, our religion will contain nothing that is mysterious or supernatural."

Pascal's Wager excerpted from Pens'ees, available on Project Gutenberg http://www.gutenberg.org/files/18269/18269-h/18269-h.htm#SECTION_III 229

This is what I see and what troubles me. I look on all sides, and I see only darkness everywhere. Nature presents to me nothing which is not a matter of doubt and concern. If I saw nothing there which revealed a Divinity, I would come to a negative conclusion; if I saw everywhere the signs of a Creator, I would remain peacefully in faith. But, seeing too much to deny and too little to be sure, I am in a state to be pitied; wherefore I have a hundred times wished that if a God maintains nature, she should testify to Him unequivocally, and that, if the signs she gives are deceptive, she should suppress them altogether; that she should say everything or nothing, that I might see which cause I ought to follow. Whereas in my present state, ignorant of what I am or of what I ought to do, I know neither my condition nor my duty. My heart inclines wholly to know where is the true good, in order to follow it; nothing would be too dear to me for eternity. I envy those whom I see living in the faith with such carelessness, and who make such a bad use of a gift of which it seems to me I would make such a different use.

It is incomprehensible that God should exist, and it is incomprehensible that He should not exist; that the soul one should be joined to the body, and that we should have no soul; that the world should be created, and that it should not be created, etc.; that original sin should be, and that it should not be. Do you believe it to be impossible that God is infinite, without parts?—Yes. I wish, therefore, to show you an infinite and indivisible thing. It is a point moving everywhere with an infinite velocity, for it is one in all places and is all totality in every place. Let this effect of nature, which previously seemed to you impossible, make you know that there may be others of which you are still ignorant. Do not draw this conclusion from your experiment that there remains nothing for you to know, but rather that there remains an infinity for you to know. Infinite movement, the point which fills everything, the moment of rest; infinite without quantity, indivisible and infinite. Infinite—nothing.—Our soul is cast into a body, where it finds number, time, and dimension. Thereupon it reasons, and calls this nature, necessity, and can believe nothing else. Unity joined to infinity adds nothing to it, no more than one foot to an infinite measure. The finite is annihilated in the presence of the infinite, and becomes a pure nothing. So our spirit before God, so our justice before divine justice.

There is not so great a disproportion between our justice and that of God as between unity and infinity. The justice of God must be vast, like His compassion. Now justice to the outcast is less vast, and ought less to offend our feelings than mercy towards the elect. We know that there is an infinite, and are ignorant of its nature. As we know it to be false that numbers are finite, it is therefore true that there is an infinity in numbers. But we do not know what it is. It is false that it is even, it is false that it is odd; for the addition of a unit can make no change in its nature. Yet it is a number, and every number is odd or even (this is certainly true of every finite number).

So, we may well know that there is a God without knowing what He is. Is there not one substantial truth, seeing there are so many things which are not the truth itself? We know then the existence and nature of the finite because we also are finite and have extension. We know the existence of the infinite, and are ignorant of its nature, because it has extension like us, but not limits like us. But we know neither the existence nor the nature of God because He has neither extension nor limits. But by faith, we know His existence; in glory, we shall know His nature. Now, I have already shown that we may well know the existence of a thing without knowing its nature. Let us now speak according to natural lights. If there is a God, He is infinitely incomprehensible since, having neither parts nor limits, He has no affinity to us. We are then incapable of knowing either what He is or if He is. This being so, who will dare to undertake the decision of the question? Not we, who have no affinity to Him.

Who then will blame Christians for not being able to give a reason for their belief since they profess a religion for which they cannot give a reason? They declare, in expounding it to the world, that it is a foolishness, stultitiam; and then you complain that they do not prove it! If they proved it, they would not keep their word; it is in lacking proofs that they are not lacking in sense." Yes, but although this excuses those who offer it as such and takes away from them the blame of putting it forward without reason, it does not excuse those who receive it." Let us then examine this point and say," God is, or He is not." But to which side shall we incline? Reason can decide nothing here. There is an infinite chaos which separated us. A game is being played at the extremity of this infinite distance where heads or tails will turn up. What will you wager?

According to reason, you can do neither the one thing nor the other; according to reason, you can defend neither of the propositions. Do not then reprove for error those who have made a choice, for you know nothing about it." No, but I blame them for having made, not this choice, but a choice, for again, both he who chooses heads and he who chooses tails are equally at fault; they are both in the wrong. The true course is not to wager at all." Yes, but you must wager. It is not optional. You are embarked. Which will you choose then? Let us see. Since you must choose, let us see which interests you least. You have two things to lose, the true and the good, and two things to stake, your reason and your will, your knowledge and your happiness, and your nature has two things to shun, error and misery.

Your reason is no more shocked in choosing one rather than the other since you must, of necessity, choose. This is one point settled. But your happiness? Let us weigh the gain and the loss in wagering that God is. Let us estimate these two chances. If you gain, you gain all; if you lose, you lose nothing. Wager, then, without hesitation, that He is.—" That is very fine. Yes, I must wager, but I may perhaps wager too much."—Let us see. Since there is an equal risk of gain and of loss, if you had only to gain two lives, instead of one, you might still wager. But if there were three lives to gain, you would have to play (since you are under the necessity of playing), and you would be imprudent, when you are forced to play, not to chance your life to gain three at a game where there is an equal risk of loss and gain. But there is an eternity of life and happiness.

And this being so, if there were an infinity of chances, of which one only would be for you, you would still be right in wagering one to win two, and you would act stupidly, being obliged to play, by refusing to stake one life against three at a game in which out of an infinity of chances there is one for you, if there were an infinity of an infinitely happy life to gain. But there is here an infinity of an infinitely happy life to gain, a chance of gain against a finite number of chances of loss, and what you stake is finite. It is all divided; wherever the infinite is and there is not an infinity of chances of loss against that of gain, there is no time to hesitate, you must give all. And thus, when one is forced to play, he must renounce reason to preserve his life, rather than risk it for infinite gain, as likely to happen as the loss of nothingness. For it is no use to say it is uncertain if we will gain, and it is certain that we risk, and that the infinite distance between the certainty of what is staked and the uncertainty of what will be gained, equals the finite good which is certainly staked against the uncertain infinite. It is not so, as every player stakes a certainty to gain an uncertainty, and yet he stakes a finite certainty to gain a finite uncertainty, without transgressing against reason.

There is not an infinite distance between the certainty staked and the uncertainty of the gain; that is untrue. In truth, there is an infinity between the certainty of gain and the certainty of loss. But the uncertainty of the gain is proportioned to the certainty of the stake according to the proportion of the chances of gain and loss. Hence, it comes that if there are as many risks on one side as on the other, the course is to play even, and then the certainty of the stake is equal to the uncertainty of the gain, so far is it from the fact that there is an infinite distance between them. And so our proposition is of infinite force when there is the finite to stake in a game where there are equal risks of gain and of loss, and the infinite 6 to gain. This is demonstrable, and if men are capable of any truths, this is one." I confess it. I admit it. But, still, is there no means of seeing the faces of the cards?"—Yes, Scripture and the rest, etc." Yes, but I have my hands tied and my mouth closed; I am forced to wager and am not free. I am not released and am so made that I cannot believe it. What, then, would you have me do?" True. But at least learn your inability to believe, since reason brings you to this, and yet you cannot believe. Endeavour then to convince yourself, not by increase of proofs of God, but by the abatement of your passions.

You would like to attain faith and do not know the way; you would like to cure yourself of unbelief and ask the remedy for it. Learn of those who have been bound like you and who now stake all their possessions. These are people who know the way which you would follow and who are cured of an illness of which you would be cured. Follow the way by which they began: by acting as if they believed, taking the holy water, having masses said, etc. Even this will naturally make you believe and deaden your acuteness.—" But this is what I am afraid of."— And why? What have you to lose? But to show you that this leads you there, it is this which will lessen the passions, which are your stumbling blocks. The end of this discourse.—Now, what harm will befall you in taking this side? You will be faithful, honest, humble, grateful, generous, a sincere friend, truthful. Certainly, you will not have those poisonous pleasures, glory, and luxury, but will you not have others? I will tell you that you will thereby gain in this life and that, at each step you take on this road, you will see so great certainty of gain, so much nothingness in what you risk, that you will, at last, recognize that you have wagered for something certain and infinite, for which you have given nothing." Ah! This discourse transports me, charms me."

If this discourse pleases you and seems impressive, know that it is made by a man who has knelt, both before and after it, in prayer to that Being, infinite and without parts, before whom he lays all he has, for you also to lay before Him all you have for your own good and for His glory, that so strength may be given to lowliness. If we must not act save on a certainty, we ought not to act on religion, for it is not certain. But how many things do we do in uncertainty, on sea voyages, in battles? I say then we must do nothing at all, for nothing is certain, and that there is more certainty in religion than there is as to whether we may see tomorrow; for it is not certain that we may see tomorrow, and it is certainly possible that we may not see it. We cannot say as much about religion. It is not certain that it is, but who will venture to say that it is certainly possible that it is not?

Now, when we work for tomorrow and so on an uncertainty, we act reasonably, for we ought to work for an uncertainty according to the doctrine of chance, which was demonstrated above. Saint Augustine has seen that we work for uncertainty, on the sea, in battle, etc. But he has not seen the doctrine of chance, which proves that we should do so. Montaigne has seen that we are shocked at a fool, and that habit is all-powerful, but he has not seen the reason for this effect. All these people have seen the effects, but they have not seen the causes. They are, in comparison with those who have discovered the causes, as those who have only eyes are in comparison with those who have intellect. For the effects are perceptible by sense, and the causes are visible only to the intellect. And although these effects are seen by the mind, this mind is, in comparison with the mind which sees the causes, as the bodily senses are in comparison with the intellect.

The book entitled Pascal's Pensées is, after reading the Bible cover-to-cover five or more times and committing all the Bible's teachings and wisdom to long-term memory to benefit you for the remainder of your life, one of the most amazing and enlightening guides to a fantastic and God-blessed life, that is based on the writings and thoughts of one of the great genius minds in world history, Blaise Pascal. Pascal's Pensées, right after the Bible, is an enlightening and phenomenal read, in the opinion of this book's author, who read the book of Pascal while completing his undergraduate university education.

What Makes People Most Fulfilled in Life: Parenting (Mother & Father combination, Single Mother, Single Father)

Parenting experience and how parenting is delivered to children are as diverse as the stars in the sky. Is it imperative to use a rigid and single formula for best parenting to raise children in the best and most successful manner? The answer is no. This should be obvious. Many of us, including the author of this book, know of or are friends or colleagues with multiple individuals with astonishingly diverse backgrounds and, in many cases, radically different upbringings, and in select circumstances, had parents who employed, successfully or unsuccessfully, shocking parental behavior and unproven or unjustified, or just pure reckless and irresponsible parenting traits and failed trials. Despite these spellbinding stories and historical accounts told to us by our friends, most of these individuals (but not all) navigated the tumultuous and tempestuous storm, persevered, and were able to exit their stormy upbringing, educate and enlighten themselves, thereby effecting a metamorphosis and transformation of themselves (children in dire circumstance into adults with unlimited potential and auspicious futures) into amazingly successful, benevolent, and Godly human beings!

Even though there is not one formula that applies to or fits all parents and instructs them how to raise their child or children properly, there are standard features and methods that should be known and employed to make parenting children less stressful, more satisfying, most efficient and effective, and generate love, respect, assurance, positive self-esteem, self-confidence, and life-long love and appreciation for God and all God-respecting family members. Christian parenting principles benefit everyone on this planet, including agnostic and atheist parents and families, because they employ strategies that have been proven to be successful for thousands of years and because when parents are mature, responsible, and wise enough to entrust the safety and well-being of their children to God and the church community, they and their children, will immediately experience the relief, serenity, peace, humility, positive self-esteem and self-confidence that results from learning Godly values and principles, such as caring and loving others as much as or more than yourself, to receive God's blessings for you as parents and for your children.

All parents, of any culture, religion or no religion, and from any country, will benefit from the true pearls of God's parenting guidelines and principles to raise healthy and happy children who are the most confident and prepared to meet all challenges in life, navigate all life's storms, and successfully contribute, in a positive way, to the betterment of society:

- Love And Honor God Above All Others.
- Love Your Children As Jesus Loves You.
- Be a Faithful Steward.
- Do Not Provoke Your Children.
- Teach God's Word.
- Train Your Children To Follow Jesus.
- Be Humble.

- **LOVE AND VALUE YOUR CHILDREN:** *Fathers, do not provoke your children to anger, but bring them up in the discipline and instruction of the Lord.* Ephesians 6:4

- **POINT CHILDREN TO SCRIPTURE:** *All Scripture is breathed out by God and profitable for teaching, for reproof, for correction, and for training in righteousness, that the man of God may be complete, equipped for every good work.* 2 Timothy 3:16-17

- **TEACH CHILDREN THE LORD'S CHARACTER***: Come, O children, listen to me;*

   I will teach you the fear of the Lord. Psalm 34:11

- **PROTECT CHILDREN'S INNOCENCE:** *Let no one despise you for your youth, but set the believers an example in speech, in conduct, in love, in faith, in purity.* 1 Timothy 4:12

- **CHARACTER TRAINING COMES FIRST:** *The fruit of the righteous is a tree of life,*

   and whoever captures souls is wise. Proverbs 11:30

- **TEACH TO CHILDREN'S GIFTING:** *Now there are varieties of gifts, but the same Spirit; and there are varieties of service, but the same*

Lord; and there are varieties of activities, but it is the same God who empowers them all in everyone. 1 Corinthians 12:4-6

- **MAINTAIN PERSPECTIVE:** *Woe to you, scribes and Pharisees, hypocrites! For you tithe mint and dill and cumin and have neglected the weightier matters of the law: justice and mercy and faithfulness. These you ought to have done, without neglecting the others.* Matthew 23:23

- **PRACTICE WHAT YOU PREACH:** *He did in all things as Joash, his father, had done.* 2 Kings 14:3b

- AN INTENTIONAL PARENTING BOOK: …that you may tell the next generation that this is God, our God forever and ever. He will guide us forever. Psalm 48:13b-14

  - Get in God's Presence
  - Make the Bible Your Authority
  - Lead by Example
  - Set Standards and Keep Them
  - Win Their Hearts

- Become a Family of Sojourners (Be a Christian Family in this world, but not of this world. Live by Godly standards as set forth in the Bible.)

  - Give Presence More than Presents.
  - Know and Honor Your Child
  - Prioritize unity

How do you raise a child in a godly way?

1) Lead by example.
2) Show them critical thinking skills.
3) Teach them how to love by loving them unconditionally.
4) Help them serve others.
5) Share your faith with them through scripture.
6) Pray with them.
7) Allow them to have their own faith.

How to be a good parent according to the Bible?

Discipline your children, and they will give you peace; they will bring you the delights you desire" Proverbs 29:17. It's not irritating, aggravating, disheartening, or provoking children to anger. "Fathers do not embitter your children, or they will become discouraged" Colossians 3:21.

- How to Biblically Discipline Your Children
- Seek your kids out, then educate and enlighten them with kindness.
- Ask good and positive questions.
- Calmly state the consequence of their action.
- Discipline with compassion.
- Be willing to make hard decisions when necessary and required.
- What makes Christian parenting different?

Christian parents should be ready and willing to express love to their children. Christian parents attempt to provide their children with a tangible example of God's love for them. When people are truly loved and cared for by their parents, they get a small glimpse of what God's love for us looks like.

- What is the role of a godly mother to her children?
- A Godly Mother Encourages Children to Seek Jesus.

Yet, you direct their attention to Jesus through it all. You show them their identities aren't in what they do but who they are in Christ. Psalm 127:3-4 says, "Behold, children are a heritage from the Lord, the fruit of the womb is a reward.

- What makes godly parents?

Respect, reverence, and worship are the key ingredients to fearing the Lord. Joseph said, "With me in charge," he told her, "my master does not concern himself with anything in the house; everything he owns he has entrusted to my care. No one is greater in this house than I am.

- What are the biblical duties of a proper parent?

- Parents should teach their children the gospel. The Lord warned that if parents do not teach their children about faith, repentance, baptism, and the gift of the Holy Ghost, the sin will be upon the heads of the parents. Parents should also teach their children to pray and obey the Lord's commandments.

- What does Jesus say about parenting?

- "Jesus said, 'Let the little children come to me, and do not hinder them, for the kingdom of heaven belongs to such as these.'

- What are biblical parental roles?

- The Bible strongly emphasizes parents' influence as a child's initial teacher. The Bible emphasizes that parents' primary duty is to nurture and guide their children from an early age while discussing the significance of parenting in a child's upbringing (Proverbs 22:6; Deuteronomy 6:7).

- How should parents treat their children biblically? Psalm 103:13: "As a father shows compassion to his children, so the Lord shows compassion to those who fear him." The Good News: Fathers, nurture your children with compassion so they do not become afraid of you.

- What does God say about a disobedient child?

- Proverbs 29:17 says this to parents: "Discipline your child, and he/she will give you rest; he/she will give you delight to your heart." A

Scripture from Proverbs 13:24 reads thusly: "He who spares the rod hates his son, but he who loves him is careful to discipline him."

- Does the Bible say you hate your children if you don't discipline them?

• The Bible says if you love your child, you'll discipline them. And you'll do it in love and not anger. Don't buy into the idea that good parents don't discipline their children because they 'love them too much.'

- What is God's attitude towards single parenting?

• Single parents need to hear that they are fine, just as they are, and just as capable of raising children well as any other family. Be clear that God holds single parent families in high regard. Psalm 68:5 says this: A father to the fatherless, a defender of widows is God in his holy dwelling.

- What does a godly mother look like?

• She is confident that He will meet her physical, material, or emotional needs. Instead of focusing on what she lacks, she speaks of God's sufficiency in her life and is grateful whether He provides much or little. A godly mother is generous. Even if she has little to share, she willingly offers it to others.

How to be a godly stepmom?

• If you are a stepmom– Pray and ask God to help you to love well. Ask Him to show you ALL of your children's hearts and how to love them better and to teach you how to pray specifically for your family....

• If you know someone who is a stepmom, then pray and ask God how you can help support your friend and her family.

- What is a biblical example of a godly mother?

• The most well-known mother in the Bible, Mary conceived Jesus, the Son of God, through the Holy Spirit. She was visited by the angel

Gabriel, who informed her of her unique privilege of bearing God's Son. She responded in humility, rejoicing in the Lord's greatness, and He blessed her greatly.

- What is the message of godly parenting?

- Godly parenting is to revolve the family around the centrality of God. Psalm 78:4 We will not hide them from their descendants; we will tell the next generation the praiseworthy deeds of the Lord, his power, and the wonders he has done. Children are not the highest value – God is.

- What does healthy parenting look like?

- In a nutshell, positive parents support a child's healthy growth and inner Spirit by being loving, supportive, firm, consistent, and involved. Such parents go beyond communicating their expectations but practice what they preach by being positive role models for their children to emulate.

- What are the traits of a Godmother?

- These characteristics: shielding, comforting, birthing, protecting, and hovering are all Godly characteristics, features, qualities, and specific examples of Godly behavior and actions manifest in mothers because all mothers on this earth are of Him, from Him, and by Him.

Chapter Four:

How Does An Individual Develop Hercules-like Strength, Fortitude, And Determination to Accomplish All Goals And Concomitantly Gain Ever-Increasing Positive Self-Confidence, Self-Esteem, And Motivation For Benevolent Purpose-Driven Occupational And Family or Friend Relationships Strengthening Aspirations?

Synopsis: From birth, or at the earliest age possible, obtain a "weightlifting set of weights" that includes a weightlifting bar and barbells and start doing push-ups, pull-ups, and abdominal crunches. Purchase a lifetime gym membership at the lowest price possible from the best gym closest to your house.

When Winston was growing up in a tiny country town, there were no commercial gyms available to work out in or to sign up and become a member of. There was only the weight room at the local high school, which was only available to high school students and too busy and crowded to accommodate outside town and community members. This was very disappointing to Winston. Winston's philosophy from birth was as follows: If the whole house, all doors, all windows, and even the dog flap in the back door is all locked up and inaccessible, forget trying to enter that silly house and build your own house which is available and accessible twenty-four hours a day, seven days per week, and 52 weeks per year!

Winston entered kindergarten one year earlier than 96% of his classmates, at four years of age. Thus, most of his classmates were 1-2 years older than Winston and 1-2 years physically stronger, smarter (supposedly, but never in reality), and often taller than Winston. Winston immediately realized the advantages of working out as a very young child. Winston completed thousands of bench presses, upper extremities curls for biceps and triceps, sit ups (now Winston recommends abdominal crunches instead, with thighs held up 90 degrees [perpendicular to back/spine] and legs maintained at this elevated position and parallel to the back/spine), and push-ups on his bedroom carpet in his home from about 5 years old and thereafter, when he woke up in the morning, before school each weekday and on weekends, then showered, and went to grammar school or proceeded with his weekend chores (mopping all the floors in the house and dusting everything in every room or vacuuming all the carpets in every room of the house; these chore choices alternated each weekend with Winston's older [eighteen months older] brother who shared in these pleasurable (not) chores, but provided both Winston and his older brother with small allowances (money), so that they could at least buy an occasional soda and candy bar once a week at one of the only two tiny food stores in town that were both walking distance from out small and humble dwelling (home). Winston felt and looked stronger (at least in his very young mind!) after every workout session each day. He also noted he had a more positive and upbeat attitude, was more energetic, and could concentrate on and memorize more of what he was studying and supposed to be learning in school each day!

Winston also joined his church pastor for early morning runs whenever Winston was free to join him at the 700 am start time. These runs were usually about 5 miles long and involved running repeated circles around a four-city-block route, multiple tabulated or calculated times until the 5-mile distance had been successfully achieved or completed! Winston found these runs exciting and exhilarating and had many great communications with his pastor throughout the duration of all these runs. What a great learning and exercising opportunity for young Winston throughout his childhood as a grammar school student of only single-digit ages.

Winston derived priceless wisdom from his pastor's guidance during these runs, which benefitted Winston until he graduated from university many years later and, in truth, for the remainder of his life! Brain-derived neurotrophic factor (BDNF) and Endorphins are created within the body due to regular or daily vigorous aerobic exercises (e.g., jogging, running, running upstairs, circuit weight training). If you have not heard of circuit training, it is a combination of six or more exercises performed with short rest periods between them for either a set number of repetitions or a prescribed amount of time.

Circuits can also be a great way to build muscle mass. Circuits that incorporate strength training can help you build lean muscle while keeping your heart rate up at the same time. Usually, there will be 8-10 exercises in a circuit, although this number can vary depending on how much time you have. You can perform a certain number of "reps" (repetitions) for each exercise (8-20 reps), or you can time each exercise (30-60 seconds per exercise). Circuit training may be shorter and faster, but it is not easy. It requires stamina and may not be suitable for beginners or people with low fitness levels. Disadvantages of circuit weight training include exhaustion from the rapid workout, which, if not careful and monitored by you, can make your form suffer or even increase the risks of an injury, again if you are not paying attention to performing the exercise with optimal form to maximize muscles fitness and decrease the risk of injuries.

Circuit training is a mixture of or combines strength and cardiovascular, or cardio, training. The average circuit training workout usually involves 8 to 12 different workout stations where you work different muscle groups. Since circuit training is a particularly high-intensity workout that quickly pushes your entire body to its limits, it should not be done too many times a week. Two or three times a week is a good benchmark to aim towards. Anywhere from 10–45 minutes is ideal for circuit training. The shorter the workout, the harder you should be pushing. Moreover, since you are alternating which body part you are working on during each move or exercise set, there is no need to rest for excessive periods between exercises. One or two minutes of rest between sets is usually more than enough.

- **Strength training.** Strength training is also referred to as anaerobic exercise, which would be a short burst of energy for movement. Think of a push-up or pull-up. These exercises help build and tone muscles.

- **Aerobic Exercise.** "Aerobic" means "needs oxygen." Your heart rate increases to get oxygen where your body needs it, thus the word "cardio." Running, biking, or jumping jacks would be examples of aerobic exercise.

The thing about a circuit is that you actually perform or execute both categories during this type of optimal zenith workout. Presses and lunges fall into strength training. Jumping jacks are cardio. **With circuit training, you build muscle and burn fat while building stamina.**

If you are limited by time for your workout session and are therefore forced to choose only one, then pick strength training: when you strength train, you break your muscles down, and your body needs to work extra hard over the next 24-48 hours to rebuild those muscles (with increased calories burned).

Individuals should choose their own various workout machines or exercises to include in their circuit weight training, suited to their desires and body parts that need the most strengthening and maximal functioning or rehabilitation after minor or major injuries.

Winston's own preferences for circuit training exercises in the gym (please work up gradually and slowly to these levels if you wish to copy Winston's circuit training routine) include a minimum of 100 total pull-ups each session (e.g., five sets of twenty or any other pattern, such as a tapering pattern is also acceptable, especially when starting this regimen), 100 or more bar dips per session, three sets of maximum weight biceps curling (15 curls per set), 150 chest (e.g., pectoralis major and minor muscles), shoulder muscles (e.g., rotator cuff muscles), and back muscles (e.g., rhomboids and trapezius) (3 sets of 50 each), 21 (3 sets of the maximum stack of weights tolerable, and keep progressively increasing weight amount until the entire stack of weights is being used for back exercises, (you may start with 7 repetitions per set of the back (trapezius, deltoids, rhomboids, and rotator cuff muscles, then work up to three sets of 50 per set), 400-800 crunches per session (either sets of 200 each, or 100 each x 8 sets). Winston performs workouts approximately three days per week, then runs 18 to 30 miles (approximately 6 miles per day) on days he is not working out in the gym.

Winston considers the running days an additional exercise type or component of his circuit exercise training overall program! Add hobby sports that are unpredictable or expensive vacation-type sports (e.g., tennis, volleyball, water skiing, snow skiing, rock climbing, hiking, or others) to this regular weekly exercise routine, and you will have the most enhanced, amazing, and fantastic brain function and physical strength you could ever hope for!

Chapter Six:

Living Life to the Fullest: Happy, Successful, Supportive, Safe, Secure, Content, Ambitious, and Healthy.

What is it that makes people happy in life? Psychological flexibility is a critical and essential factor to greater happiness and well-being. For instance, allowing yourself to be open to emotional experiences and learning to experience and gracefully adapt to, tolerate, and then overcome or recover from periods of discomfort can allow you to be more resilient and less fearful in life, empowering and enabling you to move more rapidly towards your goals and aspirations, resulting in a more rewarding, meaningful, and fulfilling existence throughout the duration of your life. The author and reader of this book should realize and know that there is no single answer to this question. There are myriad factors to consider.

Top Ten Factors Determining Differences In What Makes People Most Fulfilled in Life:

1) Age: Goals that transition from early life to mid-life to late-life ages
2) Parenting (Mother & Father combination, Single Mother, Single Father)
3) Education
4) Exercise
5) Diet
6) Health
7) Religion, Church Community, and Friends
8) Sleep
9) Music, Sports, Healthy Hobbies, and Other Recreational Activities
10) Love

What Makes People Most Fulfilled in Life?

Goals that transition from early life to mid-life to late-life ages.

Age and age-adjusted realistic goals are "all-important," but they are different in every stage of life. Infants, young children, adolescents, teenagers, young single adults, young married couples, middle-aged individuals, retired and senior citizen individuals will have vastly different priorities, goals, and aspirations, often determined by what they have already done or not done, goals they have accomplished or not accomplished, and their expected life duration and time they have or expect to have to prepare for and accomplish those distinct age-related goals.

Infants and young children have age-related goals that are quite basic but labor-intensive for those around them who are raising them. Among their top priorities are safety, security, and help with tasks they do not yet realize or know are essential to existence, dangerous, and a legitimate threat to their survival and existence. They require visual, audible, and actionable benevolent role models as parents, siblings, relatives, and other contacts to show them, teach them, and demonstrate to them what a daily routine life looks like, feels like, and how it ends with a good night of sleep. They require mentors who are supreme listeners, wise and succinct responders, slow to anger, and rapid to teach all life lessons required each day, such that the child learns that learning something new and helpful about living a good life is not only possible but expected and achievable, each and every day until that infant or young child dies one-hundred or more years later, hopefully!

Adolescents require additional distinct goals that must be transitioned to from prior infant and young children goals. When adolescents interact for the first time with church school classmates, regular school classmates, older classmates or adults, or any of these groups that have one or more members with poor discretion, poor judgment, non-Christian or otherwise sinful or evil intent, attitudes, and immoral behavior, suggestions, or peer pressure, it is vitally important and essential, ideally, that each child already possesses (or develops as soon as possible), an inner set of moral, ethical, Godly values. These age-related goals and priorities will then allow that individual adolescent to have an inner sense of self-worth, self-confidence, and a sense of who they are, want to be, and need to be to implement and achieve a successful Jesus Christ-like magical and benevolent existence in this world. These age-related goals and priorities will also enable that adolescent to avoid being negatively or adversely affected or swayed to emulate, join in, or deceptively be convinced by evil influencers that whatever bad behavior is being touted is anything other than immoral, illegal, ill-advised, wrong, dishonest, or a threat to the integrity and health of that individual or others.

The adolescent may then avoid distractions or distractors who intend to hinder that individual's honest and ethical attitude, education, behavior, improving self-esteem and self-confidence, all of which would have potentially been detrimental to that adolescent and counterproductive to the most desirable goal of being an outstanding adolescent student, church, and family member who is a role model for others (of all ages) by the moral, ethical, honest, and Godly behavior demonstrated by that adolescent child. Peer pressure is a significant risk factor for adolescents who are not taught Godly values by reading a traditional children's (non-woke) Bible at the earliest age possible and for children who have not been schooled in and educated about Godly values in church school or during regular church services by the pastor of the church. Adolescents also greatly benefit from strong, moral, and ethical male fathers and female mothers, who may serve as parental role models and mentors who teach these young developing humans who are transitioning from children to adolescents, and eventually teenagers, many essential life skills differences in males and females, puberty education, menstruation education, and God's definition of males, females, and marriage which is defined as the lifelong union, blessed by God, of a male to a female. In single-parent families, adolescents may learn these essential definitions of males and females and their differences, as defined by God, by other male and female role models and mentors within the church community by attending church youth group classes, campouts, summer and winter church gatherings and retreats, weekly Bible studies, and "Fellowship of Christian Athletes" weekly or monthly meetings in grammar school and high school. A single mother with children or a single father with children may and should seek out mentors within the church who can and are willing to be strong father or mother replacement role models for their children, which is easier than one might expect, simply by becoming more involved in weekly church youth group gatherings, Bible studies, church choir, church brass ensemble, church ministries in the local community and abroad, and various church summer camps, winter snow retreats, "Vacation Bible School" during summer school breaks, or any other church activities or sports (softball team, baseball team, basketball team, church ski group trips, church rock climbing, bike rides, water skiing, or various other church ministries: nursing home ministry, juvenile hall ministry, prison ministry, and many others.

Teenagers are a whole different ball game! Anyone who has either been a teenager (most of us) or raised teenagers, or even watched others who have or are raising teenagers knows very well that this age group is an extremely unique and independent, yet dependent, group of individuals who are deeply in need of guidance and reassurance that the path they are pursuing is the right, straight, and narrow Godly path for their life, but often too proud, independent (or at least hoping to be), or overwhelmed by school classmates' peer pressure being applied upon their shoulders like the yoke upon the back of an Ox. All individuals must always aim to have as their goal to agree to sound logic and reason and abide by and be directed by Godly principles during their lives. Hopefully, they were taught these Godly principles each Sunday in church while growing up as a child, and if not, they may be learned by attending church each week as an adult. With proper and constant reassurance that a Godly lifestyle and Christian teachings and principles, as taught in the Bible and church, are the ultimate, optimal, and most efficient means of having a fulfilling, benevolent, purpose-driven life, developing and maintaining a lifelong positive and caring attitude, and the most accurate and enduring life guide to achieving the most happy, fulfilling, and successful life, parents and mentors in the church may rescue their teenagers from unwise and unsuccessful rebellions based on misleading or deviant peer pressure from other non-God-revering classmates or evil influencers, or better yet, prevent altogether their teenagers from being distracted or diverted from God's loving, caring, protective path and guidance for their life!

College-age (teenagers and soon-to-be young adults, young professionals, or other trade specialists) individuals encounter immense peer pressure to abandon their Christian upbringing, lifestyle, and Bible-based life perspective and principles. Understanding that no human is perfect or sinless in this life (the author included), parent's best hope for their child or children should always be that the Christian and Bible principles taught to their children and young developing adults, both directly by the parents and with the assistance and guidance provided by the church community, will help guide their college or professional or other job trade specialist-bound high school graduates to make wise, reverent, holy decisions about all the temptations that arrive at and within this new age group. Decisions about sexual behavior (or, per the Bible, misbehavior if prior to marriage), alcohol and illicit drug abuse (which destroy the brain, body, and Godly soul of all individuals, rapidly and progressively with continued abuse), kind, honest, ethical, moral behavior, and caring, loving, compassionate, merciful, humble behavior versus alternative or opposite behavior and attitudes, all become poignant and highly relevant issues and guiding life principles in this age group, all depending on whether these choices are made with Bible-based education and wisdom and God's guiding principles in mind, or whether this age group chooses to shun all the wisdom and guidance available in the greatest book ever written and most widely published and read book in the world, the Bible!

Young married couples or young unmarried couples have age-related goals that are amazingly similar overall. If both groups follow the path of seeking out God's direction and guidance by attending church each week, enrolling their children in church youth group classes and activities, and, preferably, getting married if parents are not married initially with the birth of their first or multiple children, then both group can receive God's richest blessings, safety, and guidance for their entire family throughout their lives.

Middle-aged individuals, single, married, or divorced, have unique and varied goals depending on their marital or widow status, the stability and success of their children, and the strength of God's influence on their life and whether they feel thankful and grateful for God's guidance or resentful and bitter for what they might interpret as God's ignoring them, neglecting them, or God's absence from their life, either by their own choice and decision or, perhaps, if they feel (controversially and with improbable justification) that God purposely abandoned them or neglected to come to their rescue or fulfill their needs at the lowest or darkest time or period in their life when they needed God the most. Some middle-aged individuals look at the "first half" of life with regret that they made bad choices (e.g., sexual, alcohol or drug abuse, criminal, atheist, agnostic) and missed out on God's blessings. Others look back on the "first half" of their life with immense satisfaction, contentment, joy, and without regret due to their feeling blessed by God's guidance and protection throughout the tumultuous and tempestuous trials and temptations they faced and were able to overcome via the grace, mercy, and loving-kindness of their God and creator, whom they placed all their trust and loyalty in and with, in hopes of having a God-blessed life of happiness to the greatest extent possible, as determined by God.

Senior citizens and individuals who sense they are near the end of their life, young or very old or middle-aged, have the difficult decision to make, if not made years earlier or as a young child, to either believe God is and always has been their creator and savior, or to firmly believe, as agnostics or atheists, that God is a myth, neither created them nor has any power over their life, death, or after-life.

Blaise Pascal was a genius. In the first half of his life, he lived a wild life of drinking, carousing, and gambling. During and after a near-death experience, Blaise Pascal underwent a conversion experience and found

God. He lived the remainder of his life as a God-respecting, God-fearing, and Godly man. Blaise Pascal abandoned his past wild, reckless, unhealthy, and Godless lifestyle and sinful behavior and activities. He then created or developed an argument ("Pascal's Wager") in hopes of converting as many of his past friends and colleagues who were continuing on a downward spiral of ungodly and unhealthy alcohol abuse, not sleeping, and excessive gambling to the Godly conversion and transformation that brought Blaise Pascal so much joy and peace in the second half of his life. Pascal's Wager was explicitly focused on gambling odds and his hopes of convincing and persuading even his most stubborn atheist or agnostic past gambling, alcoholic, drug-abusing, sexually inappropriate or abusive, and sleep-deprived friends, who were rapidly killing themselves progressively each day by their ungodly life activities, habits, addictions, self-destructive behavior, negative attitude, lack of God's guidance and blessings in their lives, and overall unhealthy life choices that results from this sad and disappointing path in life that Blaise Pascal was once on with these friends, but then, by God's grace and mercy, was saved by God in a conversion experience that brought even more wisdom and enlightenment to Blaise Pascal, adding spiritual genius to Pascal's already impressive academic accomplishments and genius status that God blessed him with earlier in his life.

Blaise Pascal: The Penseés is a collection of philosophical fragments, notes, and essays in which Blaise Pascal explores the contradictions of human nature in psychological, social, metaphysical, and, above all, theological terms.

Pascal's Wager is a philosophical argument presented by the seventeenth-century French mathematician, philosopher, physicist, and theologian Blaise Pascal (1623–1662). It posits that human beings wager with their lives that God either exists or does not. Pascal's Wager, originally proposed by Blaise Pascal (1623–1662), takes a more pragmatic approach. Pascal thought that evidence cannot settle the question of whether God exists, so he proposes that you should bet, or Wager, on God because of what is at stake: you have lots to gain and not much to lose. Pascal was a French philosopher, scientist, mathematician, and probability theorist (1623-1662) and argued that if we do not know whether God exists, we should play it safe rather than risk being sorry. Blaise Pascal suggested that God is infinite and eternal. Human understanding is incapable of grasping these concepts through reason. Therefore, God cannot be understood by reason. "If one submits everything to reason, our religion will contain nothing mysterious or supernatural."

Pascal's Wager excerpted from Pens'ees, available on Project Gutenberg http://www.gutenberg.org/files/18269/18269-h/18269-h.htm#SECTION_III 229

This is what I see and what troubles me. I look on all sides, and I see only darkness everywhere. Nature presents nothing to me which is not a matter of doubt and concern. If I saw nothing there which revealed a Divinity, I would come to a negative conclusion; if I saw everywhere the signs of a Creator, I would remain peacefully in faith. But, seeing too much to deny and too little to be sure, I am in a state to be pitied; wherefore I have a hundred times wished that if a God maintains nature, she should testify to Him unequivocally, and that, if the signs she gives are deceptive, she should suppress them altogether; that she should say everything or nothing, that I might see which cause I ought to follow. Whereas in my present state, ignorant of what I am or of what I ought to do, I know neither my condition nor my duty. My heart inclines wholly to know where the true good is to follow it; nothing would be too dear to me for eternity. I envy those I see living in the faith with such carelessness and who make such a bad use of a gift, which it seems I would make such a different use of. It is incomprehensible that God should exist, and it is incomprehensible that He should not exist; that the soul should be joined to the body, and that we should have no soul; that the world should be created, and that it should not be created; that original sin should be, and that it should not be. Do you believe it impossible that God is infinite, without parts?—Yes. I wish, therefore, to show you an infinite and indivisible thing. It is a point moving everywhere with an infinite velocity, for it is one in all places and is all totality in every place. Let this effect of nature, which previously seemed to you impossible, make you know that there may be others of which you are still ignorant. Do not draw this conclusion from your experiment that there remains nothing for you to know, but rather that there remains an infinity for you to know. Infinite movement, the point which fills everything, the moment of rest; infinite without quantity, indivisible and infinite. Infinite—nothing.—Our soul is cast into a body, where it finds number, time, and dimension. Thereupon, it reasons and calls this nature a necessity and can believe nothing else. Unity joined to infinity adds nothing to it, no more than one foot to an infinite measure. The finite is annihilated in the presence of the infinite and becomes a pure nothing. So our spirit is before God, so our justice is before divine justice. There is not so great a disproportion between our justice and that of God as between unity and infinity. The justice of God must be vast, like His compassion. Now, justice to the outcast is less vast and ought less to offend our feelings than mercy towards the elect. We know that there is an infinite and are ignorant of its nature. As we know it to be false that numbers are finite, it is therefore true that there is an infinity in numbers. But we do not know what it is. It is false that it is even; it is false that it is odd, for the addition of a unit can make no change in its nature. Yet it is a number, and every number is odd or even (this is certainly true of every finite number). So, we may well know that there is a God without knowing what He is. Is there not one substantial truth, seeing there are so many things which are not the truth itself? We know then the existence and nature of the finite because we also are finite and have extension. We know the existence of the infinite, and are ignorant of its nature, because it has extension like us, but not limits like us. But we know neither the existence nor the nature of God because He has neither extension nor limits. But by faith we know His existence; in glory we shall know His nature. Now, I have already shown that we may well know the existence of a thing, without knowing its nature. Let us now speak according to natural lights. If there is a God, He is infinitely incomprehensible since, having neither parts nor limits, He has no affinity to us. We are then incapable of knowing either what He is or if He is. This being so, who will dare to undertake the decision of the question? Not we, who have no affinity to Him. Who then will blame Christians for not being able to give a reason for their belief since they profess a religion for which they cannot give a reason? They declare, in expounding it to the world, that it is a foolishness, stultitiam; and then you complain that they do not prove it! If they proved it, they would not keep their word; it is in lacking proof that they are not lacking in sense. "Yes, but although this excuses those who offer it as such and takes away from them the blame of putting it forward without reason, it does not excuse those who receive it." Let us then examine this point and say, "God is, or He is not." But to which side shall we incline? Reason can decide nothing here. There is an infinite chaos which separated us. A game is being played at the extremity of this infinite distance where heads or tails will turn up. What will you wager? According to reason, you can do neither the one thing nor the other; according to reason, you can defend neither of the propositions. Do not then reprove for error those who have made a choice, for you know nothing about it. "No, but I blame them for having made, not this choice, but a choice; for again, both he who chooses heads and he who chooses for tails are equally at fault; they are both in the wrong. The true course is not to wager at all." Yes, but you must wager. It is not optional. You are embarked. Which will you choose then? Let us see. Since you must choose, let us see which interests you least. You have two things to lose, the true and the good, and two things to stake, your reason and your will, your knowledge and your happiness, and your nature has two things to shun, error and misery. Your reason is no more shocked in choosing one rather than the other since you must, of necessity, choose. This is one point settled. But your happiness? Let us weigh the gain and the loss in wagering that God is. Let us estimate these two chances. If you gain, you gain all; if you lose, you lose nothing. Wager, then, without hesitation, that He is. "That is very fine. Yes, I must wager, but I may perhaps wager too much."—Let us see. Since there is an equal risk of gain and of loss, if you had only to gain two lives instead of one, you might still wager.

But if there were three lives to gain, you would have to play (since you are under the necessity of playing), and you would be imprudent, when you are forced to play, not to chance your life to gain three at a game where there is an equal risk of loss and gain. However, there is an eternity of life and happiness. And this being so, if there were an infinity of chances, of which one only would be for you, you would still be right in wagering one to win two, and you would act stupidly, being obliged to play, by refusing to stake one life against three at a game in which out of an infinity of chances there is one for you, if there were an infinity of an infinitely happy life to gain. However, there is an infinity of an infinitely happy life to gain, a chance of gain against a finite number of chances of loss, and what you stake is finite. It is all divided; wherever the infinite is, and there is not an infinity of chances of loss against that of gain, there is no time to hesitate; you must give all. Thus, when one is forced to play, he must renounce reason to preserve his life rather than risk it for infinite gain, as likely to happen as the loss of nothingness. For it is no use to say it is uncertain if we will gain, and it is certain that we risk, and that the infinite distance between the certainty of what is staked and the uncertainty of what will be gained equals the finite good which is certainly staked against the uncertain infinite. It is not so, as every player stakes a certainty to gain an uncertainty, and yet he stakes a finite certainty to gain a finite uncertainty without transgressing against reason. There is not an infinite distance between the certainty staked and the uncertainty of the gain; that is untrue. In truth, there is an infinity between the certainty of gain and the certainty of loss. However, the uncertainty of the gain is proportioned to the certainty of the stake according to the proportion of the chances of gain and loss. Hence, it comes that if there are as many risks on one side as on the other, the course is to play even, and then the certainty of the stake is equal to the uncertainty of the gain, so far is it from the fact that there is an infinite distance between them. Thus, our proposition is of infinite force when there is the finite to stake in a game where there are equal risks of gain and of loss and the infinite to gain. This is demonstrable, and if men are capable of any truths, this is one." I confess it, I admit it. However, still, is there no means of seeing the faces of the cards?"—Yes, Scripture and the rest, etc. "Yes, but I have my hands tied and my mouth closed; I am forced to wager and am not free. I am not released and am so made that I cannot believe it. What, then, would you have me do?" True. However, at least learn your inability to believe since reason brings you to this, yet you cannot believe. Endeavour then to convince yourself, not by increasing proofs of God, but by the abatement of your passions. You would like to attain faith and do not know the way; you would like to cure yourself of unbelief and ask for the remedy. Learn of those who have been bound like you and who now stake all their possessions. These are people who know the way which you would follow and who are cured of an illness of which you would be cured. Follow the way by which they began: by acting as if they believed, taking the holy water, having masses said, etc. Even this will naturally make you believe and deaden your acuteness.— "But this is what I am afraid of."— And why? What have you to lose? But to show you that this leads you there, it is this which will lessen the passions, which are your stumbling blocks. The end of this discourse.—Now, what harm will befall you in taking this side? You will be faithful, honest, humble, grateful, generous, a sincere friend, truthful. Certainly, you will not have those poisonous pleasures, glory, and luxury, but will you not have others? I will tell you that you will thereby gain in this life and that, at each step you take on this road, you will see so great certainty of gain, so much nothingness in what you risk, that you will, at last, recognize that you have wagered for something certain and infinite, for which you have given nothing. "Ah! This discourse transports me, charms me." If this discourse pleases you and seems impressive, know that it is made by a man who has knelt, both before and after it, in prayer to that Being, infinite and without parts, before whom he lays all he has, for you also to lay before Him all you have for your own good and for His glory, that so strength may be given to lowliness. If we must not act save on a certainty, we ought not to act on religion, for it is not certain. But how many things do we do in uncertainty, on sea voyages, in battles? I say then we must do nothing at all, for nothing is certain, and that there is more certainty in religion than there is as to whether we may see tomorrow; for it is not certain that we may see tomorrow, and it is certainly possible that we may not see it. We cannot say as much about religion. It is not certain that it is, but who will venture to say that it is certainly possible that it is not? Now, when we work for tomorrow and so on an uncertainty, we act reasonably, for we ought to work for an uncertainty according to the doctrine of chance, which was demonstrated above. Saint Augustine has seen that we work for an uncertainty, on sea, in battle, etc. However, he has not seen the doctrine of chance, which proves that we should do so. Montaigne has seen that we are shocked at a fool, and that habit is all-powerful, but he has not seen the reason for this effect. All these people have seen the effects, but they have not seen the causes. They are, in comparison with those who have discovered the causes, as those who have only eyes are in comparison with those who have intellect. The effects are perceptible by sense, and the causes are visible only to the intellect. And although the mind sees these effects, this mind is, in comparison with the mind, which sees the causes, as the bodily senses are in comparison with the intellect.

The book entitled Pascal's Pensées is, after reading the Bible cover-to-cover five or more times and committing all the Bible's teachings and wisdom to long-term memory to benefit you for the remainder of your life, one of the most insightful and enlightening guides to a fantastic and God-blessed life, that is based on the writings and thoughts of one of the great genius minds in world history, Blaise Pascal. Pascal's Pensées, right after the Bible, is an enlightening and phenomenal read, in the opinion of this book's author, who read the book of Pascal while completing his undergraduate university education.

What Makes People Most Fulfilled in Life: Parenting (Mother & Father combination, Single Mother, Single Father)

Parenting experience and the manner in which parenting is delivered to children is as diverse as the stars in the sky. Is it imperative to use a rigid and single formula for best parenting to raise children in the best and most successful manner? The answer is no. This should be obvious. Many of us, including the author of this book, know of or are friends or colleagues with multiple individuals with astonishingly diverse backgrounds and, in many cases, radically different upbringings, and in select circumstances, had parents who employed, successfully or unsuccessfully, shocking parental behavior and unproven or unjustified, or just pure reckless and irresponsible parenting traits and failed trials. Despite these spellbinding stories and historical accounts told to us by our friends, most of these individuals (but not all) navigated the tumultuous and tempestuous storm, persevered, and were able to exit their stormy upbringing, educate and enlighten themselves, thereby effecting a metamorphosis and transformation of themselves (children in dire circumstance into adults with unlimited potential and auspicious futures) into amazingly successful, benevolent, and Godly human beings!

Even though there is not one formula that applies to or fits all parents and instructs them how to raise their child or children properly, there are common features and standard methods that should be known and employed to make parenting of children less stressful, more satisfying, most efficient and effective, and generate love, respect, assurance, positive self-esteem, self-confidence, and life-long love and appreciation for God and all God-respecting family members. Christian parenting principles benefit everyone on this planet, including agnostic and atheist parents and families, because they employ strategies that have been proven to be successful for thousands of years and because when parents are mature, responsible, and wise enough to entrust the safety and well-being of their children to God and the church community, they and their children, will immediately experience the relief, serenity, peace, humility, positive self-esteem and self-confidence that results from learning Godly values and principles, such as caring and loving others as much as or more than yourself, to receive God's blessings for you as parents and for your children. All parents, of any culture, religion or no religion, and from any country, will benefit from the true pearls of God's parenting guidelines and principles to raise healthy and happy children who are the most confident and prepared to meet all challenges in life, navigate all life's storms, and successfully contribute, in a positive way, to the betterment of society:

- Love And Honor God Above All Others.
- Love Your Children As Jesus Loves You.
- Be a Faithful Steward.
- Do Not Provoke Your Children.
- Teach God's Word.
- Train Your Children To Follow Jesus.
- Be Humble.

LOVE AND VALUE YOUR CHILDREN: *Fathers, do not provoke your children to anger, but bring them up in the discipline and instruction of the Lord.* Ephesians 6:4

POINT CHILDREN TO SCRIPTURE: *All Scripture is breathed out by God and profitable for teaching, for reproof, for correction, and for training in righteousness, that the man of God may be complete, equipped for every good work.* 2 Timothy 3:16-17

TEACH CHILDREN THE LORD'S CHARACTER: *Come, O children, listen to me; I will teach you the fear of the Lord.* Psalm 34:11

PROTECT CHILDREN'S INNOCENCE: *Let no one despise you for your youth, but set the believers an example in speech, in conduct, in love, in faith, in purity.* 1 Timothy 4:12

CHARACTER TRAINING COMES FIRST: *The fruit of the righteous is a tree of life, and whoever captures souls is wise.* Proverbs 11:30

TEACH TO CHILDREN'S GIFTING: *Now there are varieties of gifts, but the same Spirit; and there are varieties of service, but the same Lord,* *and there are varieties of activities, but it is the same God who empowers them all in everyone.* 1 Corinthians 12:4-6

MAINTAIN PERSPECTIVE: *Woe to you, scribes and Pharisees, hypocrites! For you tithe mint, dill, and cumin, and have neglected the weightier matters of the law: justice, mercy, and faithfulness. These you ought to have done without neglecting the others.* Matthew 23:23

PRACTICE WHAT YOU PREACH: *He did in all things as Joash, his father, had done.* 2 Kings 14:3b

AN INTENTIONAL PARENTING BOOK: …*that you may tell the next generation that this is God, our God forever and ever. He will guide us forever.* Psalm 48:13b-14

- Get in God's Presence
- Make the Bible Your Authority
- Lead by Example
- Set Standards and Keep Them
- Win Their Hearts

Become a Family of Sojourners (Be a Christian Family in this world, but not of this world. Live by Godly standards as delineated, outlined, and set forth in the Bible.)

- Give Presence More than Presents.
- Know and Honor Your Child
- Prioritize Unity

How do you raise a child in a godly way?

1) Lead by example.
2) Show them critical thinking skills.
3) Teach them how to love by loving them unconditionally.
4) Help them serve others.
5) Share your faith with them through scripture.

6) Pray with them.
7) Allow them to have their own faith.

How to be a good parent according to the Bible?

"Discipline your children, and they will give you peace; they will bring you the delights you desire" Proverbs 29:17. It is not irritating, aggravating, disheartening, or provoking children to anger. "Fathers do not embitter your children, or they will become discouraged" Colossians 3:21.

- How to Biblically Discipline Your Children
- Seek your kids out, then educate and enlighten them with kindness.
- Ask good and positive questions.
- Calmly state the consequence of their action.
- Discipline with compassion.
- Be willing to make hard decisions when necessary and required.
- What makes Christian parenting different?

Christian parents should be ready and willing to express love to their children. Christian parents provide their children with a tangible example of God's love for them. When people are truly loved and cared for by their parents, they get a small glimpse of what God's love for us looks like.

- What is the role of a godly mother to her children?
- A Godly Mother Encourages Children to Seek Jesus.

You direct their attention to Jesus at all times. You show them their identities are not in what they do but who they are in Christ. Psalm 127:3-4 says, "Behold, children are a heritage from the Lord, the fruit of the womb is a reward.

What makes godly parents?

Respect, reverence, and worship are the key ingredients to fearing the Lord. Joseph said, "With me in charge," he told her, "my master does not concern himself with anything in the house; everything he owns he has entrusted to my care. No one is greater in this house than I am.

What are the biblical duties of a proper parent?

Parents should teach their children the gospel. The Lord warned that if parents do not teach their children about faith, repentance, baptism, and the gift of the Holy Ghost, the sin will be upon the heads of the parents. Parents should also teach their children to pray and obey the Lord's commandments.

What does Jesus say about parenting?

"Jesus said, 'Let the little children come to me, and do not hinder them, for the kingdom of heaven belongs to such as these.'

What are biblical parental roles?

The Bible strongly emphasizes parents' influence as a child's initial teacher. The Bible emphasizes that parents' primary duty is to nurture and guide their children from an early age while discussing the significance of parenting in a child's upbringing (Proverbs 22:6; Deuteronomy 6:7).

How should parents treat their children biblically? Psalm 103:13: "As a father shows compassion to his children, so the Lord shows compassion to those who fear him." The Good News: Fathers, nurture your children with compassion so they do not become afraid of you.

What does God say about a disobedient child?

Proverbs 29:17 says this to parents: "Discipline your child, and he/she will give you rest; he/she will give you delight to your heart." A Scripture from Proverbs 13:24 reads thusly: "He who spares the rod hates his son, but he who loves him is careful to discipline him."

Does the Bible say you hate your children if you do not discipline them?

The Bible says if you love your child, you will discipline them. Moreover, you will do it in love and not anger. Do not buy into the idea that good parents do not discipline their children because they 'love them too much.'

What is God's attitude towards single parenting?

Single parents need to hear that they are fine, just as they are, and just as capable of raising children well as any other family. God holds single-parent families in high regard. Psalm 68:5 says this: A father to the fatherless, a defender of widows is God in his holy dwelling.

What does a godly mother look like?

She is confident that He will meet her physical, material, and emotional needs. Instead of focusing on what she lacks, she speaks of God's sufficiency in her life and is grateful whether He provides much or little. A godly mother is generous. Even if she has little to share, she willingly offers it to others.

How to be a godly stepmom?

If you are a stepmom– Pray and ask God to help you to love well. Ask Him to show you ALL of your children's hearts and how to love them better and to teach you how to pray specifically for your family....

If you know someone who is a stepmom, ask God how you can help support your friend and her family.

What is a biblical example of a godly mother?

The most well-known mother in the Bible, Mary conceived Jesus, the Son of God, through the Holy Spirit. She was visited by the angel Gabriel, who informed her of her unique privilege of bearing God's Son. She responded with humility, rejoicing in the Lord's greatness, and He blessed her greatly.

What is the message of godly parenting?

Godly parenting is to revolve the family around the centrality of God. Psalm 78:4 We will not hide them from their descendants; we will tell the next generation the praiseworthy deeds of the Lord, his power, and the wonders he has done. Children are extremely important but not the highest focus or value, which is always reserved for God, who will also care for and watch over all parents' children, along with their parent or parents, if the parents first respect and follow God's teachings and guidance as their number one priority and goal every minute of their existence.

What does healthy parenting look like?

In a nutshell, positive parents support a child's healthy growth and inner spirit by being loving, supportive, firm, consistent, and involved. Such parents go beyond communicating their expectations but practice what they preach by being positive role models for their children to emulate.

What are the traits of a Godly mother?

These characteristics: shielding, comforting, birthing, protecting, hovering are all Godly characteristics, features, qualities, and specific examples of Godly behavior and actions, and are manifest in mothers because all mothers on this earth are of Him, from Him, and by Him.

Parental responsibilities include:

- Providing a safe living environment.
- Protecting the children from abuse and other dangers.
- Paying child support as ordered.
- Fulfilling the children's basic needs (food, water, shelter)
- Disciplining the children.
- Investing in the children's education.
- Knowing the children's interests.
- to protect your child from harm.
- to provide your child with food, clothing, and a place to live.

- to financially support your child.
- to provide safety, supervision, and control.
- to provide medical care.
- to provide an education.

Making Tough Decisions That Are Not Popular. If your child doesn't get angry with you at least once in a while, you're not doing your job.

- Teaching Your Child to Function Independently.
- Holding Your Child Accountable.
- Going Along for the Ride.
- Doing Your Best.
- What is the biblical role of a mother?

- Motherhood is sanctifying, but it is also sweet. Scripture teaches mothers to point children toward Christ by praying for them, modeling faith and character, and training them in wisdom (Prov 1:8, 29:15).

The Role of a Mother According to the Bible

According to the Bible, the role of a mother is to love and care for her children. She is to teach and train, nurture, and discipline. A godly mother is to model holy living for her children and care for all those in her home. She is also to care for and help her husband.

How does God want us to parent?

The fundamental goal for Christian parents should be to guide their children to a saving faith in Christ and to set them on a path to maturity, bringing them to the full measure of his glory (Eph 4:13). Parenting is one of God's most important callings. Children are a gift and blessing from God (Psalm 127:3-5).

How do you connect with parental blessings?

You can access your parental blessings by loving your parents and appreciating them. You need to do tangible and intangible things for them and live a lifestyle that will make your parents proud of you. You cannot have parental blessings if the people who have parental authority over you are sad with you.

God does hold children who don't learn from their parents' mistakes accountable.

What does the Bible say about parents not provoking their children?

"And you, fathers, do not provoke your children to wrath, but bring them up in the training and admonition of the Lord" (Eph. 6:4 NKJV)

In Christian discipline, we bring words and actions, warnings and consequences, into our children's situations to keep them on track.

How to Discipline a Child

- Time-Out.
- Losing privileges.
- Consider, only if appropriate, ignoring mild misbehavior.
- Logical consequences.
- Natural consequences.
- Rewards for good behavior.
- Praise for good behavior.
- What is biblical encouragement for single parents?

"Do not fear, for I am with you; do not be dismayed, for I am your God. I will strengthen and help you; I will uphold you with my righteous right hand." "A father to the fatherless, a defender of widows, is God in his holy dwelling."

The Bible consistently asks followers to honor and love their mothers. Examples are Exodus 20:12, "Honor your father and your mother," and Leviticus 19:3, "Every one of you shall revere his mother and father."

What does the Bible say about a mother's love for her child?

Isaiah 66:13: "As one whom his mother comforts, so I will comfort you." Isaiah 49:15: "Can a mother forget her nursing child? Can she feel no love for the child she has borne?" Proverbs 31:25: "She is clothed with strength and dignity; she can laugh at the days to come."

How do you honor an ungodly parent?

Here are six ways Christians can honor and show respect for ungodly parent(s):

- Forgive them. Jesus taught his disciples to pray, "Forgive us… as we forgive those who sin against us." (Mt 6:12)
- Pray for them.
- Address them honorably.
- Be thankful for what they did (or did not do).
- Welcome them and be kind to them.
- Provide support if necessary.

What is the heart of a godly mother?

A God-fearing mom is intimately connected with God. She maintains a prayer and devotional life to keep a discerning heart. She intentionally grows her knowledge of the truth by reading her Bible daily and committing Scripture to memory. She prays to seek God's wisdom and guidance for each day.

What are the challenges of godly parenting?

Our children need love, time, guidance, discipline, and boundaries. They need to learn about values, virtues, and the importance of a strong work ethic. They need to be taught about God and the importance of prayer and be helped to value life and to love their faith.

What are the 4 C's of good parenting?

The 4Cs are principles for parenting (Care, Consistency, Choices, and Consequences) that help satisfy children's psychological, physical, social, and intellectual needs and lay solid foundations for mental well-being.

What are the 3 F's of positive parenting?

They are firm, fair, and friendly. These F's emphasize the importance of being consistent with your children, setting clear boundaries and expectations, and maintaining a positive relationship with them.

What are the five positive parenting skills?

Being a parent comes with its share of challenges and woes. The five positive parenting skills are being encouraging, being responsive, setting an example, setting boundaries, and being interactive.

What are the five issues that affect parenting?

The Evolution of Parenting: Five Biggest Challenges Faced by Parents Today

- Balancing family and career.
- Being afraid to say 'NO'
- A culture of blame.
- Ensuring children receive a quality education.
- Overload of information.

What are the seven roles of a father?

- friend, encourager, teacher, leader, protector, helper, provider.

What makes a good parent?

- Parents who make time to listen, take children's concerns seriously, provide consistent support, step back and let kids solve problems on their own (or not), and allow ample free time for play, can help children thrive.

What is inadequate parenting?

- Neglect and neglectful parenting:
- Neglectful parenting is a parenting style defined by a lack of parental interest or responsiveness to a child. These parents are similar to permissive, indulgent parents who lack control over their children.

What is the accountability of a parent?

- Accountable parenting means your decisions need to be explainable. You need to be able to justify your actions and your decisions, and so do your kids. You also need to be in control of your decisions.

What are the five moral responsibilities of parents?

- Parents must provide their children shelter, food, clothes, education, and medical care until they are old enough to care for themselves. They also need to impart emotional and social nurturing so that their children can grow up to be responsible and empathetic individuals in society.

What are the five roles of the father?

5 Roles of a Father You Must Learn to Do Well

- Motivator. As a dad, you are a helper, coach, and a friend.
- Enforcer. Fatherlessness is a significant concern in our society today.
- Encourager. Every child loves positive fatherly encouragement.
- Trainer.
- Counselor.

Stressors faced by single-parent families.

- Visitation and custody problems.
- The effects of continuing conflict between the parents.
- Less opportunity for parents and children to spend time together.
- Effects of the breakup on children's school performance and peer relations.

Disruptions of extended family relationships.

Seven parenting mistakes that may adversely affect a child's mental health, strength, and fortitude:

- Minimizing your kid's feelings.
- Always saving (or preventing) them from experiencing failure in life.
- Overindulging your kids.
- Expecting perfection.
- Making sure they always feel comfortable.
- Not setting parent-child boundaries.
- Not taking care of yourself.

Signs of emotionally neglectful parents

- Speak with a cold and unfriendly tone.
- Unresponsive to the child's feelings.
- Dismiss the child's emotions.
- Don't talk to the child very much.
- Spend little time with the child and make them feel unwanted.
- Less positive feedback or praise.
- Express less affection.

How does an angry parent affect a child?

- It can make them misbehave or get physically sick. Children react to angry, stressed parents by being unable to concentrate, finding it hard to play with other children, becoming quiet and fearful or rude and aggressive, or developing sleeping problems.

5 Common Parenting Struggles

- Fear. When parents struggle with fear, it often causes them to think of the worst-case scenario.
- Anger. Kids don't always listen and can drive us to the edge.
- Doubt. Do you second-guess everything and worry you've made the wrong choice?
- Control.
- High expectations.

What are three signs a child is being neglected?

- A child's basic needs, such as food, clothing, or shelter, are not met, and/or they aren't properly supervised or kept safe. A parent doesn't ensure their child receives proper and maximum possible education, which would/will benefit them for the remainder of their life. Children don't receive the nurturing and stimulation they desire and require, as evidenced by their parents' actions or inactions of ignoring, humiliating, intimidating, or promoting or encouraging the unnecessary isolation of their children.

What is the best parenting style?

- The parenting style that is best for children is the supportive style. It's a style where you are warm, loving, and affectionate, but you also create structure and boundaries for your children and guide their behavior.

What Generates Happiness and Makes People Most Fulfilled in Life: Education

It has been proposed that there are perhaps four essential and basic premises and purposes for school and education of all humans:

academic (intellectual), political and civic purposes, socialization, and economic purposes,

People often underestimate the importance of education to happiness and fulfillment, especially in regard to non-monetary life satisfaction, contentment, tolerance, flexibility, and kindness traits that are a direct result of higher levels of education. Happiness can be generated in many distinct ways and by many different means. One way that happiness is achieved is via learning and implementing, on a daily basis, pure and selfless attitudes and actions.

One definition of happiness might be described, in real-life terms, as a state of peace in which there is no upheaval, violence, excessive or extreme anger, discouragement, depression, anxiety, fear for one's safety or future well-being, jealousy, guilt, regret, and no ill or evil attitude, intent, or hatred of or directed toward others in your life. Kind, positive, uplifting, encouraging, graceful, merciful, tolerant yet not condescending or compromising (e.g., defending and encouraging ethical and moral attitudes, communications, and actions at all times), constructive words, phrases, and communicated sentences create happier humans, and thus a more merry and wonderful world (the song by the famous trumpet player, singer, and actor Louis Armstrong, "It's a Wonderful World" comes immediately to mind)! When one is content with oneself, happiness is inextricably involved and always, by definition, present. The relationship between education and happiness is multifaceted and complex. Education strongly correlates with future happiness.

Happiness and positive emotions create dopamine and serotonin. When these substances are released into the brain, they positively affect and enhance our memory and our brain's ability to learn. These chemicals also increase the brain's capacity to make connections and make connections faster. Happiness comes from what we do. Fulfillment comes from why we do it.

Education may have both a direct effect on overall happiness and an indirect one through the social and financial benefits it affords. Happiness, in this case, is defined as satisfaction with how one's life is proceeding and progressively improving and becoming more satisfying, adding to one's overall happiness, contentment, fulfillment, and serenity. Research suggests that the more education you have, the happier you tend to be or are. The effect can also be positive and negative, depending on your age and position in life. Education fosters control of one's own environment, a higher level of self-esteem, and a positive perspective on the future. These three factors affect well-being positively and could be potential mechanisms linking education and well-being.

Does the highest possible level of education, that each individual pursues and successfully completes, make that individual happier or the happiest they can be? Although the answer to this question will always be open to debate, and rightly so, in general, the general consensus is, and probably always will be, that trade or professional school-educated and college or university-educated adults tend to live happier lives with a greater sense of fulfillment, serenity, and both a greater willingness and likelihood to be both financial and attitudinally inclined to contribute back to society in myriad positive ways.

These positive contributions, often made during mid-career or later in the career of persons of the highest level of education and professional expertise, may manifest in many distinct ways that eventually become apparent to the general population of "world citizens" throughout the world. Examples of these positive contributions, again the result of higher education levels in the individuals, include: parents being more capable of educating their children throughout their life, instilling better judgement and decision-making skills in their kids, based on their own higher education level and experiences in the world (e.g., after world studies or world travel in, during, or after college, e.g., in the midst of their career experience and work-related travel responsibilities), being able to retire at earlier ages and writing novels that benefit society or become involved in charitable groups, societies, organizations, other institutions (e.g., increased local church involvement [youth group leadership roles, Deacons, Elders, Bible study members or leaders]), missionary trips, as well as signing up for or volunteering for memberships and proactive roles in: Lion's Club, Elks Club, The Masons, Kiwanis Club, Big Brothers & Big Sisters organizations, Nursing and Assisted-Living Facilities, Juvenile Hall or Prison Ministries, as a National Parks supporter or volunteer, becoming a Green Peace supporter, and involvement in other local and worldwide charitable and benevolent organizations.

Individuals with higher levels of education tend to exhibit greater levels of confidence, a better sense of independence, and stronger feelings of control over their lives. Graduates of college or university-level education and training programs tend to be more resilient and less depressed. The highest possible education level that all individuals can and should be encouraged to pursue and attain will not only benefit those individuals but also ultimately benefit everyone they interact with and the society they live in. Now, in the age of the worldwide internet and international news and media companies, individuals with the highest education level possible may instantly, powerfully, and most importantly, positively influence, motivate, and inspire individuals, societies, and countries throughout the world and universe (perhaps individuals in international space stations, the moon, or on Mars in the future)! Education, independent of innate ability, helps spur innovation and technology and contributes to productivity and economic growth. A key element in this process is that education is essential to adopt the technology that produces innovation and, ideally, effects positive, benevolent, Godly aspirations, purpose-driven life tasks and pursuits, making the world a safer, kinder, more graceful, compassionate, merciful, better overall, and easier place to love others and live in peace, humility, and with zenith happiness and serenity.

Why is learning important for success? Learning new things gives us a feeling of accomplishment, which, in turn, boosts our confidence in our own skills, knowledge, and other capabilities; you'll also feel more ready to take on challenges and explore new business ventures. Acquiring new skills will unveil new opportunities and help you find innovative solutions to problems. What defines fulfillment in life is and should always be open to suggestions, modifications, and improvements but has been described in the past, seemingly accurately and concisely, as involving, amongst many other possible components and definitions, the following factors or descriptive phrases: "focus on others," "unfolded self and life," "worthwhile life," and "positive impact and legacy." Fulfillment in life may often be rapidly realized and felt first-hand by focusing on others and how an individual or collective, organized group might bring greater ease and happiness to other human beings' lives, e.g., volunteer work or other ministries offering help, encouragement, or services to other, expecting never to be repaid and nothing in return for that which was given or performed with a generous and caring attitude, perspective and intent.

Eight Important Aspects or Factors to Realize and Achieve Happiness & Fulfillment

1. Be with others who make you smile. Humans are happiest when around those who are also happy, but do not ignore or neglect those in need of help or happiness.
2. Hold on to and do not compromise your values.
3. Accept good, recognize bad in life, and always attempt to maximize good.
4. Imagine and envision, in every life scenario, how to arrive at the best outcome.
5. Obtain the highest level of education possible, studying and completing assignments and examinations you may not enjoy to prepare, qualify, and enable you to pursue, later in life, occupations and hobbies that you love that will positively impact the world and that you are passionate about.
6. Seek or create Godly, specific, focused, executable, achievable, purpose-driven life aspirations, attitudes, behavior, communication, occupation(s), and goals.

7. Look, Listen, Feel, or Sense God's direction, guidance, protection, and reassurance that you were created in God's image. Realize that happiness, success, safety, serenity, and generous and altruistic behavior and actions are God's intentions for you and that God will help you store and forever demonstrate to others in your life these benevolent features and world-enhancing qualities, intentions, and actions which will define you and remain with you throughout your life, deep within your heart, soul, mind, and for the entire duration of your physical presence and existence on Earth.
8. Have the highest, strictest, most demanding standards of ethics, morals, integrity, honesty, and work ethic for yourself, and thereby set and define an example of best behavior, most positive aspirations, motivations, intent, outlook, attitude for those who know you or do not know you but are around you, to positively motivate and inspire others to follow or emulate your life philosophy of: "positive actions and attitudes" inspire and motivate other humans that you interact with more than "negative actions, attitudes, comments and criticisms."

How does education make a difference in life? Education helps people become better citizens, obtain better-paid jobs, and helps individuals better decipher the differences between good and evil intent or aspirations, attitudes, behavior, selfishness, and selflessness.

Education enlightens individuals regarding the vital importance of hard work and the need for perpetual daily continuing self-education to maximize an individual's ability to adapt to changes in life and constantly update and improve their activities and performance to achieve success in life, no matter what changes or new circumstances they are forced to confront, analyze, overcome, or improve to achieve success and efficiency in completing their short and long-term goals.

A God-focused education from birth to physical death also may result in an auspicious, magnificent, and gracious society whereby all members have the most tremendous potential to live righteously and respectfully by knowing and respecting rights, laws, and regulations, based on Biblical teachings and values, established by God, the creator of all humans on Earth, this and other universes, whether specific individuals choose, adversely, to ignore or disregard this truth, or, hopefully, properly educated and enlightened individuals discover on their own or are taught by the parents or church communities. How does life satisfaction affect happiness?

The relationship between life satisfaction and happiness is an essential area within the field of positive psychology. The obvious and positive link between life satisfaction and happiness is hard to ignore. By definition, "happiness" is considered a short-term or day-to-day variable and essentially an emotional state or feeling. In contrast, the concept of "life satisfaction," is regarded to be a more general and long-term life perspective, goal, aspiration, or mindset, and is more closely linked to and based on critical thinking, philosophical, and cognitive processes in each individual's mind, heart, and soul. Higher or highest education levels that individuals should be encouraged to seek out and achieve by parents, friends, church or other community members and mentors include (amongst many other benefits not listed here) potential and high probability of positive achievements, successes, contentment, well-being, satisfaction, fulfillment, auspicious or unlimited choices for occupations and higher chances of job satisfaction, and, in general, flourishing in life.

How does education save lives? Highly educated people are much less vulnerable to health risks and are likelier to make healthier choices for themselves, their children, and their family members and, hopefully, share their vitally important knowledge and education with everyone in their communities. Attainment of the highest level of education possible or feasible enables a person to experience more positive health outcomes by being able to more efficiently and effectively navigate their own healthcare journey through life and to make wiser and more prudent decisions related to personal health choices, behaviors, and avoiding deleterious and harmful or fatal behaviors.

Learning has been shown to help improve and maintain our well-being. It can boost self-confidence and self-esteem, help build a sense of purpose, and foster connections with others. It has been asserted that lower education levels are potentially or can be associated with "a lack of psychosocial resources," including less or suboptimal levels of a sense of control, resilience, less ability to delay gratification, less access to cultural activities, all of which may increase that individual's levels of daily stress, frustration, and discouragement. In summary, lower levels of life-long education attainment are often associated with a lack of control and resilience and higher stress levels. This can negatively impact a person's mental health and lead to psychiatric and psychological conditions such as anxiety, depression, or even schizophrenia or bipolar disease and many other personality disorders and other psychiatric diagnoses. Therefore, education can be the key to success and a better life outcome, both in a physical health sense and mental health sense. Is education more important than mental health? Your excellent grades, education, and accomplishments in life that resulted, at least in part from your education, will always seem to be of supreme importance. However, your mental health is and will always be more important.

Luckily, the more you study, the better your brain will function, and your mental health may improve. What a wonderful fact! Why does education affect life expectancy? The longer individuals continue to educate themselves, progressing to the highest possible level of education and expertise in one or more fields of study (e.g., master's degree or doctoral degree or higher), their life expectancy has a much greater chance of being extended to older ages, possibly due to several suggested reasons including: higher levels of income (e.g., can afford to make healthier choices in diet such as organic vegetables and afford health and dental insurance), health/"healthier lifestyles" (higher educated individuals are less likely to be smokers because they know smokers often die of lung cancer, chronic obstructive pulmonary disease [COPD], emphysema, head and neck cancer, heart attacks [myocardial infarctions], and strokes [cerebrovascular accidents]), better-paying/more stable jobs that may provide health insurance or lessen the premium payments required to have an excellent health insurance plan that covers preventive health interventions in addition to routine payment of unexpected medical diagnoses or accidental injuries.

Longer years and duration of education in school have been proven to be associated with a statistically significant decrease in depression symptoms and complaints. Low educational levels are associated with increased levels of both anxiety and depression. How does learning improve the brain? Learning changes the physical structure of the brain. These structural changes alter the functional organization of the brain. Learning, thus, organizes and reorganizes the brain. Different parts of the brain may also be ready to learn at different times.

Does stress affect education? Not exercising while studying in school (and thus not naturally ridding or eliminating stress from your body while in school) may be counterproductive to an individual's intentions, desires, and wishes to be the best student they can possibly be and to attain the highest or zenith level of education possible.

When stress is not dealt with, or when stress is allowed to accumulate or fester in the body and mind, it can then rise to overwhelming levels (school-related stress) that may then actually reduce an individual's desire and motivation to proficiently complete school work, thus negatively impacting that individual's overall academic performance, accomplishments, and achievements, or, in the worst case scenario, potentially increase the odds of that student dropping out of school. Stress can also cause health problems such as depression, poor sleep, substance abuse, and anxiety.

What are several common and well-known reasons that students have anxiety problems that, more often than not, may be managed successfully with regular exercise and other forms of relieving the body and mind of excessive or extraordinary stress? In some children, fear and worry associated with school anxiety are related to a specific cause, e.g., being bullied by other students or teachers or some other traumatic, disruptive, or otherwise unpleasant event at school.

Other students may experience anxiety, which is more general in nature or related to social reasons, phobias, performance anxiety, or sundry other reasons. Can the brain change without learning? This question can be succinctly and precisely answered by studying the importance of brain connections and synaptogenesis. Connections between neurons, through synapses, especially when in an educational environment or situation such as school and during learning new concepts and ideas every day of your life (the goal) for the remainder of your life, are constantly changing throughout all of our life and are predominantly responsible for continuing learning and memory maintenance, sustenance, and preservation throughout your life, in the brain.

What Makes People Most Fulfilled in Life: Diet, Exercise, Sleep, Positive & Frequent Socialization & Love

Chapters one, four, and five discuss and comprehensively review, list reference books, and elucidate the importance of proper, updated diet information and new exercise recommendations to achieve and maintain optimal physical and mental strength, function, stability, and outperformance, compared with uneducated or under-educated individuals who are either unaware of or are purposely defying or shunning fantastic and healthy advice and recommendations to optimize their energy level, enhance their life performance in all categories, and to extend their longevity.

A great and quick read for all individuals, read and memorized many years ago by the author while still in school, is a book (copyright 1999, with online updated information over many years now) entitled, "Living to 100, Lessons in Living to Your Maximum Potential At Any Age" by Thomas T. Perls, M.D., M.P.H. and Margery Hutter Silver, Ed.D., and

John F. Lauerman." Below is a summary or synopsis of sorts, describing the enormous and immense value and wisdom contained in the findings and descriptions in this book of the research that was done to learn every facet and idiosyncrasy of the history, background, lifestyle, health habits, issues or substances used or avoided in life, social habits, exercise, sleep, dental hygiene (e.g., toothbrushing and dental flossing), exercise, indulgence in sinful, poisonous, toxic habits, abuses, dependences (e.g., overuse or abuse of prescription medications, use of illicit drugs that are toxic to brain and body [alcohol, smoking of tobacco, marijuana, cloves, cocaine, others, chewing tobacco, excess consumption of fat, sugar, protein or too frequent eating habits versus more healthy intermittent fasting]), and assimilated all the research they obtained from interviews, surveys, family member histories regarding all persons worldwide that reached the age of one-hundred years old or older.

"Living to 100, Lessons in Living to Your Maximum Potential At Any Age" by Thomas T. Perls, M.D., M.P.H. and Margery Hutter Silver, Ed.D., and John F. Lauerman." (1999)

Centenarians, once a rarity, are the world's fastest-growing age group: there are currently about 50,000 people over 100 in the United States alone, almost three times as many as in 1980. Centenarians are setting the gold standard for healthy aging. What can we learn from these pioneers? How can people decades younger apply the centenarians' longevity lessons to their own lives? These are the questions Harvard scientists Thomas Perls and Margery Hutter Silver set out to answer when they launched the New England Centenarian Study. As they probed beyond disease to identify the parameters of an energetic later life, Perls and Silver realized that the key to preserving health and vitality lies not in learning how people stay young but in understanding how they age well. By identifying lifestyle patterns, vitamins, and medications that contribute to aging well -- and may even help slow down the aging process -- they show how all of us can maximize the healthy portion of the lifespan. Filled with personal profiles, informational sidebars, and quizzes, Living to 100 offers inspiration and solid scientific information to the more than seventy-five million people alive today who can look forward to their ninth and tenth decades.

The importance of sleep to health, longevity, happiness, and fulfillment cannot be overstated.

Getting enough rest can help reduce stress, improve your mood, and boost your energy levels. Unfortunately, with the busy lifestyles that many people lead, rest is often put on the back burner. This is why maximizing rest is essential for optimal health and happiness. It's no secret that sleep is an important part of a healthy lifestyle, but getting a good night's shut-eye could also be the key to feeling contented.

How does sleep affect the quality of life? Sleep or lack of sleep may positively or adversely, respectively, affect nearly every tissue type, all organs, all physiologic processes, all chemical reactions, and the short-term and long-term health of and longevity of our body and physical, mental, social, and spiritual life. Sleep affects growth hormones, stress hormones, our immune system, appetite, breathing, blood pressure, and cardiovascular health. Is sleep the most important thing in life? Some might argue that the answer to this question is yes because a good night's sleep recharges humans and prepares them for optimal functioning the following day. Others might argue that sleep is the second most important thing in life, "taking second seat or second fiddle" only to the productive use of our daytime school or work hours available.

Daily decisions are best executed with the most wisdom and discernment after a good night of restful and deep, restorative sleep. Wise decisions, choices, exercise, and other school or work activities that occupy our daytime, daylight, or night shift awake hours are most efficiently and effectively executed and consistently performed daily following restful sleep each preceding evening. Sleep, thus, is vital to preserving the integrity and maximum health of our bodies and uninterrupted continuation of errorless myriad chemical processes, neurotransmitter functions, and other physiologic processes occurring each second in our amazing and miraculous human bodies, all created by God and created in the image of God.

Sleep is essential to every process in the body, affecting our physical and mental functioning the next day, our ability to fight disease and develop immunity, and our metabolism and chronic disease risk. Sleep is truly interdisciplinary because it touches every aspect of health. How does sleep contribute to happiness? Sleep gives us more energy and improves our mood and libido. And for men, getting enough sleep is also linked to the ability to achieve and maintain an erection. Does lack of sleep affect the quality of life?

Lack of sleep or sleep deficiency is linked to many chronic health problems and increases various major health risks and the incidence and frequency of such conditions as heart disease, kidney disease, high blood pressure, diabetes, stroke, obesity, depression, infections, and is also linked to a higher chance of injury in adults, teens, and children. There is no 100% consensus on how many hours of sleep each individual needs at every stage of life, and the optimal number of sleep hours may vary considerably in different individuals and may be dependent on the activities and intensity or strenuousness of those activities of that individual that particular day. However, average healthy adults generally need at least seven hours (eight hours may be optimal) of sleep per night. Babies, young children, and teens need even more sleep to enable their growth and development. Other factors may complicate these simple generalizations of necessary sleep hours, where more than eight hours or less than seven hours may be preferred for various health reasons, e.g., someone who is ill and did not receive any deep and restful sleep the previous night may require more hours of sleep. Someone who took a four-hour nap earlier that day may not require a full hour of sleep later that day and night to feel fully rested the next morning. Why is sleep important emotionally?

Sleep stages include stages one and two (considered light sleep, but not fully restorative and restful stages of sleep; interestingly, people who consume alcohol, caffeine [e.g., coffee or chocolate], or certain nonprescription or nonessential prescription medications [e.g., taking narcotic pain meds just before sleeping when their pain level is minimum and does not require narcotic pain medication]), can relegate that patient to being trapped in stage one or two sleep all night, instead of being able to enter into the restful and restorative deep sleep stages known at stage 3, stage 4, and R.E.M. (rapid eye movement) stage. Sufficient deep and restful sleep, especially stage 3, stage 4, and R.E.M. sleep facilitates the brain's processing of emotional information. During sleep, the brain works to evaluate and remember thoughts and memories, and it appears that a lack of deep stages of restful and restorative sleep is especially harmful to the consolidation of positive emotional content. In one study, which is neither all-inclusive nor proof of universal truth for every individual on Earth, participants who slept seven hours and six minutes rated themselves as "perfectly happy."

People who slept seven hours rated themselves as "mostly happy," and those who slept for six hours and 54 minutes reported themselves as "somewhat happy."

Take what you wish from this study's findings and results, although always with a grain or larger chunk of salt when indicated.

Having a broader set of social contacts, which leads to a greater and more significant number of satisfying relationships and faithful, positive, and supportive friends, is vitally important and essential for happiness, longevity, and fulfillment in life. Social interactions and relationships, positive and negative, can all be educational and contribute to an individual's valuable lessons in navigating stormy waters in this world, also known as this tumultuous and tempestuous world we live in.

Relationships are indelibly connected to some of the strongest (and potentially most positive, life-invigorating, motivational, and inspirational) emotions individuals can and should experience in life. Even negative relationships, which should be avoided whenever possible (especially abusive, unethical, immoral, or other evil relationships), can make an individual more resilient in the life path they will navigate, hopefully with the great wisdom and insight they learned and acquired from their past relationships, positive and negative. Social connections make people happier, more content, and calmer. Satisfying relationships are also associated with better health and greater longevity.

Benefits of Socialization:

What is socialization, and why is it important? Social interaction is a basic human need, just as food, shelter, and water have been considered life-sustaining basic human requirements for centuries. Simply stated, the more socializing an individual engages in, the greater that individual's chances are of living longer, especially when these interactions are with great mentors. What defines "great mentors"? Great mentors are highly educated, "healthy-diet-consuming," exercising, "non-sexually-immoral" (or otherwise unethical, criminal, dishonest, selfish, or ungodly) individuals, and non-alcohol or drug-abusing individuals.

These great mentors are defined by their life example and daily behavior of being reliable, honest, benevolent advisors who seek to enhance the spiritual, mental, social, and physical health of all their advisees, e.g., persons being advised by someone, e.g., their mentor(s). Human interactions are of vital importance to rapidly and most efficiently and effectively helping our brain and body experience, interpret, and then comprehensively analyze and understand what is going on around us and what events and human reactions result from our interactions and communications, then filing these experiences and episodes of learning, one file at a time, in mental and physical file cabinets that categorize and organize these events and define the context of each of these human interactions and consequences, helping individuals, much like a supercomputer would or like the processes of quantum computing, that ultimately result in these individuals becoming progressively more intelligent, more innovative, wiser, more sophisticated, and analogous to a complex quantum computer with ever-increasing critical reasoning skills, problem-solving ability, agility, prowess, and expertise, with every subsequent problem they encounter in the course of their lives.

Moreover, when relationships are unexpectedly negative, disappointing, discouraging, or even devastating, and thus challenge an individual right up to the perceived limit of that individuals maximum breaking point (keep in mind, however, that God, in the Bible, states that humans will never be tested beyond the limits he bestowed on his creations, e.g., humans, and that he had empowered them with to withstand and overcome, because of God's love for all humans), then these adverse experiences and human interactions, can ironically and counterintuitively actually immensely and instantly help us expand and extend what that individual previously considered as their personal limitation level for handling or dealing with stressful or dire circumstances, persevering through that life-challenging event, and ultimately expanding, dramatically, how that individual sees the world and the new near-invincible, within reason, potential they have to deal with future unexpected and surprising challenges in life. Socialization affects an individual's stress levels in many ways. For instance, socialization increases a hormone (serotonin) that decreases anxiety levels and makes us feel more confident in our ability to cope with stressors. Socialization, by definition, requires individuals to seek out, listen to, and act on the needs of others to establish and maintain those friendships; put another way, focusing our energy outward as opposed to inward, producing a less self-centered and selfish individual and concomitantly initiating a type of metamorphosis, e.g., changing a single-colored, crawling caterpillar into a beautiful multicolored and flying butterfly, in that human.

Ways to Create, Maintain, And Sustain Long-Term Connections With Other Individuals

1. Smiling, as simple and effortless as that may sound and seem, is very successful and satisfying.

2. Make direct eye contact and be sincere and honest in all communications.
3. Schedule significantly long and effective meetings or gathering times for deep discussions.
4. Listen intensely, proactively, and in a fully engaged manner, which demonstrates true concern.
5. Actively show and demonstrate, not just by words but via your actions, your support, and your love.
6. Communicate sensitively, sincerely, and efficiently, covering necessary topics in the time allotted.
7. Seek always to encourage, support, motivate, inspire, and reassure, demonstrating your loyalty.
8. Whenever possible, focus on helping and uplifting others above and beyond, focusing on self.
9. Always strive to be authentic and kind versus elite and condescending or otherwise unkind
10. Respect other individuals' boundaries
11. Attempt always to remain focused on the present and future more than the past.
12. Spend minimal time on meaningless, insignificant, or inconsequential topics.
13. Be equitable in listening and speaking during the conversation, as necessary, required, and recommended.
14. Offer admiration when appropriate and discouragement of bad ideas as well.
15. Seriously interpret on a minute-to-minute basis how you make others feel.
16. Show empathy by listening to others' points of view before ever responding.
17. Listen to the feelings and intentions of words spoken or written between the lines.
18. Offer and be open to receiving, when appropriate, honest and sincere feedback.
19. Be willing, prepared, and committed to creating and nurturing relationships.

20. Have an aspiration and intent to give rather than receive most often, if possible.
21. Always be open to new relationships, especially those that are positive, supportive, moral, ethical, and holy, and thus, will enhance one's inner peace, serenity, and health.

An essential aspect of human society is the fact that an individual's life is positively enhanced, intertwined, and inseparable (at least in regard to optimizing longevity) from, preferably positive more than negative, interactions and social relationships with other diverse individuals from all different backgrounds, cultures, and countries. Full social participation is such a fundamental human need and desire. It has been suggested that a lack of any social connections may significantly increase an individual's odds of premature death, possibly up to or by as much as 50%. Social connectedness, more often than not, leads to longer life, better health, and improved well-being. One definition of social connectedness is the degree to which people have and perceive a desired number, quality, and diversity of relationships that create an overall sense of belonging to a meaningful group of other humans and being cared for, valued, and supported by the group.

Socialization prepares people to participate in social groups by teaching them the norms and expectations of those groups. Socialization's three primary goals include teaching impulse control while developing a conscience, preparing and training people to perform specific social roles, and education by cultivating shared sources of meaning and value specific to each social group. The family has been said to be (this has been confirmed over thousands of years now) the most important agent of socialization for children. Children feel secure and loved when they have strong and positive family relationships. Positive family relationships engender a sense of security, safety, and serenity to all family members.

The educational impact and life-long value of life aspects and strategies that are tried, practiced, and proven on a daily basis in positive communicating family members are often understated or even completely ignored by some individuals, much to their detriment. Families members in Godly, church-attending neighborhoods and communities learn to effectively and efficiently resolve conflict through attentive listening and using wisdom and sound judgment in determining right versus wrong attitudes, aspirations, and motivations of the individuals involved in each conflict. These same family members can then work as a team to prevent future unnecessary conflicts or disputes to the best extent possible and thereby enjoy each other's company in an immensely more satisfying manner than if proper conflict resolution is not properly addressed or ignored altogether.

Positive family relationships are built on quality time spent with all members of the family on an equitable basis to the best extent possible, communication (e.g., intense and attentive listening without talking or with minimal verbal responses until someone has finished stating their reasoning for the actions they took or the things they said), teamwork (e.g., group problem solving with all family members input, preferences or recommendations being honestly and seriously considered and implemented in final conflict resolutions), and appreciation of each and every family member with equal and large amounts of love being graciously or mercifully given to each family member (sometimes more deserved than other times). Parents' values and behavior patterns profoundly influence those of their daughters and sons. Suggested goals of socialization are many, such as self-regulation, a sense of self, motivation and cultural beliefs and morality, and both physical and mental benefits, including increased cognitive ability, good mental health, communication skills, independence, and improved physical health, from infancy to centenarian!

Individuals who practice and perfect peaceful, moral, ethical, and otherwise positive social relationships, in general, are known to exhibit or possess better mental health or fewer mental health problems, e.g., fewer psychological or psychiatric issues, conditions, or diagnoses. Social activity helps an individual discover and learn, hopefully, more about healthier lifestyle habits such as the mind, body, and soul health benefits of more frequent and more vigorous exercise and a better diet. Staying social throughout one's life also helps individuals periodically or intermittently "blow off steam" or "de-stress." Socialization by individuals, learned at the earliest age possible, such as in preschool, ideally, has been demonstrated throughout time and is now commonly known to stave off feelings of loneliness, sharpen memory, hone and enhance cognitive skills, increase one's sense of happiness and well-being, improve that individual's mood, generate feelings of joy, lower that individual's risk of dementia, with a resultant and concomitant benefit to the individual of expected or anticipated increased longevity (socialization helps you live longer)! It has been said that people who are isolated face a 50% greater risk of premature death than those who have stronger social connections. Furthermore, positive social interactions promote a sense of safety, belonging, and security and are thus highly beneficial to the development and maintenance of that individual's brain health.

Lastly, socialization enables and allows individuals to confide in others and lets them confide in you, which is like an imaginary, but real in this case, super vitamin for that individual's mental health, allowing excessive positive emotions to be shared with others (benefitting all involved) and prevents the accumulation and buildup of negative emotions, by allowing excessive negative emotions to be vented, so that they may safely exit that individual's body and mind, and not fester or build up in pressure and force, as that of a volcano or earthquake just before the eruption or cracks/explosions, respectively, commence, often with precarious or disastrous and perilous results and outcomes.

Social support may reduce your blood pressure amidst or during stressful tasks and boost your immune system. It has been observed and well-documented that spouses with strong social support networks had better immune system functioning than those with low support levels or fewer support networks when caring for a partner with cancer.

Chapter Eleven:

What is the Purpose of Life? What are "The Rapture" and "The Second Coming?" Does Anyone Really Believe That There Is Not An Optimal Godly Attitude, Faith, Manner, And Method Of Living Life? Does Anyone Really Believe There Is Not Or Will Never Be Dire And Severe, Eternal Consequences For Their Evil or "Ungodly" Behavior, Especially If They Neither Acknowledge God's Existence Nor Repent Their Sins Nor Request God's Forgiveness Of Their Sins? What is Godly Behavior, And How Does the Bible Define Godly Living?

Just as the first coming of Jesus Christ, the Messiah (i.e., the Anointed One, the Son of God) was literal, so will be the Second Coming.

Q: What is the Rapture?

A: There are many Christians who believe that the second coming of Jesus Christ will be in two phases. First, He will come for believers, both living and dead, in the "rapture" (read 1 Thessalonians 4:13-17). In this view, the Rapture—which is the transformation and catching up of all Christians, dead or alive, to meet Christ in the air—will be secret, for it will be unknown to the world of unbelievers at the time of its happening.

The effect of this removal, in the absence of multitudes of people, will, of course, be evident on Earth. Then, second, after a period of seven years of Tribulation on Earth, Christ will return to the Earth with His Church, the saints who were raptured (Matthew 24:30, 2 Thessalonians 1:7, 1 Peter 1:13, Revelation 1:7). He will be victorious over His enemies and will reign on the Earth for 1,000 years (the millennium) with His saints, the Church.

After 1,000 years, living unbelievers and the wicked dead now raised to life will be judged at the great white throne judgment. They will then be cast into the lake of fire, while <u>the saved will live forever with Christ</u> in a new heaven and Earth (Revelation, chapters 19-22).

Be ready to meet Christ by giving your life to Him today.

Many other evangelical Christians believe that Christ's return and the Rapture will not occur until the seven years of the Tribulation have ended. As far as the latter view is concerned, the Rapture will not be secret since it will be part of Christ's visible and triumphant return to end this present evil age (1 Thessalonians 4:13-17). At this point, interpreters differ as to whether there will be a literal thousand-year reign of Christ on Earth or whether the white throne judgment and the new heaven and Earth will immediately appear.

All Christians do not agree on every detail of what will occur in the final events of this world's history. Some of these events and their order of occurrence have simply not been made clear in the Bible. What is important is that all Christians hold in common that Christ will ultimately return bodily, visibly, and gloriously to reign and rule with His resurrected and transformed saints forever and ever. The details of this great event will be made known in God's own time.

>> Are you Rapture ready?
WHAT IS THE RAPTURE?
By R. Robert Creech, PhD

Will there be a time when all Christians suddenly disappear from Earth?

"Warning! In case of Rapture, this car will be unmanned!" the bumper sticker on the car in front of you proclaims. *What's that supposed to mean?* You wonder.

Perhaps you've seen the trailer for the movie *Left Behind*. In the film, the world is plunged into chaos after the Rapture takes all Christian believers from Earth. They simply vanish—right in the middle of whatever they were doing.

The whole idea that millions of people could suddenly disappear without a trace may seem a bit ... well, creepy. So what is the Rapture, and what exactly do Christians believe about it?

Dispensationalism and the Rapture

The idea of the Rapture developed as part of a larger movement in nineteenth-century England called "dispensationalism." Led by John Nelson Darby, a former priest in the Church of Ireland, a group known as the Plymouth Brethren began to study the Bible in an attempt to map out the future of the world. They divided history into seven "dispensations" or ages.

WHAT IS DISPENSATIONALISM?

A literal interpretation of Scripture that divides history into seven "dispensations" or ages, with the belief that there are two "peoples of God:" Israel and the Church.

Darby endeavored to read the Bible as literally as possible and believed that Jesus Christ would soon physically return to the world.[1] However, in his study, he found several seeming contradictions within the Bible. This was particularly true in regard to the promises made by God to Israel through the Old Testament prophets, such as a rebuilt temple of immense proportions.[2]

To help reconcile such instances, Darby formed some theological conclusions that influenced his teachings, including:

- The belief that there are two "peoples of God:" Israel and the Church
- God has separate plans for each of them.

---

[1] "John Nelson Darby," *Christian History*, August 8, 2008, http://www.christianitytoday.com/ch/131christians/pastorsandpreachers/darby.html.

[2] See *The Holy Bible,* New International Version © 2011, Ezekiel 40–48.

In order for God to fulfill all his promises to the nation of Israel, there must be a time in the future when the Church is no longer present, and the Jewish temple in Jerusalem can be rebuilt.

According to Darby, the Church Age (the time in which we are now living) is a kind of parenthesis in God's plan. At the end of the Church Age, the Church will be taken out of this world. God will then continue with his plans and promises to Israel.

The Rapture is not to be confused with the Second Coming of Christ; rather, it is a secret coming for the Church.[3] Darby taught that Jesus' actual return would occur approximately seven years later, following a period called the Great Tribulation, which Christians will escape. During the Great Tribulation, a series of plagues will be sent to the Earth, as understood from a literal reading of Revelation chapters 6–9 and 16–18.

The Spread of Dispensationalism

During one of his visits to England in the 1870s, American evangelist Dwight L. Moody met some of the Plymouth Brethren.[4] Impressed by their piety, he invited some of them to America to teach in his Bible schools. As conferences in Bible prophecy grew in popularity, the Moody Bible Institute was founded and began training Christian leaders in this way of thinking.

In fact, Darby himself visited the U.S. more than once. Through his influence, the Sixteenth and Walnut Avenue Presbyterian Church in St. Louis, pastored by James H. Brooks, became a center for dispensationalism in the United States.

---

[3] Bruce David Forbes and Jeanne Halgren Kilde, eds., *Rapture, Revelation, and the End Times: Exploring the Left Behind Series* (New York: Palgrave Macmillan, 2004), 53.

[4] Martyn McGeown, "The Life & Theology of D. L. Moody," accessed January 22, 2015, http://www.cprf.co.uk/articles/moody.htm#.VMFow3bBwu1.

In St. Louis, a Presbyterian layman named Cyrus I. Scofield adopted Darby's beliefs. He then became the pastor of a church in Dallas, Texas, and eventually helped found Dallas Theological Seminary.

In 1909, Scofield published a Bible with annotations explaining the dispensational interpretation of Scripture. The notes provide a schematization of complex biblical materials by relating each passage to Darby's teachings. Known as the Scofield Reference Bible, the work became quite popular and did much to spread dispensationalist views among the Bible-reading public.[5]

As dispensationalism grew, passionate preachers and writers—such as R. A. Torrey, J. W. Chapman, A. C. Dixon, A. J. Gordon, and A. T. Pierson—drove home Darby's teachings from the pulpit with their evangelistic fervor.

The Second Coming of Christ or the Rapture of the Saints?

However, throughout history, other Christians have thought differently about these matters. They believe that **there is only one "people of God,"** comprised of both Jews and non-Jews who place their faith in Jesus as the Messiah. They believe that Jesus himself will one day return to complete the kingdom he launched with his life, death, and resurrection.[6]

The first followers of Jesus believed that Jesus might be back even within their lifetime.[7] The Apostles' Creed, an early declaration of Christian faith that dates back to the second or third century, states, "I believe in Jesus Christ … and he will come to judge the living and the dead." [8] That is, early Christians believed that Jesus would return

---

5   LeAnn Snow Flesher, "The Historical Development of Premillennial Dispensationalism," *Review & Expositor* 106, no. 1 (December 1, 2009): 35–45.

6   Forbes and Kilde, 35. Also see *The Holy Bible,* Matthew 24:30–31, 36–39.

7   See *The Holy Bible,* 1 Corinthians 15:51–57 and 1 Thessalonians 4:13–18.

8   The Apostles' Creed is cited by many Christian denominations, sometimes with slight variations in wording for the purpose of clarity. The one we are using here is from the Church of England. "The Lord's Prayer and the Apostles' Creed,"

to the Earth personally, would raise all the dead to life, and that each person would give an account of their life to him.[9]

Those who hold this traditional understanding do not believe that God will snatch up believers from the world and then go on with other things on Earth. Rather, they believe that Jesus will come a second time to set the world right. He will renew heaven and Earth, raising the dead to live forever in a world in which God's reign of love and peace is complete.

Is the Rapture in the Bible?

But what does the Bible say about all this? Well, dispensationalists point to several biblical passages as evidence of the Rapture, while non-dispensationalists interpret these verses differently.

For example, 1 Thessalonians 4:15–17 reads:

According to the Lord's word, we tell you that we who are still alive, who are left until the coming of the Lord, will certainly not precede those who have fallen asleep. For the Lord himself will come down from heaven, with a loud command, with the voice of the archangel and with the trumpet call of God, and the dead in Christ will rise first. After that, we who are still alive and are left will be caught up together with them in the clouds to meet the Lord in the air. And so we will be with the Lord forever.

The expression "caught up together" is understood by dispensationalists to refer to the Rapture. In fact, in the Latin version of the text, the word translated as "caught up" is *rapiemur*, from which the word "rapture" comes.

However, non-dispensationalists have traditionally understood this text as a promise that when Jesus returns and raises the dead, the living will join them in the new life he brings.

The Church of England website, http://www.churchofengland.org/prayer-worship/worship/texts/daily2/lordsprayercreed.aspx.

9   See *The Holy Bible*, Matthew 25:31–46; John 5:28–29, 14:1–3.

Sometimes, dispensationalists refer to a statement Jesus made regarding his return: "Two men will be in the field; one will be taken and the other left. Two women will be grinding with a hand mill; one will be taken and the other left." [10]

They view those "taken" as the followers of Jesus and those "left behind" as the nonbelievers. Others object that reading the passage in its context shows the opposite.

Let's tack on the previous three verses:

As it was in the days of Noah, so it will be at the coming of the Son of Man. For in the days before the flood, people were eating and drinking, marrying and giving in marriage, up to the day Noah entered the ark, and they knew nothing about what would happen until *the flood came and took them all away.* That is how it will be at the coming of the Son of Man. Two men will be in the field; *one will be taken*, and the other left. Two women will be grinding with a hand mill; *one will be taken* and the other left.[11]

Jesus says that just as those in Noah's day were "taken away" by the flood, so it will be at the coming of the Son of Man. In this context, it appears that those "taken away" are nonbelievers who are taken away to judgment. Those "left behind" are believers.

Living in Frightening Times Unquestionably, we live in a difficult and frightening period of history. The threat of nuclear destruction has been hanging over our heads for seventy years. Human carelessness, consumption, and waste threaten life on the entire planet.

War never ceases, and terrorism spreads. Violence is intense and held before our eyes in daily doses. Racial tensions are high, and economic

---

10   Ibid., Matthew 24:40–41.

11   Ibid., Matthew 24:37–41, emphasis added.

fears loom large. A rapidly changing society has unleashed crises of morality and faith. These are difficult days.

It's no wonder that in times like these, people—both dispensationalists and non-dispensationalists—look for hope in a different future. And they pray that this future will come quickly.

In fact, the promise of Jesus' return to Earth is described in early Christian writings as "the blessed hope" of his followers.[12] Although the Bible encourages believers to live with perseverance in the face of difficulties, they are to do so with the hope and faith that God's future for the Earth is one worth waiting for.[13], [14]

The Rapture in 2 Thessalonians 2:1–10
Myron J. Houghton, Ph.D.

The Context

In verses one and two, Paul states: "Now we beseech you, brethren, by the coming of our Lord Jesus Christ, and by our gathering together unto him, That ye be not soon shaken in mind, or be troubled, neither by spirit, nor by word, nor by letter as from us, as that the day of Christ is at hand." (All Bible quotations are from the King James Version.)

Several things may be said about these verses. (1) Paul is writing to the Thessalonian believers about the Rapture. "The coming of our Lord Jesus Christ" is further described in verse one as "our gathering together unto him." (2) He writes to them because they were in danger of being

---

[12] Ibid., Titus 2:13.

[13] For further information on Christian beliefs regarding the second coming of Christ, please see: A. J. Conyers, *The End: What Jesus Really Said About the Last Things* (Downers Grove, IL: InterVarsity Press, 1995); Philip Edgcumbe Hughes, *Interpreting Prophecy: An Essay in Biblical Perspectives* (Grand Rapids, MI: Eerdmans, 1976); and William H. Stephens, *The Bible Speaks to End Times* (Nashville: Convention Press, 1993).

[14] Photo Credit: Carl Zoch / Stocksy.com.

troubled, and this disturbance was being caused by three things: "by spirit" (a false prophet—cf. 1 John 4:1), "by word" (a false preacher—cf. 1 Cor. 1:18) and "by letter, as [if] from us" (a false letter with Paul's forged signature). (3) The false teaching which these three sources presented, and which disturbed the Thessalonians was that "the day of Christ" had come. (Some Greek texts read "day of the Lord" rather than "day of Christ," but in either case, this "day" refers to the time when Christ will directly intervene in human affairs by bringing destruction upon the world.) (4) Furthermore, the verb that is translated as "is at hand" is in the perfect tense and thus signifies completed past action with present results. Thus, the false teaching was that the day of Christ, the Lord had arrived and was now present. (5) This "day" refers not to the Rapture (obviously, the Thessalonians would know that the Rapture had not yet taken place) but to the Tribulation, Second Coming, and the Millennium (Zechariah 14:1–4, 9, cf. J. Dwight Pentecost, Things To Come, 229–231). Thus, the issue which disturbed the Thessalonians was that they were being told that they were now in the end-time Tribulation. We know from 2 Thessalonians 1:4 that these believers were already suffering persecution, so this conclusion was not farfetched.

Paul's purpose, then, in 2 Thessalonians 2:3–10, is to show these believers that they were not in the Tribulation. In v. 3, he states that two things must occur before the Tribulation can begin— (1) the "falling away," and (2) the revelation of the man of sin. For those aware of Daniel's prophecy (9:26) that "the prince that shall come" will confirm a covenant with many for seven years and then break it "in the midst of the week," the lawless man of sin is made known when he confirms the covenant, not when he breaks it. II Thessalonians 2:4 indicates the identity of this man rather than the time of his revelation by relating him to Daniel's prophecy.

The Removal of the Restrainer is the Rapture

There have been various views concerning the identity of the restrainer. Dr. Pentecost lists five of them as follows: (1) the restrainer was the

Roman Empire, (2) the restrainer was human government and law, (3) the restrainer is Satan, (4) the restrainer is the Church, and (5) the restrainer is the Holy Spirit (Pentecost, Things To Come, 259–62). Several comments should be made about these views. First, the restrainer could not be the Roman empire because such a view limits the restrainer to the past, while Paul indicates that the one being restrained (the man of sin) will live in the future, during the day of the Lord. Second, human government will continue to exist even when the man of sin is revealed; therefore, human government cannot be the restrainer since the man of sin is revealed AFTER the restrainer is removed (2 Thessalonians 2:7, 8). Third, Satan cannot be the restrainer because a house divided against itself will fall. Fourth, the Church alone cannot be the restrainer because the one being restrained has "all power and signs and lying wonders" (2 Thessalonians 2:9). Nevertheless, in verse six, something is doing the restraining, while in verse seven, the restrainer is a person, so the Church could be involved in the restraining process. Fifth, the Holy Spirit is the restrainer because only a member of the Godhead is able to restrain this man of sin who is empowered by Satan.

While all three Persons of the Godhead are omnipresent, the Father is resident in heaven, and the Son is resident at the Father's right hand. It is the Holy Spirit, the third person in the Godhead, who came on the Day of Pentecost. Carefully notice the promise of the Lord Jesus Christ to those who believe in Him: "If any man thirst, let him come unto Me and drink. He that believeth in Me, as the scripture hath said, out of his belly shall flow rivers of living water" (John 7:37–38). The inspired interpretation of this promise is given in the very next verse: "But this spake He of the Spirit, which they that believe on him should receive; for the Holy Ghost was not yet given, because that Jesus was not yet glorified." On the Day of Pentecost, the Holy Spirit came to create the Body of Christ by placing believers into that Body (1 Corinthians 12:13a), and He came to indwell the physical bodies of every member of that Body (1 Corinthians 12:13b).

2 Thessalonians 2:7 tells us the restrainer will restrain "until he be taken out of the way." Some have said this expression cannot refer to a

spatial removal but only to a stepping aside (cf. The MacArthur Study Bible note at 2 Thessalonians 2:7). However, A Greek English Lexicon of the New Testament (2nd ed., revised and augmented by F. Wilbur Gingrich and Frederick W. Danker from Walter Bauer's 5th ed., 1979) lists this very verse as an example of this word's use "to denote change of location" (page 159, bottom right-hand column). The third edition of this work, published in 2000, gives 2 Thessalonians 2:7 as an example of the sixth use of the word: "to make a change of location in space" (bottom of page 198 and top of 199). The removal of the restrainer, then, refers to the departure of the Holy Spirit in the Rapture of the Church.

The "Falling Away" is the Rapture

Two possible solutions have been presented as to the identity of the "falling away." The first solution is the one traditionally given and is still the most popular view today. It understands the "falling away" as a great apostasy or departure from the faith. Almost any standard commentary will defend this position. For a detailed defense of this view, see The Thessalonian Epistles by D. Edmond Hiebert. Basically, the argument is that the Greek word translated as "falling away" means a religious apostasy. The second solution, which is possible, understands the "falling away" as a reference to the Rapture of the Church. This view is defended by E. Schuyler English in his book, Re-Thinking the Rapture.

There are four reasons which, when taken together, seem to indicate that Paul was referring to the Rapture when he mentioned this term.

Reason # 1: The word, which is translated as "falling away," can refer to a physical departure. Note that this argument does not say that the word always or even normally has this meaning. "Departure, disappearance" is the second meaning given for this Greek word in A Greek-English Lexicon, by Liddell & Scott, I, 218. Part of the problem here is that this word is used only twice in the New Testament——here and also in Acts 21:21, where Paul is told that some accuse him of teaching a departure from Moses. In this latter passage, this word is used in the sense of a religious apostasy. In the LXX (the Greek translation of the Old Testament), this word or an older form is found in Joshua 22:22, 1 Kings 21:13, 2 Chronicles 29:19, 33:19, Isaiah 30:1, and Jeremiah 2:19. In these cases, the word also has the idea of religious departure. However, either the context or a descriptive phrase is used to indicate that a religious apostasy is meant. Therefore, it might be argued that the word itself was more general.

In the New Testament, the verb form of this word is used fifteen times (Luke 2:27, 4:13, 8:13, 22:29; Acts 5:37,38, 12:10, 15:38, 19:9, 22:29; 2 Corinthians 12:8; 1 Timothy 4:1, 6:5; 2 Timothy 2:19; and Hebrews 3:12). Of the fifteen references, only three have reference to a religious departure, and these three are qualified by context (Luke 8:13) or by a descriptive phrase (1 Timothy 4:1—" from the faith" and Hebrews 3:12—" from the living God"). It is clear from some of the remaining references that a physical departure is meant (the angel who delivered Peter from prison departed from him—Acts 12:10, and Paul prayed that a thorn in the flesh might depart from him—2 Corinthians 12:8.) This word is translated departynge by William Tyndale (c. 1526), by Cranmer (1539), and by the Geneva Bible (1557). Beza (1565) translated it as departing.

Reason # 2: The use of the definite article ("the") lends support to the view that the falling away is the Rapture. The basic function of the article "is to point out an object or to draw attention to it. Its use with a word makes the word stand out distinctly" (Dana and Mantey, A Manual Grammar of the Greek New Testament, 137). Paul is not speaking of A falling away but THE falling away. In all probability, Paul is referring to some subject he has previously discussed with the Thessalonians. Robertson agrees with the use of the article in this verse. He states: "And the use of the definite article (the) seems to mean that Paul had spoken to the Thessalonians about it." (Word Pictures in the New Testament, IV, 49). Now, if this is the use of the article in 2 Thessalonians 2:3, one would expect to find a place, either in 1 or 2 Thessalonians, where Paul previously referred to a departure from the faith. This writer knows of no such reference. However, there is a previous reference to the Rapture of the Church in 1 Thessalonians 4:13–17 and 2 Thessalonians 2:1.

Reason # 3: Paul's style of writing in this chapter also lends support to the idea that the "falling away" is the Rapture. In verse 3, Paul states that two events must occur before the day of the Lord can come, namely (1) the "falling away" and (2) the revealing of the man of sin. Paul's reference to this second event seems to be more fully described in verses 8–9. If, indeed, this is Paul's style, then verses 6 and 7, which describe the removal of the Holy Spirit and the Church, would be a more detailed explanation of the first event in verse 3 (the "falling away").

Reason # 4: Paul's purpose in writing lends support to the view that the "falling away" is the Rapture. Remember the setting. The Thessalonian believers were being persecuted for their faith, and they thought they were in the Tribulation. Paul writes to tell them that they can't possibly be in the Tribulation because two things have to occur before the Tribulation can begin: the "falling away" and the revelation of the man of sin. If religious apostasy is a means by which Paul expects the Thessalonians to know whether or not they are in the Tribulation, then he has failed to prove his point because there has always been religious apostasy, even in the time of the apostle Paul, and the Thessalonians were not in a position to distinguish any present apostasy from "THE apostasy." However, if Paul was referring to the Rapture of the Church, then the Thessalonians could know with certainty that they could not yet be in the Tribulation.

Conclusion

If both the removal of the restrainer and the "falling away" refer to the Rapture of the Church, then II Thessalonians 2:1–10 offers two proofs for the Rapture occurring before the Tribulation.

Eschatology, which is also known as "end times" theology, is an area of biblical study that has captivated the masses for more than two millennia. Over time, various interpretations and theories have emerged surrounding Christ's return and the end of the world as we know it. These ideas have been embedded in contemporary books and films as believers look to entertainment — and current events — for clues surrounding what's to come.

But what does the Bible really say about the end times? There are, in fact, many Bible verses about the end times that speak about the future return of Christ and the events and conditions that will one day come to fruition. These verses and themes are explored in countless films that you can watch right now on Pure Flix.

Read Also: *11 Christian Movies About The End Times*

"The Dark: Great Deceiver" and "The Coming Convergence," among other feature films, were inspired by events described in the Book of Revelation, the prophetic book that concludes the New Testament.

And while the Book of Revelation is the most well-known set of Bible verses about the end times, for most Christians, when studying end times prophecy, it is far from the only place in Scripture that describes what will unfold during the "last days."

If you're interested in learning more about what the Bible says about the end times, here are some additional key passages for you to take into consideration:

Bible Verses About The End Times

1 Thessalonians 4:13-18 (KJV)

"But I would not have you to be ignorant, brethren, concerning them which are asleep, that ye sorrow not, even as others which have no hope. For if we believe that Jesus died and rose again, even so them also which sleep in Jesus will God bring with him. For this, we say unto you by the word of the Lord, that we which are alive and remain unto the coming of the Lord

shall not prevent them which are asleep. For the Lord himself shall descend from heaven with a shout, with the voice of the archangel, and with the trump of God: and the dead in Christ shall rise first: Then we which are alive and remain shall be caught up together with them in the clouds, to meet the Lord in the air: and so shall we ever be with the Lord. Wherefore comfort one another with these words."

Matthew 24:40-41 (KJV)

"Then shall two be in the field; the one shall be taken, and the other left. Two women shall be grinding at the mill; the one shall be taken, and the other left."

2 Timothy 3:1-5 (KJV)

"This know also, that in the last days perilous times shall come. For men shall be lovers of their own selves, covetous, boasters, proud, blasphemers, disobedient to parents, unthankful, unholy, Without natural affection, trucebreakers, false accusers, incontinent, fierce, despisers of those that are good, traitors, heady, high minded, lovers of pleasures more than lovers of God; Having a form of godliness, but denying the power thereof: from such turn away."

Matthew 24:6 (KJV)

"And ye shall hear of wars and rumours of wars: see that ye be not troubled: for all [these things] must come to pass, but the end is not yet."

Watch: The "Left Behind" trilogy is available on Pure Flix. Stream the whole trilogy with a free trial today. "Left Behind," "Left Behind: Tribulation Force," and "Left Behind: World At War" are available today!

Mark 13:32 (KJV)

"But of that day and [that] hour knoweth no man, no, not the angels which are in heaven, neither the Son, but the Father."

Matthew 24:7 (KJV)

"For nation shall rise against nation, and kingdom against kingdom: and there shall be famines, and pestilences, and earthquakes, in divers places."

1 Corinthians 15:52-54 (KJV)

"In a moment, in the twinkling of an eye, at the last trump: for the trumpet shall sound, and the dead shall be raised incorruptible, and we shall be changed. For this corruptible must put on incorruption, and this mortal must put on immortality. So when this corruptible shall have put on incorruption, and this mortal shall have put on immortality, then shall be brought to pass the saying that is written, death is swallowed up in victory."

1 Timothy 4:1 (KJV)

"Now the Spirit speaketh expressly, that in the latter times, some shall depart from the faith, giving heed to seducing spirits and doctrines of devils."

Watch: The "Apocalypse" franchise. All five movies are available on Pure Flix – be sure to get your free trial to stream "Apocalypse," "Apocalypse 2: Revelation," "Apocalypse 3: Tribulation," "Apocalypse 4: Judgment," and "Apocalypse 5: Deceived."

Joel 2:28-32 (KJV)

"And it shall come to pass afterward, [that] I will pour out my Spirit upon all flesh, and your sons and your daughters shall prophesy, your old men shall dream dreams, your young men shall see visions: And also upon the servants and upon the handmaids in those days will I pour out my Spirit. And I will shew wonders in the heavens and in the Earth, blood, and fire, and pillars of smoke. The sun shall be turned into darkness, and the moon into blood, before the great and the terrible day of the LORD come. And it shall come to pass, [that] whosoever shall call on the name of the LORD shall be delivered: for in mount Zion and in Jerusalem shall be deliverance, as the LORD hath said, and in the remnant whom the LORD shall call."

Matthew 24:21 (KJV)

"For then shall be great tribulation, such as was not since the beginning of the world to this time, no, nor ever shall be."

Ezekiel 36:24 (KJV)

"For I will take you from among the heathen, and gather you out of all countries, and will bring you into your own land."

These Bible verses about the end times only scratch the surface when it comes to biblical prophecies. When learning about eschatology, it is important that we always remember that no one knows the day nor the hour. We must also specifically remember the words of Jesus in Matthew 24:44 (KJV), "Therefore be ye also ready: for in such an hour as ye think not the Son of man cometh."

To watch any of the end times movies mentioned above — as well as hundreds of other family movies, documentaries, and shows — try Pure Flix during your free trial.

Also, if you're looking for a quick explainer on the Rapture, the Tribulation, and other concepts related to the biblical end times, consider downloading our free eBook, "End Times Movies and the Theology That Inspired Them."

Billy Hallowell has been working in journalism and media for more than a decade. His writings have appeared in Deseret News, TheBlaze, Human Events, Mediaite, and on FoxNews.com, among other outlets. Hallowell has a B.A. in journalism and broadcasting from the College of Mount Saint Vincent in Riverdale, New York, and an M.S. in social research from Hunter College in Manhattan, New York.

Revelation 20
New International Version

The Thousand Years

20 And I saw an angel coming down out of heaven, having the key to the Abyss and holding in his hand a great chain. **2** He seized the dragon, that ancient serpent, who is the devil, or Satan, and bound him for a thousand years. **3** He threw him into the Abyss and locked and sealed it over him to keep him from deceiving the nations anymore until the thousand years were ended. After that, he must be set free for a short time.

4 I saw thrones on which were seated those who had been given authority to judge. And I saw the souls of those who had been beheaded because of their testimony about Jesus and because of the word of God. They[a] had not worshiped the beast or its image and had not received its mark on their foreheads or their hands. They came to life and reigned with Christ for a thousand years. **5** (The rest of the dead did not come to life until the thousand years were ended.) This is the first resurrection. **6** Blessed and holy are those who share in the first resurrection. The second death has no power over them, but they will be priests of God and of Christ and will reign with him for a thousand years.

The Judgment of Satan

7 When the thousand years are over, Satan will be released from his prison **8** and will go out to deceive the nations in the four corners of the Earth—Gog and Magog—and to gather them for battle. In number, they are like the sand on the seashore. **9** They marched across the breadth of the Earth and surrounded the camp of God's people, the city he loves. But fire came down from heaven and devoured them. **10** And the devil, who deceived them, was thrown into the lake of burning sulfur, where the beast and the false prophet had been thrown. They will be tormented day and night forever and ever.

The Judgment of the Dead

11 Then I saw a great white throne and him who was seated on it. The Earth and the heavens fled from his presence, and there was no place for them. **12** And I saw the dead, great and small, standing before the throne, and books were opened. Another book was opened, which is the book of life. The dead were judged according to what they had done as recorded in the books. **13** The sea gave up the dead that were in it, and death and Hades gave up the dead that were in them, and each person was judged according to what they had done. **14** Then death and Hades were thrown into the lake of fire. The lake of fire is the second death. **15** Anyone whose name was not found written in the Book of Life was thrown into the lake of fire.

Footnotes

a. Revelation 20:4 Or *God; I also saw those who*

Revelation 21
New International Version

A New Heaven and a New Earth

21 Then I saw "a new heaven and a new earth," [a] for the first heaven and the first Earth had passed away, and there was no longer any sea. **2** I saw the Holy City, the new Jerusalem, coming down out of heaven from God, prepared as a bride beautifully dressed for her husband. **3** And I heard a loud voice from the throne saying, "Look! God's dwelling place is now among the people, and he will dwell with them. They will be his people, and God himself will be with them and be their God. **4** 'He will wipe every tear from their eyes. There will be no more death' [b] or mourning or crying or pain, for the old order of things has passed away."

5 He who was seated on the throne said, "I am making everything new!" Then he said, "Write this down, for these words are trustworthy and true."

6 He said to me: "It is done. I am the Alpha and the Omega, the Beginning and the End. To the thirsty, I will give water without cost from the spring of the water of life. **7** Those who are victorious will inherit all this, and I will be their God, and they will be my children. **8** But the cowardly, the unbelieving, the vile, the murderers, the sexually immoral, those who practice magic arts, the idolaters, and all liars—they will be consigned to the fiery lake of burning sulfur. This is the second death."

The New Jerusalem, the Bride of the Lamb

9 One of the seven angels who had the seven bowls full of the seven last plagues came and said to me, "Come, I will show you the bride, the wife of the Lamb." **10** And he carried me away in the Spirit to a mountain great and high, and showed me the Holy City, Jerusalem, coming down out of heaven from God. **11** It shone with the glory of God, and its brilliance was like that of a very precious jewel, like a jasper, clear as crystal. **12** It had a great, high wall with twelve gates, and with twelve angels at the gates. On the gates were written the names of the twelve tribes of Israel. **13** There were three gates on the east, three on the north, three on the south, and three on the west. **14** The wall of the city had twelve foundations, and on them were the names of the twelve apostles of the Lamb.

15 The angel who talked with me had a measuring rod of gold to measure the city, its gates, and its walls. **16** The city was laid out like a square, as long as it was wide. He measured the city with the rod and found it to be 12,000 stadia[c] in length and as wide and high as it is long. **17** The angel measured the wall using human measurement, and it was 144 cubits[d] thick.[e] **18** The wall was made of jasper, and the city of pure gold, as pure as glass. **19** The foundations of the city walls were decorated with every kind of precious stone. The first foundation was jasper, the second sapphire, the third agate, the fourth emerald, **20** the fifth onyx, the sixth ruby, the seventh chrysolite, the eighth beryl, the ninth topaz, the tenth turquoise, the eleventh jacinth, and the twelfth amethyst.[f] **21** The twelve gates were twelve pearls, each gate made of a single pearl. The great street of the city was of gold, as pure as transparent glass.

22 I did not see a temple in the city because the Lord God Almighty and the Lamb are its temple. **23** The city does not need the sun or the moon to shine on it, for the glory of God gives it light, and the Lamb is its lamp. **24** The nations will walk by its light, and the kings of the Earth will bring their splendor into it. **25** On no day will its gates ever be shut, for there will be no night there. **26** The glory and honor of the nations will be brought into it. **27** Nothing impure will ever enter it, nor will anyone who does what is shameful or deceitful, but only those whose names are written in the Lamb's Book of Life.

Footnotes

a. Revelation 21:1 Isaiah 65:17
b. Revelation 21:4 Isaiah 25:8
c. Revelation 21:16 That is about 1,400 miles or about 2,200 kilometers.
d. Revelation 21:17 That is about 200 feet or about 65 meters.
e. Revelation 21:17 Or *high*
f. Revelation 21:20 The precise identification of some of these precious stones is uncertain.

Revelation 22
New International Version

Eden Restored

22 Then the angel showed me the river of the water of life, as clear as crystal, flowing from the throne of God and of the Lamb **2** down the middle of the great street of the city. On each side of the river stood the tree of life, bearing twelve crops of fruit, yielding its fruit every month. And the leaves of the tree are for the healing of the nations. **3** No longer will there be any curse. The throne of God and of the Lamb will be in the city, and his servants will serve him. **4** They will see his face, and his name will be on their foreheads. **5** There will be no more night. They will not need the light of a lamp or the light of the sun, for the Lord God will give them light. And they will reign forever and ever.

John and the Angel

6 The angel said to me, "These words are trustworthy and true. The Lord, the God who inspires the prophets, sent his angel to show his servants the things that must soon take place."

7 "Look, I am coming soon! Blessed is the one who keeps the words of the prophecy written in this scroll."

8 I, John, am the one who heard and saw these things. And when I had heard and seen them, I fell down to worship at the feet of the angel who had been showing them to me. **9** But he said to me, "Don't do that! I am a fellow servant with you and with your fellow prophets and with all who keep the words of this scroll. Worship God!"

10 Then he told me, "Do not seal up the words of the prophecy of this scroll, because the time is near. **11** Let the one who does wrong continue to do wrong; let the vile person continue to be vile; let the one who does right continue to do right; and let the holy person continue to be holy."

Epilogue: Invitation and Warning

12 "Look, I am coming soon! My reward is with me, and I will give to each person according to what they have done. **13** I am the Alpha and the Omega, the First and the Last, the Beginning and the End.

14 "Blessed are those who wash their robes, that they may have the right to the tree of life and may go through the gates into the city. **15** Outside are the dogs, those who practice magic arts, the sexually immoral, the murderers, the idolaters, and everyone who loves and practices falsehood.

16 "I, Jesus, have sent my angel to give you[a] this testimony for the churches. I am the Root and the Offspring of David and the bright Morning Star."

17 The Spirit and the bride say, "Come!" And let the one who hears say, "Come!" Let the one who is thirsty come, and let the one who wishes take the free gift of the water of life.

18 I warn everyone who hears the words of the prophecy of this scroll: If anyone adds anything to them, God will add to that person the plagues described in this scroll. **19** And if anyone takes words away from this scroll of prophecy, God will take away from that person any share in the tree of life and in the Holy City, which are described in this scroll.

20 He who testifies to these things says, "Yes, I am coming soon."

Amen. Come, Lord Jesus.

21 The grace of the Lord Jesus be with God's people. Amen.

Footnotes

    a.   Revelation 22:16 The Greek is plural.

Bible Verses About the End of Time

The Bible says that in the end times, Jesus will return in glory to judge the heavens and the Earth. Preceding Jesus' return, there will be wars, rumors of wars, and great calamities such as famine, natural disasters, and plagues. The antichrist will arise to deceive people and lead them astray. Those who refuse to accept Jesus as their savior will suffer eternal punishment.

These verses about the end of time help us to see that God's ultimate plan is for our redemption and happiness. The Bible encourages Christians to "keep watch" as the end approaches and not fall back into a life of sensual pleasure.

The book of Revelation says that when Christ returns, he will conquer evil. "He will wipe away every tear from their eyes, and death shall be no more, neither shall there be mourning, nor crying, nor pain." (Revelation 21:4). Jesus will govern God's kingdom with righteousness and justice.

The Return of Jesus Christ

Matthew 24:27

For as the lightning comes from the east and shines as far as the west, so will be the coming of the Son of Man.

Matthew 24:30

Then will appear in Heaven the sign of the Son of Man, and then all the tribes of the Earth will mourn, and they will see the Son of Man coming on the clouds of Heaven with power and great glory.

Matthew 26:64

Jesus said to him, "You have said so. But I tell you, from now on, you will see the Son of Man seated at the right hand of power and coming on the clouds of Heaven."

John 14:3

And if I go and prepare a place for you, I will come again and will take you to myself, that where I am you may be also.

Acts 1:11

And said, "Men of Galilee, why do you stand looking into Heaven? This Jesus, who was taken up from you into Heaven, will come in the same way as you saw him go into Heaven."

Colossians 3:4

When Christ, who is your life, appears, then you also will appear with him in glory.

Titus 2:13

Waiting for our blessed hope, the appearing of the glory of our great God and Savior Jesus Christ.

Hebrews 9:28

So Christ, having been offered once to bear the sins of many, will appear a second time, not to deal with sin but to save those who are eagerly waiting for him.

2 Peter 3:10

But the day of the Lord will come like a thief, and then the heavens will pass away with a roar, and the heavenly bodies will be burned up and dissolved, and the Earth and the works that are done on it will be exposed.

Revelation 1:7

Behold, he is coming with the clouds, and every eye will see him, even those who pierced him, and all tribes of the Earth will wail on account of him. Even so. Amen.

Revelation 3:11

I am coming soon. Hold fast what you have, so that no one may seize your crown.

Revelation 22:20

He who testifies to these things says, "Surely I am coming soon." Amen. Come, Lord Jesus!

When will Jesus Return?

Matthew 24:14

And this gospel of the kingdom will be proclaimed throughout the whole world as a testimony to all nations, and then the end will come.

Matthew 24:36

But concerning that day and hour no one knows, not even the angels of Heaven, nor the Son, but the Father only.

Matthew 24:42-44

Therefore, stay awake, for you do not know on what day your Lord is coming. But know this, that if the master of the house had known in what part of the night the thief was coming, he would have stayed awake and would not have let his house be broken into. Therefore, you also must be ready, for the Son of Man is coming at an hour you do not expect.

Mark 13:32

But concerning that day or that hour, no one knows, not even the angels in Heaven, nor the Son, but only the Father.

1 Thessalonians 5:2-3

For you yourselves are fully aware that the day of the Lord will come like a thief in the night. While people are saying, "There is peace and security," then sudden destruction will come upon them as labor pains come upon a pregnant woman, and they will not escape.

Revelation 16:15

"Behold, I am coming like a thief! Blessed is the one who stays awake, keeping his garments on, that he may not go about naked and be seen exposed!"

The Rapture

1 Thessalonians 4:16-17

For the Lord himself will descend from Heaven with a cry of command, with the voice of an archangel, and with the sound of the trumpet of God. And the dead in Christ will rise first. Then we who are alive, who are left, will be caught up together with them in the clouds to meet the Lord in the air, and so we will always be with the Lord.

The Tribulation

Matthew 24:21-22

For then there will be great tribulation, such as has not been from the beginning of the world until now, no, and never will be. And if those days had not been cut short, no human being would be saved. But for the sake of the elect, those days will be cut short.

Matthew 24:29

Immediately after the tribulation of those days, the sun will be darkened, and the moon will not give its light, and the stars will fall from Heaven, and the powers of the heavens will be shaken.

Mark 13:24-27

But in those days, after that tribulation, the sun will be darkened, and the moon will not give its light, and the stars will be falling from Heaven, and the powers in the heavens will be shaken. And then they will see the Son of Man coming in clouds with great power and glory. And then he will send out the angels and gather his elect from the four winds, from the ends of the Earth to the ends of Heaven.

Revelation 2:10

Do not fear what you are about to suffer. Behold, the devil is about to throw some of you into prison, that you may be tested, and for ten days, you will have tribulation. Be faithful unto death, and I will give you the crown of life.

Signs of the End Times

Joel 2:28-31

And it shall come to pass afterward, that I will pour out my Spirit on all flesh; your sons and your daughters shall prophesy, your old men shall dream dreams, and your young men shall see visions. Even on the male and female servants in those days, I will pour out my Spirit. And I will show wonders in the heavens and on the Earth, blood and fire and columns of smoke. The sun shall be turned to darkness, and the moon to blood, before the great and awesome day of the Lord comes. And it shall come to pass that everyone who calls on the name of the Lord shall be saved.

Matthew 24:6-7

And you will hear of wars and rumors of wars. See that you are not alarmed, for this must take place, but the end is not yet. For nation will rise against nation, and kingdom against kingdom, and there will be famines and earthquakes in various places.

Matthew 24:11-12

And many false prophets will arise and lead many astray. And because lawlessness will be increased, the love of many will grow cold.

Luke 21:11

There will be great earthquakes, and in various places, famines and pestilences. And there will be terrors and great signs from Heaven.

1 Timothy 4:1

Now, the Spirit expressly says that in later times, some will depart from the faith by devoting themselves to deceitful spirits and teachings of demons.

2 Timothy 3:1-5

But understand this, that in the last days, there will come times of difficulty. For people will be lovers of self, lovers of money, proud, arrogant, abusive, disobedient to their parents, ungrateful, unholy, heartless, unappeasable, slanderous, without self-control, brutal, not loving good, treacherous, reckless, swollen with conceit, lovers of pleasure rather than lovers of God, having the appearance of godliness, but denying its power. Avoid such people.

The Millennial Kingdom

Revelation 20:1-6

Then I saw an angel coming down from Heaven, holding in his hand the key to the bottomless pit and a great chain. And he seized the dragon, that ancient serpent, who is the devil and Satan, and bound him for a thousand years, and threw him into the pit, and shut it and sealed it over him, so that he might not deceive the nations any longer until the thousand years were ended.

After that, he must be released for a little while.

Then I saw thrones, and seated on them were those to whom the authority to judge was committed. Also, I saw the souls of those who had been beheaded for the testimony of Jesus and for the Word of God and those who had not worshiped the beast or its image and had not received its mark on their foreheads or their hands.

They came to life and reigned with Christ for a thousand years. The rest of the dead did not come to life until the thousand years were ended. This is the first resurrection.

Blessed and holy is the one who shares in the first resurrection! Over such, the second death has no power, but they will be priests of God and of Christ, and they will reign with him for a thousand years.

The Antichrist

Matthew 24:5

For many will come in my name, saying, 'I am the Christ,' and they will lead many astray.

2 Thessalonians 2:3-4

Let no one deceive you in any way. For that day will not come unless the rebellion comes first, and the man of lawlessness is revealed, the Son of destruction, who opposes and exalts himself against every so-called God or object of worship so that he takes his seat in the temple of God, proclaiming himself to be God.

2 Thessalonians 2:8

And then the lawless one will be revealed, whom the Lord Jesus will kill with the breath of his mouth and bring to nothing by the appearance of his coming.

1 John 2:18

Children, it is the last hour, and as you have heard, that antichrist is coming, so now many antichrists have come. Therefore, we know that it is the last hour.

Revelation 13:1-8

And I saw a beast rising out of the sea, with ten horns and seven heads, with ten diadems on its horns and blasphemous names on its heads. And the beast that I saw was like a leopard; its feet were like a bear's, and its mouth was like a lion's mouth. And to it, the dragon gave his power and his throne and great authority. One of its heads seemed to have a mortal wound, but its mortal wound was healed, and the whole Earth marveled as they followed the beast.

And they worshiped the dragon, for he had given his authority to the beast, and they worshiped the beast, saying, "Who is like the beast, and who can fight against it?"

And the beast was given a mouth uttering haughty and blasphemous words, and it was allowed to exercise authority for forty-two months. It opened its mouth to utter blasphemies against God, blaspheming his name and his dwelling, that is, those who dwell in Heaven.

Also, it was allowed to make war on the saints and to conquer them. And authority was given it over every tribe and people and language and nation, and all who dwell on Earth will worship it, everyone whose name has not been written before the foundation of the world in the book of life of the Lamb who was slain.

The Day of Judgment

Isaiah 2:4

He shall judge between the nations and shall decide disputes for many peoples, and they shall beat their swords into plowshares, and their spears into pruning hooks; nation shall not lift up sword against nation, neither shall they learn war anymore.

Matthew 16:27

For the Son of Man is going to come with his angels in the glory of his Father, and then he will repay each person according to what he has done.

Matthew 24:37

For as were the days of Noah, so will be the coming of the Son of Man.

Luke 21:34-36

"But watch yourselves lest your hearts be weighed down with dissipation and drunkenness and cares of this life, and that day come upon you suddenly like a trap. For it will come upon all who dwell on the face of the whole Earth. But stay awake at all times, praying that you may have strength to escape all these things that are going to take place, and to stand before the Son of Man."

Acts 17:30-31

The times of ignorance God overlooked, but now he commands all people everywhere to repent because he has fixed a day on which he will judge the world in righteousness by a man whom he has appointed; and of this he has given assurance to all by raising him from the dead.

1 Corinthians 4:5

Therefore, do not pronounce judgment before the time, before the Lord comes, who will bring to light the things now hidden in darkness and will disclose the purposes of the heart. Then, each one will receive his commendation from God.

2 Peter 3:3-7

Knowing this, first of all, that scoffers will come in the last days with scoffing, following their own sinful desires. They will say, "Where is the promise of his coming? For ever since the fathers fell asleep, all things are continuing as they were from the beginning of creation." For they deliberately overlook this fact, that the heavens existed long ago, and the Earth was formed out of water and through water by the Word of God, and that by means of these, the world that then existed was deluged with water and perished. But by the same Word, the heavens and Earth that now exist are stored up for fire, being kept until the day of judgment and destruction of the ungodly.

2 Peter 3:10-13

But the day of the Lord will come like a thief, and then the heavens will pass away with a roar, and the heavenly bodies will be burned up and dissolved, and the Earth and the works that are done on it will be exposed. Since all these things are thus to be dissolved, what sort of people ought you to be in lives of holiness and godliness, waiting for and hastening the coming of the day of God, because of which the heavens will be set on fire and dissolved, and the heavenly bodies will melt as they burn! But according to his promise, we are waiting for new heavens and a new earth in which righteousness dwells.

Revelation 11:18

The nations raged, but your wrath came, and the time for the dead to be judged, and for rewarding your servants, the prophets and saints, and those who fear your name, both small and great, and for destroying the destroyers of the Earth.

Revelation 19:11-16

Then I saw Heaven opened, and behold, a white horse! The one sitting on it is called Faithful and True, and in righteousness, he judges and makes war. His eyes are like a flame of fire, and on his head are many diadems, and he has a name written that no one knows but himself. He is clothed in a robe dipped in blood, and the name by which he is called is The Word of God. And the armies of Heaven, arrayed in fine linen, white and pure, were following him on white horses. From his mouth comes a sharp sword with which to strike down the nations, and he will rule them with a rod of iron. He will tread the winepress of the fury of the wrath of God the Almighty. On his robe and on his thigh, he has a name written: King of kings and Lord of lords.

Revelation 22:12

Behold, I am coming soon, bringing my recompense with me, to repay everyone for what he has done.

Preparing for the End Times

Luke 21:36

But stay awake at all times, praying that you may have the strength to escape all these things that are going to take place and to stand before the Son of Man.

Romans 13:11

Besides this, you know the time that the hour has come for you to wake from sleep. For salvation is nearer to us now than when we first believed.

1 Thessalonians 5:23

Now, may the God of peace himself sanctify you completely, and may your whole Spirit and soul and body be kept blameless at the coming of our Lord Jesus Christ.

1 John 3:2

Beloved, we are God's children now, and what we will be has not yet appeared, but we know that when he appears, we shall be like him because we shall see him as he is.

Promise of Deliverance

Daniel 7:27

And the kingdom and the dominion and the greatness of the kingdoms under the whole Heaven shall be given to the people of the saints of the Most High; their kingdom shall be an everlasting kingdom, and all dominions shall serve and obey them.

Zechariah 14:8-9

On that day, living waters shall flow out from Jerusalem, half of them to the eastern sea and half of them to the western sea. It shall continue in summer as in winter. And the Lord will be king over all the Earth. On that day, the Lord will be one, and his name one.

1 Corinthians 15:52

In a moment, in the twinkling of an eye, at the last trumpet. For the trumpet will sound, and the dead will be raised imperishable, and we shall be changed.

Revelation 21:1-5

Then I saw a new heaven and a new earth, for the first Heaven and the first Earth had passed away, and the sea was no more. And I saw the holy city, new Jerusalem, coming down out of Heaven from God, prepared as a bride adorned for her husband.

And I heard a loud voice from the throne saying, "Behold, the dwelling place of God is with man. He will dwell with them, and they will be his people, and God himself will be with them as their God. He will wipe away every tear from their eyes, and death shall be no more, neither shall there be mourning, nor crying, nor pain anymore, for the former things have passed away."

And he who was seated on the throne said, "Behold, I am making all things new." Also, he said, "Write this down, for these words are trustworthy and true."

A graduate of Asbury Seminary, Nathan co-founded Christ Community Church with a fervent mission to serve the poor while making disciples of all nations. In 2017, he started Bridgetown Ventures, a ministry that empowers the marginalized to be architects of change in their own communities. In his transformative book <u>Storm the Gates</u>, Nathan invites readers to embody the core values essential to fulfilling the Great Commission, serving as a clarion call for compassion, faith, and global discipleship.

What is Godly behavior, and how does the Bible define Godly living?

Romans 12:2
New International Version

2 Do not conform to the pattern of this world, but be transformed by the renewing of your mind. Then, you will be able to test and approve what God's will is—his good, pleasing, and perfect will.

1 Peter 1:3
New International Version

Praise to God for a Living Hope

3 Praise be to the God and Father of our Lord Jesus Christ! In His great mercy, he has given us new birth into a living hope through the resurrection of Jesus Christ from the dead, 100 Bible Verses About Godly Living

Romans 12:2

Do not be conformed to this world, but be transformed by the renewal of your mind, that by testing, you may discern what is the will of God, what is good and acceptable and perfect.

2 Timothy 3:1-9

But understand this, that in the last days, there will come times of difficulty. For people will be lovers of self, lovers of money, proud, arrogant, abusive, disobedient to their parents, ungrateful, unholy, heartless, unappeasable, slanderous, without self-control, brutal, not loving good, treacherous, reckless, swollen with conceit, lovers of pleasure rather than lovers of God, having the appearance of godliness, but denying its power. Avoid such people.

1 Peter 2:11

Beloved, I urge you as sojourners and exiles to abstain from the passions of the flesh, which wage war against your soul.

Romans 12:1

I appeal to you, therefore, brothers, by the mercies of God, to present your bodies as a living sacrifice, holy and acceptable to God, which is your spiritual worship.

2 Corinthians 5:17

Therefore, if anyone is in Christ, he is a new creation. The old has passed away; behold, the new has come.

Galatians 5:22

But the fruit of the Spirit is love, joy, peace, patience, kindness, goodness, faithfulness,

1 Timothy 4:7

Have nothing to do with irreverent, silly myths. Rather, train yourself for godliness;

2 Timothy 3:16

All Scripture is breathed out by God and profitable for teaching, for reproof, for correction, and for training in righteousness.

1 Peter 2:2

Like newborn infants, long for the pure spiritual milk, that by it you may grow up into salvation—

Ephesians 4:1

I, therefore, a prisoner for the Lord, urge you to walk in a manner worthy of the calling to which you have been called,

John 14:6

Jesus said to him, "I am the way, the truth, and the life. No one comes to the Father except through me.

Galatians 5:16

But I say, walk by the Spirit, and you will not gratify the desires of the flesh.

James 1:1-27

James, a servant of God and of the Lord Jesus Christ, To the twelve tribes in the Dispersion: Greetings. Count it all joy, my brothers, when you meet trials of various kinds, for you know that the testing of your faith produces steadfastness. And let steadfastness have its full effect, that you may be perfect and complete, lacking in nothing. If any of you lacks wisdom, let him ask God, who gives generously to all without reproach, and it will be given him.

John 3:16

"For God so loved the world, that he gave his only Son, that whoever believes in him should not perish but have eternal life.

Hebrews 13:5

Keep your life free from the love of money, and be content with what you have, for he has said, "I will never leave you nor forsake you."

Psalm 119:105

Your Word is a lamp to my feet and a light to my path.

Romans 6:23

For the wages of sin is death, but the free gift of God is eternal life in Christ Jesus our Lord.

1 John 2:15-16

Do not love the world or the things in the world. If anyone loves the world, the love of the Father is not in him. For all that is in the world—the desires of the flesh and the desires of the eyes and pride of life—is not from the Father but is from the world.

1 Corinthians 11:1-34

Be imitators of me, as I am of Christ. I commend you because you remember me in everything and maintain the traditions even as I delivered them to you. But I want you to understand that the head of every man is Christ, the head of a wife is her husband, and the head of Christ is God. Every man who prays or prophesies with his head covered dishonors his head, but every wife who prays or prophesies with her head uncovered dishonors her head since it is the same as if her head were shaven.

Matthew 6:24

"No one can serve two masters, for either he will hate the one and love the other, or he will be devoted to the one and despise the other. You cannot serve God and money.

James 1:26

If anyone thinks he is religious and does not bridle his tongue but deceives his heart, this person's religion is worthless.

Philippians 4:13

I can do all things through him who strengthens me.

Proverbs 16:3

Commit your work to the Lord, and your plans will be established.

Galatians 2:20

I have been crucified with Christ. It is no longer I who live, but Christ who lives in me. And the life I now live in the flesh, I live by faith in the Son of God, who loved me and gave himself for me.

John 10:10

The thief comes only to steal, kill, and destroy. I came that they may have life and have it abundantly.

Genesis 2:7

Then the Lord God formed the man of dust from the ground and breathed into his nostrils the breath of life, and the man became a living creature.

Matthew 5:16

In the same way, let your light shine before others so that they may see your good works and give glory to your Father who is in Heaven.

Psalm 23:1-6

A Psalm of David. The Lord is my shepherd; I shall not want. He makes me lie down in green pastures. He leads me beside still waters. He restores my soul. He leads me in paths of righteousness for his name's sake. Even though I walk through the valley of the shadow of death, I will fear no evil, for you are with me; your rod and your staff, they comfort me. You prepare a table before me in the presence of my enemies; you anoint my head with oil; my cup overflows.

1 John 1:9

If we confess our sins, he is faithful and just to forgive us our sins and to cleanse us from all unrighteousness.

1 John 5:20

And we know that the Son of God has come and has given us understanding, so that we may know him who is true; and we are in him who is true, in his Son Jesus Christ. He is the true God and eternal life.

James 1:19-20

Know this, my beloved brothers:
Let every person be quick to hear.
Slow to speak.
Slow to anger, for the anger of man does not produce the righteousness of God.

Matthew 7:21-23

"Not everyone who says to me, 'Lord, Lord,' will enter the kingdom of Heaven, but the one who does the will of my Father who is in Heaven. On that day, many will say to me, 'Lord, Lord, did we not prophesy in your name, and cast out demons in your name, and do many mighty works in your name?' And then will I declare to them, 'I never knew you; depart from me, you workers of lawlessness.'

James 4:11-12

Do not speak evil against one another, brothers. The one who speaks against a brother or judges his brother speaks evil against the law and judges the law. But if you judge the law, you are not a doer of the law but a judge. There is only one lawgiver and judge, he who is able to save and to destroy. But who are you to judge your neighbor?

1 Corinthians 6:19-20

Or do you not know that your body is a temple of the Holy Spirit within you, whom you have from God? You are not your own, for you were bought with a price. So glorify God in your body.

Philippians 4:8

Finally, brothers, whatever is true, whatever is honorable, whatever is just, whatever is pure, whatever is lovely, whatever is commendable, if there is any excellence, if there is anything worthy of praise, think about these things.

Ephesians 4:32

Be kind to one another, tenderhearted, forgiving one another, as God in Christ forgave you.

John 11:25-26

Jesus said to her, "I am the resurrection and the life. Whoever believes in me, though he dies, yet shall he live, and everyone who lives and believes in me shall never die. Do you believe this?"

Proverbs 28:20

A faithful man will abound with blessings, but whoever hastens to be rich will not go unpunished.

James 4:1

What causes quarrels, and what causes fights among you? Is it not this, that your passions are at war within you?

James 2:14-24

What good is it, my brothers, if someone says he has faith but does not have works? Can that faith save him? If a brother or sister is poorly clothed and lacking in daily food, and one of you says to them, "Go in peace, be warmed and filled," without giving them the things needed for the body, what good is that? So also faith by itself, if it does not have works, is dead. But someone will say, "You have faith, and I have works." Show me your faith apart from your works, and I will show you my faith by my works.

Ephesians 4:26

Be angry and do not sin; do not let the sun go down on your anger,

Jeremiah 29:11

For I know the plans I have for you, declares the Lord, plans for welfare and not for evil, to give you a future and hope.

Genesis 1:20

And God said, "Let the waters swarm with swarms of living creatures, and let birds fly above the earth across the expanse of the heavens."

John 8:12

Again, Jesus spoke to them, saying, "I am the light of the world. Whoever follows me will not walk in darkness but will have the light of life."

John 7:38

Whoever believes in me, as the Scripture has said, 'Out of his heart will flow rivers of living water.'"

Hebrews 4:12

For the Word of God is living and active, sharper than any two-edged sword, piercing to the division of soul and of Spirit, of joints and of marrow, and discerning the thoughts and intentions of the heart.

Matthew 6:33

But seek first the kingdom of God and his righteousness, and all these things will be added to you.

1 Timothy 4:8

For while bodily training is of some value, godliness is of value in every way, as it holds promise for the present life and also for the life to come.

Ephesians 4:1-6

I, therefore, a prisoner for the Lord, urge you to walk in a manner worthy of the calling to which you have been called, with all humility and gentleness, with patience, bearing with one another in love, eager to maintain the unity of the Spirit in the bond of peace. There is one body and one Spirit—just as you were called to the one hope that belongs to your call— one Lord, one faith, one baptism.

John 6:35

Jesus said to them, "I am the bread of life; whoever comes to me shall not hunger, and whoever believes in me shall never thirst.

Luke 11:28

But he said, "Blessed rather are those who hear the word of God and keep it!"

Proverbs 14:27

The fear of the Lord is a fountain of life, that one may turn away from the snares of death.

Genesis 2:9

And out of the ground, the Lord God made to spring up every tree that is pleasant to the sight and good for food. The tree of life was in the midst of the garden, and the tree of the knowledge of good and evil.

1 Timothy 6:12

Fight the good fight of the faith. Take hold of the eternal life to which you were called and about which you made the good confession in the presence of many witnesses.

1 Thessalonians 5:22

Abstain from every form of evil.

Galatians 6:1-3

Brothers, if anyone is caught in any transgression, you who are spiritual should restore him in a spirit of gentleness. Keep watch on yourself, lest you too be tempted. Bear one another's burdens and so fulfill the law of Christ. For if anyone thinks he is something when he is nothing, he deceives himself.

Romans 12:17-21

Repay no one evil for evil, but give thought to do what is honorable in the sight of all. If possible, so far as it depends on you, live peaceably with all. Beloved, never avenge yourselves, but leave it to the wrath of God, for it is written, "Vengeance is mine, I will repay, says the Lord." On the contrary, "If your enemy is hungry, feed him; if he is thirsty, give him something to drink; for by so doing, you will heap burning coals on his head." Do not be overcome by evil, but overcome evil with good.

Matthew 4:4

But he answered, "It is written, "'Man shall not live by bread alone, but by every word that comes from the mouth of God.'"

Isaiah 41:10

Fear not, for I am with you; be not dismayed, for I am your God; I will strengthen you, I will help you, I will uphold you with my righteous right hand.

Proverbs 18:21

Death and life are in the power of the tongue, and those who love it will eat its fruits.

Genesis 1:1

In the beginning, God created the heavens and the Earth.

Revelation 1:1

The revelation of Jesus Christ, which God gave him to show to his servants the things that must soon take place. He made it known by sending his angel to his servant John,

James 2:8

If you really fulfill the royal law according to the Scripture, "You shall love your neighbor as yourself," you are doing well.

Colossians 3:5-10

Put to death, therefore, what is earthly in you: sexual immorality, impurity, passion, evil desire, and covetousness, which is idolatry. On account of these, the wrath of God is coming. In these, you, too, once walked when you were living in them. But now you must put them all away: anger, wrath, malice, slander, and obscene talk from your mouth. Do not lie to one another, seeing that you have put off the old self with its practices.

Romans 12:1-2

I appeal to you, therefore, brothers, by the mercies of God, to present your bodies as a living sacrifice, holy and acceptable to God, which is your spiritual worship. Do not be conformed to this world, but be transformed by the renewal of your mind, that by testing, you may discern what is the will of God, what is good and acceptable and perfect.

Romans 5:10

For if while we were enemies, we were reconciled to God by the death of his Son, much more, now that we are reconciled, shall we be saved by his life.

1 Peter 3:10

For "Whoever desires to love life and see good days, let him keep his tongue from evil and his lips from speaking deceit;

1 Peter 2:11-12

Beloved, I urge you as sojourners and exiles to abstain from the passions of the flesh, which wage war against your soul. Keep your conduct among the Gentiles honorable so that when they speak against you as evildoers, they may see your good deeds and glorify God on the day of visitation.

James 2:12-13

So speak and so act as those who are to be judged under the law of liberty. For judgment is without mercy to one who has shown no mercy. Mercy triumphs over judgment.

James 2:1

My brothers, show no partiality as you hold the faith in our Lord Jesus Christ, the Lord of glory.

James 1:22-27

But be doers of the Word, and not hearers only, deceiving yourselves. For if anyone is a hearer of the Word and not a doer, he is like a man who looks intently at his natural face in a mirror. For he looks at himself and goes away and at once forgets what he was like. But the one who looks into the perfect law, the law of liberty, and perseveres, being no hearer who forgets but a doer who acts, he will be blessed in his doing. If anyone thinks he is religious and does not bridle his tongue but deceives his heart, this person's religion is worthless.

Hebrews 1:3

He is the radiance of the glory of God and the exact imprint of his nature, and he upholds the universe by the Word of his power. After making purification for sins, he sat down at the right hand of the Majesty on high,

2 Timothy 3:16-17

All Scripture is breathed out by God and profitable for teaching, for reproof, for correction, and for training in righteousness, that the man of God may be complete, equipped for every good work.

1 Timothy 3:15

Few of the aspects of character

Colossians 3:23

Whatever you do, work heartily, as for the Lord and not for men,

Philippians 4:8-9

Finally, brothers, whatever is true, whatever is honorable, whatever is just, whatever is pure, whatever is lovely, whatever is commendable, if there is any excellence, if there is anything worthy of praise, think about these things. What you have learned, received, heard, and seen in me—practice these things, and the God of peace will be with you.

Deuteronomy 30:19-20

I call Heaven and Earth to witness against you today that I have set before you life and death, blessing and curse. Therefore choose life, that you and your offspring may live, loving the Lord your God, obeying his voice and holding fast to him, for he is your life and length of days, that you may dwell in the land that the Lord swore to your fathers, to Abraham, to Isaac, and to Jacob, to give them."

Leviticus 24:17-18

"Whoever takes a human life shall surely be put to death. Whoever takes an animal's life shall make it good, life for life.

Genesis 3:22-23

Then the Lord God said, "Behold, the man has become like one of us in knowing good and evil. Now, lest he reach out his hand and take also of the tree of life and eat, and live forever—" therefore the Lord God sent him out from the garden of Eden to work the ground from which he was taken.

Colossians 3:23-24

Whatever you do, work heartily, as for the Lord and not for men, knowing that from the Lord you will receive the inheritance as your reward. You are serving the Lord Christ.

Philippians 2:14-16

Do all things without grumbling or disputing, that you may be blameless and innocent, children of God without blemish in the midst of a crooked and twisted generation, among whom you shine as lights in the world, holding fast to the Word of life, so that in the day of Christ I may be proud that I did not run in vain or labor in vain.

2 Corinthians 5:21

For our sake, he made him to be sin who knew no sin so that in him we might become the righteousness of God.

Romans 3:23

For all have sinned and fall short of the glory of God,

Colossians 3:12-14

Put on then, as God's chosen ones, holy and beloved, compassionate hearts, kindness, humility, meekness, and patience, bearing with one another and, if one has a complaint against another, forgiving each other; as the Lord has forgiven you, so you also must forgive. And above all, these put on love, which binds everything together in perfect harmony.

Philippians 3:18-19

For many, of whom I have often told you and now tell you even with tears, walk as enemies of the cross of Christ. Their end is destruction, their God is their belly, and they glory in their shame, with minds set on earthly things.

Ephesians 5:5

For you may be sure of this, that everyone who is sexually immoral or impure, or who is covetous (that is, an idolater), has no inheritance in the kingdom of Christ and God.

Romans 8:18

For I consider that the sufferings of this present time are not worth comparing with the glory that is to be revealed to us.

Hebrews 12:1

Therefore, since we are surrounded by so great a cloud of witnesses, let us also lay aside every weight and sin which clings so closely, and let us run with endurance the race that is set before us.

2 Timothy 1:7

For God gave us a spirit not of fear but of power and love and self-control.

Philippians 2:3

Do nothing from selfish ambition or conceit, but in humility count others more significant than yourselves.

Romans 7:1-25

Or do you not know, brothers—for I am speaking to those who know the law—that the law is binding on a person only as long as he lives? A married woman is bound by law to her husband while he lives, but if her husband dies, she is released from the law of marriage. Accordingly, she will be called an adulteress if she lives with another man while her husband is alive. But if her husband dies, she is free from that law, and if she marries another man, she is not an adulteress. Likewise, my brothers, you also have died to the law through the body of Christ so that you may belong to another, to him who has been raised from the dead, in order that we may bear fruit for God. For while we were living in the flesh, our sinful passions, aroused by the law, were at work in our members to bear fruit for death.

John 15:13

Greater love has no one than this, that someone lay down his life for his friends.

Matthew 19:26

But Jesus looked at them and said, "With man, this is impossible, but with God, all things are possible."

Galatians 5:19-21

Now the works of the flesh are evident: sexual immorality, impurity, sensuality, idolatry, sorcery, enmity, strife, jealousy, fits of anger, rivalries, dissensions, divisions, envy, drunkenness, orgies, and things like these. I warn you, as I warned you before, that those who do such things will not inherit the kingdom of God.

Proverbs 11:12-13

Whoever belittles his neighbor lacks sense, but a man of understanding remains silent. Whoever goes about slandering reveals secrets, but he who is trustworthy in Spirit keeps a thing covered.

Psalm 118:1-29

Oh, give thanks to the Lord, for he is good, for his steadfast love endures forever! Let Israel say, "His steadfast love endures forever." Let the house of Aaron say, "His steadfast love endures forever." Let those who fear the Lord say, "His steadfast love endures forever." Out of my distress, I called on the Lord; the Lord answered me and set me free.

1 John 4:1

Beloved, do not believe every Spirit, but test the spirits to see whether they are from God, for many false prophets have gone out into the world.

Ephesians 2:20

Built on the foundation of the apostles and prophets, Christ Jesus himself being the cornerstone,

Romans 8:28

And we know that for those who love God, all things work together for good, for those who are called according to his purpose.

John 3:16-17

"For God so loved the world, that he gave his only Son, that whoever believes in him should not perish but have eternal life. For God did not send his Son into the world to condemn the world, but in order that the world might be saved through him.

Unless otherwise indicated, all content is licensed under a Creative Commons Attribution License. All Scripture quotations, unless otherwise indicated, are taken from The Holy Bible, English Standard Version. Copyright ©2001 by Crossway Bibles, a publishing ministry of Good News Publishers. Contact me: openbibleinfo (at) gmail.com. **Cite this page**: Editor: Stephen Smith. Publication date: July 9, 2023. Publisher: OpenBible.info.

Chapter Seventeen:

Definitions of "Father" and "Father's Eyes" in the most published book in this universe and the greatest book ever written, the Holy Bible. "Satan worshipers," atheists, agnostics, and "world citizens" of every religion, culture, society, and country in this universe and all universes may all benefit from, and what's more, prosper and maximize their accomplishments and "endeavors success stories" by studying, understanding, and then employing in real life the attitudes, perspectives, definitions, principles and concept or gestalt of "Father" and "Father's Eyes" as described and defined in this fascinating and life-changing chapter.

Characteristics of a Godly Father

(https://answersingenesis.org/train-up-a-child/raising-godly-children/characteristics-of-a-godly-father/)

by Scot Chadwick on June 17, 2016

Father's Day is designated as a time to celebrate fathers, yet we live in a culture where fathers are often ridiculed and dismissed as deadbeats. The portrayal of dads in pop culture is more than embarrassing. One journalist writes in an article titled, "Dumbing Down Dad: How Media Present Husbands, Fathers as Useless." It's not hard to find. If you watch TV, then you've most likely witnessed the portrayal of the modern-day husband and Father as lazy, incompetent, and stupid. Just these three characteristics are sure to bring to mind one commercial or sitcom that personifies this type of man.[1] How should Christians respond to this mindset toward fathers? And how should a father act by a biblical standard?

Children Walking in the Truth

Holidays like Father's Day and Mother's Day provide excellent opportunities to remember important principles and events, repent of personal failures, recalibrate toward the good and the right, and resolve to persevere toward righteousness. Father's Day should remind us that God-fearing parents of all ages have been concerned that their children would walk in the truth.

Father's Day should remind us that God-fearing parents of all ages have been concerned that their children would walk in the truth.

In the Bible, the patriarch Abraham was chosen by God to "command his children and his household after him to keep the way of the Lord, by doing righteousness and justice" (*Genesis 18:19*). Over 2,000 years later, the Apostle John celebrated the faith of his spiritual children, saying, "I have no greater joy than to hear that my children are walking in the truth" (*3 John 4*).

Raising godly children remains the burden and responsibility of all parents, especially fathers, as the Scripture says, "Fathers, do not provoke your children to anger, but bring them up in the discipline and instruction of the Lord" (*Ephesians 6:4*; cf. *Proverbs 22:6*). This commitment emulates the desire of our heavenly Father who seeks "godly offspring" from the covenantal marriage of a man and a woman (*Malachi 2:15*), and hopes that those children will pass along the faith to the generation after them (*Deuteronomy 6:2, 5–7*; *2 Timothy 2:2*).

Ungodly Influences

We live in a crazy, mixed-up world that is often anything but godly. Christians need to be wise to the fact that our secular culture is trying to influence us and our children to reject God and live however we please.

This ungodly, sinful desire is nothing new, but we need to discern these powerful influences.

Ever since our first parents disobeyed God, human societies have been corrupted with all kinds of sin in thought, Word, deed, attitude, and affection. The generations leading up to God's judgment in the Flood exhibited such gross defilement that God chose to judge the whole Earth, sparing only righteous Noah and his household:

The Lord saw that the wickedness of man was great on Earth and that every intention of the thoughts of his heart was only evil continually.

Now, the Earth was corrupt in God's sight, and the Earth was filled with violence. And God saw the Earth, and behold, it was corrupt, for all flesh had corrupted their way on the Earth (Genesis 6:5, 11–12)

Even after the Flood, God knew that "the intention of man's heart is evil from his youth" (*Genesis 8:21*), and this truth hasn't changed throughout human history. The Apostle Paul warns us that wicked human behavior and godless morality will become more prevalent as we proceed "in the last days":

But understand this, that in the last days, there will come times of difficulty. For people will be lovers of self, lovers of money, proud, arrogant, abusive, disobedient to their parents, ungrateful, unholy, heartless, unappeasable, slanderous, without self-control, brutal, not loving good, treacherous, reckless, swollen with conceit, lovers of pleasure rather than lovers of God, having the appearance of godliness, but denying its power. Avoid such people. (2 Timothy 3:1–5)

The wise parent seeks to protect children from sinful influences such as evil company (*1 Corinthians 15:33*) and worldly wisdom (*James 3:14–16*), helping them to pursue righteousness and practice self-control as they recognize the judgment to come (*Acts 24:25*). But it's not enough simply to isolate our children from evil—we must help our children discern between good and evil (*Hebrews 5:14, 12:7–11*) and encourage them to love and pursue the good (*Psalm 34:14; 2 Timothy 2:22*). As we help them, we should remember that "more is caught than taught." What our children see in us regarding our attitudes, affections, choices, words, and behavior can significantly influence them toward godliness or ungodliness.

While Paul might not have had any physical children, he certainly had many spiritual descendants. For example, he regarded the church in Corinth as his "beloved children":

I do not write these things to make you ashamed but to admonish you as my beloved children. For though you have countless guides in Christ, you do not have many fathers. For I became your Father in Christ Jesus through the gospel. I urge you, then, to be imitators of me. That is why I sent you Timothy, my beloved and faithful child in the Lord, to remind you of my ways in Christ, as I teach them everywhere in every church. (1 Corinthians 4:14–17)

A Model to Follow

One of the prevailing concerns Paul had in writing his second letter to his protégé Timothy was that Timothy would "not be ashamed of the testimony about our Lord, nor of me his prisoner, but share in suffering for the gospel by the power of God" (*2 Timothy 1:8*). In the context of an evil and unbelieving world, Paul wanted Timothy to "be strengthened by the grace that is in Christ Jesus" (*2:1*). Paul fully recognized that his life provided a model for Timothy and others to follow. He carefully lived his life in Christ, knowing that others were observing him.

You, however, have followed my teaching, my conduct, my aim in life, my faith, my patience, my love, my steadfastness, my persecutions and sufferings that happened to me at Antioch, at Iconium, and at Lystra— which persecutions I endured; yet from them all the Lord rescued me. Indeed, all who desire to live a godly life in Christ Jesus will be persecuted. (2 Timothy 3:10–12)

In this brief commendation in *2 Timothy 3:10–12*, Paul identified several observable aspects of his life to which all fathers should pay careful attention:

- **Teaching:** Sound teaching from God's Word should flow from the lips of a godly father so he can instruct, reprove, correct, and train himself and his family in righteousness. He should adhere closely to the Scriptures, meditating upon it constantly, speaking it to address particular needs, and ordering his life according to the Bible. This is a challenge, fathers: get into the Word and let the Word get into you.
- **Conduct:** A father's daily practice should match his eternal position in Christ, indicating he has been freed from bondage to sin and can now live in a manner pleasing to God. His behavior should be excellent in the sight of God and man, and his mode of everyday living must conscientiously declare that Jesus is Lord of his life.
- **Aim in Life:** With humble submission to our gracious heavenly Father's goodwill, a godly father lives intentionally according to principles derived from God's Word. He has decided beforehand how he will handle temptations and has resolved to pursue the righteousness of God.
- **Faith:** A godly father trusts and obeys the Scripture as the written record of God's revelation. He confidently rests upon the Bible for all matters of truth, recognizing that the eternal and all-knowing God has documented the foundation of everything we need to know for this life and the life to come.

A godly father does well to pay attention to his own example, knowing that his children and others are watching and may follow his lead.

- **Patience:** In the difficulties of life, a godly father keeps a cool spirit and bridles his tongue. Though he may become angry, he speaks and acts to promote peace. When troubles are beyond his

- control, he entrusts himself to a just God who directs all things according to His time and purposes.
- **Love:** A godly father exhibits growing affection for God by delighting in His Word, drawing near to Him in prayer, and resting in His sovereignty. His love for God translates into love for others such that he purposely and selflessly serves others according to their needs and best interests, beginning with his own wife and children.
- **Steadfastness:** Owing to his trust in and obedience to God, a righteous father endures challenging people and situations with hope, knowing that God sanctifies us through trials. He keeps moving forward in faith, knowing that following Christ is a long journey full of joys and sorrows, culminating in the glory to be revealed with Christ.
- **Persecutions:** Fully believing that the world hates God and those who stand for Him, a faithful father will embrace suffering for His sake and for the gospel of Jesus Christ. He is willing to struggle valiantly for the truth while aggressively loving opponents, believing that God may bring them to repentance.
- **Sufferings:** A godly father might not seek to suffer hardship for God, but he welcomes painful circumstances for His sake so that he can be purified through suffering, and this may give him opportunities to comfort others who are likewise afflicted.

A godly father does well to pay attention to his own example, knowing that his children and others are watching and may follow his lead. Paul had earlier exhorted Timothy, "Keep a close watch on yourself and on the teaching. Persist in this, for by so doing you will save both yourself and your hearers" (*1 Timothy 4:16*). This is why it breaks our hearts here at the ministry to see fathers mixing their Christianity with the religion of evolution and ignoring the doctrine of creation. It sets a bad example for the children of the next generation. Our mindset as physical or spiritual fathers should follow Paul's perspective: "Be imitators of me, as I am of Christ" (*1 Corinthians 11:1*).

Fruit for Your Labor

While paying careful attention to these things, a godly father also remembers that his own performance is no guarantee of his child's faith, but neither are his failures a guarantee of his child's spiritual catastrophe. We and our children can turn from our sin, and our gracious heavenly Father is so willing to forgive and cleanse a penitent soul. Just as godly Hezekiah begat vile Manasseh (who later repented), so wicked Amon also begat righteous Josiah. A father's influence can powerfully affect others, and he must faithfully fulfill his responsibilities, but we must leave the ultimate results to our gracious God. Happy Father's Day, and may the Lord give you fruit for your labor.

Footnotes

1. Sarah Petersen, "Dumbing Down Dad: How Media Present Husbands, Fathers as Useless," Deseret News, February 27, 2013, http://www.deseretnews.com/article/865574236/Dumbing-down-Dad-How-media-present-husbands-fathers-as-useless.html?pg=all.

Below are enlightening references and verses from the Bible, defining and further clarifying the concept of "Father's Eyes."

The Bible, New International Version, Acts Chapter 17, Verses 22-31:

22 Paul then stood up in the meeting of the Areopagus and said: "People of Athens! I see that in every way, you are very religious. **23** For as I walked around and looked carefully at your objects of worship, I even found an altar with this inscription: to an unknown god. So you are ignorant of the very thing you worship, and this is what I am going to proclaim to you.

24 "The God who made the world and everything in it is the Lord of Heaven and Earth and does not live in temples built by human hands. **25** And he is not served by human hands, as if he needed anything.

Rather, he himself gives everyone life and breath and everything else. **26** From one man he made all the nations, that they should inhabit the whole Earth; and he marked out their appointed times in history and the boundaries of their lands. **27** God did this so that they would seek him and perhaps reach out for him and find him, though he is not far from any one of us. **28** 'For in him we live and move and have our being.' [a] As some of your own poets have said, 'We are his offspring.' [b]

29 "Therefore, since we are God's offspring, we should not think that the divine being is like gold, silver, or stone—an image made by human design and skill. **30** In the past, God overlooked such ignorance, but now he commands all people everywhere to repent. **31** For he has set a day when he will judge the world with justice by the man he has appointed. He has given proof of this to everyone by raising him from the dead."

The Bible, New International Version, Romans Chapter 8, Verse 28

And we know that in all things, God works for the good of those who love him, who have been called according to his purpose.

A Godly father reveres God's Word (the Bible). Your role as a father is to guide and direct your children toward God, their creator, and to demonstrate by your actions that you are not only aware of what a Godly father is like but that you are making every attempt possible to be a Godly father as Jesus Christ demonstrated during his time on Earth, after God sent his Son, Jesus, to be an example of a Godly human, before being sacrificed and crucified (even though sinless), so that he could take on the sins of all present and future humans, who if they repent, will then have a pathway to Heaven, because of God's grace and mercy in allowing his Son, Jesus, to be the "sacrificial lamb" to erase the sins of those humans who repent of their sins before their death and honestly and earnestly live a Godly "reborn (in Christ Jesus) life" as soon as they learn of Jesus Christ, the Holy Spirit, and God the Father (also known as the "Holy Trinity"). A Godly father will show his children where to go for answers in their times of need, every second of every day, namely, God's Word or The Bible. In the Bible, James 1:5 states, "If any of you lacks wisdom, let him ask of God, who gives to all liberally and without reproach, and it will be given to him."

A Godly father teaches his children, in every aspect of life, Godly lessons that will benefit them and society during their generation and all future generations. "Train up a child in the way he should go," so that "even when he is old he will not depart from it" (Proverbs 22:6). This Bible verse applies to parent's children in general, sons and daughters.

What are the six characteristics of a godly child or adult in "Father's Eyes"?

In the Bible, in chapter 1 Timothy 6:11–12, the Bible clearly answers this question. "But as for you, O man of God, flee these things. Pursue righteousness, godliness, faith, love, steadfastness, and gentleness. Fight the good fight of the faith.

(Below Paragraphs From: 5 Character Traits Godly Men Value - Kerusso.com; July 23, 2020)

Five Character Traits Godly Men Value

The Greek philosopher Socrates is credited with having said, "The unexamined life is not worth living."

This school of thought, formed almost 2,500 years ago, still has relevance for modern believers of Christ. So, what does it mean to be a godly man?

Godly Men Characteristics

In 1 Timothy 6:11–12, the Bible reads, "But as for you, O man of God, flee these things. Pursue righteousness, godliness, faith, love, steadfastness, and gentleness. Fight the good fight of the faith. Take hold of the eternal life to which you were called and about which you made the good confession in the presence of many witnesses."

Just before these words, Timothy explained that those who argue for the sake of arguing and who refuse to hear the Word of Christ when in the temple for the sermon lack righteousness. He encourages us to pursue godly gain and avoid an unhealthy obsession with extreme wealth. He doesn't encourage poverty either, even discussing the food and clothing each person should have.

In verses 11 and 12, Timothy switches gears to a more positive tone. Instead of telling the reader what to avoid, he succinctly explains what a godly man embodies. The godly man expresses his belief in God publicly "in the presence of many witnesses," and his personality consists of six traits:

- righteousness
- godliness
- faithfulness
- love
- steadfastness
- gentleness

Of course, we're describing what makes a man godly, so we've already included godliness, but let's consider the other five items and a few more verses that offer an even more well-rounded look at God's kind of guy.

A passage in Titus adds to these traits (Titus 2:1–15). Verse 2 directs older men "to be sober-minded, dignified, self-controlled, sound in faith, in love, and in steadfastness."

Younger men get a different set of instructions in verses 6–8, which directs them to be "self-controlled… a model of good works, and in your teaching show integrity, dignity, and sound speech that cannot be condemned." So Titus adds to the list of ideal personality traits:

- sober-minded
- dignified
- self-controlled

- showing integrity
- of sound speech

With these passages, we've built a pretty full picture of a godly man. He's an honest gentleman who proudly declares that he loves God. He also shows love for others and speaks with restraint. The Bible describes the kind of nice guy you can rely on to be a good man.

Let's explore a few of the traits of a godly man a bit more in-depth. Five character traits rise to the top since they imbue more than one of the traits above and represent a few of the aspects of character worth cultivating.

A godly man is honest.

- In Proverbs 19:1, God's Word says, "Better is a poor person who walks in his integrity than one who is crooked in speech and is a fool."
- As men after God's own heart, it is vital for us to examine our words, deeds, and actions to see that they align with God's instructions for living to fulfill His good plans for our lives. Walking with integrity takes practice because we're faced with temptations to lie every day. Some lies make our lives easier, but to develop integrity, a godly man must develop honesty that he uses consistently.

A godly man is responsible.

- Romans 14:12 says, "So then, each of us will give an account of ourselves to God."

- Believers in God should set a goal to leave lasting value, impact others for eternity, and ultimately take responsibility for the legacy we are leaving in the name of Jesus. Whether our neighbor knows if we behaved irresponsibly shouldn't concern us as much as the fact that God knows. As we learn in James 4:17, we've sinned if we know the right thing to do but fail to do it.

Those verses make it easy to understand that a godly man can't embody a steadfast nature and righteousness and shirk his responsibility.

A godly man is generous.
2 Corinthians 9:6 says, "Remember this: Whoever sows sparingly will also reap sparingly, and whoever sows generously will also reap generously."

God's Word, the Bible, shows us that generosity can and should extend not just within our own family or our most familiar community but also to others who look, think, and act differently than we do. Throughout God's Word, we're admonished to generously give, such as in Acts 20:35. We're not to worry about doing so, but to give cheerfully (2 Corinthians 9:7) because God sees what we do and returns our generosity to us in the same measure (Luke 6:38). That doesn't mean dollar for dollar; it means in a pay-it-forward sense that when we do something to help someone, in the future someone will do something to help us (2 Corinthians 9:11). In Luke 12:33, God's Word explains that He will provide us with eternal life and treasure in Heaven for the good we do on Earth.

A godly man is patient.
Exodus 14:14 says, "The Lord will fight for you; you need only to be still."

When people refer to someone as having "the patience of Job," they say that for a reason. The godly man, Job, lost everything, but he didn't take matters into his own hands to seek justice for what he had lost. He fell to his knees and worshipped the Lord, and then he was still. In the quiet of his soul, Job knew God had a plan, and in the end, God restored to Job twice as much as he had in the beginning.

When things go wrong, it gets tough to remain patient since we're just ready for things to improve. The Bible admonishes us in Romans 12:12 to "be patient in tribulation," and Colossians 3:12 reminds us that as one of God's chosen ones, we each need to develop patience. Throughout the Bible, God reminds us that He only wants good things to happen to us, and if we'll only pray to Him, speaking our heart's desire, He'll open the door. Matthew 7:7, Philippians 4:6, and Jeremiah 29:11 all tell us essentially that.

A godly man is humble.

Philippians 2:3-4 says, "Do nothing from selfish ambition or conceit, but in humility count others more significant than yourselves. Let each of you look not only to his own interests but also to the interests of others."

Christ may have been born in a stable, but the Son of our Creator God was anything but ordinary. He lived a humble life, working as a carpenter while conducting His mission work. The miracles he performed showed us what it means to be a humble servant leader among men. He washed the feet of His followers, a task intended for one of the lowest servants in a household.

In John 13:1-38, we can read of His last night of freedom before the Romans took him into custody. He takes off the garments He wears when preaching and ties a towel around himself to wash the feet of His disciples, saying His goodbyes with full knowledge of what will occur in the following days.

The man of God strives to emulate Christ, doing for those around him without bragging about himself. True humility may go unnoticed because you won't call attention to it, but what greater humility is there?

Expressing Yourself as a God-Fearing Man

How you develop your godly character traits remains up to you. A godly man is a man who strives to become a better, godlier person, but only the Bible can properly tell you how to do that. We know from Scripture that a godly man prays and pursues spiritual growth.

As a godly man, wearing clothing that quietly exudes your faith can offer you another way to glorify God. Of course, we want every godly man to look good, too, so our T-shirts and hoodies offer simple reminders like "Hold Fast" and "Choose Joy." These pre-shrunk ring-spun cotton shirts offer a semi-fitted cut.

Are you living for the Lord and want to respectfully share your faith and belief in Christ with others?

(Above Paragraphs From: 5 Character Traits Godly Men Value – Kerusso.com ; July 23, 2020)

What does the Bible say about good fathers?

- **Ephesians 6:4:** "Fathers, do not provoke your children to anger, but bring them up in the discipline and instruction of the Lord."

- **Proverbs 1:8:** "Hear, my son, your father's instruction, and forsake not your mother's teaching."

- **2 Corinthians 6:18:** "And I will be a father to you, and you shall be sons and daughters to me, says the Lord Almighty."

- **Psalm 103:13:** "As a father has compassion on his children, so the Lord has compassion on those who fear him."

- **Proverbs 22:6:** "Start children off on the way they should go, and even when they are old, they will not turn from it."

- **2 Samuel 7:14-15:** "I will be a father to him, and he'll be a son to me. When he does wrong, I'll discipline him in the usual ways, the pitfalls and obstacles of this mortal life. But I'll never remove my gracious love from him."

- **Proverbs 23:22:** "Listen to your father, who gave you life, and do not despise your mother when she is old."

- **Proverbs 23:24:** "The father of a righteous child has great joy; a man who fathers a wise son rejoices in him."

- **Psalm 32:7-8:** "You are my hiding place; you will protect me from trouble and surround me with songs of deliverance."

- **Proverbs 4:11-12:** "I will guide you in the way of wisdom, and I will lead you in upright paths. When you walk, your steps will not be hampered, and when you run, you will not stumble."

- **Luke 15:20:** "But while he was still a long way off, his father saw him and was filled with compassion for him; he ran to his son, threw his arms around him, and kissed him."

- **Deuteronomy 1:31:** "There you saw how the Lord your God carried you, as a father carries his son, all the way you went until you reached this place."

- **Malachi 4:6:** "He will turn the hearts of the fathers to their children, and the hearts of the children to their fathers."

- **Hebrews 12:7:** "Endure hardship as discipline; God is treating you as sons. For what son is not disciplined by his father?"

- **Psalm 103:13:** "As a father has compassion on his children, so the Lord has compassion on those who fear him."

- **Proverbs 22:6:** "Start children off on the way they should go, and even when they are old, they will not turn from it."

- **2 Samuel 7:14-15:** "I will be a father to him, and he'll be a son to me."

- **Proverbs 4:1-2:** "Hear, children, fatherly instruction; pay attention to gain understanding. I'll teach you well. Don't abandon my instruction."

- **Proverbs 3:11-12:** "Don't reject the instruction of the Lord, my son; don't despise his correction. The Lord loves those he corrects, just like a father who treats his son with favor."

- **Proverbs 15:5:** "A fool doesn't like a father's instruction, but those who heed correction are mature."

- **Proverbs 23:24:** "The father of the righteous will be very happy; the one who gives life to the wise will rejoice."

- **Matthew 26:53:** "Or do you think that I'm not able to ask my Father, and he will send to me more than twelve battle groups of angels right away?"

- **Psalm 68:5:** "Father of orphans and defender of widows is God in his holy habitation."

- **Hebrews 12:9:** "What's more, we had human parents who disciplined us, and we respected them for it. How much more should we submit to the Father of spirits and live?"

- **1 Corinthians 13:7:** "Love puts up with all things, trusts in all things, hopes for all things, endures all things." (Note: Fatherhood means offering, without expecting anything in return, unconditional love, and like God, it means exhibiting trust, hope, endurance, constancy, and resilience.)

- **3 John 1:4:** "I have no greater joy than this: to hear that my children are living according to the truth."

- Luke 15:31: "Then his father said, 'Son, you are always with me, and everything I have is yours.'"

- Psalm 103:13: "Like a parent feels compassion for their children — that's how the Lord feels compassion for those who honor him."

- Luke 12:32: "Don't be afraid, little flock, because your Father delights in giving you the kingdom."

- Proverbs 4:11-12: "I teach you the path of wisdom. I lead you in straight courses. When you walk, you won't be hindered; when you run, you won't stumble."

- Psalm 127:3-5: "No doubt about it: children are a gift from the Lord; the fruit of the womb is a divine reward. The children born when one is young are like arrows in the hand of a warrior. The person who fills a quiver full with them is truly happy!"

- Proverbs 3:3-4: "Don't let loyalty and faithfulness leave you. Bind them on your neck; write them on the tablet of your heart. Then you will find favor and approval in the eyes of God and humanity."

- Proverbs 20:7: "The righteous live with integrity; happy are their children who come after them."

- Proverbs 14:26: "In the fear of the Lord is strong confidence and refuge for one's children."

- Deuteronomy 1:31: "And as you saw him do in the desert, throughout your entire journey, until you reached this very place, the Lord your God has carried you, just as a parent carries a child."

- Proverbs 1:8: "Listen, my son, to your father's instruction; don't neglect your mother's teaching."

- Ephesians 6:4: "As for parents, don't provoke your children to anger, but raise them with discipline and instruction about the Lord."

- Deuteronomy 6:6-7: "These words that I am commanding you today must always be on your minds. Recite them to your children. Talk about them when you are sitting around your house and when you are out and about; when you are lying down and when you are getting up."

- Psalm 78:4: "We won't hide them from their descendants; we'll tell the next generation all about the praise due the Lord and his strength — the wondrous works God has done."

- Psalm 103:8: "The Lord is compassionate and merciful, very patient, and full of faithful love."

- Jeremiah 31:3: "The Lord appeared to them from a distance: I have loved you with a love that lasts forever. And so, with unfailing love, I have drawn you to myself." (Note: God's love is forever, as should be the love of parents, father and mother included.)

- Lamentations 3:22: "Certainly, the faithful love of the Lord hasn't ended; certainly, God's compassion isn't through!" (Note: The Lord's consistent love, protection, and guidance are in perpetuity, as should be the love, protection, and guidance provided by parents ("Father's Eyes") to and for their children.)

- 2 Samuel 7:14-15: "I will be a father to him, and he will be a son to me … I will never take my faithful love away from him…" ("Father's Eyes" provide unwavering love and support in good times, but especially during bad times or after mistakes have been made or severe losses have been experienced, or when periods of trials and tribulations have begun in this tumultuous and tempestuous world, and continue to provide consistent unwavering love and support to each and every generation.)

• 2 Corinthians 6:18: "I will be a father to you, and you will be my sons and daughters, says the Lord Almighty." (**Every** human being must acknowledge and remember that we were and are all born equally loved and cherished by God as God's children and miracles of blessed existence in this universe, and will continue to have this irrevocable holy and blessed status each and every day, provided we acknowledge God's existence and live our lives as instructed by the Bible, as God's guide to humans on how to live God-like or Godly lives.)

• Proverbs 17:6: "Grandchildren are the crown of the elderly, and the glory of children is their parents."

• John 15:9: "As the Father loved me, I too have loved you. Remain in my love."

• Romans 8:14: "All who are led by God's Spirit are God's sons and daughters."

• 1 John 3:1: "See what kind of love the Father has given to us in that we should be called God's children, and that is what we are! Because the world didn't recognize him, it doesn't recognize us."

What are the Traits of a Godly father?

• Integrity, Worship, Purity, Prayer, Marriage,

• Constantly:

• Doing good works

• Striving to be righteous as defined by God in the Bible, the greatest & most published and read book ever.

• Truthful in all their daily activities and behavior

• Honest in their adherence to God's commandments

• Dedication to the Godly development, growth, health, and positive and joyous spiritual maturation of their family members preclude their selfish pursuits.

- Desires to develop in himself and all his family members, seven Godly attributes.

- What are examples of 7 godly attributes?

- Aseity. The aseity of God means "God is so independent that he does not need us." It is based on Acts 17:25, where it says that God "is not served by human hands, as if he needed anything" (N.I.V.) (Godly fathers should not need, require, or expect to receive thanks, love, or rewards for the loving deeds done for and on behalf of their family members, yet these always are God's blessings when received)

- Eternity (seeks for all his family to be reunited with God, their Creator, for eternity)

- Goodness

- Graciousness

- Holiness

- Immanence (the state of being present as a natural and permanent part of something)

- Immutability (unchanging over time or unable to be changed; Godly reliability and dependability)

- Impassibility (the theological *doctrine that God does not experience pain or pleasure from the actions of another being*)

What are the characteristics and features of Godly fathers with God-inspired and God-Guided leadership skills and attributes?

- servant attitude, love, kindness, peace, purity, truth, integrity, faithfulness, modesty, bravery, respect, and humility

What are considered the four pillars of a Godly man, a Godly father's heart, "biblical manhood (or Godly parents in general)," also known as "Father's Eyes," in the specific case of this book?

- The Four Pillars:
- 1) The Servant King,
- 2) The Tender Warrior,
- 3) The Wise Mentor, and
- 4) The Faithful Friend

11 Qualities of a Christian Father
by <u>DAVID PEACH</u>

Article by <u>David Peach</u>

<u>David Peach</u> has been in full-time mission work with the Deaf since 1994. He has started several deaf ministries in various countries and established a deaf church in Mexico. David now works as Director of Deaf Ministries for his mission board.

DAVID HAS WRITTEN *207* ARTICLES ON WHAT CHRISTIANS WANT TO KNOW!

Read more: <u>https://www.whatchristianswanttoknow.com/11-qualities-of-a-christian-father/#ixzz892SWSONF</u>

Billy Graham once said: "A good father is one of the most unsung, unpraised, unnoticed, and yet one of the most valuable assets in our society."

We can find many qualities of a good Christian father in the Bible. But we must start with the father simply being present. One statistic I read from the Department of Health and Human Services said that in 1996, 42% of single-mother households lived below the poverty level. Yet only 8% of households with married parents were considered poor. If the absence of <u>a father</u> from home makes that drastic difference in the finances, surely his absence affects so many other areas. Fathers, for the sake of your children and their future, be there for them.

But there is much more to being a godly Christian father than simply living in the same house. Here are 11 characteristics from the Bible that every Christian father should have.

Love God

Deuteronomy 6:4-9 "Hear, O Israel: The Lord our God is one Lord: And thou shalt love the Lord thy God with all thine heart, and with all thy soul, and with all thy might. And these words, which I command thee this day, shall be in thine heart: And thou shalt teach them diligently unto thy children, and shalt talk of them when thou sittest in thine house, and when thou walkest by the way, and when thou liest down, and when thou risest up. And thou shalt bind them for a sign upon thine hand, and they shall be as frontlets between thine eyes. And thou shalt write them upon the posts of thy house and on thy gates."

The classic passage on training children starts with loving God above all else. Our Jewish friends call this passage *Shema Yisrael* (which means "Hear, Israel"). It is the centerpiece of the Jewish prayer time. All of Israel is instructed to love God above all others. Then, parents are instructed to teach their children God's law. The promise in verse 2 of this chapter is a long life to those fathers and children who learn to obey and trust God.

This commandment is repeated in Mark 12:29 and 30. To be a good father, you must learn to love God above all else.

Love Others

Mark 12:31: "And the second [commandment] is like, namely this, Thou shalt love thy neighbor as thyself. There is none other commandment greater than these."

The first commandment is to love God, and the second is to love others. Without this, you cannot be a good Christian, and you cannot be a good father. To be a good Christian father, you must have the characteristic of love for others and demonstrate that love in your communications, behavior, and actions. This is not just for your own children but for all people. If you do not have this love, it will show in your life and negatively influence your children.

Besides being a good Christian characteristic, it is a command from our Lord. This even includes our enemies, as Jesus taught in the sermon on the mount (Matthew 5:43-48).

Mentor

Proverbs 22:6 "Train up a child in the way he should go: and when he is old, he will not depart from it."

"A good father is one of the most unsung, unpraised, unnoticed, and yet one of the most valuable assets in our society."

There is much discussion on this verse as to whether it is a promise or a principle. Regardless of your take on the topic, it should be clear what the command is. The command is to train children. That is something that I, as a father, can make a decision to do. But it is not just a command to train and teach because we are always modeling for our children how to live; it is a command to train, teach, and guide them in the way they should go. Train them in the right way. Be a mentor to them.

Patient

Ephesians 6:4: "And, ye fathers, provoke not your children to wrath: but bring them up in the nurture and admonition of the Lord."

Along with mentoring, it requires patience to train a child correctly. Do not provoke or frustrate your children with unreasonable demands. Losing your patience with your children creates tension for everyone.

It is very difficult and challenging for them to learn in such a caustic and chaotic environment.

Good Worker

Genesis 2:15: "And the Lord God took the man, and put him into the garden of Eden to dress it and to keep it."

God put Adam in the garden and gave him instructions to work. This was before the fall of Adam and Eve. From the very beginning, God planned that man would have a job to do. The difference after the fall is that work would become difficult.

Paul teaches in 2 Thessalonians 3:10-12 that men who are lazy and refuse to work should not be allowed to eat. Be careful with this passage. This does not mean that people who can't work shouldn't eat. It says that those who "would not work," meaning that they could, but they choose not to.

The following several characteristics are from the guidelines for pastors and deacons. While not all fathers need to be pastors to be considered godly fathers, it should be understood that only the best fathers with the best qualities would be qualified to be <u>pastors or deacons</u>.

Sober and Self-Controlled

1 Timothy 3:2: "A bishop then must be blameless, the husband of one wife, vigilant, sober, of good behavior, given to hospitality, apt to teach;"

We can conclude many things from the following verses, but let's focus on a few that are essential today in fathers.

In this context, sober means being self-controlled and not "flying off the handle" at their children or others.

One of the godliest examples in my life as a young man was my school principal. He was always very calm and even-tempered. It was rare for him to raise his voice, even when trying to get people's attention. That didn't mean things never bothered him; it is just that he did not show it outwardly by a display of extreme emotion. Any of his children would tell you he was not afraid to dole out punishment when necessary, but it was never out of anger. When my classmates, his children, or I ever got punished, we always felt it was because he loved us and he wanted us to turn out to be the best servants of God that we could be. Oh, that I could be a father like him.

Sober – Not a Drunkard

1 Timothy 3:3: "Not given to wine, no striker, not greedy of filthy lucre; but patient, not a brawler, not covetous;"

Paul says of deacons in verse 8, "Not given to much wine." Both of these are talking about drunkenness. The Bible teaches that a wise man will avoid alcohol completely (Proverbs 23:29-35). A quality of a Christian father should be one who avoids alcohol. Certainly, no drunk individual should ever be considered to be showing godly characteristics.

Blameless

1 Timothy 3:2, 10 "A bishop then must be blameless, the husband of one wife, vigilant, sober, of good behavior, given to hospitality, apt to teach;… And let these also first be proved; then let them use the office of a deacon, being found blameless."

This does not mean that the person has never done wrong but that he lives in such a way that when accusations come, people don't immediately assume they are true. And I am not talking about politicians here who pay people to clean up their past messes and shift the blame to others. I am talking about a man who people can trust because they don't see fault in this man and his character.

Do you know how you sometimes sense a bad or otherwise unfavorable feeling or feelings about someone after meeting them and communicating with them for several minutes? Do you begin to suspect they are hiding something? Try not to be that man. Live in such a way that people do not immediately jump to a guilty verdict when they hear a false accusation against you.

Worthy of Respect

1 Timothy 3:7: "Moreover he must have a good report of them which are without; lest he fall into reproach and the snare of the devil."

This whole passage points to people you could respect. Of course, children are supposed to obey and honor their parents (Ephesians 6:1, 2). The idea of honoring their parents is the idea of respect. 1 Timothy communicates the aspiration and concept of being a man that others can and should respect.

A couple of years ago, we began attending a church in the new town that we had moved to. Within a few weeks, a young couple left the church because of a job transfer. Everyone was sad to see Brian and his wife move. Though I had not met Brian at that point, I learned to respect him. Brian is about 15 years younger than I am. Yet, men 20 and 30 years older than me speak very highly and respectfully about Brian. Now, when Brian and his wife visit the church, there is a crowd in the back of the auditorium gathered around them. I would dare say that if he ever entered the ministry, he would have a church ready to hire him because of the excellent reputation he has built among the people.

Not a Lover of Money

1 Timothy 6:6-11 "But Godliness with contentment is great gain. For we brought nothing into this world, and it is certain we can carry nothing out. And having food and raiment let us be therewith content. But they that will be rich fall into temptation and a snare, and into many foolish and hurtful lusts, which drown men in destruction and perdition. For the love of money is the root of all evil: which while some coveted after, they have erred from the faith and pierced themselves through with many sorrows. But thou, O man of God, flee these things; and follow after righteousness, Godliness, faith, love, patience, meekness."

The qualifications of a deacon or preacher say that he should not be a lover of money. The verses above, which come from later in 1 Timothy, say that a man of God is a man who is content with what he has. Of course, we need money to live and care for our family, but that should not be the focus of our existence. Our focus should be on Godliness and training our children to value the same.

Manifest the Fruit of the Spirit

Galatians 5:22, 23: "But the fruit of the Spirit is love, joy, peace, longsuffering, gentleness, goodness, faith, meekness, temperance: against such there is no law."

There are characteristics in these two verses that should have been mentioned previously. As a Christian father whom the Holy Spirit guides and controls, you should manifest His work in your life by having these characteristics—and many more.

Take these 11 qualities of a Christian father and work on them. You may do well in some areas but not in others. Make it a point to do better in these lacking areas. Comb the Bible for other attitudes and character traits that you can implement in your life so that you can lead your family well.

7 Tips for the Christian Father
by DAVID PEACH

https://www.whatchristianswanttoknow.com/7-tips-for-the-christian-father/#ixzz892UdObh9

Fathers, it is important that we consider ourselves role models for our children. This is not something we can take lightly. It always bothers me when public figures say that they are not role models and should not be looked up to for how to live. However, they are a model by virtue of being a public figure. People will look up to them for leadership. They may or may not be a good one, but people are going to follow their lead. The same is true with fathers for our children. They will always look to us as an example of how to live. Saying "do as I say and not as I do" will not change the fact that you have young eyes watching your every move.

Here are seven tips for Christian fathers that I hope will be a help and blessing to you.

Love Your Wife

Loving the mother of your children is important to being a good dad. Children derive security and stability from knowing their parents are unified and <u>love one another</u>. Your children should see you doing special things for your wife. This is a good example of how they should treat their future spouse. It also gives them a chance to see a good relationship. With TV, music, and movies today, your children are being taught that many horrible relationships exist in the world. Your family does not need to be one of those.

Your children will copy what they see you doing, not just what you think you are doing.

Be a Role Model

As I mentioned in the introduction, realize that you are a role model. You should conscientiously and gladly perform that task. Your children will copy what they see you doing, not just what you think you are doing. Smile. Use good manners. Show respect to others—at all times. Your children live with you and see you every day. That also means they see you when you mess up. Admit your mistakes and use them as a teaching opportunity.

Respect Your Children

Ephesians 6:1 is a favorite verse of parents. It says that children should obey their parents. As fathers, we like that. The next verse says that they should honor and respect their parents. This chapter is getting better and better by the verse. Verse 4 then talks to fathers. It states that fathers (parents) are not to provoke their children to wrath. This means that you should not badger them. In other words, you should respect your children the same way they are supposed to <u>respect you</u>.

Give them rules to obey and expect them to comply. When this is done, without yelling and screaming, your kids know their limits and can easily live within the confines of those rules. You may think children hate rules and regulations and won't obey them. Turn that around and think how frustrated and provoked you are when you are unsure of what is expected of you at work. Each day, the boss changes his rules or expectations. It becomes a minefield just to step into the office. Would it not be much better to have written policies that everyone knew and that were enforced? Think how much less frustration there would be for you and your children if they knew what was expected of them. This puts a structure in place so that you can respect one another. But that respect is destroyed when you are not consistent with the rules you have agreed upon.

Talk With Your Children

Depending on the age of your children, it may or may not be easy to talk with them. At certain ages, they want to share everything with you. During those times, you need to be a good listener. This will help them know you care about them and the things going on in their lives. When the time comes that they are less likely to share with you, they will remember that you took the time to listen when their conversations were petty and immature.

As your children grow older, try to find and learn their interests along the way and during their winding path and journey to adulthood. This will give you a common ground for conversation. There will be rough years when you feel like they are not talking to you as much as you would like, but make sure they have your attention when they do talk. It will open up more opportunities in the future.

Take Your Children to Church

One of the best ways to find common ground with your children is to <u>share your faith</u> with them. They should grow up knowing that you love the Lord. There are an endless number of conversation topics if you both have a love for God's Word. Don't expect the church to do all the work in instilling this love. Going to church together is a tremendous and significant step in building love for God and giving you common beliefs.

Realize Each Child is Different

Understand that each child you have is different. Don't try to treat them all the same. If one child is strong-willed, then take the time to mold them into someone who will stand strong and firm for the right things. Help them to see that they need to be more gracious with others who don't see or currently experience the world the same as they do. You may find your next child is compliant and wants to please everyone. Help develop their sensitivity to the needs of others in a good way. However, they must also learn to stand up for themselves and what is right.

You cannot always expect that the teaching you give or provide to one child will necessarily work or be efficient and effective for all your other children. Treat each child as a unique individual and child of God, and you will raise godly children who honor the Lord.

Let Your Children Be Children!

<u>Be patient</u> with your young ones. They don't have the physical or mental maturity that you do. Allow them to be kids and make mistakes. That does not mean you should never push them to do their best, but also

realize their best may be far less than your best. One of the ways that parents can frustrate their children and provoke them to wrath is to set unrealistic expectations for them.

(The Above Articles were written by David Peach.)

David Peach has been in full-time missions work with the Deaf since 1994. He has started several deaf ministries in various countries and established a deaf church in Mexico. David now works as Director of Deaf Ministries for his mission board.

DAVID HAS WRITTEN *207* ARTICLES ON WHAT CHRISTIANS WANT TO KNOW!

Read more: https://www.whatchristianswanttoknow.com/11-qualities-of-a-christian-father/#ixzz892SWSONF)

What are examples of "Father's Eyes" spiritual disciplines? Prayer, Meditation, Confession, Worship, Forgiveness, Grace, Mercy, Compassion, Empathy, Humility, Generosity, Kindness, Joy, Contentment, Study, Simplicity, Guidance, Celebration, Thankfulness, Service

What Scripture honors fathers and mothers and requires or demands respect and reverence for "Father's Eyes"?

Exodus 20:12

"Honor your father and your mother so that your life will be long on the fertile land that the Lord your God is giving you." (Note: It's one of the Ten Commandments for an excellent and Godly reason, specifically, because God bestows the blessing and miracle of every human's birth on each individual's parents, Dad and Mom, so that you could be born as a blessing and creation of God, thus affording each human the opportunity to live a Godly life and thereby honor their Creator and savior, Jesus Christ, fulfilling God's vision for their life, fate, and destiny, and simultaneously enabling and facilitating all God's children to return to heaven to spend a blissful and miraculously joyful eternity with their originator or Creator, "Father's Eyes," also known as God and many other names in the Bible.)

Many Different (Selected) Names of God in the Bible

- The personal name of God YHWH (pronounced with the vocalizations Yahweh or Jehovah): Yahweh. Meaning: "I AM WHO I AM" or "the LORD"
- Hebrew titles: Elohim, Adonai, El-Shaddai, Abba / Father
- Elohim (Hebrew: אֱלֹהִים, romanized: ʾĔlōhīm: [(ʔ)elo'(h)im]), the plural of אֱלוֹהַּ (ʾĔlōah), is a Hebrew word meaning "gods" or "godhood". Although the word is plural, in the Hebrew Bible, it most often takes singular verbal or pronominal agreement and refers to a single deity, particularly the God of Israel.
- Adonai Meaning: "Lord" or "Master"
- El Shaddai Meaning: "God Almighty" or "God the All-Powerful" or "The All-Sufficient One."
- Ancient of Days
- Abba / Father, which is Hebrew, "Most High"
- Jehovah Chereb Meaning: "The LORD the sword"
- Jehovah Gibbor Meaning: "The LORD the mighty warrior."
- Jehovah Hashopet
- Jehovah Hoshiah
- Jehovah Kanna
- Jehovah-Nissi (The Lord My Banner)
- El-HaNe'eman (The God Who Is Faithful)
- El Sela (God My Rock)
- Jehovah-Rapha (The Lord Who Heals)
- Jehovah-Jireh (The Lord Who Provides)
- Rofeh
- Yahweh Rohi
- Yahweh Shammah
- Yahweh Shalom
- Yahweh Tsidkenu

What are the seven powerful names of God?

Tetragrammaton, Adonai, El, Elohim, Shaddai, Tzevaot; some also include I Am that I Am. In addition, the name Jah—because it forms part of the Tetragrammaton.

What are examples of good fathers in the Bible?

Adam was a good father, as described in the Bible in Genesis, but by no means was he perfect or sinless, as is the case with all humans on this earth and in this universe. Noah was an amazing and fantastic example of a Godly father, who despite being asked by God to build "Noah's Ark (actually God's Ark)," which likely sounded crazy to both his family members and humankind at that time, proceeded faithfully to construct the ark which ultimately allowed God to wipe out the evil path followers on earth, and start anew, with God-respecting and God-following humans who would once again, not only acknowledge God as their Creator, but also accept the fact that God desires (but does not need or require) his human creation's love and affection, and that God wishes to bless all humans that seek God, repent of their sins, and live Godly lives as taught by the life of Jesus Christ in the Bible. The possibility of dramatic, excessive, and continuous unrelenting rain that would not only result in a devastating and lethal flood to all inhabitants of earth, was beyond the imagination of his contemporaries and the society in which Noah lived and was a member of. However, much like many other biblical stories and accounts of other Godly fathers that have been God-inspired, God-fearing, and God-guided, Noah obeyed God's command for him to build the ark, which resulted in God's blessings, including the survival of Noah's family and all God's creations that God considered, rightly so, holy and Godly in their demonstration of their faith in God or merely by their innocence and non-participation in evil behavior and activities, again as defined ever so clearly in the Bible, in its entirety.

(Below paragraphs are from: <u>7 Great Fathers in the Bible - Manhood Journey</u>

; https://manhoodjourney.org/fathers-in-the-bible/#:~:text=While%20Adam%20had%20to%20learn,and%20their%20families%20from%20destruction.)

7 Great Fathers in the Bible - Manhood Journey

About the Author: Bob Bunn

Bob Bunn has spent more than twenty years in Christian publishing as a writer and editor. He currently serves as a content editor for the adult Bible study curriculum at Lifeway Christian Resources in Nashville, Tennessee. Bob holds B.S. and M.S. degrees in journalism and earned his M.Div. and an Ed.D. from The Southern Baptist Theological Seminary. He and his wife, Mary, are active members of Nashville's First Baptist Church, Nashville, Tennessee, where they raised their three children.

7 FATHERS IN THE BIBLE:

1) **Adam: When there's no instruction manual (Genesis 1–4).** As literally the first man on the earth, Adam was the first famous father in the Bible. But that also means he had no example to follow when his kids came along. He had to lean into his relationship with his heavenly Father, and that's not a bad place to be. When you feel like you're making it up as you go, turn to Him for direction.

2) **Noah: When God doesn't make sense (Genesis 6–8).** While Adam had to learn on the fly, Noah had to do something that had never been done—and it probably sounded a little crazy. Rain, much less a flood, was beyond the imagination of his culture. But like a lot of biblical fathers, he obeyed just the same. As a result, he saved his sons and their families from destruction.

3) **Abraham: When patience doesn't feel like a virtue (Genesis 12–21).** Like Noah, Abraham obeyed God even when the instructions seemed odd. But he also had the additional

challenge of waiting several decades before the Lord fulfilled His promise. Chances are that your kids aren't exactly what you'd like them to be just yet. But remember, God is at work even while we wait. We trust Him one step at a time and do our best to be faithful—just like Abraham.

4) **Job: When we lose it all (Job 1).** Job reflected many of the same qualities as other famous dads in Scripture. He loved his kids, and he even prayed for them regularly. But his greatest example came once he lost everything, including his children. Life is filled with tragedy and disappointment. During those situations, we probably teach our kids more about God and faith than all the other times combined. Those seasons aren't fun, but they can be teachable moments.

5) **Jehonadab: When you want to leave a legacy (2 Kings 10:15-17; Jeremiah 35).** Jehonadab probably doesn't roll off the tongue when you think about famous fathers in the Bible, but his impact on his family lasted for generations. We first see him helping King Jehu fulfill God's plan of wiping out Baal worship in Israel. But years later, long after Jehonadab was gone, Jeremiah met with some of his ancestors—the Rechabites—and they were still honoring him through their lives and their commitment to the Lord. Every dad leaves a legacy. We want to strive to live in a way that models Jehonadab.

6) **Joseph (Jesus's earthly dad): When your reputation is at stake (Matthew 1:18-25).** Joseph loved Mary but was also confused about what was happening. He wanted to do the right thing, but he wasn't sure what that right thing was—until God stepped in. Once he heard from the Lord, Joseph put all his fears and concerns behind him. Like Mary, he probably heard the snickers behind his back and saw the scowls of those who didn't believe his story. His reputation probably took a shot, but obeying God and getting the chance to help raise the Son of God was worth the trouble.

7) **Jairus: When your best isn't good enough (Mark 5:21–43; Matthew 9:18–26; Luke 8:40–56).** Jairus did everything the right way. When his daughter was on the brink of death, he turned to Jesus for help. But his world still fell apart. Like many biblical fathers (and contemporary dads), he faced a challenge of faith at that moment. He could give up or choose to keep trusting Jesus. <u>He remained faithful, and it made all the difference in the world.</u>

THE ONLY PERFECT EXAMPLE OF A FATHER

Of course, the most famous Father in Scripture isn't human at all. The Bible refers to God as our heavenly Father, and He provides the example we all need to follow. Even the best of us will fall well short of His perfection, but the stories He provides and describes of the joy and struggles of biblical fathers can help us become more like Him in our lives and our roles as dads.

How many books are in the Bible? This is a common question. The generally accepted answer is as follows below.

66 (is the generally accepted answer)

A number of biblical canons have since evolved. Christian biblical canons range from the 73 books of the Catholic Church canon, and the 66-book canon of most Protestant denominations, to the 81 books of the Ethiopian Orthodox Tewahedo Church canon, among others.

The below paragraphs are from:

<u>**Why Are Protestant and Catholic Bibles Different?**</u>

<u>Text & Canon Institute</u>

https://textandcanon.org/why-the-catholic-bible-has-more-books-than-the-protestant-bible/

November 7, 2021

JOHN D. MEADE

John (Ph.D., The Southern Baptist Theological Seminary) is a professor of the Old Testament, codirector of the Text & Canon Institute at Phoenix Seminary, and a contributor to the Hexapla Project. He is the author (with Ed Gallagher) of *The Biblical Canon Lists from Early Christianity* and *y Scribes and Scripture: The Amazing Story of How We Got the Bible* (con Peter Gurry).

canon

Why Are Protestant and Catholic Bibles Different?
Knowledge of the Bible's history clears away the caricatures and misinformation swirling around this common question.

John D. Meade
NOVEMBER 7, 2021

Why do Catholic Bibles contain more books than Protestant ones? Few questions provoke more curiosity (and angst) about the history of the Bible than why and how the two major Western branches of Christianity have different books in the Book. The Roman Catholic Bible has 73 books, while the Protestant Bible contains 66.

Both groups claim the Bible functions as their authority for doctrine, though admittedly in different ways. That is, Protestants and Catholics claim the Bible is their canon or authority for faith and morals. Before we can understand how each group reads their Bible, we need to learn the differences between the Bibles they read. To do that, we will detail the major differences, describe the history of the canon, and then show why the question matters.

The Differences

Catholics and Protestants have the same 27-book New Testament. Thus, the differences between their Bibles concern the boundaries of the Old Testament canon. In short, Catholics have 46 books, while Protestants have 39. Therefore, Catholics have seven more books and also some additions within shared books: Tobit, Judith, Wisdom of Solomon, Ecclesiasticus / Sirach / Ben Sira, 1–2 Maccabees, Baruch, and the additions to Daniel and Esther.

Protestants call these books collectively "the Apocrypha," while Catholics refer to them as "the Deuterocanon." Here, "Deuterocanon" does *not* mean second in authority but second only in reception in time. The Protestant Old Testament agrees with the narrower contents of the Hebrew canon (though not the ordering and numbering of books), while the Catholic Old Testament contains these same books plus the deuterocanonical books.

How the Different Canons Arose

At the start, several simplistic answers need to be avoided. These include the notion that Protestants *removed* books from the Bible or that Roman Catholics finally *published* their Bible pure and simple at the Council of Trent. As we will see, the Old Testament's history from the beginning of the Christian era to the 16th century was quite complex. One must understand the early history of the relationship of the canon to these other books before making sweeping statements about what happened in the 16th century.

Early Christian History (100–400 AD)

Early Christians answered the question "What is the Old Testament?" differently as they recognized the voice of their Shepherd in the Jewish writings that remained. Jesus and the Apostles did not leave behind a list of authoritative books for the earliest church, and there were various spiritually significant books and different opinions about them. The complete Greek Bible codices of the fourth century (Vaticanus,

Sinaiticus, Alexandrinus) contained many of the deuterocanonical books alongside the others. They were integrated alongside the rest of the Old Testament.

Christians were clearly copying and reading these books. Whether they considered them as having authority or not is a separate question, as we will see. Furthermore, in the third century, Christians began to cite the deuterocanonical books as "scripture." Clearly, they considered these works important. Although the New Testament and second-century authors never cite the deuterocanonical books *as Scripture*, they do allude to them, showing awareness of them. (See, for example, the allusion to the Jewish martyrs of 2 Maccabees 6–7 in Heb. 11:35.)

But Paul's statement in Romans 3:2, "the Jews were entrusted with the oracles of God," probably led many early Christians to conclude that the church's Old Testament canon should match the Jewish canon. The earliest, second- and third-century lists of Melito of Sardis, Bryennios list, Origen of Alexandria, and the fourth-century Greek lists (e.g., Cyril of Jerusalem, Athanasius of Alexandria, Gregory of Nazianzus) omitted almost all of the deuterocanonical books (e.g., some still included Baruch as part of Jeremiah).**1**

These Christians and others beside did *not* outright reject the deuterocanonical books. Rather, they considered them useful for believers to read for edification, but not authoritative for doctrine. That is, their first-tier-canonical books established doctrine for the church, while second-tier-readable books illustrated piety for believers. That is a crucial distinction that is sometimes lost today.

First-tier books established doctrine, while second-tier books illustrated piety for believers.

However, in the Latin West, another development was underway. Instead of asking whether a book was part of the Jewish canon, some early Christians accepted a book into the canon if the churches read and received that book. Augustine of Hippo and Pope Innocent I, for example, clearly accepted the deuterocanonical books based on this consideration. But other Latin Christians, such as Jerome of Stridon and Rufinus of Aquileia, continued to promote the narrower canon, placing the deuterocanonical books in a secondary list of edificatory books that did not establish church doctrine.

What this short survey shows is that fourth-century Christians were divided over the criteria for the Old Testament canon. Based on the canon lists, most Christians would have followed the Hebrew canon criterion for determining what belonged in their own. But others determined the Christian Old Testament by looking at what books the churches were reading in public and accepting. The two views agreed on the Hebrew canon but disagreed on the status of the deuterocanonical books, with some relegating them to a secondary, edificatory status and others integrating them with the rest of the books. The issue was still debated in the early Reformation period and into the period of the Roman Catholic response in the Council of Trent (1546).

Reformation Period and Council of Trent

Although the Council of Florence around 1445 included a list of Old Testament books that incorporated the deuterocanonical books, the list did not have a dogmatic definition. This means that Catholics before the Council of Trent were still debating the Old Testament canon in different ways. For example, Cardinal Ximénes (best known for his role as Grand Inquisitor), Cardinal Cajetan (known for his role as a reviewer of Martin Luther's teachings at the Diet of Augsburg in 1518), and the great Catholic scholar Erasmus would have probably agreed with the early Protestants on the contents of the Old Testament and the distinction between the canonical books and the edificatory deuterocanonical books. But other Catholic theologians were persuaded that Pope Innocent, Pope Eugenius, and the Council of Florence, among others, included the deuterocanonical books in the canon.

When the Council of Trent convened in 1546 to discuss the matter of the canon of Scripture, they committed to printing the list of books of the Council of Florence, but they did not believe they were settling once and for all the debate between Augustine and Jerome—a live debate at the time between Humanist and Protestant scholars on the one hand and Catholics on the other.

But when the council published its decree on the canon, the text did not clearly reflect this live debate. Instead, it came with an unqualified list of books that included the deuterocanonical books on the same tier as the other books. But the minutes and papers of the Council of Trent's meetings suggest a different story. They show that the theologians and church leaders believed they were not settling the long-held debate over the deuterocanonical books despite the fact that their decree published the wider list of books without any qualification or explanation. As one recent Catholic historian says, "In this case at least, the council itself must be held responsible for the misunderstanding." **2**

From this point forward, Catholic apologists, who should have known better, began to defend this canon as part of Roman Catholic identity. For their part, Protestants also understood Trent's decision as a way to include the deuterocanonical books that supported some of their doctrinal positions.

In 1566, Roman Catholic theologian Sixtus of Sienna coined the term "Deuterocanonical" to describe these books together with a few others that Christians would not call Deuterocanonical today (e.g., Revelation). By "Deuterocanonical," Sixtus means second in time of reception—not second in authority and dignity. These books were slower to be received into the church's canon of Scripture, and therefore, he called them deuterocanonical, while Protestants continued to call these books "Apocrypha," clearly preserving the ancient distinction between them and the canonical books.

Do the Differences Matter?

As early as 1519, the differences between these canons could be felt. At a debate in Leipzig, Martin Luther and Catholic Johann Maier von Eck debated the doctrine of Purgatory and the role of indulgences, among other issues. As Luther questioned the scriptural authority for Purgatory, he noted that 2 Maccabees 12:43–45 might offer some opinion, but "since Maccabees is not in the canon," it is only effective for the faithful and does not furnish such authority. Only books in the canon could establish doctrine. If a book's canonical status was disputed, as all the deuterocanonical books were, then it was not a sufficient authority. In this, Luther was appealing to Jerome's view.

In 1547, one year after Trent's decree on the canon, John Calvin, in his *Antidote*, argued that the leaders at Trent "provide themselves with new supports when they give full authority to the Apocryphal books. Out of the second of the Maccabees, they will prove Purgatory and the worship of saints; out of Tobit satisfactions, exorcisms, and whatnot. From Ecclesiasticus, they will borrow not a little. For from whence could they better draw their dregs?" **3**

These early Protestants understood clearly that the Apocryphal books taught different doctrines than the canonical books, and once the Roman Catholic Church lent full authority to them, many of their teachings could then find full support, too. Clearly, the differences between the two canons are not trivial. Canon means authority, and thus, an authoritative support for the church's teachings.

Clearly, the differences between the two canons are not trivial. Canon means authority, and thus, an authoritative support for the church's teachings.

Conclusion

Today, because of the different canons, Catholics and Protestants have different scriptural authorities. Opening up the history of the matter shows that Catholics at Trent did not think they were solving the canon debate or publishing the Catholic Bible once and for all, even if the decree had that effect.

Similarly, the history of the matter shows that Protestants were not removing books from the Bible, for their canon was not only traditional but, in so far as it cohered with the Hebrew canon, actually had the more ancient precedent. Knowledge of the Bible's history clears away the caricatures and misinformation swirling around this question.

JOHN D. MEADE

John (Ph.D., The Southern Baptist Theological Seminary) is a Professor of the Old Testament, Codirector of the Text & Canon Institute at Phoenix Seminary and a contributor to the Hexapla Project. He is the author (with Ed Gallagher) of *The Biblical Canon Lists from Early Christianity* and *y Scribes and Scripture: The Amazing Story of How We Got the Bible* (con Peter Gurry).

The Definitive, Divine Definition And True Life-Enhancing Significance Of "Father's Eyes":

"All that is necessary for triumph of evil is that good men do nothing."

"If you were indicted for being a Christian, would there be enough evidence to convict you?"

"True democracy makes no inquiry about the color of the skin, or the place of nativity, or any other similar circumstance." – Salmon P. Chase

"Focusing on diversity, while ignoring commonality, will never lead to or result in unity."

This generation is currently obsessed, in an ill-advised manner and with an extremely short-term perspective, with the phrase "Diversity, Equity, and Inclusion (D.E.I.)." "Father's Eyes" cautions this generation, and all past and future generations, that this D.E.I. phrase and abbreviation could very well be not only destructive but disastrous and devastating in its unexpected or unanticipated "end result" and consequences. "Diversity, Equity, and Inclusion (D.E.I.)," with more careful and thoughtful scrutiny, might be more accurately and surprisingly characterized by a completely different set of three words, especially when referring to this phrase's devastating "end result" and disastrous annihilation of and complete disregard for the concepts and principles of motivation, inspiration, work ethic, color-blind world skin color perspective, commonality of all humans as children and ever-expanding and maturing adults with progressively more discernment and wisdom each day of their God-guided life. Three such words that accurately characterize the harmful and dangerous "end result" of those who might otherwise naively embrace the phrase "Diversity, Equity, and Inclusion (D.E.I.)" are the following three words: Divisive, Embezzlement, and Invasion (or Implosion) (D.E.I.)."

Diversity in the acronym and phrase D.E.I. is more accurately the word "Divisive" and, in both the short-term and long-term, will result in the resurrection of evil racism that Martin Luther King, Jr. fought so brilliantly and bravely to defeat and wished to eradicate from this universe, from his birth until his untimely and tragic death.

Martin Luther King Jr. (born **Michael King Jr.**; January 15, 1929 – April 4, 1968) was an American Baptist minister and activist who was one of the most prominent leaders in the civil rights movement from 1955 until his assassination on April 4, 1968. A Black church leader and a son of early civil rights activist and minister Martin Luther King Sr., King advanced civil rights for people of color in the United States through nonviolence and civil disobedience. Inspired by his Christian beliefs and the nonviolent activism of Mahatma Gandhi, he led targeted, nonviolent resistance against Jim Crow laws and other forms of discrimination in the United States.

King participated in and led marches for the right to vote, desegregation, labor rights, and other civil rights.[1] He oversaw the 1955 Montgomery bus boycott and later became the first president of the Southern Christian Leadership Conference (SCLC). As president of the SCLC, he led the unsuccessful Albany Movement in Albany, Georgia, and helped organize some of the nonviolent 1963 protests in Birmingham, Alabama. King was one of the leaders of the 1963 March on Washington, where he delivered his "I Have a Dream" speech on the steps of the Lincoln Memorial. The civil rights movement achieved pivotal legislative gains in the Civil Rights Act of 1964, Voting Rights Act of 1965, and the Fair Housing Act of 1968.

The SCLC put into practice the tactics of nonviolent protest with some success by strategically choosing the methods and places in which protests were carried out. There were several dramatic standoffs with segregationist authorities, who frequently responded violently.[2] King was jailed several times. Federal Bureau of Investigation (F.B.I.) director J. Edgar Hoover considered King a radical and made him an object of the F.B.I.'s COINTELPRO from 1963 forward. F.B.I. agents investigated him for possible communist ties, spied on his personal life, and secretly recorded him. In 1964, the F.B.I. mailed King a threatening anonymous letter, which he interpreted as an attempt to make him commit suicide.[3]

On October 14, 1964, King won the Nobel Peace Prize for combating racial inequality through nonviolent resistance. 1965, he helped organize two of the three Selma to Montgomery marches. In his final years, he expanded his focus to include opposition to poverty, capitalism, and the Vietnam War. In 1968, King was planning a national occupation of Washington, D.C., to be called the Poor People's Campaign, when he was assassinated on April 4 in Memphis, Tennessee. His death was followed by national mourning, as well as anger, leading to riots in many U.S. cities. King was posthumously awarded the Presidential Medal of Freedom in 1977 and the Congressional Gold Medal in 2003. Martin Luther King Jr. Day was established as a holiday in cities and states throughout the United States beginning in 1971; the federal holiday was first observed in 1986. Hundreds of streets in the U.S. have been renamed in his honor, and <u>King County</u> in <u>Washington</u> was rededicated to him. The <u>Martin Luther King Jr. Memorial</u> on the <u>National Mall</u>

The National Mall is a landscaped park near the downtown area of Washington, D.C., the capital city of the United States of America.

In Washington, D.C., was dedicated in 2011.

The word diversity (more accurately, divisive) has been nefariously used in the past. It is also currently being used in a wicked and nefarious manner and with the deceptive, inaccurate, and untruthful supposition that specific skin colors should be given board seats or director positions on company rosters merely because they are female, transgender, gay, lesbian, black, brown, yellow or other skin colors or ethnicities or have a disability or psychiatric disease of one more types.

This errant mentality discards the merit-based system of advancement in life through honest and hard work, as defined by education, skills development, and perfection of performance of duties which qualify that individual to be considered worthy of a higher position of responsibility, respect, and leadership based on their already demonstrated professional education, communication skills, and ability to inspire and motivate their colleagues and coworkers by their life-long preparation and performance, which rightfully made them qualified to be interviewed and obtain the position they aspired to be assigned and worked so hard to be hired for.

When individuals are selected in a predetermined, biased, unethical manner which is not merit-based or based on the qualifications that make those individuals the best performers in those job positions being filled by the "highest-skilled and best-qualified" candidates for, e.g., a highly skilled and highly paid job of great importance and significance, and merely because they are different from other company directors or company board members or otherwise anomalous or distinct in one or more ways (e.g., female gender [versus male gender], transgender, gay, lesbian, black, brown, yellow or other skin colors or ethnicities or have a disability or psychiatric disease of one more types), yet without any identifiable skills or qualifications that would confirm or substantiate that they are a better candidate for that position than someone else who is "plain and ordinary" (e.g., similar to other highly educated and skilled directors or board members of the company), but highly skilled and best qualified for that job position, then this hiring of the "diversity" individual is not only racist, prejudicial, unjustified, unwarranted, but also unethical, immoral, dishonest, irresponsible and insulting to all the other job candidates who earnestly worked to be and were the best candidates for that job, but were discarded with disdain and disrespect, because they were not of the prejudged (unethically), "diversity" outlier group.

This application and interpretation of the word diversity is a travesty and a sin. This application and interpretation of the word diversity also stimulates hate, steals human motivation to work hard toward their occupational goals, makes college-educated students with hundreds of thousands of dollars in undergraduate or graduate school loan payments due, to wonder why they studied so hard and long, only to have their top occupation or job position given to someone else who was either unqualified or less qualified or less capable to carry out and perform the job role that they were hired to perform, again, merely because the competing job applicant was deemed to be in the prejudged pseudo-righteous "diversity" category or group, despite the truthful fact that the more competent and capable job applicant or applicants (in the "plain and ordinary" highest skill and performance group), was or were all simply banished and exiled from the job interview and company for the aforementioned evil and misguided reasons.

Is it not more wise and prudent to encourage all individuals to educate themselves to the greatest extent possible and receive the highest training available to obtain and perfect specific job and occupational skills and qualifications in order to effectively compete and then win, based on their own merit and qualifications, the job they seek and are interviewing and applying for, not based on their "diversity" (a.k.a., divisive quality or aspect), but rather based solely on and righteously and honestly on the years and effort they put into their preparation to be the very best candidate for and winner of that job interview and subsequent hiring for that job position? "Father's Eyes" greatly admires those who work diligently, honestly, and earnestly to achieve their goals without receiving special considerations, favoritism, prejudgments (that are not based on merit or qualifications), or other special advantages or privileges, all of which are unethical, immoral, and motivation and inspiration killers to those dreamers who thought their goals would be achieved and realized if they worked long enough and hard enough to become the best at what they do to obtain their dream job. "Diversity (a.k.a., Divisive)" is thus devastating to the "American Dream" (e.g., those who work the hardest can improve their position in life based on their effort, education, and training, and this earned higher position is unlimited in its potential upside) and is literally blinding to "Father's Eyes."

With regard to the word "equity" (a.k.a., embezzlement) in the phrase "Diversity, Equity, and Inclusion (D.E.I.)," this word is in direct defiance and contradictory to the very premise of the American Declaration of Independence! The United States of America is famous for both its founding fathers and their sagacity and brilliance in carefully constructing and "proof writing," and proofreading the American Declaration of Independence (which inspired them during the American Revolution to free themselves from England, enabling America to become an independent and free nation.

The second paragraph of the first article in the Declaration of Independence contains the phrase "Life, Liberty, and the pursuit of Happiness." (Note: Jefferson's original rough draft is on exhibit in the Library of Congress, in the city of Washington D.C., within the United States of America.)

We hold these truths to be self-evident, that all men are created equal, that they are endowed by their Creator with certain unalienable Rights, that among these are Life, Liberty and the pursuit of Happiness.

As a result of this masterpiece document, the Declaration of Independence, America won its independence from "Great Britain." It then subsequently enabled and empowered the same authors and others to create a subsequent masterpiece document known as the American Constitution, which then, as such the remarkable document that this was, encouraged, inspired, allowed for, and enabled (and currently enables) people from the entire world to legally immigrate to the United States of America to potentially pursue and achieve the "American Dream" (e.g., those who work the hardest can improve their position in life the most, based on their effort, education, and training, and this earned higher position is unlimited in its potential upside).

One must pay close attention to details to realize and comprehend the subtle brilliance of the content of the American Declaration of Independence. Note, most importantly, that this document did not unethically or ignorantly suppose, assume, or try to manipulate or dictate that all Americans should be granted, undeservedly, "equity." Any rational, reasonable, educated, logic-loving, truth-inspired, and motivated American knows that "equity" for all Americans is not a realistic, appropriate, reasonable, or practical goal, not on a daily, weekly, monthly, or yearly basis or in any circumstance or situation. Why is this? "Father's Eyes" acknowledges that while all children are born with equal worth and value, and as such, should show care, love, and respect to each other (regardless of what country, society, or "world citizens" they might have been born in and amongst) throughout their lives, as siblings of the same family of God, their "Father's Eyes" creator, protector, guidance counselor, and judge of their behavior, throughout their life and in "end times."

The subtle but profound brilliance of the American Declaration of Independence resides in the fact that this document contains the phrase "Life, Liberty and the **pursuit of** Happiness" (**not** "the guarantee of equity or equal Happiness among everyone, e.g., every "world citizen.") The reason is simple. All "God's children" born into this world ("humankind") must navigate their path in this life, and all individuals will have varied and distinct adventurous paths, with some paths being more tumultuous and tempestuous in nature than the paths of others.

Happiness, achievements, health, safety, confidence, choices to embrace morality and ethical, honest behavior versus running from or ignoring such values, principles, and behavior will largely be affected and dependent on how early in life all God's children born into this world, can find "Father's Eyes" trusted mentors who have the qualifications and ability to provide for them the God-intended and God-guided education they need and deserve, and to enlighten, inspire, and motivate them to seek out and embrace God's love for, God's direction for, and God's support for all his equally respected and created children.

Those who find God at the earliest age possible and acknowledge God and "Father's Eyes" importance to their lives and overall happiness will then be inclined, based on Bible teachings and stories of great wisdom and enlightening concepts, attitudes, and life perspectives, to work hard and diligently and fervently toward making their life, their family's life, and life of all those "children of God" and "world citizen" members around them and in their communities, better, stronger, healthier, happier, more educated, ethical, moral, inspired, and motivated to achieve unparalleled success that only God ("Father's Eyes") can facilitate and make feasible and possible.

The word equity should never equate to stealing money, salaries, or income from those most qualified and educated job applicants, often who spent hundreds of thousands of dollars for the higher levels of education and training, (e.g., Master's Degree or Doctorate Degree), to be the best job candidates that they are and have become as a direct result of their long and expensive education and training pathway, only to give these jobs to less qualified, less educated, individuals with documented evidence of less training, experience, and less evidence of skills expertise, based solely on prejudicially and biased decisions by company administrators who wish to select job candidates by, e.g., skin color, income level, or other fringe and radical criteria, such as transgender, gay, or lesbian sexual orientation or purported self-designated sexual preference status, by radical, misguided, deviant, or extremists ("Diversity, Equity, and Inclusion") job applicants with inferior training, judgment, and experience.

Inclusion, the third word in the deceptive and evil, misleading phrase, "Diversity, Equity, and Inclusion (D.E.I.)," which pretends to be benevolent in intent, yet is ungodly, disastrous and devastating in the potential future demolition and destruction of our God-blessed world, especially when misinterpreted and laced with evil intent to replace Godly society values with superficial, racial, prejudice, distorted perceptions of what determines an individual's worth and value on planet earth, from the time of their creation by God, and as God's children while growing up, until their final year of maturation and eventual death as a "senior child of God." When inclusion means you must hire ungodly sexually deviant and irreverent individuals who claim to be transgender, gay, or lesbian, or that you must hire a job applicant simply because they are a particular skin color (always prejudiced when important, vital, and essential decisions are inappropriately based on this meaningless factor), rather than determining who is the most qualified regardless of their sexual orientation or skin color (which is called "ethical and honest hiring"), then inclusion can only be equated, accurately and honestly, to the two words, "invasion" or "implosion." Invasion because sexual preferences or sexual orientations and skin color have invaded ethical, merit-based job hiring practices and protocols which are just, moral, ethical, honest, honorable, and Godly. Implosion is relevant because companies who hire unqualified individuals for job positions solely because of their supposed sexual preferences or based only on their skin color, in fact, is a "recipe for disaster and company implosion." When previously efficient companies are invaded by and then full of employees who are unqualified or the least qualified to perform their job (especially compared with the more qualified job candidates who were bypassed or passed over because they were too ordinary, too normal, too qualified, too competent, too capable, too talented, too educated, too skilled, and clearly had better judgment, common sense, and moral, ethical, hard-working attitudes, and Godly lifestyles, traits, and characteristics), these companies will then constantly be in danger of failure and bankruptcy due to the hiring of the least qualified job candidates versus the most motivated, dedicated, and qualified job candidates that they could have, should have, but chose not to hire, all due to their distorted, unwise, and prejudiced hiring perspectives, attitudes, and inappropriate actions in hiring unqualified job applicants.

Humans will always be young children of God, at any age, due to God's transcendence of the time spectrum and concomitant existence in the past, present, and future, thus outside the confines or limits of time, and always infinitely older, wiser, omniscient, omnipotent, and omnipresent, thus the greatest "Father's Eyes" that all his children could ever wish, hope, or ask for in our finite life and time on this earth before being reunited with our "Father's Eyes" in perpetuity in heaven, granted that we repent of our sins while on earth, as early as possible, live a Godly life, accept that Jesus Christ is our path to heaven, taking away our burden of sins, as God's gift (through the painful God/Human sacrifice of Jesus Christ, God's only son, being crucified on the cross, literally and symbolically, to take on the sins of all humans to the grave, for God's imperfect children, so that God's children can then enter, sinless, into heaven. God desires (without need of us, but God does unconditionally love and care for us) to be reunited with all his children shortly after their life journeys and mission (of spreading the word of God's salvation to all other humans on earth) are completed. After these journeys by all God's children are completed, God will joyously welcome all his children back (the reunion) to their heavenly home for eternity.

Inclusion, in the phrase "Diversity, Equity, and Inclusion (D.E.I.)," has already been tainted by Satan and evil influencers who have no respect, reverence, or belief in God's existence and benevolence, nor in God's inevitable and eventual judgment of the behavior, beliefs, and other actions of all his children born into this world, in the "end times." Those who do not seek God's word, guidance, and instructions as delineated clearly in the Bible at the earliest opportunity in life, and those who knew of God and the Bible but rejected both and denied their importance or relevance to or in their life, and those who fail to repent of their sins, fail to live a Godly life or fail to accept Jesus Christ as their savior, who died for their sins by crucifixion, despite never having sinned, so that all humans may return sinless to heaven, to be reunited with God, their Father and "Father's Eyes" in perpetuity, will be judged harshly and righteously in "end times" (e.g., the Rapture, Tribulation, Millenium, Second Coming eras described in the Bible in the book of Revelation), which is clearly communicated throughout the Bible, the greatest book ever written and the most published and read book ever!

Satan and evil, ungodly individuals would like to have you believe or will attempt to intimidate or violently protest or attempt to attack you and kill you if you do not believe and support their false and ungodly narrative that the word "inclusion" means that all Christians and Godly individuals should accept transgender, gay and lesbian individuals as the new normal instead of the "lost and misdirected, misguided children of God that they are and will always be, who need only repent of their sins against God their creator, and start living the Godly life that was intended for them as instructed in the teachings of the Bible, and seek proper and clinically indicated psychology assistance and psychiatric treatment and counseling for gender dysphoria issues they have that led them to sinful and ungodly choices to embrace being a gay, lesbian, or transgender individual rather than God's "Father's Eyes" intention for them to celebrate and rejoice and relish their birth gender and develop into the boy or girl they were born as, and bless God and their families and communities by being the best and most well-behaved God-respecting and God-fearing, holy male or female child of God that "Father's Eyes" determined they would be, again male or female only, at birth and remain as for the duration of their life. God does not make mistakes regarding the gender he assigns to all his children born to parents who are blessed with the gift(s) of God to have one or more children!

Inclusion (e.g., Invasion or Implosion) must never be equated with "children of God" and Christians compromising their Godly values, ethics, morals, as clearly taught in the Bible, to either accommodate or pacify those exerting "peer pressure" (more accurately in this specific case, "Satan pressure"), on them or toward them, or those evil individuals trying to convince the Godly Communities and Christians of this world that transgender, gay, lesbian, bestiality, or other promiscuous behavior such as fornication is anything but the truth, ungodly and sinful behavior, gender dysphoria requiring psychology or psychiatric counseling, education, therapy, and other treatment, including Bible reading to attain and retain, for life, God's wisdom and priceless guidance and teachings that are contained within the pages of this greatest and most enlightening book, inspired and blessed by God, that was ever written!

Against, and in critically important and direct defiance of those evil individuals in this universe who will constantly attempt to "divide and conquer" (e.g., deceptively steer all human beings ["world citizens"] toward hatred, jealousy, envy, and division based on nonsensical differences such as skin color, culture, or country of origin), a righteous battle must be waged and won by Christians each day of their existence, over these evil and ungodly individuals attempting to destroy our

God-created and God-blessed world and universe(s). God's kingdom, which is made up of all God's equally loved and cherished children who are born in each generation and created equal in "Father's Eyes," is constantly being attacked, covertly and overtly, by evil warmongers who reject and resent God, their Creator. Thus, a God-guided battle must be fought and won each and every day of every Godly human being's existence.

The clear and unified goal must be that all God's children (e.g., all humans worldwide or "world citizens") must defend against deceptive and sinister means, methods, and attacks that are waged by evil, God-rejecting, and God-defiant individuals or groups, on Godly individuals, communities, churches, values, and moral/ethical behavior and principles as taught clearly and unequivocally in the Holy Bible, "Father's Eyes."

For centuries now, these Satan-like, Satan-loving, Satan-worshiping individuals have been constantly and innovatively devising new means and methods to broach or penetrate and breach Godly values and God's fortress, in order to attack God's children, individually or in large groups, to accomplish their despicable goals and aspirations of subtly, inconspicuously, or even overtly and blatantly separating all God's children away from their beloved and loving Creator.

All God's created and beloved humans (a.k.a., "world [and all universes] citizens created by God"), who are equally valued, cared for, protected, respected, and loved by God, must remain strong and united in their Godly purpose and intent, to defeat their evil opponents in every battle waged and won, by God's omnipotence, oversight, direction, and protection.

God sent his son, Jesus Christ, down from heaven to live as a human role model and example of Godliness and to be sinless. God and Jesus Christ both were aware that Jesus would have to be crucified (murdered) so that all sinful humans may be forgiven of their sins if they acknowledge God, repent of their sins, and accept Jesus Christ as their savior, who voluntarily died to be a human sacrifice for all the sins of humanity in perpetuity. God's son, Jesus Christ, was crucified unjustly and used as a scapegoat (e.g., accused and unjustly charged with crimes he never committed) by his jealous and evil opponents who refused to recognize him as God's son and savior of the world. God sent his son, with and in love, to redeem and educate all God's human creations, e.g., God's children, that they could be saved by repenting of their sins, living a Godly life, and allowing Jesus Christ to take on and then wash clean all their human transgressions or sins, because (and despite the required fact that) Jesus was unjustly crucified (becoming a sinless sacrifice to God the Father for the dreadful and myriad sins of every human in every generation by this selfless sacrifice agreed to by Jesus Christ in order to be the savior of all God's children, sinful as they may be and are), and then, after achieving his savior mission and gift to all God's children who acknowledge and accept this sacrifice and savior event of Jesus Christ, underwent resurrection to be reunited with his loving God the Father, or "Father's Eyes."

God refuses to reject his human children creations, whom he loves unconditionally and regardless of the country, society, or community in which they are born, and despite their many imperfections, sins, defiance, rejections, evil attitudes, and evil behavior demonstrated by some of God's misguided and spiritually immature children. Knowing of this behavior, God sent his only son, Jesus Christ, to die for and accept the miserable and tortuous, painful task of dying (being crucified, a brutal and unwarranted, unjust execution he did not merit or deserve) for all humans and their sins in perpetuity, and for all generations, to give all God's creations (humans), a pathway to be reunited with their God and Creator in heaven.

Despite all human being's sins and imperfections, God created a pathway for their forgiveness and redemption so they can live with their loving Father and Creator throughout eternity. God only asks that his children repent of their sins, accept Jesus Christ, who sacrificed himself on God's behalf, and immediately start living a Godly life in order to spend eternity with God in heaven. God's wish and desire (note that the word "need" was and never will be specifically mentioned with regard to God, who wishes us to be reunited with him in heaven but is in no need of any one individual to exist and proceed throughout time, continuing in his role of "Father's Eyes," granting through his benevolence and Godliness, blessings and protection for all his children creations born into this world), is to be forever in love with and reunited with all his creations (e.g., every human being and child of God that he created and gave birth to via their assigned parents), both while they exist on earth and during the Second Coming, Tribulation, Millenium, and Rapture, as described in the Bible, the book of Revelation. After each of God's children and adults, having received God's and Jesus Christ's messages of salvation, have had the opportunity to share this uplifting message with each and every human they come in contact with during their life on earth and in this universe, and after all God's children or adults have repented of their sins and accepted Jesus Christ as their martyr and savior, only then may God's children and adults enter into heaven to be forever reunited with their compassionate, graceful, merciful, living, loving, Creator, who was, is, and always will be, forever, omnipotent, omnipresent, omniscient, and who will rejoice and unconditionally love and celebrate the return of his Godly children and adult creations from earth to heaven, and cherish their godly "Father's Eyes" transformation in perpetuity!

Winston Anselm Irons

(The above excerpts/chapters are from the book "Father's Eyes: Daily Devotions To Life Happiness, Health, And Fulfillment.")

CHAPTER FOURTEEN:

Analysis Of Fifty Superheroes Who Became The Truly Elite And Honorable During This Century Or Past Centuries And Synopses Of Their Endeavors And Life Achievements Along With Their Profile Portraits And Classic Statements, Communications, Brief Descriptions Of Their Demonstrated Superhero Perspectives, Attitudes, Actions, Behaviors, And Their Other Messages To This World For This Generations And All Future Generations! All Readers Who Seek To Learn From These Superhero Mentors To Become Superheroes During Their Own Lifetimes Have The Potential To Become Superheroes Themselves If Exceptional Steadfastness, Ethical/Moral/God-Respecting Behavior, And Earnest Effort, Work, Courage, and Resilience To Accomplish Their Benevolent Aspirations, Goals, And Glorious Superhero Destinies Are Pursued With Unwavering Determination. With Regard To Superhero Status Achievements In Life, There Has Never Been A More Succinct And Precise Synopsis Statement or Philosophy To Inspire, Motivate, And Induce Or Initiate A Gestalt And Paradigm Shift In Every Individual Who Chooses This Endeavor And To Embark On This Magnificent Zenith Goal In Life To Be A Superhero And Mentor For And To All "World Citizens" In This Generation And Future Generations: "It takes one to know one ('Superhero')."

This Concluding Chapter Will Enlighten All Readers By Means Of Its Concise Yet In-Depth Study And Analysis Of 50 Real-Life And Real-World Superheroes That Became Truly Elite And Honorable, Thus Mentors To All "World Citizens," As A Result Of Their Perspectives, Aspirations, Goals, Endeavors, Resilience, Courage, Fortitude, And Magnificent Accomplishments.These Truly Elite And Honorable Superheroes Also Are All Characterized By Their Ethics, Morality, Honor, Bravery, Respect for Democracy, Human Rights, Freedom, And Defense And Protection Of The Independence, Health, And Well-Being Of All World Citizens In The Last Several Centuries. Below Is An Introductory List Of These Surperheroes That We Will Discover, Explore, Study, And Analyze In Depth To Attain Priceless And Life-Transforming Knowledge Of Their Surprisingly Near-Identical Characteristics, Qualities, Perspectives, Attitudes, And Traits, In The Paragraphs That Follow This List, That Empowered All These Superheroes From The Past Several Centuries To Be Acknowledged, Recognized, And Honored To Be Included On This List Below.

1) Winston Churchill
2) Abraham Lincoln
3) George Washington
4) Martin Luther King Jr.
5) Nelson Mandela (1918-2013)
6) Mohandas Karamchand Gandhi ("Mahatma Gandhi," 1869-1948)
7) Dalai Lama
8) Mother Theresa
9) Dr. Albert Schweitzer
10) Dietrich Bonhoeffer
11) C. S. Lewis
12) Billy Graham
13) D. L. Moody
14) Watchman Nee
15) Blaise Pascal
16) Desmond Tutu

17) Oskar Schindler (1908—1974)
18) Harriet Tubman
19) Rosa Parks (1913-2005)
20) Frederick Douglas (1818-1895)
21) Susan B. Anthony
22) Eleanor Roosevelt
23) Cesar Chavez
24) Corrie ten Boom
25) Anne Frank
26) Florence Nightingale
27) Jackie Robinson
28) Ruby Bridges
29) Katherine Johnson
30) Leonardo da Vinci
31) Sir Francis Bacon
32) Albert Einstein
33) Amelia Earhart
34) Chief Joseph (1840-1904)
35) Irena Sendler
36) Raoul Wallenberg
37) Malala Yousafzai
38) Vaclav Havel
39) Wangari Maathai
40) Neil Armstrong
41) Sally Ride
42) Joan of Arc (Jeanne d'Arc)
43) Aung San Suu Kyi
44) Lech Walesa
45) Emmeline Pankhurst
46) Luis Palau
47) William Wilberforce
48) John Stott
49) A. W. Tozer
50) CharlesSwindoll

1. Winston Churchill

Winston Churchill (1874-1965) was the Prime Minister of the United Kingdom during World War II. His leadership and oratory skills were crucial in rallying the British people during the darkest days of the war. Churchill's steadfast resolve and inspiring speeches helped to maintain British morale and resistance against Nazi Germany, ultimately contributing to the Allied victory[1] [2].

---

1   https://en.wikipedia.org/wiki/Winston_Churchill

2   https://www.britannica.com/biography/Winston-Churchill

2. Abraham Lincoln

Abraham Lincoln (1809-1865) served as the 16th President of the United States. He led the nation through the Civil War, preserved the Union, and issued the Emancipation Proclamation, which began the process of freedom for America's slaves. Lincoln's leadership and dedication to equality and democracy have left an enduring legacy[3] [4].

---

[3] https://en.wikipedia.org/wiki/Abraham_Lincoln

[4] https://www.history.com/topics/us-presidents/abraham-lincoln

3. George Washington

George Washington (1732-1799) was the first President of the United States and is often referred to as the "Father of His Country." He led the Continental Army to victory over the British in the American Revolutionary War and presided over the Constitutional Convention of 1787. Washington's leadership set many precedents for the new nation[5][6].

---

[5] https://en.wikipedia.org/wiki/George_Washington

[6] https://www.britannica.com/biography/George-Washington

4. Martin Luther King Jr.

Martin Luther King Jr. (1929-1968) was a Baptist minister and civil rights leader who played a pivotal role in the American civil rights movement. He advocated for nonviolent resistance and led numerous campaigns to end racial segregation and promote equality. His famous "I Have a Dream" speech remains a symbol of the fight for civil rights[7] [8].

---

[7] https://en.wikipedia.org/wiki/Martin_Luther_King_Jr

[8] https://www.britannica.com/biography/Martin-Luther-King-Jr

5. Nelson Mandela

Nelson Mandela (1918-2013) was a South African anti-apartheid revolutionary and political leader who served as President of South Africa from 1994 to 1999. He was the country's first black head of state and the first elected in a fully representative democratic election. Mandela's leadership in dismantling apartheid and fostering reconciliation and peace earned him global admiration and the Nobel Peace Prize in 1993.

6. Mahatma Gandhi

Mahatma Gandhi (1869-1948) was an Indian lawyer, anti-colonial nationalist, and political ethicist who employed nonviolent resistance to lead the successful campaign for India's independence from British rule. His philosophy of nonviolence and civil disobedience has inspired movements for civil rights and freedom across the world.

7. Dalai Lama

Dalai Lama is the spiritual leader of Tibetan Buddhism and a symbol of peace and compassion. The 14th Dalai Lama, Tenzin Gyatso, has been a tireless advocate for the rights and autonomy of the Tibetan people and has promoted nonviolence, interfaith dialogue, and human values globally. He was awarded the Nobel Peace Prize in 1989.

8. Mother Teresa

Mother Teresa (1910-1997) was a Roman Catholic nun and missionary who founded the Missionaries of Charity, a religious congregation dedicated to helping the poorest of the poor. Her selfless work in the slums of Calcutta (now Kolkata) brought her international recognition and numerous awards, including the Nobel Peace Prize in 1979.

9. Dr. Albert Schweitzer

Dr. Albert Schweitzer (1875-1965) was a theologian, organist, writer, humanitarian, philosopher, and physician. He is best known for founding the Albert Schweitzer Hospital in Lambaréné, Gabon, where he provided medical care to the local population. Schweitzer's philosophy of "Reverence for Life" and his dedication to humanitarian work earned him the Nobel Peace Prize in 1952.

Superheroes

10. **Dietrich Bonhoeffer**

Bonhoeffer Dietrich Bonhoeffer (1906-1945) was a German Lutheran pastor, theologian, and anti-Nazi dissident. He was a founding member of the Confessing Church, which opposed the Nazi regime.

11. C. S. Lewis

C. S. Lewis (1898-1963) was a British writer and lay theologian, best known for his works of fiction, including "The Chronicles of Narnia," and his Christian apologetics, such as "Mere Christianity." Lewis's writings have inspired millions and continue to be influential in both literary and religious circles.

12. Billy Graham

Billy Graham (1918-2018) was an American evangelist and a prominent Christian figure of the 20th century. He conducted numerous crusades, preaching to millions around the world and reaching even more through radio and television. Graham's message of salvation and his efforts to promote social justice and racial equality have left a significant legacy.

13. Dwight L. Moody

Dwight L. Moody (1837-1899) was an American evangelist and publisher who founded the Moody Church, Northfield School, and Mount Hermon School in Massachusetts, as well as the Moody Bible Institute and Moody Publishers in Chicago. His dynamic preaching and commitment to education and evangelism had a profound impact on American Christianity.

14. Watchman Nee

Watchman Nee (1903-1972) was a Chinese church leader and Christian teacher who founded the Local Churches movement. His extensive writings on Christian living and church practice have influenced millions of Christians worldwide. Despite being imprisoned for his faith, Nee's legacy continues through his books and teachings.

15. Blaise Pascal

Blaise Pascal (1623-1662) was a French mathematician, physicist, inventor, writer, and Catholic theologian. He made significant contributions to the fields of mathematics and science, including the development of Pascal's Triangle and Pascal's Law. His philosophical work, "Pensées," remains a seminal text in Christian apologetics.

Superheroes

16. Desmond Tutu

Desmond Tutu (1931-2021) was a South African Anglican bishop and social rights activist. He was a leading figure in the fight against apartheid and was awarded the Nobel Peace Prize in 1984 for his efforts. Tutu's advocacy for peace, justice, and reconciliation has left a lasting impact on South Africa and the world.

17. Oskar Schindler

Oskar Schindler (1908-1974) was a German industrialist and member of the Nazi Party who is credited with saving the lives of 1,200 Jews during the Holocaust by employing them in his factories. His efforts to protect his Jewish workers from deportation and death have been immortalized in the book "Schindler's Ark" and the film "Schindler's List."

18. Harriet Tubman

Harriet Tubman (1822-1913) was an American abolitionist and political activist. Born into slavery, she escaped and subsequently made some 13 missions to rescue approximately 70 enslaved people, including family and friends, using the network of antislavery activists and safe houses known as the Underground Railroad. Tubman also served as a scout and spy for the Union Army during the Civil War

19. Rosa Parks

Rosa Parks (1913-2005) was an American civil rights activist best known for her pivotal role in the Montgomery Bus Boycott. Her refusal to give up her seat to a white passenger on a segregated bus in Montgomery, Alabama, in 1955 sparked a city-wide boycott and became a symbol of the fight against racial segregation and injustice.

Superheroes

20. Frederick Douglass

Frederick Douglass (1818-1895) was an American social reformer, abolitionist, orator, writer, and statesman. Born into slavery, Douglass escaped and became a national leader of the abolitionist movement in Massachusetts and New York. His powerful speeches and writings, including his autobiography "Narrative of the Life of Frederick Douglass, an American Slave," were instrumental in advocating for the end of slavery and the advancement of civil rights.

21. Susan B. Anthony

Susan B. Anthony (1820-1906) was an American social reformer and women's rights activist who played a pivotal role in the women's suffrage movement. She co-founded the National Woman Suffrage Association and tirelessly campaigned for women's right to vote, which was eventually granted with the passage of the 19th Amendment in 1920.

22. Eleanor Roosevelt

Eleanor Roosevelt (1884-1962) was an American political figure, diplomat, and activist. She served as the First Lady of the United States from 1933 to 1945 and was a key advocate for civil rights, women's rights, and the rights of World War II refugees. Roosevelt also played a significant role in the drafting of the Universal Declaration of Human Rights.

23. Cesar Chavez

Cesar Chavez (1927-1993) was an American labor leader and civil rights activist who co-founded the National Farm Workers Association, later known as the United Farm Workers (UFW). Chavez dedicated his life to improving the working conditions and wages of farm workers through nonviolent means, including strikes, boycotts, and marches.

24. Corrie ten Boom

Corrie ten Boom (1892-1983) was a Dutch Christian watchmaker and author who, along with her family, helped many Jews escape the Nazi Holocaust during World War II by hiding them in their home. Her book "The Hiding Place" recounts her experiences and her unwavering faith in the face of adversity.

25. Anne Frank

Anne Frank (1929-1945) was a Jewish girl who hid with her family during the Nazi occupation of the Netherlands. Her diary, written while in hiding, provides a poignant and powerful account of her life and the horrors of the Holocaust. "The Diary of Anne Frank" has become one of the most important and widely read books in the world, symbolizing the resilience of the human spirit.

26. Florence Nightingale

Florence Nightingale (1820-1910) was an English social reformer and the founder of modern nursing. She gained fame for her work during the Crimean War, where she significantly improved the unsanitary conditions at a British base hospital, reducing the death count. Nightingale's pioneering work laid the foundation for professional nursing.

27. Jackie Robinson

Jackie Robinson (1919-1972) was an American professional baseball player who became the first African American to play in Major League Baseball (MLB) in the modern era. Robinson broke the baseball color line when he started at first base for the Brooklyn Dodgers in 1947. His courage and talent helped pave the way for the integration of professional sports in America.

28. Ruby Bridges

Ruby Bridges (born 1954) was the first African American child to desegregate an all-white elementary school in the South. At the age of six, she bravely walked past angry mobs to attend William Frantz Elementary School in New Orleans in 1960. Her courage played a crucial role in the Civil Rights Movement and the fight against segregation in education.

29. Katherine Johnson

Katherine Johnson (1918-2020) was an American mathematician whose calculations of orbital mechanics were critical to the success of the first and subsequent U.S. crewed spaceflights. Her work at NASA's Langley Research Center helped send astronauts to the Moon and ensured their safe return. Johnson's contributions were highlighted in the book and film "Hidden Figures."

30. Leonardo da Vinci

Leonardo da Vinci (1452-1519) was an Italian polymath whose areas of interest included invention, painting, sculpting, architecture, science, music, mathematics, engineering, literature, anatomy, geology, astronomy, botany, writing, history, and cartography. His masterpieces, such as the "Mona Lisa" and "The Last Supper," and his numerous inventions and scientific studies have left an indelible mark on the world.

31. Sir Francis Bacon

Sir Francis Bacon (1561-1626) was an English philosopher, statesman, scientist, jurist, orator, and author. He served as Attorney General and as Lord Chancellor of England. Bacon is best known for developing the scientific method and for his works on empiricism, which laid the groundwork for modern scientific inquiry.

32. Albert Einstein

Albert Einstein (1879-1955) was a German-born theoretical physicist who developed the theory of relativity, one of the two pillars of modern physics (alongside quantum mechanics). His equation ($E = mc^2$) has been dubbed "the world's most famous equation." Einstein's work has had a profound impact on the understanding of the universe and has influenced countless scientific advancements.

33. Amelia Earhart

Amelia Earhart (1897-1937) was an American aviation pioneer and author. She was the first female aviator to fly solo across the Atlantic Ocean. Earhart set many other records, wrote best-selling books about her flying experiences, and was instrumental in the formation of The Ninety-Nines, an organization for female pilots. Her mysterious disappearance during an attempt to circumnavigate the globe remains one of the greatest unsolved mysteries in aviation history.

34. Chief Joseph

Chief Joseph (1840-1904) was a leader of the Nez Perce tribe who is best known for his resistance to the U.S. government's attempts to forcibly remove his people from their ancestral lands in the Pacific Northwest. His eloquent and dignified leadership during the Nez Perce War of 1877 and his subsequent advocacy for Native American rights have made him a symbol of the struggle for justice and equality.

35. Irena Sendlerowa

Irena Sendlerowa (Irena Stanislawa Sender, 1910-2008) was a Polish social worker and humanitarian who served in the Polish Underground during World War II. She is credited with saving the lives of approximately 2,500 Jewish children by smuggling them out of the Warsaw Ghetto and providing them with false identity documents and safe housing. Sendler's bravery and compassion have made her a celebrated figure in Holocaust history.

36. Raoul Wallenberg

Raoul Wallenberg (1912-1947) was a Swedish architect, businessman, diplomat, and humanitarian. During World War II, he is credited with saving tens of thousands of Jews in Nazi-occupied Hungary by issuing protective passports and providing shelter in buildings designated as Swedish territory. Wallenberg's efforts have earned him recognition as one of the Righteous Among the Nations.

37. Malala Yousafzai

Malala Yousafzai (born 1997) is a Pakistani education activist and the youngest-ever Nobel Prize laureate. She gained global attention after surviving an assassination attempt by the Taliban for advocating for girls' education. Malala continues to campaign for the rights of girls to receive an education worldwide through the Malala Fund.

38. Václav Havel

Václav Havel (1936-2011) was a Czech statesman, playwright, and former dissident who served as the last President of Czechoslovakia and the first President of the Czech Republic. Havel was a leading figure in the Velvet Revolution, which peacefully ended communist rule in Czechoslovakia. His commitment to democracy and human rights has left a lasting legacy.

39. Wangari Maathai

Wangari Maathai (1940-2011) was a Kenyan environmental activist and the first African woman to receive the Nobel Peace Prize. She founded the Green Belt Movement, which focused on tree planting, environmental conservation, and women's rights. Maathai's work has had a profound impact on sustainable development and environmental stewardship in Africa.

40. Neil Armstrong

Neil Armstrong (1930-2012) was an American astronaut and aeronautical engineer who became the first person to walk on the Moon on July 20, 1969, during the Apollo 11 mission. His famous words, "That's one small step for man, one giant leap for mankind," marked a significant milestone in human space exploration and inspired generations of scientists and explorers.

41. Sally Ride

Sally Ride (1951-2012) was an American astronaut and physicist who became the first American woman to travel into space in 1983 aboard the Space Shuttle Challenger. Ride's historic flight broke barriers for women in science and space exploration. She later dedicated her life to education and inspiring young people, especially girls, to pursue careers in science, technology, engineering, and mathematics (STEM).

42. Joan of Arc

Joan of Arc, also known as **Jeanne d'Arc,** was a remarkable figure in French history. Born around 1412 in Domrémy, France, she claimed to have received visions from saints instructing her to support Charles VII and help drive the English out of France during the Hundred Years' War1 2.

At just 17, Joan led the French army to a pivotal victory at the Siege of Orléans in 1429, which significantly boosted French morale and paved the way for Charles VII's coronation1 2. Despite her successes, she was captured by the Burgundians, allies of the English, in 1430 and handed over to the English1 2. Joan was tried for heresy and witchcraft, and she was burned at the stake in 1431 at the age of 19 1 2.

In 1456, a posthumous retrial cleared her of all charges, and she was canonized as a saint by the Roman Catholic Church 19201 2. Joan of Arc remains a symbol of courage, faith, and patriotism.

(1. en.wikipedia.org, 2. history.com, 3. worldhistory.org, 4. worldhistory.org, 5. newworldencyclopedia.org)

43. Aung San Suu Kyi

Aung San Suu Kyi (born 1945) is a Burmese politician, diplomat, and author who has been a prominent figure in the struggle for democracy and human rights in Myanmar. She was awarded the Nobel Peace Prize in 1991 for her nonviolent efforts to bring democracy to Myanmar. Despite facing house arrest and political challenges, Suu Kyi remains a symbol of peaceful resistance.

44. Lech Wałęsa

Lech Wałęsa (born 1943) is a Polish statesman, dissident, and Nobel Peace Prize laureate who co-founded and led Solidarity (Solidarność), the Soviet bloc's first independent trade union. His leadership in the movement for workers' rights and political reform played a significant role in the end of communist rule in Poland and the broader Eastern Bloc.

45. Emmeline Pankhurst

Emmeline Pankhurst (1858-1928) was a British political activist and leader of the British suffragette movement, which helped women win the right to vote. She founded the Women's Social and Political Union (WSPU), known for its militant tactics. Pankhurst's relentless campaigning and advocacy were instrumental in achieving women's suffrage in the United Kingdom.

46. Luis Palau

Luis Palau (1934-2021) was an Argentine-American evangelist who played a significant role in the global Christian evangelical movement. Known for his large-scale evangelistic campaigns, Palau preached to millions of people around the world, spreading messages of faith, hope, and salvation. His work has had a lasting impact on Christian communities globally.

47. **William Wilberforce**

William Wilberforce (1759-1833) was a British politician, philanthropist, and leader of the movement to abolish the slave trade. His tireless efforts in Parliament and his advocacy for social reform led to the passage of the Slave Trade Act of 1807, which ended the British transatlantic slave trade. Wilberforce's legacy is celebrated for his commitment to human rights and social justice.

48. John Stott

John Stott (1921-2011) was an English Anglican priest and theologian who was a leading figure in the worldwide evangelical movement. He was known for his influential writings, including "Basic Christianity," and his role in shaping modern evangelical thought. Stott's emphasis on biblical teaching and social justice has left a profound impact on Christian communities around the world.

49. A. W. Tozer

A. W. Tozer (1897-1963) was an American Christian pastor, author, magazine editor, and spiritual mentor. Known for his deep and insightful writings on the Christian faith, Tozer's works, such as "The Pursuit of God" and "The Knowledge of the Holy," have inspired countless believers to seek a deeper relationship with God. His legacy continues through his many published books and sermons.

50. Charles Swindoll

Charles Swindoll (born 1934) is an American evangelical Christian pastor, author, educator, and radio preacher. He is the founder of Insight for Living, a popular radio ministry, and has written numerous books on Christian living and leadership. Swindoll's practical and encouraging teachings have reached millions, helping them to grow in their faith and navigate life's challenges.

References:

1. en.wikipedia.org
2. britannica.com
3. en.wikipedia.org
4. history.com
5. en.wikipedia.org
6. britannica.com
7. en.wikipedia.org
8. britannica.com
9. comicbook.com
10. hollywoodreporter.com
11. collider.com
12. comiccrusaders.com
13. screenrant.com
14. history.com
15. en.wikipedia.org
16. history.com
17. britannica.com
18. americanhistorycentral.com
19. historynet.com
20. britannica.com

PHOTO GALLERY

50 Superheroes From This Century And Centuries Past

Photos With Essential Educational, Inspiring, Motivating, Insightful, Wise Superhero Mentors' Advice, And Enlightening History, Statements, And Quotes From These Superheroes, Historians, And Biographers.

51 Real-Life Superheroes: The Truly Elite And Honorable Characterized By Their Ethics, Morality, Courage, Honor, Bravery, Respect for Democracy, Human Rights, Freedom, And Defense And Protection Of The Independence Of All World Citizens The Last Two Centuries

Daniel Joseph Cyrus

Winston Churchill

Superheroes

Abraham Lincoln

George Washington

Superheroes

Martin Luther King Jr.

THE TIME IS ALWAYS **RIGHT** TO DO WHAT IS **RIGHT**

It takes empathy, patience, and compassion to overcome anger, hatred, and resentment.

Nelson Mandela (1918-2013)

Mohandas Karamchand Gandhi ("Mahatma Gandhi," 1869-1948)

Daniel Joseph Cyrus

Dalai Lama

---- *Superheroes* ----

Mother Theresa

Daniel Joseph Cyrus

Dr. Albert Schweitzer

Superheroes

Dietrich Bonhoeffer

C. S. Lewis

Billy Graham

Superheroes

Dwight L. Moody

Watchman Nee

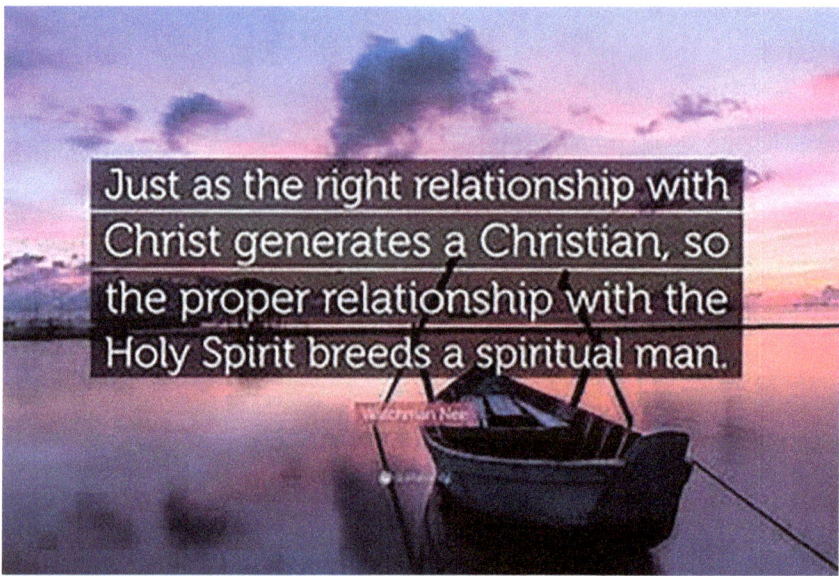

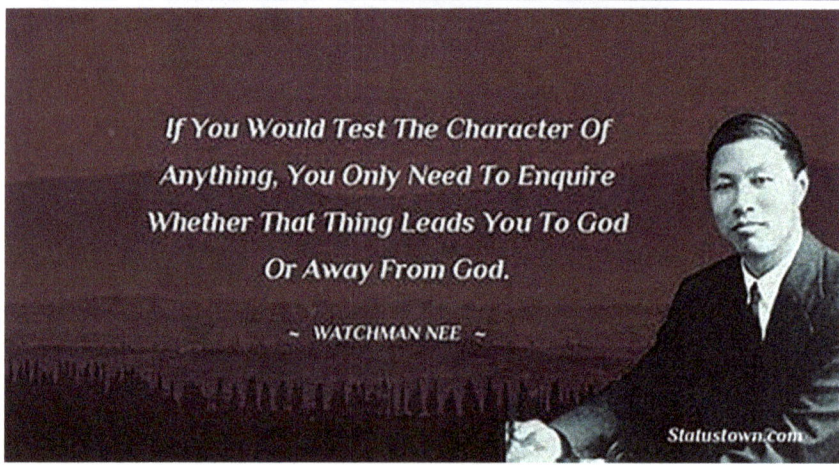

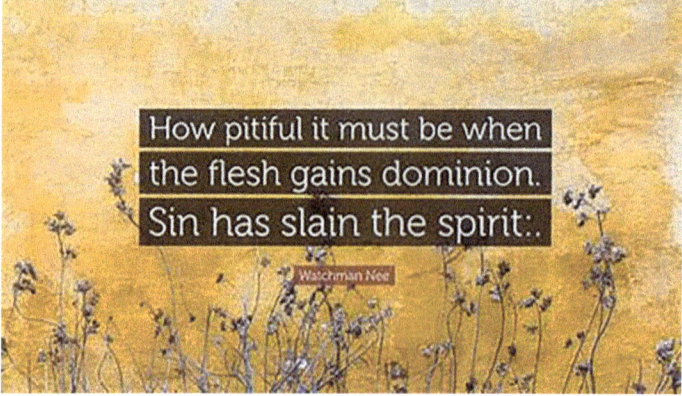

Superheroes

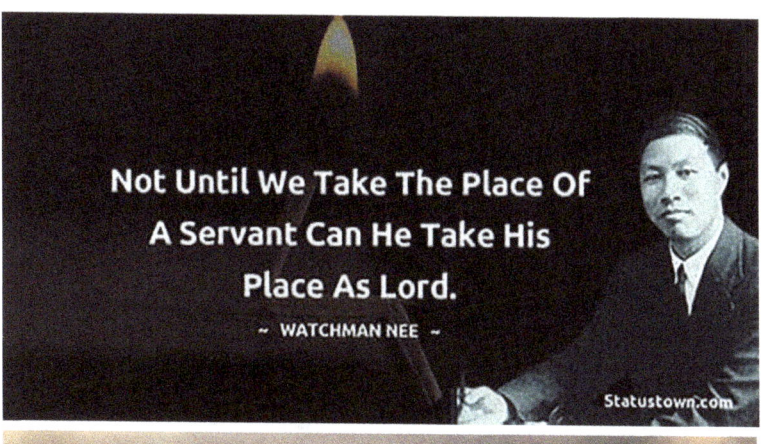

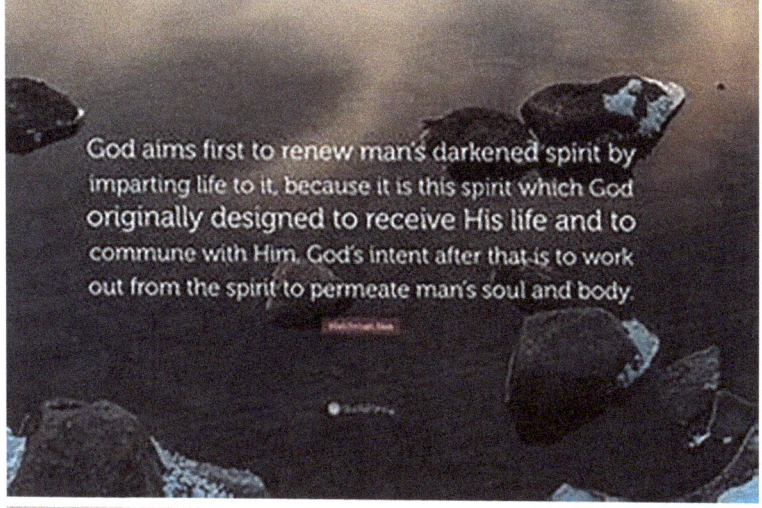

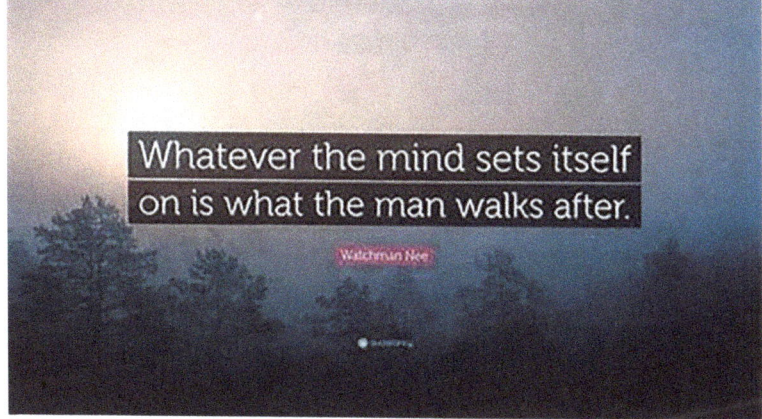

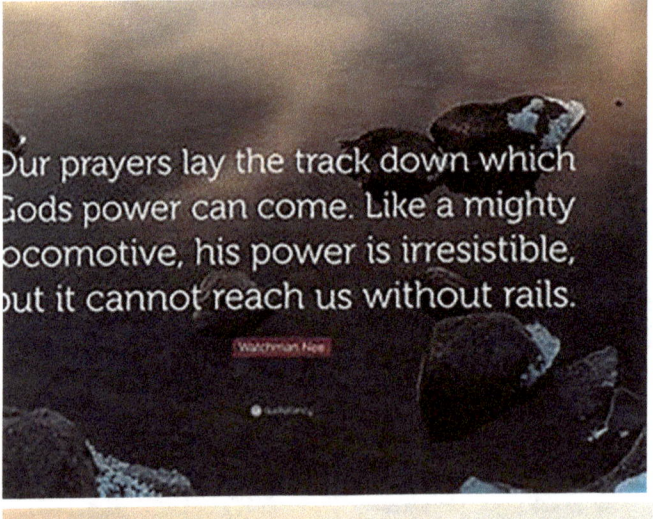

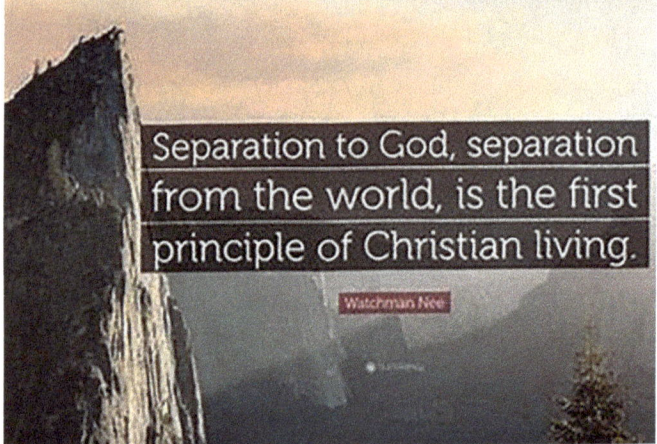

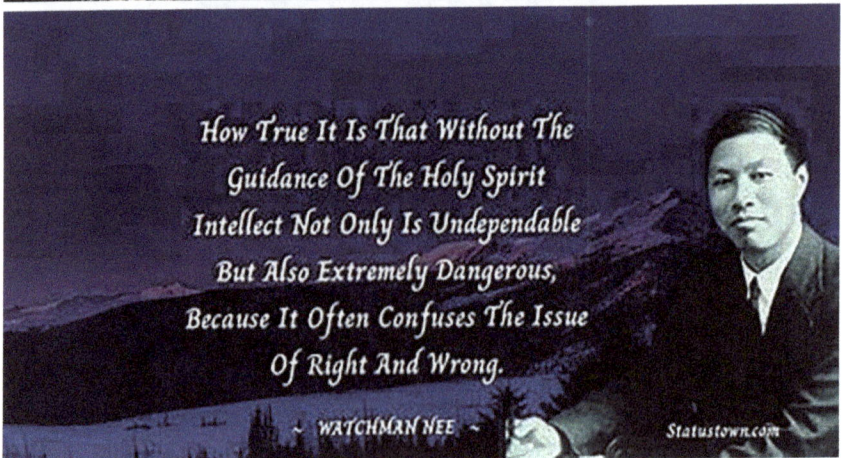

Superheroes

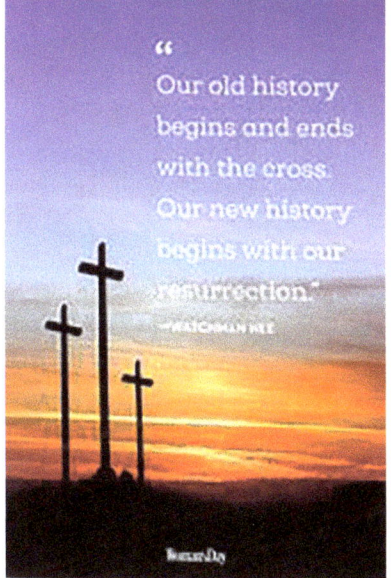

Daniel Joseph Cyrus

Blaise Pascal

―――― *Superheroes* ――――

Desmond Tutu

Superheroes

Oskar Schindler (1908—1974)

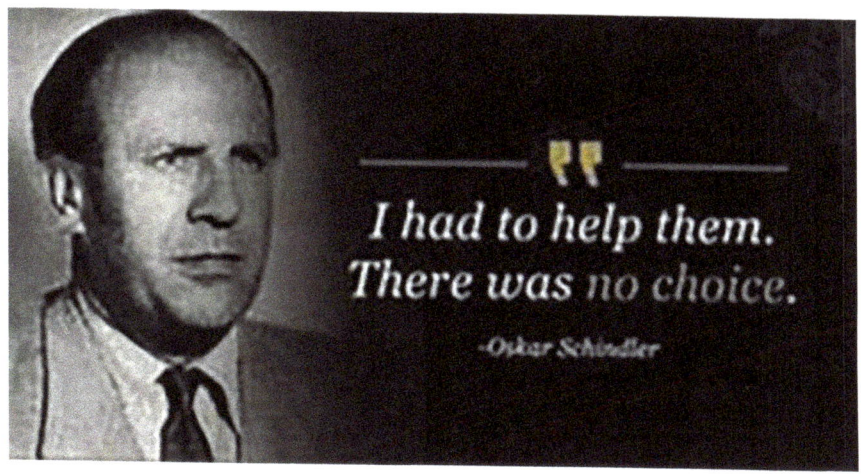

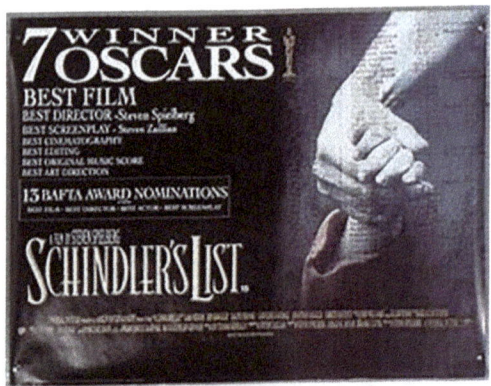

Harriet Tubman

I never ran my train off the track, and I never lost a passenger.

Rosa Parks (1913-2005)

―――― *Superheroes* ――――

Frederick Douglas (1818-1895)

Susan B. Anthony

———————— *Superheroes* ————————

Eleanor Roosevelt

Cesar Chavez

Cesar Chavez

- César Chávez was a Mexican American farm worker, labor leader, and civil rights activist who founded the United Farm Workers.
- His work led to numerous improvements for union laborers.
- His work focused on unskilled migrant laborers.
- He used non-violent protests like Martin Luther King, Jr.

Superheroes

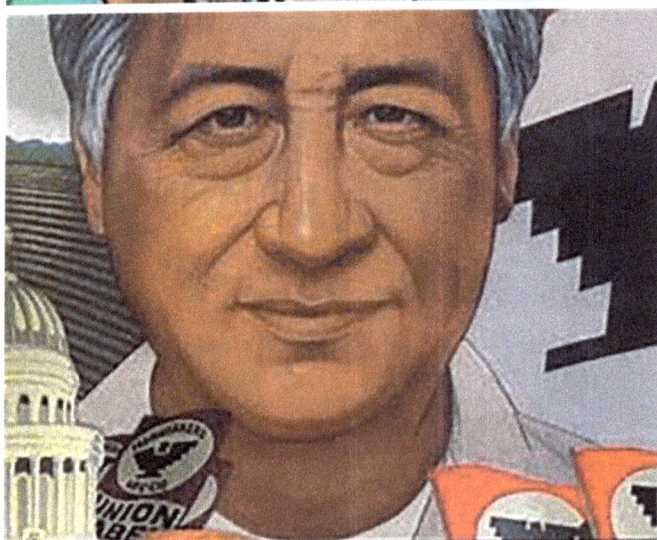

Superheroes

Corrie ten Boom

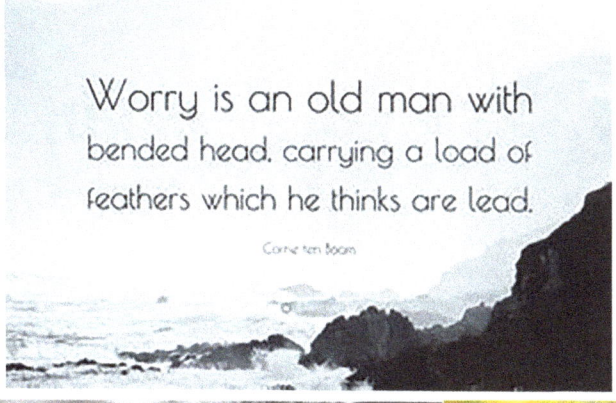

Worry is an old man with bended head, carrying a load of feathers which he thinks are lead.

Corrie ten Boom

Corrie ten Boom
1892-1983

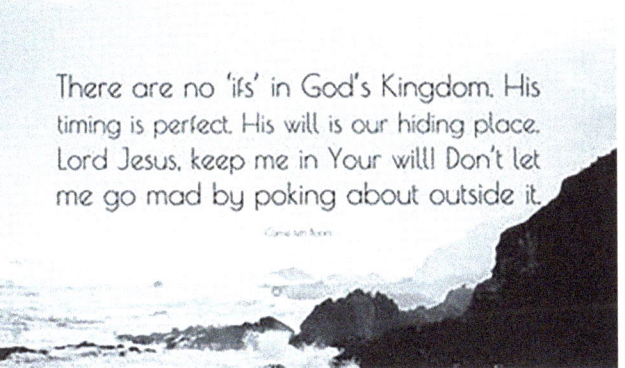

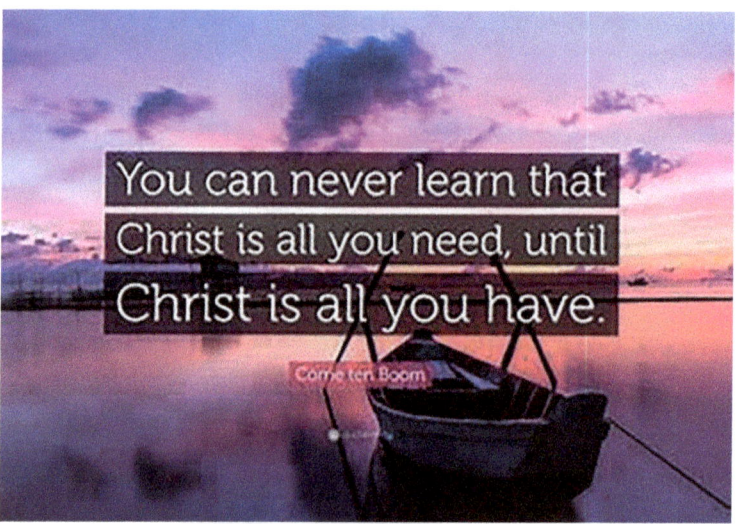

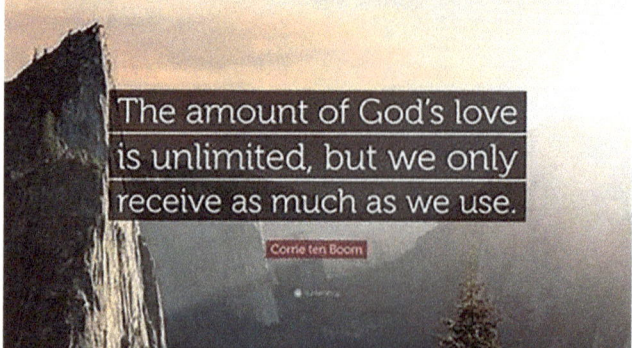

Superheroes

"Today I know that such memories are the key not to the past, but to the future. I know that the experiences of our lives, when we let God use them, become the mysterious and perfect preparation for the work He will give us to do."

Corrie ten Boom

Forgiveness is the key that unlocks the door of resentment and the handcuffs of hatred. It is a power that breaks the chains of bitterness and the shackles of selfishness.

Corrie Ten Boom

"The measure of a life, after all, is not its duration, but its donation"
—Corrie Ten Boom

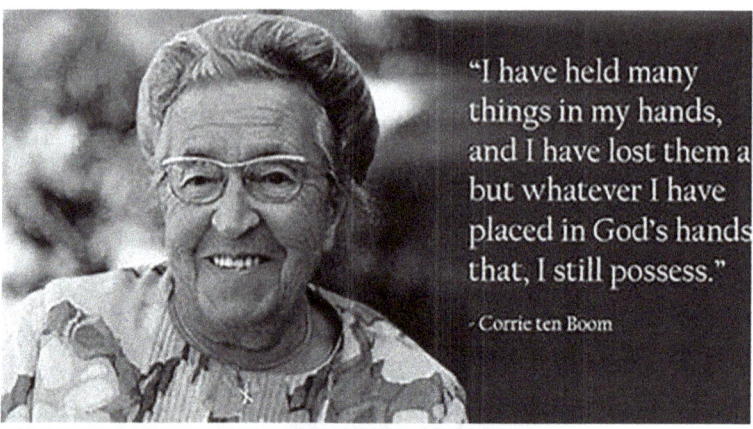

Superheroes

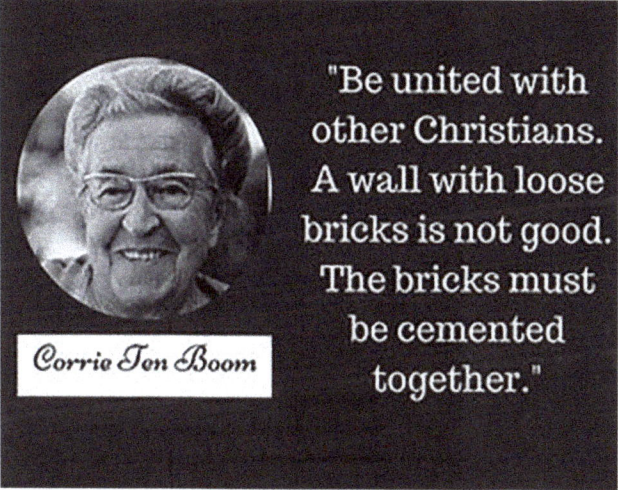

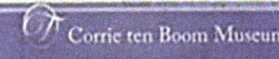
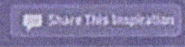

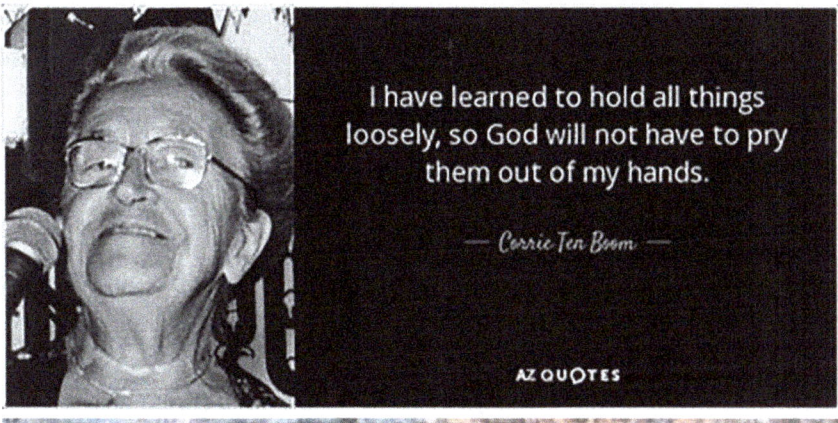

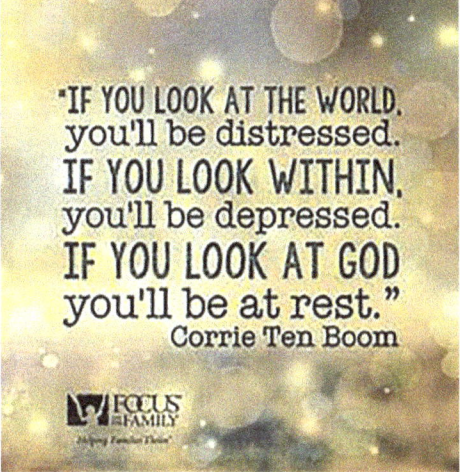

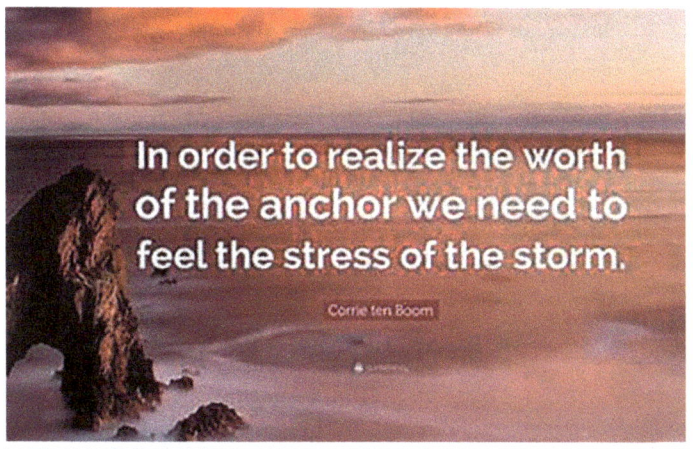

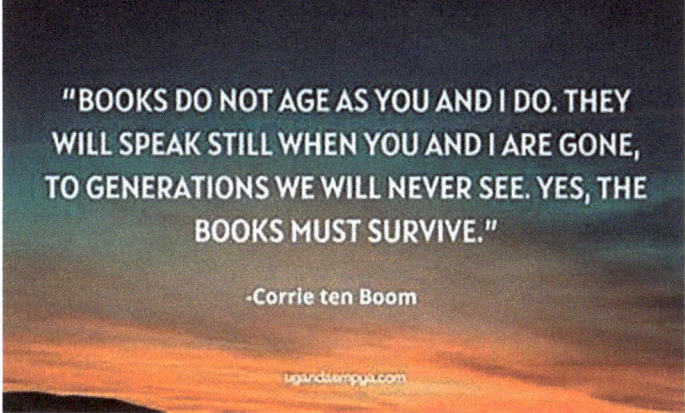

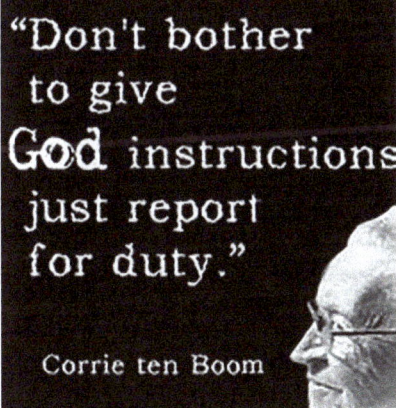

Anne Frank

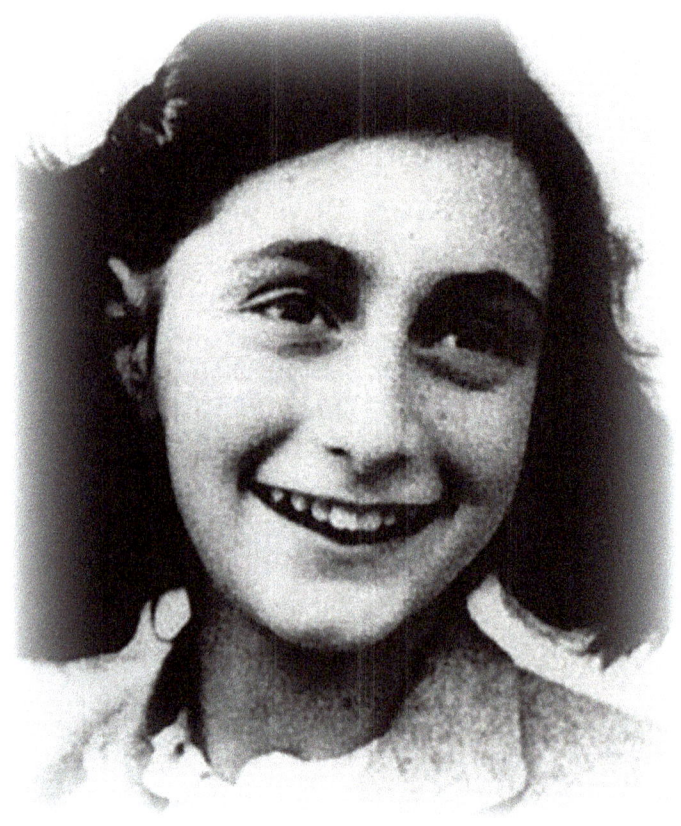

Superheroes

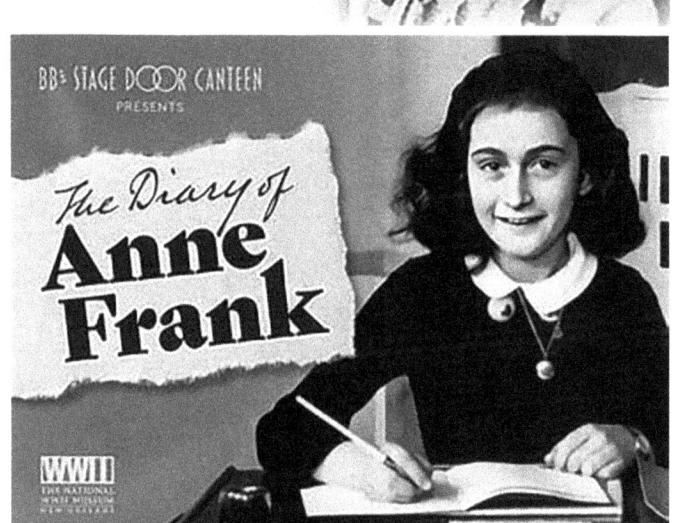

Florence Nightingale

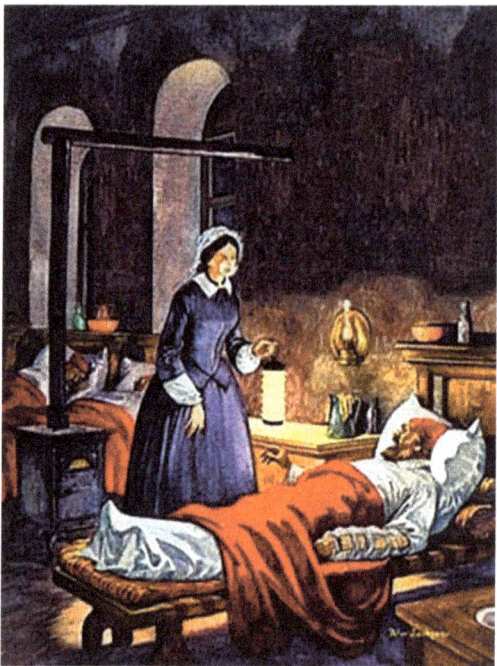

Superheroes

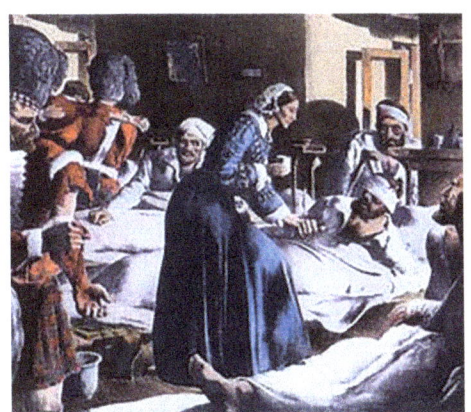
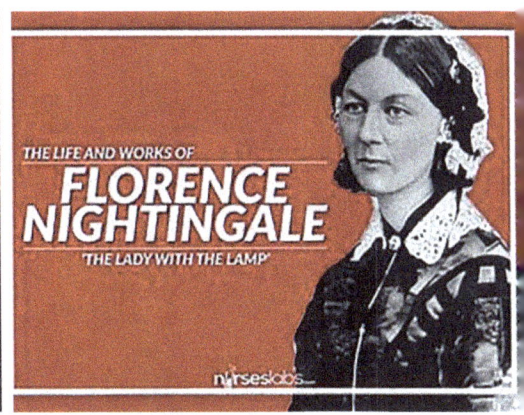

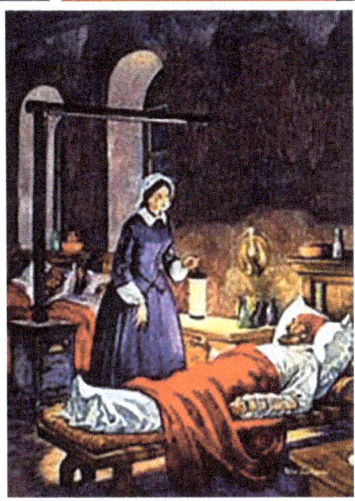

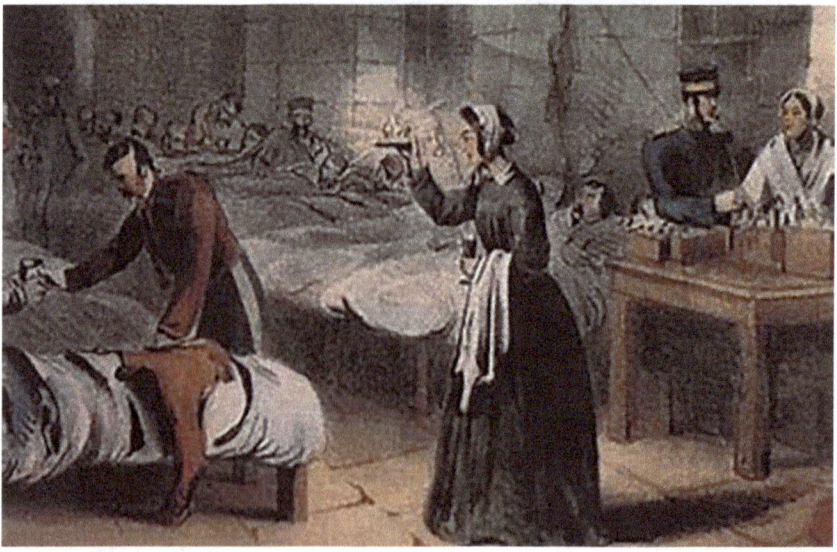

Superheroes

Jackie Robinson

Ruby Bridges

RUBY BRIDGES
THIS IS YOUR TIME

Katherine Johnson

Superheroes

Leonardo da Vinci

Sir Francis Bacon

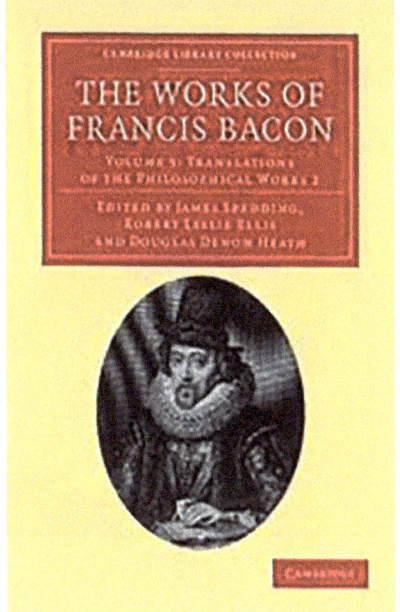

Albert Einstein

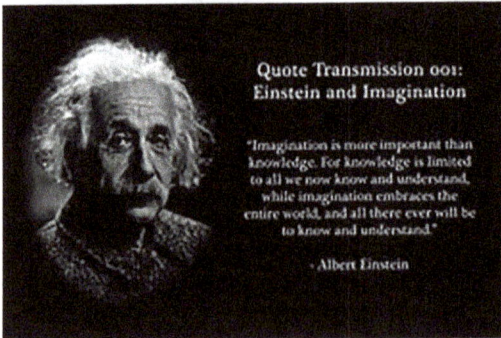

— Superheroes —

Amelia Earhart

Superheroes

Chief Joseph (1840-1904)

Daniel Joseph Cyrus

Irena Sendler

Raoul Wallenberg

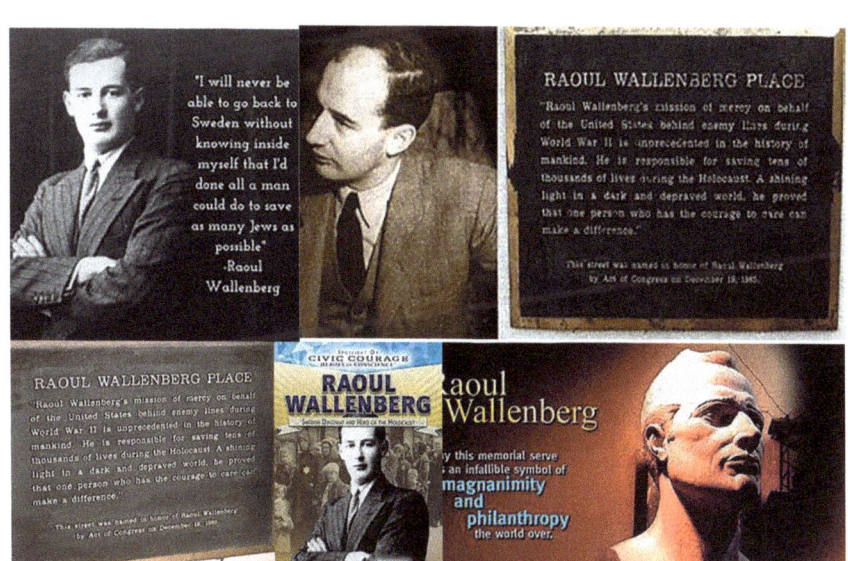

— Superheroes —

Malala Yousafzai

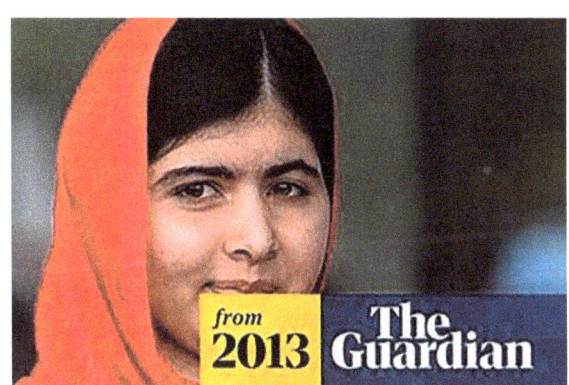

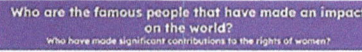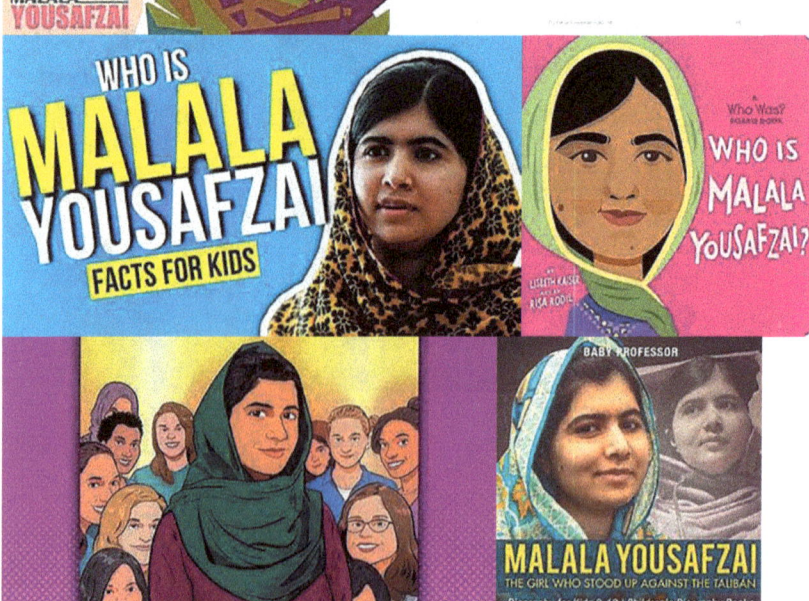

Superheroes

Vaclav Havel

Wangari Maathai

Superheroes

Neil Armstrong

Superheroes

Daniel Joseph Cyrus

Sally Ride

Superheroes

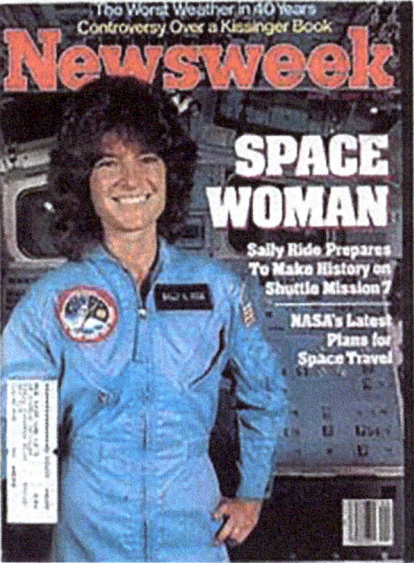

Joan of Arc (Jeanne d'Arc)

Superheroes

Aung San Suu Kyi

Superheroes

Lech Walesa

Emmeline Pankhurst

Emmeline Pankhurst

Emmeline Pankhurst (née Goulden; 15 July 1858 – 14 June 1928) was a British political activist and leader of the British suffragette movement who helped women win the right to vote. In 1999 Time named Pankhurst as one of the 100 Most Important People of the 20th Century, stating "she shaped an idea of women for our time; she shook society into a new pattern from which there could be no going back". She was widely criticised for her militant tactics, and historians disagree about their effectiveness, but her work is recognised as a crucial element in achieving women's suffrage in Britain.

Born in Moss Side, Manchester to politically active parents, Pankhurst was introduced at the age of 14 to the women's suffrage movement. On 18 December 1879, she married Richard Pankhurst, a barrister 24 years older than her known for supporting women's right to vote;

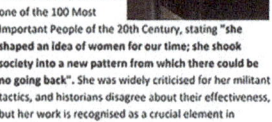

Background

- Emmeline was born on the 15th of July 1858
- She was the oldest girl of 10 children.
- Her father, Robert Goulden was a successful business man with strong political beliefs. He took part in campaigns against slavery.
- Her mother Jane was a feminist and began taking Emily to meetings when she was very young.

Luis Palau

Luis Palau
1934-2021

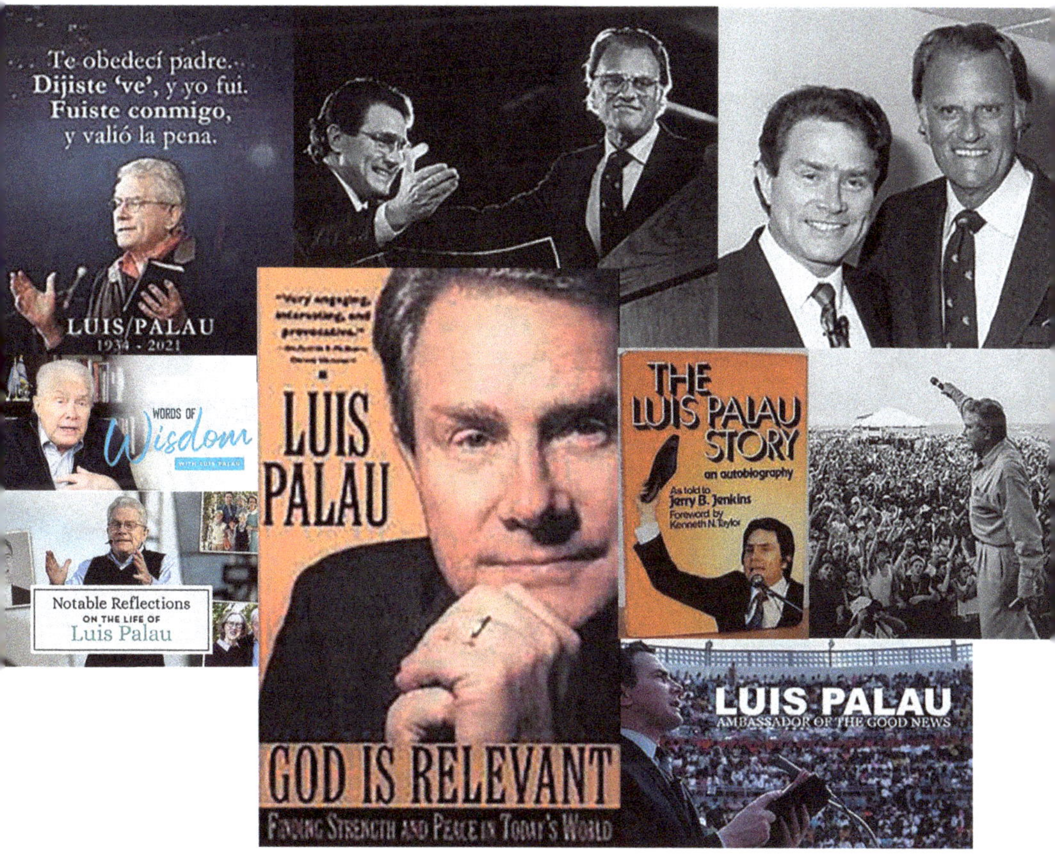
Te obedecí padre.
Dijiste 've', y yo fui.
Fuiste conmigo,
y valió la pena.
LUIS PALAU
1934 - 2021
WORDS OF
Wisdom
Notable Reflections
ON THE LIFE OF
Luis Palau
"Very engaging, interesting, and provocative."
LUIS PALAU
GOD IS RELEVANT
FINDING STRENGTH AND PEACE IN TODAY'S WORLD
THE LUIS PALAU STORY
an autobiography
As told to
Jerry B. Jenkins
Foreword by
Kenneth N. Taylor
LUIS PALAU
AMBASSADOR OF THE GOOD NEWS

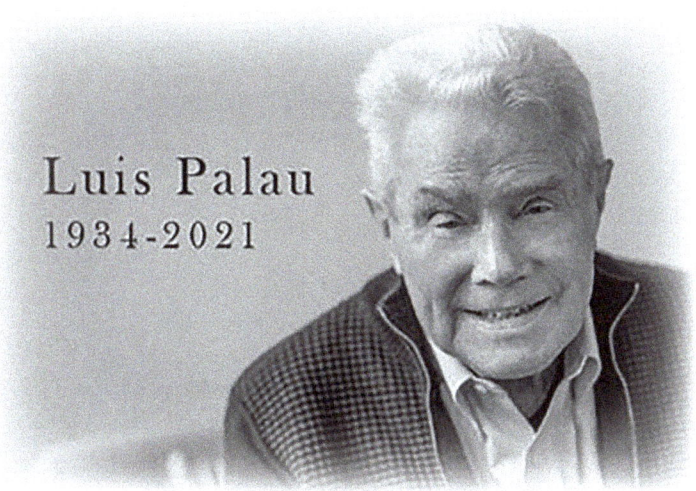

William Wilberforce

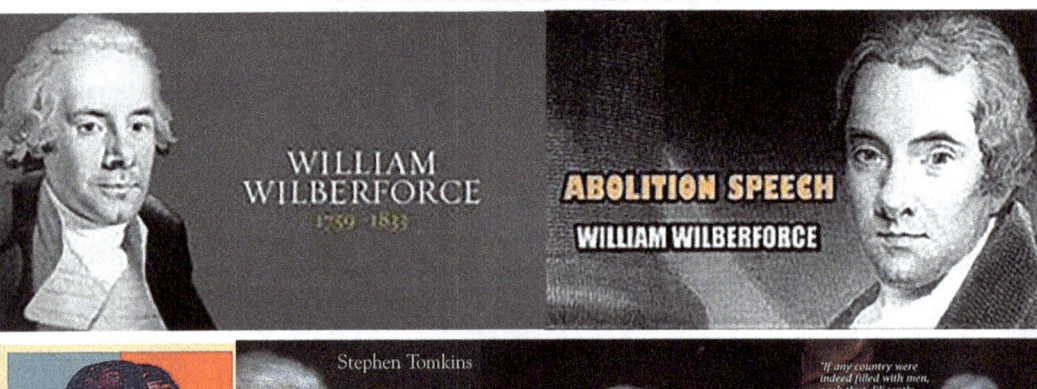

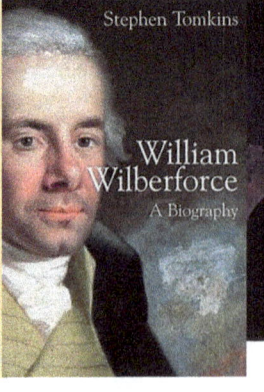

John Stott

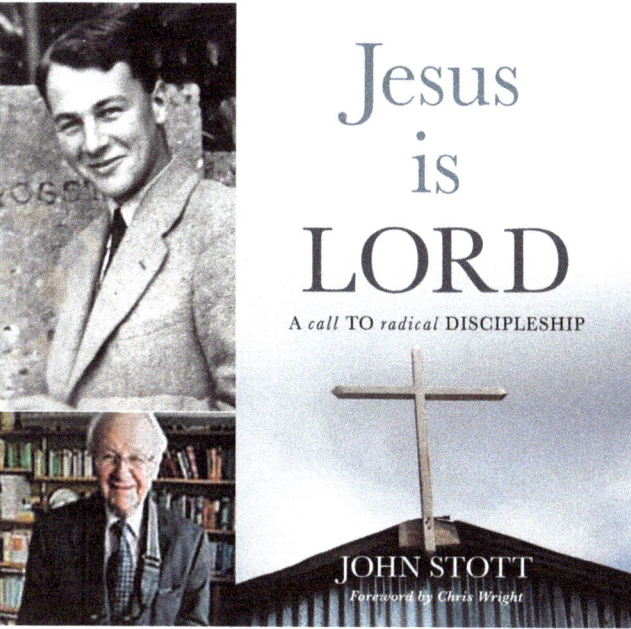

A. W. Tozer

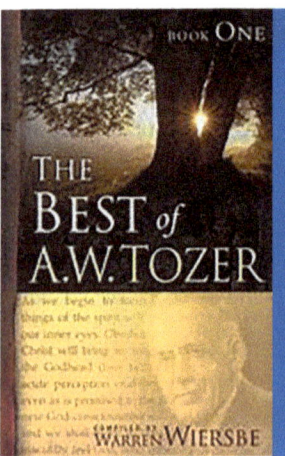 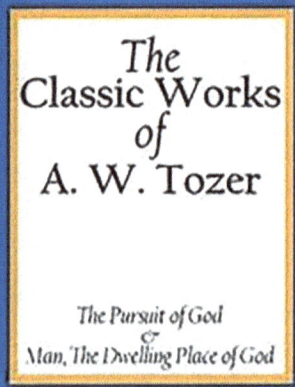 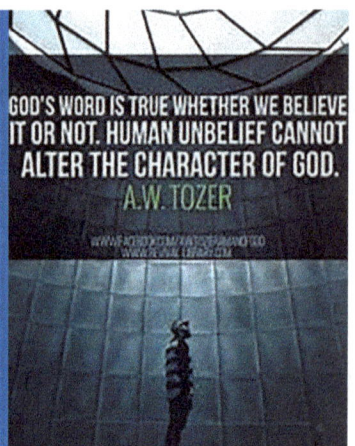

Superheroes

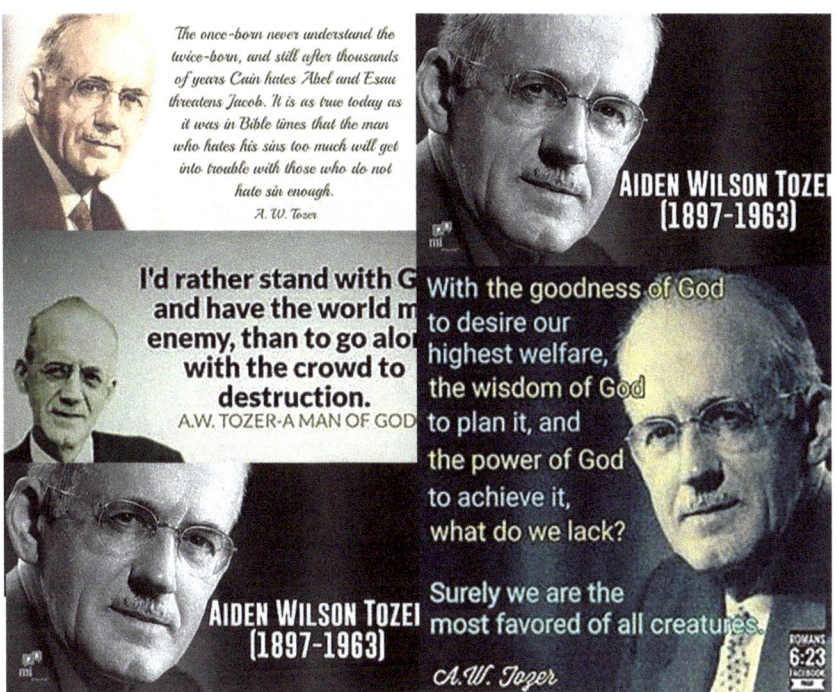

Charles Swindoll

Superheroes

CHARLES SWINDOLL

He said, "The longer I live, the more I realize the impact of attitude on life. Attitude, to me, is more important than facts. It is more important than the past, than education, than money, than circumstances, than failures, than successes, than what other people think or say or do. The remarkable thing is we have a choice every day regarding the attitude we will embrace for that day. We cannot change our past. We cannot change the fact that people will act in a certain way. We cannot change the inevitable. The only thing we can do is play on the one string we have, and that is our attitude. I am convinced that life is 10% what happens to me and 90% how I react to it. And so it is with you. We are in charge of our attitudes."

81.

CHARLES SWINDOLL

He said, "The longer I live, the more I realize the impact of attitude on life. Attitude, to me, is more important than facts. It is more important than the past, than education, than money, than circumstances, than failures, than successes, than what other people think or say or do. The remarkable thing is we have a choice every day regarding the attitude we will embrace for that day. We cannot change our past. We cannot change the fact that people will act in a certain way. We cannot change the inevitable. The only thing we can do is play on the one string we have, and that is our attitude. I am convinced that life is 10% what happens to me and 90% how I react to it. And so it is with you. We are in charge of our attitudes."

81.

Attitude
By Charles Swindoll

The longer I live,
the more I realize the impact of attitude on life.
Attitude, to me, is more important than
the past, than education, than money,
than circumstances, than failures, than successes,
than what other people think or say or do.
It is more important than appearance,
giftedness, or skill.
It will make or break a company...
a church... a school... a home.
The remarkable thing is we have a choice every day
regarding the attitude we will embrace for that day.
We cannot change our past...
we cannot change the fact
that people will act a certain way.
We cannot change the inevitable.
The only thing we can do
is play on the one string we have,
and that is our attitude.
I am convinced that life
is 10% what happens to me

CHARLES R. SWINDOLL

"The longer I live, the more I realize the impact of attitude on life. Attitude, to me, is more important than facts. It is more important than the past, than education, than money, than circumstances, than failures, than successes, than what other people think or say or do. It is more important than appearance, giftedness or skill. It will make or break a company...a church...a home. The remarkable thing is we have a choice every day regarding the attitude we will embrace for that day. We cannot change our past...we cannot change the fact that people will act in a certain way. We cannot change the inevitable. The only thing we can do is play on the one string we have, and that is our attitude...I am convinced that life is 10% what happens to me and 90% how I react to it. And so it is with you...we are in charge of our attitudes."

16.

"The secret lies in how we handle today, not yesterday or tomorrow. Today... that special block of time holding the key that locks out yesterday's nightmares and unlocks tomorrow's dreams."

Charles Swindoll

When God's in it, it flows. When the flesh is in it, it's forced. If he is in it, it's remarkable how approval will be granted, how our growing interest will percolate, and how the timing will fall right into place. It will come together, almost in spite of you.

Charles R. Swindoll
Daily Christian Quote Website

Each **day** of our lives, we make **deposits** in the **memory** banks of our **children.**

- Charles **Swindoll**

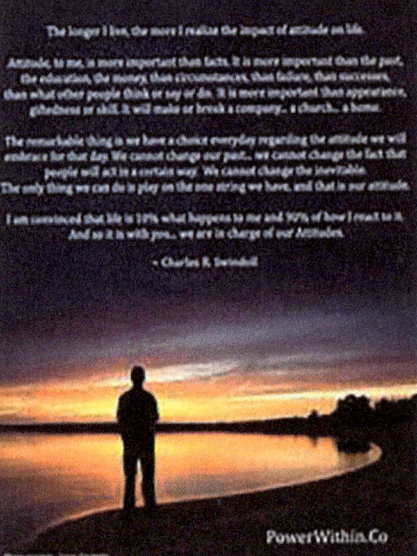

OVERCOMING UNFAIR TREATMENT

The LORD is righteous within her;
He will do no injustice.
Every morning He brings His justice to light;
He does not fail.
But the unjust knows no shame.
— *Zephaniah 3:5*

Dear Lord, we want You to find a polished and quiet spirit within us. To make that happen, we need You to come in like a Small Occupy or like water filling empty spaces. Occupy reserved portions of our lives where anger is brewing and the secret places where grudges are being stored. Sweep through the houses of our hearts ... don't miss out nooks or a single area — cleanse every dark closet, look under every rug. Let nothing go unnoticed as You take full control of our motives as well as our actions. Deep within our hearts, carry us clean of blame and revenge, of self-pity and keeping score. Enable each one of us to be big enough to press on, regardless what unfair treatment we've had to endure. Take away the scars of ugly treatment and harsh words. Keep us from licking our wounds. Forgiveness comes hard ... but it's essential. Help us forgive, even

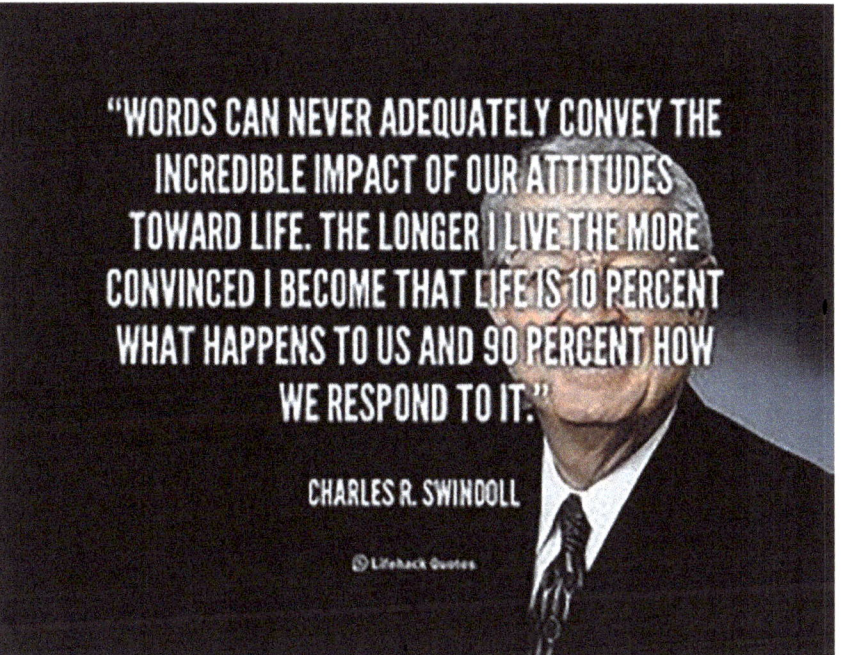

CONCLUSION

Superheroes: Becoming The Truly Elite And Honorable

When Morality, Ethics, Acknowledgement Of Unalterable Divine Birth Gender, and Respect For Each Country's Conservative And Godly Religious Society Values-Based Enlightenment, Motivation, And Inspiration Are Embraced by Every Society Member And Each Citizen Of Every Country, These "World Citizens" Will Then Inevitably Merit, Attain, And Achieve "Superhero" Status, A Realization That Is Satisfying, Highly Desirable, Fulfilling, Eternal, And That Will Be Experienced By Each and Every One Of These Transformed "World Citizens" In Every Country Throughout The World.

A Final Message And Blessing To All Future Endeavoring Superheroes: Embrace And Cherish The Opportunity To Become The Truly Elite And Honorable, For Every "World Citizen," Culture, Society, And Country In This World Will Ultimately, Infinitely, Eternally, And Reverently Respect And Be Indebted And Forever Thankful For You, In Addition To Your Certain Attainment Of God's Grace, Mercy, And Blessings While On Earth And In Heaven With God In Perpetuity!

Daniel Joseph Cyrus

www.ingramcontent.com/pod-product-compliance
Lightning Source LLC
Chambersburg PA
CBHW072339220125
20519CB00002B/38